D1033001

MARIA EDGEWORTH

Letters from England
1813–1844

MARIA EDGEWORTH

From a daguerreotype taken in 1841 (see p. 593). She wears a dark wig quite unlike the light brown hair of her youth.

MARIA EDGEWORTH

Letters from England
1813–1844

EDITED BY
CHRISTINA COLVIN

OXFORD
AT THE CLARENDON PRESS
1971

Oxford University Press, Ely House, London W. 1

GLASGOW NEW YORK TORONTO MELBOURNE WELLINGTON
CAPE TOWN SALISBURY IBADAN NAIROBI DAR ES SALAAM LUSAKA ADDIS ABABA
BOMBAY CALCUTTA MADRAS KARACHI LAHORE DACCA
KUALA LUMPUR SINGAPORE HONG KONG TOKYO

PRINTED IN GREAT BRITAIN

To M. S. B.

and to the memory of

H. J. B. and H. E. B.

CONTENTS

LIST OF PLATES

INTRODUCTION

I. *Maria Edgeworth in England*

LIKE Lady Clonbrony in her novel *The Absentee*, Maria Edgeworth was 'Henglish born in Hoxfordshire';[1] the home of her mother Anna Maria Elers was at the manor house of Black Bourton, near Witney, and it was there that the latter on New Year's Day 1768[2] gave birth to her eldest daughter and third child. Maria's father, Richard Lovell Edgeworth, was a lively, ebullient, and warm hearted young Irish gentleman from County Longford. Though for well over half a century Maria's home was at Edgeworthstown in Ireland the greater part of her first rather unhappy fourteen years were passed in England. After the death of her mother in 1773 and her father's marriage to Honora Sneyd the family went for two years to Ireland and sixty-five years later Maria spoke of this period of her childhood and

how unhappy she was. She remembered in Dublin getting out of the garret window on the window stool when she was about six years old and some passenger running in and telling the maid of the child's danger. When the maid said as she took her in 'Do you know you might have fallen down and broken your neck and been killed?', Maria answered, 'I wish I had—I'm very unhappy.'[3]

Because of her stepmother's ill health she was sent late in 1775 to Mrs. Latuffiere's school in Derby,[4] and early in 1781, after R. L. Edgeworth's third marriage (Mrs. Honora Edgeworth died in April 1780), she was moved to Mrs. Devis's establishment in Upper Wimpole St., London, fashionable, but to Maria very uncongenial. An English childhood thus gave her a familiarity with English life and she never wrote of it as an

[1] For a detailed account of ME's childhood and of her life in Ireland see M. S. Butler, *Maria Edgeworth: A Literary Biography* (forthcoming); *Memoir of Maria Edgeworth*, ed. A. Hare (1894); H. J. and H. E. Butler, *The Black Book of Edgeworthstown* (1926); and E. Inglis Jones, *The Great Maria* (1959). For a full bibiography, see *The New Cambridge Bibliography of English Literature*, vol. iii (1969).

[2] For this revised date, see *Notes & Queries*, Sept. 1971.

[3] Harriet Butler (*née* Edgeworth) to her brother M. Pakenham Edgeworth, Aug. 1838.

[4] For an account of school life as at Derby, see ME's 'The Bracelets' in *The Parent's Assistant* (1796).

outsider. She had, however, only a conventional boarding-school education with nothing bluestocking about it and with few of the advantages of family life and home teaching on which she and her father later put such stress in their successful book *Practical Education* (1798).

The more important phase in Maria Edgeworth's upbringing only began when the Edgeworths moved to Ireland in 1782. In Ireland for the first time she now had a happy family life and her family and home became, and remained ever after, the centre of her existence. Moreover, partly because of her stepmother's ill health, she was her father's companion as he rode about the country; she learnt from him the business of running an Irish estate and shared with him his interest in the ways of life and the manner of speech of his tenants. It was at this time that there grew up between them the close relationship which shaped her thoughts and actions to the end of her days. Richard Lovell Edgeworth set himself to supplement his daughter's conventional education as an English young lady, and the basis of what he taught her in these early years in Ireland was also predominantly English. He was himself half English; he had been to an English as well as to an Irish school, to Corpus Christi College, Oxford, as well as to Trinity College, Dublin; and he had lived in England almost entirely for the previous twenty years, occupying himself with science and engineering. These scientific interests he passed on to Maria as well as giving her a knowledge and understanding of polite literature. From the beginning of her Irish life R. L. Edgeworth also encouraged his daughter to write, starting, however, not with Irish tales, but with a translation of a story by Madame de Genlis.[1]

By the time the Edgeworths were again in England in the autumn of 1791 Maria was writing steadily, if only for the amusement of the growing circle of children in the family.[2] Though she spent most of the two years' stay at Clifton outside Bristol, helping to look after her young brothers and sisters, R. L. Edgeworth, a devoted but not a possessive father, arranged

[1] Letters from ME to Fanny Robinson: mid-nineteenth-century copies in the Edgeworth papers (originals in the Huntington Library, California).

[2] R. L. Edgeworth had twenty-two children, the youngest born in 1812, the eldest in 1764.

that his daughter should pay a long visit to London with the widow of his old friend Thomas Day. Maria, until many years after shy and all too conscious of her own insignificant appearance and diminutive size, commented: 'I dare say that if I go I shall be amused for a time and happy in Mrs. Day's society but I *do not* think of the Journey with pleasure for I shall find neither Father nor Mother ni Amant assurément in the wide Town of London. But however I shall have learnt from *experience* how happy compared with other situations my Home is and that is all the good I expect.'[1] Mrs. Day died and Maria was invited instead to stay with her school friend Fanny Robinson who had married the banker Charles Hoare. Her earlier forebodings about London society were unfortunately realized: Mrs. Hoare was 'kind to me but not as kind as possible'.[2]

I spent most of my time as I liked. I say most because a great deal of it was spent in company where I heard of nothing but of chariots and horses curricles and tandems. Oh to what contempt I exposed myself in a luckless hour by asking what a Tandem was! I know my dear Aunt you will say 'This will do Maria a great deal of good' and so I believe it will. I believe it must enlarge the mind and improve the manners, though at the moment it may be disagreeable to hear opinions diametrically opposite to all one has been used to and to see a variety of characters entirely different from those we have been used to love and admire.[3]

Mrs. Hoare's society provided her with none of the warmth of feeling or the intellectual interests which she found at home, and an unreasonable distaste for the fashionable world which this visit confirmed is apparent in almost all her novels and many of her letters. In 1811 she wrote to Etienne Dumont, '*un grand succès* in *society* would add very little to my happiness. I have tried Paris and Edinburgh and Dublin and know pretty well what the pleasure of seeing and hearing and being seen and heard amount to, and I enjoy amusement and compliments and flattery all in their just proportion, but they are as nought in my scale, compared with domestic life.'[4] After her visit to London

[1] ME to Mrs. Ruxton, n.d. 1791.

[2] ME to Sophy Ruxton, 17 Oct. 1792.

[3] ME to Mrs. Ruxton, 6 Nov. 1792.

[4] ME to Etienne Dumont, 9 July 1811 (Bibliothèque Publique et Universitaire, Geneva).

as a literary lion in 1813 she admitted that for a writer 'there is a security, and a sense of reality in studying from the life which the most inventive imagination can never attain',[1] but she returned home 'loving my own friends and my own mode of life preferably to all others after comparison with all that is fine and gay and rich and rare'.[2] Though her adverse attitude of 1792 had been slightly modified by having the company of some of her family and by the enjoyment of a wider panorama, right up to the end of her last visit in 1844 she continued to express her relief in getting away from London and returning home. This is not to deny that she was often well amused, for as her letters show she had a disposition for making herself happy.

It was the bustle, the insincerity, and the superficial contacts of her London life that Maria disliked; her attitude was always determined by the people in any place and not at all by its physical character. Till late in her life she had little visual taste or interest and was no 'traveller in search of the picturesque'. She greatly preferred country life to that in Town: 'there are more materials for thinking in Town but less time for thought —More presented to the mind but less exertion of the mind itself—At least so my mind has always felt it. I am so much amused and in such admiration of others that I cannot feel any necessity for exertion of my own.'[3] In Town 'I have always felt deep regret when I have transiently seen, and been obliged to part from any one who might on further acquaintance have become friends and this is one of the evils of a town life: people are doomed to meet in such crowds or with so many circumstances of constraint or theatric decoration, that they cannot in ten years become as well acquainted as they could in ten days, or ten hours in a private family in the country.'[4] Thus her country-house visits were what she specially enjoyed in England and these produced her most attractive letters home.

Maria Edgeworth was a sociable person by nature. Her first stepmother Mrs. Honora Edgeworth recorded that 'Maria when 3 years old used to wish to grow a woman that she might *make tea*. She retained this idea and at ten years old the amusement

[1] ME to Dumont, 7 Aug. 1813.
[2] ME to Mrs. Ruxton, n.d. 1813.
[3] ME to Mrs. Lazarus, n.d. 1831.
[4] ME to Dumont, 9 July 1811.

she liked best was to play with baby tea things.'[1] Twenty years later, in *Practical Education,* Maria condemned her own early pleasure in baby tea things and gossiping tea parties[2] and till after her father's death in 1817 her sociability was very much confined to her close friends and relations in Ireland. In 1813, literary celebrity though she then was, she went to London as a shy and reluctant visitor, well content to move in the wake of her lively and not very popular father. 'In her father's lifetime when she came up to London she was like a sealed fountain', wrote Isaac D'Israeli in 1822, 'but now being on her own bottom she pours down like the falls of Niagara.'[3] She had not only acquired the power to talk and to enjoy English social life, but her successful visits to England, France, and Scotland as chaperone to her sisters gave to her a self-confidence of a kind she never had in R. L. Edgeworth's lifetime. Of all his children perhaps Maria had been the most dependent upon his forceful and flamboyant character, but it was she who now acquired the capacity to take her father's place, in fact if not in name, as the active head of the family.[4]

II. *Maria Edgeworth's English Friendships*

Anyone reading these letters must be struck by the range of Maria Edgeworth's acquaintance. Socially she belonged to the middling country gentry[5] and her career as an author might have been expected to lead her into literary circles, but she met also and made friends among Midland industrialists, among scientists, economists, and politicians, and even, despite her lack of aesthetic taste and knowledge, among artists and sculptors, such as Wilkie[6] and Chantrey.

Some of Maria's most historically interesting friendships were inherited from her father. Between 1766 and 1782 Richard

[1] MS. notebook of the Edgeworth children's sayings and doings compiled by Mrs. Honora E *c.* 1779.

[2] *Practical Education* (1798), chap. I, Toys.

[3] *Letters and Journals of Lord Byron,* ed. Prothero (1901), vi. 86 n.

[4] See below, introduction to visits of 1830–1 (p. 414) and 1840–4 (p. 569).

[5] See below, p. xxxii.

[6] Wilkie's genre pictures, e.g. *The Rent Day,* often portray in paint the same kind of scene as ME described in her books, e.g. in chap. xii of *The Absentee.*

Lovell Edgeworth had been a member of the Lunar Society of Birmingham, a group of people especially interested in the practical application of scientific discoveries.[1] The society included Erasmus Darwin, physician and poet, Josiah Wedgwood the potter, James Watt the engineer, and the chemist James Keir, as well as Thomas Day, the eccentric author of *Sandford and Merton*, who was perhaps R. L. Edgeworth's greatest friend in England. Connected too with the group was William Strutt, the cotton spinner and engineer, whom the Edgeworths visited in Derby in 1813.[2] After R. L. Edgeworth's death in 1817 only two of the original Lunar group survived, James Watt, of whom we catch a last glimpse in a letter of 1819,[3] and James Keir, but with the Strutts and with the next generation of Darwins and Wedgwoods Maria, partly for old time's sake, kept up some relationship for many years. Her friendship with James Keir's daughter was of a different order. The Edgeworth's first contact with Amelia Keir seems to have been in 1799 when they took her to London with them and somewhere about this time Maria's brother Lovell appears to have been attracted to her. However in 1801 she married John Lewis Moilliet, a Birmingham banker and merchant of Swiss origin,[4] and in 1819 they were living at Smethwick Grange, near Birmingham, conveniently near the route from Holyhead to London. They were rather surprising friends; their slow ways were in great contrast to the quick wits and rapid speech of most of the Edgeworths. Although they kept up contacts with intelligent industrial society in the Midlands and were well-informed people, they were not themselves creative, as the members of the Lunar Society had been. Maria, however, and the rest of her family, was won over by their exceedingly warm hearts and, despite the unsatisfactory experiment of sending the Moilliet's son to Lovell Edgeworth's school, the friendship lasted all their lives.

Another very different Midland family with whom the Edgeworths kept up right into the 1840s, was that of the Sneyds of

[1] For the Lunar Society, see Robert E. Schofield, *The Lunar Society of Birmingham* (1963).

[2] See below, p. 25.

[3] See below, p. 176.

[4] J. L. Moilliet had settled in England before he was 20 but he kept up his Swiss connection, partly for business reasons, and in 1820 entertained Maria at his house, Chateau de Pregny, near Geneva.

Byrkley Lodge, near Lichfield. Edward Sneyd was the elder of the two brothers of Mrs. Honora and Mrs. Elizabeth Edgeworth and was a well-to-do country gentleman belonging to a cadet branch of the Sneyds of Keele.[1] His wife had been a schoolfellow of Maria's at Derby. With their daughter Emma, they were polite, rather reserved, and highly conventional. Kind as they were in 1818–19, their relationship with the Edgeworths was never entirely wholehearted, although Maria sometimes did not know, and certainly never explained in her letters, the cause of the trouble. Probably the initial difficulty lay in the scandal created by R. L. Edgeworth's marriage with Elizabeth Sneyd, the sister of his deceased wife Honora.[2] Later it is likely that they resented the decision of Edward Sneyd's surviving sisters, Mary and Charlotte, to live at Edgeworthstown and not at Byrkley Lodge.[3] By 1831 Maria Edgeworth visited Byrkley Lodge only to please the aged and much beloved Aunt Mary[4] and in 1844, when her aunt and Mr. and Mrs. Sneyd were all dead, she found Emma Sneyd repulsively cold to her.

All these friendships had their origin in a period long before the visits described in these letters. When the Edgeworths came to London in 1813 they entered what was for Maria a new kind of English society. Her letters of 1813–22 are full of the names of Society hostesses who invited her to their houses because she was a literary lion. Among such hostesses were Lady Spencer, who prided herself on her literary connections,[5] Lady Stafford,

[1] His money came more from his father's judicious investment in the development of canals than from landed property.

[2] It was widely supposed, quite wrongly, that R. L. Edgeworth had lived with Elizabeth before their marriage. Major Sneyd refused his daughter her dowry but evidently afterwards forgave her as he left legacies to her children.

[3] It must be remembered that many of the letters printed below which describe the Sneyds were designed to be fit for the eyes or ears of Charlotte or Mary Sneyd. The Misses Sneyd had left Edgeworthstown in 1817 in fulfilment of a promise to live with their brother after RLE's death, but they returned to Ireland in November 1819. Even those who did not approve altogether of its owner found Edgeworthstown a very lively place (see C. K. Bushe, quoted in E. Œ. Somerville and Martin Ross, *Irish Memories* (new ed. 1925), 49), and Frances Beaufort (later Mrs. Edgeworth) wrote when staying with the Edgeworths' cousins at Fox Hall in 1797, 'they appeared as flat after those we had just left [at Edgeworthstown] as boiled chicken after venison': Frances Beaufort to the Revd. William Beaufort, 2 July 1797.

[4] See below, p. 554.

[5] ME and her father had corresponded with Lady Spencer at least since 1803 and ME's *Leonora* (1806) was dedicated to her.

and Lady Bathurst.[1] Rather more amusing were the 'esprit parties' given by the bluestocking hostesses Lydia White and Lady Davy, both old acquaintances who had visited Edgeworthstown in 1809 and who had eccentricities of character to delight any novelist. Follies and nonsense, whims and inconsistencies diverted Maria, like Elizabeth Bennet, although no one could suppose that her first object in life was a joke. Her suspicion that this was sometimes Sydney Smith's first object marred her opinion of him, even if it did not spoil her enjoyment of his exuberant conversation.[2]

Connected both with the world of fashion and with intellectual circles were the Hopes. Mrs. Hope belonged to an old Irish family. She was the youngest daughter of William Beresford, Archbishop of Tuam, first Lord Decies, and brother of the first Marquess of Waterford. Her husband Thomas Hope came from a rich Amsterdam merchant family and was a noted connoisseur and collector, author of *Household Furniture* (1809), a book containing designs from ancient models, many of which he adapted for his own magnificent houses in Duchess St., London, and at the Deepdene. Hope did not find his entry into the fashionable world easy; he lacked *savoir faire* in society and was shy, with a bad manner and ugly voice. It was probably as a lion that the Hopes first invited Maria Edgeworth to their house and partly for this reason that they invited her so often afterwards. But Maria would not have gone on visiting them if she had not found Mrs. Hope 'good humoured and unaffected'[3] and if she had not discovered that despite his shyness Mr. Hope's conversation was full of interest. His esoteric taste, like a good many other more knowledgeable people, she could not share, but he had been a great traveller, particularly in the Near East, and was full of the solid information and characteristic national anecdotes that the Edgeworths so much appreciated.

[1] Lady Stafford, afterwards Duchess of Sutherland, was later unfavourably known for her part in the Highland Clearances. Her house, Trentham, was, like Lady Bathurst's at Cirencester, conveniently situated on ME's itinerary.

[2] See below, p. 597.

[3] D. Watkin, *Thomas Hope, 1769–1831, and the Neo-classical Idea* (1968), 18. The description is Mary Berry's. ME's disapproval of Mrs. Hope at the end of her life was due to a social slight to her sister Fanny. ME was sensitive to the not unnatural tendency of those who entertained her to treat her sisters as mere author's appendages and not as persons worth cultivating on their own account.

Lady Elizabeth Whitbread, Lord Carrington, and Lord Lansdowne[1] belonged to the same great world, but Maria Edgeworth's relationship with them was less superficial. Of all Maria's aristocratic acquaintance she had perhaps the greatest respect and liking for Lord Lansdowne. He was the second son of the first Marquess, a Whig from birth, Chancellor of the Exchequer when he was only twenty-six, and a leader of the opposition from 1807 for twenty years. As W. H. Lyttelton wrote, 'a more unvenal, and I think, unambitious soul never existed in the breast of a public man'. He was 'a sagacious counsellor, a courteous and liberal host, a valued friend, a cultivated companion, and a munificent patron'.[2] At Bowood and at Lansdowne House he, with his agreeable but less forthcoming wife, entertained a society which was perhaps only second to that at Holland House in intellectual distinction.[3] With more fire, and perhaps a less yielding temper, he might have been Maria Edgeworth's ideal public character. Lord Carrington was not, like Lord Lansdowne and most of the Edgeworths' political friends, a liberal Whig, though he too voted with the opposition after 1806. A banker, he had received his peerage for financial assistance and advice to the younger Pitt. He had, however, literary interests: he was vice-president of the Literary Fund and a Fellow both of the Society of Antiquaries and the Royal Society. When he visited Edgeworthstown in 1813 Maria described him to her aunt as 'most amiable and benevolent, without any species of pretension'.[4] As with the Moilliets it was his great kindness of heart that won her.

Qualities of character, rather than of mind, were also what attracted Maria to Lady Elizabeth Whitbread, with whom she

[1] Lord Carrington, Lord Lansdowne, and Samuel Whitbread's nephew, Mr. Gordon, all visited Edgeworthstown in 1813 or 1814. This suggests that the Whitbreads, Lord Carrington, and Lord Lansdowne all found RLE's company enjoyable, though London society in general found him unlikeable. ME's devotion to her father strongly predisposed her towards those who appreciated him.

[2] Quoted in *Complete Peerage*. For Lord Lansdowne as a host, see *Memoirs, Journals and Correspondence of T. Moore*, ed. Lord John Russell (1853), and J. Britton, *Autobiography* (1849–50).

[3] Lady Holland was not received in fashionable society because of her position as a divorcée, and ladies were not generally entertained at Holland House.

[4] *Mem.* i. 292. He gave tangible proof of his benevolence in 1818 by securing for MPE a cadetship in the service of the East India Company.

stayed many times in Kensington. Lady Elizabeth, widow of the radical M.P. Samuel Whitbread who committed suicide in 1815, was the sister of the great Earl Grey, associated through her husband with the left wing of the Whig party, but born a member of the old Whig aristocracy. Harriet Edgeworth described her as 'very romantic and when earnest on anything quite eloquent but I should think weak and not sensible in the conduct of her own affairs. In short though a very interesting person I should not like to tie myself to her.'[1] But to Maria her old fashioned politeness and impulsive warmth were irresistible; she resembled her adored Aunt Ruxton.[2] This was why she felt so much at home at Grove House.

A similarly home-like atmosphere was to be found at Maryon Hall, Frognel, where lived T. W. Carr, solicitor to the Excise. Mr. Carr and his wife had a large affectionate family,[3] something of a counterpart to the large family at Edgeworthstown, and they lived on intimate terms with the considerable intelligentsia of Hampstead, including particularly Joanna and Agnes Baillie, with whom the Edgeworths also stayed. Joanna Baillie, though almost unknown today, had in her time a certain *succès d'estime*, particularly for her *Plays on the Passions* (1798, 1802), and she was a well-loved figure with a wide circle of literary acquaintance in both England and Scotland.

The Baillies and the Carrs made the middle-class society in Hampstead very agreeable, but it had nothing to compare with the interest of the conversation of the utilitarian legal reformers Sir Samuel Romilly and Sir James Mackintosh. Mackintosh had a brilliance unequalled in Maria's opinion by anybody but her old friend Etienne Dumont, Lord Lansdowne's former tutor. Dumont had also been librarian and intellectual adjutant to Lord Lansdowne's father, the first Marquess, formerly Lord Shelburne. Despite his great ability 'il avait besoin, pour combattre, du bouclier d'autrui'. Lord Shelburne (later Lansdowne), the French politician Mirabeau, and Jeremy Bentham all owed him a considerable debt. He was the great popularizer and interpreter of Bentham's utilitarian ideas, particularly on the Continent. Less brilliant in their conversation but almost equally

[1] Harriet E to Harriet Beaufort, 7 Feb. 1822.

[2] See below, p. xxxvi.

[3] 'This *family* family', as Harriet E put it.

satisfying were the political economists T. R. Malthus and the candid and warmhearted David Ricardo, the charm of whose rather unpolished family life overset Maria's notions of what a civilized circle ought to be.[1] If she never lost her value for the old fashioned politeness of her Aunt Ruxton, she learnt that she could sometimes do without it.

The strongest common interest among the Edgeworths, from the unsatisfactory eldest son Richard to the very literary and philosophical Francis, was in science. Their father's delight in science had started in his boyhood and all his children, daughters as well as sons, shared his taste for it. Maria was more readily responsive to scientific than to literary imagination. In April 1822 she wrote to her aunt, 'We have been to Almacks and to Lady Londonderry's—very entertaining—Mais à quoi cela mène t'il ? à—nothing. But something always remains from sensible society and often more even than information—friendship.'[2] She was referring here chiefly to the society she met at the houses of Mrs. Marcet, the writer of scientific children's books, and of the much more distinguished Mrs. Somerville, the mathematician. Here she found Pond, the Astronomer Royal, Kater the physicist and surveyor with his charming musical wife, the philosophical radical M.P., Warburton, with his sound sense and high integrity, and, best of all, the latter's great friend, William Hyde Wollaston. Wollaston completely enthralled them with his profound and varied scientific knowledge and, like Mrs. Marcet, won their respect because he 'never went one point beyond what he could vouch for truth and never practised any of the little arts of professed conversationalists to hide the bounds of their knowledge or to excite sensation or surprise'.[3] To this society also belonged Captain Francis Beaufort, later Hydrographer Royal, Mrs. Edgeworth's brother. When Fanny Edgeworth married in 1829, she lived very much in the same society as her uncle and thus her eldest sister had additional opportunities of keeping up with and adding to the acquaintance she had made earlier.

[1] See below, p. 257. [2] See below, p. 390.

[3] See below, p. 308. This description of Mrs. Marcet may be compared with Charles Babbage's description of Wollaston: 'The most singular characteristic of Wollaston's mind was the plain and distinct line which separated what he knew from what he did not know' (*D.N.B.*).

The scientific friendship of her later years which gave Maria Edgeworth most pleasure was that of John Herschel, the astronomer. Many years before, in 1799, R. L. Edgeworth and his wife and daughter had visited Slough to see William Herschel's great telescope, but Maria's friendship with Sir John and his wife belongs chiefly to the last ten years of her life when he was at the height of his career and had already received his baronetcy. More Catholic in his knowledge than his distinguished father, he passed some of his leisure time in translating Schiller, Burger, Homer, and Dante, but 'he never lost his taste for simple amusements; was in his element with children, loved gardening, and took interest in all technical arts'.[1] He was besides interested in education and was a man of complete integrity whose scientific genius was 'absolutely untainted by the egotism of the discoverer'. Maria Edgeworth asked no more. Nothing illustrates better her undiminished intellectual power in the last years of her life when she had almost ceased to write than her lively interest in Herschel's explanations of his scientific discoveries.

In the nature of things many of those Maria Edgeworth met and liked in England were mere passing acquaintances but when one examines the real friendships she made for herself everywhere it is clear that to her what mattered in her friends was first of all warmth of heart and personal integrity, combined with some degree of intellectual tastes. Wit alone did not hold her for long,[2] and those for whom she expressed the greatest admiration, such as James Watt, William Strutt, Dumont, Lord Lansdowne, David Ricardo, Dr. Wollaston, Mrs. Marcet, Mrs. Somerville, and Sir John Herschel, were all persons with achievements to their credit in the world of engineering, of politics, or of economic or scientific knowledge. Except for Sir Walter Scott, she did not have the same kind of feeling for comparable figures in the literary world.

III. *Character Sketch of Maria Edgeworth*

A character sketch of Maria Edgeworth drawn from her published works would not only be incomplete but misleading, and

[1] *D.N.B.*

[2] See her unkind portrait of Horace Churchill the wit in her novel *Helen* (1834), partly drawn from Samuel Rogers.

very different from the picture presented by her family letters. At first glance her books suggest a bluestocking, rational and considering, with an enjoyment of 'chemistry, mechanics and political economy, . . . vile cold hearted trash in a novel', as Lord Dudley called it.[1] Her readers would not be surprised at her pleasure in the practical business of life: 'her father employed her as an agent and accountant; an employment in which she showed marvellous acuteness and patience . . . The exactness of arithmetical calculation, far from disgusting her by its dryness, was agreeable to the honesty of her mind'[2] and she showed great efficiency in more than one financial crisis. A closer look at the books of course gives glimpses of something warmer, for example in the spirited descriptions of individuals and the many lively Irish scenes in *Castle Rackrent* and *The Absentee*, but in general many people would agree with what Lord Byron said of her as an author—'Oh! *heart*—she has no more heart than a post but she writes well and cleverly'.[3]

This verdict, however, is totally misleading when applied to her as a person. Her family letters show very clearly that her dominant traits were an impulsive warm-heartedness and generosity. These too were the qualities which she most admired in others, in her family and friends, and in the Irish people. The cool and rational side of Maria displayed in her books and in her conduct in major crises is at variance with her aspect in everyday family life: 'Nobody who has seen her in small alarms, such as the turning of a carriage or such things could believe the composure, presence of mind and courage she showed in our great alarm today' [a fire at Edgeworthstown],[4] wrote Honora Edgeworth in 1828. Maria herself was aware that she sometimes appeared volatile to the rest of the family and in 1841 when she and her sister were re-reading a series of letters beginning nearly sixty years earlier she was delighted to find herself 'the

[1] *Letters to 'Ivy' from the First Earl of Dudley*, ed. S. H. Romilly (1905), 250.

[2] *Mem.* i. 14–15.

[3] Leslie Marchand, *Byron* (1957), ii. 486–7. For another aspect of the contrast between ME and her books, see Harriet E to Mrs. E, 18 Nov. 1820: 'They [Princess Galitzine etc.] agreed that they were astonished when they saw Maria, for that they had always supposed her to be exceedingly tall and very severe and grave.'

[4] *Mem.* iii. 5.

same in my friendships and in my views of what did then and has always made me happy—the love of those I love and domestic life—For a person apparently so full of words and so *impressionable* as I must probably appear to those who only hear me talk. . . .'[1]

Her strong family feeling, her adoration for her father in particular and for her half-sister Fanny, is tedious to read of today and was sometimes seen as a weakness by contemporaries. It was too the only vulnerable place in her armour against flattery; she swallowed compliments to her family whole, whereas she either laughed at or was nauseated by compliments to herself, according to the degree of good taste and sincerity of the speaker.[2] She did not care much for reputation and there was nothing of the literary *poseur* about her. When Maria was in Paris in 1820 her nineteen-year-old sister Harriet who was with her wrote home,

> I did not know the extent of her talents—the extent of her modesty I was well acquainted with. But the best idea I can give you of her is to say that after displaying all that is most brilliant to Princesses and peers, or after the deepest arguments with the most celebrated and the most scientific she goes to order our gowns or to continue a new habit shirt or to talk nonsense or sense with us. How astonished some of her solemn admirers would be if they were to see her rolling with laughter at some egregious folly and still more would some of the brilliant wits be surprised at the quantity of fancy and talent she wastes on us.[3]

Her conversational powers were probably what struck her contemporaries most in the latter part of her life. When she went to London in 1813 'she was much sought for' out of 'curiosity to see a person much celebrated for her works', but in 1819 she was 'invited by those who wish to have the pleasure of her conversation'.[4] Thomas Moore described her then as 'delightful, not from display but from repose, the least pretending person

[1] ME to Fanny Edgeworth (then Mrs. Wilson), Xmas 1841; Harriet E (then Mrs. Butler) to MPE, 11 Dec. 1841.

[2] Harriet E to Harriet Beaufort, 7 May 1820; *Thoughts on Bores: Tales and Novels of Maria Edgeworth* (1833), xvii. 319.

[3] Harriet E to ? Harriet Beaufort, 4 June 1820. As late as 1846 MPE's young wife described ME as 'a regular jolly old bird': Christina E to her brother Norman Macpherson, 3 Apr. 1846.

[4] *The Farington Diary*, viii (1928), 217. Society was 'glad to have somebody that amused them and was the fashion': Harriet E to Mrs. Ruxton, 30 May 1822.

in the company'.[1] By contrast, in 1831 he complained of her loquacity,[2] a fault of which she was herself conscious: 'What a blessing it is sometimes to have an impassive countenance and to have a refuge in *usual* silence. Silence in me always proclaims that there is something wrong or extraordinary. God help me!'[3] Most people, however, enjoyed her 'perfume of wit'.[4] Sir William Rowan Hamilton, the Irish mathematician, spoke of her great talent for drawing people out and making them talk on whatever they were best acquainted with. 'In her conversation she is brilliant and full of imagery to a degree which would in writing be a fault. She knows an infinite number of anecdotes about interesting places and persons, which she tells extremely well and never except when they arise naturally from the subject.'[5] The comments could be multiplied, but perhaps the most suggestive picture of all comes from a letter written by Harriet Edgeworth (by then Mrs. Butler) to her sister Fanny telling of the 'perfume of happiness' Maria brought with her on her return from England in 1831:

> I must say I never saw Maria more perfect than she is . . . she . . . is in such good spirits and so perfectly free from feverishness or overtalking or undertalking or laughing or anything and is so delightfully and unceasingly entertaining. It really is a new existence to be with her again—There's nothing like her after all in the world.[6]

IV. *The Letters*

'I have not the pen of our friend Maria Edgeworth who writes all the while she laughs talks eats drinks and I believe though I do not pretend to be so far in the secret all the time she sleeps

[1] *Memoirs, Journals and Correspondence of T. Moore*, ed. Lord John Russell (1853), ii. 169.

[2] Ibid. vi. 187. It seems to have been a case of too many wits competing to speak and ME won. The tales she told in her letters are sufficient evidence that she could listen as well.

[3] ME to Mrs. E, 16 Jan. 1829.

[4] *Memoir of the Rev. Sydney Smith* by Lady Holland (3rd ed. 1855), 446.

[5] R. P. Graves, *Life of Sir W. R. Hamilton* (1882–9), i. 162 (27 Aug. 1824).

[6] Harriet E (then Mrs. Butler) to Fanny E (then Mrs. Wilson), St. Swithin's Day (15 July) 1831. When ME was reproached for not writing in her later years, Conversation Sharp said 'She is too busy being happy' (ME to Mrs. Lazarus, n.d. 1831). Cf. ME to Charlotte Sneyd, 19 Apr. 1813 (below, p. 17), for a very similar description of RLE by ME.

too.'[1] So wrote Sir Walter Scott after visiting Killarney in her company. Over 2,000 letters survive to her family alone. She did not, however, write letters to obtain reputation as a letter writer:

> If that were my object I would adapt my means to my end. I would commence a correspondence with some of the '*fetchers and carriers of bays*', whose suffrage and services are to be had at a cheap rate by one who has any literary name. I might, with full security that they would give them publicity in society, address brilliant epistles to the Miss B[erry]s or Miss W[hite], or Lady C[? ork] or Lady D[avy] or Sir Harry E[nglefield] or Messieurs J[effrey] R[ogers] S[? mith] T[? ennant] or any of the bel-esprit characters of the alphabet. But I utterly disdain, and detest the commerce of literary affection and flattery. Such a waste of time—such a waste of talent! I would not be at the trouble of corresponding with any, except those whom I really consider as friends.[2]

Nevertheless, her surviving letters to people in the outside world are numerous enough. They are, however, mostly very different from those she wrote to her family—careful, punctuated, over-polite and rather sedate.[3] The letters to her family, on the other hand, are spontaneous, informal, and often ungrammatical and incorrect over facts ('As to accuracy, I can compare myself only to the sailor who "would never quarrel for a handful of degrees" ').[4] Though her essays and novels are composed in an elegant and well controlled style, the letters she wrote in the later part of her life are so conversational and parenthetical that no one could turn them into correct English without substantial re-writing.

It would not be true to say that if she was careless in composition she was also careless of what she said. 'I beg you will not *hawk* my letters about. I could not write to you with ease if I did not feel sure that I was writing for *you* only and my aunt of course',[5] she wrote to her cousin Sophy Ruxton as early as 1802. In 1805 she put it more plainly:

[1] *The Letters of Sir Walter Scott 1825–1826*, ed. H. J. C. Grierson (1935), 237.

[2] ME to Etienne Dumont, 7 Aug. 1813.

[3] The only letters I have read which at all resemble her family letters are those addressed to Sir P. Crampton, now in the Library of Trinity College, Dublin.

[4] *Private Letter Books of Sir Walter Scott*, ed. Partington (1930), 269–70: letter of ME, 8 Apr. 1825.

[5] ME to Sophy Ruxton, 25 Sept. 1802.

> My dear kind aunt! She thinks, 'Such a letter will do my little niece Maria credit, and I *will* show it'. But what is the consequence of this? Maria when she writes to aunt Ruxton must look before she leaps, which is a thing she does not like to do and she must consider whether such and such a thing is fit to be said to Mrs. This and Mrs. T'other as well as to aunt Ruxton and whilst she is weighing consequences the genius of nonsense takes his flight and instead of that open-hearted open-mouthed laughter loving little fellow comes one, trim, spruce, full dressed with cautious and mincing gait, the genius of familiar epistles.[1]

But she continued to suffer from her letters being shewn.[2] In a period when communications were relatively poor it was inevitable that the letters from absent members of a household should be circulated to supplement the newspapers and the Edgeworths at home complained to Maria's younger companions as well if their letters were not 'public enough'.

Maria Edgeworth disapproved strongly of the publication of letters and left strict instructions against the publication of her own.

> What I wish to have published I write for publication—but not private letters. Those are always for the persons to whom I address them only. I think the publication of letters may lead to all manner of affectation in letter writing and to the destruction of all private confidence. In my own case I am sure I could not write naturally or with any ease or pleasure if I even *thought* of my letters being published—One eye squinting to the public and celebrity and the other looking or pretending to look only to my dear friend or correspondant.[3]
>
> I own it is a sacrifice to give up the chance of reading some admirable private letters. But why is this reading so delightful? Because we flatter ourselves we get behind the scenes into the private life and character and inmost souls of the writers. Had they thought we should read how differently would they have written. *So* I have no objection

[1] ME to Sophy Ruxton, 26 Feb. 1805.

[2] See below, p. 47, and also ME to Dumont, 7 Aug. 1813, and Dumont to ME, 6 Sept. 1813: 'recevant une lettre d'Edgeworthstown, j'ai lu un paragraphe ou deux pour faire comme, tout le monde, et ne pas refuser ce qui etoit attendu ou [? et] desiré.' The tone of a few letters suggests they were written for circulation, e.g. the account of Newgate (pp. 373–5).

[3] ME to A. Cunningham, 27 July 1842 (National Library of Ireland MS. 8145 (IX)). The letter is apropos of Cunningham's desire to publish her letters to David Wilkie.

to treat myself to reading very old letters which come from old receptacles heaven knows how and when I can wash my hands at all events of any share in the treachery.[1]

With a justified mistrust of contemporary editors she said: 'Garbling destroys the value, not only the texture but the value of *wholeness*, the *integrity*, the unity of purpose, sentiment, mind.'[1]

There must, however, have been pressure on the family to provide some kind of biography fairly soon after Maria's death in 1849. Mrs. Edgeworth with her daughters Harriet Butler and Lucy Robinson set to work and in 1867, two years after Mrs. Edgeworth's own death at the age of ninety-six, *A Memoir of Maria Edgeworth* appeared in a privately printed edition. The bulk of the work on the letters can only have been done by Harriet and Lucy, though the earlier parts of the connecting narrative at any rate must be based on material which Mrs. Edgeworth provided. The *Life and Letters* published by Augustus Hare in 1894 is almost entirely drawn from this earlier book. He had had no access to the manuscript family letters which had passed from Harriet (Mrs. Richard Butler) and Lucy (Mrs. Robinson) to the daughter of their brother Pakenham, Harriet Jessie (Mrs. A. G. Butler); the latter felt herself still bound by the original ban on publication.

In preparing their book, Maria's two sisters had distorted the text, partly by the process of selection, partly by correcting the English, and partly in order to avoid hurting the feelings of living persons. 'On lui saurait gré for all her charity', wrote Harriet once, 'when one sees how she could tomahawk.'[2] Harriet and her sister would print, for example, no unfavourable remark about the Pakenhams, their connections and neighbours in County Longford; the reader may infer that the Duke of Wellington was less than kind to his wife Kitty Pakenham, but is not told that Maria feared that the Duchess had wept his affections away. Their selection of the letters, moreover, was dictated by the character of Maria as they knew her, and even their mother Mrs. Edgeworth did not know her till she was thirty years old.

[1] ME to Mrs. Lazarus, 22 Mar. 1827.
[2] Harriet Butler to MPE, 11 Dec. 1841.

Their attractive account can be much supplemented from the surviving letters of the other Edgeworths, the material for an enormous family chronicle. Life at Edgeworthstown was not static. In the sixty-seven years Maria lived there the circle round her was constantly changing as children were born, grew up, went into the world or died. And neither the personalities nor the opinions of Richard Lovell Edgeworth and his daughter remained unaltered during the period.

Subsequent writers on Maria Edgeworth have been restricted by the limitations of their own knowledge and by their own tastes and those of the period in which they wrote. What I have tried to do in editing these letters is to allow Maria Edgeworth to speak for herself, and not to interpose subjective editorial judgements of my own; her over-enthusiastic comments on some people, e.g. on her Sneyd connections and on Lady Elizabeth Whitbread, may seem tedious at times but they are part of the whole picture. With such a mass of material available some principle of selection had to be adopted if the result was to be a book of manageable size. Although the letters written from Maria's home contain much that is of interest on the writing of her books, three-quarters of them concern domestic life at Edgeworthstown House. Those which she wrote while travelling have a far more concentrated interest and give a vivid picture of a much wider range of society as well as of their writer, even if they provide little information about her books, and by their nature obscure the fact that Maria Edgeworth's family and her Irish home meant more to her than anyone or anything else.

I have begun with a visit of 1813 because the earlier letters written from England[1] are almost completely if inaccurately printed in the *Memoir* and by Hare. For reasons of space it has not been possible to reproduce the letters as a whole, and I have omitted passages concerning: (*a*) prospective itineraries; (*b*) postal arrangements; (*c*) news of Edgeworthstown servants settled in England; (*d*) some, but not all, shopping arrangements; (*e*) repetitious matter (when letters to two people were

[1] A fairly full selection of the letters from Scotland in 1823 was printed in R. F. Butler, 'Maria Edgeworth, Unpublished Letters and Sir Walter Scott', *Review of English Studies*, N.S. ix, no. 33 (Feb. 1958). I hope to publish the letters from France at some later date.

written on or about the same date and one is omitted this has sometimes meant losing a few minor remarks which were not repeated); (*f*) long effusions of family sentiment and purely family news, e.g. Fanny's love affair in 1819 and her health throughout.[1] For the purpose of setting the scene I have left in rather more family affairs in the earlier than in the later letters. When any other type of material has been left out I have indicated its nature. At the end I have added a small arbitrary selection, mostly of new material, from the letters written on visits of 1840–1 and 1843–4. Maria Edgeworth was then an old woman; she moved in a much more restricted social circle and her letters, never compressed, became tiresomely long-winded, even if on occasion she could write as well as ever.[2]

v. *Maria Edgeworth's Family Circle 1813–1844*

(These notes are intended merely to give sufficient biographical detail to explain references in the letters.)

Richard Lovell Edgeworth, F.R.S. (1744–1817), her father, m. 1. Anna Maria (d. 1773), dau. of Paul Elers of Black Bourton, Oxon. 2. Honora (1751–80), dau. of Major Edward Sneyd of Byrkley Lodge, Staffs. 3. Elizabeth (1753–97), dau. of Major Edward Sneyd of Byrkley Lodge, Staffs. 4. Frances Anne Beaufort. R. L. Edgeworth described himself as a middling country gentleman; at his death in 1817 he had an income of about £3,700–£4,000 p.a., but when he moved to Ireland in 1782 it had been perhaps half that amount. While he lived in England he had been a member of the Lunar Society of Birmingham, whose primary interest was in the application of science to industry.[3] His own special interests were chiefly in transport engineering, the design of roads, and vehicles, but he was also deeply concerned with the theory of education and became a member of the Irish Committee on Education. He was co-author with his daughter of *Practical Education* and *Professional Education*. Because of his wider opportunities as a man he was a more interesting and open-minded person than Maria, but his reputation has been much obscured by the pompous prefaces which he

[1] For Fanny's love affair, see below, p. 152.

[2] e.g. the letter of 2 Feb. 1844, describing the opening of Parliament, is in its manuscript form nearly double the length of the extracts here printed.

[3] See R. E. Schofield, *The Lunar Society* (1963).

added to her works, and by the fact that, for differing reasons, he was not a popular man either in Ireland or in London society: in Ireland he was too educated and too unconvivial for his neighbours and, while participating in local and national politics, rejected their notorious venality;[1] in London he was thought by many to be an egotistic and boisterous bore.[2] But his lively mind and warm-hearted affection won him the devotion of his own family and his influence on Maria cannot be over-estimated. If he taught her to moralize he also passed on to her his own interest in the Irish, their way of life, and their turns of phrase,[3] and without his constant encouragement it is unlikely that she would have published anything.

Mrs. Frances Anne Edgeworth (1769–1865), dau. of the Revd. D. A. Beaufort. She married R. L. Edgeworth in 1798 and became, with Sophy Ruxton, Maria's greatest friend among her own contemporaries. Before her marriage she had provided some illustrations for Maria's *The Parent's Assistant* and after it she taught herself to make engineering drawings for her husband. Like Maria, she helped with the management of the estate.

Emmeline Edgeworth (1770–1847), dau. of R. L. Edgeworth and Anna Maria Elers. m. (1802) John King or Konig of Clifton, a surgeon of Swiss origin who was assistant to Dr. Beddoes of the Pneumatic Institution. She had two daughters, Zoe and Emmeline (m. Dr. Gibbons). Her father described her as 'an agreeable animal', but her letters are not stupid.

Anna Edgeworth (1773–1824), dau. of R. L. Edgeworth and Anna Maria Elers. m. (1794) Dr. Thomas Beddoes of the Pneumatic Institution, Clifton (see *D.N.B.*). She had four children, Anna, Mary, Thomas Lovell, the poet (1803–49) (see *D.N.B.*), and Henry, a sailor. She was regarded by her family, justly, as flighty, but her letters show intelligence and charm.

[1] 'He was looked on as crazed in the county of Longford': MS. marginal note in a copy of Grace Oliver's *A Study of Maria Edgeworth* (1882) which belonged to a former Edgeworthstown curate, the Revd. James Lyster.

[2] His offence seems particularly to have been in talking down the wits. Some of the sourest stories originate from Rogers and Croker and must be discounted, but there can be no denying the unpopularity.

[3] As shown, for example, in *Essay on Irish Bulls* (1802) by R. L. and Maria Edgeworth.

Lovell Edgeworth (1775–1842), only son of R. L. Edgeworth by Honora Sneyd. He succeeded his father as owner of Edgeworthstown in 1817 and set up an unusual school[1] there which took boys from both Catholic and Protestant, middle- and lower-class families. He was a gifted teacher and originally a man of some force of character,[2] but he was incompetent in estate business and his unfortunate experiences as an internee in France from 1803 to 1814 had led him to drink, which in his later years took a complete hold on him. He was so heavily in debt by 1826 that, to save the incomes of the rest of the family, Maria was obliged to take over the management of the estate from him, and after further troubles in 1833 he sold his interest in the property to his brother C. S. Edgeworth and went to live at Ruthin.

Henry Edgeworth (1782–1813), eldest son of R. L. Edgeworth and Elizabeth Sneyd. He was a doctor, educated at Edinburgh. He died of tuberculosis after a long illness, during which he was partly insane.

Charles Sneyd Edgeworth (1786–1864), son of R. L. Edgeworth and Elizabeth Sneyd. m. (1813) Henrica (Harriette) Broadhurst (d. 1846). He was a lawyer, educated at Trinity College, Dublin. Both he and his wife were valetudinarian, and after his father's death he abandoned his profession. His interests were literary and he wrote a life of the Abbé Edgeworth.

Honora Edgeworth (1791–1858), only surviving dau. of R. L. Edgeworth and Elizabeth Sneyd. m. (1838) Francis Beaufort (see p. xxxvi). She was retiring and dependable, 'everybody's confidante and councillor', but less lively than most of her half-sisters. She helped Maria with the children's books written in the 1820s, copying, editing, and correcting proofs.

William Edgeworth (1794–1829), youngest child of R. L. Edgeworth and Elizabeth Sneyd. He was a rail and road engineer (he laid out the spectacular road from Killarney to Glengariff). He was very intelligent but, like almost all Elizabeth Sneyd's

[1] See H. J. and H. E. Butler, *The Black Book of Edgeworthstown* (1927), 218–22; D. Clarke, *The Ingenious Mr. Edgeworth* (1965), 237–9; *Familiar Letters of Sir W. Scott*, ed. Douglas (1894), ii. 319–20; MS. appendix by ME to Black Book of Edgeworthstown (Irish State Paper Office).

[2] See below, p. 210 n.

children, lacked 'push', a quality very necessary in his profession at that date. He had some kind of mental breakdown of over a year in 1818–20 but recovered completely.

Frances Maria Edgeworth (Fanny) (1799–1848), eldest dau. of R. L. Edgeworth and Frances Beaufort. m. (1829) Lestock Peach Wilson. She was Maria's favourite sister. Her letters, though factually informative, are mostly very reticent and her attraction does not come through. Her chief interests were science and politics. She had bad health.

Henrietta Edgeworth (Harriet) (1801–89), dau. of R. L. Edgeworth and Frances Beaufort. m. (1826) the Revd. Richard Butler, Vicar of Trim, an Irish antiquary. Scott described her to Joanna Baillie as 'kind natured clever Harriet'.[1] She was the most vigorous and practical of the Edgeworth sisters, with a lively and impetuous tongue as well.

Sophia Edgeworth (1803–37), dau. of R. L. Edgeworth and Frances Beaufort. m. (1824) her cousin Barry Fox. She was the least intellectual of Mrs. Frances Edgeworth's children. Her four children were Maxwell, Waller, Mary Anne, and Charlotte.

Lucy Edgeworth (1805–97), dau. of R. L. Edgeworth and Frances Beaufort. m. (1843) the Revd. T. R. Robinson, F.R.S., of Armagh Observatory (see *D.N.B.*). She was for many years immobilized by a spinal complaint.

Francis Beaufort Edgeworth (1809–46), son of R. L. Edgeworth and Frances Beaufort. m. (1831) Rosa Florentina Eroles. He was at Charterhouse from 1819 to 1826 and at Trinity College, Cambridge, from Oct. 1826 to Dec. 1828. He went down without a degree, being unwilling to master the necessary mathematics, and went abroad determined to be 'a philosopher and a poet'. He eventually settled down at Edgeworthstown and acted as agent for his brother.

Michael Pakenham Edgeworth, F.R.S. (1812–81), youngest child of R. L. Edgeworth and Frances Beaufort. m. (1846) Christina Macpherson. He was at Charterhouse from 1823 to 1828 and at

[1] *Letters of Sir Walter Scott 1823–1825*, ed. H. J. C. Grierson (1935), 240.

Hertford College (Haileybury) from 1829 to 1830. He became an Indian civilian and a botanist of some distinction (see *D.N.B.*).

Mary Sneyd (1750–1841) and *Charlotte Sneyd* (1754–1822) (Aunts Mary and Charlotte), sisters-in-law of R. L. Edgeworth. They spent most of their time at Edgeworthstown.

Margaret Ruxton (1746–1830) (Aunt Ruxton), sister of R. L. Edgeworth. m. (1770) John Ruxton of Black Castle, Co. Meath. She stood almost in the relation of a mother to Maria who was devotedly fond of her. Physically she was very like her brother and shared many of his tastes but she attached much more importance to manners and to class distinctions.

Sophy Ruxton (1776–1837), elder dau. of the above. After Mrs. Edgeworth she was Maria's most intimate friend and correspondent. She was strong-minded and independent and Maria's most influential literary critic outside the Edgeworthstown circle.

Margaret Ruxton (d. 1854), younger dau. of Margaret and John Ruxton.

Richard Ruxton (1775–1840), son of Margaret and John Ruxton. m. (1807) Elizabeth Selina Staples (Bess). After inheriting money from an uncle he changed his name to Fitzherbert.

The Revd. Daniel Augustus Beaufort (1739–1821), father-in-law of R. L. Edgeworth. He was Vicar of Collon and a distinguished Irish topographer and cartographer (see *D.N.B.*).

Mrs. Beaufort (1739–1831), Mary (*née* Waller), wife of the above.

The Revd. William Beaufort (1771–1849), Rector of Glanmire, Co. Cork, elder son of the Revd. D. A. Beaufort.

Captain (*later Admiral*) *Francis Beaufort* (1774–1857), younger son of the Revd. D. A. Beaufort; K.C.B., F.R.S. m. 1. Alicia Wilson. 2. Honora Edgeworth. He wrote *Karamania* (1817) and later became Hydrographer to the Navy (see *D.N.B.*).

Henrietta Beaufort (Harriet) (1778–1865), dau. of the Revd. D. A. Beaufort. She was the anonymous author of *Dialogues on Botany* (1819) and *Bertha's Journal* (1829).

Louisa Catherine Beaufort (1791–1867), dau. of the Revd. D. A. Beaufort. She was the author of an essay on the Round Towers of Ireland for which she was elected an honorary member of the Royal Irish Academy.

Elizabeth Waller (Aunt Bess) (d. 1835), Mrs. Beaufort's sister. She lived at 31 Merrion St., Dublin, 'l'hotel d'Amitié'.

VI. *Chonological details of Maria Edgeworth's life before her English visit of 1813*[1]

1768 1 January	ME born at Black Bourton, Oxon.
1768–early 1771	The Edgeworths lived at Hare Hatch, Berks.
1771 spring and summer	The Edgeworths stayed with Thomas Day at Stow Hill, nr. Lichfield.
autumn	RLE went to France leaving his wife and family at Black Bourton. His wife joined him at Lyons in 1772.
1773 March	Death of ME's mother Anna Maria E in childbirth.
17 July	RLE married Honora Sneyd at Lichfield.
1773–early 1776	The Edgeworths lived in Ireland at Edgeworthstown, Co. Longford.
1775 autumn	ME went to Mrs. Latuffiere's school at Derby.
1776–autumn 1779	The Edgeworths lived at North-church, Herts.
1779 October–1780 April	The Edgeworths lived at Beigher-ton, Salop.
1779?	ME spent her Christmas holidays with Miss C. Sneyd at Lichfield
1780 30 April	Death of Mrs. Honora E.
summer	RLE and his children went to Scar-borough with the Sneyds.
25 December	RLE married Elizabeth Sneyd in London.
1781 February?	ME went to Mrs. Devis's school in Upper Wimpole St., London.

[1] These details are taken from *Memoir of Maria Edgeworth* (privately printed 1867); *Memoirs of R. L. Edgeworth* (1820); and the surviving family letters, which sometimes provide a different and more reliable date.

1781–1782	The Edgeworths lived first at Northchurch and then at Davenport Hall, Cheshire. ME spent some holidays at Anningsley, Surrey, at the house of Thomas Day.
1782 June	The Edgeworths returned to Ireland to live at Edgeworthstown.
1783	*Adelaide and Theodore* (translation by ME from Madame de Genlis)[1] printed but withdrawn before publication.
1791 autumn	The Edgeworths went to stay at Clifton.
1792 12 October–5 November	ME paid a visit to her school friend Mrs. C. Hoare in London, returning to Clifton via Bath.
1793 autumn	The Edgeworths returned to Edgeworthstown from Clifton.
1795	Publication of ME's *Letters for Literary Ladies*.
1796	Publication of *The Parent's Assistant*.[2]
1797 November	Death of Mrs. Elizabeth Edgeworth.
1798 31 May	RLE married Frances Anne Beaufort. Publication of *Practical Education* by RLE and ME.
1799 April	ME, RLE, and Mrs. E went to England.[3] They spent a week in the Midlands, sightseeing at various factories. They stayed at Hill Top, nr. Birmingham, with James Keir, F.R.S., the chemist. They then went south, passing through Oxford and Slough, where they saw William Herschel's great telescope.

[1] No copy of this can now be located but C. S. Edgeworth owned one volume *c.* 1860.

[2] There is no known copy of the 1st edition. It is advertised as just published in *Letters for Literary Ladies* (1795), but in an undated letter of *c.* 19 Mar. 1796 (*Mem.* i. 73) to Sophy Ruxton ME talks as if the book was not yet out.

[3] Almost all ME's letters written on this visit are missing, but some of Mrs. Edgeworth's survive.

	c. 29 April	ME, RLE, and Mrs. E arrived in London where they spent a fortnight, mostly in sightseeing. They met Mrs. Barbauld, Dr. C. Burney, Mrs. Bicknell, and their publisher Joseph Johnson.
	c. 14 May	ME, RLE, and Mrs. E left London for Clifton.
	5 June	Birth of Fanny Edgeworth at Clifton.
	end of July	ME, RLE, and Mrs. E left Clifton, travelling by Chepstow and Hereford to stay at Hill Top with James Keir. From there they visited the Darwin family at Derby.
	September	ME, RLE, and Mrs. E returned to Edgeworthstown.
1800		Publication of *Castle Rackrent*.
1801		Publication of *Early Lessons*, *Belinda*, and *Moral Tales*.
1802	October–1803 March	ME with RLE, Mrs. E, and Charlotte E visited France. Marriage proposal to ME by A. N. C. Edelcrantz. On their way from Holyhead to Dover the Edgeworths visited Josiah Wedgwood II, Erasmus Darwin's widow, and one of the Strutts, probably William.
1803	March–April	ME, RLE, Mrs. E, and Charlotte E visited Edinburgh and Glasgow.
1804		Publication of *Popular Tales*.
1805		Publication of *The Modern Griselda*.
1806		Publication of *Leonora*.
1809		Publication of 1st series of *Tales of Fashionable Life* and *Essays on Professional Education* (under RLE's name).
1812		Publication of 2nd series of *Tales of Fashionable Life*.

VII. *The Family of Richard Lovell Edgeworth*

By his 1st wife Anna Maria Elers	By his 2nd wife Honora Sneyd	By his 3rd wife Elizabeth Sneyd	By his 4th wife Frances Anne Beaufort
Richard 1764–96	Honora 1774–90	Elizabeth 1781–1800	Frances Maria 1799–1848
Lovell b. and d. 1766	Lovell 1775–1842	Charlotte 1783–1807	Sophia 1803–37
Maria 1768–1849		Henry 1782–1813	Harriet 1801–89
Emmeline 1770–1847		Sophia b. and d. 1784	Lucy Jane 1805–97
Anna Maria 1773–1824		Charles Sneyd 1786–1864	Francis Beaufort 1809–46
		William 1788–90	Michael Pakenham 1812–81
		Thomas Day 1789–92	
		Honora 1791–1858	
		William 1794–1829	

VIII. *The Text*

When Mrs. Edgeworth and her daughters compiled *A Memoir of Maria Edgeworth* they allowed themselves considerable liberties with their material; the text of letters was not only corrected, punctuated, and embellished, but letters of different dates and to different persons were conflated and no omissions of any kind were indicated. Over 100 of the letters here printed are entirely new, besides portions of many others. Except for the letters of 1813 the text is taken from the original letters in my possession.[1] The letters of 1813 are in the National Library of Ireland and are printed with the kind permission of the Director. The manuscript of a few letters given in the *Memoir* has not survived and in these cases I have used Mrs. Edgeworth's text of 1867.

Except when written to her older relations such as Mrs. Ruxton and Dr. Beaufort, Maria Edgeworth's letters to her family

[1] These letters descended through Maria's sisters Harriet (Mrs. Richard Butler) and Lucy (Mrs. Robinson) to their niece Harriet Jessie (Mrs. A. G. Butler), only daughter of M. Pakenham Edgeworth, and from her to my father Harold Edgeworth Butler.

were extremely careless. She wrote conversationally, in a hurry, and she does not seem to have re-read often before despatch; her muddles over names were a byword in the family—she mistook them, she spelt them wrongly, and not in a uniform manner; and her punctuation consisted largely of dashes. For visual reasons I have reduced the number of dashes, either by leaving them out or by substituting full stops and question marks as appropriate. I have also rationalized her use of inverted commas and sometimes disregarded her paragraphing, which appears to have little significance. Obvious English mis-spellings have been corrected but fairly consistent idiosyncratic spellings have been left. As far as possible proper names have been corrected and systematized. Dates in square brackets have been added by myself or by Lucy Robinson (*née* Edgeworth) whose additions and emendations are marked with a †. I hope I have made the minimum alterations necessary for the comfort of the reader without impairing the spontaneity of the original letters. Omissions by editor (see above, pp. xxxi–xxxii) have been indicated by three dots (. . .).

Although I have consulted a large number of people it has unfortunately not been possible to identify all Maria Edgeworth's frequently inaccurate quotations; a few of the untraced lines may have come from family verses now lost. Notes relating to persons will normally be found in the Biographical Index.

IX. *Acknowledgements*

My first debt is to my mother, Mrs. H. E. Butler, and to my aunts, the Misses O. and R. F. Butler, who made most of these letters available to me and have helped me continually with advice and family information. The Director of the National Library of Ireland not only gave permission for the publication of the 1813 letters, but very kindly deposited them temporarily in the Bodleian Library for my use and provided me with copies of letters of other members of the Edgeworth family belonging to the same period.

Maria Edgeworth's interests were very wide ranging and obviously I could not have annotated her letters without the assistance of many other people, too numerous to mention by name.

I owe much to the patient helpfulness of my husband's colleagues who have endured my questions for so long. In particular I should like to thank W. G. Moore who elucidated many of the French references, Charles Morgenstern who answered theatrical queries, Trevor Levere who provided much of the material for the scientific footnotes, my cousin Edgar Macdonald who helped with American material, J. S. G. Simmons, and Michael Hurst who was writing his *Maria Edgeworth and the Public Scene* at the same time. I am grateful to Miss Clare Weld and Miss Eleanor Chance for help with typing. Without the hospitality and resources of the Bodleian Library and the courtesy and kindness of its staff this book would have been impossible.

Finally I owe a special debt to my sister-in-law Marilyn Butler for her encouragement and for the information and advice she has given me throughout. Few people read Maria Edgeworth today and to work alongside someone else who found equal enjoyment and interest in the subject was an immeasurable stimulus in the undertaking.

x. *Abbreviations*

E	Edgeworth
CSE	Charles Sneyd Edgeworth
ME	Maria Edgeworth
MPE	Michael Pakenham Edgeworth
RLE	Richard Lovell Edgeworth
Mem.	*A Memoir of Maria Edgeworth*, ed. Mrs. Edgeworth (1867)
Memoirs of RLE	*Memoirs of R. L. Edgeworth* (1820)

1813

MARIA EDGEWORTH had seen nothing of London 'Society' since, shy and unknown, she had stayed with her school friend Mrs. Charles Hoare in 1792[1] and now, after the publication of *Tales of Fashionable Life* in 1809 and 1812, she was at the height of her reputation. Her father had long wished to visit London with his daughter but it was only in 1813 that family circumstances made this possible; no doubt, justly proud of Maria, he wanted to have the pleasure of lionizing her. With his wife and daughter he now spent three and a half months in England, visiting their family and friends as well as passing six weeks in London. Probably not all the letters written by Maria during this time survive. For example, much of what happened in the latter part of their stay we know only from Mrs. Edgeworth's summary in the *Memoir*;[2] no account remains of the day spent in the country with the Romillys, the meeting with Mrs. Abington, or the breakfast with Byron. After leaving London the three Edgeworths visited Maria's sisters Emmeline King and Anna Beddoes at Clifton and Malvern and old friends at Gloucester and Perrystone Court, Herefordshire. Finally they went to Derby to meet Sneyd Edgeworth's fiancée Henrica Broadhurst.

To Miss Mary Sneyd

Bangor Ferry, Wednesday, 31 March 1813

I will go and write a few lines of a letter to my dear Aunt Mary and—Oh why should you write *now* my dear? You have nothing

N.B. Explanations relating to persons will normally be found in the Biographical Index.

[1] See above, Introduction, p. xv. She spent some days in London in 1799 and again in 1802 and 1803 on her way to and from France but she does not seem to have gone into society on any of these occasions.

[2] *Mem.* i. 287.

new to tell her. Nothing new—but I love her and wish to write to her and if I did not love her I should be worse than Caliban. Well write only a few lines. That is just what I mean to do, and to go on with my letter at any odd place where we *stop the night*.

Honora will tell you all we saw at Howth, so I go on from Holyhead. Breakfasted with Mr. Grainger who was so agreeable that my father disordered a chaise on purpose to go on in the mail with him. This mail coach very comfortable held but four inside, so we were all to ourselves. My father says he never received so much pleasure in his life from any eatable as from a china orange which Mr. Grainger gave him just at the moment when his mouth was parched with thirst. This orange quite recovered him from the remaining effects of sea-sickness and then he was ready to converse and to enjoy this gentleman's conversation. I wish you had heard him speak of Sophy Ruxton. He says she is the most agreeable, sensible, charming young woman he has seen in Ireland. He declared he was quite enchanted with her and bid me tell her so. If he had not lived abroad he never would have ventured to speak with such enthusiasm. He says he shall go to Paris and he will I am sure do all he can for Lovell.[1] He has lived in good or at least high company abroad—Prince de Neufchatel—Berthier—and the D'Arembergs—told us a variety of entertaining anecdotes. Caulaincourt now duc de Vicenza was brought up in the family of the Prince de Condé—l'enfant de la maison the playfellow of the Duc d'Enghien. Bonaparte employed Caulaincourt to seize the Duc d'Enghien and the wretch did so and has been repaid by a dukedom. We asked how the present Empress is liked in France. 'Not at all by the Parisians. She is too haughty—has the Austrian scornful lip and sits back in her carriage when she goes through the streets.' The Parisians used to make these complaints against Antoinette.[2] On

[1] Lovell Edgeworth was a prisoner of war in France. Repeated unsuccessful attempts were made to secure his return home but he was eventually allowed to move from Verdun to Paris. It was not generally possible for the English to travel in France at this time but permits were given, for example, to some scientists (De Beer, *The Sciences were never at war* (1960)). I have not been able to identify Mr. Grainger.

[2] Queen Marie Antoinette was, like the Empress Marie Louise, an Austrian archduchess.

what small things the popularity of the high and mighty depend. Mr. Grainger thinks there will soon be a counter revolution in France.

Josephine is living very happily and amusing herself with her garden and shrubberies. It is a curious circumstance that this cidevant Empress and Kennedy & Co the London nursery man are now as Mr. Grainger says in partnership. She has a license to send him what shrubs and flower seeds she chuses from France and he has license to send her cargos in return. Mr. Grainger saw great cargos arrive from him. I dare not go on with more of his anecdotes lest they should fill all my paper. He seems a most good natured benevolent *shrewd man of the world.* He will carry over Madame Recamier's box for me and is glad to do it as M. Recamier has obliged him. We parted from Mr. Grainger at Bangor Ferry and were very sorry for it. He went on in the mail. He will see us again in London. I wrote to my aunt Ruxton this morning to say we had met Mr. Grainger.

At Bangor Ferry at the inn door we saw a most curiously packed curricle with all manner of portmanteaus and hats slung in various ingenious ways—behind the springs two baskets, the size and shape of Lady Elizabeth Pakenham's basket—A huge bunch of white feathers sticking out from one end of one of the baskets as we approached to examine out came the live head of a white peacock—a Japan peacock—On the other side a Japan peahen. The gentleman to whom the carriage belonged appeared next carrying on a perch or stand made to fasten behind the carriage a large fine macaw! The servant who was harnessing the horse would not tell to whom the carriage belonged. He always replied to all enquirers 'It belongs to that there gentleman'. An impertinent vulgarian with his chin buried in a figured yellow handkerchief went on saying 'Its the most *curous* concern ever I *seed.* I should a'thought it belonged to the Marquis of Sligo for he's the most curous man I know in all England. Only for the horse in't good enough for he.' We have not been able to settle whether the master of this equipage is a gentleman—a gentleman's gentleman or a shewer of wild beasts but my father is decided he is a man of no literature as he had never heard of Miss Edgeworth or her works.

N B. My father has left directions with Francis Beaufort about the part of patronage[1] that is to come to Dublin from Dr. Beaufort and also proper instructions about the trunk.

Tomorrow we go to the slate quarries spend morning there and sleep at Capel Curig. Good night. I am perfectly well—not the least tired—have enjoyed this fine day—had a delightful walk before dinner in a hanging wood—by the water side—pretty sheep paths—wood anemones in abundance with their white flowers in full blow—two ploughs going in a field below the wood—very chearful—the sound of the Welchmen's voices talking to their plough horses. The plough giving the idea of culture and civilization contrasted agreeably with the wildness of the wood and mountains.

We shall be at Dr. Darwin's Shrewsbury on Saturday—Good night again.

Thursday. How fortunate we have been as to the winds and weather. Last night was a violent storm of wind and thunder and lightening. This morning all was bright and after a breakfast of muffins 'very good and very hot too' we set out for the slate quarries.[2] Stopped at Mr. Worthington's nice neat house the front of which is all slate plaistered over so as to look like beautiful stone. Mrs. Worthington received us hospitably and spoke in high terms of Sneyd and William. Sneyd she said was a most amiable youth and William 'no doubt was a young man of great talents'. She added Mr. Worthington's opinion that he would certainly succeed in the world. Mr. Worthington to our disappointment was not at home; he is at Liverpool. With Mrs. Worthington was visitor a Mrs. Waterson, who had got up at 5 o clock this morning, or some morning lately, to read Vivian.[3] My father of course liked her much. We proceeded to the slate mills; in our way saw the inclined planes and little carts full of

[1] *Patronage*, a novel by ME published early in 1814. This refers to the manuscript, substantially written before she came to England, but not finally completed till after her return to Ireland. It was ME's practice to circulate her manuscripts among her relatives.

[2] At Capel Curig. There were slate quarries in Co. Longford which RLE would have liked to see reopened.

[3] *Vivian* forms vol. iv of ME's *Tales of Fashionable Life* (1812).

slates running down. Tell William that we were much pleased with the sawing mill—particularly with the screw and wheel which keep the saw down upon the blocks of slate. I will not here attempt to describe any of the machinery to you; but I *trust* I have the principal parts of it by my fathers clear explanations fixed in my memory. Tell William we saw the cutting engine and saw the men splitting the slates and took our time, full time to see every thing quite at leisure. The road to the slate mills is most beautiful. It goes by the side of a glenn at the bottom of which is a stream flowing over such rocky and uneven ground that it forms a continued cascade. The rail ways[1] are above six miles long. They are very narrow; I had formed an idea of their being much more *magnificent*; but it seems that in this country canals and rail ways are made as useful and as little splendid as possible. I was surprised to see the rail ways winding round the rocks and going over heaps of rubbish in many places where you would think a wheelbarrow could scarcely go. We went on from the Mills to the slate quarries. We had been admiring the beauty of landscape and the sublimity of the Welch mountains, my father did not say anything to raise my expectations, but when we arrived near the place he took me by the hand and led me over a hill of rubbish of slates on the top of which was a rail way. We walked on till we came between two slate *mountains* and soon found ourselves in the midst of the slate quarries. It was the most sublime sight of all the works of man I ever beheld. It is like a mine above ground. The height of slate rock on each side of the *terrace* on which we stood appeared to me about 70 feet and below us thirty feet deeper we saw men at work quarrying. The men looked like pigmies in the midst of these vast works. There is a curious cone of greyish colored slate which the workmen say is good for nothing, but it is good for something. It has a sublime and picturesque appearance. Mrs E has made a sketch of it. We saw one man with a great wooden mallet at one stroke break a mass of slate in two as large as the tea table and as thick as the great bible. While we were in the quarry (I was going to say the *mine* for it is more like a mine

[1] In 1786 RLE had had a project for transporting gravel, coal, and iron ore in Ireland on railways. He used them for carrying limestone on his own estate (*Memoirs of RLE* (2nd ed. 1821), 62–5).

than a quarry) a heavy shower of hail came on which falling between the rifts of the rocks and blown by the high wind added to the sublimity of the scene. We were comfortably sheltered in one of the slate sheds in which the workmen sit to split slates. Upon the whole I was much more pleased than I had expected. I was actually silenced with admiration of the sublime both in nature and art. I was astonished that *art* could appear sublime in the midst of the sublimity of nature. Forgive me aunt for turning up here.[1]

Finding that Mr. Worthington is at Liverpool my father has decided to go to Liverpool so we shall write to say that we cannot be at Derby or Byrkley Lodge on saturday or tuesday. We have come on to Conway at which place I now write. We proceed to Holywell and Chester. I said the weather had been favorable to us but I forgot to tell you that during the storm of last night it snowed just enough to cover the tops of the Welch mountains with white to encrease the beauty of the prospect for us. They appeared more majestic—strong contrast of bright lights and broad shades—the foreground all green—the *leaves* of the honeysuckles all green in the hedges and fine hollies bright green—primroses in abundance. It was literally 'Spring in the lap of winter'. We stopped at beautiful Aber where there was the prettiest landlady I ever saw with a beautiful sister—eat bread and butter and cheese and excellent pancakes tell Lucy. Quite refitted set out on a delightful sunshining evening to pass Penmaenmawr. My father says that the mountain has considerably altered its appearance since he knew it first—from the falling of masses of rock and the crumbling away of the mighty substance. Cultivation has crept up its sides to a prodigious height. In parts seemingly inaccessible there was pasture. A little cottage nestled just under the mountain's huge stone cap. The fragments of rock that have rolled down, some of them across the road are ten times the size of the rock in Mr. Keating's lawn and in contrast to this idea of danger are sheep and lambs now feeding quietly—the lambs not larger than kittens. One of them I particularly remarked was no larger than little Francis's poor deceased *Muff* or *Tippet*. Neither my father or Mrs. E ever went over Penmaenmawr in the evening, so

[1] This last sentence is written up the side of the page.

that they had never seen it with the western sun upon it and it appeared quite new to them.

We got to Conway in excellent time, 6 o clock in the evening. Mrs. Rous the landlady of the Harp inn recollected my father, Lovell and my aunt Ruxton. She is a nice looking old woman—very like the old mother in the print of Robin Gray. The boy to whom Lovell used to be so good, and who stopped my father the last time he went over Penmaenmawr to tell him that Lovell had given him Lazy Lawrence,[1] was drowned: he was one of many lost on the Ferry boat at Conway in a great storm 5 or 6 years ago.

The old harper who used to be the delight of travellers at this inn is now sitting in an arm chair in the little parlor within the kitchen in a state of dotage. His harp stood in the room in which I slept carefully buckled up in its green cover. At Bangor there was no harper. The waiter told us they were 'no profit to master and was always in the way in the passage so master never let none come now'.

In the midst of all the sublime and beautiful I saw this day I had also a happy mixture of the comic for we had a Welch postillion who entertained us much by his contracted vocabulary and still more contracted sphere of ideas. He and my father could never understand one another because Mr. E called *quarry* quarry and the Welchman called it querry. And continually the Welchman asked us the burthen of all he said 'if we would not like to be driven to Caernarvon'.

Friday morning. 7 o'clock dressed and ready to go on with my scribbling. Before I go on I must assure you my dear kind Aunt Mary that it is a great pleasure, not the least trouble to me to write this letter. I write at odd minutes when the horses are changing—after breakfast and after dinner for a quarter of an hour at a time. You know it is impossible that should tire me. It is worthy of observation to me at least that all my present conveniencies for writing, which are all that any lady can want [are] gifts of various Sneyds.[2] I use Miss Sneyd's pocket ink-stand which has been of continual comfort to me. My ivory cutter penknife is a gift [from] Aunt Charlotte and my little

[1] A story in ME's *The Parent's Assistant* (1796).
[2] See *ME's Family Circle* and *Biographical Index.*

Sappho seal a present of aunt Mary's. I keep them all with the letter I am writing in the ridicule[1] Fanny made for me which never quits my arm and has been, tell her, the joy of my life.

Now to go on with our journey—8 o clock a fine morning walked down to Conway Ferry—The great archway under Conway Castle covered with wall flowers in *full* blow—Very pleasant crossing the ferry. The beautiful view of Conway Castle and the country near it, which has been drawn at least a thousand times, we could not help wishing to be able to draw again just as we now saw it. I said to one of the boatmen, 'You Welchmen have a beautiful country to live in'. 'Yes Ma'am but I wish I was out of it.' 'Where else would you wish to be?' 'With the armies abroad Ma'am where I once was.' 'With whom?—and where?' 'With General Moore Ma'am at Corunna.' 'What did you think of General Moore?' 'I thought he was a brave man and I liked him.' My father then continued the conversation and as I was going ashore I heard only the concluding sentence which was framed as ingeniously for his purpose as any lottery advertisement could be. 'I wish I had some of the dollars we was obliged to throw away at Corunna or one even or a part of one even for I was overworked last night and almost done up but if I had sixpence I could set myself up again with a pot of porter.' My father gave him the sixpence which you will allow he deserved. In our way from Conway to St. Asaph nothing new. In our way from St. Asaph to Holywell we past a beautiful gateway of Wyatts belonging to a Mr. Hughes.[2] Mrs. E took a sketch of it. We went in to look at the prettiest Porters lodge I ever saw—two neat old women who shewed us the inside. Nothing could be more comfortable except that the kitchen fire smoked. 'Ah Madam,' said the old woman, 'these chimnies that be made for beauty do seldom draw well.'

She was a very chearful old woman but I would not change our own good Margery Woods for any porter-ess in Christendom. My father inquired where the iron work of these gates was made and hearing that it was made at Hardinge[3] a town a few

[1] An alternative word for reticule.

[2] Kinmel Park, designed by Samuel Wyatt for the Revd. Edward Hughes.

[3] Hawarden.

miles farther on he stopped there. It soon afterwards began to snow very hard but we stopped nevertheless at the Iron founderies at Hardinge and tell William we wished very much for him to see the boring engines and the punching machine. My father said, 'If my little Francis was three years older I should wish for him. If I live what pleasure I shall have some time in shewing him these things.' As I do not think my Dear Aunt you would wish for details of all I saw even if I were capable of giving them clearly, I will not expatiate but only note that I hope William will hear from the best authority a description of the punching machine with its perpendicular *oval* wheel. My father is to write to this foundery about his iron gates.

Have you had any snow? We had a heavy shower of snow for two hours. The snow was very obliging to us for it came in a part of the country where we had little to see. Even through the snow however we spied the green gooseberry bushes in every cottage garden in full leaf. It would be worth while to plant gooseberry bushes if only for the pleasure of seeing this earliest green bush of the spring. The white thorn—I mean the black thorn is in leaf in the hedges and for miles we have seen such beautiful hollies in the hedges! I wish my aunt Charlotte would be so kind to take a few small hollies out of Wilkinsons garden and have them planted in the new ditch between Woods and Duffy's also some cuttings of honeysuckles and some cuttings of pyracanthus. Enough can be had from my garden. I wish she would ask Deniston to repair the dashing of Connors house.

Adieu my very dear Kind aunt Mary I must finish abruptly—post going—I have been as happy and well as possible. Maria E.

To Mrs. Ruxton

Liverpool, 6 April 1813

Many times since we parted, a hundred times within this week have I wished my dearest Aunt to talk over with you the things and people I have seen. I have been very well, very happy, much entertained and interested and I have longed for my absent friends to share with me the pleasure I have felt.

To Mrs. Ruxton, 6 April 1813

Liverpool is the first great commercial town we have seen since we came to England. It is very fine and very grand and would make a glorious figure in a table of exports and imports, 'the very best town that ever was known to lend or to spend or to give in' but to *live in* the very last I should chuse. All the faces you see money making faces, every creature full drive after their own interest, elbowing, jostling, headlong after money! money! money! The wise ones say that the appearance of business in the streets is not nearly what it was. Then the people must have fairly run over one another. If you ask a question you must *buy* an answer and then it is given in the Lancashire dialect which you can't understand. There is a smell of a ship all over the town of Liverpool pursuing you even to your bedchamber, a much stronger smell of a ship then we had in the packet which brought us to England for that had very little of it. But notwithstanding all this which struck us at first sight, hearing and smell as disagreeable notwithstanding that we were much struck with the contrast between the *gentility* of Chester and Liverpool yet we had soon reason to rejoice that we had come here. My father found out Mr. Roscoe and he was so good to come to see us and he invited us to his house Allerton Hall about seven miles from Liverpool. Mr. Roscoe is a benevolent-looking chearful gentlemanlike old man tall—neither thin nor fat—with a peaked forehead—thick grey hair, *tufty* about the face—rather longer than North the hairdresser would allow it to be—looks as if it was blown by the wind in a picturesque style. He is very like the prints you may have seen of him—his bow courteous but not courtly—his manner frank and prepossessing free from pretension of any kind. He enters into conversation readily and immediately tells something entertaining or interesting—seeming to follow the natural course of his own thoughts or of yours without effort and without any desire to display. He has a quick recollective memory; speaks excellent language but with a strong provincial accent which at once destroys all idea of elegance. This at first disappoints, but in a short time his chearful kindness entirely effaces the recollection of this and even the perception of it. Mrs. Roscoe is an honest-faced, fat, *hearty*, good natured hospitable body, without the least pretensions to polish, but with a downright plain good understanding and uncommonly warm heart which throws out all her thoughts and feelings in broad Lancashire dialect—Almost as broad as Tummas and Meary. She calls her eldest son *Wully* instead of Willy or William &c but she seems so to adore her husband, to be so proud of him and so fond of her children that it is impossible not to like her. She has five sons, and two daughters. One of the sons inherits his fathers poetical talent but neither sons or daughters have any polish of manner or appearance. In short though it is in the power of a father's genius to drag a whole family up in the world, yet unless the mother be a woman of education and good manners it seems impossible to give an air of gentility to the family. Now I have written this I wish to blot it out because it seems ungrateful to make such an observation on a family by whom we were so hospitably received and among whom there appeared such genuine goodness and warm family affection as might well compensate for the want of that politeness which often only conceals the contrary defects.

Mr. Roscoe gave himself up to us the whole day. First he took us to the Botanic garden where I saw many things I had seen before and some which were new to me; but perhaps you and Sophy are well acquainted with them; therefore I shall only just mention the names and if you wish for more can give explanations hereafter—The coffee tree in *red berry*—The sago palm—The palm tree in *fruit and flower*—The cabbage tree—The banana in *fruit*—the papyrus—Venus's flytrap. This is a very curious plant of which you know the description in Darwin.[1] The very intelligent man who shewed it to us says he believes it is the only one in England. It requires much care. He shewed us the fly-catching motion of the plant—impossible to describe.

After seeing this botanic garden and the admirable manner in which it is managed we were surprised to hear from Mr. Roscoe that it has never made since its establishment a single botanist, nor do the ladies and gentlemen delight in it except as a public parade walk to shew themselves to the Prince of Wales when he came there.

From the Botanic garden we proceeded to Allerton Hall, a spacious house in a beautiful situation—Fine library—Every

[1] See Erasmus Darwin, *The Botanic Garden* (1789), Pt. II, The Loves of the Plants, Canto I, p. 139 n.

room filled with pictures, and a gallery of pictures. Some of them Mrs. E says were excellent. Many of them are presents from persons in Italy who admired his Leo the 10th.[1] The gallery tell Margaret is about the size of that of Lord Sunderlin.[2] There is a picture of Tasso so like Mr. Jephson that it might pass for his. By the by it has a sort of mad vigilance in the eyes—looks as if he saw his genius that haunted him that instant at the window. Don't be afraid my dear aunt that I should go through a whole gallery of pictures in this letter or expatiate on what I don't understand; but I may just mention that Mr. Roscoe has I think arranged his collection admirably so as to shew in chronological order and *edifying* gradation the progress of painting. The picture[3] which he prized the most was painted by one of Raphaels masters (Francesco Francia I think) not in the least valuable for its own sake but for a *frieze* below the original picture by Michael Angelo. The picture a holy family is in distemper highly varnished. The frieze about a foot deep represents the destruction of the oracles and Moses breaking the tables. It is a gray color something like the coloring of the figures at the Temple. Mr. Roscoe thinks it is one of Michael Angelo's earliest performances and he says it is *conceded* that this is the only Michael Angelo certainly original in England. Of this I know nothing, but I know that it struck me as full of genius and I longed for you and Margaret when we looked at a portfolio full of Michael Angelo's sketches, drawings and *studies*. It is admirable to see the pains that a really great man takes to improve a first idea. Mr. Roscoe is free from all the cant of a connoisseur and speaks of painting as a philosopher.[4] Turning from the drawings of Michael Angelo to a room full of Fuseli's horribly distorted figures I could not help feeling astonishment not only at the bad taste but at the infinite conceit and presumption of Fuseli! How could this man ever make himself a name? I believe he gave Mr. Roscoe these pictures, else I suppose

[1] Published in 1805.

[2] Baronstown, Co. Meath.

[3] This picture was entirely the work of Aspertini: see Michael Compton, 'William Roscoe and early collectors of Italian Primitives', *Liverpool Bulletin* (Walker Art Gallery Number), vol. 9 (1960–1), pp. 27–57. I am indebted to Mr. Hugh Macandrew of the Ashmolean Museum for this information.

[4] 'and in language which Sir Joshua Reynolds might have used but not the pronunciation' is here crossed out.

they would not be here sprawling their fantastic lengths, like mishapen dreams. Instead of *le beau ideal* they exhibit *le laide ideal.*

Towards dinner time the room filled with sons, tall black eyed bashful young men who spoke not at all. I was a considerable time before I knew them asunder. The eldest a little man a banker, with the most frightened look I ever saw was however the first to enter into conversation and we soon happily found one common subject of interest. *Wully* had been at Harrowgate and had met Mrs. Foster and the two Miss Fosters and he seemed charmed with Miss Laetitia Foster. The mother and sisters agreed with me in preferring Bess. It was very droll to hear Mrs. Roscoe complaining in the broadest of broad Lancashire dialect of the '*aldest* young lady's having so *mooch* of *the haccent* that she could scarce *understond* her at the *furst* going hoff'. The Fosters filled happily the *hanging* five minutes before dinner. Dinner in all its courses and desert excellent. At the desert I tasted a fruit that was new to me—'The forbidden fruit'[1]—size and rind of a lemon—tastes like an insipid bad lemon—or like a shaddock.

Mr. Roscoe could converse at dinner and so could a Mr. Shepherd. Darwin's poetry was mentioned and I liked the manner in which Mr. Roscoe spoke of him. He neither ran Darwin down nor cried him up but said exactly the truth that he had misapplied his great powers and had been misled in poetry by a false theory that everything should be *picture*—therefore he has not taken the means to touch the feelings. Speaking of similies and allusions Mr. Roscoe made what appeared to me at the moment to be both a new and just observation that writers of secondary powers when they are to descibe or represent either objects of nature or feelings of the human mind always begin by simile. They tell you not what the thing *is* but what it is *like.* On the contrary a man of genius makes the full representation or impression in the first place and tells you what it is like afterwards—*works it off* with a simile. My father does not agree to this and we have been discussing it ever since. I think the

[1] A form of citrus, usually identified with Citrus decumana of which grape fruit are a variety. Shaddock is often used of a grape fruit but is strictly applied to the large pear shaped varieties of the species.

French tragedians and Cato[1] are fine examples on Mr. Roscoe's side of the difference between describing passion and exciting it. Our own Shakespear too is a host on [illegible] side.

Mr. Roscoe's conversation is not *too* literary. You my dear Aunt know what I mean. It has a happy mixture of anecdote and *facts*. He has been much taken notice of by the great since he rose to celebrity and I particularly admire the simplicity with which he talks of them. He never introduces Dukes and Princes to do himself honor but to tell some characteristic anecdotes of them. The Prince of Wales was at Liverpool just after Fox's death. I have not time to tell you half the strange things he said and did but I will mention a *shabbiness*. Mr. Roscoe was to shew his Royal Highness the Botanic garden. So he walked round it with him and as they went the prince said 'Pray now Mr. Roscoe what is the quickest growing tree you know?' Mr. Roscoe mentioned a species of poplar. 'I wish you would have the goodness to send me a few to hide a wall in a new building I am making at Brighton.' Mr. Roscoe sent ten pounds worth as a present. Met the Prince afterwards in London. 'The trees are growing very well but there are not enough of them.' Mr. Roscoe sent ten pounds worth more—But I never would have done that!

As we were looking at a cameo of Brougham Mr. Roscoe told us an anecdote of the young Princess and the Queen which redounds little to the credit of either. To provoke the Queen the Princess hung up in her apartment at Windsor a cameo of Brougham and another of Sir S. Romilly on each side of a bust of Fox.[2] The Queen the moment she saw them broke the cameos to pieces. Silly! Silly! Was not it? . . .

We were talking of an exchange of prisoners and Mr. Roscoe told us that very lately a French frigate having taken an English merchantman the French Captain restored the cargo and let the English vessel go upon condition that the English Captain should procure the liberty of six French prisoners now in Eng-

[1] Joseph Addison's tragedy, produced in 1713.

[2] The King and Queen disliked Fox for what they thought was his lack of political principle, his dissolute life, and his bad influence on the Prince of Wales. Brougham and Romilly were also strong Whigs and Princess Charlotte had taken a great interest in their electoral fortunes in 1812 when both lost their seats.

land. The French prisoners were named to him and he engaged that he would obtain their liberty but upon his return and upon his application to the Admiralty and to the Transport Office he was told that it was not in their power to fulfil any such engagement. My father says this is quite right, that otherwise the Transport Office would give up to merchantmen the power to legislate for England. Mr. Roscoe is writing to the Admiralty about it but I fear he will not succeed. One of the prisoners in question is a young man of 17 who has been a prisoner 9—years. The French Captain wrote to tell him that he had purchased his liberty and the young man has written the most pathetic remonstrances to the English Captain on his breach of promise and honor.

April 9th. Saturday. I finish this my dearest aunt in the dark at Mr. Holland's at Knutsford. Since I began it we have passed a delightful day at Manchester and a day here. At Manchester we owed our chief pleasure to Dr. Ferriar and his daughter of whom I will write when I can to Sophy. I feel rejoiced to be at this clean quiet place after Liverpool and Manchester. I should dislike extremely to live in a manufacturing town. I caught cold walking at ten o clock at night in the mud in the streets of Liverpool with a dirty democrat. I have had a cough ever since. It is curious to see rich manufacturers growing into fine people with pictures and gildings and mirrors and democratic principles and aristocratic tastes! I have been told that Larry the footboy and Mrs. Rafferty's dinner[1] are nothing to what has been seen at the dinners of les nouveaux riches at Liverpool and Manchester. Adieu my dearest aunt.

I have got a candle at last and *could* go on saying a great deal more to you but I *must* not. My father says I must not write more and accuses me of scrawling forever to that Aunt Ruxton of mine of whom he says both my head and my heart are full. I admit it—and of whom next to himself ought I to think so much and with so much grateful affection as of her who has been constantly partially kind to me from the time I was a child with inflamed eyes and swelled features for whom nobody else cared. Affectionately and gratefully yours M. E.

[1] See ME's novel *The Absentee, Tales and Novels of Maria Edgeworth* (1833), ix. 125–30.

To Miss Charlotte Sneyd

Byrkley Lodge,[1] 19 April 1813

You would have heard from me sooner but that I have been too happy ever since I came here to write. I never could tear myself away from such agreeable conversation, or spare time even to tell you how much, how very much I like all I have seen and heard in this house. I wish you and aunt Mary and Honora and Sneyd and William were with us or could see in the fairy glass all that has passed since we came to this delightful place. The *desolation of the forest*[2] (of which by the by we saw the engraving at Dr. R. Darwin's) made the first view of the forest scenery about Byrkley Lodge more surprising and beautiful to us. The rich hollies are still covered with scarlet berries, the hawthorns freshly come out in delicate green and the *white* blackthorns contrasting with the dark hollies, and the oaks of giant brood are picturesque though they have not a leaf upon them. What must they be in summer or autumn! The extreme neatness, and flower-garden trimness and chearfulness about the house is just what it ought to be to combine the idea of comfort at home, with romantic scenery abroad. But altogether the place however beautiful is nothing compared with the people. I had a very agreeable recollection of Mrs. Sneyds manners, but the reality far surpasses my recollection or imagination. She is so sprightly so polite, so kind! Her manners appear to me the perfection of manners, that word which has been so much hacknied and abused by vulgarians suits and describes Mrs. Sneyd. She is truly *elegant*. She pleases from the first moment one sees her and she continues pleasing with accelerating power the more she is known. Miss Sneyd with a different grace has yet a likeness to her mother and with less gaiety she has a composure of manner and a self-possession which immediately raise the expectation of superior character and understanding—an expectation which she fully gratifies. I have had a great deal of conversation with her and the more I have had the more I have desired. She is as far as the greatest lover of originality could wish from all

[1] The home in Staffordshire of Edward Sneyd, RLE's brother-in-law. It is now demolished.

[2] A reference to F. N. C. Mundy's poem *The Fall of Needwood* (1808).

that is commonplace and yet she has none of that love of singularity and ambition for notoriety which we see in many who desire to unite the pretensions of fashion and of genius. I perceive that her mind has been much cultivated, but the power of thinking and judging for herself has not been weakened as you know my father says it often is, by cultivation. My father is at this moment reading with her '*Prometheus*'[1] and I can scarcely fix my attention on what I am writing. I love to see Miss Sneyd with my father she is so much at ease with him and seems to understand him so well.

The person in the family who is most different from what I expected is my *uncle* Sneyd. Yes my *uncle* for so he has desired me to call him. At first I thought his manner cold and reserved, but in a few hours all that wore off. I was most agreeably surprised to feel myself completely at ease with him and talking nonsense to him. He is easily amused, and laughs so heartily and seems to enjoy everything playful and comic in conversation so much that I am free from all fear in his company—free from all fear that either my own or my fathers spirits should be too much for him. Oh my dear Aunts I do wish you could see my father and Mr. Sneyd together! I know it would give you so much pleasure to see how they go on. My uncle laughs till he rolls on his chair, and claps his hands with delight at my father's sallies of wit and nonsense. My father declares he has been so happy since he came here that he does not know how time goes. I never saw him from morning till night in more delightful even spirits—quite free from effort or over-exertion, but in those easy natural spirits, which I cannot describe but which you know—and know to be the sign and proof of his being thoroughly pleased and happy. He has been perfectly well too—has slept every night, and has eaten I think more in one day here than he *could* eat poor man on his journey in three. There was such a want of *tenderness* at the inns, and such continual tenderness here. The day before yesterday after dinner something occurred about sending chaise and horses with us to Derby. Mrs. Sneyd urged that 'Mr. Sneyd does the same always for Mr. Sedley'. My father stretched his hand across the table to Mr. Sneyd

[1] Probably a translation of Aeschylus, but possibly a poem of Swift's (1724).

saying 'I am sure Edward would do as much for me in the way of kindness as for any Mr. Sedley upon earth'.

My uncle was so much touched that he was obliged to cover his eyes with his hand and he looks so like my aunt Mary! I did not perceive this likeness at first between him and my aunt Mary though my mother did. But as soon as ever I saw it from that instant I began to love him and to feel that I *knew my way through his mind.* Under the appearance of coldness and reserve I perceive he has affectionate sensibility and tenderness.

I think Mrs. E particularly pleases him and Miss Sneyd and they seem fully to understand her character. Emma (for at last I must call her Emma and I have a right to do so if I may judge by the kindness she shews me) Emma in speaking to me of Mrs. E used a strong expression 'Mrs. Edgeworth has a *fearlessness of truth* which I admire and which reminds me of her brother Captain Beaufort.' Mr. Sneyd expressed the same idea one day when we were talking of the new and good fashionable verb to *toad* (from toadeater and toadeating). Mrs. E was asked by my father for a derivation and she gave one from the French *avaler des couleuvres.* Mr. Sneyd whispered to me 'I should think Mrs. E knew nothing about it. I am sure at least she knows nothing of the practice. Mrs. E I'm clear never *toads.*' Emma says that Mrs. E's laugh is enough to make a whole house chearful. On some occasion it was questioned what Mrs. E would do and Mr. Sneyd said 'I am sure she would do always what is *just.*' The pleasure of seeing and feeling that she is so much liked and so fully appreciated very much encreases my happiness here, and I shall be very *very* sorry indeed to go away. I shall never again see people I like so well till I return home. After all kindness is more delightful than any species of entertainment.

I had been much amused by seeing variety of things and people before I came to Byrkley Lodge and I had intended to tell them all to you but I find they have so much sunk in my estimation and so faded from my memory that I cannot recall past circumstances or recover them sufficiently to describe them as I could have done I *believe* a week ago. I left off *with my aunt Ruxton* at Mr. Roscoe's. The next day we went from Liverpool to Manchester. On our way Mrs. E and my father stopped to see the four thousand acres of bog[1] which he has improved. My father would not let me run the hazard of wetting my feet so I sat in the chaise (and was not sorry for it) a full hour reading '*the Clergyman's widow*'[2] a very touching *simple* tale. At Manchester[3] my father found Alas! that Mr. and Mrs. Ewart were gone to London about some tax on cotton. However we comforted ourselves with Dr. Ferriar. He drank tea with us the first evening at our inn. He looks something like Mr. G. Knox—imagine a black-eyed dark complexioned Mr. Knox—good conversation, variety of literature and knowledge. His son and very agreeable *well-mannered* daughter walked about Manchester the next morning—shewed us a fine library—two fine libraries—wasted an hour and half at the museum of an old sadler who had collected old armour and old coins—dined at Dr. Ferriar's—excellent house—excellent dinner excellent company—Four handsome and well informed clever ladies—*two* of them not in the least conceited—Mrs. and Miss Appleby—Mr. and Miss Duckworths and Miss Hornby. Miss Hornby is a niece of Lord Derby's and we heard that Lady Derby had taken pains to form her manners. This appeared and did not appear too much. Very agreeable day—Went at night to Mr. Lee's house to see the gas lights—saw them *only* at Mr. Lee's house. They were out at the manufactory Mr. and Mrs. Lee not at home. Gas lights beautiful. (Memm. The two Miss Lee's[4] Canterbury tale writers are sisters to this gentleman and live with him. There is a melancholy history of the suicide of Miss Harriet Lee—occasioned by pure vanity. I have not time to tell it but note it here for future telling.)

Went on next morning to Knutsford. Knutsford a much prettier village-looking little Town than I had expected—interspersed with railed-in nice gardens, little *nooky* green spots, and

[1] For RLE's activities in Irish bog improvement, see *Memoirs of RLE* (2nd ed. 1821), ii. 292–8.

[2] *The Clergyman's Widow* (1812) by Barbara Hofland.

[3] RLE had written to William Strutt in March to ask him what literary and scientific people he ought to see in Liverpool and Manchester: R. S. Fitton and A. P. Wadsworth, *The Strutts and the Arkwrights* (1958), 215 n. His son William E had visited Ewart and Lee in 1811.

[4] Harriet and Sophia Lee were both alive at this date, but there were three other sisters. Two vols. of *The Canterbury Tales* came out in 1797–8 and in 1805 a further 3 vols. by Harriet Lee only.

here and there in the fields picturesque paths and cottages. Mr. Hollands house something like Dr. Beauforts only smaller. Mr. Holland—I never was more surprised!—is neither an old or an elderly man—but looks almost as young as his son. Certainly he looks more like Dr. Holland's elder brother than his father. He is a very strong resemblance of Dr. Holland. How William must have been diverted in his *snugs* by hearing me talk of *the old father*. Mrs. Holland is a young second wife, with a pleasing appearance and gentlewomanlike manners—something like Mrs. Pakenham; it struck us all three. She is *composed* and sensible and amiable and appears to be an excellent wife and mother in law. Mrs. E and she *coalesced* immediately. One of the daughters—Bess—is a sweet creature and would adorn either court or cottage. The other sister has a forbidding countenance and a manner reserved till it is *gruff*; but upon knowing her better the 2d. day I found her good and sensible. There is in the whole family a true simplicity of character and a mutual affection which touches and attaches. I admired their not pretending to be above their circumstances—giving us the style of dinners and going on just the same way that I am sure they always do when by themselves. Mr. Holland is doatingly passionately fond of his son and they are all so fond and so proud of him that it is quite delightful to see so much nature and such good nature. Their post comes in at night about ten o clock and constantly the father watched about that time in hopes of a letter from his son '*No I don't think there's a letter from him. The man stays to bar the door. He'd come up directly if there was a letter*—Ah no no! there's none!' I forgot to say that Mr. Holland was not alarmed by our not having returned his son's letters as he had copied them he was not at all anxious for the originals.

Mrs. E took several pleasant walks while she was at Knutsford; one especially to an old farmers of which she will some time give you an entertaining account. I could not walk, for I had a baddish cold and cough, caught at Liverpool, and never let go at Manchester where the Hotel, the most disagreeable I ever was in, was so noisy that I could not sleep. I rested at Knutsford deliciously and enjoyed the tranquillity of the place and the benevolence of this family contrasted with the manufacturing bustle and selfishness of Liverpool. At Mr. Holland's we found a note from Mrs. Powys begging to see us. She is at Mrs. Cholmondely's a few miles from Knutsford. We went the next morning. She was warmly and affectionately glad to see us. She is less altered than I could have expected in the course of 20 years. You know I have not seen her since the year 92. Except that her color is less of the peony red than it used to be I see scarcely any difference. Her manners and tone of voice appeared so well bred and gentle that I could scarcely find any resemblance to *the character* in Emilie de Coulanges.[1] She said 'I am much softened . . . very much softened since you knew me.' Mrs. Cholmondeley's appearance shocked me extremely. I had known her at Mrs. Devis's[2] a rosy pretty girl. She is like nothing living. She is like a corpse taken out of the grave and clothed in mourning. She cannot live long. Mr. Holland told us that both she and her sister Laetitia injured their health irreparably by the means they have taken to preserve their complexion and beauty—starving—and *taking medicines* perpetually. He knew it professionally. Mrs. H. Leicester (Laetitia Smythe) he thinks actually killed herself by it. How foolish to sacrifice health—especially when there can be no beauty without it.

We went on to Shrewsbury through a most tiresome sandy road. Dr. Darwin and Mrs. Darwin received us very kindly—their house and themselves very agreeable. He is uncommonly entertaining and so full of anecdote that he would be a treasure to me if I could remember but a tenth part of what he tells . . . Dr. Darwin has a gloriously fine boy of 9 years old . . .

From Shrewsbury came to Lichfield. On our way—opposite to Lord Bradford's house[3] my father stopped the chaise—got out and walked down to the church. We did not know what he had been doing till he returned and then he told us that he had been to Mrs. Honora Edgeworth's monumental stone. We went by ourselves. The white marble is perfectly fresh. Dined at the Swan—excellent inn—Dr. Sacheverell Darwin was with us before dinner. My father liked him much. 'Why did not Edward

[1] *Tales of Fashionable Life*, v (1812). Some traits of Mrs. Powys probably suggested the character of Mrs. Somers.

[2] A school in Wimpole St., London, attended by ME 1781–2.

[3] Weston Park, Shifnall. Mrs. Honora E's monument is in Weston church.

Darwin come to see me when he was in Ireland?' said my father. 'That is what we could never find out', said Dr. Sacheverell Darwin. 'For my part I should have thought it a *point of duty.*' My father thought this alluded to old Dr. Darwin's friendship for him and to the sense which the son has of my father's having defended his memory against the attacks of Miss Seward and others.[1] He liked the warmth with which it was said. Mr. Pole—Mrs. Darwin's son has just died. I fancy he is no great loss to the world.

We drank tea with Mrs. Greaves and Miss Greaves. The *bust* of Mrs. Greaves is still that of a fine woman. She was very glad to see us and quite animated talking over old times with my father. Miss Greaves is the very picture and reality of good nature and good humor. Two young Cavendish's sons of Lord Waterpark supped with us. The elder a pleasing young man was on his way to Lord Moira with whom he is going to India. My father gave him some good advice which Mrs. Greaves earnestly conjured him never to forget. Next morning Miss Greaves walked with us to the Close—Cathedral beautiful!—Dean of Lichfield (Woodhouse) to whom my father paid a visit, came and walked about the cathedral with us—pleasing man. A very intelligent gentleman Mr. [?][2] was also so good to shew us the Cathedral and told us a number of anecdotes about the painted windows and monuments. The painted windows[3] are the best designed I ever saw—£200!—how wonderfully cheap they were. I had expressed a desire to see the inside of the Palace[4] and Miss Greaves wrote a note to Lady Oakley who lives there and who politely invited us. The inside of the house is so modernised and beautified that I should scarcely have known it again. I wish I could have seen it in its old state. With what mixed sensations my father must have seen it!

[1] Miss Seward published a life of Erasmus Darwin in 1804. RLE had written to the *Monthly Magazine* in September 1802 in defence of Dr. Darwin; see also his letter to Walter Scott, *Memoirs of RLE* (2nd ed. 1821), ii. 245.

[2] Word illegible.

[3] The Herkenrode glass in the Lady Chapel. Sir Brooke Boothby bought the glass in Belgium for £200 and re-sold it to the Dean and Chapter for the same sum. It dates from the sixteenth century.

[4] The Bishop's Palace at Lichfield had at one time been the home of Canon Seward and his daughter Anna. Honora Sneyd was partly brought up there and was living with them when she first met RLE.

Returned to Mrs. Greaves to take leave of her. Miss Greaves was so good to take us to a house within a few doors of hers (Mrs. Simpson's I believe) to see a picture of Miss Seward. It is very handsome. It must have been done when she was very young. It is not at all like what I remember of her. A great deal of conversation passed about Miss Seward and Mrs. and Miss Greaves told us many of her latter follies of which we knew nothing. But she was a horrible woman and not worth talking about. Yes—one thing which Miss Sneyd told me I must repeat for my aunt Mary's amusement. When Miss Seward began to read Leonora[1] she was charmed with the character of Lady Olivia—said it was so eloquent! so feeling! so delightful! But when she went on with it and found that Lady Olivia is ridiculed *she was enraged with me beyond measure.*

April 20th. Came to Byrkley Lodge to dinner Wednesday last and have now been here six happy days. The weather has been delightfully fine we have walked a great deal in the forest and seen all the views of this beautiful place. Mrs. Sneyd has driven me in the nice little ass-carriage in which she used to drive aunt Mary and I wish you and my aunt Mary had just such a one. The time has passed so quickly that I hardly know how it has gone—walking—talking—laughing—continually. My uncle has been particularly cheerful. My father says he never saw him so gay. Alas! now it is all over and tomorrow morning we must go. We are *very* sorry . . . Tell Dear Sneyd that I am not ungrateful for his kindness in sending me his *Circuit Journal*[2]—I read it to the tea table and it was liked by all. I read his review of fash tales both at Knutsford and at Byrkley Lodge and it was much admired and occasioned much diversion.

(Wednesday April 21st) Derby. past 12 o clock at night! Upon looking over this long letter I am truly ashamed of the heap of confusion I have made. I do not think I have at all conveyed to you the impressions made on my own mind. Things of no consequence have swelled to an immoderate size and it is all out of proportion. But my dear aunt Charlotte I was anxious to tell you all that would interest you and there was so much

[1] *Leonora* (1806) by ME.

[2] Most of the Edgeworths kept journals when away from home. CSE was at this time a practising barrister going on circuit. For the 'review' see below, p. 24 n. 2.

that one thing, as Kitty[1] says, drove another out of my head— . . .

Oh my dear Aunts I forgot to tell you that Mr. and Mrs. Lister spent half a day at Byrkley Lodge. I like him and think him very agreeable. I was so surprised by his youthful appearance! I expected to see a man of 45—and black and grave—and he is fair and gay. We went to Mr. and Mrs. Gisborne's. Mr. Gisborne took to my father prodigiously. He seems an excellent [pri]mitive awkward soul and body but she is stiffness personified. I am convinced her back never touched the back of a chair since she was born. I am sure that as you said she thinks she is sitting for the example of the whole duties of woman.[2]

In our way here (to Derby) my father was so good to stop to let me see the Woman of Tutbury.[3] Mrs. E and he went to see her with my uncle yesterday. If I had time I could describe a fine scene but it is late at night and I can only say in general that all the *world* in these parts are now talking and writing about this fasting woman. A new watch is going to be instituted about her. Mr. Sneyd has declined having anything more to do with it. I fear that she is an imposter—and I fear still more that aunt Mary will be vexed at my thinking so but I cannot help it.

. . . .

After all I have never thanked you and my aunt Mary for the pretty gold chain and bracelets which Mrs. Sneyd gave me from you. They looked very nice with our black lace gowns. Mrs. Sneyd and Emma were in white—never wore mourning while we were there except a black spenser and pelisse at church.[4] As my father had none we have never worn mourning. It will be over or *only the tail of the shower* by the time we reach Town. Mrs. Sneyd was very obliging in all the little *pattern and direction* dress things as in all the rest and this will save us much

[1] Kitty Billamore, the old English housekeeper at Edgeworthstown.

[2] Thomas Gisborne wrote *An Enquiry into the Duties of the Female Sex* (1797). Gisborne gives an account of this meeting in a letter to Zachary Macaulay (Knutsford, *Life of Zachary Macaulay* (1900), 300–1). He supposed Sneyd's 'review' to have been published and to be serious instead of a parody.

[3] Anne Moore, who pretended to live without eating or drinking between 1807 and 1813. She made £400 by exhibiting herself after a first attempt at unmasking her in 1811, but a second stricter watch exposed her fraud in 1813.

[4] Henry, RLE's second surviving son, a doctor, died at Clifton after a long and hopeless illness. Their failure to wear mourning was ill thought of in London.

trouble in London. I forgot—ungrateful as I am—to tell you that Mrs. Sneyd and Emma have given me a most convenient red morocco writing case much better than those with drawers at the end. My father likes it almost as well as I do. Adieu. I love you all—so help me God—Maria E—past *one* o clock.

Wednesday *night*

To Honora Edgeworth

Derby. Monday, 26 April 1813

My dear Honora

. . . I felt so sorry to leave Byrkley Lodge that I could not immediately turn my mind to enjoy as I ought, and as I wished to do, all at Mr. Strutt's where everything is so different.

Do not let William utterly reprobate me for this. Now that I have been here five days my admiration and regard for his friend Mr. Strutt and for all his works would I am sure satisfy him. We have been treated with so much hospitality and kindness by him and he shews such a high esteem and I may say affection for my father that even if he had not the superior understanding he possesses it would be impossible for me *not* to like him. From the moment we entered his house he gave up his whole time to us. His servants, his carriage, everything and everybody in his family were devoted to us, and all was done with so much simplicity of generosity that we felt at ease even whilst we were loaded with favours. Mr. Strutt's house is indeed as Sneyd and William described it, quite a palace, yet there is more *comfort* than magnificence and it is plain that the convenience of the inhabitants and guests has been consulted in everything and the ostentation of wealth never appears. Tell Sneyd I slept in the blue room and had the bed chamber and dressing room which he lived in during his illness. My father and Mrs. E were in the crimson bed chamber and dressing room at the other end of the gallery. In each dressing room there was a writing desk and table with everything that could be wanted for writing—And in each bed chamber a dressing table so completely stored with all things necessary for the toilette that a beau or belle who had had the misfortune to lose his or her dressing box would have felt no inconvenience from that loss—brushes soft and hard for coat and hat—hair-brush—powder pomatum—ivory comb—tortoise shell combs of different sorts—pincushions and even papers ready cut in abundance for curling the hair—and such abundance of drawers little and large and wardrobes! And such charming beds, on their *whalebone sacking* (which by the by we all took for granted and it was the only thing in the house which we did not actually see). My mother told Mr. Strutt how William had on his return home raved of him and of all his contrivances above about and underneath for making his house comfortable and my father begged that Mr. Strutt would shew Mrs. E the house. He laughed and colored and said 'There was nothing to shew and that it seemed ridiculous to shew the house.' But with great good nature he went all over it [with] us and shewed us all William had described—The laundry, the drying room, the kitchen, the *cockle*,[1] the steam engine, the methods of supplying the hot and cold baths—of warming the house, keeping it at an equal temperature and getting rid of all kitchen smells, and bad air. My fathers expectations were more than fulfilled. He was continually calling to my mother to note *this*, and note *that*.

Seven hours of one day Mr. Strutt and his nephew Jedediah Strutt employed in shewing us the cotton mills at Belper. With infinite patience they explained to us all that must be as familiar to them as their a-b-c-. I wish my head would hold a hundredth part of what went in at my eyes and ears that morning, or even one tenth part of what I thought I understood. Tell William that since he was here many improvements have been made. A machine has been made for cleaning the cotton by wind which succeeds and saves all the time formerly employed by women and children in picking and cleaning it. This machinery supplies the place of that building which was called the panopticon.[2] . . . Now I will say no more of machinery and I daresay you will be glad of that.

[1] Mrs. Edgeworth glosses this in *Memoir of ME* as a 'Sylvester Stove'. It was a central heating apparatus invented by William Strutt and later improved and marketed by Charles Sylvester: C. Sylvester, *The Philosophy of Domestic Economy* (1819).

[2] A detailed mechanical description is here omitted.

Stay you must go with me to the Infirmary.[1] Another whole morning Mr. Strutt gave up to shewing it to us. He built it. It is a noble building—as airy and clean as any private house much more so than most private houses—hot air from a *cockle* below conveyed all over the house to produce a healthful and regulated warmth for the whole and any temperature that may be required for patients—the apartments so arranged that by shutting certain doors perfect quiet can be secured for the sick—the fever apartments safe from the rest—many contrivances for cleanliness which I cannot here explain but the effect of which is to make the whole Hospital fresh and free from every disagreeable smell. There are but two or three beds in most of the rooms—several small rooms with one only—Convalescent rooms &c—the kitchen so neat and beautifully useful as that in Mr. Strutts own house—a small steam engine supplying water continually. The housekeeper the woman who manages all this is about Mrs. Billamore's age and she seems to be just such a good steady beenvolent woman as Kitty. I wish Kitty had her health and power of moving about. She shewed that she was *in* her business and in triumph took us to *her* larder and her dairy and shewed us *her* bread. This whole institution is altogether a most noble and touching sight. Such a *great* thing planned and carried into successful execution in a few years by one man! It made us all *silent* with admiration for it was above all praise. I think any person who can think or feel might be cured and must be cured of conceit by seeing such large things!—so much good done by an individual compared with the little that is usually accomplished in a whole life. And all the time Mr. Strutt is so free from vanity that he never adverts to any thing he has done except simply to gratify others with the sight of what is well finished. My father declared that if he could have his family with him when ill he would rather be in this infirmary than in his own house. While Mr. Strutt was going on with this infirmary numbers of people in Derby were standing by expecting and some wishing to see him fail. When first the hot air flues were opened or rather when first the *cockle* was heated *word* was brought to Mr. Strutt that they would not do at all—that the hot air all escaped—impossible

[1] For a detailed description of Derby Infirmary, see C. Sylvester, op. cit. It was the model for many later hospitals.

to heat the building. 'I was frightened. I could not think what was the matter; but I went there directly threw off my coat and waistcoat and put my arm up the flues, found great holes which had been left by the carelessness of the workmen—stopped them and all was well.'

The whole hospital cost but £15,000. Every one has been now so convinced by his *success* of Mr. Strutt's merit, that he has power to do what he pleases and nothing is thought well done but what he directs. We often heard him spoken of by those who did not know we were acquainted with him and it was very agreeable to hear the general and warm expressions of esteem *from all degrees*. Certainly Mr. Strutt's house was the best place William could have come to when he was in England and Mr. Strutt the best friend he could have made. He saw at once all the respect that can be obtained and all the comforts and luxuries that can be earned by ingenuity and integrity joined in his own line of life. I do not wonder that he liked Mr. Strutt so well. There is no regard lost between them for Mr. Strutt speaks of him just as he and my father could wish. It was very agreeable to hear this family express such regard both for Sneyd and William. Every thing they had said or done was repeated to us and seemed to be as fresh in the minds of young and old as if they had happened yesterday. The young ladies are not elegant but they are friendly and obliging, cheerful and sensible enough. The eldest is not melancholy now but she seems indolent and timid. Tell Sneyd that none of the *key* work went on with Miss Lawrence about wine or any thing. All was most handsome—I might say sumptuous—but I dare not touch upon dinners or suppers because you know my mother says I always mention *eating* and *drinking*.

We all three like Miss Lawrence. I think the best thing in her favour is that her pupils have confidence in her and are attached to her. Miss Lawrence took with admirable temper some remarks of my father on her pronunciation.

We dined at Mr. Joseph Strutts; his daughters are better looking and more polished than their cousins. One of them Isabella is very pretty. We also went to Mr. George Strutts but saw only his daughters pleasing young women. He and Mr. Henry Strutt whom I believe William knew are gone to

Edinburgh. I will name the people we met at Derby for W and Sneyd will like to hear who we saw. Dr. Forester—his brother Mr. French—Miss French who has agreeable manners and good taste. *This* last she proved to our satisfaction by various compliments she paid to Sneyd—Miss Broadhurst[1]—not *my* heiress tho' she says that after the publication people used to turn their heads whenever her name was announced and ask if she was Miss E's Miss Broadhurst. She met Sneyd in Dublin—has been lately at Kilkenny—admired Mr. Rothe's acting of Othello[2] &c. Saw a good deal of Mr. Higginson and Mr. Sylvester. Mr. Sylvester I think is a man of surprising abilities and of a calm fearless mind that will never be awed from pursuing and speaking on any subject what he thinks the truth. It is as impossible to put him out of temper as to daunt him in argument . . .

We have been at the Priory.[3] Mrs. Darwin was at first much out of spirits. Besides the death of her son she has just lost a grand child—infant and her daughter Harriet Mrs. Maling has just sailed with her husband for the Mediterranean. This daughter always slept in her room and was her constant companion till she married. Mrs. Darwin pointed to her little bed and said with tears in her eyes 'There Harriet always slept'.

The Priory is a beautiful place and looked cheerful, the grass just mowed before the windows and Mrs. Darwin &c raking it together—Emma Darwin very beautiful! but in weak health—took us to see a nice Botanic garden she is making. What different occupations they have and [what] different lives the Darwins lead from the Strutts. All their views and the whole turn of their minds different—Yet each good in their way and all different from our own—and as different as possible from all at Byrkley Lodge. I think one of the greatest advantages of travelling and seeing the world as it is called, arises from this perception of the various ways in which people may be good and happy.

[1] Later Mrs. C. Sneyd Edgeworth. Miss Broadhurst is the name of a character in *The Absentee: Tales of Fashionable Life*, v and vi (1812).

[2] This is a reference to the private theatricals held at Kilkenny in 1802–19. Mr. Rothe belonged to a well-known Kilkenny family and was a regular actor there. Othello was his best part: *The Private Theatre of Kilkenny* (priv. print. 1825). ME was at Kilkenny in 1810 (*Mem.* i. 237).

[3] Breadsall Priory, Derbyshire.

It teaches us to separate what is essential from what is not essential to happiness . . .

Tuesday the 27th. With much regret we left Mr. Strutt's . . .[1]

Cambridge. Wednesday . . . My mother will tell you the history of our night travels over the bad road between Leicester and Kettering, my father holding the lantern stuck up against one window and my mother against the other the bit of wax candle Kitty gave me. Kitty will be very glad to hear how useful it was. I don't think we could have got on without it. Pray tell her this and put her in mind of her laughing when I snatched it from the chimney piece and said I would put it in my box for that it might be of vast use to us at some odd place or other.

In passing through Loughborough,[2] we talked to the landlady of the Three Crowns about poor Lord Moira. Donington you know is near Loughborough and the *whole town* of Loughborough belonged to Lord Moira. He has been obliged to sell it all! It brought she said above a hundred thousand pounds. My father says it must have sold for a great deal more, but every thing was sold below its value as is always the case when people are in distress. She says it was the Prince of Wales who ruined him—who used to come and live at Donington for months with 40 wasteful servants and horses innumerable. This however would have gone but a little way to his ruin if the prince had not *borrowed* money from him and if Lord Moira had not been so profuse in his generosity to the French princes. He is ruined by ill placed and I fear ostentatious generosity. Our landlady spoke of him with great pity—said he was universally loved in the neighbourhood—'He was the kindest gentleman! His servants all told her so—not a servant but he gave something to in the midst of his distress before he set off—found situations for some and *give* money to others. But he could not speak to them scarce at all—only just to say "There's something for you"—or "there's something done for you". He could not bear to come through

[1] The *Memoir* (i. 269–70) here adds: 'We breakfasted at Markeaton with Mr. Mundy: he is a charming old gentleman, lively, polite, and playful as if he was twenty. He was delighted to see my father, and they talked over their schooldays with great zest. My father was, you know, Mr. Mundy's horse, "Little Driver" ' (*Memoirs of RLE* (2nd ed. 1821), i. 44–5). The MS. of this portion of the letter is no longer extant.

[2] For an earlier and contrasted visit to Loughborough, see *Mem.* i, 114–15.

Loughborough *after* by day light, he came through by candle-light and to this very house—poor gentleman!' . . .

8 o clock Thursday morning. My dear Honora I think I shall have no time at night to finish this so now to conclude I must huddle together 3 anecdotes of children which otherwise I should forget to tell you if I put it off till next letter.

A little girl in Derby, one of the manufacturing children whom a lady was teaching to read met with some story about a bee. By her mode of reading the lady thought she did not understand what she was reading. The lady questioned her. The childs answers were unintelligible—'Do you know what a bee is? Did you ever see a bee?' 'No never.' 'What do you think it is like?' 'Something like a cow!'[1]

Another child in repeating part of its catechism was to say the words 'the Father, Son and Holy Ghost' but forgetting one yet having a vague notion it was something about *the sun* she said 'the Father *moon* and Holy Ghost'.

Now you will not laugh at the next so you may all rest the risible muscles. A clergyman who had instructed the children at a large manufactory (I believe at Manchester) was to quit the place and when he was going away the children resolved to earn some money to give him at parting some token of their gratitude. It was settled that they should each subscribe a certain sum to buy a silver cup for him. One girl of about 11 year old sat up many nights to earn her subscription and when she had earned that she found that there were several girls less than herself who were not able to earn any money though they wished it much. She went on working at over hours and never ceased till she had earned sufficient for each of the little children and she gave the money to each that they might have the pleasure of subscribing for themselves.[2]

Thursday Evening. I must end abruptly and affectionately Maria E.

[1] ME used this incident in *Early Lessons Continued* (1814), ii (The Bee and the Cow).

[2] This is the basis of 'The Silver Cup' (ibid. i).

To C. Sneyd Edgeworth

(Please take this in small doses—but not fasting)

1 May 1813
Collin's Hotel, Conduit St., London
4 o clock

Now the post has gone out and taken Grattan's frank to Edgeworth's town, I may go on quietly and begin again a letter to my dear Sneyd. Let us go back if you please to Cambridge. Thursday morning we went to breakfast with Mr. Smedley. It had been a dreadfully rainy night, but luckily the rain ceased in the morning, and the streets were dried, by the wind, on purpose for us. In Sidney College we found your friend Mr. Smedley in neat cheerful rooms, with orange fringed curtains, pretty drawings, and prints—a breakfast table as neatly and plentifully prepared as you would have had it for his friends—Coffee, tea, tongue, cold beef, exquisite bread and many *inches* of butter. I suppose *you* know, but no one else, at home, can guess why I say *inches* of butter. All the butter brought to the Cambridge market must be stretched into rolls a yard in length, and an inch in diameter, and these are sold by inches and measured out by compasses, in a truly mathematical manner worthy of an University. Mr. Smedley made us feel at home at once, Mrs. E made tea—I coffee. Mr. Smedley talked of Sneyd—called him *Sneyd* and my father seemed quite happy and shewed so quickly that he was pleased that Mr. Smedley could have no doubts on that point. After having admired the drawing of Warwick Castle and a picture of Cromwell and Fanny's kettle-holder[1] we sallied forth to see Cambridge with our friendly guide. My father and Mrs. E had taken a walk the preceding evening in the rain, under favor of an umbrella: had seen the outside of various colleges, and had walked in Clare Hall, and Trinity gardens; but I had as yet seen nothing, and was glad I had not drizzled with them. *Now* it was quite fine, and sunshiny and the gardens and the academic shades were really beautiful. We went to the

[1] Smedley carried on a joking flirtation with 14-year-old Fanny E about this date: see his letters to CSE, now in the library of Sidney Sussex College, Cambridge.

University Hall[1] to see the statue of Pitt—very stiff—*Somerset* very fine. An election of a new professor for Chemical lecturership was going on. Farish was one of the candidates—The man of whom John Leslie Foster used to talk in such raptures when first he came from Cambridge—the man who lectured on arches and whose mechanical paradox of the one-toothed wheel[2] William will recollect. My father was introduced to him—invited him to dine with us. Mr. Farish accepted the invitation. We sat down with a few other ladies on one of the benches. A number of *Fellows* and scholars with black tiles on their heads walked up and down the hall whispering occasionally to one another; and in five minutes Mr. Smedley said 'The election is over. I must go and congratulate Mr. Professor Farish.'

Never was election so quickly, or so silently conducted. In this hall there is the beautiful statue of Newton by Roubiliac.[3] We next proceeded through the University library which is not nearly so fine as the Dublin-College library. Saw Edward 6th's famous little manuscript *exercise* book. Hand good and *ink* admirable. Shame to the chemists of modern days who cannot make half as good ink! Saw Faustus's first printed book and one printed 5 years afterwards. Saw various other College curiosities viz a Persian letter to Lord Wellesley—An Oriental MS.—an Indian Idol said to be made of rice and looking like white marble. I lifted it and found it as heavy as marble. Mr. Smedley smiled at my being so *taken* with this idol; and I told him that I was curious about this *rice-marble* because we had lately seen at Derby a vase of similar substance, about which there had been great debates. Some denied that it could be rice, because it was so heavy. Mr. Smedley then explained to me that the same word in Persian expresses *rice* and the composition of which these idols &c are made. Hence the mistake has arisen. Honora I believe

[1] The Senate House. The statue of Pitt is by Nollekens and had been placed there in 1812.

[2] This is probably a reference to James Ferguson's Mechanical Paradox, described in his *Select Mechanical Exercises* (1773), 46–57 and Plate V. It was part of the mechanism of an orrery. ME has a long reference to the autobiographical part of this book in *Frank: A Sequel* (1822), ii. 148–98. I am indebted to the Science Museum for identifying the Mechanical Paradox.

[3] This statue was and is in Trinity College Chapel.

has a set of teacups and saucers of this composition. We saw the *MS* written on papyrus leaves. We had seen the papyrus tree growing at the botanic garden at Liverpool and I had then wondered how the stiff bark could be rolled up. I now found that it is not rolled up. It is cut in stripes and fastened together with strings through holes in each end (like my sandal-wood fan)—the stripes about as broad and very like a common green flagger dried—written all over in the smallest characters, indented into the leaf. I describe this, not for your amusement, my dear Sneyd, who have seen it but for those who have not. The only things we saw besides in this library worth of note, were three casts taken after death. How or why they came there I don't know; but they were very striking—a cast taken from the face of Charles the 12th of Sweden and the hole in the forehead where the bullet entered, while he was urging the engineer to hasten the works at the siege of Frederickshall—A cast from Pitt—very like a statue taken from the life and like all the prints I have seen of him—A cast of Fox—shocking! not in the least like any bust or picture of him and said to be so unlike what he *was* in health that none could know it to be him—no character of greatness or ability—nothing but pain, weakness, or imbecillity. We cannot help looking at casts taken after death with curiosity and interest and yet it is not probable that they should mark the real, natural, or habitual character of the person; they often can only mark the degree of bodily pain or ease felt in the moments of death. I think these Casts made me pause to reflect more than any thing I saw this day.

Went next to Trinity College library—beautiful! I liked the glass doors opening to the gardens at the end and the trees in full leaf! The proportions of this room excellent and every thing except the ceiling which is *quite* plain (too plain) we thought extremely *handsome* as Mr. Hampton says. The bust of Bacon and Newton excellent but Bacon looks more like a courtier than a philosopher—his ruff is elegantly plaited in white marble. By Cipriani's painted window, with its glorious anachronisms we were much amused; and I regret that it is not recorded in the essay on Irish bulls.[1] It represents the presentation of Sir Isaac

[1] *An Essay on Irish Bulls* (1802) by RLE and ME. A bull is an expression involving a ludicrous inconsistency unperceived by the speaker (*O.E.D.*).

Newton to his Majesty *George the 3rd* seated on his throne—*Bacon* sitting on the steps of the said throne, writing! It seems that the foreign artist was not guilty of *all* the blunders in this picture. Cipriani had made the king, Henry the 8th; but the fellows of the college thought it would be pretty to pay a compliment to his gracious Majesty king George the 3d so they made Cipriani cut off Henry the 8th's head, and stick George the 3d in his place. This is still to be seen in the first design of the picture. The junction is covered with a pasted paper cravat, like the figure that changes dresses in Sophy or Lucy's or little Henry's book.

Saw Milton's original MS of his lesser poems and letters and plan of a tragedy on the subject of the Paradise Lost, which tragedy I rejoice that he did not write. If there had been time I should have liked to have examined the alterations and the various emendations, which Milton made in these MS: I hear, that these corrections are all printed; and, if so, I do not see much value in the MS, except just to satisfy curiosity by shewing the handwriting of Milton. But I have not such delight in seeing the writing of great authors and great folk as some people have. Besides, by this time, I had become very hungry; and was right glad to accept of Mr. Smedleys proposal that we should *re*journ to his room, and take some sandwiches. Rested—eat—talked—looked at the engravings of Clarkes[1] marbles and read the account of the manner in which these ponderous marbles had been transported to England. We saw the marbles themselves.

The famous head of Ceres is in a sad mutilated condition. It must have belonged to a gigantic statue and perhaps at a great height might have produced a great *sensation*. There is no face yet Clarke I hear strokes it and talks of its beautiful *contour*. The appearance of the head in front is exactly like Lucy's or Sophy's doll whose face had peeled off. The hair is *fine*; and the figure from its vast size may be sublime. If you get the little pamphlet describing these marbles I think you will have a more sublime idea of them than I have who have seen them. When you get the pamphlet observe that the *sitting* figure is dressed up by

[1] A collection of statues and fragments of Greek sculpture presented to Cambridge University in 1803 by Dr. E. D. Clarke (see below, p. 43).

Flaxman and not the least like the original bust. There were several other mutilated stones on which great value was set; but I felt that I could not pump up any enthusiasm for them. I only wondered how anybody could think it worth while to bring them so far or even to allow them house room when brought. How a true antiquarian would despise me for this—but truth is truth—and I have no taste for these *hideous* old stones. My father saw Dr. Vince in his lecture room and reproached him nicely for not having done him justice in his essay in the Cyclopaedia[1] about the application of springs to carriages.

After having recruited our strength with sandwiches, and by talking, and laughing, we set out again to the Vice chancellor Davie's, to see a famous picture of Oliver Cromwell.[2] As we knocked at his Vice-Chancellorship's door Mr. Smedley said to me, 'Now Miss E if you would but settle in Cambridge! Here is our Vice-Chancellor a batchelor . . . *do* consider about it.'

We went up stairs—found the Vice Chancellor's room empty; had leisure before he appeared to examine the fine picture of Cromwell, in which there is more the expression of greatness of mind and of determination, than the usual character of Presbyterian hypocrisy. This portrait seems to say '*Take away that bauble*' not '*I am seeking the lord—(that is looking for the cork-screw)*'.

The Vice chancellor entered—and such a wretched pale, unhealthy object I have seldom beheld! He seemed crippled, and writhing with rheumatic pains, and scarcely able to walk. After a few minutes had passed, Mr. Smedley came round to me, and whispered 'Have you made up your mind?' 'Yes—quite—thank you.' Saw the vice Chancellor's fine apartments and the

[1] RLE had published 'An Account of some Experiments on Wheel Carriages' in *Trans. Royal Irish Academy* ii (1788). His *Essay on the Construction of Roads and Carriages* came out later in 1813. The Cyclopaedia is probably Rees's *Cyclopaedia* (1802–19), but I have not been able to trace Dr. Vince's article.

[2] Now in the hall of Sidney Sussex College. It was given to the College by Thomas Hollis and is attributed to Samuel Cooper. Hume in his *History of England* (Oxford English Classics (1826), vii. 234) tells the story that one day the Protector dropped a corkscrew and immediately his courtiers flung themselves on the floor to find it. 'Cromwell burst out a laughing. "Should any fool," said he, "put his head at the door, he would fancy, from your posture, that you were seeking the Lord; and you are only seeking a corkscrew."'

Chapel[1]—He poor man shivering (as well he might) with the cold; My father comforted him by suggesting that the whole building, and the eating hall, could be warmed with hot cockles for £50—made our curtsies—bows and thanks and walked off. Mr. Smedley desired me to tell you that this Vice Chancellor was a year and half ago, a healthy hale country curate. High College living and the change from an active to a *sedentary* life have brought him suddenly to this sad pass. Now to the beauty of Cambridge, the beauty of beauties!—King's College Chapel! I had seen prints of it in Britton,[2] and had heard much of it from many of its admirers; but it far surpassed my expectations. On the first entrance I felt silenced by admiration. I never beheld any thing at once so beautiful and so sublime. The prints give a good idea of the beauty of the *spandrilled* ceiling with all its rich, and light ornaments; but no engraved representation can give an idea of the effect of size, height and *continuity* of grandeur in the whole building. Besides the idea of *duration* the sublime idea of having lasted ages is more fully suggested by the sight of the real building, than it can be by any representation or *description*—For which reason I merely tell you the effect it had upon my mind. The organ began to play an anthem of Handel's while we were looking at the chapel. I wished for you particularly at that moment Dear Sneyd. Your friend took us up the hundred stairs to the roof—where *he* was delighted with the sound of the organ and the chaunting, rising from the choir below, and my father was soon absorbed in the contemplation of the mechanical wonders of the roof—that stone roof, of which you know Sir Christopher Wren said 'Shew me how the first stone was laid and I will shew you how the second is laid'. Mr. Smedley exclaimed 'Is not the sound of the organ fine?' To which my father, at cross purposes, answered, speaking to Mrs. E, 'Yes—the iron was certainly added afterwards'. Mr. Smedley at once confessed, that he had no knowledge or taste for mechanics; but he had the patience, and good nature to walk up and down this stone platform three quarters of an hour. I wished that William had been in his place and I daresay he would have

[1] Designed by James Essex (1776–82). It has twice been remodelled since the Edgeworths saw it.

[2] E. W. Brayley and J. Britton, *The Beauties of England and Wales*, ii (1801).

had no objection. He stood listening and observing Mrs. E very eager examining with my father the defects in the wooden roof which covers this stone roof and pointing out where the wood had been cut away to admit the stone, as proof that the stone-roof was an after-thought of the architect's who had probably first intended to leave the wooden roof open to view like that in Westminster Abbey.[1] Smedley at last turned to me, with a look of astonishment, and said 'Mrs. E seems to have this taste for mechanics *too*!' He spoke of it as a kind of mania I thought. So I nodded at him very gravely and answered 'Yes—you'll find we are all tinctured with it, more or less.'[2]

At last, to Mr. Smedley's great joy, he got my father alive off this roof, and on his way to Downing,[3] the new College, of which John L Foster talked so much, and which, I thought he told us was to be like the Parthenon. Shockingly windy walk to it! Thought my brains would have been blown out! Passed Peter-house, and saw the rooms in which Gray lived,[4] and the irons of his *fire escape* at the window. Warned Mr. Smedley of the danger of my fathers being caught by a coach-maker's yard, which we were to pass. My father overheard me—laughed—contented himself with a side glance at the springs of gigs, and happily passed the danger. I nearly disgraced myself as the company were admiring the front of Emmanuel College by looking at a tall man stooping to kiss a little child. Got at last, in spite of the wind, and coachmaker's yards, within view of Downing College—and was sadly disappointed! It can never stand a comparison with King's College Chapel which is Alas! too near it.

Home to dinner with an excellent appetite—excellent dinner—Mr. Farish and Mr. Smedley were very agreeable and entertaining and *did* very well together, though such different persons. Mr. Farish is the most primitive, simple hearted man I

[1] The wooden roof had been built first but a stone vault was in the original design.

[2] In 1843 ME said that her brother-in-law Richard Butler took no interest in mechanical processes: 'this seems to me like wanting a sense'.

[3] Built 1807–20 to the designs of William Wilkins.

[4] Thomas Gray is said to have moved from Peterhouse to Pembroke because of a practical joke playing on his fear of fire. There were iron bars outside a window at Peterhouse which were traditionally supposed to have been supports for a rope ladder which he had ordered just before he left the college.

ever saw—of the *Alison*—species. I must, for my aunt Mary's amusement mention one of his speeches. At the beginning of dinner my father said to Mrs. E 'My dear Fanny a stranger who sees you picking out tender morsels for me with such care and putting this bit and that on my plate, must say to himself "What an epicure that old man must be! And what a tyrant! And how I pity that young wife of his for being obliged to humor him."' 'That is not exactly the conclusion I should draw' replied Mr. Farish speaking with a very *deliberate* Scotch accent, 'And I should not think it owing to my own dullness neither.' Smedley and all of us were much diverted—but maybe this won't sound droll to you. So different do things appear said warm at the moment, and written in cold blood.

The bells were ringing in honor of Professor Farish's election, or as Smedley said, at the Professor's expense. Farish insisted upon it, very coolly, that they were not ringing for him, but for a *shoulder of mutton*. 'A shoulder of mutton! What do you mean?' 'Why a man left to the University a shoulder [of] mutton for every thursday, on condition the bells should ring for him always on that day. So this is for the shoulder of mutton I say.'

The bells reminded him of another story. 'Did you, Mr. E, ever happen to hear of the late Bishop of Elphin?' We all exclaimed that we knew him and loved him. 'Aye he was an excellent man, and very clever. He told me this story of himself. When he was young, he was travelling through some village in Scotland, where they have an odd custom, once a year, of gathering together to strive who should tell the biggest lie or *lig* as they call it and they lie for a prize; and whoever tells the biggest, is to have a hone for his prize. So they stopped the Bishop's carriage and opened the door and told him he must get out and lie too. But he pleaded that he was a clergyman and could not lie. But that would not do—he must come out and *lig* for the prize. So he did not know what to do but he said he was not in the habit of *ligging*. He declared that he had never told a lie—in his life. On this they all roared out "Oh! that's the biggest. Gi' him the prize! Gi' him the hone. That's the biggest lie of all!"' Mr. Farish seemed as much at ease with us this evening, as if he had known us all his life; and sat exactly as I am sure he does by his own fireside, with his feet on the fender, and every now and then leaning his head down on his hand, resting his elbow on his knees in an absent fit, thinking probably of some dear mathematical problem till recalled to attention by something that made him laugh or smile which he was always very ready to do. He paid no compliments, in words but his coming to spend the evening with us, the day of his election, when I suppose he might have been feasted by all the grand and learned in the University, was I think the greatest honor my father has received since he came to England—and so he felt it.

Whilst my father was talking mechanics and mathematics to Mr. Farish—of bridges—of tunnels—of the experiment not well tried, between the pendulum and the mountain[1]—of Mr. Strutt and the top &c—Smedley went on talking to me of Rokeby[2]—admires it exceedingly—admires Matilda particularly, for what do you think? For her generosity, her gentleness her politeness certainly—Yes—but particularly for . . . her *paleness.* He is charmed with Scott for making his heroine *pale.* She is the only pale heroine he remembers to have heard described. Matilda it is said is drawn from a Mrs. Russel of Northumberland—a charming woman—but she Alas has married a rich coalmerchant who has not a literary idea.[3] I can't help it.

Among a variety of anecdotes which Smedley told me and told exceedingly well, he told the history of Russian Dr. Clarke's marriage—first regretting as we all did, that the said Dr. Clarke was not this day at Cambridge. Mr. Cripps to whom Clarke was travelling companion (a very rich man and, by all I can understand, something of a blockhead) came to Clarke one day and said with a very solemn face 'Clarke do you know I have fallen in love with Angelica Rush!'

Now Clarke was at this moment desperately in love with Angelica Rush. So he answered 'Oh you will be the most miser-

[1] This probably refers to the experiments of Nevil Maskelyne, Astronomer Royal, who in 1774 measured the direction of a plumb-line on either side of the mountain Schiehallion in Perthshire in order to find the density of the earth and hence its mass. I am indebted to Mr. H. R. Calvert of the Science Museum for this information.

[2] Walter Scott's *Rokeby* had been published earlier in the year.

[3] Matilda was probably drawn from Scott's early love, Wilhelmina Belsches: Scott to ME, 10 May 1818, *Letters of Sir Walter Scott, 1817–19*, ed. Grierson (1933), 145; Lockhart, *Life of Scott* (1850 ed.), chap. xxv, 223. She married Sir William Forbes.

able man alive if you fall in love with such a vixen. Why! you would never have a moment's peace if you married Angelica Rush. You'd much better think of her sister, who is a good quiet soul.' Accordingly Cripps fell out of love with Angelica, and into love with her sister, and married her and Clarke married his Angelica. And we all laughed at the dramatic trick; and then Farish and my father discussed the morality of the joke, and we all concluded that we hoped it was *only* a good story.

How much the circulation of newspapers as well as books contribute to give subjects of conversation in common to people in the most distant parts of different countries. Do you recollect our seeing in the news-paper an account of a man who poisoned several racehorses by putting arsenic in the water-troughs? Also an account of a horrid woman who made her servant boy murder her husband; and ordered him to go back and *finish him* as composedly as if she had told him to kill a pig?

Smedley tells me that it is strongly suspected, that the horse poisoner had an accomplice or instigator of high rank—a nobleman well known at Newmarket. I will not mention the name as Smedley scrupled to mention it and as you would not give a farthing perhaps to hear it. To the last moment the *unhappy* man expected a reprieve. The day before he was to be executed Lord Francis Osborne went to see him and asked if there was anything he wished for particularly. 'Yes one thing—but I shan't ask it for it is not likely to be granted.' Lord Francis pressed him at all events to make the request. 'Well then I want to see Jack—(naming the kings evidence by whose means he had been convicted). I want to see him alone in my cell *for* my only wish in the world now is to eat his heart for my supper.' Smedley says he can vouch for the truth of this anecdote. When this man was brought out for execution, he was more cool and composed than any other person present. When the cord was to be put about his neck it was perceived that it was too short and that it could not well reach him. He pointed to the hassock on which he had been kneeling and made a sign to them to put it under his feet!

The woman who murdered her husband was an extraordinary compound of insensibility and sensibility. While sentence was pronouncing upon her, she shewed no symptom of feeling, but from the moment she was condemned she would not let any creature see her face. She kept it constantly hid, even till she was executed. On hearing the sermon the evening before her execution she wept and sobbed bitterly yet in the morning seemed quite insensible and eat a hearty breakfast. These sound like newspaper paragraphs, yet they are facts in human nature which I thought you would like to know and Smedley vouches for them.

I suppose you know he has published minutes of the trial of that Mr. Kendal who was accused of having set fire to Sidney-College and who, though *brought off* by the talents of Garrow on the trial was so generally thought to be guilty and to have escaped only by a quirk of law, that he has been expelled the University. What a strange thing that at Cambridge and Dublin trials of incendiaries should take place within a short time of each other. It seems as if the fashion of certain crimes prevailed at certain times. I did not intend to give you this page on crimes and punishments and I am quite surprised at seeing what was said in a few instants requires so much time and space to write. When these horrid stories unluckily came across my memory I was going to have told you something quite different—That Smedley when he saw Mrs. E and I, in a great hurry getting our *Government* frank to Honora ready to go this evening good-naturedly sat down to pour out coffee and tea for us; and by that means, without interrupting my father and Mr. Farish, *we*, at another table, accomplished our purpose. They staid till eleven; and a few minutes after they were gone, as I was sitting by the fire, and boasting of my strength and of the certificate of strength I had obtained for seven hours walking and just as my father was saying to me 'You would have been killed with half this cold wind or a hundredth part of this exercise at Edgeworthstown' I grew suddenly sick—so sick and with such pain in my stomach that I could scarcely walk across the room and upstairs to my room. The greater part of the night I was so violently sick that I thought I could not possibly have gone on with our journey in the morning but at last I had a few hours sleep—quite refreshed and brisk again by nine o'clock in the morning! And then we talked over, of course, what could have been the cause of the sickness, *mushrooms* eaten in Scotch Collops? or cold on the roof of Kings College Chapel? Unable to settle the point. All I can tell is, that it is all over; and I am now, and have been as well as ever, ever since. Smedley breakfasted with us, and kindly stayed with us till the last moment, when he packed us into our chaise. Just before we parted my father said

'Certainly my son Sneyd does make the best friends in the world but he has too many good friends. It is a great misfortune to him to have such good and agreeable friends.' 'How so?' cried Smedley. 'Because it must diminish his motive for exertion. He *has* every thing he wants . . . the dog! He knows he is esteemed and beloved. What motive can he have?'

Smedley answered and we all supported his opinion, that the motive for exertion, and for good conduct of all kinds is much encreased by a person's having early in life a number of good friends to whose opinion he looks up. It binds him to society. Smedley exclaimed, 'I am sure whenever I do a silly thing, or one that I don't quite approve, I always say to myself, I'm glad Sneyd's a hundred miles off. What would Sneyd think of this?' I need not tell you that my father liked your friend for this. Goodbye Mr. Smedley—I hope you liked us half as well as we liked you. My father and Mrs. E invited him warmly to Edgeworthstown and I think he will *come* or *go* whichever it should be.

Now I am fairly got away from Cambridge I think the antithetical speech comparing Cambridge and Oxford is *just—'Oxford is a university in a Town—Cambridge a Town in a university'*. Upon the whole we thought it well worth our while to have come 30 miles out of our way to see Smedley and Cambridge and you had the thanks of all the party for your advice.

In passing through the village of Trumpington and just as we came within sight of Dr. Clarke's house I urged my father to call upon him. 'Without an introduction! With two ladies with me! No. With all my impudence my dear Maria I can*not* do that.'

'Oh *do*! You'll repent it afterwards if you don't. We shall never have another opportunity of seeing him.'

'Well, at your peril then be it!' (He let down the glass, and ordered the postillion to drive up to Dr. Clarke's house.) I *quailed* in the corner, the moment I heard the order given, but said nought. Out jumped my father and during two or three minutes, whilst he was in the house, and my mother and I waiting in the carriage at the door I was in an agony! But it was soon over, for out came little Dr. Clarke, flying to us, all civility, and joy and gratitude . . . and *honor*! and *pleasure*! and *pleasure* and *honor*, and *ashamed* and *obliged* &c went on between us as he handed us up the steps and into a very elegant room with fine drawings, paintings, books.

I am not sure whether you ever saw Dr. Clarke? Certainly neither printed portrait nor description had ever given me the least idea of him. From the print I had imagined he was a large man, dark eyes and hair with a penetrating countenance. No such thing. He is a square pale flat faced goodnatured looking fussy man with very intelligent eyes, yet great *credulity* of countenance and still greater benevolence. In a moment he whisked about to different rooms, upstairs and down, and got together Angelicas drawings (She draws beautifully and I like him for being proud of her drawings)—Ruins—sketches—books everything that could please us. Angelica herself is a timid, dark, soft-eyed woman, with a good figure—I thought very pretty—but my mother was disappointed in her looks. I am told that some say it is very rude to say a person is *very clean* but, on the other hand, I am told, that Mr. Mundy who is a man of taste and politeness declares he prefers my heroines because they are *clean*. So I may venture to praise Angelica for looking elegantly clean brilliantly white—with a lace Mary Queen of Scots cap like that which I am sure *you* remember on Lady Adelaide Forbes. She received us with timid courtesy. Her timidity soon wore off and the half hour we spent here made us wish to have spent an hour. Dr. Clarke seemed highly gratified by finding that his travels in Greece[1] had interested us so much—shewed us original drawings of Moscow &c and a book of drawings of the ruins of Athens done by the draughtsman who went out with the Duc de Choiseul-Gouffier. These were beautifully done—mere outlines—perfectly distinct and giving I think better architectural ideas, than we have from more finished and flattered drawings. With Dr. Clarke was a tall, dark eyed fine fashionable looking gentleman—grave and seemingly on good terms with himself. He was introduced to us as Mr. Walpole and I perceived that he thought and every body [*sic*] that 'not to know him argued ourselves unknown'.

[1] *Travels in Various Countries of Europe, Asia and Africa* (1810–23).

I concealed as well as I could that I did not in the least know what might be his claims to celebrity. My father and he entered into conversation. My father talked of Captain Beauforts having been lately in the Mediterranean—Grecian Isles—Coast of Caramania.[1] Mr. Walpole seemed to know the merit of Captain Beaufort and appeared uncommonly desirous to know whether he was likely to publish his notes. Indeed he hinted that he wished to have them to incorporate with some work of travels which he is preparing.[2] He asked my father for Captain Beaufort's direction and my father wrote before he slept to Captain Beaufort to beseech him to publish for himself and by himself and not to give up his notes or merge his credit in that of any other persons pretensions.

We were sorry not to see more and very glad we had seen this little of Dr. Clarke and his Angelica and his nice little boy about 5 years old—not at all shy. I said to him 'Do my dear go into the next room and tell Mrs. E that I wish she would come into the hall to look at a picture.'

He ran directly and took her by the hand as little Francis takes Aunt Mary after dinner 'You must come into the next room, will you? . . . to look at a picture.'

It is very foolish to tell you such little things—I know—but little things often please me more than large ones. As we passed through the hall Dr. Clarke shewed us the *lyre* and the *testudo*. I wish I had had your lines—Apropos—or mal apropos. . . .

But to proceed—Where was I? Leaving Dr. Clarke's. In the hall Dr. Clarke between Mrs. E and I had given a hand to each and seemed a little puzzled how to get us both into the carriage at once . . . or which first—for it was evident that my rights of seniority had at first sight impressed him with the idea that I was *Mrs.* Edgeworth and it was not right clear in his head *how* it *was*—but in his distress he called to Mr. Walpole 'Walpole put this lady into the carriage will you' and with a *Meadows*[3] air he obeyed.

[1] Francis Beaufort published *Caramania* in 1817.

[2] Mr. Walpole's *Travels in various countries of the East* (1820) included travels by Morritt, Sibthorp, and Hunt.

[3] The blasé coxcomb, the 'insensiblist', in Fanny Burney's *Cecilia*.

Now we are again on the London road and except fine corn fields—broad wheeled wagons and gentleman's fine seats of which my mother always would ask the names, nothing interrupted our perusal of *Pride and Prejudice* for the remainder of the morning and till we reached Epping Place[1] by dinner time. I am desired not to give any opinion of *Pride & Prejudice* but to beg you all to get it directly and read it and tell us what yours is.

Slept at Epping place and my father and Mrs. E wrote letters before they slept but they would not let me because I had been sick the night before and because my stomach was sore and for no better reasons!

Arrived in Town the next morning. The whole road is *Town* for some miles before you come to London. I do not remember seeing so much of this when I was here ten years ago. We stopped and sat half an hour within a few doors of Johnson's[2] shop whilst my father went in to speak to him and to inquire for letters. Mrs. E and I were much amused by the continually flowing crowd all with faces intent on their own interests and minding us and our chaise no more than if we and it had not existed.

My father returned with my aunt C's letter and Mr. Wakefields. We went on to Mrs. Griffiths—found she had taken apartments for us at No. 19 Collins Hotel Conduit St.—came here—rooms small and dear and dark—£1-17 a week. My father is gone in search of better rooms.

this sunday morning 3 oclock.

The trunk is come safely and in our possession but not unpacked. I will write to dear good Dr. Beaufort when I have looked at Patronage and at his corrections, but we do not unpack the trunk because we are going to change our lodgings. And now goodbye my dear Sneyd. My mother is scolding me for writing so much and I must have done. This is the last *long* letter I daresay I shall have it in my power to write while in London and so much the better for I agree with my mother that it is very foolish to write such long letters. But I got up early to it

[1] The home of Lestock Wilson, father-in-law of Mrs. Edgeworth's brother, Francis Beaufort. The house was called The Grove.

[2] The shop in St. Paul's Churchyard of Joseph Johnson, the Edgeworth's publisher who had died in 1809. The business was carried on by his nephews John Miles and Rowland Hunter, of whom the latter remained ME's publisher till 1827.

for I was determined foolish or not to shew you my dear brother that I am not ungrateful for all the trouble you took to write to me everything that could interest or entertain me.

Miles has been here. Churchill stopped printing my fathers Ms. on wheel carriages because it was not *punctuated* to his fancy but it is to go on tomorrow and tell Ho the Appendix is to be printed so her labor won't be lost. Miles said he never had had such beautiful drawings of machinery sent to him to be engraved as my mothers.

. . . .

We are *incog* till we have carriage—servant—dress—and lodgings. Tell my aunts mourning will be no trouble to us as it will be over next sunday. My father has his black coat. Love to my own dear *packer and gauger*[1] Fanny. I will write to her next.

To C. Sneyd Edgeworth

No. 10 Holles Street, Saturday morning,
8 April [May] 1813

My dear Sneyd . . .

One word I must add in the midst of my hurry—that I do entreat you my dear brother *not to shew my letters to any body* except my two aunt Sneyds and William Honora Fanny and Sophy Ruxton when she is at Edgeworthstown. It is not my dear that I am afraid of my literary reputation but I know the mischief that may be done by repeating opinions of persons &c given so freely and often so rashly as I write them to my intimate friends. They must repair by their discretion my indiscretion or else I must totally refrain from giving my opinions of persons—characters and manners. *Then* I should be *shut up*—frozen, *unnatural*—and there would be an end of all *confidence* and all entertainment from my letters. You then might as *well* or much better read my printed books.

I *know* that my first impressions of persons are often erroneous and to express these to any but the friends who will not repeat them and who can assist me in forming better judgments

[1] In 1689 Sir John Edgeworth was made Searcher, Packer, and Gauger to the port of Dublin.

would be in the highest degree unjust and injurious. For example I am shocked when I see *reflected* back to me the strong impression I have given at Black Castle[1] and at Edgeworthstown of poor Mrs. Roscoe's vulgarity. It is true she is not polished and I was struck with it at the moment much more than I ought. She was most hospitable and kind to me, to all of us and the real *strong impression left upon my mind* was of her *goodness*—her open heartedness—her independance of spirit which treated Duke of Gloucester and Prince of Wales with less attention than the friends she loved. This impression I fear I have failed to give to any one and consequently I have been unjust and ungrateful. What I said I cant recollect but I perfectly recollect that in the last letter I wrote you I expressed various opinions of Clarke and other persons which ought not to be repeated. Farewell my dear Sneyd I hope I have made my motives intelligible and I trust entirely to you to comply strictly with my request. About *things* read or repeat what you will but not a word about persons. Send this letter home when you have a frank because it will serve for an answer to my aunt Charlotte who asked whether I had any objection to my letters being sent to Black Castle or different friends. I do not like to have *that* done. I believe it is unnecessary to say *how* well I love my aunt Ruxton but she would read to Bess Ruxton and she to all *the world*. I trust to the discretion of the person to whom I write always or else I could not write freely. I have been brought nearly to tears by the just scolding my father and Mrs. E have given me for expressing too [gap in MS.].

I will write again soon to Aunt Mary about Patronage but put her kind heart at ease by telling her that it is safe in the trunk that I have never had time to look at it—that my father seems in no hurry about it—that Miles says since it cant come out in June he does not want it till October. So *that* point is gained and my own opinion is that it will not be published till spring and that I shall bring it back with me. Mrs. Clifford dear good *well bred soul* is continually with us—Davy and Lady kind as kind can be—Dumont *scarcely handsome* in person—beautiful in mind. . . .

[no signature].

[1] The home near Navan of ME's aunt Mrs. Ruxton.

To Sophy Ruxton

[Monday, 16 May 181

My dear friend, I have true pleasure in writing to you because I know you do not shew my letters and I can therefore write just as freely as I would speak to you if I were sitting over the fire with my feet on the fender at Caroline Hamilton's dangerous hour of the night. Our common history and of the sights we have seen, and of the kindness and pleasure we have received from various friends and acquaintances on our *journey* to London I have written ten accounts to various friends, but for you my own dear Sophy I have reserved the subjects which interest *me* most and in which I am ever secure in your sympathy and confidence. . . . (Pray mind the words *private* and *public* in all that follows and always look before you leap.)

Mrs. E has been much diverted by my meeting with Sweden, its king, or its courtiers wherever I go and to whomever I talk.[1] In the most unexpected way this flashes upon me continually in company. But I don't care about it now in the least—only when Madame de Stael[2] comes I shall ask her a few questions but I only ask for information sake, totally damn me &c.[3]

I fear Madame de Stael's arrival may be put off till we have left Town. I hear now that she is not to come till the beginning of June. The Edinburgh Review of her last book[4] has well prepared all the world for her arrival. It is a flourish of trumpets before her entrance on the stage. I think the praise of transcendant genius indisputably hers and no more is given to her in that Review than is justly due but I think the review itself paradoxical and disheartening. It is written by Jeffrey; it has been the general subject of conversation here among all the beaux esprits and some extol and some decry it violently. I dont care much about it. Dumont detests it as he detests every thing

[1] This is a reference to the Swedish Abraham Niclas Clewberg Edelcrantz who had proposed to ME in Paris in 1802. For many years after she regretted her hasty refusal.

[2] The Baron de Stael Holstein was a Swede.

[3] A family phrase, several times used by ME in letters. I do not know its origin.

[4] *De la littérature considerée dans ses Rapports avec les Institutions Sociales* (1812), reviewed *Edinburgh Review*, xli (Feb. 1813).

paradoxical and sophistical. What do I think of M. Dumont? I will tell you not only what I think but what I have thought. What I may think hereafter it is out of my power to predict.

The evening of the day after our arrival, I had a dreadful *customary* headache and had gone to lie down. Mrs. E came to summon me downstairs. 'Do come if you possibly *can* for M. Dumont has come a long way on purpose to pay his respects to you.' I was so sick and in such pain I could hardly bear to move. However I crawled down and a most wretched figure I must have made, for I could scarcely speak and I would have given five guineas well counted that he had not called this unlucky evening but so it was and there he was! A fattish, Swiss-looking man in black, with monstrous eyebrows and a red large face like what the little robbins described the gardener's face when it looked down upon them in their nest.[1] I felt at once que l'amour n'avoit jamais passé, et ne passeroit jamais par là. Au reste, he is and will be always to us an excellent friend, a man of first rate abilities, superior in conversation to anyone I have met with except Sir James Mackintosh. Dumont lives the life of a French savant in society—wants nothing more and seems to have sold himself to Bentham as Dr Faustus sold himself to the devil. This point settled, *completely*, I will now my dear Sophy go on with our public history and you are at liberty to read any parts of what follows to who ever you please. *That* I leave to your discretion but don't send my letters about, for I hate it.

The first persons who came to see us were Sir H and Lady Davy. They have been uniformly and zealously kind and attentive to us and Davy is just the same in his manners as he always was. We have been frequently at their dinners and parties. They see all the world of wit, and much of the world of fashion and rank. I should fill a roll as long as that genealogy of the Appreece's[2]

[1] See *The History of the Robins* (*Fabulous Histories*, 1786) by Selina Trimmer.

[2] In 1757 Samuel Foote produced *The Author*, a two-act comedy. It contained a caricature of a Mr. Aprice as a man ridiculously ambitious of being thought a patron of the arts (W. Cooke, *Memoirs of Samuel Foote* (1805)). In Act II, Scene I, Cadwallader (Aprice) unrolls his pedigree, saying 'There it is; there, Peter, help me to stretch it out. There's seven yards more of Lineals, besides three of Collaterals, that I expect next *Monday* from the Herald's Office.' RLE had known Foote many years before.

which Foote unrolled across the stage, if I were to give you the list of the names of those to whom we have been introduced at her house but I will just name a few of the most conspicuous in both classes—Lord Byron, Malthus, 2 Smiths (Rejected addresses[1])—Miss Baillie—Mrs. Opie—Mr. Morritt of Rokeby—Mrs Marcet—Mrs. Morris Ld. Erskine's daughter—Mrs. Dixon Smeaton's daughter—Sir James and Lady Mackintosh—the Miss Berrys—Miss Fanshawes—Lady Crewe—Mrs. Weddell—Lady Carysfort, Lord and Lady Carrington—Lord Lansdowne—Mr. and Lady Elizabeth Whitbread—Miss Fox—Lord and Lady Darnley—Lord and Lady Hardwicke—Lady Charlemont—Lady Charlotte Lindsay—Lord Gower—Lord Somerville—Dutchess of Somerset. I am tired and so are you of this list of names. Of Lord Byron[2] I can yet tell you nothing but that his appearance is nothing that you would remark in any other man. He stood behind the door all night with the Dutchess of Somerset who penned him up effectually and I hear he complained that he could not get out but all the time I am sure he was flattered by it. Nobody but her Grace heard him say one word. This is an imitation of Lady Hertford and P. Regent. We are to breakfast quite in private with Lord Byron in a few days and then I shall be able to tell you what I think of him. Malthus is plain and sensible in conversation and agreeable notwithstanding a sad defect in his pronounciation—the two Smiths—nothing but the Rejected addresses. One of them is better than the other but it is scarcely worth making a distinction—Horace in London[3] has undone them—Mrs. Marcet, *plain* and sensible and good natured but I have yet seen her only in great parties—she will I am sure appear to far more advantage in a select society—Mrs. Opie—my curiosity is satisfied—The Miss Berrys all that you have heard of them from people of various tastes, consequently you know they are well bred and have nice tact in conversation. Miss Catherine Fanshawe I particularly like. Altogether I think her one of the most agreeable and unaffected women of talents I have seen. She has delightful talents—far

[1] H. and J. Smith, *Rejected Addresses* (1812).

[2] For Byron's weathercock opinions on the Edgeworths see *Letters and Journals*, ed. Prothero (1901), v. 109, 178, 179, 440, etc.

[3] H. and J. Smith, *Horace in London* (1813).

superior even to what I expected. Her drawings have charmed my mother—full of invention as well as of taste. Her *Village school* and *Village children at play* are beautiful compositions and her drawings for the Bath guide[1] full of humour and character without vulgar caricature. But her manners and conversation are what I most like—perfectly a gentlewoman, her appearance, well bred, not labouring at the oar of Bel Esprit or at any oar, but quite easy, natural and sprightly. Yes indeed I should be flattered by its being thought that I had any resemblance to such a woman. Lady Crewe has still the remains of much beauty—*Buff and blue and Mrs. Crewe*[2]—I looked at her with Charles Fox in my head. Except her dress which happened to be blue there appeared to be nothing else *blue* about her. The difference between her really fashionable air and manner and that of the *strugglers* and imitaters struck me much but as to the little I heard of her conversation it was nothing that marked talent. Her *style* is something like Mrs. Fortescue's—quiet—rather reserved—wishing to have people exert themselves for her amusement—with the air of an idol long used to be worshipped and expecting it but still a well bred idol.

Lady Elizabeth Whitbread in one word delightful and I wish we may like her as well on further acquaintance as I did the first evening I saw her. Lady Darnley has been very polite in her attentions to us and *of course* we like her. She asked kindly for the *Staples*.[3] Miss Fox[4]—very agreeable—converses at once—without preface or commonplace—Lady Charlotte Lindsay Ditto. Lady Hardwicke was much more pleasing than I had expected to find her and both her Ladyship and her Lord peculiarly gracious to us.

[1] [Christopher Anstey], *New Bath Guide* (1766). These drawings, like those of John Sneyd (see below, p. 141), were done for private amusement, not publication.

[2] After the Westminster election of 1780 'Mrs. Crewe gave a splendid entertainment. . . . On this occasion the ladies, no less than the men, were all habited in blue and buff [the Whig colours]. . . . After supper, a toast having been given by his Royal Highness, consisting of the words, "True blue and Mrs. Crewe", which was received with rapture, she rose, and proposed another health, expressive of her gratitude and not less laconic, namely, "True blue and all of you" ' (Wraxall, *Memoirs* (1884), 350). Fox was the successful candidate.

[3] ME's cousin Richard Ruxton married Elizabeth Staples.

[4] The Hon. Caroline Fox.

Private. Lord Somerville is so much charmed he says with Lady Delacour and Lady Geraldine[1] whom he pronounces to be perfect women of fashion and who he says are in high repute in the *Equerry's* room at court that you know I cannot help being charmed with his Lordships good breeding in return. He was quite indignant against certain pretenders to fashion; Lady Derby[2] he says is always *acting*—that there is continually a stage *aside* which betrays her. I told him the remark of a friend of ours that a gentleman or gentlewoman cannot be made in less than two generations. 'In less than *five* Ma'am I think it is scarcely possible.' *end of Private.*

Lady Lansdowne taking in beauty, character, conversation, talents and manners I think superior to any woman I have seen —perfectly natural—daring to be herself—gentle, sprightly, amiable, and engaging—the style of dear Mrs. Parkinson Ruxton but in figure, beauty and talents far superior. I long to see more of her and feel afraid I shall like her so much that I shall be sorry to part with her.

Private. Lady Spencer—dined at her house—clever and in the Lady Granard-style—taking snuff and pulling her lace shawl and giving her opinions of Windham—Fox—Pitt &c &c in a *loudish* quality voice—laughing at what she says herself and *tres capable.* In elegance she is not all I expected—but mum-mum. I am charged and conjured not to give my opinions in writing because we have found they *come round* so strangely and dangerously. Lord Spencer puts me I cant well tell why in mind of my uncle Ruxton—not in figure—he is thin and unlike him—but in his reserved quiet way of enjoying conversation in his snugs. I was quite at ease with him and placed quite to my satisfaction between him and Lady Lansdowne. The dinner au reste was stupid tho' very grand—24 candles on the table in superb branches—sideboard of gold plate at one end and silver at the other end. Private—a prodigiously fine desert—of which no creature eat. It was like the Barmecide feast. I mean *literally* that nobody touched any thing except a biscuit. This I perceive is *an air*—Very ridiculous! Lady Georgiana Spencer very pretty—

[1] Characters in ME's *Belinda* (1801) and *Ennui* (*Tales of Fashionable Life,* (1809)).

[2] Lady Derby was Eliza Farren, the actress.

Lady Sarah Lyttleton the other daughter I am told is uncommonly well informed and had a prodigious desire to be acquainted with me for whom she had the highest admiration &c *but* she seated herself on a sofa at a distance from me and never *could* cross the room or speak one word to me. But they were one and all *potent* starers and so near sighted as to be compelled to have frequent recourse to their glasses. All this is only my first impression. When we go there again perhaps I may find it all different. Lady Bessborough was there—her manner soft and sentimental—beseeching you to like her with voice and with eye. We are to go there and shall see more.

Private. Lydia White has been very kind to us and eager to bring together people who could suit and please us—very pleasant dinner at her house. She conducts her *esprit parties* as they are now called very well. Her vivacity breaks through the constraint of those who *stand* upon their great reputations and are afraid of committing their precious souls. Met at Lydia Whites Mr. Hallam Lord Byron's friend—mentioned in his notes[1]—very agreeable man but not a first rate—very scarce those! Met at Lydia White's by appointment Lady Crewe—saw her granddaughters or nieces the Miss Grevilles—like Admiral Pakenham's daughters—colts taken up late from grass—open faced and open hearted but heads and shoulders not well drilled.

Public. Charming! Amiable Lady Wellington! As she truly said of herself '*She is always Kitty Pakenham to her friends*'. She received us just as she would have done at Pakenham Hall. After comparison with crowds of others, beaux esprits, fine ladies and fashionable *scramblers* for notoriety her dignified graceful simplicity rises in ones opinion and we *feel* it with more *conviction* of its superiority. She let us in in the morning, talked about her children, shewed them to us and the little Wellesley. What a contrast to her children! delightful children! I could go on but I must not fill this letter with Lady Wellington because I can tell you nothing of her but what you *know*. Lord Longford just come to town. Met us yesterday (Saturday) at the exhibition of

[1] Byron satirized Henry Hallam in *English Bards and Scotch Reviewers* (1809), ll. 547–51.

Sir Joshua Reynolds' pictures[1] (Some of these pictures excellent —His children from the sublime infant Samuel to the arch gipsey child are admirable).

We have been to one of Mrs. Siddons readings—*Measure for measure*. It did not come up to my expectations—fine attitudes but I did not think she pleaded as a sister would have pleaded for a brother. Her voice expressed indignation and reproach admirably, but the tones of tenderness and sorrow were wanting and the looking through spectacle glasses at the book from time to time breaks all illusion. We are to see her *act* in the gamester[2] on the 25th. She acts for the benefit of decayed actors. In settling with Sheridan *she came short* 10 or 12 thousand pounds and her *Readings* are to make up this defalcation.[3] . . .

We have been to a grand night at Mrs. Hopes—furniture Hope[4]—rooms really deserve the French epithet *superbe*! All of beauty rank and fashion that London can assemble I believe I may say in the newspaper style was there and we observed that the beauties past fifty bore the belle. The Prince Regent stood holding converse with Lady Elizabeth Monck one third of the night—she leaning gracefully on a bronze table in the center of the room in the midst of the sacred but very small space of circle etiquette *could* keep round them. The other two thirds of the night he sat in a window sofa with Lady Harcourt [Hertford].† They staid till half past three till every body else was gone and Mrs. Hope tired to death. About 900 people were at this assembly—The crowd of carriages so great that after sitting an hour waiting in ours, the coachman told us there was no chance of our getting *in* till two o'clock unless we got *out* and walked. A good natured coachman *backed* his horses to *favor* us and we crossed bravely and got into the house and up the staircase but no power

[1] A commemorative exhibition of Reynolds's paintings opened at the British Institution on 8 May.

[2] *The Gamester* (1633) by James Shirley. Mrs. Siddons was acting for the benefit of the Theatrical Fund.

[3] At the Argyll Street Rooms. According to J. Boaden, *Memoirs of Mrs. Siddons* (1827), iii. 383, her readings were to supplement her income.

[4] Thomas Hope of Deepdene published in 1809 *Household Furniture*, a book of adaptations of ancient designs, mainly Greek and Egyptian, for modern use. He was a plain man, his wife a beauty, and a disappointed artist, Antoine Dubost, in 1810 exhibited a portrait of them entitled *La belle et la bete* (D. Watkin, *Thomas Hope, 1769–1831, and the Neo-Classical Idea* (1968), 19).

of ours could have got on had it not been for the gloriously *large* body and good natured politeness of the Archbishop of Tuam who fortunately met us at the door recognised us just as he would have done at Mrs. Bushe's in the County of Longford and made way for us through the crowd in the *wake* of his greatness we sailed on prosperously and he never stopped till he got us up to his beautiful daughter to whom he presented us and who received us with a winning smile. It is fortunate that the mistress of such a house should be so beautiful. I don't think Mr. Hope is at all a bête though she is a belle but perhaps I only think well of his taste and understanding because he was very civil to us. I asked him who somebody was who was passing and he answered 'I really don't know. I don't know half the people here nor do they know me or Mrs. Hope even by sight. Just now I was behind a lady who thought she was making *her speech* to Mrs. Hope but she was addressing her compliments to some stranger.' Among the old beauties the Dutchess of Rutland held her preeminence and looked the youngest. When you write to Edgeworthstown say that Lady Rancliffe and Lady Levinge at Mrs. Hopes and everywhere have been particularly obliging in their attentions to us. They seem really glad to see us there. We are going to dine at Lady Levinge's this day to meet Lady S: Bayley a daughter of Lady Jerseys[1]—like her mother in person and as unlike her in mind I understand as her friends could wish.

And now my dear Sophy I have done with the chapter of Lords and Ladies with which my letter is filled. Pray do not think because I name these fine people and their civilities that my poor little head is turned or turning with them. Be assured that the whole panorama passes before me as a panorama. It amuses me but I no more would pass my *life* in this way than spend it looking at a panorama. I feel that my own way of life and my own friends are all in all to me and among those dear Aunt Ruxton foremost now as ever in my affection. Yesterday we heard something that will give her pleasure and at the risk of my uncle's thinking me a lump of vanity I must tell it to you. But I must go back a little and tell you that a few days after we came to Town we were told by Mr. Wakefield that there was

[1] Lady Jersey was notorious for her former connection with the Prince Regent.

to be at the Freemason's Tavern a Lancasterian[1] meeting at which there was to be Sir James Mackintosh—Whitbread—Lansdowne—Dukes of Kent and Sussex—that it was expected they would all speak and as the subject was education and the Reports of the Irish Commissioners of Education to be alluded to my father determined to go and we were anxious to go as many ladies go to this meeting to hear public speaking which in this country they have scarcely any other opportunity of hearing. We went. The Secretary on our being named invited my father to the Committee room and we ladies were ushered into a fine large hall filled with green benches as for a lecture room—raised platform at one end for the *performers*—that is for the gentlemen of the Committee and for those expected to speak—arm chairs for the Royal Dukes empty common chairs for common men. Waited an hour and were introduced to various people—among others to the Mr. Allen who is so famous for his generous benevolence who lives most economically and gives thousands as easily as others would give pence. Dumont seated himself between Mrs. E and I. Consequently the hours waiting was so filled with conversation that it seemed but 5 minutes. Enter Royal Dukes preceded by stewards with white staves—gentlemen of the committee ranged at the back of the theatre, one row in front on each side of Dukes seated—Lord Lansdowne—Mr. Whitbread—Mr. Lancaster—two or three others and Mr. Edgeworth. The object of the meeting to effect a junction between the Bell and Lancasterian systems and parties.[2] It had been previously agreed that Lancaster should have his debts paid and should retire and give up the schools to the committee. *Private*. He has I think a bad countenance and I have a notion is not the *right thing*. *Public*. Lord Lansdowne spoke extremely well—manner and matter. When he adverted to the Board of Education he turned to my father whom he called 'a most distinguished member of that Board' and called upon him to speak to support his assertion that the dignified clergy among those Commissioners had acted with liberality. It had been previously

[1] The Royal Lancasterian Society was founded to promote the education of the poor on a non-sectarian basis according to the principles of Joseph Lancaster.

[2] Bell's system of education was that pursued by the National Society for promoting the Education of the Poor. It was strongly Church of England. The proposed junction did not take place.

agreed in the Committee room that my father should move the vote of thanks which had been prepared for the ladies who had forwarded by their exertions the Lancasterian schools and education in general.

Thus called upon my father got up to speak. When he first rose and when I heard the Duke of Kent say in his sonorous voice 'Mr. Edgeworth—gentlemen' I was so frightened I dared not look up but I was soon reassured. My fathers speaking was next to Lord Lansdowne's the best I heard and loud plaudits convinced me that I was not singular in this opinion. The account of the meeting will appear and if I can get the paper you shall have it. The Duke of Kent speaks well and makes an excellent chairman. The best thing these dukes do is the attending these meetings.

Yesterday my father was invited to a Lancasterian dinner—No ladies at the dinner. For an account of it I should like to refer you to Lord Fingall next to whom my father sat but as perhaps you will not see Lord Fingall immediately I must tell you that my fathers health was drank and when his name was mentioned and given by the Duke of Kent loud applauses ensued as I am told by a gentleman who was present. The Duke of Bedford rose after dinner and after speaking of the Irish Board of Education and the excellence and liberality of the 14th Report[1] pronounced an eulogium upon 'that excellent letter which is annexed to that report, a letter full of liberality and good sense on which indeed the best part of the Report seems founded I mean the letter of Mr. Edgeworth to whom this country as well as Ireland is so much indebted'.

Private Mr. Wakefield, poor Mr. Wakefield! Whatever his faults and whatever may be his sins of omission or commission[2] has shewn us this day such warmth of heart and honest gratitude that I can never forget it. He came early in the morning all red and radiant with joy to tell my mother and I how much my father's speech (and what he said in reply to the Duke of Bedford) had been applauded and was really approved. My dear

[1] *14th Rep. from Commissioners of Bd. of Education of Ireland*, H.C. 21, p. 221 (1812–13), vi.

[2] Wakefield was author of *Ireland: statistical and political* (1812). The Edgeworths had taken great trouble in revising the information in his manuscript, but they were not satisfied with the book.

Sophy you and my aunt would be delighted if you saw how *good* my father is in all companies. You would not believe as he desired me to tell my aunt how pretty behaved he is. What a comfortable thing it is to see our dearest relations *look* and act like gentlemen and gentlewomen. Mrs. E is so much liked and appreciated by everybody who has head, heart or eyes! I often hear whispers about her from those who don't know that I have quick ears but I am no listener—only when I can't help hearing you know I can't . . . As I have half an hour before the cursed mantuamaker, I beg her pardon *dressmakers* appointment I will tell you all we did yesterday between the times of writing 3 pages of this epistle. But first I must note because I shall forget it if I don't that there are no such things as governesses any more than mantuamakers in the world. Governesses are all *ladies who conduct the education* of Miss so and so— . . . Coach at the door—'Put on hat this minute Maria and come out and pay our visits for we shall meet some of these people tonight or tomorrow.'

To save myself trouble I enclose the list of the visits which we made just as Mrs. E wrote them on the card by which we steered. (God knows how I should steer without her.)

The three crosses X mark the three places where we were let in and though we were always sorry when the step was let down yet we regularly got into the carriage again saying 'I am *very* glad we were let in there'. Lady Milbanke is very agreeable and has a charming well informed daughter. Mrs. Weddell is a perfectly well bred most agreeable old lady—sister to Lady Rockingham—who lived in the Sir Joshua Reynolds set—tells anecdotes of Burke Fox Windham—has the last century at her fingers ends and plays it well—magnificent house—fine pictures—as much above them all as Lady Elizabeth Pakenham would be and as much too proud to be vain—not reserved manners—gentle voiced and cheerful and affable without the affectation of affability. We spoke of having just seen Sir Joshua Reynolds's exhibition of pictures. 'Perhaps if you are fond of painting you would take the trouble of walking into the next room and I will shew you what gives me a particular interest in Sir Joshua's pictures.' Large folding doors opened—large room full of admirable copies from Sir Joshua Reynolds—In crayons—done by

Mrs. Weddell herself. Mrs. E says they are quite astonishing. Her conversation as good as her painting—passed through many books lightly and with *touch and go* ease in a quarter of an hour. I began with mentioning a curious anecdote of Madame d'Arblay—that when she landed at Portsmouth a few months ago and saw on a plate at Admiral Foleys a head of Lord Nelson and the word *Trafalgar* she asked what *Trafalgar* meant. She actually (as Lady Spencer told me who had the anecdote from Dr. C. Burney) did not know that the English had been victorious at Trafalgar or that Lord Nelson was dead. This is the mixed effect of the recluse life she led and the care taken in France to keep the people in ignorance of certain events. From this I mentioned a similar instance recorded in Thiebault[1] of the chevalier Mason living at Potsdam during the 7 years war and not knowing any thing of it when the King of Prussia returned. Then Mrs. Weddell went through Thiebault and Madame de Bareith's[2] memoirs and then she asked me if I had ever happened to meet with an odd entertaining book Madame de Bavière's[3] memoires. How little I thought when my dear Aunt Ruxton gave me that book to read that it would stand me *in stead* at Mrs. Weddells 5 years afterwards. We talked it over and had a great deal of laughing and diversion. Mrs. Weddell is the Mrs. Weddell who formerly lived in Yorkshire and whose pictures Dr. and Mrs. Beaufort went to see—who had such a charming society there *and* who was so much attached to her husband. She is now huge and very plainly dressed old fashionedly but she must have been beautiful and graceful formerly. Her picture of her sister Lady Rockingham is charming—but I must leave her (only till Wednesday).

Came home—Papa dressing to dine at Sir Samuel Romillys—Lady Romilly just recovering from *confinement*—birth and death of child. They only see gentlemen as yet. We two were to dine at Lady Levinge's. While we were dressing long note from Miss Berry sent by her own maid to apologise for a mistake of her

[1] Dieudonné Thiebault, *Mes souvenirs de vingt ans à Berlin, ou Frederic le Grand, sa famille, etc.* (1804).

[2] *Memoirs of the Margravine de Bareith, sister of Frederick the Great, written by herself* (1812).

[3] Madame de Bavière (Elizabeth Charlotte, Princess Palatine), *Fragments de lettres originales* (1788).

servants who had said *not at home* to us, entreat we would *look in* this evening—much hurried dressing. Lady Levinge's dinner (which was not on table till 8 o'clock) very entertaining because quite a new set of people. I have only time to name Lady S Bayley—Most beautiful—Mr. Bayley sat by me—very conversible —Mr. Byng son of Lord Torrington—Lord Killeen—Lord and Lady Rancliffe &c.

Called in the evening at Miss Berry's—Without any comparison the most agreeable house I have seen in Town—quite like French society—met there persons innumerable—among them Augustus Foster—Henry Pakenham and Lord Caledon from Ireland. Had a great deal of conversation with Lady C. Lindsay who is as agreeable as all the Norths are said to be. Mr. Ward was there but I did not hear him. *Private. Mrs. Scott of Kilkenny here and flirting finely*.

Went—shamefully late—to Mrs. Sneyds. Home. Found my father in bed. Stood at the foot and heard his account of his dinner at Sir Samuel Romillys with Dr. Parr Dumont Malthus &c —very entertaining but I have not time to tell you more. I have been standing in my dressing gown writing on the top of a chest of drawers and now my mother will positively not let me write any more. I must dress for a breakfast at Lady Davys where we are to meet Lord Byron and nobody else to be admitted.

I must just say that half an hour we spent with Lady Wellington yesterday was by far the most agreeable part of the day. Lord Douro has been ill but we saw him *looking* a great deal better and able to stand full half an hour which if very weak he could not do as I know from experience. Lady Wellington diverted us by an account of the serious and friendly counsels she has had from many not to neglect her dress.

'My dear Lady Wellington' said one lady 'How many times a day do you think of your dress?'

'Why three times—Morning, evening, and night besides *casualties*.'

'But this won't do you must *think* of it seriously—at other times and when you go into the country always dress to keep the habit my dear Lady Wellington.'

Sir W Farquhar told Lady Wellington that the Dutchess of Rutland every day at home and when sure of seeing no creature is dressed at all points to keep up the habit. He saw her one day *alone* at breakfast with her little son dressed as if for company and the same care which the conscious sylphs would have paid to the drapery and the ringlets—her Grace going to the glass to arrange the ringlets and looking back over her shoulder at the effect of drapery behind. Goodbye I must go and do likewise. Your ever affectionate (if you write to me) friend Maria E

To Fanny Edgeworth

Tuesday morning, 18 May 1813,
Before breakfast—up at half past 7

My own dear Fannikin, This morning and many a morning since I came to London have I blessed you for going without your breakfast for me seven years ago with so much good humor as you did. You cured me completely of lying in bed till *the last moment* and now I have the advantage of it every day of my life so it is but fair that you should have some little pleasure from it yourself. My dear packer and gauger I wish you could know how often I have thanked you in my own mind and sometimes aloud when I am dressing in a desperate hurry, for all the care you took in putting up my clothes and all my jingembobs so nicely for me that day and night when I was lying disabled in my bed. I remember well the *tired red spot* you had in your cheek when you stood at the foot of my bed and wished me a good night at last and I assure you that your good humor when I sent you of a 100 different messages at once was not lost upon me. I recollect that I was almost in the same state in which I desired Mrs. Hoare's[1] maid *to put everything at top*. I believe my mother has told you the sad history of the loss of my dressing box with every trinket and keepsake which all my friends had given me; Madame Recamier, and Mrs. Stewart and Mr. Hartegan and the garnets which you or Sophy (I forget which) were to inherit, and the gold chains which my aunts had taken such pains to get

[1] See above, Introduction, p. xv.

for me and which I had worn but two or three times all! all! gone! But all! all! come again! The honest landlady at Market Harborough sent it to me and wrote a very civil letter and never claimed the 2 guineas reward which I offered. She said it was the fault of the postillion and it was but just that I should be at no loss. Tell Honora my *old man's* box is very useful to me and I don't know what I should do without the portfolio she made for me. So much for my thanksgivings. No I have not done yet. I must tell you that Mrs Hunter (Johnsons-Hunters wife) having heard that I liked rhododendrons sent me a present of a fine large one taller than myself (think how tall that must be!) and broader than my two aunts and you and Honora standing close together. It is at this moment standing in our middle bow window with 16 bunches of flowers upon it each bunch in rich blow. My dear father is so kind as to water it night and morning. Thank Honora for all she has done for me in my garden. I am sure I shall return with fresh taste for it. I am much amused by all the fine things and fine people I see here and enjoy the panorama by day light and candle light as much as any of my friends or acquaintance could wish but I would not for any consideration live always such a rantipole life. Some of the pleasantest time is coming home in the carriage at night and talking with Mrs. E when we are going to bed. She makes a dressing room of my bedchamber which is a fine large one in which we have two dressing tables, two chests of drawers and everything comfortable. I should not have been nearly so happy if she had not dressed in the room with me. Do you remember how happy you and Honora and I were in the same room in Dublin and how we used to waken you every night by our talking? *That* was delightful! Tell Honora that Mr. Whishaw was quite disappointed when he found that she was not with us. He really asked very kindly for her and I must tell you that Mr. Whishaw appears to much greater advantage here than he did in Dublin. He is much esteemed I find by the cleverest people and by the best, and in company with numbers he looks like a gentleman and converses well and does not *roll about* nearly so much as he did *and* he is very goodnatured to us and brought Malthus to see us. We dined yesterday at Mrs. Marcets with Mr. Whishaw, Malthus, Mrs. Malthus and her sister, Mr. Dumont and Mr. Haldimand, brother in law to Mrs. Marcet and an old *old* Mr. Haldimand *father to the brother in law* . . .

Our dinner and evening at Mrs. Marcet's was very agreeable. Mrs. Marcet herself is plain, and has not an agreeable voice or fashionable appearance, but she is sensible in conversation and unaffected. She has two nice children 5 and seven years old—girls. They came smiling up to me, and kissed me, and shewed that they were prepared to like me. They are the nicest children I have seen since I left home. Mrs. Marcet said that she was quite surprised by my father's having ventured to give 'Conversations of Chemistry'[1] to a girl of 9 years old. My mother told how it had been read and explained bit by bit. 'Ah' said Mrs. Marcet 'Who but Mr. E would or could do that!' Mr. Malthus is a perfectly unaffected amiable, gentlemanlike man, who really *converses*; that is, listens, as well as talks, and follows the ideas of others as well as produces ideas of his own. Mrs. Malthus is a charming domestic amiable woman with a pleasing voice and manner—well dressed and well looking—perfectly a gentlewoman. Miss Eckershall is not the sister William danced with. That sister remembers William well, and they asked after him. The Miss Eckershall he danced with, is, as they told me a *Female Forrester*,[2] but she is *curing* of her singularities. Dumont is very entertaining; and of his abilities you have heard so much that I need say no more. He is uniformly kind to us.

After our dinner and evening at Mrs. Marcet's we went to Anna's friends the Horners at eleven o'clock—a larg*ish* party—Mrs. Horner is certainly like Honora but much handsomer—not so genteel but walks much better. She is beautiful, and natural, and engaging; and my father is charmed with her and talked to her about her darling only child. She seemed much pleased with my father and promised to follow his advice about arithmetic for her child. At Mrs. Horners we met in a crowd of sattins and laces whom we did not know, Mrs. and Miss Roget, who asked kindly for Lovell and Sneyd—and Mr. Cullen, Sneyd's friend, who was delighted to find that Sneyd had made him known to

[1] *Conversations on Chemistry* by Mrs. Marcet was published in 1806.

[2] The uncouth hero of a story in ME's *Moral Tales* (1801). He is supposed to have been based on Lord Ashburton but his character probably also owes something to the eccentricities of Thomas Day.

us by description. My father was very gracious to him and said that he always liked Sneyds friends. Mr. Leonard[1] Horner, the great man, was there but I did not *hear* him. We met another of Sneyds friends at Lydia White's, twice—Mr. Kingston—Mr. Kingston is very conversible. There was such a crowd and so many people speaking to us that I could see no more—Mrs. Kingston is pretty and pleasing . . .

But you will expect to hear about the sights we have seen. The *mint* which Mr. Lawson shewed us I dare not attempt to describe to you because it would fill two pages and be unintelligible perhaps afterwards. Tomorrow we are to go to Mr. Brunel's to see the machine for cutting blocks[2] &c. Westminster Abbey—sublime Westminster Abbey—we have seen and seen in the most agreeable manner, in company with Sir James Mackintosh. We breakfasted at his house which is close to the Abbey with a delightful Mr. and Mrs. Abercromby and then he went with us and at every step some new idea or some apposite allusion or quotation from French English or classical poets rose to his recollection. If I had ever doubted of the superiority of rational associations for the memory, over Feinagle's system[3] of bad punning Sir James Mackintosh, as a practical example, would have convinced me of it. . . .

The only sights we have seen besides Westminster Abbey, and the Mint are some exhibitions of pictures—with Mrs. Sneyd and Emma—Sir Joshua Reynolds; and that of modern painters at Somerset House. Sir Jo's are beautiful—the others below par—except one admirable portrait of old Mr. Watt's. We are to dine with Mr. Watt.

My father has dined with Sir S Romilly along with Dumont Malthus and Dr. Parr &c. Dr. Parr and he had a battle about the Bishop of Elphin whom my father warmly defended.[4] Dr. Parr ended by saying 'Sir I like your warm heart; send me the

[1] Anna Beddoes's friends were Leonard Horner and his wife. 'Leonard' must be a slip of the pen for 'Francis' who was the 'great man' of the Horner family.

[2] Machinery for making ships' blocks was patented by Brunel in 1797 and he built sawmills with improved machinery 1805–12 (see below, p. 203).

[3] Gregor von Feinagle, *The New Art of Memory* (English trans. 1812).

[4] This was presumably the incident referred to by Byron in his comments on the *Quarterly Review*'s venomous article on RLE's *Memoirs* (*Letters and Journals* (1901), ed. Prothero, v. 109). It places the matter in a different light. ME herself met Dr. Parr at the Horners (*Mem.* i. 287).

epitaph on the Abbé Edgeworth and I'll correct it for you'. Dr. Parr *plays* Dr. Johnson in society . . .

Mrs. Siddons' reading of 'Measure for Measure' did not answer my expectations. We are to see her act Mrs. Beverley in the Gamester the 25th. It was very difficult to get a box; but one was most handsomely given to our name; and we have been able to oblige Mr Mrs. and Miss Sneyd with places. I am very, *very* glad they go with us. We have *also* given places in this box to Lady Charleville and her daughter (who is very pleasing), to Lord Tullamore (her son) and a certain Russian Prince, Prince Kutaslo. I know nothing of him but that he is short and fat and looks good humored and like two men bound in one. He says he has a great desire to pay me his *hommage*. If he throws himself at my feet he will never be able to get up again. I hope that none of these people will talk so as to prevent me from hearing Mrs. Siddons . . .

Yesterday—tuesday we dined with Miss White—very entertaining dinner. Company were—Lady Charlotte Lindsay, Mr. Frederic Norths sister—*most* agreeable!—Sir James and Lady Mackintosh—Miss Berry—the famous Berry (she is all that is said of her!)—Mr. and Mrs. Morris (rich and fashionable friends of Mrs. Inchbalds, who have invited us to meet her there)—Miss Grattan daughter of Grattan the great—Mrs. Grattan is a delightful old lady—Rejected-addresses-Smith—a man who is said to converse better than any man in England—*Mr. Sharp*; he is called *conversation-Sharp*. I sat beside him, and thought all the World was right for once.

In the evening at Miss White's the rooms were crowded with company. A list of their names would be no diversion to you therefore I will only mention those who talked most to me; and whom I thought the most agreeable—viz Lady Charlotte Lindsay—Lady Charleville—Mrs. Broderip—Sir W. Phipps—Mr. Tennant—Mr. Whishaw—Lady Milbanke and daughter—daughter is a prodigious heiress—£12,000 per Annum—William look sharp! I should like her much for my sister-in-law (as far as I could see in morning visit and evening rout)—very handsome—18—quite unaffected—sensible conversation—*and* she holds up her head! Oh my dear Fannikin I thought of you, and wished that at her age yours may be held as well. I have continually thought of you in public rooms, where numbers are gathered together, and where all has been done that milliners and mantuamakers, and money, and mothers can do for the appearance of daughters; and all this is nothing compared with what they can do for themselves, by taking thought in time to add at once to their stature and their grace—by holding up their heads and stepping-out well when they walk. *Backs* are what distinguish gentlewomen more than *faces* in public and vulgarity or gentility sits on the shoulders. My dear Fan if I did not love you truly, I could not spare time to lecture you at this moment when I have 100,000,000,000 other things to do and my dress for dinner imperiously demands my consideration. The Duke of Bedford is to be here in an hours time, and in his Grace's presence I *must do nothing*. Today we dine at Mr. Solly's mothers (very rich)—go in the evening to a Mrs. Weddell's; I have described her in a letter to Sophy Ruxton who will tell you about her . . .

We are invited to Lady E Whitbreads—where I wish to go —to Lady Cork's where I do not wish to go—to the Dutchess of Sussex or Lady Augusta Murrays whichever she is to be called—*but* there are great doubts whether we *ought* to go.[1] I mention these engagements and names for my aunts diversion—We are to go to Lord and Lady Darnleys and Lord and Lady Carringtons. Lord Carrington sent me an excellent sermon of Dr. Fawcetts which I wish I had seen before Vivian[2] was published as there is an x passage in it on *false shame* which Russell might have quoted . . .

Believe me my dear friends my head is not turned by this vortex, though the hurry in which I write may naturally lead you to suspect that it is. I love you all after more extensive comparison better than ever; and prefer the life we lead at home and that state of life to which it has pleased God to call me to any other upon earth—happy equal marriage only excepted—marriage such as your mothers is, and such as I hope may one day be your lot my dear. Remember I say *happy equal* marriage—nothing *less*. I would rather see you in your grave than see

[1] Her marriage was null and void under the Royal Marriages Act of 1772.

[2] *Vivian* is one of the second series of ME's *Tales of Fashionable Life* (1812). Russell was tutor to the hero.

you as I see many—many who are in fine houses and fine coaches.

. . . Good b'y'e my dear Fan. Ever affectionately your friend—and *sister*.[1] That last, Nature made you. The first you have made yourself and I thank you for it; and think it will add to your happiness as well as to mine Maria E . . .

To Fanny Edgeworth

Monday, 31 May 1813

My dear Fan—While my father and mother are gone out to buy some colors to paint a scene for Mrs. Marcets play, which is to be acted tomorrow I am allowed to have the pleasure of writing a tiny note to you in a frank which my mother intended to fill.

Without preface I will begin with what is freshest in my memory—the history of yesterday. Went at 11 o clock to pay a visit to Lady Wellington, who had sent to beg to see us—sat a delightful half hour with her. Her little boy is getting quite well. Tell Sophy Ruxton I asked if there was any print of her children. She said 'There is none but if there was one I would certainly send it to Miss Ruxton.' There is a pretty little *drawing* of them *designed* not drawn by herself—one boy riding on a cushion and the other standing beside him and trying to draw a sword from the scabbard. This was in the exhibition last year and Lady Wellington thinks that this gave rise to the report Sophy heard of there being a print. The more we see of Lady Wellington the more we both admire and love her and the more comparisons we make with others the more we feel her easy, graceful superiority—but no more about her, or I shall forget every body else. At one o clock went with Madame Achard and M. Dumont to Kensington to pay a visit to a Mrs. Mallet, whose voice, and conversation were so strikingly like Mrs. Tuite's that my mother and I could hardly wait till we got downstairs to say so. I need not tell you that we thought Mrs. Mallet very agreeable. Went to Kensington gardens but a shower came

[1] The number 1 is inserted above 'friend' and 2 above 'sister'.

on and all the dressed groups were forced to take shelter under trees and parapluies.[1] Everything unfortunate is picturesque. Nevertheless I was sorry it rained. Madame Achard is a clever, rich, benevolent Swiss lady with a screeching voice which my father cannot endure. Tell my aunt Mary that M. Dumont is very plain, very fat and as far from sentimental as any human being can be. Au reste he has in conversation all the abilities his letters promise. He is an excellent critic, full of anecdote—entertaining and instructive—Just a French homme de lettres laid out for that kind of life—The mornings spent in writing and reading—dining out regularly. For the last 4 years it is said he has never dined at home. He has been very friendly whenever he has met us, but from his disliking crowded parties and our happening to be engaged on the days when he was invited to dine at the same places we have not seen much of him. I do not think he will ever come to Ireland though he still says he will. He seems to have bound himself for ever and ever to Bentham.

After our return from Kensington my father and Mrs. E paid a visit to Dean and the Miss Allotts and after various tickets had been left at various doors, which I forgot to mention, we dressed for dinner and went to dine at Lady E Whitbreads. Tell Sneyd I quite agree with him in thinking her agreeable—perhaps the more so because she was uncommonly attentive to us. The company were Sir H and Lady Davy—Mr. and Mrs. Ponsonby—Mr. Freeling—Mr. Brougham—Mr. Rogers (Pleasures of memory)[2]—*and* Sheridan. Sheridan came in late—sat next to Rogers, who was sitting next to me—whispered to Rogers and made him tell *who* every body was; then bid him introduce him to me and stretching across said 'Mr. Rogers has used me very ill and Lady E Whitbread has broke her compact with me, for I had bargained that I should sit next to Miss E'. Mr. Sheridan conversed a great deal both with my father and with me, with the ease and freedom of a man who had no character for wit to sustain. He looks bloated but his eye is an eye of inextinguished and inextinguishable fire—dark, very prominent, more like the eye of an ostrich than of a man. Some say it is very alarming;

[1] 'sols' is written above 'pluies', making the alternative word 'parasols'.

[2] Samuel Rogers, *The Pleasures of Memory* (1792).

but I did not feel it so. Indeed I always think it less alarming to talk to persons of the first abilities, than to fools. The fools are always trying to shew their wit by finding faults. People of abilities are in general more indulgent and better able to balance accounts. Tell my aunts that Mr. Sheridan talked to me much of Mrs. Honora E who, as he said he had heard was the handsomest woman of her day and he had heard that she bore some resemblance to his first wife—Miss Linley, whose picture by Sir Joshua Reynolds is now in the exhibition. I do not see the resemblance. Sheridan seemed to *feel* whilst he spoke of his first wife. A gentleman told me that he saw him go into the exhibition room after all the company had left it one day lately to look at her picture. He talked of Miss Seward and Major Andre &c.[1]

After dinner when the ladies went upstairs Lady E Whitbread shewed us her house, which is both magnificent and *comfortable* 4 large rooms on a floor and a delightful boudoir and below a library looking into a garden. Company in the evening—Miss Grant a friend of Anna's—Lord and Lady Grey—*both* very agreeable—an old dowager Lady Grey—Lady Asgill her sister Mrs. Bouverie (agreeable) Miss Ogle in a fur cap sister in law to Sheridan—Miss Berrys—Mr. Atkins and two or three *persons unknown*. The party not being too large it was very pleasant —broke into small conversation groupes sitting and standing. Lady E Whitbread said 'There is no chance you know of Sheridan's coming up till one o clock.' But lo! he made his appearance before eleven, took a little stool and sat down in the middle of our group consisting of Lord and Lady Grey Mrs. Ponsonby and Mrs. E. The stool cracked under him so he was forced to take a chair, but his elevation did not make him the less agreeable. I don't think he had drank up to his wit-point, but he was perhaps much the more agreeable to ladies. The moment he came in, Lady Elizabeth whispered to Mr. Whitbread 'Order supper soon, and plenty of punch, for Sheridan will want it'. We were very sorry we could not stay to supper. We were engaged to Miss White and after a delightful hour, when we got up to go Sheridan held us back and said 'You are not going, you *must not* go'. But alas we were in duty bound to go away so we went,

[1] Supposed to have been engaged to Honora Sneyd, RLE's second wife.

and Miss White was much obliged to us for the sacrifice we made. There we found a crowd of people—among them Mrs. Opie Lady Crewe and a Mrs. Broderip, whom I mention for future description—Lady Asgill (again) and her sister Mrs. Wilmot who came and had waited an hour on purpose to be introduced to us. My aunts will recollect *who* Mrs. Wilmot is—the lady who modelled the cow for Lady Holte[1]—She appears to me by far the most sensible of the family . . .

. . . As I have more time than I expected I will go back my dear Fan to some of our last week's operations and mention our interview with Mrs. Inchbald tho' I rather think my mother has already written you all an account of it. With much difficulty Mrs. Morris a friend of hers prevailed upon her to come so far into the world again as to dine at her house to meet us (Then Alas we were engaged). But we went in the evening—found the rooms absurdly crowded—as thick as pins in a pincushion—made our way through pinioned forms to a recessed window where at last we saw the waving black plumes of Mrs. Inchbalds bonnet. The recess was dark and till I pushed fairly into it I could see no more. She was in black and muffled but well dressed for effect—a tall commanding figure much handsomer face (as well as I could see) than I expected—prodigious fire and expression in her eyes and whole countenance—A theatrical yet not an affected manner (or at least affectation become natural)—quick feeling and the same originality and openness and carelessness about *committing* herself—and confidence in the sympathy of others—the same freedom from pride that apes humility and the same frank readiness to praise and to be pleased which appear in her letters to us. She talked a great deal (for our gratification) about the Simple story[2] and told us that the price she had been originally offered for it was Oh shameful! Oh incredible—*two* guineas! How my aunt Mary will lift up

[1] A great friend of Mrs. Elizabeth E. According to Farington (*The Farington Diary*, i (1923), 58) Mrs. Wilmot also modelled horses.

[2] ME was particularly fond of Mrs. Inchbald's *A Simple Story* (1791) and the two authoresses corresponded until 1817 when ME was deeply offended by Mrs. Inchbald's unfeeling letter on RLE's death. Speaking of her meeting with ME, Mrs. Inchbald wrote, 'She [Madame de Stael] talked to me the whole time: so did Miss Edgeworth whenever I met her in company. These authoresses suppose me dead, and seem to pay a tribute to my memory' (J. E. Boaden, *Memoirs of Mrs. Inchbald* (1833), ii. 190 (letter of 26 Aug. 1813)).

her hands and eyes! . . . Your affectionate sister Maria Edgeworth

To Mrs. Ruxton

[25 June 1813]

Malvern Links. Friday morning *before breakfast*

My Dearest Aunt,

. . . The grand panorama of London closed and the visions of dukes duchesses and countesses vanished from our sight, no regrets are left on our minds, we cast no longing lingering look behind, but all our thoughts looks and feelings are towards home, dear home. I have enjoyed more pleasure more amusement, of all kinds, infinitely more than I expected, received a thousand times more attention, more *kindness* than I could have thought it possible would be shewn to me. I have enjoyed the delight of seeing my father esteemed and honored in his age by the best judges in England, I have felt the pleasure of seeing my true friend and mother (for she has been a mother to me) appreciated in the best society and now with the fullness of content I return home loving my own friends and my own mode of life preferably to all others after comparison with all that is fine and gay—and rich and rare . . . Affectionately yours Maria E

To Miss Mary Sneyd

[June 1813]

[beginning missing] . . . The *one* day we spent with Anna was filled as full of pleasure as it could be. In the morning we all went out in one of the job sociables—went to see Samuel Essington[1] at the Essington Hotel. At first he thought it was a carriage full of strangers and came out to let down the step. I wish you could have seen the delight that glowed in his face and the tears that stood in his projecting eyes when he beheld my father.

[1] A former Edgeworthstown servant.

'Master! Master I declare!—Oh Sir Ma'am! Miss—Mrs. Beddoes! Miss Edgeworth how glad I am!' He shewed us his excellent house—walked us round his beautiful little lawn and shrubberies all of his own making—cut roses moss roses and blush roses for us with such eagerness and delight—all of his own planting. 'And all all owing to you Sir! that first taught me! Five admirals Sir would you believe it were at the laying out of this house.'

Poor Samuel walked and talked and perspired and with a face breadthened and shining with joy told my father the rise and progress of his fortunes and shewed the wonders he had done—All which you shall hear of viva voce. Went on to the house of a Mrs. Barry mother to Colonel Barry—Redmond Barry—beautiful place! Where Samuel Essington had been employed to lay out the walks. *Capability* Brown and picturesque Price and Knight[1] could not have laid them out better had they put their three heads and 6 eyes together and the *creation* of the shrubberies all in full flower and fragrance was quite surprising and delightful in this wild place. My father wrote on one of the pillars of the [ve][2]randa '*A paradise amid the wild*'.

We went into the house and with many mixed feelings (tell my dear Sophy) saw Mr. Redmond Barrys beautiful drawings.

Drove on through wild and beautiful lanes to see a fine [house] with a frightful name—*Castle ditch*[3]—belonging to Lord Somer[s] [? father] to the gallant Colonel Cocks who was Lord Wellingtons friend and who when he lost his [life] was so much regretted. One of the younger sons is I believe a friend of Sneyds. Their place is fit for Mrs. Radcliffe's or Mrs. Beauforts[4] powers of description—The castle they are building more superb than anything Vivian ever imagined but they fortunately have a fortune equal to the expense. Lady Somers came out from the house in which they now dwell at the foot of the terrace of the

[1] Lancelot Brown (1715–83), landscape gardener; Sir Uvedale Price (1747–1829), author of *An Essay on the Picturesque* (1794); Richard Payne Knight (1760–1824), author of *The Landscape* (1796) and *Analytical inquiry into the principles of style* (1808).

[2] Manuscript torn.

[3] Now Eastnor Castle, begun 1812 in the Norman style to the designs of Robert Smirke.

[4] e.g. in *The Mysteries of Udolpho* (1794). Mrs. Beaufort, Mrs. Edgeworth's mother, wrote very vivid letters, some of which are among the Edgeworth papers.

castle and invited us in—Very polite—shewed us fine pictures and gave us fine strawberries &c.[1]. . . Your ever affectionate Maria E.

[1] The last two paragraphs may be supplemented by a letter of 18 Sept. 1813 to Dumont (Bibliothèque Universitaire et Publique, Geneva) in which ME describes her meeting at Perrystone with Sir James Mackintosh: '. . . during the few days I passed with him, at Mrs. Clifford's in the country, I saw a great deal of Sir James Mackintosh. I admired his incomparable memory, and the splendid display of his abilities and acquirements—Splendid, beyond what I had ever before seen of conversational powers. Yet I was sometimes inclined to close my eyes "blasted with excess of light". When I went to bed, I used to feel actually fatigued with admiration, and attention. I recollect one night in particular, my sister followed me to my room, and throwing herself into a chair, with a doleful length of face, and exhausted tone, said "My dear Maria, how very strong you are grown! not to be tired!" "My dear Anna you are quite mistaken, I am tired to death, tired, as if I had been seeing a first rate actor the whole day."

'What surprised me, and provoked me with myself, was to find, that notwithstanding my full perception of Sir James Mackintosh's transcendant talents, I was but little interested about him. I am not envious, I hope. I generally am enthusiastically fond of superior abilities, and I saw my father transported with admiration of Sir James—Yet I do not care if I never see him again while I exist—except for my father's sake, or my brothers. They wish to see him. On the contrary, I have an earnest desire to see and know more of Sir Samuel Romilly. He seized strong hold of my mind, I should be less happy, I should think less well of myself if I were to forfeit his esteem—which I *know* that I possess, though he never told me so. If I were to describe the two men, I should say—The one is more root than flower—the other, more flower than root. . . .'

HONORA EDGEWORTH

From a skiagram ($\frac{1}{3}$ original size)

1818

RICHARD LOVELL EDGEWORTH died in June 1817, and before his death he had made his eldest daughter promise to complete and publish his memoirs as soon as possible after his death. Maria completed a draft of the second volume almost a year later. Her father's own lively first volume was written in a way which offended convention and it was with understandable misgivings about the reception of the work that she decided to submit it to the criticism not only of her family in Ireland but of various people in England, in particular Francis Beaufort and Etienne Dumont, who was expected to visit his former pupil Lord Lansdowne in the course of the summer. She left Ireland in the middle of August, taking with her her shy and reluctant half-sister Honora[1] to give her a chance to meet a world outside the restricted circle of her Irish acquaintance. Maria had other family business to transact: to settle with her brother-in-law in Bristol, Mr. King, about final payments of her sister Emmeline's dowry; to find a suitable school for her nine-year-old half-brother Francis; and, more harassing, to help arrange about a mental home for William Edgeworth who had a serious breakdown just after she and Honora left Ireland. The necessity of writing on these subjects to some extent restricted the range of the letters written in 1818.

To Fanny Edgeworth

Bangor, Monday, 17 August 1818

My dear Fanny, We went on board at 7 oclock on Saturday Evening. Mr. Hutton went to Howth to meet us—put us and

[1] Honora wrote (24 Aug. 1818) of 'this journey which before had not promised too many charms to me' and (from Bowood, 13 Sept. 1818) 'all the risk I run is that of being thought very stupid, which is perhaps better than the discovery which would be made if I opened my mouth more frequently—that I am a fool'.

the carriage on board—saved us all trouble in the kindest manner.

We had a passage of upwards of 40 hours but the sea was so calm and the motion so very easy that neither Honora nor I were more sick than you and I were on the dear river at Black Castle. We landed at 12 oclock this day. Captain Davies of the Countess of Liverpool was our captain. You have heard Lord Forbes speak of him as a sensible man and such we found him and most kind he was to us. We wished *not* to meet with any one on board whom we knew, We met only one gentleman whom we had ever seen before—Mr. Ellis. He was good natured and serviceable. He had under his protection a Mrs Currie and her two children —a boy of 10 and a girl of 8—nice well bred children and she a most interesting woman in deep mourning—gentle manners soft voice—widow of the *last officer* who fell at Waterloo—Aide de Camp of Lord Hill. His family continue friends to her and her children—much to their honor. We asked her to sit in our carriage on deck which she did and today let us carry by turns her boy and girl a stage each in the open carriage. She accepted in the most gracious and graceful manner that attention which was her due. Honora liked her much and had satisfaction in shewing her this little kindness. Honora enjoyed the fresh air this charming day. The Welch mountains with the sun shining upon them were most beautiful—like one of my mothers crayon drawings looking so soft as if we could with a touch of the finger rub them out or rub all the various colors together . . . [end missing]

To Fanny Edgeworth

Bath, 2 Nelson Place, 31 August 1818

My very dear Fanny . . . Anna who is, as you said *'a darling creature to be with'* has contrived so as to lodge and receive us all (George [Bristow] inclusive) between her new and old house. We have been to see her new house—and now let me *insense* you about that house. It is not at the top of the wearisome hill as you think but half way down the hill just at the corner of Cavendish Buildings. It has a delightful view of fields hills trees and trim flowery gardens and a wee wee triangle garden of its own. It is but a small house I confess but it exactly *fits* and suits Anna and her family—the dining parlor cheerful—the two drawing rooms opening one into another with a balcony and windows to the ground. The rooms are crooked but the crescent is a sufficient excuse to the minds eye and nice furniture supplies all deficiencies. Anna is furnishing it by degrees elegantly and prudently so as to do honor at once to her taste and judgment—and there's a fine sentence for you! She will not remove to it till the beginning of October. I am sorry she should not receive my aunts in it as it is so much nicer than her present lodgings. She has it for £70 rent + £15 taxes. For her lodgings here she pays a hundred but then she has the advantage of the woman of the house to cook. Old George is as happy as a king here all day and there all night. I dont mean anything to the scandal of old Mrs. Pallmer the old dame who keeps the house and who is so careful a dame and so afraid of wasting anything of Anna's that she eats her bacon and greens out of a wooden bowl rather than hazard a plate and drinks from the running spout rather than endanger a cup or glass. She does use the new kitchen table but not without reluctance. To his infinite amusement Henry found her the other day at dinner with one of Toms sheets for her tablecloth. Tom and Henry[1] are precisely what my mother described—Cupid in jacket and trowzers and a professor of 15. I have made Tom talk and smile however more than I expected. He had the gallantry to escort us to Clifton and after returning home to come again for us on the day we left Clifton.[2] We went in the Landaulette open and he between us and we plaguing him with pistol questions half the way. How he felt or how he bore it is hard to say but I made the corners of his mouth frequently relax against his will into a smile of which he seemed ashamed as much as I was proud. Did I tell you that Honora enjoyed this open carriage even more than I expected on her journey. It is in every respect comfortable. I cannot tell you how kind Mr. Hutton was to us about it. One instance of his *politeness* I must mention—he had our arms painted on the carriage that we might he said consider it completely as our own—No accident—except the breaking of a spoke which is well mended—and two bolts—replaced.

[1] Thomas Lovell Beddoes, the poet, and his brother Henry.
[2] ME's sister Emmeline King lived at Clifton.

Mrs. Guillemard the wisest of Annas friends is still here. I like her much and the more for liking you and my mother as she does. My niece Anna I like as you did. I think her much improved in everything but appearance. Her figure surprised me. I had expected to see a much taller person but she is like a figure in *dough* that has been made tall and well proportioned and squeezed down into a hoddy-doddy shape. Little Mary prettyish and pleasing. She is quite taken up with two canary birds whom she is teaching to eat out of her hand—and a very pretty succession of pictures she and her birds continually make. We walked for 5 hours yesterday over Bath and saw all its Alps on Alps and crescents on crescents. Some foreigner exclaimed on seeing them 'Here is a cascade of crescents!'

. . . Did anybody tell you that we breakfasted with Mrs. Chandler—she was very kind. The Smiths—her son and daughter in law are in Italy. So now I am come to the end of my paper and have not told you one entertaining thing. All of that description that I can at this moment recollect is that the last Bath bride Miss Brownlow who has just married Mr. McNeill of the Isles sat up a whole night to read Ormond[1]—she *says*—but what is more certain is that she ordered for her wedding dresses sixty two dresses being a new morning and evening gown for every day of the honey moon and she has transparent night chemises of the thinnest muslin and *gauze*—some striped some spotted—with bows of white satin ribbon and other absurdities which if they make you smile will do some good—*Mrs McNeill of the Isles*! a Scottish chieftains lady. Consider how times and manners change. . . . Maria E.

To Mrs. Edgeworth

2 Nelson Place, Tuesday, 1 September 1818

. . . I will take it for granted that from Fanny you will hear all our adventures up to our return from Clifton. You will rejoice that all there went on and off so well. The first day after we received your good news we went out in glorious spirits to

[1] *Ormond, a tale* by ME (1817).

kill off our visits—Mrs. Doctor Percival—Not at Home—Miss Pilot—not at home—Mrs. Holroyd—at home—most gracious and charmed to see us. This queen of the Bath blue stocking society seems at 80 happier than I could have conceived that anybody leading this kind of life could be. She is well bred—active and delighted with herself and the Queen and the Princess of Hesse Homberg and the candlestick the Queen gave her and the letters of the Princess—and innocently and happily vain of having sat on the sofa with the Queen and having had troops of Royal and noble friends and gifts of drawings from innumerable *gifted* ladies of quality and lady artists. I observed a pretty view of a cascade in Wales reminding me on a diminished scale of your Tivoli and I was surprised to hear it was Mrs. Henry Hamiltons drawing. She is so little vain that we really know *her* without knowing her accomplishments.

Mrs. Holroyd *of course* brought out a parcel of letters and set me to read some of them to the company—Luckily only ourselves and 2 Annas Mrs. Guillemard and Ho. It is a torturing trial to read difficult and new handwriting of fine letters and never did any idiot hobble and gobble and blunder as I did—Especially, to my shame and Mrs. Holroyd's discomfiture when I came to some favorite sentimental *insertions* of poetry or soidisant poetry. I called *mercy*—misery—and so on—and read them again to do better and did the very same again! Then without knowing what letters or words were before my eyes or what came out of my mouth I hurried on through a fine description of Swisserland—Oleanders!—Mont Jura! Mont Blanc! While Mrs. Holroyd sat with hands occasionally uplifted acting *barberdash* admiration till—Oh disgrace to my family!—at the most sublime and beautiful part where 'the *sensations* made the *heart* nearly *burst*' I read *twist* instead of *burst* and this made the two Annas and Honora ready to burst with laughter and I knew how it was with them and was in the most dreadful danger of laughing uncontrollably myself. I went on struggling with the weakness of fear and suppressing laughter—in violent perspiration I assure you through another page till at last, when the woman was looking over me and at the much expected name of *Gibbon*[1] I could not pronounce it from the state I was in and was forced

[1] Mrs. Holroyd had been a great friend of Gibbon.

to stop short! My huge fashionable bonnet luckily covered my face so that as I sat on the sofa profile to her Mrs. Holroyd could only see that I was in some kind of convulsive distress. Anna and Mrs. Guillemard and Ho assure me that if they had not known *me* they should have thought I was crying. Mrs. Holroyd read over my shoulder for me and Honora with admirable presence of mind, though she was as white as ashes with fright, began to say something about *Oleanders* and I made an effort to get out something about a pomegranate that I had seen the day before but my voice would not have done for anyone who *knew* me. I have seldom struggled or suffered more confusion in 5 minutes. However I recovered without quite disgracing my *famally*[1] and it was all as well and smooth as possible and I talked away afterwards and I believe Mrs. Holroyd was delighted with us all and *me* in particular—reprobate as I was. Much pressing to spend an evening but we declined—'Only come to Bath for a few days' etc. . . .[2]

. . . in years I could yet get over if I were quite sure of the *steadiness* of his attachment and of his having a temper and character fit to secure domestic happiness. Some of his letters however which she has shewn me so far from giving me this hope *frighten* me. I doubt whether he wishes to be her husband. I think he wishes to make her passionately in love with him and to play at fast and loose—if no worse—and even if he wished to be and were her husband I think he would make her a very bad one and besides they would not have enough to live upon—even if his debts were paid which I am sure never will be paid—by him—and his elder brother will not be so obliging to die. So much the better for it and I will do my best to make her think so. His last letter has quite roused her pride and she will not write again—she *says*—and I *hope*.

. . . Heaven preserve me from a Bath life—or an amateur literary tittle tattle-life at Bath or in any other part of the globe. Those who have lived with real friends and superiors as I have cannot bear to live with *worshippers* and inferiors. Near or at a distance I equally detest that sort of life.

[1] Deliberate Irishism.

[2] Half a page cut out, presumably about the private affairs of Anna Beddoes. I have not been able to identify her suitor.

Yesterday evening we went to see gaslight and a gazometer and gas apparatus in an ironmongers shop here. I never heard any person shew or explain anything better. I wished for Francis and Pakenham. He shewed us pretty little *fireworks* of gas made in the easiest manner. The gas coming through an old *brass* top of a lamp which was in the shape of the spout of a watering pot with many holes formed a beautiful appearance—like a sea urchin with spiracles of flame green lilac and yellow—a tulip variegated with its leaves fanned about by the wind appeared when the man lit the gas through another bit of old pipe of another shape—and the poor man appeared so happy and so innocently and rationally happy that it was impossible not to sympathise with him. Many a beauty and many a grand philosopher eaten up internally with envy and jealousy might have been glad to change places with him could they know their own interests.

I like Mrs. Guillemard—she is a steady sensible woman and does Anna credit in the choice of a friend. To us she is most kind. She seems to live but to oblige us—spends all her days walking about the streets advising us in purchases or shewing us the way to all we want. Her conversation tho never literary is *never-the-less* agreeable and the more new and instructive to me. From her brother she has learnt a great taste for science and in odd ways has seen a great deal of life. Yesterday she gave us an account of a Bristol turtle feast at which she lately was and saw turtle on the table in 8 different forms—turtle soup—a shell of turtle—turtle patties and I forget the rest but she says the quantity of these and other dishes took away from her all appetite and she never was so tired in all her life as in sitting it out for 3 or four hours—Marvelling as she did at the capacity of the stomachs of the worshipful company. Her husband is now in Italy and she conducts all his business.

Apropos to *honey* at breakfast—in answer to my asking whether she had read and believed Huber[1] on bees and whether she credited or discredited what one of the men in '*Les Ecoles Normales*'[2] says that there is not such a thing as a queen bee Mrs. Guillemard told me that there certainly are queen bees—

[1] François Huber, *Nouvelles Observations sur les abeilles* (1792).

[2] Probably a textbook for a French teachers' training college.

that she has seen them often—that she and her brother had been long attentive observers of bees—that they had hives made of many stages for their bees and that one year after removing one of the upper stages and taking away in it all the last years honey they observed a great commotion in the under hive that remained. All were in battle and confusion. She thought they must have lost their queen. She went to look in the stage of the hive she had taken off—found the queen half smothered in honey—carried her to her subjects. They shewed joy—buzzed round her—cleaned her—fed her and the tumult was appeased among her loyal subjects. The queen is not only longer than other bees but has more rings on her body . . . Adieu. I have written to the last moment. Maria E.

To Mrs. Ruxton

8 September 1818, Tuesday

Bowood—Yes my dearest Aunt, Honora and I are actually at Bowood,[1] and never were people more kindly, more cordially received. Could we forget the contrast between everything around us and everything at home we might enjoy all the comforts and luxuries, and smiles and politeness by which we are surrounded. We came here yesterday to dinner and all I can say to you, my dear friends who were so anxious about us is that I am sure you would have been pleased and gratified. Lady Lansdowne had written me word that there was to be no company for some days—only one lady a Miss Carnaguy—two gentlemen who were to go away this day—Sir George Paul and a Monsieur Cottu a French judge belonging to some of the *superior courts* of appeal who is travelling in England and going all the circuits to see the British modes of justice. This French judge is as leste[2] a looking little personnage as ever you saw and as little like a judge much more like a petit maitre of secondary ton in a French play. All he has learnt by going circuit in England is as he says to admire more the French method of doing these things. Sir George Paul is the man who has done so much about prisons of late years—conversible. I sat beside him at dinner—

[1] Lord Lansdowne's house in Wiltshire.

[2] Adroit, smart.

Honora between the young judge and Lady Lansdowne. She had had a headache well over the day before we came to Bowood and was quite well and looked pretty and genteel. Lady Lansdowne and she might pass for sisters. Lady Lansdowne was very attentive to her. There was no other company except a lady whose name I have never yet been able to hear. She is staying in the house and is a conversible woman. The Judge and Sir George set off at 7 oclock this morning and now we are to have a few days to ourselves . . .

Anna wrote to you I know a day or two after we arrived. I have always liked her company but it never was so agreeable to me as during this fortnight. It was impossible for any creature to be kinder. We saw very few people at Bath. When we first arrived we were in such anxiety we could not and when better accounts came from home we were too much hurried with preparations for coming here and too glad of an excuse for having our evenings to ourselves to accept any invitations.

Mrs. and Miss M. Ruxton you know are at Cheltenham. Mrs. Nugent was very attentive and kind to us—Mrs. Stewart has written to her about us. Mrs. Holroyd came repeatedly to see me and I paid her two long morning visits and saw her letters from the Queen and Princesses &c. She is an agreeable old lady —especially when she talks of the Pakenhams. We breakfasted one day with Dr. Haygarth and Miss Haygarth sister and father to that Mr. Haygarth who wrote the poem of '*Greece*'[1] which I talked of so much to you. Dr. and Miss Haygarth are both well informed and agreeable and the family seemed much attached. We saw all Mr. Haygarth's drawings taken in Italy—Greece—Switzerland—The Tyrol &c. They are admirable sketches. Mr. Haygarth himself was not at home or rather he is at his own home—has settled on his own estate in Hampshire. I hope we may meet him *when, or if* we go to London. This was the *only* invitation I accepted at Bath. I was desirous to lay the foundations of an acquaintance in this very amiable family. What more have I to tell my dear aunt that can amuse or please her? Nothing—but that M. Dumont read a French play last night and put me in mind of the happy time when Mr. Knox read one—But tho M. Dumont reads exquisitely well I found my attention

[1] *Greece, a poem* (1814) by William Haygarth.

often wandering. The play was not Moliere's but one of Dancourt's—second rate—La *femme* or la société bourgeoise[1] or some such title. The young French judge who was starting up from the sofa or curling his hair on the hearth every 5 minutes appeared to me to be nearly the coxcomb M. le Comte of the play—with the change of fashion of a few years.

Lady Lansdowne's 3 children—Lord Kerry 8 or 9 years old a fine intelligent boy—Lady Louisa—about 6—a very lively natural engaging little creature—Lord Henry about 3. Lady Lansdowne obviously is as intent upon their education as a mother can be but this does not spoil her for society. She is not one of the stupid good mothers whom *M. de Stendhal*[2] reprobates. A great deal was said last night by M. Dumont Lord Lansdowne and Sir G. Paul worth remembering but it is all gone out of my poor head. I can only recollect that Madame de Stael's last book[3] was talked over and admired and that all agreed in preferring it to her Allemagne. The character of Bonaparte they think particularly well done. Madame de Stael saw a good deal of Lord Byron at Coppet[4] and said that there is one striking characteristic resemblance between his countenance and Bonapartes—that the different parts of the physiognomy never agreed in expression. When the mouth smiled the eyes did not smile.

I have not yet seen any thing of this place except from the windows and as we drove up to it. The approach is not prepossessing. I ought not to judge yet but the grounds appear to me to be made fine in spite of nature. The water which I see from my windows though with banks fringed with trees appears to me to be made-water. The house is a magnificent pile of building added to and extended from century to century and therefore more agreeable than any regular mansion. We have as yet scarcely got acquainted with the suite of rooms. The library *tho* magnificent is a most comfortable habitable looking room. Our own rooms opening one into the other just as we wished are only too handsome and luxurious for us. One is quite a sitting

[1] *Les bourgeoises à la mode* (1693).

[2] Probably a reference to *Rome, Naples and Florence* (1818), 179, 218.

[3] *Considérations sur la révolution française* (1818). Her *De l'Allemagne* came out in 1810.

[4] Madame de Stael's house near Geneva.

room dressing room with a canopy sofa bed—the other our spacious bedchamber with a bed in which Honora and I might lose ourselves. Old George has a nice little room within reach of us. He is well and looks very respectable.

And now my dear aunt you know as much of us as if you were with us . . . [end missing]

To Harriet Edgeworth

Bowood, 8 September 1818

I have not time to write *well* enough for Pakenham therefore must address this to his guardian angel. At Collon I promised him a book of pictures to color if he would cure himself for one whole day of answering *I dont know* when asked any question that he could answer. You told me that he fulfilled the conditions. I enclose a little book for him to prove to him that I have not forgotten his promised reward. People should be very exact in this respect with children. I send another book for dear Francis—The art of speaking on the fingers . . .

Wednesday 4 oclock September 9th

Just returned from a delightful walk with charming and amiable Lady Lansdowne. How few women deserve both these epithets but how well they do in conjunction. She is just the same as she was at her own walk over the potatoe field in Edgeworthstown[1] and has been reminding me of every little incident that passed while she was with us—made me describe you to her and marked all the differences *and* she wore this morning a brown spencer delightfully like Honora's. Her natural lively happy children came walking skipping running along with us calling to Mamma at every yard Mamma Why?—and Mamma What—and Mamma when and Mamma may I? Light little Lady Louisa flying about with her green persian sash floating and her long reed whip bending in her hand and her thick auburn curls over her face is as engaging a child as I am sure her mother was at her age—Lord Kerry slight figure a head taller than Francis—a year younger—many years less manly but very amiable. It is agreeable to see how early the habits of good breeding are

[1] The Lansdownes visited the Edgeworths in Aug. 1813.

taught and learned. 'Kerry my dear dont take Miss Honora on the wet grass. You know Kerry when you are walking with a lady you should always consider what the lady likes not merely' &c. She tutors well and playfully. I never saw a happier mother wife and woman altogether—with everything this world can give to make her happy and every disposition to enjoy and give enjoyment to others. It is delightful to see that so much happiness still exists in the world and so much goodness. It keeps up hope.

We have just been my dear H to the cascade you mentioned and in consequence of your desiring me to see it. It is beautiful —a full foam and fine fall. The sun from under a dark cloud came full out as we had the first view and it looked like a fairy tale cascade of diamonds glittering in the sun and with force and rapidity scattered far and wide in dazzling succession. We almost felt as if we could grasp them—and . . .

But—Lord Grenville's coach and four has just driven to the door—ladies maids and imperials out—and in—and I must go and dress. Honora has everything correct and fitting admirably. Everybody likes her and she—Goodbye—I hear Lord Grenville's ministerial or antiministerial foot[1] treading grand in the *corridore*.

Maria E

Mr. Grenville of whom Franklin gives such a well drawn character[2] is come too. Who Miss Carnaguy or Carnagey a Scotch fashionable or elegante is I dont know but she is well skilled in French and French literature and seems intended to stay here. Lady Lansdowne seems to be very intimate with her calls her Elizabeth.

Goodbye again—*Dear* Harriet

[1] After the fall of the ministry of All the Talents Lord Grenville and his followers had voted with the opposition until 1817. They then broke away owing to differences over the control of radical agitation, over which they supported the government.

[2] Franklin said Grenville appeared 'a sensible, judicious, intelligent, good tempered and well instructed young man . . . his conversation always polite and his manner pleasing . . .'. Grenville as a young man was appointed to treat with Franklin in the peace negotiations after the War of American Independence: *Private correspondence of Benjamin Franklin*, ed. W. T. Franklin (1817), 332.

To Mrs. Edgeworth

[September 1818]

I concluded my note to Harriet if I remember rightly just when Lord and Lady Grenville had arrived. You will be very angry with me when I tell you that that day we were late for dinner. The footman with his terrible knock at our door came with—'Dinner, Ma'am—all sat down'. All sat down and we had to march into that vast dining room and take our seats—mine left between Lady Grenville and her brother-in-law Mr. Thomas Grenville—Honora's between Lord Grenville and Dumont. Lady Grenville was superbly dressed at all points—a fat little woman not quite so protuberant as Miss Kitty M[alone] or Lady F[? arnham] but in very good case—rosy good-humored unmeaning little face. Except for the quantity of Mechlin lace you might have taken her for any body's housekeeper—bowed her head to me, as I took my seat, though not introduced and as soon as I had the use of my eyes through the mist of confusion and remorse and in the dead silence that prevailed I looked round to discover who was who and what was what. Lord Grenville with his dark eyes and huge Foster[1] eyebrows first fixed my attention but he was like an iron mask—the Primate's[2] silence *speaks* in comparison with his—and there was no secret promise of humor lurking about the eyes. Mr. T. Grenville's first look is that of a methodist preacher with his eyes squeezed close but in his face there was a promise of humor—since faithfully kept. The dinner was stupid notwithstanding the most meritorious efforts of Lord and Lady Lansdowne pour engrainer[3] quelque conversation. They both applied to me more than once in the most polite manner, but always unluckily about things of which I knew nothing—new bridge in Dublin and pier of Howth I endeavored to answer about—but believe me I was insufferably stupid and overpowered with remorse for being late and with the sense that all these people were averse to me as I knew they had been to Madame de Stael and were to *Patronage* etc.

[1] The family of Lord Oriel and of the Bishop of Clogher.

[2] William Stuart (1755–1821), Archbishop of Armagh. The character of Lord Oldborough in ME's *Patronage* (1814) is partly based on him.

[3] An old spelling for engréner, used figuratively for 'to begin'.

You recollect that it was at a dinner at Lord Grenville's that the lemon juice intercepted letters[1] were discussed and reprobated. My silence and *shyness* (the breakfast table will be so good not to laugh at my applying that word to myself) were I believe of more service to me than the finest things I could have said for before the desert was ended Mr. T. Grenville began to feed me with ripe figs which I hate and barberry drops which I love and Lady Grenville so far conquered the *fear* or aversion which I acknowledge she seemed to have of me as to take the golden scissars from my hand and cut grapes for me. Honora all the time looked very pretty and genteel and as well dressed as any body except Lady Lansdowne. This was a comfort to me even in my disordered state. After dinner at coffee time—sitting on the bed of roses before a nice blaze of wood, Lady Grenville began to chatter away about Where is My Lord this and my Lady that and is such a person at Longleat and is such another at Ampthill[2] &c. When *les Messieurs* arrived the silence recurred. It was hard heavy work when Lord Grenville took his seat in the chair by the fire and all took their seats—Political economy—and the law of evidence Lord Lansdowne tried upon him in vain. Dumont I saw from the first disliked him and sat with his mouth shut up. Deadly heavy evening—glad to go to bed and through our open bedchamber and dressing room doors to talk to one another.

Lord Grenville added as little to the pleasures of society during the three days he was here as it was possible and yet he seemed a good natured man and Lady Lansdowne resolved it all into *natural shyness*—ill cured in childhood. Whenever Lord Grenville did let out anything it was very correct—deep and strong—in a slow—low—house of Lords voice and with his eyes always directed to Lord Lansdowne—God bless him. I am glad I *have* seen him for 3 days, but I never wish to see him

[1] *Patronage, Tales and Novels of Maria Edgeworth* (1833), xiv. 138. Lord Grenville's guests disapproved of the whole affair of the intrigue between English ministers and a foreign court, not only of the letters in cipher and lemon juice (used as invisible ink): Dumont to ME and RLE, 26 Jan. 1814 (MS. in Library of University College, London). *Patronage* was not popular with the critics but it sold well, the first three editions totalling 6,000 copies (*The Farington Diary*, vii (1927), 227).

[2] The seats of Lord Bath and Lord Holland.

again. The only thing I can remember from him is—'Baffin's Bay! That is a curious conclusion My Lord they have drawn about Baffin's—Because Baffin in his journal writes I have examined this bay and find no passage further some have concluded that no such bay exists and would proceed to erase it from the Charts.' He spoke once with some enthusiasm to me about Barrow's eloquence.[1] You will recollect it was Lord Grenville who wrote the preface to Lord Chatham's letter to Lord Camelford[2] which my father liked so much and which is indeed admirable.

Next morning Lady Grenville superb in Valenciennes lace—ruffs and scarf and cap—did not walk under less than 200 guineas—and the drollest trit-trot little walk she has—turning at short angles, to be brisk and airy, the wind taking the skirts of her pelisse. Her Ladyships very handsome baruche and four bright bays came to the door at one to take the select an airing. Lady Lansdowne said *her* landau was too heavy for the occasion. I was asked by Lady Lansdowne to accompany them and Honora was consigned to the walkers—Miss Carnagy, and Mr. Dumont &c. Away we rolled over the downs and the black faced black legged sheep looked up as we passed and presently we got out and saw beautiful views—and then arrived at the place where the battle of Roundway[3] was fought and where Prince Rupert and the king's troops had their last advantage over Cromwell—vide Rapin—Hume and Clarendon.[4] Lady Lansdowne who is very well informed and perfectly easy and agreeable in communicating information shewed and told all about it while Lady Grenville was as well as she could keeping her great white crape bonnet from being blown off by the high wind. Into all manner

[1] John Barrow, secretary to the Admiralty, published in 1818 *A Chronological History of Arctic Voyages* and proposed to Lord Melville voyages for the discovery of a NW. passage. Baffin in his journal was unusually vague in his information about the situation of the bay and so misled later geographers.

[2] *Letters written by the late Earl of Chatham to his nephew, T. Pitt, Esq.* (*afterwards Lord Camelford*), *then at Cambridge*, ed. Lord Grenville (1804).

[3] The Battle of Roundway Down, 1643, at which Wilmot routed the Parliamentary forces under Sir William Waller who was besieging Devizes, then precariously held by Royalist troops under Sir R. Hopton (Clarendon, *History of the Rebellion* (1849 ed.), iii. 100–3).

[4] Paul de Rapin, *History of England* (1726–31), the standard history of England till the appearance of David Hume's *History of Great Britain* (1754–7).

of strange shapes it was blown and she bore it very well. And then we were to drive on to see the Mardyke[1] a curious dyke raised by the Saxons. So we drove and drove and we were to have met the gentlemen who were to have shewed us the way but we missed them and missed our road and at last in a ravine where the white chalky ruts were deep even to the nave of the wheel and crossing and sloping with a perilous descent the coachman stopped and Lady Lansdowne (who is as brave as a lion and as gentle as a lamb) asked if he was afraid that we could not go on.

'*Why my Lady—it is rather impossible*'

We got out and walked one after another picking our way down the ravine while the velvet capped postillions dismounted and unharnessed the horses and the gold laced scarlet fellow was obliged to assist in dragging the carriage down and turning into a lane which led back to the castle—Very cold—desperately sharp wind—shawls blowing—muslin gown—thin shoes. I had a little headache before I set out. It grew so bad before we reached home that I feared I could not go down to dinner—hurry of dressing—sick twice while putting on the white satin and muslin fineries but into them I did get and down I went for I knew it would be shockingly disagreeable to Honora if I did not and would lead to many disagreeable *sorrows and fears*. I never was nearer fainting in my life than at this dinner. I could neither swallow nor see or hear. I recollect just seeing Miss Carnagy and Lady Lansdowne look at me frightened but they were so good natured as to let me alone seeing I did not wish to be noticed. Horribly frightened I was. I knew that I could not stand if I tried to get up. Mr. Grenville was good natured and talked to his next neighbor and Dumont's shoulder *covered* me and I recovered by degrees and *did not disgrace my family*. Lady Lansdowne and Lady Grenville and Miss Carnegie the moment we went into the drawing room got round me declaring they never had seen any creature look so ill and that at one time I was so white that they were certain I was *gone* but I tell you I did not *disgrace my famully* [*sic*]. By managing myself admirably I got through the whole evening! But what any body said I don't very well know.

[1] The Wansdyke.

Next morning—sick and wake [*sic*] but able to appear. It was very agreeable in the delightful library after breakfast this day—groupes round various tables—books and prints. Lady Lansdowne found the battle of Roundway for me in different histories and Lord Lansdowne shewed me a letter of Waller's[1] to Lord Hopton on their quarrel after this battle and Lord Grenville shaking his leg and reading was silent and I suppose happy. The third day the Grenvilles were to go away. There was great pressing for their staying to meet the Bathursts who are to be here on tuesday but they were engaged to Longleat (Lady Baths) so they went away after breakfast—Lord Grenville coasting sideways the whole length of the library, looking out of the corner of his eye like a shy horse and giving at last one nod sideways to those he left behind but speaking to no one. I never heard a sound more joyous than their parting wheels. After *lunch* we set out on a walk. Dumont and I walked on together and for the first time this week we had some comfortable conversation. 'Diable cet homme! Je ne le comprend pas. C'est un homme de glace—de fer. Et la femme—The first time I did see her I did think he had married somebody out of his house. She is no better than somebody's housekeeper—sister of Lord Camelford too! Bon! Bah!'

We went on to our own business. Dumont I told you had been very much pleased with my father's MS.[2] He had by this time read a good deal of mine—likes it—says he cannot attempt to cut it till he has read it all and looked over it a second time. He hates Mr. Day in spite of all his good qualities. He says he knows and *cannot bear* that sort of man 'who has such pride and misanthropies about trifles and who raises a great theory of morals upon an amour propre blessé. Now he is one who if he should take it into his head a woman should not wear powder in her hair would raise a great discourse to prove that the woman who should be *capàble* to wear powder should be *capàble* to commit murder.'

Our thoughts began to thaw and our spirits to boil the moment the dead pressure of the Grenvilles was taken off. But I

[1] Not listed in *B.M. Cat. Lansdowne MSS.* or in *R. Hist. MS. Comm. Lansdowne* but the reference is perhaps to Waller's moving letter to his old friend of 16 June 1643, a draft of which was partly printed in *Clarendon State Papers*, ed. Scrope and Monkhouse (1773): *F.T.R. Edgar, Sir Ralph Hopton* (1968), 99.

[2] Manuscript of vol. i of *Memoirs of RLE*, published in 1820.

forget to tell you that one of them remained behind. To my surprise when the baruche had driven off I saw Mr. Thomas Grenville Lord Grenville's brother return into the library and here he has been ever since. He is an old bachelor and an oddity—takes long walks of 14 and 20 miles by himself—and has opened wonderfully from the silent methodist preacher looking man into a person of grave but sly humor—saying in a low drawling English gentlemanlike sleepy tone the drollest and keenest things without moving his head to the right or the left or changing a muscle of his countenance except those about his mouth which he permits to smile in a certain fashion. He has a great deal of literature—no vanity but I suspect a good deal of dried pride—a vast deal of anecdote—lived with Sheridan Burke Fox &c—asked if I knew *Lewis O Beirne*—was very much surprised to hear he was a *strict* bishop—told me various anecdotes not to be trusted to paper. He was it seems quite the delight and *butt* of that society for certain inconsistencies.[1] Mr. T. Grenville says that Sheridan was often silent and seldom brilliant in conversation except when half drunk. I asked about the comedy of *Affectation*[2] of which the Bishop of Meath told us. 'Yes—he did half write it. I met him one day when he was in great pecuniary embarrassments. He shook my hand joyfully. "It is all settled and I have made a provision for Tom—£200 a year." "Indeed! How?" "An annuity from the money I am to get for the new comedy I am finishing!"' It never went further.

But Sheridan has drawn me away from my business. Now I will tell you how we pass our day. Morning—7 oclock—I get up and write (this morning at half after six for the pleasure of writing to you my dearest mother. Be satisfied I never write a word at night and I cannot have any pleasure so great as writing what I hope may even for a few minutes amuse you).

Breakfast ½ after nine—Breakfast very pleasant tho a servant waits—but he is an Italian a Milanese—seems like a machine who understands only what relates to *his service*—stands by a

[1] The Bishop of Meath acquired his see as a reward for services as a government pamphleteer and as private secretary to two Viceroys of Ireland. The pliable, courtier-like aspect of his personality is portrayed in the character of Councillor Falconer in ME's *Patronage* (1814).

[2] For details of this projected comedy, see T. Moore, *Memoirs of the Life of the Rt. Hon. Richard Brinsley Sheridan* (1835 ed.), 157–63.

round table placed in front of a stand of flowers—on this table large silver lamp tea urn—Coffee urn and all necessary for tea and coffee to be made by him. On the large round table at which we sit there appears what looks like an elegant gouter—mixed cut glass and beautiful china—meat sweetmeats—honey—cakes —buns—rolls &c little in each dish or china basket—numbers of cut glass cream ewers and jugs and cut glass sugar basons. Milanese watches all who enter—*salvers* them with tea and coffee—and the cups are changed and all continually supplied withouten hands crossing or any *I'll trouble yous*. I am a convert which I thought I never should be to this system. Conversation goes on delightfully and one forgets the existence of the *dumb waiter*.

After breakfast we all *stray* into the library for a few minutes —settle when we shall meet again for walking. Then Lady Lansdowne goes to her dear dressing room and dear children—Dumont to his attic—Lord Lansdowne to his out of door works and we to our elegant dressing room—Miss Carnagy to hers. Between one and two—luncheon—then walk—happy time! Lady Lansdowne is so chearful and polite and easy—just as she was in her walks at Edgeworthstown—but very different walks are these—Most various and delightful—from dressed flower knots shrubbery and park walks to fields with inviting paths—wide downs—shady winding lanes happy cottages—not *dressed* but naturally well placed and with evidence in every part of their being suited to the inhabitants. The women in their blue bodices and black flat hats and men often in carters frocks look as if they were picturesque decorations in the lanes.

After walk dress and make haste for dinner—but well dressed you must be. You were very right indeed my dear mother and Fanny. We never could have got through without Venn and Briscoe and Wilkinson to boot. We do very well and hope we are neither above nor below what is fit.

Dinner always pleasant because Lord Lansdowne and Lady Lansdowne converse so agreeably—Dumont also towards the desert. After dinner we find the children in the drawing room. Surely I described the children to you. I have not time to repeat but I will add that I like them better the more I see of them. One day and but one Miss de Lally their governess appeared in the evening when we were quite alone—more of her hereafter.

When there is company one card table—party of whist for gentlemen—Dumont in particular who goes to sleep Lady Lansdowne says if he does not play or read. While they go to cards Lord Lansdowne sits down at a round table with us, takes up one of the many books and reads or talks to us as we work. When the Grenvilles were gone and before they came Dumont read French plays to us in the evening. The first evening he read two of Dancourts—very indifferent—Quite a pity to waste his reading on them—one of Corneille's—Le Florentin[1]—beautiful and admirably read. Last night we ladies all begged for one of Moliere's. Dumont hung back with '*D'ailleurs*—Eh—Mais—Vous les connoissez—vous devez les sçavoir aussi bien que moi'. We pressed till at last poor Dumont took refuge with Lord Lansdowne and I heard him say to him that it was impossible to read Moliere without a quicker eye than he had pour de certains propos. Lady Lansdowne and I reproached one another and were ashamed and took to our work and Lord Lansdowne and Dumont went to the library and brought at last as odd a choice as could well be made with Mr. T. Grenville for chief male auditor.

'*Le Vieux Celibataire*'[2]

An excellent play—interesting and lively throughout with continual new situations and the old bachelor himself a charming character. Dumont read it I think as well as Tessier could have read it but there were things that seemed as if they had been written on purpose for le celibataire who was listening and the Celibataire who was reading—so that Honora and I dared scarce look at one another across the table et j'etois tres embarrassée de ma contenance as the reader continually looked at me for audience and I could not dare to stir even at the most *shrinking* passages of Madame Everard and the Celibataire's tete a tete. I had one comfort that I was certain others were in as bad a plight as myself but to look back at Mr. Grenville sitting bolt upright in his chimney corner was what I dared not, though I longed to see how it was going with him. He was very

[1] *Le Florentin*, a one-act comedy by La Fontaine and Champmeslé (1683).

[2] *Le Vieux Celibataire* (1792), a comedy by Jean François Collin d'Harleville.

good humored about it and very much entertained. Pray do not imagine from what I have said that the Celibataire is as *bad* as Moliere—No it is all very elegant and proper. The *shrinking* or what Harriet would call the *squadgy*[1] feeling arose from the dreadful appositeness. No more about it—Too much already but it is fresh from last night in my mind and consequently in talking to you I was forced to empty my mind of it before I could get on to any thing else.

I forgot to tell you that the last day that Lord and Lady Grenville were here there arrived to dinner two young gentlemen suppose about twenty or four and twenty—brothers—Sir William and Mr. Hort—sons of the Sir J. Hort my father and Aunt Ruxton knew—were wards of Lord Lansdowne—reside in the neighbourhood—fine estate—Sir William a very pleasing young man—but that is a phrase à la Neckar[2] that will give you no ideas—dark eyes—round good natured face—gentlemanlike figure—middle sized—good manners—no conceit—or *ennui*—not so well as Lord Forbes but far above most of the young men of the present day—Literature enough for conversation—no pretension—a very good mechanic. At dinner one day Lord Grenville and all the gentleman except himself were talking nonsense about the new magnetic perpetual motion. He modestly asked a question or two which shewed he understood that it was all nonsense and even the authority of Lord Grenville's eye and contradictory belief could not frighten him from his understanding. He saw that Honora and I understood him and we became acquainted and to a certain degree intimate from that time forward. He always sits *where he ought to do at dinner*. I draw no conclusions *for* I fear both brothers are going away today. The youngest may go as soon as he pleases—not because he has the misfortune to be the youngest but because he is not worth talking of. He is like any other young man that you would never think of.

Let me see if I can recollect any of the multitude of entertaining things I have resolved to remember for you when I heard them in conversation.

Lord Lansdowne when I asked him to describe Rocca to me

[1] Squadgy, squangy, family adjectives meaning socially uncomfortable.

[2] Madame Necker had a reputation for being prim and governessy.

said he heard him give an answer to Lord Byron which marked the indignant frankness of his mind. Lord Byron at Coppet[1] had been going on abusing the stupidity of the good people of Geneva. Rocca at last turned short upon him 'Eh! Milord pourquoi donc venez vous vous fourrer parmi ces honnetes gens.'

I must jumble anecdotes together as I recollect them.

When Madame de Stael was here[2] Mr. Bowles the poet or as Lord Byron calls him the sonneteer was invited to dine here. She admired his 'Sonnets' and his '*Spirit of Maritime discovery*'[3] and ranked him high as an English genius. In riding to Bowood that day he fell from his horse and sprained his shoulder but still came on. Lord Lansdowne willing to shew him to advantage alluded to this in presenting him before dinner to Madame de Stael. He is a simple country curate-looking man and rather blunt and when Madame de Stael in the midst of the listening circle in the drawing room began to compliment him and herself upon the effort he had made to come to see her he replied 'Oh Ma'am say no more about it for I would have done a great deal more to see so great a *curiosity*'. Lord Lansdowne says it is impossible to describe the shock in Madame de Stael's face—the breathless astonishment—and the total change produced in her opinion of the man and her manner towards him. She said afterwards to Lord Lansdowne 'Je vois bien que ce n'est qu'un curé qui n'a pas le sens commun—quoique grand poète.' She never forgot it. Two years afterwards she spoke of it to Lord Lansdowne at Geneva and wondered how it was possible that un tel homme could exist.

Yet on many occasions she showed more want of *tact* herself considering the better opportunities she had had as Neckar's daughter and residing half her life at Paris. Lady Lansdowne told me that once when Lord Bathurst was here at the time when the news from Lord Wellington was anxiously expected one of the red despatch boxes was brought in to Lord Bathurst. All the company retreated of course to leave the minister to look at his

[1] Madame de Stael's house near Geneva.

[2] In 1813.

[3] *Sonnets, written chiefly on picturesque spots* (2nd ed. 1789); *The Spirit of Discovery; or the Conquest of Ocean* (1804).

papers. Lord Bathurst retired to a recessed window. Madame de Stael followed him. '*De quoi s'agit t'il Milord?*' His Lordship was surprised and shocked almost beyond the power of diplomatic answer and complained indignantly afterwards of this want of good breeding.

Dumont told me another instance in which she received a good retort courteous. 'Madame de Stael etoit toujours fort embarrassée pour la conversation avec les femmes. Se trouvant un jour aux prises avec une très belle femme et ne sçachant que lui dire elle commençait en lui parlant de ses diamans et elle avoit l'indiscretion de lui en demander le prix. Puis soudaine—se corrigeant, sçachant que c'étoit la une sottise "Eh Pardon Madame—c'est une curiosité fort indiscrète mais vous savez que c'est la un défaut de *notre sexe*". "Eh Madame!—la curiosité! J'ai toujours cru que c'etoit un défaut *des femmes*."' I have heard a great many more of these repartees but I cannot recollect them and they seem to me and probably will seem to you not to do quite so well in slow cold writing as in warm quick conversation—Therefore no more about them.

Mr. Bowles dined here the other day and perhaps thought me a *curiosity* but did not tell me so. He is a simple—not curate but rector—full of his poems and his church music and his house at *Bremhill*. Now there is a village of Bromham also in the neighborhood which Lady Lansdowne had taken me to see the morning of the day he dined here and all dinner time he and I and Lord Lansdowne and Dumont were making confusion in French and English between these two names and two places, both of which had pretty churches &c. Mr. Bowles was puzzled almost out of his wits and temper because Lady Lansdowne had promised to take me to *Bremhill* when he was at home and he suspected we had gone that morning. Still he could not believe Lady Lansdowne would use him so and he could not possibly make her hear or venture to put a question to her from one end of the table to the other encompassed too as she was by Grenvilles. He colored and fretted and questioned me and at every one of my blundering answers changed his opinion backwards and forwards. The moment he was released from the dining room and could get to Lady Lansdowne he went to complain that for the life of him he could not make out whether Miss E had been at Brem Hill or Bromham and that very morning he had received a letter from a Member of parliament a member of a Committee reprimanding him as vicar of *Bromham* for something of which he was innocent and ignorant he being vicar or rector of Bremhill you know.

Next day being sunday Lady Lansdowne set all to rights by taking Honora and me and Mr. Grenville to church at Brem Hill—a real country church that put me sorely in mind of the church at Ross to which dear mother we went together and with another in happy days.[1] So it is!—that in this as in thousands of instances the most pleasing things are now blasted with melancholy and the more striking for coming unexpected upon the mind.

Mr. Bowles is not like the clergyman that read prayers and preached that day at Ross. Mr. Bowles tho simple has no dignity and is too full of himself. He preached extempore and kept one in painful sympathy lest he should never get through it. After church went to his very pretty old parsonage newly *done up*—with good taste—walked over his little shrubbery—stuck full of inscriptions and grottoes and bowers and came at last to the weary hermitage where apropos to a hermits inscription the question came plump upon me '*Have you read my poem of the Missionary?*'[2] 'No.' The good natured author helped me out by saying 'No. It was published at first without my name.' He gave me a copy and all's well that ends well. So ended our visit to Brem Hill. A happier man in a house and place more suited to him I never saw. Lord Lansdowne made him the happy creature he is. His wife is a plain woman something like Mrs. Alison, who has the good sense understands the affairs of this world and is just the wife necessary for a poet. He was desperately in love with her sister—a most beautiful creature who died of a consumption. This sister comforted him and he married her and has never repented.

Now there is a trait of this man's character which from all that you have heard you would never guess. He is one of the greatest cowards existing—afraid in a carriage—afraid in a room by himself—afraid in a large room—afraid of a large bed—afraid like a child of 4 years old. One night at Bowood when

[1] With RLE in 1813.

[2] [W. L. Bowles], *The Missionary, a poem* (1813).

he was to return home in his carriage in the dark he fell into agonies exclaiming that he should certainly die of it if he got into the carriage. Lady Lansdowne asked him to stay all night. So he did—but in the morning he came down all pale to breakfast. He had been so *frightened* when he wakened and found himself in so large a room—so large a bed. He would never sleep at Bowood again. *Moral*—He was not educated as Francis and Pakenham have been. Excellent boys—how good it is of them to be happy at home after all the amusement and indulgence they had at Castle Forbes and what comfort they must be to you. I will try to get a plan of this house for Francis. I hope P has received the little books I sent him. I enclose the prints of another book I got for him but the letterpress was so silly I could not send it. These prints are only for the amusement he used to like of coloring them.

Just when I was writing this Lady Lansdowne came to my room and paid me half an hours visit. She brought my fathers Mss in its *Solander*.[1] I had lent it to her to read. She was exceedingly interested in it. She observed that his leading taste for mechanics had governed his destiny. She says it is not only entertaining and interesting but useful in shewing *how* such a character was formed and in encouraging others to hope that even without early favorable circumstances they may distinguish themselves. 'When he was settled after his first marriage at Hare hatch he seemed then as much out of fortune's way as man could be and yet he found occupations that led to distinction and that friendship for Mr. Day which was so honorable to both.' She admires and loves Mr. Day as much as Dumont dislikes him. Had she seen him she would not have endured his manners however 24 hours. . . .[2] Her own manners are charming. She has simplicity of character—and delightful to see so much happiness as she enjoys—Husband—children—friends—fortune—youth—beauty—talents—character—*temper* and *benevolence*—Everything that a human can have. Every person about her seems to love her. No indeed I do not repent coming here but shall all my life rejoice that I have seen so much goodness and happiness in a castle where both can exist as well as in a cottage.

[1] A box made in the form of a book (*O.E.D.*)

[2] A few lines are cut out of the MS. here.

But I must dress for dinner because I am not in a cottage. Goodbye. I have just seen that I have written 3 sheets and fear you will say I have written too much but it has all been since before breakfast not a candlelight word. My eyes are much better. I shall not write again for some time because I have much to get ready for Dumont . . .

Sir W. Hort did not appear so agreeable when I saw more of him. Sir H. Bunbury who was secretary to Lord Bathurst and is nephew to Mrs. Inchbald's Sir C Bunbury has been here these 3 days—fashionable and tells things that entertain me—because out of my line—but he is nothing extra—is married Lady Lansdowne says to a pretty goose—glad not here. He says that when the Duke of Clarence first saw his wife he turned about and observed 'Not so d—d ugly as I expected'. The Princess of Hesse was received at her German home by 80 soldiers to make a grand shew—all in different shabby uniforms. Sir H Bunbury knew *Henri* de la Roche Jacquelein—quite enthusiastic about him and Madame and M. de L'Escure and all that book[1]—But as it often happens when one thinks one shall hear something more nothing new came out except from Lord Lansdowne that the cause of the uncertain conduct towards the Vendeans was that Windham and Pitt disagreed about the conduct to be pursued. Windham was for assisting the Vendeans at all hazards and to the utmost extent. Pitt having it always in view to make peace with the then ruling powers in France on *certain* terms did not like to commit himself so far by assisting the Vendeans as to preclude this possibility. So that Windham whenever he could act encouraged the Vendeans with promises which Pitt contrived to make null and void.[2]

Thank you my dear Sophy for the Jewess's[3] letters and for the ginger sugar receipt. Adieu my dear mother. You see this is merely for your *own* self as there is not a word in it can interest any other mortal. Honora is well. So am I. She does wear flowers in her head and looks very pretty. Natural Hollyhocks

[1] *Mémoires* (1815) of the Marquise de la Rochejacquelein.

[2] Windham was secretary at war 1784–1801 and a strong supporter of the French royalists.

[3] Rachel Mordecai, later Mrs. Lazarus. Her letter of protest about the portrait of the Jewish coachmaker in ME's *Absentee* (1812) started a long correspondence between ME and herself (1815–39).

all gone—Plants all come or coming in on great barrows into the superb greenhouse. I wish I could get a Sparmania[1] for Lady Lansdowne who never saw one . . .

The book sur la peinture by Mr. Beyle Alias Count de Stendhal[2] diverts Lord Lansdowne every evening delightfully. It is so conceited—so absurd and yet such sparkling mica of talent. Sir H Bunbury has just brought a book which all are devouring —Voyage en Autriche a la suite de l'armee Francaise en 1809 par le Chevalier cadet de Gassicourt.[3] He was Bonaparte's apothecary. Tell me if Lady G[ ] can . . . [end missing]

To Sophy Ruxton

19 September 1818

My dear friend, . . . I take it for granted then that you know all our history up to friday or saturday last the day on which Lord and Lady Grenville left Bowood. Since that time we have had remaining of the first *batch* of visitors Mr. T. Grenville, le vieux celibataire—two Horts—Sir William and his brother—Mr. Gally Knight—Lord and Lady Bathurst and Lady Georgiana and Lady Emily Bathurst. Mr. T. Grenville left us yesterday. The Horts are also just departed. All the rest are going today . . . Sir William Hort was a good humored young man and that was all. Nothing came out on further acquaintance—the brother fat and good humored but *coarsish* and heavy. Mem. he gave me two pebbles! People *will* give me pebbles wherever I go—unworthy and ungrateful as I am.

Lord Bathurst is a chearful formalist with smiling usage of the world sufficient to be an *agreeable* diplomatist—*flat* but not stiff backed—dry faced—of the old school—of the class of man in appearance to whom Mr. Edward Sneyd belongs—the first rank of that class. We saw him only for a day and half. He was ministerially obliged and very sorry to be obliged, to return to Town the second day. It is curious that we have seen within the course

[1] A greenhouse evergreen shrub from S. Africa, first introduced in the late eighteenth century.

[2] *Histoire de la peinture en Italie* (1817).

[3] C. L. Cadet de Gassicourt, *Voyage en Autriche, en Moravie, et en Bavière fait à la suite de l'armée française pendant le campagne de 1809* (1818).

of a week one of the heads of the ministerial and the Ex-ministerial party. In point of ability Lord Grenville is far superior I think to any one I have seen. Lord Lansdowne with whom I had a delightful tete a tete walk yesterday told me that Lord Grenville can be fully known only when people come to do political business with him. There he excels. You know his preface to Lord Chatham's letters. His manner of speaking Lord Lansdowne says is not pleasing in the house. From being very near sighted he has a look of austerity and haughtiness. As he cannot *see* all he wants to see he throws himself back as he stands with chin up determined to look at none. Lord Lansdowne gave me an instance, I might almost say a *warning* of the folly of judging hastily of *character* at first sight from small circumstances. In one of Cowper's letters[1] there is an absurd character drawn of Lord Grenville in which the poet represents him as a petit maitre. Lord Lansdowne says this arose from Lord Grenville's taking up his near sighted glass several times to look at different objects during a morning visit he paid Cowper. There cannot in nature or art be a man further from a petit maitre—But he is taking up too much of my paper.

Mr. Gally Knight is a rich amateur both in taste and bel esprit. He has a great deal of anecdote and being well acquainted with the Sneyds coalesced well with us.

Lady Bathurst is a very well bred, well drest, well rouged, affable without being offensively affable woman of the world and of the court—talking with a happy ease of all that is great and fine in this world in a low *proper* voice—never going beyond her own sofa table talk and seated on a bed of roses at the round table all evening with a low candle to herself nets and spangles with great delicacy and diligence a purse which will never be *used* by any mortal. She is remarkably obliging to me and seems to have no natural or artificial repugnance to me as being an author tho she neither has nor pretends to any literature. We have many subjects in common—Her brother the Duke of Richmond and all Ireland[2]—Her aunt Lady L. Connolly Miss E Napier—All the Pakenhams, and the Duchess of Wellington—

[1] *The Life and Letters of William Cowper* by William Hayley (new ed. 1809), ii. 190: letter of 29 March 1784 to Revd. John Newton.

[2] The Duke of Richmond was Lord Lieutenant of Ireland 1806–13.

Very communicative and *confidential* on that last subject, and I am very sorry from all the anecdotes she told me to be convinced that the duchess has been more hurt by her friends than her enemies and more by herself than both put together—but still if she does not quite wash out his affections with tears they will be hers during the long autumn of life. He lately said to Mrs. Pole 'After all *home* you know is what we must look to at last.' . . . Lady Emily the youngest is pale, scarcely handsome but unaffected and obliging. Lady Georgiana Bathurst is a very pretty and I need scarcely say fashionable looking lady of about 22—easy agreeable and quite unaffected. Her mother being rather sickly and indolent has employed Lady Georgiana to do the honors for her both at home and at those famous Argyll Rooms.[1] She has been in Paris—speaks French well and *enough* French air and French flowers—not too much. The simplicity of their dress indeed struck us particularly after all the turmoil the Bath ladies and Bath dress-makers make in vain about this business—plain French white silk frocks with a plain short full sleeve like Fannys and plaited blond round the neck and a blond flounce and thats all—a crescent of white july-flower or scarlet carnations on the head—morning dresses more shewy—young ladies with a profusion of flowers in straw bonnets and matrons with blond caps and crape bonnets and [more] profusion of lace than anything my poor countrified imagination could have conceived—Lady Lansdowne's taste—brilliant in cleanliness—finest materials muslin or lace and work white as the driven snow—But I am sure there must be a warehouse of morning gowns to supply her for I never saw her in the same twice. Tell my dear Fanny she was quite right in her representations and exhortations to us and we are right glad we took hers and my mothers advice. We do very well. Honora always looks elegant and talks agreeable to all and I never listen to her but look sometimes in the faces of those to whom she is speaking to see the impression and am always pleased with it. Upon the whole my dear Sophy I think she is at present better here than she could be anywhere else—and far from repenting—the visit to Bowood has hitherto

[1] Argyll Rooms, Regent St., said to have been established by Colonel Greville for balls, concerts, and masquerades. Associated with the Harmonic Institution and rebuilt about this time by John Nash.

surpassed my expectations in every respect[1] . . . [Lady Lansdowne] is so amiable and so desirous to make others happy that it is impossible not to love her. The most envious of mortals I think would have the heart opened to sympathy with her. They are so fond of one another and shew it and do *not shew* it in a most agreeable manner. His conversation is very various and natural and full of information given for the sake of those to whom he speaks—never for display. What he says lets us into his feelings and character always and *therefore* interests me. *Besides* he convinces me in the most polite and delicate manner that he likes me and her manners are so affectionate and caressing to me that I cannot feel that I am a stranger. When I feel her hands resting on my shoulders and hear the kind tones of her voice I feel almost as if I were with my mother or aunt Ruxton . . . [end missing]

To Mrs. Edgeworth

Grove, Epping,[2] Sunday, 4 October 1818

My dearest Mother . . . After having written so much on business it is time I should think of something to amuse you my dearest mother and to draw a smile if I can from the dear breakfast table. *Who* is at it? Only Mamma—Lovell and Sophy? Or are the young ones all returned from Black Castle? I may safely say I love you *all* whoever you be. Now let me see—What shall I tell to win a smile from you all?

Lord Lansdowne shall win it for me. Among the many pretty little anecdotes he used to give me when I sat beside him at dinner he told me one of his own childhood. It was brought out by my observing that children had very early a great desire to produce an *effect*, a *sensation* in company and that when they see that they have made a change in any grown person's countenance even if they do not know the cause they are delighted and persist if not from *malice* from curiosity and a desire to try and experiment and see what will happen.

[1] For an account of the meeting of T. Moore and ME at Bowood on 19 Sept. 1818, see *Memoirs, Journal and Correspondence of Thomas Moore* (1853), ii. 166–70.

[2] The house of F. Beaufort's father-in-law, Mr. Wilson.

Yes said Lord Lansdowne I remember distinctly having that feeling and acting upon it once in a large and august company when I was a young boy. It was at the time of the French revolution when the French nobility began to emigrate and among the first the Duke and Duchess de Polignac[1] came to England and with all their suite came to Bowood where my father was anxious to receive these illustrious guests with all due honors. One Sunday evening when they were all sitting in state in the drawing room my father introduced me and I was asked to give the company a sermon. I had a little time given me for consideration and then I began. The text I chose—quite undesignedly was '*Put not your trust in Princes*'. The moment I had pronounced the words I saw my father's countenance change and I saw changes in the countenance of the duke and duchess de Polignac and of every face in the circle. I saw I was the cause of this and though I knew my father wanted to stop me I would go on to see what would be the effect and I repeated my text and preached upon it and made out as I went on what it was that affected the congregation.

Afterwards Lord Shelburne desired him to go round the circle and wish the company a good night. But when he came to the Duchesse de Polignac he could not resolve to kiss her he so detested the patch of rouge on her cheek. He started back—Lord Shelburne whispered a bribe in his ear '*I'll give you a shilling*'. No—he would not—and they were obliged to let him off and to laugh it off as well as they could—his father very much vexed. The duchesse de Polignac not a woman as Lord Lansdowne observed accustomed to have her advances slighted or her kisses refused was somewhat surprised at the event and I suppose set it down to the account of English rusticity—bien anglois!

Another days dinner anecdotes—We were talking of Glenarvon[2] and I said we had thought the Princess of Madagascar—Lady Holland—the best part of the book—so good that we

[1] The duchesse de Polignac had been a favourite of Queen Marie Antoinette and governess to the royal children. She and her husband fled to England at the outset of the Revolution.

[2] *Glenarvon*, a novel published anonymously in 1816 by Lady Caroline Lamb. The novel is not very tightly constructed and the episode of the Princess of Madagascar is irrelevant to the main plot.

fancied it had been inserted by a better hand. Lord Lansdowne said 'It is certainly written by Lady Caroline Lamb and she was provoked to it by a note of good advice from Lady Holland.[1] At the time when Lady Caroline Lamb knocked the page on the head with the hearth broom and when he was in imminent danger of dying in consequence of the blow and her Ladyship obliged to hide herself waiting the event, she wrote to Lady Holland who was at that time high on her list of friends. She wrote to thank her for having as she heard defended her on this occasion against the world's abuse. Lady Holland answered that she had indeed defended her Ladyship by positively denying the whole story as she never had believed one word of it till she was to her astonishment assured of its truth by Lady Caroline's own note. She added that she advised Lady Caroline in her then dreadful circumstances to think less of what the world said and more of the pain she had given her mother by her conduct and of the *horrible risk she had run*. This incensed Lady Caroline to such a degree that she immediately went and wrote the Princess of Madagascar.'

When I said we thought the book stupid and that we could hardly get through it Lord Lansdowne said that unless from curiosity to know what would be said of particular people he was not sure that he could have got to the end of it. 'But' added he 'besides this *natural* curiosity about my friends and acquaintance I expected to meet myself and to find myself abused for just at that time I had given her Ladyship sufficient provocation according to her manner of judging. I met her, to my sorrow one morning at the corner of some street where there was a great mob—I think at the time of somebodys election.[2] She was riding, I was walking. She jumped off her horse—came up to me took me by the arm and declared I should carry her through the mob to Sir Francis Burdett who was in some house at the farthest end of the street—But I positively refused declaring it was quite impossible.' Another time there was a set of gentlemen met on Sir S Romilly's election committee she would go to it tho no other woman was to be there and tho she was told there

[1] For Lady Holland's relations with Lady C. Lamb, see *The Home of the Hollands, 1605–1820* by the Earl of Ilchester (1937), 267–71.

[2] The Westminster election of 1818.

would be a mob. Lord Lansdowne met her there and remonstrated. She made her way up to a poor tame sheepish looking old curate 'Reverend Sir you shall protect me! Under your protection what harm can befall me. I am sure you will protect me' and she fastened upon his arm and walked him up and down till his heart was like to break. Another time she went to a quaker meeting—

But Francis calls and says I *must* come out to walk and that he hates foolish letters . . .

half after 4

Returned from a pleasant walk—on the gravel walk with Francis. Though it had rained torrents all morning 5 minutes sunshine had made the walk quite dry—it is so well made—rounded like a bed well tucked-up. Francis has shewn us all the varieties of trees and shrubs which have been stowed into this small compass and which he now has revealed to view—The tulip tree and acacia and variegated oak and the varieties of maple and ash and the variegated rhododendron and Chinese dwarf elm and all that you and Fanny may remember seeing here *and* he abused old Black at every turn—especially for leaving *two* leaders instead of one to his trees, thereby occasioning them to fork and rot . . . I wish I had time to write to Harriet. As for Lovell I both love and admire him and I recommend to him 'Report of the minutes of the evidence before H of C on Education'—price 15 shillings.[1] It contains much that will interest him on schools.

I recommend Harriet and Fanny to read in the third part of Sir W Temples Miscellanea 'A Defence of the essay on antient and modern learning'.[2] It contains a good view of history in small compass. This whole book of Sir W. T's Miscellanea was recommended to me the last evening I spent at Bowood and lent to me to read on my journey by a Mr. Denman a very sensible lawyer—the man who defended the Derby prisoners.[3] Lord

[1] *Report from the Select Committee on the Education of the Lower Orders* (*Parl. Deb.*, vol. xxxviii, cols. 1207 et seq.).

[2] Sir W. Temple, *Miscellanea, The Third Part* (ed. Swift, 1701) contains 'A Defence of the Essay upon Ancient and Modern Learning' (published in the Second Part).

[3] At the summer assizes in 1816 Denman defended 'Captain' Jerry Brandreth,

Lansdowne brought him in for one of his [? boroughs]†. He came the day before we left Bowood. I was sorry we saw no more of him. As we sat down to dinner hearing me say I was going next day to Mrs. Joanna Baillie's he asked me after her and I asked if she was an acquaintance of his. 'I am proud to say I am a relation of hers and I am proud to say I am a friend of hers.' From this beginning a friendship between Mr. Denman and me soon grew—as high as it could in a few hours. He is brother to Dr. Baillie's wife—only a *connexion.* I wish gentlemen would be accurate. He talked much of Mr. W. Strutt. . . . Yours affectionately Maria E

To Mrs. Edgeworth

Saturday—after breakfast, 13 October 1818—*exact Madam!*

Enclosed is a letter from Lady Spencer—Read it dear mother before you go farther—

Mr. Lestock Wilson was present when I received this letter and when I was talking to Francis about it at breakfast. He is connected with the Directors of St. Pauls School and tells me that if you should wish either of your sons to have this appointment he can procure it. *But* tho the schooling is *free* it is merely a day school in fact for the boys board at their own expense—the expense amounts to near 80 Guineas per annum. *And* there are no regular boarding houses, nor any play ground belonging to the school. The boys all of them board where they can some at 2 or 3 miles distance—walk morning and night home by themselves through the streets. I think this would be an insuperable objection to you. I answered Lady Spencer with grateful thanks and declined her offer saying that one of our friends had offered you this appointment but that notwithstanding the pecuniary advantage of an *exhibition* securing £100 per annum for 7 years there were disadvantages (stating them) which I thought would be insuperable. Mr. L. Wilson tells me that he and others have been trying to persuade the directors to remove the school to a scite where there might be play ground and

leader of the Luddite riot of June that year, and his associates Turner and Ludlam. All were convicted and hanged.

proper boarding houses. They are now obliged to repair the old school house and it will cost to do this as many thousands as to build or purchase a new one. But the directors as Mr. L. Wilson expressed it 'are so pig headed that they will not be convinced that their charter allows them liberty to do this though the clause before their eyes is as strong as words can make it by the wise and good founder leaving all to their conscience to do as times may alter whatever is most beneficial for the school'.[1] Pray read this in the reports.

There are hopes that the rational part of the Directors may in time open the understandings of the irrational and that the new school house may be had in the course of a year or two. *Therefore* consider whether you would like it for Pakenham. Francis intends to send his eldest boy there. Francis says that if you should like it an arrangement—Pooh! It is not worth my writing more about it for I am almost sure you will not like it and that you will prefer the Charter-House—Therefore to *that* all my thoughts are directed. I will write this day to Lady E. Whitbread and if she encourages to Lord Grey. I will also write *straight* impudent creature! as I am to the Bishop of London. I can but be refused and then I am just where I was—no—better —because I shall have nothing to reproach myself with hereafter for having omitted any application.

Francis laughs at me for my wish to go and *see* the Charterhouse and Mr. Russell. He says Mr. Russell has nothing to do with boys of Francis's age and that I should do no sort of good by this visit. Nevertheless if you my dear mother would feel it any satisfaction I shall do it if Francis and all the world *grinned* at me. Therefore I pray you to answer me distinctly will it be any satisfaction to *you* . . .

I wrote to Mrs. Bicknell asking whether she would rather that I should go to her at Greenwich or whether she would like to come to me as kind Joanna invited her to spend the day and look over the parts of *the* MS. in which she and her husband are mentioned.[2] This morning I received her answer. 'I cannot

[1] St. Paul's School was at this time on the eastern side of St. Paul's Churchyard. It was rebuilt in 1823 but did not remove from its City site till 1880.

[2] Mrs. Bicknell was Sabrina, one of the orphans brought up by Thomas Day as a possible wife for himself (*Memoirs of RLE* (2nd ed. 1821), i. 209). After her husband's death she became housekeeper to Dr. Burney.

come to you my dear Miss E for I have had these 5 months an abscess in my back which prevents me from bearing the motion of a carriage. I am but just recovering &c.' Then she goes on to say that she must prepare and pack the clothes of a boy who is going to the university on Wednesday and therefore prefers seeing me on Thursday (as I had mentioned two days). There she is with an abscess in her back doing all this mending and packing. Well may it be said that half the world don't know how the other half live.

Now, after my brag of cheerfulness to turn if I can to cheerful subjects. Honora and I had a pleasant drive the other day in Mr. Lestock Wilson's gig to look for Mr. Day's old residence at Stapleford Abbot.[1] We passed through pretty lanes and saw fields green as those of green Erin and hedgerows rich with fine old oak and elm such as I hope Erin will have—some hundred years hence. Mr. L. Wilson shewed us the road he had ridden with Fanny the first ride I believe she took—a ten mile ride—and another 14 mile ride he described and regretted that he had not a decent horse to mount her. Nevertheless he says she got through it very well. We stopped at cottages to inquire about Mr. Day but no man under 40 knew more than that there had been such a person. Mr. Wilson was going to go and make inquiries and to leave the reins in my hand but to this I totally objected with an earnestness which diverted him and Honora much. At last we found a half gentleman who was proud to tell us that the fee simple of the property formerly Mr. Day's was now his *property* and a farmer Ainsworth occupied it and there was a *pass* and *a gate* which though his *property* we might go through &c. So proud of his property he directed us. I had described to my companions the place and as we drove up missing the wood before the house and seeing a house quite unlike what I remembered I thought it could not be the right place but as we got to the top of the [? hill] the wood discovered itself below. I got out and crossed the dirty yard in spite of a dog barking and springing to the length of his chain longing to eat me. A woman and children appeared staring as if stuck though with amazement—Then a *charming* old grey headed man leaning on crutches, but with ruddy cheeks and smooth forehead and fine large

[1] 5 miles from Epping.

dark eyes which lighted up and sparkled with pleasure and with affection the moment I mentioned the name of *Day*!

Day! know him Aye sure I do and have good right so for to do for very good he was to me. Please to walk in—pointing with his crutch—Did he live here? Aye in this very house—no not this very house for the house he lived in was all pulled down every bit except yon brick wall and this has been built by me just to live in. We went in and he seated himself in his elbow chair by the kitchen fire with his arms resting as easily you may see by Honora's sketch of him. She made that sketch while I kept him talking. He spoke in the most grateful manner of poor Mr. Day and of Mrs. Day who had sent wine to his wife when she lay in and who said she would send more but I said there was plenty and plenty. Oh Mr. Day was a *good* man and did a power of good to the poorer sort. I was one of his days-men (day laborers) at first and then he helped me on and when he was tired of this here farm and wanted to settle at his other place, he offered me this but I said Sir I am not able for it—but he said Ainsworth if I help you a bit you'll then be able wont you?

It was quite touching to me to hear the manner in which this worthy old man spoke of Mr. Day. I asked him if he remembered a servant Mr. Day had who ploughed the sandy field 16 times. He instantly answered 'George Bristow! Oh aye I remember him well enough and a very honest good servant he was—always I liked George Bristow.' 'He is now our servant and came here with us.' 'Why! I thought he went to live with a family in Ireland.' 'So he did with our family.' '*Oh!* you comes from Ireland and he with you. I wish he had comed here today with you.' 'So do I indeed but he is gone to see his friends at Eton.' 'Well well he was an honest man that G. Bristow—very unlike Mrs. Walker the housekeeper.' Pray tell Molly this. The old man wanted to have entered into particulars about Mrs. Walker and her *child* but I would not understand him—*So* he finished with 'I am very sorry I have nothing fit to offer a lady to drink.'

I begged from his daughter a few acorns from the oaks formerly Mr. Days and I will bring them home for my aunt Ruxton and Lovell to plant in honor of him. This old man is 84—his 8 children married and unmarried all good to him and he is one of the most chearful looking creatures and most lively at his age I ever beheld (I never saw your grandfather[1]).

He regretted that the old house had been pulled down—But them workmen, masons and carpenters overpersuaded him that he might get 4 or 500 £ for the bricks and timber—so down it came every stone and stick and he did not get over £100. I mentioned the buried money[2] and he sensibly answered 'But if it was *in* the house it must have comed out of the walls when them pulled 'em down'. Farmer Ainsworth wore a carters frock well stitched and very easy he was in it—as much at his ease and as fine and polite a looking benevolent countenance as the Archbishop of Tuam and as happy tho he never tasted turbot or turtle in his born days. So much for Farmer Ainsworth. I hope you will like his portrait.

We had a delightful drive yesterday from Epping through various chearful villages and heaths and pretty by roads (We came by Tottenham). What amazing difference between the scene and the inhabitants of the country here and in Wales! I could not help recollecting and contrasting with the country and people we now saw, those sublime scenes in Wales and the simple picturesque peasantry in their blue wool and black hats. For 6 or 7 miles as we approached Hampstead the whole country seemed to be what you might call a *citizens paradise*—not a *fools* paradise though a fastidious man of taste or an intolerant philosopher might think them synonymous terms. No here are means of *comfort* and enjoyment more substantial than ever were provided in any fools paradise. Then such *odd* prettinesses—Such a variety of little *snuggeries* and such green trellices and bowers and vinecovered fronts of houses that look as if they had been built and painted in exact imitation of the cottages in the front and side scenes of Drury-lane—the vines spreading over squares like a paper-hangers vine paper—And all the houses so slight—as if each proprietor had said to himself 'Now I'll run me up a box in the *country* and be rural and happy!'

[1] The Revd. Daniel Cornélis de Beaufort (1700–88).

[2] '. . . apprehending a general Bankruptcy, Mr. Day had sold several Thousand Pounds out of the Funds during the late war and deposited it under the boards': Thomas Lowndes to RLE, 25 Oct. 1789 (Edgeworth MSS.).

Carriages of all sorts running and rolling past—Landaus—gigs—garden carts—ass carts—ass carriages—low wheeled—very pretty—numbers of riding parties—children especially on asses and ponies looking so happy!—schoolboys rising in their little stirrups and lending their little souls to the delight of the sunshine holiday. At one house as we passed we saw a groupe a line of white robed ladies mother aunts and sisters I am sure who on Hampstead Heath had just come out of their house without hat or bonnet to see the first mounting and performance on horseback of an urchin of 7 year old who was on horseback I suppose for the first time—he was in a blue jacket and trowzers *the moral*[1] of Pakenham—on a little long tailed poney—first walking then trotting manfully backwards and forwards to the delight of mother sister and aunt, under a row of shady trees. Fool! why waste your time describing this. The number of *Cockney Castles* however I must mention diverted me exceedingly. There are such a variety of miniature castles with towers and battlements such as Milton and Scott never dreamed of and with all their imagination could never conceive—No nor Vivian[2] neither.

Why we came back to Hampstead in the middle of our visit to Epping is explained in a letter to Fanny which has reached or will reach you in a day or two after this. Be patient and take it for granted we are right and mirrors of prudence.

Joanna Baillie and her sister the most kind cordial warm hearted creatures came running down their little flagged walk to welcome us and thank us for thinking it worth while to come back for 4 days. I would not have done otherwise for any consideration. Half an hour after we arrived morning visitors—a Miss Montgomery sister to a Colonel Montgomery Irish—niece to Lady Gosford. She went to Spain, how or why Lord knows with her brother—lived there some time—formed a romantic friendship with a Spanish lady—Colonel Montgomery fell in love with her friend—never told his sister till it was all settled lest she should be blamed as the contriver of a match which he knew would displease all his friends at home. He

[1] Symbolical figure (*O.E.D.*).

[2] ME's *Vivian, Tales of Fashionable Life* (1812). Vivian ruined himself by building a Gothic mansion: see *Tales and Novels of ME* (1832–3 ed.), viii. 36 ff.

married and brought home his bride. She is not such a person as you or aunt Ruxton would picture to yourself from the sound of a Spanish lady and a romantic story. She is simple looking—dark complexion—not dignified—nothing that gives an idea of birth or good breeding or poetry. She was *bourgeoise* I suspected from the first and I learned afterwards I suspected rightly—Miss Montgomery a very interesting really romantic not sham romantic or affectedly romantic person—evidently a very warm hearted friend—an intimate friend of Lady Byron.[1] Of course hates Lord Byron properly. She assured me that the account we have heard of his chief motive for marrying being revenge she believes to be true. 'There were mixed motives I grant—money—she was reputed to have a much larger fortune than she really possessed. Lord Byron was distressed for money. To be sure he could have had other fortunes but then there was vanity. Miss Milbanke was just then in London the heiress who made the best figure. When he first proposed for her he had seen her only half a dozen times in public places and large parties. Her answer was as courteous and gentle a refusal as possible—that she admired his poetry and his talents but that she really could not trust her happiness with a person of whose character she knew so little. He smothered his rage and for two years dissembled and acted as well as he could all the virtues and the part of a lover to perfection. But literally no sooner was the ceremony over than the fiend broke out. As her father handed her into the carriage he swore a terrible oath at him and no sooner was he seated in the carriage with his bride than he turned to her as they drove off and asked How she dared, how she could ever venture to marry a man whom she had refused!'

Miss Montgomery met him lately abroad. He is grown fat and quite vulgar looking she says, he has quite embruted. The ladies abroad say that he has had no success in gallantry there—nothing but what his money has purchased. Miss Montgomery saw a letter of his written just after he had received the purchase money of an estate he has sold. He wrote that he was pefectly happy for that

[1] At this period ME collected from Lady Byron's friends a number of stories against Lord Byron, but in later letters she expressed the opinion that Lady Byron was cold-hearted. For an account of Byron's married life, see M. Elwin, *Lord Byron's Wife* (1962), chaps. 9–11.

now he had money 'and money is power and pleasure and happiness'. Lord Lansdowne told us also that he appears quite gay and without any touch of remorse. It is not worth saying more of him.

Mrs. Hunter wife to the celebrated John Hunter and aunt by marriage to the Miss Baillies was engaged to dine here yesterday to meet us. She is 78—a fine tall figure—plump not fat—fair—very fair—not a wrinkle in her forehead—hair in curls light as a flaxen dolls—but her own hair made into a front—a smiling lively countenance tho with white eyebrows and eyelashes so white that she seems as if she had none—rouged! I'm sorry for it but I cant help it—bright pink. Now her eyesight has failed a little she puts on too much. This is the only thing that is disagreeable about her but when she converses we forget it as we did with Mrs. Lefanu. She speaks well—is polite and agreeable. She wrote Mary Q of Scots lament and the Son of Alknomook shall never complain.[1] She entertained me exceedingly and as she went away she stopped on the stairs to say to Joanna '*I like Miss E exceedingly*'. So you see why I liked her exceedingly. No you dont yet see *all* the reasons. I mentioned to her that my father had been an admirer of Mr. Hunters talents—that he used to meet him at Slaughters coffee house.[2] I told her that he has recorded the circumstance that passed at the trial of Sir T. Boughton's laurel water &c.[3] She was much

[1] Mrs. Hunter's poems were published in 1802 with a second edition in the following year. 'The Son of Alknomook shall never complain' is one of the variants of the refrain of 'The Death Song', written for and adapted to an original Indian air.

[2] There were two Slaughter's Coffee Houses in St. Martin's Lane. Old Slaughter's occupied Nos. 74 and 75 and was opened in 1692. It was frequented especially by literary men (e.g. Pope, Dryden, and Goldsmith) and by artists (e.g. Hogarth, Gainsborough, Roubiliac, Richard Wilson, and Wilkie), but it was also the meeting place of the St. Martin's Club, a parish society. Old Slaughter's was demolished in 1843: *Survey of London, Vol. XX* (1940), 117, Pl. 102; Wheatley and Cunningham, *London Past and Present* (1891), iii. 252–3; J. McMaster, *Short History of . . . St. Martins-in-the-Fields* (1916), 225; *The Farington Diary*, ii (1923), 78 n. New (or Young) Slaughter's Coffee House occupied No. 82 St. Martin's Lane. It was opened in 1760. From 1767–71 and 1781–2 RLE frequented there a society of literary and scientific men which included John Hunter the surgeon, Sir Joseph Banks, Captain Cook, and Smeaton: *Survey of London, Vol. XX*, 117; *Memoirs of RLE* (2nd ed. 1821), i. 183–6, 375.

[3] In 1781 Captain Donnellan was tried at Warwick for alleged poisoning of his brother-in-law Sir T. Boughton with laurel water. John Hunter was criticized by the judge for his hesitancy over the toxicity of laurel water: *D.N.B.*; *Memoirs of RLE* (2nd ed. 1821), i. 184–6.

interested. She never knew my father herself but spoke handsomely of him.

Both Joanna Baillie and her sister have a great deal of agreeable and *new* conversation—not old trumpery literature over and over again and reviews &c but new anecdotes of people, and circumstances worth telling apropos to every subject that is touched upon and frank free observations on character without either ill nature or fear of committing themselves—Quite *safe* companions—no blue-stocking tittle-tattle or habits of worshipping or being worshipped—Domestic affectionate creatures—good to live with—without fussing, continually doing what is most obliging and whatever makes us feel most at *home*. They have asked Mr. Whishaw and Mr. Denman here to dine tomorrow . . .

M. Dumont left at Hunters for me his last translation of Bentham Tactique des assemblees[1] &c—on the first page wrote Miss Maria E de la part de son sincere et inalterable ami E. Dumont—and yet either as you say from monkish or philosophical principles never did man part with a friend with less appearance of feeling—*sincere* I believe and *inalterable* I am sure and clear I am that we are not suited to each other except as author and critic. I am most grateful for his criticism . . . Yrs. affectionately Dearest mother Maria E

To Mrs. Edgeworth

Hampstead,[2] Thursday, 15 October 1818
8 oclock before breakfast

My dearest mother, The happiest time of my day is when I am writing to you and flattering myself that I am giving you some minutes of pleasure or *respite* from pain and you see I write in broad daylight not wearing out any of my eyes by candlelight. I believe I left off on tuesday when we were just going to the vale of health[3] to see Mrs. Hunter in her baby house cottage—

[1] *Tactique des Assemblées Législatives . . . ouvrage extrait des manuscrits de J. Bentham* (1816). Dumont's often charming letters to ME (MS. in Library of University College, London) would lead one to suppose that they were on easy and intimate terms, but he seems almost always to have been rather stiff with her when they met.

[2] ME was staying with Joanna and Agnes Baillie at Bolton House.

[3] An area of Hampstead Heath.

Very nice it is with a swarm of singing birds in cages in the trelliced room and an open book of mathematics which Miss Hunter was reading on the table. She is a pleasing unaffected sensible girl with wonderfully good manners. Mrs. Hunter was much gratified by your *kind* message to her and *'to her nice little daughter'*. When we were going away I whispered a request to kind Joanna, to whom almost as readily as to yourself I can say anything, and she invited Miss Hunter to spend the next evening with us; she asked Mr. Hunter also to bring his daughter. Two ladies Mrs. and Miss Milligans spent *Tuesday evening* here —relations of Miss Baillies—rich and agreeable—I dont mean rich and *consequently* agreeable. They live in the Miss Berry's house while they stay abroad and from their intimacy with the Miss Berrys and others of notoriety have good store of anecdote. They made the evening pass well.

Wednesday morning. Breakfast time in this house is very pleasant. These two good sisters look so neat and chearful when we meet them in the morning—delicately white tablecloth—*Scotch marmalade*—Excellent tea and coffee—Everything at breakfast and at dinner at all times so neat and suitable!—and comfortable and with such good will and real politeness—without fussing or officious civility. The two sisters seem to live but to oblige us yet never seem to go an inch out of their way in doing it. I mention particularly their neat and nice mode of living because *this* far surpassed my expectations. For kindness and hospitality I *was* fully prepared. A tidy maid servant waits at dinner—But stay—I am not at *dinner* yet—I was at *breakfast*. At breakfast they converse—very agreeably—New things always in their conversation—Anecdotes both of Scotch and English friends—*passages* of their former lives—feelings and opinions—all arising from what *went before* in conversation, not prepared or dragged in. They told us the history of Mrs. Fry the quaker who goes to reform the people at Newgate. They know her intimately. She is very rich—very handsome a delicate madona-looking woman—married to a man who adores her and what is much more to the purpose supplies her with money and lets her follow her benevolent *courses* (I did not say *whims*) as she pleases. She has a great deal of worldly good sense, Joanna B says, mixed with her enthusiasm; and knows how to carry her own purposes into effect without running across other peoples prejudices or interests. She is sister to *Mr.* Gurney—They also rich benevolent people who have done a world of good of which I ought to have known but never heard before. I was further ashamed to have forgotten what I suppose I have heard of Mr. Saml. Hoare—a distant relation of *my* Mr. Hoares the banker. It was he who with Mr. Buxton—Fowell Buxton during the scarcity last year by their own munificence and by devoting their whole time to managing the contributions of others, saved from famine, or from rising in rebellion for want of food, *twenty thousand of the weavers of London.*[1] These excellent men are friends of Miss Baillie's. Unluckily these people are all absent but they would have been delighted to see us I am told and am fond to believe. But pray don't think that the Miss Baillie's conversation is *all* about *stupid good* people. They have a great variety I assure you and in one word they are the most agreeable persons to *live* with—ready to converse at right times and then to employ themselves and be silent. I am grown so fond of them I shall be *very* sorry to part with them—dear affectionate souls. (Remember that I tell you an anecdote of a dutchess of Bedford in Charles 1st's time who ordered the butler to hide the family plate—which he did so effectually it has never been found since.)

Wednesday morning after breakfast. Went with Joanna to Stoke Newington to see Mrs. Barbauld (I see you smile with approbation)—a fine sunshiny day—Pleasant drive from that gay gaudy *teadrinkingest* place Hampstead to Stoke Newington—On the road there observed some of the fine charitable institutions *Vaccine hospitals—Asylum for the blind—Asylum for deaf and dumb*[2]—all *by voluntary contribution* in proud large letters inscribed on the buildings. As Miss Baillie said these institutions

[1] From 1808 Buxton had taken an interest in charitable undertakings in Spitalfields, especially in education, the Bible society, and the sufferings of the weavers. In 1816 at a Mansion House meeting for the relief of starving weavers he gave a vivid factual account of their situation and over £43,300 was raised to set up a well-organized system of relief.

[2] The Small Pox Hospital at Battlebridge (King's Cross); The Asylum for the Indigent Blind, St. George's Fields; The Deaf and Dumb Asylum, Old Kent Rd. It seems most improbable that ME saw these institutions on *this* journey, though the dust heaps she mentions just afterwards were in Holloway (cf. *Our Mutual Friend*) and may well have been on her route.

are worthy of England's *'princely merchants'* and are mostly promoted and supported by them. Next we passed (such is the strange mixture in human affairs) a mean looking mount of coal ashes and rubbish, 'high as the house and higher'—broad as the house and broader than *Edgeworthstown* house! This heap of rubbish is the property of one man who has for some years kept coalmen and dustmen in his pay to bring here their refuse. It is now worth a thousand a year to him. He sells it again to the roadmenders and gardeners. This coal mount put me in mind of the crockery mount, the mount of broken china in or near Rome[1] which I have heard aunt Ruxton describe. What a dismal place Stoke Newington is!—with its rows of pointed poplars veiled in smoke and its swampy Dutch appearance with its ditchy-canal called the *new River*![2]—and such a smell of mixed coal-smoke, and brick-kiln, and Oh! Oh! Oh!—pull up the window! Poor Mrs. Barbauld! Her house and her white wainscotted room is so forlorn-looking yet *finish* too—like the finery in the cabin of a ship. We waited some time before she appeared and I had leisure, my dear mother to recollect everything that could make me melancholy[3]—The very sofa that you recollect still *there* and the very same where you and my father sat. I was quite *undone* before Mrs. Barbauld came in but was forced *to get through it*, and to talk. She was *very* kind and I do believe was much gratified by our visit. I said every thing for you that you could have wished. Mrs. Barbauld looks much better and better dressed than she used to do and was very agreeable. *But* I forget almost all she said—for I was stupified all the time I was there. Opposite to me sat fixed as in a dream Miss Hamond—a long-faced, hard faced wooden-cut of a head. I asked for her brother. He is well and their affairs are going on better. I felt as if I had lived 2 or 3 lives and as if I was a hundred years old and had been left alive here on earth by mistake. But the mind has wonderful elasticity and the fresh air has more power over the spirits than I could have believed till I had felt it—on *some* occasions, where

[1] Monte Testaccio, Rome, a mound over 100 ft. high and over 900 yds. round, composed entirely of potsherds.

[2] The New River was a canal cut by Sir Hugh Myddelton in 1613 to supply London with water. Beginning near Ware, it passes by Enfield, Hornsey, and Stoke Newington to Islington.

[3] ME had visited Mrs. Barbauld with RLE in 1813. See also below, p. 266 n.

no reasoning or philosophy will do. When we drove away I was glad we *had* paid the visit and I am sure you will approve. I forgot to tell you that the day before this we saw Mrs. Carr and Miss Carr—as kind and agreeable as ever. They inquired with real interest for *all* of you and asked innocently many painful questions and *were sorry to hear that poor William had not recovered his health.*

Miss Carr dined here, we like her very much. She is a particular friend of Lady Byron's—travelled with her in England the year Lord Byron left her—went with her to the very place where Lady Byron had been married. She gave us a most touching account of Lady Byron's conduct—of her struggles to repress her feelings—of the absurd conclusion some people drew from her calm manner and composed countenance that she did *not feel.* Remember that I tell you of Lady Byron's coming as if in her sleep into Miss Carr's room that night in the dead of night and sitting on the side of her bed—wishing *to be able to cry.* I cannot write it all—but I am sure I shall remember to tell it you. It made too great an impression ever to be forgotten. Miss Carr is a most engaging unaffected truly feeling young woman and she is extremely well informed and accomplished. She was so good at my request to let her servant bring with her this evening two books large as Allen's Town[1] print-books of her drawings —sketches she made in 1816 on a tour through Germany Swisserland and Italy. Honora was delighted with them. Miss Carr as we turned them over gave most entertaining notes explanatory—telling us anecdotes of places and people and manners. When we came to Italy and Florence we found that she there had met Lord and Lady Lansdowne, who are friends of hers and Lady Lansdowne and she took sketches together. She admires and likes Lady Lansdowne as much as we do. These drawings and conversation afforded us delightful entertainment all evening. She used to sketch in any way she could as the carriage went on and at every stage to reform and touch up the memorandums. It seems as if every beautiful spot on the banks of the Rhine had been sketched by her. How I did wish that you and Fanny could have seen them! Some are merely sketched like etchings with pen and ink on white paper or brown. Others are

[1] Mrs. E's mother's family, the Wallers, lived at Allenstown, Co. Meath.

shaded with white chalk or white paint on brown paper. The white paint 'tips with silver every mountains head'[1] and has fine effect in Swisserland in representing the glaciers—Needles —Mer de Glace &c. She has promised me a drawing or two so you shall not be put off with my tantalizing description.

Hunter and his nice little girl came; and I was glad they had the pleasure of seeing these drawings. Hunter told me that Mr. Scott brother to Lady Oxford called on him yesterday to praise Caramania.[2] He was Consul at Venice. He had some time ago written to Hunter to say that the father of the Armenian Convent there was delighted with the book and most anxious to obtain some of the inscriptions which Francis has still unpublished. The father says that if Captain Beaufort will send them to him he will send them to Armenia and get them translated for him. When I see Hunter again I will get a clearer account. His was confused and mine unintelligible—no matter. The *result* was that the fame of Caramania spreads far and wide.

This morning Thursday we went to Greenwich to see Mrs. Bicknell. She was glad to see me and I am *very* glad I went to see her and that I went through the reading of all the passages in both my father's MS. and my own. Her eyes were bad and she could not read herself she said. It was disagreeable to me as you may guess—especially to read about the *foundling hospital.* She wishes that part to be left out on account of her sons.[3] Her son is now a solicitor in good business and lives next door to her in a good house, with garden—greenhouse and all befitting £2000 per annum. He was dreadfully shocked a few years ago by meeting with his origin or his mothers origin in Miss Sewards life of Darwin.[4] He was just then in weak health. He had never heard the circumstances before. So much for the wisdom of concealment! He came to his mother in such a state of irritation as she could not describe. He has high spirit and was violently

[1] Pope, *Homer's Iliad*, Book VIII, l. 674.

[2] Francis Beaufort's book, published in 1817.

[3] See *Memoirs of RLE* (2nd ed. 1821), i. 209–13. The episode has been so reworded that it is not clear that Mrs. Bicknell came from a foundling hospital. Mrs. Bicknell had been adopted by Thomas Day, who wished to educate a wife for himself. The story has been told many times, e.g. S. Scott, *The Exemplary Mr. Day* (1935).

[4] Anna Seward, *Memoirs of the Life of Dr. Darwin* (1804).

enraged with Miss Seward. They had a furious paper war. To my surprise neither he or Mrs. Bicknell are aware that Mr. Keir in his life of Day[1] had told all the circumstances. I can easily alter a sentence or two so as to avoid repeating or tearing open the wound. In some magazine lately he met with a half true, half false history of Mr. Day and his mother which ended with saying *she was dead*. He was again enraged with this. How glad I am that I went to Mrs. Bicknell and heard and saw all her feelings. She was pleased with Honora—said *her* mother[2] was extremely plump when she first saw her and had one of the prettiest bosoms she ever beheld.

I was struck with a great change in Mrs. Bicknells manner and mind. Instead of being as Mr. Day thought her helpless and indolent she is more like a stirring housekeeper—all softness and timidity gone! She spoke of Mr. and Mrs. Keir with great resentment and of Mr. Day as having made her miserable—*a slave* &c! It was a very painful visit to me. I was very glad Honora was with me. Poor soul!—she saw nothing that was pleasant at Greenwich. We had only this one object and saw nothing—nothing literally but Mrs. Bicknell!—and came back not content—except with ourselves.

Thursday dinner

Mr. Whishaw dined with us—was very friendly—spoke of you most kindly—never asked for William. He knew from Dumont's letters that he was very ill. He talked a great deal evidently to amuse us. He took an opportunity of speaking about the MS. Had heard of it from Dumont who thought well of it. I said it wanted still much correction and that I was but just beginning to be able to judge of it. '*I advise you to lay it by for some time and then look at it again.*'

In the evening came Mr. and Mrs. Carr and 2 Miss Carrs—Miss Mulso (Chapone's niece) a Mr. Morris (not our Morris but some rich grand traveller) and Mrs. Morris—*personnage muet*. I was much tired by the morning business and they were all like flitting images before me. I was stupified but they all talked happily except Miss Mulso who sat mum-chance or *grum*

[1] James Keir, *Account of the Life and Writings of Thomas Day* (1791).
[2] Mrs. Elizabeth E (*née* Sneyd).

chance in a dirty white satin turban—whom Mrs. Baillie regretted I did not speak to her. I never knew her name was *Mulso* till she was gone. When introduced I thought they said Miss *Mercer* but it's all one—I could not have talked to her I was so stupid . . .

We saw Mr. Samuel Hoare father of the gentleman mentioned in the beginning of this letter as having saved 20,000 poor by his and Mr. Buxton's exertions. Mr. Hoare told us many entertaining anecdotes of Crabbe the poet who is with him. I just note for future telling you—*history of his letter to Lord Thurlow* and *speech to his patron* the Duke of Rutland about *Coursing*.[1]

I packed up the cap box marvellous well! in my own conceit. *Friday morning 8 oclock.* Miss Carr came to breakfast and to take leave of us. I have not seen any young lady in England I like so well. As to Joanna Baillie and her sister!—I can only say I *rejoice* we came back to them. I would not have missed seeing so much goodness and receiving so much kindness for any consideration. I am sure we have not found what Madame de Stael describes of London houses being closed boxes[2] . . .

Friday morning continued. We went round by *London* to Epping that we might see the principal Dentists—collect all their advice and opinions and carry them with us to Epping to decide *what* and *who* to follow. My dear mother, imagine if you can how strange—how melancholy to me it was to drive about London without you or anyone to direct! But the necessity pressed and it was done—better too than I could have expected. Mr. L. Wilson who is a most *serviceable* person sent us horses and a most excellent postillion from London to Hampstead by 9 oclock. Mr. L. Wilson had warned him that he was to carry us to various places in Town. He knew the Town well. Thank goodness! George Bristow was not with us. He is at Eton with

[1] Lord Thurlow and the Duke of Rutland both helped Crabbe in his clerical career and he was for some time domestic chaplain to the Duke, who was well known in the sporting world. When Crabbe made his first attempt at coursing, he was so upset by the cry of the hare that he abandoned the sporting activities customary among the clergy of the Belvoir neighbourhood.

[2] 'le *chez soi* (home) est le goût dominant des Anglais . . . Chaque ménage a sa demeure separée, et Londres est composé d'un grand nombre de petites maisons fermées comme des boîtes, et ou il n'est guère plus facile de pénétrer . . .' (Madame de Stael, *Considérations sur la révolution française,* Pt. 6, vi, De la société en Angleterre).

his brother. The carriage was *open* and the driver stopped before we went into London and asked what places we wished to go to. I had made (after your dear good fashion) a list on a card[1] which I read to him and he settled which to go to in order as follows—

Mr. Thompson Dentist—George St. Hanover Square
Parkinson Dentist—Sackville St.
Dumergue—12 Albemarle St.
Henderson 33 Charlotte St. Rathbone Place
Waite Old Burlington St.
Hopkinson & sons High Holborn—Pallmer & Wilson—Kings Arms Yd. Coleman St.

We found not the least difficulty except about *Mr. Waite*. The number Alicia had given us was 5. We found no such person at 5 *old* Burlington St.—tried *New* Burlington Street—no such person! and very extraordinary!—no creature we asked could direct or had *ever heard* of *Mr. Waite* dentist. We tried apothecary's shop—No—We bought a 5 shilling *directory*—not a dentist in it. But we were determined not to give up because the only commission Francis had given me was to bring him a box of tooth powder *from Waite's*. At last at the *coachmakers* I got a *Court* guide in which *he* suggested that the dentists must be and we found Waite No. 2 not 5. Blockhead! we had trusted to a woman who said there was no Waite in that street. The drivers patience looked nearly exhausted. 'To go back a mile and a half!—from the coachmakers in High Holborn!' But back we went—maid only at home—*Mr. Waite out of Town Ma'am till monday*. But we got the box of tooth powder and this satisfied us.

The dentists differed much in opinion about Honora's teeth. Thompson and Dumergue advised the taking out the two front teeth which they said cannot *last*—advise inserting two—rivetting them. Thompson thought there may be some little inflammation of the gum in consequence of taking out *one* of the teeth of which the nerve is *dead*—cost of the *two*—6 Guineas—Parkinson Ditto—Ditto—expense Ditto. Dumergue was most bold and decided—engaged that there was no hazard. She might travel directly afterwards—a little pain not much. It would be a very great improvement to her mouth. He could lessen the

[1] See above, p. 59.

projection—in short strenuously advises rivetting in two teeth —price ten guineas. Henderson on the contrary abhors all rivetting—says it will be *impossible* in her case because the stump of one tooth is not sound. The rivets will not hold. Filing the teeth across to get them out will be extremely painful operation—will be followed by inflammation—impossible to travel for a week or 10 days afterwards! The false teeth when *rivetted* will be very troublesome and *offensive*. If she were to have artificial teeth he would recommend, not human teeth but those which he makes of Hippopotamus teeth. He fastens with gold wire—shewed me how—like Lady Granards—to which I strongly objected. Then he shewed me how they could be notched with a bit of the bone itself behind the other teeth and made to take in and out every day.

Henderson was against her having artificial teeth at present. Hers may last some years—advised filing them shorter and covering behind and before with a waxy looking composition—daily—can shew how to apply it. If she chuses to have new teeth from him price is *2 guineas*. I fear he could not make Hippopotamus teeth match in color with hers. What to decide when Doctors disagree is difficult. I wish you were here to help us, my dear *Irresolue*.[1] We paid nothing to any of these people for their opinions; but promised to write from Epping if anything is to be done—to appoint hour &c—on the 22d. They were all very civil—Henderson was the most of a *quack* in manner and *least* of a genteel-coxcomb-quack. In conduct Henderson was the most downright and candid—repeatedly saying 'Dont trust to my opinion *alone*—Consult others—Consult others'. Since I cannot have you with me dearest friend you see I ease my mind by telling you *all* that passes. I hope I don't tire with details? They prove that I write only for you. Who else could bear them?

We went to Mr. Huttons civil coachmaker. Honora bespoke a trunk which will fasten under George's Dickey—price 2 Guineas. We are to send the carriage as soon as we go to Town. He lets us have another with coach box for the day or days we stay. I think we must have one because we could never find our way or walk the distances we want to go. Horses and coachmen we must manage to get and *pay* for. *Mr. L. Wilson—Good at need—*

[1] Probably a reference to the play of that name by Destouches, translated by Murphy in 1778 as '*Know your own mind*'.

will manage that for us. No one can be more usefully obliging. Francis has advised us to go to Mr. Lestock Wilsons house of business at the end of our morning's work and Mr. Wilson had promised to have horses ready bespoke to carry us to Epping. We went to his house of business Kings Arms Yd. Coleman St. a very good house. He had sandwiches &c prepared for us and after resting half an hour we went on—a fine evening—carriage open—delightful drive to Epping and most refreshing after the Dentists and the turmoil of London streets with all the city drays coalcarts &c.

Could I four years ago have believed if it had been prophecied to me that I poor little i should this day have been driving about London with Honora *alone*? *Yet* during the time I had scarcely leisure for astonishment. I regretted much that Honora in driving through so much of London had no one with her to tell her what any place or building was. How I wished for your head!

We were right glad to feel ourselves with Francis and Alicia[1] and the children at *quiet* Epping again. This *quiet*, which I once hated is *now* so agreeable! How we change in feelings! . . . You ask whether the drawing room here is furnished. At this moment Francis is unrolling carpets just bought for drawing room and Mrs. Wilsons room—very pretty—his choice—brown leaves something like our own on a blue ground. He hopes to have the rooms carpetted and rugged by tuesday to surprise and delight Mrs. Wilson who has so much wished it.

Sunday morning—18th October

I send you Brougham's pamphlet.[2] I think Lovell will like to read it particularly. Perhaps it will come at a moment when you may be *horribly* busy and melancholy but the time *will* come afterwards when you will want employment for your thoughts. I therefore send also the account of Sir Patrick Hume and his admirable Griselda.[3] I beg it may be given to my dear sister

[1] Francis Beaufort's wife, daughter of Mr. and Mrs. Wilson.

[2] *Speech of Henry Brougham in the House of Commons, May 8, 1818, on the education of the poor and charitable abuses*. For Lovell Edgeworth's interest in education, see above, p. xxxiv.

[3] Sir Patrick Hume was a strong Presbyterian and Whig. In 1684 his 12-year-old daughter, afterwards Lady Grisel Baillie, kept him secretly supplied with food when he was in hiding in the church vault at Polwarth. The work referred to is perhaps G. Rose, *Observations on the historical work of the late Rt. Hon. C. J. Fox* (1809).

Harriet. I think it a present worthy of her. The rest of the book is little worth. It will arrive however with some parcel of books hereafter at Edgeworthstown and shall be sewed together and bound for her. Ethereal substance soon unites again.[1]

Adieu—yours my dear mother with as much affection and esteem as ever was felt by a daughter in law.[2] I will not presume to say by a daughter because you have 4 who would give me the lie direct.

Maria Edgeworth.

Sunday Evening half after 4. Just returned from a very pleasant walk through the fields towards Coopersale home by the forest—the two boys very happy driving and hunting Mr. L. Wilson through the wood. There are great variety of pleasant walks here.

Odd Replies to ODD *questions*

I asked the Baillies[3] about the princesses—The princess Sophia is not insane—only nervous and weak—this is the truth and *nervous* is not here used as a soft equivocal word.

The princess Amelia[4] was said to have died a martyr to the King's evil and all scars and sores—absolutely false. Dr. Baillie saw her during all her illness—*after death*—told his sister that her neck and every part of her was free from all scar or sore or swelling or any symptom of that disease. She died of atrophy—really worn out—anxiety of mind accelerating or producing it—all about her children true—Fitzroy her husband I *think* she said but am not sure—was not always kind to her.

The princess [Sophia][5] is married it is believed to General Garth. Miss Baillie says you would be surprised at her choice if you saw him.

All the stories about the King's apartments being stuffed to prevent cries being heard is false. Dr. Baillie says the rooms are

[1] Pope, *Rape of the Lock,* Canto III, l. 152, parodying Milton's *Paradise Lost,* Bk. VI, on Satan cut asunder by the Archangel Michael.

[2] Step-daughter.

[3] Dr. Matthew Baillie was physician to the royal family.

[4] The Princess is said to have died of tuberculosis, perhaps complicated by erysipelas. The story of her marriage and her children is not generally accepted.

[5] Princess Sophia had an affair with General Garth and is said to have had a child by him.

just as they always were. As to the Queen no mortal knows whether she will die tomorrow or live months. All the physicians say she may die any hour or may hold out a month or 2.[1] Dr. Baillie never sees her—never has seen her since her illness.

To Mrs. Edgeworth

Epping, Friday, 23 October 1818

Dearest mother . . . My last letter if it has reached you must have informed you of our visits to the London dentists. Now be it known to you that Mr. Waite whom we did not see is the man whom we think by Francis's account we shall prefer. He is a filer and stuffer and abhors artificial teeth and rivetting. Francis has decided Honora to be decided by Waite's opinion. She has written and made an appointment to be with him on Monday next the 26th one oclock . . .

I forgot to tell you that the new carpet is down in the two drawing rooms all the same—looks very handsome Mrs. Wilson much pleased with it and with F's kind attention in covering her footstools with the same—spick and span for her return.—The only inconvenience that being the same as carpet none but lynx eyes can see them and they will break all shins. I hope Alicia will not stumble over them—The red morocco strip round them and brass nails thereon her only chance of escape. Even the poor old gentleman just articulated '*Very soft*'. Once to me he said 'Do you like this house *Mrs.* Edgeworth?' 'Very much indeed Sir. It is very much improved.' 'That is all Captain Beaufort's *merit*' he replied speaking with great difficulty. I answered 'Captain Beaufort does not think so.' But my words and my sentiment were lost in empty air. The understanding was by that time gone again and the look fixed in vacancy. The library is fitted up with nice book cases—Francis' ship turkey carpet on the floor. Francis Alicia Honora and I inhabit it—most comfortably. I now write at Francis' desk *in* the end window a delightful nook. [no signature]

[1] The Queen died on 17 Nov. 1818.

To Mrs. Edgeworth

31 Harley Street,[1] 29 October 1818

My dearest mother, We have spent two days and half in Town—sleeping at Harley St. and at every other moment that we could spare from *business* with dear kind Mrs. Marcet. She had two bedrooms opening into each other prepared for us and would hardly permit us to sleep any where else. We have been as busy as possible—1st morning I went to the Charter House with Mr. L Wilson—Mr. Russell exceedingly obliging—a very gentle sedate sensible man—inquired for Lovell kindly—Shewed us all the Charter House—fine play ground—recommended a boarding house now repairing for Francis—will put him under the care of Tom Beddoes. Each Boarding house has a monitor answerable for a certain number. We saw Tom and Henry.[2] They look forward to Francis's coming with pleasure. All I saw and heard convinced me that it is wise to send Francis to this school—I mean all I saw of Mr. Russell. As to the rest I could know nothing but that bedchambers and play ground are good.

I took the decided step of putting his name on the list. There will be a vacancy at Xmas. The 2d. Wednesday in January is I think the day when he should be at the Charter House. I have written it down with other particulars but have not now time to look for the paper. I will send it next packet.

Honora's teeth have been filed and cleaned by Waite[3]—a great coxcomb but a good dentist—cost £5. Francis and she persuaded me to let Alexander see my eyes. He says there is no danger of my losing them[4]—that all I feel proceeds from having overstrained them. This has brought on a disease in the absorbent vessels of lids. He has given an ointment I fancy same as yours...

Yesterday at Mrs. Marcets dined Mr. Whishaw—Sir John Sebright—2 Mr. Prevots—Evening Mr. and *new* Mrs. Mallet—Dr. Wollaston the preceding day.

Dr. Marcet gave us introduction to Museum this morning and we went with Mrs. Marcet and a party to see the Phigalian[5] and

[1] The Wilson's house in London.

[2] Beddoes.

[3] Waite appears as the fashionable dentist in ME's *Helen* (1834).

[4] ME as a child had been threatened with the loss of her eyesight (*Mem.* i. 11).

[5] Greek marbles of the fifth century B.C. from Bassae in Arcadia.

Elgin marbles and all you and I saw before in the Museum. We had the pleasure of taking Mr. L Wilson and his brother with us. Honora was pleased but had scarcely time to see or enjoy 1/100000th part—Mr. Smith one of the *Orderers* of Museum amazingly civil—Shewed Honora the fine volumes of Rembrandts and Antonios[1]—prints. We went from Museum to call on Mrs. Griffiths—returned to Harley St. to take up baggage. I write this while the trunks are putting on . . .

Now the purpose for which I got this frank was to send you patterns of cloth I obtained yesterday from Otley. There is no black *Vigonia*[2]—the Vigonia wool will not take black dye. Tell me which you prefer the Merino or the Queens cloth. The prices and width you will see. The queens cloth comes to a guinea the dress cheaper. The Merino looks much the best in the piece. Otley will send it to me when I know your decision.

Poor Mrs. Wilson is so weak that I think she cannot last long. She does not seem to suffer much. . . .

Your affec Maria E

To Mrs. Ruxton

Kensington Gore,[3] 29 October 1818

My dearest Aunt, I got up at half after six this morning to ensure this happy leisure hour for writing to you. Knowing your kind faith in me, and depending entirely upon your assurance that you had rather I should write always to my mother when I could not have time to write to both you and her I have acted accordingly. But this one letter I must address to your own self because in the first place I am anxious to hear from you how my uncle does. Fanny says that he was in bed with a cold and eresipelas when she and all the flock whom you have sheltered left Black Castle. I hope you will tell me that he was convalescent and sitting up or lying at full length on the wheeled-round sofa in the dear drawing room when this reaches you and I think I

[1] Van Dyck.

[2] A latinization of vicuña, a S. American animal related to the llama, with a fine silky fleece (*O.E.D.*).

[3] At the house of Lady E. Whitbread (Grove House).

see him smiling with his wonted benevolence when you tell him 'Here is a letter my dear from your little niece Maria for you' and snugging himself up on his elbow to hear news of us. I wrote to my mother a few scrambling lines yesterday while the trunk &c were putting into the carriage. I leave London and of that and of all our history up to that moment I take it for granted you will have heard from Edgeworthstown before this reaches you.

We arrived here between 4 and 5. Lady Elizabeth Whitbread's house is next door to Mr. Wilberforce's. A porte cochere entrance let us into a small kind of court-lawn with poplars and little grass plot—The house like any good looking house at Kensington with jutting out bow windows and large panes—windows opening French Spagniolettes[1] &c—an odd up and down house inside—Library—the room into which we were shewn a large long low room with a book case the whole length at one side under a kind of corridore of low wooden pillars. *The books* were evidently belonging to former times—this was the first thing that struck us. Lady Elizabeth Whitbread was not in the room but we were most kindly received by a lady who was her governess and now is her friend and companion—Miss Grant—The Spagniolette bow window at the end of the room open to a view of a very pretty and good sized back lawn with a willow acacia and several fine trees—The lawn about the size of the lawn at Black Castle in front of the house as far as Suzy Clarke's. Lady Elizabeth after a time came in and from the moment she appeared lawn, house, books and every thing but herself was forgotten. She was in second mourning. I used to think her rather plain but her countenance has been so softened by grief and has such an interesting charming expression that she is quite handsome. Smiling through her tears which she struggled to conquer, not hide she came to me and pressed me in her arms in a most affectionate manner. 'This meeting must bring painful recollections to us both[2]—but *pleasurable* too. Thank you for coming to me. You do not know how much I

[1] An espagnolette is a bolt running the full length of the (French) windows and with a hook at each end. At a suitable height from the ground it has a handle hinged in two places.

[2] A reference to the deaths of Samuel Whitbread (1815) and RLE (1817).

have looked forward to this day but my friend there can tell you I am speaking the plain truth.'

She tried in vain to go on with different beginning of conversations but there was such sweet kindness in her looks that there was no need for words *but* very great need Honora and I felt to get out of the room that we might not encrease her grief by our own tears. When we said something about going to dress she instantly wiped away her tears and with a chearful light step followed us and would shew us to our rooms herself. She staid but a moment and left us in a largish good bedchamber opening into another little room. As we looked round the truth instantly struck us from the sight of the furniture of the room that this was her own bedchamber—fine old dark mahogany wardrobe half as large again as that in my mothers dressing room—tables—long rolling toilette glass and every piece of furniture belonging to better times—jars of old china—black and gold framed profiles of her family—and a full length print of her husband in a plain black frame. Concieve my dear aunt *how* we must have felt when we found that she had gone out of her own bedchamber for us and nooked herself into some little den of a room!

'Your *party* at dinner today' said she when we went down 'will be no *party*, for you said you did not wish for company but some of your friends and mine—My friend Mr. Robert Talbot for one—he met you at an aunt's house—Black Castle—I think —just before you left Ireland. He has talked to me much of the pleasures of that place and that visit. A rainy day I think prevented his seeing you again.'

This may give you an idea of her kind politeness. Besides Mr. Talbot there was her nephew Mr. Gordon who had spent some days with us at Edgeworthstown in former happy times and Charles Sheridan son to Brinsley Sheridan by his last wife. You know it was at a dinner given at Mr. Whitbreads that we met Sheridan[1] when we were last in England! Everything at dinner so elegant and yet so simple and proper—*brought down* to her present circumstances—with a kind of dignified humility and resigned chearfulness and sweetness in her whole manner—the most touching I ever saw—so perfectly free from affectation or

[1] See above, pp. 69–70.

ostentation of *humility* or of any sentiment but true natural feeling and exquisite politeness of the heart.

'Mr. Talbot—eat of this dish (of Scotch collops). You know you are kind enough to like it.' (Then turning to me) 'Just after my friend Miss Grant and I came to live here Mr. Talbot came unexpectedly to see me and found this one dish on the table, between us.' Two old *family* servants waited—One Scotch, one Irish. Of both when they had left the room she told us characteristic anecdotes.

I forgot to tell you that the conversation at dinner was very agreeable among the gentlemen but Lady Elizabeth was so much more interesting than anything else I cannot remember a word of it except what *she* said. She was amused by Honora's replying to some question Mr. Gordon asked that she had been in London *many* years ago. 'That young creature talking of *many* years ago. If she were older she dare not do that but with blooming countenance she may.' From this moment she called Honora *Mine antient* and with a variety of nice playful polite allusions continually referred to her and *brought* not dragged her into notice most agreeably by shewing that she liked her particularly and had discovered that she was no commonplace young lady. I have not seen any person our own relations excepted who has shewn such *distinguished* liking for Honora since we came to England as this lady nor has Honora ever been placed and attended to so much to my satisfaction at any dinner or in any company as this day. All the three gentlemen worshipped properly and like well bred gentlemen. Mr. C. Sheridan speaks remarkably well. Mr. Talbot you know is gravely agreeable and Mr. Gordon blushing up to the eyes tho' a travelled man fresh from France and Italy was the more interesting from not being more assured.

In the course of the evening when the ladies were alone Lady E. Whitbread gave us entertaining accounts of the Mr. Talbot on lake Erie nearly what I have heard from you and Sophy with some particulars of his visit to London and of his remarks on modern manners and dinners which I must keep for fireside talk when we meet or it would lead me through 20 pages. But pray do not let me forget to tell of the dandy officers who sleep with cabbage leaves over their mouths and mustachios.

From grave to gay Lady E. Whitbread passed frequently in a manner most graceful and touching. How my mother would like her and how she would love my mother! There would be such sympathy between them and such approbation of each other—in conduct—taste—propriety and dignified affection. When we were quite alone she spoke of her husband—never *naming* him but alluding to past times which seemed like a '*dream of happiness*'. She had not latterly been happy. She foresaw what *must* be. She saw too much *pressed* upon that great mind. She often tried to prevent him from working so hard but it sometimes came to his saying 'Dont speak to me my Love—I *must* go on. It can't be helped. I have not time to listen to you'. Then afterwards he bitterly regretted that he had not listened to her and that he had not withdrawn from the accumulation of public business and of persons crowding round him for assistance when he most wanted it himself.

Once she started up from the sofa and walked up and down the room very much agitated saying 'If one could look back calmly or fix one's recollection at all upon *some* things it might be borne better. It is not death—not the death of those most dear—that is most terrible but the circumstances preceding.' She was then at the far dark end of the room and she was relieved by a burst of tears and in a minute or two came back to us and turned the conversation to some chearful subject. She has you perceive taken possession of my imagination entirely. Her kindness, her most affectionate manner to myself I suppose prepossessed me irresistibly. When she regretted in a tone which I *must* believe to be the tone of truth that she could not see more of me and urged me to return if possible and spend some time with her I felt strongly tempted to do so. I took that opportunity to speak of her having left her room and said I would never promise to come again unless she would promise that she never would never again etc.—She promised that she never would—that she would put us into 'any little room and treat us just as if we were her own family' . . .

I am sure I have not found English houses and London houses as Madame de Stael described them little boxes well closed and impossible to get into. In no less than 3 friends houses in London were beds prepared for us and the houses offered to us to use literally as our own—Dr. and Mrs. Baillies—Mrs. Marcets and 31 Harley St. which is in London what 31 Merrion St.[1] was to us in Dublin in many respects . . .

At the end of my last hurried scribble to my mother I said that we were just going to see Angersteins pictures. We saw them—had the house to ourselves and full time. Honora enjoyed them exceedingly. Mr. Gordon says that in Italy he was often asked about Mr. Angersteins *collection* of pictures of which foreigners seem to know the merit.

Farewell my dearest aunt. I must end abruptly. I have not been since seven oclock *fasting* for the good lady's maid who I am sure is an old attached servant like our own Kitty tho' not like her in the least in face or figure came up to me at 8 oclock 'Ma'am will you let me bring you up a cup of tea from the housekeepers room where we are now at breakfast. My lady always takes one when she gets up early and you won't breakfast till half after ten.' . . . After Breakfast—Miss Grant has just been telling me more about Mr. Whitbread. For a month before the dreadful blow his wife had been saying to her 'I feel that something horrible is hanging over me but I dont know in what shape it will come'. He *said* many things that might have opened their minds to the state of his intellects but they had been so accustomed to look up to him and all about him had been so much in the habit of looking to him as a superior mind that must ever stand collected in itself and commanding that they did not dare to believe or *imagine* the truth. There was no doubt that he had been insane for at least a month before the horrid catastrophe.

[no signature]

To Mrs. Edgeworth

Bowood Park, 3 oclock Tuesday, 3 November 1818

I write a few lines my dearest mother only to tell you where and how we are—well—and happy—this moment returned to dear Bowood . . . We went to Wimbledon friday last to dinner and staid till Monday—after breakfast went away. Lady Spencer was

[1] The home in Dublin of Mrs. Edgeworth's aunt, Miss Waller.

very attentive and courteous to us and we had all the honors of Wimbledon. She is by far the cleverest woman I may say the cleverest person I have seen since I came to England but I have seen many, *many* more agreeable and more interesting. I feel not the slightest symptom of affection for her and yet she was amazingly condescending—I wont say *flattering* because she is too proud to flatter. I thanked her in your name about Francis and St. Pauls. She never mentioned you or your dear father or Francis or Caramania.[1] That vexed me. I mentioned your father and Francis once but afterwards was as proud as Francis himself would have wished about him. At parting she God blessed me and requested her *dear* Miss Edgeworth whether I determine to stay or not to stay till spring to write immediately and let her know.[2]

I have not time to give you a regular history of our adventures at Wimbledon this day but will write au long by a Ward packet. I will only tell you who were there—Lady Anne Bingham her sister—a mincing *baashful* lady who flattered me amazingly—Lady Jones—Sir W. Jones widow—a thin tall dried old lady—velvet bonnet-ed nutcracker chin and nose—penetrating benevolent and often smiling black eyes—and her nephew a young Mr. Hare. Young as he is he has just accomplished making himself a fellow of Cambridge. He is about the size and figure of John Bushe when first we saw him but quite serious—yet unaffected—his hair as Lady Spencer observed too long and stood up as if with fright ever since reading for the fellowship but he is not pedantic and *is* goodnatured. After hearing me speak about little Francis and the Charter House he told me that he had been there for 6 years—that he thinks it an excellent

[1] Lady Spencer's family, the Binghams, were distantly connected with the Beauforts.

[2] Honora wrote to her brother Sneyd from Wimbledon, 31 Oct. 1818: '. . . Lady Spencer received Maria graciously—is certainly a very clever woman and converses in an uncommonly entertaining manner—But she does not please me—There is something haughty yet coarse about her—My dear Sneyd—how you would dislike her laugh, which if not belonging to a Countess I should say was vulgar . . . Maria is certainly received here, I mean in England, altogether with a kindness which is most gratifying, not with admiration for the author, but with a feeling of respect and attention for the woman which makes it perfectly comfortable and gratifying to her sister to be in her train and to pick up the crumbs—In this house there is less of the feeling for the person than anywhere we have been—but still nothing offensive. . . .'

school—and most kindly at parting from me he repeated what he had twice said that whenever Francis comes to the Charter House he will go and see him and that he will directly on his return to town go to the Charter House and secure a good safe friend for him a brother of one of his school fellows whose name he begged me to write down *Starr* . . . affectionately your Maria E

To Mrs. Edgeworth

Bowood Park, 4 November 1818

The newspapers have told you the dreadful catastrophe—the death and the manner of death of that great and good man Sir Samuel Romilly.[1]

My dearest mother there seems no end of horrible calamities. There is no telling how this has been felt in this house. I did not know till now that Mr. Dugald Stewart had been so very intimate with Sir Samuel and so much attached to him—40 years his friend! And now to lose him in this shocking manner at the moment most dangerous for Mr. Stewart's own mind. Mr. Stewart has been dreadfully shocked. He has not been able to sleep these two nights. He wanders about the house walking most feebly, leaning on his daughter a melancholy spectacle. He was just getting better—enjoyed seeing us—conversed with me quite happily the first evening and I felt reassured *as to his mind* but what may be the consequence of this stroke none can tell. His amiable daughter and Mrs. Stewart shew great resolution and judgment. I rejoice that we came—they say I am of use conversing with him. The only thing to which he has been able to turn his mind is the MS of my fathers life. He says that it is *very* interesting to him. This morning he read the preface and all the history of childhood. His affectionate manner of speaking of him and you at *this time* is very touching. When he read the account in the papers and Dumonts evidence and *Sir Samuels letter to Dumont*[2] he cried bitterly and Mrs. Stewart said that relieved

[1] Sir Samuel committed suicide on 2 Nov., distraught by the death of his wife on 29 Oct.

[2] See *Romilly Edgeworth Letters, 1813–1818,* ed. S. H. Romilly (1936). Sir Samuel had written to Dumont on 27 Sept. saying: '. . . I apprehend the worst . . . With all this do not suppose that I have not quite resolution enough to undergo

him much. Lord Lansdowne did not sleep Lady Lansdowne says and looks wretchedly. He was extremely attached to Sir Samuel and beside private friendship as he says the public loss is irreparable. Lord Lansdowne can hardly speak on the subject without tears notwithstanding all his efforts. The first thought both of the Stewarts and ourselves was to leave this house to leave Lord and Lady Lansdowne to themselves but Lord Lansdowne to whom I spoke directly assured me in the most affectionate manner that instead of being any constraint it was a comfort to him and to Lady Lansdowne to have people with him who as he knows *feel* as they do. How excessively Sir Samuel Romilly was beloved as well as respected. Poor Dumont! how unjust to think he wanted feeling! His letter to Lord Lansdowne during the time of Lady Romilly's illness and all his conduct to them shew the tenderest feeling.

November 5th

This morning Lord Lansdowne has shewn me a letter he has just received from good Mr. Whishaw. Sir Samuel on the 4th October added a codicil to his will appointing Mr. Walsham Lady Romilly's brother his executor and guardian to his children. Lady Romilly had formerly been sole guardian. In case of this gentleman's death or declining to act Sir Samuel appoints Mr. Whishaw and Lord Lansdowne his executors and guardians to his children. Mr. Walsham—he changed his name from *Garbett* for some estate—Lady Romilly's brother cannot act he is in such bad health. It is thought he will die. It is evident from this codicil that Sir Samuel at that time gave up hope of Lady Romilly. What resolution he shewed in writing it. He has settled all his affairs properly. From his calling for *that sheet of paper* and from his efforts to write it was feared that he had left no will . . . Maria E

Memorandum for future

The people that *have been* here—2 young Mr. Smiths relations of Lord Lansdowne's—Mr. and Mrs. Ogden—he clever and rich—she—the strangest of beauties. Pray get me a piece of bog

everything, and to preserve my health for my children's sake . . .' Dumont stated at the inquest that Sir Samuel had had no sleep for about six weeks and had two or three times expressed to him his fear of mental derangement.

oak for turning for Mr. J. Wilson. I have *promised* it. Pray write to your brother William and ask him to inquire if a portrait of Spenser can be had at a certain *Castle Saffron* near Cork now a ruin but in which there was the only portrait known of Spenser except one in some Scotchman's possession.[1] Does Dr. Beaufort know of any other? I promised Lady Spencer to ask. I have never received your drawings. I have written to Ward. Mrs. D. Stewart tells me that Wilkie saw the sketch she has of the Irish dance[2] and was delighted with it—did not know whose it was—said it was *admirable*.

To Miss Waller

Byrkley Lodge, 24 November 1818

My dear Miss Waller,

I *seem*, but only *seem*, to have been very ungrateful in never having written since we left your hospitable house or parted from your most friendly self . . . I will forbear to allude further to any of the horrible events that have happened since we parted, except to tell you with respect to the Romillys that I had a letter a few days ago from Lady Lansdowne, in which she says that Lord Lansdowne, who is one of Sir Samuel's executors and guardian to his children, went to see them, and 'was very much struck with Miss Romilly's self-command'. He saw all the family at Mrs. Davies's, Lady Romilly's sister, 'all endeavouring to exert themselves for the sake of one another'.

In the gloom which that terrible and most unexpected loss cast over the whole society at Bowood during the last days we spent there I recollect some minutes of pleasure. When I was consulting Mr. Dugald Stewart about [erasure in MS.] in my fathers MS I mentioned Captain Beauforts opinion at some

[1] A portrait of Spenser was in the possession of the Earl of Kinnoull at Dupplin Castle. Lady Spencer had a copy of it by Raeburn at Althorp. I am indebted to the National Portrait Gallery for this information. J. N. Brewer in his *Beauties of Ireland* (1826), ii. 427, states on the authority of Dr. C. Smith (*Ancient and present state of the County and City of Cork*, 1750) that there had been an original portrait of Spenser preserved at Castle Saffron, near Doneraile; it had disappeared by 1826.

[2] A drawing by Charlotte Edgeworth (d. 1807). It was engraved, rather badly, as an illustration to *Memoirs of RLE*, ii.

point. The moment his name had passed my lips, Mr. Stewart's grave countenance lighted up, and he exclaimed, 'Captain Beaufort! I have *the very highest opinion* of Captain Beaufort ever since I saw a letter of his, which I consider to be one of the best letters I ever read. It was to the father of a young gentleman who died at Malta to whom Captain Beaufort had been the best of friends. The young man had excellent qualities, but some frailties. Captain Beaufort's letter to the father threw a veil over the son's frailties and without departing from the truth placed all his good qualities in the most amiable light. The old man told me' continued Mr. Stewart 'that this letter was the only earthly consolation he ever felt for the loss of his son. He spoke of it with tears streaming from his eyes and pointed in particular to the passage that recorded the warm affection with which his son used to speak of him.' It is delightful to find the effect of a friends goodness thus coming round to us at a great distance of time and to see that it has raised the esteem of those we most admire and love for our friend even while personally a stranger. Mr. Dugald Stewart has not yet recovered his health. He is more alarmed I think than he used to be, by the difficulty he finds in recollecting *names* and circumstances that passed immediately before and after his fever. This hesitation of memory I believe everybody has felt—more or less—after any painful event. In every other respect Mr. Stewart's mind appears to me to be exactly what it ever was, and his kindness of heart even greater than we have for many years known it to be. Miss Stewart is a charming girl. I feel hopes that they will come to see us in Ireland. Mr. Stewart is so fond of Lovell and seems so well inclined to cross the sea, that if his health recovers sufficiently during the winter I think he will certainly be in Ireland next summer. He will spend the winter in Devonshire. We are now happy in the quiet of Byrkley Lodge where we have been received with much kindness. Mrs. Sneyd with not only a very polite but warm and cordial manner has urged us to make this our home as long as we can . . . My aunts are pretty well but there are strong traces of her severe illness still in my aunt Charlotte's appearance and my aunt Mary is much thinner than when I saw her last. They are, as you may guess delighted to have Honora with them again. This moment Mr. John Sneyd who is here is saying to

Honora 'Will your aunts go back to Ireland? Their hearts seem to be so much with you in Ireland that I often think they will go back to you all.' Of this I have no hope but it is most agreeable to hear them speak of their friends in Ireland. *You*, and all *of yours* would I am sure be pleased.

Mr. John Sneyd is very agreeable. I had heard so much of him before I saw him that I was afraid I should not like him *sufficiently*. But on the contrary he far surpasses my expectations. He has a sort of quiet well bred wit and humor which wins upon one gradually—perfectly easy. I prefer his style of conversation to that which is more brilliant, but betrays more effort. He has shewn me his drawings for Castle Rackrent[1] of which I had heard so much and which, as well as himself far surpass my expectations. It is wonderful how he never having been in Ireland could form such good notions of Irish people and *clothe* his ideas so well. He has made *portraits from imagination* of your friend *old Thady*—Sir Tallyhoo—very good—*Sir Patrick and Thady drinking his health—Sir Murtagh and his skinflint lady* just before the fatal quarrel—excellent *skinflint* lady—*Captain Moneygawl*—admirable—a drawingroom hero condescending to lower himself to the level of the ladies capacities—Mrs. Jane—with her damaged bonnet—*entirely good*—Lady Rackrent of Mount Juliets Town—and Sir Condy just when he is bringing her the back way home—when she is exclaiming 'angels and ministers of grace &c'—*The Gossoon*—on his return with the candles—an excellent gossoon. Mr. J. Sneyd admires very much Charlotte's drawings especially the Irish dance.

We have not yet seen any visitors since we came here and have paid only one visit to the Miss Jacksons. Miss Fanny you know is the author of Rhoda—Miss Maria Jackson the author of Dialogues on botany and a little book of advice about a *gay garden*.[2] I like the gay garden lady best at first sight but I will suspend my judgment prudently till I see more. I am not allowed to *say* more for I am summoned out by a multitude of counsellors . . . Yours affectionately Maria Edgeworth.

[1] Published anonymously by ME in 1800. For the drawings see also below, pp. 553–4.

[2] *Rhoda. A Novel.* By the author of 'Things by their right names' (1816). I have not been able to find Miss Maria Jackson's books; a book called *Dialogues on Botany* was published anonymously in 1819 by Mrs. E's sister Harriet Beaufort.

P.S. I have just heard a true story worthy of a postscript even in the greatest haste. Two stout foxhunters in this neighbourhood who happened each to have as great a dread of a spider as ever fine lady had or pretended to have chanced to be left together in a room where a spider appeared crawling from under a table at which they were sitting. Neither durst approach within arms length of it, or touch it even with a pair of tongs. At last one of the gentlemen proposed to the other who was in thick boots to get upon the table and jump down upon his enemy—which was effected to their infinite satisfaction. I am glad we ladies are this story to the good against the courageous sex.

I was very glad to hear from Mrs. Henry Hamilton that she liked Walter Scott—no love lost for he wrote to me[1] in delight with both Mrs. and Mr. Henry Hamilton—thanking me for making him acquainted with them—very pleasant to me!

[fragment 15 or 17 December 1818]

I cannot refrain from penning down an anecdote I have just heard. A middle kind of drinking squire in Derbyshire consulted Dr. Darwin about an inflammation in his eye. Dr. Darwin prescribed and ordered total abstinence from spirituous liquors. Some time afterwards Dr. Darwin saw the gentleman again the inflammation still continued and Dr. Darwin said he suspected his orders had not been obeyed and that unless they were the eye could not get well. 'Why then Doctor I will tell you what. If this eye wont agree with rum punch it is no eye for me.'

Did you ever answer about Sir—something Dillon and his character?

It is whispered that Mr. H[? enry] P[akenham] is attached to or attaching himself to a Miss Rigby who is very clever and understands—I dont know how many languages.

To Sophy Ruxton

Byrkley Lodge, 17 December 1818

My *best* and *dearest* friend—It does not always happen that these two epithets go with truth and justice together but in this instance they certainly do . . .

[1] *Letters of Sir Walter Scott 1817–1819*, ed. Grierson (1933), 198.

Now leaving all these matters in the mighty bosom of futurity I will bring the history of the past up to the present moment. I believe when I left off writing to my dear aunt I was form*ing* an opinion of Mr. Broadhurst[1] and I have not form*ed* it quite yet though we have since dined slept and spent a day and half at his house. His manners are wonderfully good and easy *considering*—rather too nonchalant—languishing and poco curante. His voice would be agreeable if he did not speak as if he was more than half asleep—his abilities good but not so good as he thinks them—the violence of his temper he speaks of with candor. That is the thing I like best yet I am not quite sure that I have seen to the bottom of the character nor does it signify for I do not think we shall see much more of him or at least that we shall ever be interested in forming any further judgment. Our visit to Foston was very pleasant. The house is very handsome and very handsomely furnished drawing room and dining room full of pictures some good—some indifferent—4 of Glovers[2]—One Teniers or copy from—very good—one of the fairs of which we have the Le Bas print—Some of Morlands and one of Turners said to be valuable. I think the whole expense—pictures—furniture—establishment—altogether was above what a man of good sense—good taste and good feeling would in his circumstances display. So theres an end of that chapter.

We met no one there but a Mr. Frederick Anson brother of Lord Ansons who had years ago been a rejected lover of Miss Sneyds and who has since consoled himself with a wife and '6 squalling brats'. How easily affairs of the heart are settled with most men. Poor Sir Samuel Romilly! That dreadful recollection crosses my mind often when least expected.

We have been to Sudbury[3]—Lord Vernons—morning vis—House old—built by Inigo Jones—Thick walls—*tower* chimneys—old furniture—*massive* old pictures—old everything—perfect contrast to modern Mr. Broadhursts—a long gallery 130 feet long reminded me of Kilkenny-castle gallery. It is lined with old family pictures full lengths on every side. Here the great and the

[1] Brother of Mrs. Sneyd E, with whom he was not always on good terms. He was intermittently insane.

[2] John Glover (1767–1849), landscape painter.

[3] Sudbury Hall was begun *c.* 1613 and completed 1660–90. The architect is unknown.

virtuous may moralise their fill and may look by turns at Lord Clarendon—Chancellor More and Killigrew[1]—and at Charles the 2ds three mistresses all side by side at full length—*Duchess of Cleveland—Duchess of Portsmouth* and *Nell Gwynn* in her laced nightshift. Barring the nightshift *which same* is slipping off Nell is, 'God bless us!' as Molly Coffey would say 'Ma'am *almost* as naked as ever she was born'—but quite at ease playing with a dog and looking at the spectators for admiration through her pretty curls.

Lord Vernon not at home—Company in the house—Mr. and Mrs. Brooke Boothby. He is nephew of Sir Brooke and married to a daughter of Lord Vernon's by former wife—a merry jesting young man of fashion after the style of Tom Sheridan. There was also a Mrs. Granville Vernon a charming young woman who delighted me by her unaffected well-bred good manners and gratified me in particular by her praise of *Harry and Lucy*[2] which she said had been of real use to her little children. She spoke the truth I believe. She knew the glossary intimately. I wish to see more of this lady but she has left Sudbury. She reminded me of those lines of Lord Byron's in Beppo[3] describing our feelings of regret at seeing flitting forms of excellence that pass us in our passage through life—excite peculiar sympathy and are no more seen, or heard of, tho they may be the very people particularly suited to our tastes.

Another style of *character* I have seen quite new to me and very entertaining though exciting no sort of sympathy—a young fox

[1] Edward Hyde, 1st Earl of Clarendon, Lord Chancellor to Charles II 1660–7; Sir Thomas More, Lord Chancellor to Henry VIII 1529–32; and either Thomas Killigrew (1612–83) or Sir William Killigrew (1606–95), both dramatists and courtiers.

[2] Published in *Early Lessons* (1801) and *Continuation of Early Lessons* (1814). These sections of the books were largely the work of RLE.

[3] *Beppo* (1818), Stanza XIV:

> 'One of those forms which flit by us, when we
> Are young, and fix our eyes on every face;
> And, oh! the loveliness at times we see
> In momentary gliding, the soft grace,
> The youth, the bloom, the beauty which agree,
> In many a nameless being we retrace,
> Whose course and home we know not, nor shall know,
> Like the lost Pleiad seen no more below.'

hunting squire[1] of an antient family who would have suited squire Western in every respect except in speaking in modern Foxhunting terms. He is possessed with a genuine Foxhunting enthusiasm. I enclose a copy of a note from him which was received a few days ago and which I copied verbatim. You must not shew it to Bess because it might work round through Cavendishes.[2] I will read it for my dear uncle in the man's genuine voice when I come back. This most entertaining *and tiresome*, rattling man dined here yesterday with a heavy companion of his a Mr. Cod*r*ington from Wiltshire worth 15,000 a year and in my opinion not worth his dinner. How my aunt would have been put out of all patience with his impassive face! It is like a spoiled plaister of Paris bust of an Apollo ending in a swelled jaw and an inhuman underhung mouth like a child's bad attempt at a mouth. My delightful foxhunter meantime dashing through thick and thin in conversation ran down and killed off all manner of game in France—Spain—Portugal—Italy—West Indies Bermudas, Canary Islands all in a breath! has been shipwrecked —tied to a Raft—thrown from a curricle—broke his leg—Set it again—wrong way—'lame for life—never mind—Yet don't pretend not to mind neither—if one of *your-fairies* were to come and stand before me and say to me Sir will you have your leg *so* or as it was before I'd say, I dont deny I should rather have it—of the two—you understand *as it was before*—But I can dance still—danced the dances at the ball t'other night—confounded pain the first—always is till sinews warm—like mail coach horse' &c &c &c. But in the midst of all this rattle there is in this man an excellent heart. He could hardly be brought to explain *how his accident* happened because the man who drove the curricle at that time was the stupid friend who now was sitting in the room opposite to us never moving a muscle of his white plaister of Paris face.

[1] This foxhunting squire presumably suggested Squire Squires Rogers in ME's *Frank: A Sequel* (1822). A number of incidents in vols. i and ii of this book were clearly suggested by experiences during this English visit. ME's letters written at this time were being read aloud to the family while it was being composed.

[2] Bess (*née* Staples) was the wife of ME's cousin Richard Ruxton. Her half-sister Anna Maria was stepmother-in-law to Lord Waterpark's brother, the Hon. George Cavendish.

The foxhunting youth told us one fact quite new to me. I dont remember it in any book or to have heard it from any traveller —that in the Canary Isles they often send dogs in among the sugar canes to kill the rats which destroy the canes but there is a kind of dust or fine fibres blown from the canes which blind the dogs in the course of a few weeks. Great numbers of terriers are sent out from England to these Islands to supply the place of those who perish in this way. 'You could not send Ma'am a more acceptable present than a terrier to the Canary Isles.'

I went to bed entertained and tired to death of this man but I hope I shall see him again. He has a very large fortune and he is desperately in love with a most elegant and well informed young lady—I hear—who is cruel but maybe wont be long so. I have never seen her and don't quite envy her tho I think there is better making of a husband in this man than in half those who would finely despise him.

Mrs. Sneyd and Emma have been this morning to pay a Vis to Lady Waterpark but I would not go because her Ladyship has not been to see me—only sent a nonsensical apology by her son. When Lady Waterpark heard of the Duke of Leinsters marriage with Lady Harrington's daughter she exclaimed 'There's a woman who has married her daughter to a Duke and never gave a good dinner in her life'. . . .

Honora has been practising quadrilles every evening with Emma and Mrs. Sneyd and I have been dancing posts for them. Emma dances well and very much like a gentlewoman and *teaches* admirably well and kindly. Mr. Sneyd danced with us till he was seized with the cramp in his leg and now he plays on the violin for us every night. He has learned all the quadrille tunes on purpose—*Pantalone*, *L'Eté*, *La Poule*—*La Pastorale*—La Frenise—La Carnivale &c. Two young Mr. Vernons Lord Vernon's sons and Mr. Boothby are to dine here tomorrow on purpose to dance quadrilles all evening so you see that Honora is at last likely to have a little of what you would wish for her. It is impossible to be more kind to her than her uncle aunt and cousin are to *her*—and to *me*. They seem to like my company *so much* that I am quite surprised and gratified for they shew me something of the fondness of Black Castle. They let me do just as I please and I am quite at ease—and talk nonsense. My dear aunts Mary and Charlotte are pretty well and they say that we enliven them much. This makes me solidly happy. All the morning till luncheon time I spend in my own room. I get up at half after seven *now*—that is *within this last week*, because *now* I have got my *fathers* MS back from Mr. Dugald Stewart and I am going on with a fresh revisal of it. I look at the notes of all my friends at every page. Honora takes it after me and this I hope will make it correct for the press. Mr. Stewart thought it extremely interesting and entertaining. He has marked some passages for omission. He and Francis Beaufort both have advised the leaving out *the passage* about Richard and some others about my mother.[1] After day and night balancings I have at last decided *to leave them out*. But I will not enter upon this subject which would lead me too far for this letter. I only wish you to know that I am not idle or losing sight of my great object. I put my own MS *by* for some time to recover power to judge and elasticity of mind after heavy and various load of criticisms. Depend upon me. I will do it well at last.

Friday morning with a better pen

My dear Sophy I am ashamed of all I wrote last night by candlelight and with a desperate pen which I could not see to mend. But I have not time to *write* it *fair*. So my Fair ones, you and Margaret must decipher it as you can and I give you leave to curse me—*loud*—but not *deep*.

Now that I am awake I must tell some things I forgot to mention in their proper places last night. Go back to Sudbury to Lady Vernon. I forgot to tell you that she is a sensible plain mannered woman—more housekeeper-looking than lady-like but worth 100 fine ladies for goodness of heart. She was one of three heiress sisters, daughters of an eminent lawyer Sir John Whitefoord—Scotch—one married that Colonel Cunningham who had his underjaw shot off in Spain or Portugal. She had been engaged to him. She had the highest admiration of his heroism and stood to it and was his wife for eleven years. He never could eat in company—was forced to lie down on a sofa to be fed. With

[1] RLE's marriage to Maria's mother, Anna Maria Elers, was unhappy and in his *Memoirs* he spoke of her with more frankness than was considered decent. He educated his eldest son Richard according to the principles of Rousseau and the boy proved very undisciplined. Very little was in fact left out.

a quill nourishment was put into his mouth and got down by his wife Heaven and she know how. It was in the time of cravats over the chin and his was so adjusted with a thick stuffing of bran underneath to receive the saliva which he could not swallow and to hide all that the veiled prophet himself could not have shewn. These bandages would, as you must conceive, have been insufferably offensive if they had not been changed every hour almost. He used to go about with her into company. Mrs. Sneyd has met him with her at the play and the opera. He looked like anybody else when *cravatted*—only deadly pale. He could not articulate intelligibly but his wife understood him with wonderful quickness. She never quitted him—slept in the same room with him till the hour of his death and her affection seemed to encrease instead of diminishing. What will not affection do in good minds! She was admired and courted as a widow but she faded away—said she knew she should die—and died a year after her husband. Another of these sister heiresses is married to Mr. Cranstoun Mrs. Dugald Stewarts brother so you comprehend this connects us a little with Lady Vernon. She does not personally know Mr. or Mrs. Dugald Stewart but has heard much of them and admires and loves their characters. She took to me most kindly the morning she first saw me and told Honora she liked me. Lord Vernon has just returned from Town. I have never seen him yet.

Friday Evening.

While I have been copying for you my rare foxhunters note a Concerto has been playing—Emma Sneyd on the harp—Mr. Sneyd—*violin*—Mr. Boothby *violincello*—Mr. Vernon—*the flute* and the *harpsichord* (I beg its pardon the *pianoforte*) would not accord with the flute therefore Honora who was *pianoforte* is not playing which I regret (but in the morning she did). They are a merry and agreeable set of musicians; and Mr. Boothby in particular is very diverting. He is calling out at this instant 'Now! No more jokes, no more laughing! Let us be serious in "*Life let us cherish*", and then, if we dont murder it we shall be "*Within a mile of Edinburgh Town*". Oh mercy! I played a bit of "*Within a mile of Edinburgh Town*" to your "Life let us cherish". Miss Sneyd! Henry Vernon! Do recollect to *rest*. *Stop* before you begin. This pause puzzles me to death. I have never known where we begin &c &c.'

Now my dear Sophy you know all that is going on, and the style of it, as if you were with us. This Mr. Boothby is son to the *Mr. Boothby*—formerly a lover of *the lady* who turned pale as death when my aunt Ruxton named him to her accidentally. If you will put me in mind when we meet again at dear Black Castle I will give you a description of the Minorca lady he married who used to say in her broken English 'I am very jealousy' . . . Just as I had written this Mr. G. Vernon made some wondrous and to me quite inexplicable discovery in his flute, which caused it agree at last with the pianoforte so Honora has been called to play and they are all playing in grand concert 'The Hunters rest'. Even to my dull ears it is so delightful, that I cannot *rest* without listening more. So goodbye, my dear Sophy.

Saturday morning

They had dancing after their concert and quadrille dancing till bed time—went through *Pantalon—Poule—Eté—Pastorale—Frenise—Carnival* with much diversion. To give you an idea of Mr. Boothby's sort of humor—At supper he was complimenting John Vernon a young lad of 19 who danced but *so so*. He concluded with 'And he did it all with such an unpretending unassuming manner! Dear me! I wish *I* could be so unassuming! But you know I can't.' What *nothings* in conversation please and make one laugh in conversation and when repeated and taken out of the place they fitted in conversation how inevitably they lose their effect and make one say as you do now 'Hum! Is that all! Very flat'.

I am called away to pay a morning visit to the Whole duty of Woman. That will be *flat* indeed I fear.

I have returned and did not see the whole duty[1]—only her husband and his beautiful, really beautiful drawings and his *frightful*, really frightful squinting eyes and his sons Ditto Ditto . . . [no signature]

[1] Mrs. Gisborne. See above, p. 24.

To C. Sneyd Edgeworth

Elford,[1] 21 December 1818

My dear Sneyd

This little pebble brooch will reach you I hope just in time for you to give it with my true love to Harriette for a Christmas box —a very *very* little one it is—but it is that which you preferred and it has been set exactly like the others and by the same person, Gray.

We have spent a very pleasant day and a half Mr. and Mrs. Sneyd Emma Honora and I at this delightfully neat pretty place with Mr. John Sneyd, who *notwithstanding* all I had heard beforehand of his agreeableness does not disappoint me but as far exceeds my expectations. His humor is so easy and joined with such quiet good breeding that it always pleases as much as it amuses and never goes a hairsbreadth too far nor half a note nor a hundredth part of a note too high for the most delicate soul of sympathy. He has treated us to the sight of a great number of his own drawings which are admirable in the style of Bunbury[2] or rather in an original style of his own. Ist course served to us was a set of designs for Castle Rackrent. These he shewed me at Byrkley Lodge. I expressed a wish to have possession of a striking likeness of Captain Moneygawl a charming officer whose condescending smile *becomes* the hero lowering himself to the level of the ladies' capacity. Mr. J. Sneyd said he would copy this for me if he could but to my surprise when we came here I found he had made a complete set of copies of all the Castle Rackrent designs for me. He next shewed us his designs for Tom Jones—then a set for Crabbe's tales[3]—excellent—but I do not know Crabbe well enough to feel their merit. I will take a course of Crabbe on purpose to understand these designs. Those he has done for the Bath Guide[4] are admirable. How I wish we could have seen all these things together my dear Sneyd and Harriette! And particularly I wish we could have looked over together a portfolio of drawings and etchings from drawings of Lady

[1] The Revd. John Sneyd was incumbent of Elford.
[2] Henry William Bunbury (1750–1811), artist and caricaturist.
[3] *Tales in Verse* (1812).
[4] [Christopher Anstey], *New Bath Guide* (1766). See above, p. 52.

Caroline Wortley's—the parting of Hector and Andromache and a representation of Andromache with her child and alone the hour after the parting—also Coriolanus and his wife and many others that reminded me of Flaxman[1] and of Sneyd's tracings from them. He shewed me these in consequence of my shewing him some tracings I had made from Charlotte's[2] drawings which he much admired. I consulted him on the propriety of publishing a few specimens of these in my fathers life. He much approved. The extreme neatness comfort and ingenious luxury and elegance of various contrivances at Elford reminded me of the Vicarage at Collon but this is far superior in *trellices*—porches—greenhouses—pheasants—swans &c—dining room hung with choice drawings and paintings opening with glass doors into a jewel (for I would not say a *bijou*) of a little greenhouse perfuming not overcoming the air with [? Oleas] &c. We have not half time to examine or enjoy all the luxuries of this sweet place where 'the sun always shines'. Literally they say it is never winter here and assuredly on this 21st December I never could have told by anything I see or feel in this room that it is not the middle of summer—blinds down to keep out the too bright too hot sun—grass fresh green and flowers in greenhouse in blow all conspire to deceive the eye and smell and feeling—Sneyds motto from Dryden is quite applicable to *this sweet place* . . . [end missing]

[1] Flaxman made illustrations for the *Iliad* and the *Odyssey* for Mrs. Hare Naylor. Engravings from them were first published in 1793.

[2] ME's half-sister (d. 1807).

1819

AT the beginning of 1819, when Lovell Edgeworth brought little Francis over to school in England, he also brought Fanny Edgeworth, Maria's favourite half-sister and 'almost her child'. In the previous year Fanny had met Lestock Wilson, Francis Beaufort's brother-in-law. He had proposed to her and she was much attracted to him, admiring his 'honorable character, active habits and steady, clear good sense', but the older Edgeworths were unenthusiastic; Lestock rather bored them, he spoke little, had no particular intellectual tastes and his connections were mercantile. Fanny was pretty and clever and not yet twenty and they thought she could do better. Her visit to England was to allow her to see more of the world before she made up her mind. Unfortunately she was dazzled by the company to which she was introduced and she let herself be persuaded by Maria, a good deal influenced by Lady Elizabeth Whitbread, that she would be throwing herself away in making such a match. She refused Lestock in the middle of April. She was much upset by her decision, her health suffered, and her feeling for him was too strong to allow her ever to look at any one else; she finally married him nearly 10 years later. Maria and the rest of the family came to realize that, though he was inferior to Fanny 'in what is called genius' and his abilities were 'nothing extraordinary', his character was 'first rate'.[1] In 1819 Maria was so engrossed in conscientious reporting on Fanny's affairs that her account of much of the society she met is unusually sketchy.[2]

[1] Description of General Clarendon in ME's *Helen* (1834), i. 54, 58.

[2] Her sisters' letters are sometimes fuller and we can only regret that Maria gives, for example, no sketch of Brougham and his conversation.

FRANCES MARIA EDGEWORTH (FANNY

From a skiagram ($\frac{1}{3}$ original size)

To Harriet Edgeworth

Derby, New Kings Head, 1 January 1819

This is my 51st birthday and this first day of the new year I cannot begin in any way more to my own satisfaction than by writing to my beloved, my excellent sister Harriet. A happy year and many happy years to you, my dear sister. And if you live I think you *must* be happy *because you will make others happy* . . . Farewell. Your true friend Maria Edgeworth. . . .

I wish I could draw the figures passing before me. Pray persevere as you have done dear Harriet in drawing. Whenever you travel you will reap the advantage. At this moment there is the most excellent view of *Market day* from this window—a perfect Teniers—coach going off—Town-house standing askew in beautiful perspective—coal carts unloading—*flapping leather hooded* horse and team—delightful old women and old men talking and bargaining together—for picturesque tête à tête worth all the prettiest young ladies that figured in last nights quadrilles.

To Mrs. C. Sneyd Edgeworth

[*c.* 1 January 1819][1]

I had a pleasant ball because Honora danced a great deal and was much taken notice of by civil and military. Emma danced with a Mr. Codrington a *great fortune* from Wiltshire (but nothing more that I can discern)—Mr. Chetwynd and Mr. Hartop—Honora with Mr. Griesley—*Captain* (I believe) Leslie and Captain Freeman of the 18th—Scotch gentlemanlike men. Mr. Chadwick the great foxhunter I believe you know. As he is lame he could not dance, but he told me it would rest him very much to sit by Miss Honora Edgeworth at supper and he had that refreshment. Honora and Emma were dressed as nearly the same as possible—both in black crape trimmed with bugles and black flowers in their hair. The most genteel people were in black. Mrs. Sneyd unknown to us had had the bugle trimming put on Honora's crape while we were at dinner so that she found it

[1] Fragment; beginning and end missing.

ready on her bed when she went to dress. Mr. Brooke Boothby (Junr.) and Mr. Henry Vernon dined here and drank tea. Mr. Brooke Boothby is what is aptly called an entertaining *rattle*. He has really a good deal of humor. There was a battle between some ladies about quadrille dancing and country dances. The country dances had the best of it and . . . [top of page missing] at her departure and it would have done your heart good to have seen Captain Freeman tying the string of her cloak while Messrs Boothby Vernon and Captain Leslie were looking on. We slept soundly but Honora has not as far as I can find dreamed of any of these things or persons. The only new thing I learned is that a dandy who is not *correct* or who is in any way extraordinary among his fellows is by them called a *tiger dandy*.

Among the people of note were Mr. and Mrs. Littleton—Mrs. Littleton still very handsome tho not so brilliantly fresh as I saw her 5 years ago. Alas! What changes 5 years may make!

To Mrs. Edgeworth

St. Helens,[1] Sunday, 3 January 1819

My dearest mother, . . . I enclose a civil note from Lady Stafford. The moment I knew dear Fanny was coming I wrote to prepare way for her. Mr. and Mrs. Sneyd seem delighted with the thought of this visit and I am delighted to be in some degree the means of accomplishing what they wish. They have never been at Trentham before except for one morning vis. I see more and more that the *ranks* in society are more separated in England than in Ireland . . .

Honora and I went yesterday to the Priory[2]—arrived there at half past 10—stayed till two. Mrs. Darwin was very affectionate in her manner and enquired most kindly for you—looks ill and very melancholy—poor creature. She has never recovered the loss of that beautiful Emma and even that dolt of a son John was a *loss* to *her* for she loved him so as to fancy he was like Dr. Darwin! He is however no loss to any other creature. He drank himself to death with gin and other spirits swallowed in the lowest company in the meanest public houses in Derby. His bill for

[1] ME was staying with the Strutts.

[2] Breadsall Priory, Derbyshire.

spirits the last year of his existence was above £200. His father a little before his own death discovered this creatures taste for drinking, found empty bottles concealed in some part of his room and was shocked and much enraged—But all in vain! All too late! The early care was wanting. Mr. Strutt observed to me, 'All the sons of the first Mrs. Darwin turned out well—all the sons of the second ill. Does not this prove how much depends upon the mother's care in early education, and does not it show us of what consequence mothers are?' . . . I liked Mrs. Maling much better than I expected. She is much more feminine than I expected in person and manner—has a sweet voice and excellent things to say with it. She appears to have a large portion of her fathers genius and her mothers strength of character. Captain Maling a large handsome sea officer—nothing extraordinary—Knew Captain Beaufort. [no signature]

To Harriet Edgeworth

Trentham,[1] Sunday morn 10th January 1819

My dear Harriet . . . Lovell called for Francis at 8 oclock and poor Fanny and he parted and Fanny was as pale as a turnep. Lovell took him to Byrkley Lodge to spend some hours with my Aunts. I have written to Lady Jones to ensure her seeing or rather her nephews seeing Lovell and Francis when they call upon her in London. Her nephew promised to introduce F to a good safe friend at Charter House and I am the more anxious for this because (*private except to my mother*) I understand from Anna that Tom Beddoes has by his temper and nonconformity to subordination displeased Mr. Russell who had my sister written to by one of his ushers to say that unless he made up his mind to behave better he, *Mr. R.*, advised Anna not to send him again as he would necessarily be sent away from the school. Anna I believe has brought him to reason or temper but as I cannot now feel as secure as I did of his being a proper guide schoolfellow for Francis I am anxious for a more safe guide philosopher and *friend* . . . Yours truly and affectionately in the *last* capacity not [1 line cut out for autograph]

[1] Lord Stafford's house in Staffordshire.

To Mrs. Edgeworth

Trentham, Monday 11 January 1819

My dearest mother, . . . As far as I can see, and judge Honora and Fanny appear as well in point of ease of manners and gentility as your heart could wish and just like the best bred of the young ladies here. Lady Stafford's daughter Lady Elizabeth Gower is beautiful and I think altogether the most engaging, graceful, unaffected person I ever saw with a great deal of conversation and talents without pretensions. Lady Stafford rises in my opinion the more I hear of her sentiments and the more I attend to her character. She justifies my fathers judgment. *How much* I wish you were here and how often at every fresh thing I see or hear that I know would please you I cannot express. While Lord Stafford was shewing us the pictures in particular I missed you—missed you for Fanny. How much you would tell her that she cannot learn without you.

We were fortunate in finding Lady Harrowby here—but Lord Harrowby and Lord and Lady Ebrington went the day we came. Lady Stafford says she regrets that we did not see Lady Ebrington and that Lord Harrowby is a most entertaining agreeable man. Lady Harrowby Lord Stafford's sister is all Madame de Stael describes *très spirituelle*—very easy and conciliating in her manner—not affected—but with less dignity and strength of character than Lady Stafford. She was very particularly obliging to me and pressed me to come to Town and to let her know—whenever—wherever &c—and at taking leave again desire Fanny to remind me and to remember that she should also be glad to see *her* with me. Besides Lady Harrowby we have had her daughter Lady Mary Ryder very pretty with hair parted and in curls like Charles 2d's beauties—very like a fair haired picture at Kilkenny castle and Lady Elizabeth like a dark haired soft dark eyed beauty of the same time—such a mouth! Mr. J. Sneyd, son to Mr. Sneyd of Keele is here—a very pretty finish young man with talents and fashion and a high opinion of both—very full of Lords and Ladies &c.

Mr. Standish also is here who is a famous person in the world of fashion. Lady Stafford says he is one of the *exquisites* and that her maid told her that his toilette is the thing best worth seeing in the house—all gilt plate—and such dressing boxes and essences and apparatus as make the ladies maids and the gentlemen's gentlemen bless themselves. He has a very nice patch on his lip and such gales of perfume blow from him—and his cambric is so exquisite. But I am sure 9/10ths of his toilette is lost upon me. I should not know him from any common Dandy. He is ugly-ish—very entertaining and easy in conversation when he is not too much intent upon his worthless person to give his mind fair play. He is—however incongruous it may sound—a great sportsman—very fond of the chace. In speaking of this passion to me and deprecating my contempt he said 'I know it's all folly. I tell myself so. But in short C'est plus fort que moi.' I played off upon him some of the foxhunting terms which I had learned from Mr. Chadwick much to his surprise and diversion.

The Sunday when we went to church (which by the by joins the house and you walk from the house into it) we found that Mr. Butt nephew to Dr. Butt is the clergyman—preaches well—tall—thin—handsome—dined here—a mixture of simplicity and a good opinion of himself and great intentness on his own objects and thoughts. Mrs. Cameron is now on a visit to him and we will go and see her tomorrow . . . Your ever affec and most obliged Maria E . . .

To Mrs. Edgeworth

Trentham, Thursday, 14 January 1819

You see we are here still. Mr. and Mrs. Sneyd and Emma returned home on tuesday but Lord and Lady Stafford expressed such an earnest wish that we should stay a little longer that finding that Mrs. Sneyd would not take it unkindly I consented. Lady Elizabeth when I told her I had determined to stay leaped from the ground at least 18 inches and no eyes could doubt the expression of joy in her beautiful countenance nor could any ear mistake the sound of the clapping of her hands. She is so kind to Honora and Fanny and seems to value them so justly and so to enjoy their company that even independently of Lord and Lady Stafford I would have staid for her sake. But before I go on any farther let me put your mind at ease dearest mother about Fanny's health. Her cold is going off—her own looks are coming on. The pink shell color is gaining and spreading over the turnep cheek and the pleased and pleasing expression is lighting in those eyes of which Admiral Pakenham said—nothing but the truth. She has ridden out these last two mornings on a nice poney with Lady Elizabeth . . . Lord Francis is very clever and original and simple and affectionate and fond of his sister and as far from a dandy of any kind—solemn or vain—as can be conceived. His drawings and his poetry would both be excellent even if a Lord did not own the happy lines. I am afraid you will think I am exaggerating and that I have fallen too suddenly in love with all these people but I assure you I have not colored even to the life in representing their kindness—nor have I nor dare I repeat to you half the handsome things Lady Stafford has said to me of Fanny . . . I have not time to attempt any description of the beauties or magnificence of this Park or House—pictures or whole establishment. That must be for hereafter but just N B—10 livery servants and four servants out of livery—in black. These last only appear in the sitting rooms or stand in the hall and antichambers con-ti-nu-ally. But the magnificence does not interfere with the comfort. It is *splendid happiness*, not *splendid misery* . . . Yours affectionately Maria E

To Mrs. Ruxton

Byrkley Lodge, 20 January 1819[1]

Dearest, kindest, and most polite of aunts,

I see my little dog on your lap, and feel your hand patting his head, and hear your voice telling him that it is for Maria's sake he is there. I wish I was in his place, or at least on the sofa beside you at this moment, that I might in five minutes tell you more than my letters could tell you in five hours.

I have scarcely yet recovered from the joy of having Fanny actually with me, and with me just in time to go to Trentham, on which I had set my foolish heart. We met her at Lichfield. Conceive the pleasure I felt when, after we had all given it up, driving into Lichfield, passing the George inn, we saw that

[1] MS. missing; printed from *Mem.* ii. 25–8.

frightful little Head standing in the gateway! Never did sight of beau or belle give me more pleasure. We spent the evening at Lichfield—the children of four different marriages all united and happy together. Lovell took Francis on with him to Byrkley Lodge, and we went to Trentham.

When Honora and I had Fanny in the chaise to ourselves, ye gods! how we did talk! We arrived at Trentham by moonlight, and could only just see outlines of wood and hills: silver light upon the broad water, and cheerful lights in the front of a large house, with wide open hall door. Nothing could be more polite and cordial than the reception given to us by Lady Stafford, and by her good-natured, noblemanlike lord. During our whole visit, what particularly pleased me was the manner in which they treated my sisters: not as appendages to an authoress, not as young ladies merely *permitted*, or to fill up as *personnages muets* in society; on the contrary, Lady Stafford conversed with them a great deal, and repeatedly took opportunities of expressing to me how much she liked them and valued them for their own sake . . .

Lady Elizabeth Gower is a most engaging, sensible, unaffected, sweet pretty creature. While Lady Stafford in the morning was in the library doing a drawing in water colours to show Honora her manner of finishing quickly, Fanny and I sat up in Lady Elizabeth's darling little room at the top of the house, where she has all her drawings, and writing, and books, and harp. She and her brother, Lord Francis, have always been friends and companions: and on her table were bits of paper on which he had scribbled droll heads, and verses of his, very good, on the Expulsion of the Moors from Spain. Lady Elizabeth knew every line of these, and had all that quick feeling, and *colouring* apprehension, and *slurring* dexterity which those who read out what is written by a dear friend so well understand.

Large rooms filled with pictures, most of them modern—Reynolds, Morland, Glover, Wilkie; but there are a few ancient: one of Titian's that struck me as beautiful—Hermes teaching Cupid to read. The chief part of the collection is in the house in town. After a happy week at Trentham we returned here, and found a letter from Lovell saying he had placed Francis at the Charterhouse.

. . . The morning after Mr. Standish's arrival, Lady Stafford's maid told her that she and all the ladies' maids had been taken by his *gentleman* to see his toilette—'which, I assure you, my lady, is the thing best worth seeing in this house, all of gilt plate, and I wish, my lady, you had such a dressing box.' Though an exquisite Mr. Standish is clever, entertaining, and agreeable. One day he sat beside me at dinner, we had a delightful battledore and shuttlecock conversation from grave to gay as quick as your heart could wish: from L'Almanach des Gourmands[1] and *'le respectable porc'* to Dorriforth and the Simple Story.[2]
[Printed from *Mem.* ii. 25–8. MS. missing.]

To M. Pakenham Edgeworth

Byrkley Lodge, 26 January 1819

Is there in Bewick a bird called the *Storm bird*?[3] It has another name the *Thrice-Cock*. A few days ago at breakfast Miss Sneyd gave us an account of it which I wished that you could have heard. It is the largest kind of thrush. Its cry is never heard except before a storm. When a dark black cloud threatens a heavy shower of rain and when the wind blows hard then the Storm-cock cries or screams.

After we had talked about the storm-cock Mrs. and Miss Sneyd began to *tell about birds* of different sorts. Mr. Glover the painter who has taught Miss Sneyd to draw has been often at Byrkley Lodge in summer time. He is almost as fond of birds as of painting. He knows so well the ways of birds that he can get acquainted with them let them be ever so wild or shy. There was a hawk in the forest here which had been tamed to live in the garden, but which had been lost in the wood. The day after Mr. Glover came here he came home from walking with the hawk on his finger. He had a little bird of his own in a cage in

[1] A French treatise on cookery, reviewed both by the *Edinburgh* and the *Quarterly Reviews*. The current numbers of the *Edinburgh* and *Quarterly Reviews* are very often the key to the conversation reported by ME.

[2] Dorriforth is the chief male character in Mrs. Inchbald's *A Simple Story* (1791), one of ME's favourite novels.

[3] *History of British Birds* (1797 and 1804), engravings by Bewick and text by the Revd. Mr. Cotes. A storm cock is a missel thrush.

London. He let it out by accident and it flew into some bushes in a *square* in the neighbourhood (Ask Harriet or Kitty what is meant by a *square* in a Town). Mr. Glover went into the square and whistled as he used to do when he called the bird and the bird came back to his hand. I think he must be a good natured gentleman.

We have two bird cages in this room and I wish Kitty could hear the birds singing as they did this very fine day. I will soon send you three or four acorns from an Ilex which grows at Trentham. Lady Stafford gathered them for me to send to you. You must sow them in a pot and put them in the greenhouse and take care that the cat does not claw them up and that the mouse in Mamma's dressing room does not eat them. If you do not recollect what sort of a tree an Ilex is, walk up towards Fanny's garden and just as you turn from the Dingle walk towards Sneyds old garden you will see an Ilex on your left hand on the grass and an Ilex on your right hand in the border next the garden wall. To the height of such trees as these your acorns may in time grow.

Lady Stafford asked me if my little brother Pakenham had ever tried to blow a potatoe flower in a hyacinth glass. She says that when she was young she tried this. She put a potatoe into such a glass as you have seen Mamma use for hyacinths. The potatoe grew very tall and its flowers nearly touched the ceiling of the room in which it grew. When Mamma and Harriet come home ask them to let you try this. Give my love to Kitty. I know you are alone with her and I am sure you are very good—obedient and kind to her. Honora and Fanny send their love to you and her. We heard of Francis last night. He is very well tell Kitty and all who see him and know anything of him say he is good. I am yours affectionately Maria Edgeworth.

To Mrs. Edgeworth

Byrkley Lodge, 28 January 1819

Since I have taken your child from you I must console you for her absence by bringing the ideal presence before you as often and as strongly as I possibly can. She *herself*, Honora and

Mrs. Sneyd all wrote to you last night and I am sure told you all that could be known about us up to this day. And this day we have been all sitting together in the drawing room going on with our various little employments—Mrs. Sneyd by turns making net for one of the Miss Leicesters and a pantin[1] for one of the Leicester children—Emma rummaging in a box for new ribbons from Lichfield to find what will suit half a dozen nets—all the ribbons so pretty they make one's eyes water—Fanny in the library by her recluse philosophical self for some time—Then joining the vulgar herd in the drawing room—Honora on Fanny's appearance quitting her drawing table where she was copying Mr. J. Sneyd's Captain Moneygawl and joining Fanny on the sofa and reading out of one book (and that book too small for any one person) Ariosto, translating it much to their mutual satisfaction both saying the lines at a time and hoping 'Aunt Sneyd and Maria we don't disturb you'—coming at last to the old virgin and flower that has been hackneyed so long and that flourished for the last time in the beggars opera.[2]

Enter Mr. Sneyd, to whom as if he was just fresh landed from Naples both the Italian scholars ran with their book and 'Oh uncle! Oh Mr. Sneyd! You'll explain this'—A loud laugh about some naivetés of Fanny respecting said old virgin. N B Mr. Sneyd likes Fanny very much and he laughs till his eyes close and he shakes himself and pats her on the shoulder. *We* altogether do him more good I am clear than the whole college of physicians so don't you begrudge our living upon him as we do. His face and voice continually say

'You are kindly welcome
Welcome to me
Kindly welcome every one'—

and we have many fat hens tho we are none of us *Mrs. Bride* Alas!

But to go on with our story my aunt Mary was all this time conning over the little copy of verses I wrote yesterday and

[1] A puppet.

[2] Ariosto, *Orlando Furioso*, Canto I, Stanzas 42–3; *Beggar's Opera*, Act I, Scene VIII (*Poetical Works of John Gay* (O.U.P. 1926), 493). The verses in *The Beggar's Opera* come directly from *Dioclesian, or the Prophetess* as altered by Betterton from Beaumont and Fletcher (W. O. Schutz, *Gay's Beggar's Opera* (1923)).

knitting a garter for me and listening to me consulting about the insertion or omission of one of Mr. Day's letters in my fathers life—Aunt Charlotte writing a letter and then making me dictate to her a charade which Anna gave me and which I believe I sent you on *Car-mine*.

Luncheon and a bowl of paste for Mrs. Sneyd's *pantin*.

Luncheon—damson pie—pork pie—mutton steaks—hot mashed potatoes x—puffs—unnoticed—brawn untouched—cold roast beef on sideboard—seen too late! Observation by Mrs. Sneyd—Not well bred ever you know to put the gravy on the meat when you serve any body—No because you should leave the person at liberty to eat it or not as they please—Just like butter on and *off* vegetables it should be—Yes and just like love which you should be allowed to take or leave. With such nonsense as this and much laughter that must appear *causeless* in writing we go on most happily.

Then comes Mrs. Sneyd who is always producing some thing new from her stores with a box, a maroon colored barrel-like box like one of Honora's containing little white balls seemingly of mortar size of marble. 'Do you know these?' 'Not I.' 'What are they?' 'The French exploding bullets (detonating balls—in miniature) forbidden to be used.'

'Oh let us see them.'

'Mr. Sneyd! come then come into the Hall and throw one down for us against the floor.'

'Are they Prince Rupert's drops?'[1]

'Not at all not at all.'

Mr. Sneyd desired Dan to go out of the way lest he should be hurt or frightened out of his wits for he is a sad coward but in vain Dan was advised ordered chaced away on one side or the other into Drawing room and dining room. Return he would and push between his master's legs to see. So the first bullet was thrown. Nought ensued—a second and third O—O. 'Oh they are spoiled all.' But after 4 trials one *went off* as it struck the floor with the sound of a pocket pistol and a little flash and Dan and I ran away—He in earnest trembling I only in jest upon my word Ma'am.

[1] Glass drops with long slender tails, which burst into pieces, on the breaking of these tails in any parts (*O.E.D.*).

It is so dark I must stop especially as I have nothing more to tell you except that I like a miracle of virtue went out to walk by myself this foggy day and presently out came dear Fan—Virtue rewarded! quoth I. So we walked up and down the long gravel walk in the garden (fat gardener fanning out an apricot tree on which last year there were 20 dozen of apricots). Fanny said this straight walk reminded her of the day when years and years ago I walked up and down the long walk in our garden *upon guard* for Sophy and her who were not allowed to be in the garden without me—She and Sophy all the time up in an apple tree broiling or cooking upon a *gridiron* made of the bottom of an old basket the figure and spikes of which I have this minute *in* my eye or before my eye which is rather better. 'How patient you were Maria' said Fanny 'to walk up and down all that time for us.' Fanny is the most grateful young person I have ever in the course of my life had the happiness to know.

Exit Mrs. Sneyd saying '*Nobody* must touch this table. *There is a man in press.*' I must exit for the 2d bell has rung.

All the time I was dressing acted Waite the dentist[1] for Fanny and made such a stomping about the room that Mr. Sneyd could not think what was the matter—Laughing all—and all the way down stairs—scarcely recovered for *Grace.*

N.B. The *man in press* alluded to above was a man two cubits high—two of *my* cubits high at least—a jolly fiddler, whose rosy cheeks grinning teeth blue waistcoat and suitable small cloths Emma had been painting all morning—Excepting always the time when she was tuning her harp and giving me an admirably clear description of the mechanism of a newly invented harp which never or seldom needs tuning.

Grace and dinner—Dinner! a circumstance not to be lightly passed over. I am always allowed to feed Dan who sits up on my chair with his head close to my elbow and eats from a silver fork as genteelly as any gentleman and more genteelly than many I have seen and drinks out of a glass too—without much sputtering . . .

I hope and trust in Heaven and the mail coach that Lovell will receive and convey safely to you the following articles Black

[1] See above, p. 129.

cloth for a pelisse—superfine *Pinna*—2¼ yards wide [ ][1] at 30 shillings. 2 pieces of striped muslin. These tho' coarse I think will do for morning gowns for the younkers. Mrs. Sneyd wears the like in summer at home on the principle that it's better to have plenty of coarse and clean than few fine and dirty. But if, precedent and principle notwithstanding you think these *too* coarse for Harriet Sophy and Lucy keep them for me and I will make *happy people* with them—at my peril. I don't mean them as *presents* to my sisters. They are too cheap for that. They cost but *one* shilling a yard! 2 pieces contain 10 yards each—¾ *wide*—scarcely—but I suppose they will make 3 gowns.

But to go on with the contents of my parcel. The parcel will also contain a black velvet gown and spencer. I have rolled it up on the principle for packing velvet which I think you told me—to *crumple* rather than *crease*—not to flatten the *nap whatever you do.* I fear this principle will ill agree with the trimming and lace; but I have taken an average in the interests of *lace velvet* and *satin* and I hope I am *wise*—and I hope still more that the gown and spencer will fit you dearest mother. It is made by the very best dressmaker in Paris by a pattern body which I got my dear Fan to take from a gown of yours and sent last summer to Mrs. Jos Wedgwood. I have a gown and spencer the same myself only my lace is unluckily rather handsomer. The connoisseurs here and all who have seen mine pronounce them to be the handsomest gowns that have been brought from France. Madame Gautier said she was determined to send me the best specimen of Parisian manufacture and Parisian taste. Now my dear friend! my dearest friend! don't redden and scold me in my absence at first *sight* and first *thoughts* of these gowns but *accept graciously* as you will know how to do and consider that I *never* should have had so handsome a gown for myself *but* for the consideration that it was the only way of making the fellow gown comfortable to you. Now the having this *respectable* dress at this time for myself has been of real comfort. When I have not had time to think about it and yet wanted to make a good appearance often I have popped into my black velvet suit with such joy at Trentham &c—sure of being *right* and of being admired and—*envied.* Think how comfortable! *Too besides* it will last my life and I daresay

[1] Word illegible.

be worth leaving in my will like the Duchess of Marlborough's *suits.*[1] Now I *trust* I have said so much that I shall have answered all your arguments and worn out your indignation before the arrival of the parcel.

Now to go on with the history of our day. After post time we adjourned to the drawing room. Emma and I lay down foot to foot at each end of the great delighful old fashioned black sofa and Fanny came and sat on the sofa beside me sideways so as to skreen the light of 4 lamps from my eyes and read the newspaper. I am more and more convinced of the wisdom of my fathers advice to me to read the papers constantly—to keep up the knowledge of all the *real* interests of the world and to exercise the judgment daily upon the great subjects on which the minds of the first people in the country are exercised. This is particularly necessary to a dealer in fiction. How happy I am to have Fanny who is so kind to read to me when my eyes are tired and who is interested in all the subjects I like. This day's paper contained the discussions on prisons—Mr. Buxton—penal laws —Mr. Bennet's speech about *your* man who was to be *exported* transported for forging a frank.[2] It is consoling to see that Sir Samuel Romilly gave an impulse to the public mind which is now acting upon the best and wisest in the country. (Newspaper finished)

Coffee and tea—Florence Macarthy[3] till bed—the Irish parts performed by M.E.—The English alternately by Fanny and Mr. Sneyd. What a shameful mixture in this book of the highest talent and the lowest malevolence and the most despicable disgusting affectation and *impropriety*—and total disregard of the consequences of what she writes. I love O Leary—and wish *that* admirable original character could be taken out of this heap of trash. I do not think the Crawleys *well* done except perhaps some part of Old Crawley. Vulgar as he is and incredible as I perceive it is to the English that such a man could be admitted

[1] Sarah, Duchess of Marlborough left her *clothes* to three of her attendants. This is, however, probably a punning reference to her innumerable lawsuits.

[2] On 25 Jan. Alderman Wood presented a petition for a revision of the criminal code and Mr. Bennet a petition from Dr. Halloran, an elderly ex-clergyman sentenced to transportation for forging a frank; on the transport ship *Baring* he with 18 others was put into a space only 19 ft. square.

[3] *Florence Macarthy* (1816) by Lady Morgan. Lady Morgan's father was an actor-manager and she had been brought up in the atmosphere of the theatre.

in company there are such in Ireland. My general feelings in closing the book are shame and disgust and the wish never more to be classed with *novel* writers when the highest talents in that line have been so disgraced. Oh that I could prevent people from ever naming me along with her—either for praise or blame. Comparisons are indeed odious. God forbid as my dear father said I should ever be such a thing as that! It was for want of such a father she has come to this . . . Your affectionate M E . . .

To Harriet Edgeworth

Byrkley Lodge, 29 January 1819

My dear Harriet, I often think with twinges of compassion of your little widowed Pakenham and of the difficulty you must feel in supplying to him the loss of his Francis. How can he get through the long day—even with your assistance? I wish I could help you to any scraps of amusement for him. He is so very good by all accounts that he deserves to have even the enclosed *beautiful* Lanthorn fly. It is a vile colored print which I espied yesterday as Mrs. Sneyd was turning over a portfolio of scraps and I seized upon it for Pakenham—same time ran away with the charming ladies in the dress of 1780 with their hats sticking on their heads by miracle—No—but by the help of steel pins as long as my arm and longer.[1]

There is an account of the Lanthorn fly in a note to Lalla Rookh[2] which I remember is interesting and if Lalla Rookh is not at hand I dare say Rees[3] will tell you about him. Goldsmith's animated nature[4] will not—more shame for that inspired ideot. I was amused by the account Lovell and my mother gave of the different choice Francis and Pakenham made of the heroes and great men Nelson—and Sir J. Reynolds. I enclose the first copy of some rhymes which I have just written at Mrs. Sneyd and Emmas request for them to send to a little girl of 6 or seven

[1] This enclosure survives. It is a print published in Oct. 1780 by Fielding and Walker of Paternoster Row. It seems to have been torn out of a book.

[2] *Lalla Rookh* (1817), best selling poem by Thomas Moore. There is no note on the Lanthorn fly but this is perhaps a reference to the nest of the Indian Gross-beak which lights up the chambers of its nest with fireflies (*Lalla Rookh* (1860 ed.), 134).

[3] *The New Cyclopaedia* (1802–20), ed. Abraham Rees.

[4] *Animated Nature* (1774).

years old Laura Leicester with a box of colors and portfolio. If you think they would divert Pakenham and suit his genius for *painting* pray read them to him though I am afraid his poetical genius will be above them especially as he is so nice in requiring *sense* in his own lines. Thank him for those he wrote on my birthday—the sense and kindness of which I relished much. I happened to be beside Lady Stafford when they came to my hands and she looked so good naturedly at me and seemed so glad that I had a letter from home that I could not help reading them to her. She was delighted with them (you will not tell him *this* I am sure) and *that* was the reason she gathered the Ilex acorns for him and sent him the message I wrote to him about the potatoe flower in hyacinth glass.

The little girl Laura Leicester who is supposed to speak the rhymes is very lively and flies about from one thing to another just as represented. Emma Sneyd told me an anecdote of her which will give you an idea of her character. When the family were in London, upon some visit when the party were to be carried home in sedan chairs the child said to her mother 'Mamma let me give orders to the chairman myself—or else you know what shall I do when I grow up if I dont learn to order when I'm a child.' The mother agreed that she should order the chairman. So she ordered him to carry her home to Portman Square—such a number—'And be sure you *jump me* as high as you can all the way.'

The little sketches of towers and trees enclosed are what Emma was doing last night on bits of covers of letters while reading was going on—just like my mother. I seized upon them for Pakenham.

In Crabbe you will find some lines in the description of 'the *dwellings of the poor*' which admirably describe *weeds.*[1] Pakenham I think would like them. I never knew or *felt* the merit of Crabbe till I re-read him lately. It is not the merit of fine *Scott* or *Byron* or Pope poetry but of strong thought and strong feeling and minute observation in an original style—the thoughts forcing on the rhymes till you quite disregard them. Pray after having put all *Scott* and all desire of comparisons out of your head read Crabbe again *by* himself and *for* himself—*The*

[1] *The Borough* (1810), Letter XVIII, ll. 290–303.

Confidante[1]—*The Parish Clerk*—and in *Prisons*[2] pray read the last pages—the female condemned prisoner and the man. The man's dream is I think the most beautiful dream I ever read. Extracts from these poems of Crabbes would be excellent for the poor. Fanny is now writing out some for Lovells school.[3] Pray read Crabbes *Schools* to my mother; I know she will like it. There are some admirable lines addressed to the venders of immoral books.[4] What a different use Crabbe and Lord Byron make of the talents God gave them.

Pray look at my edition of Cowper and see whether it contains a little poem called the Colubriad—the battle of a snake and a cat. If it be there read it to Kitty. If it be not there be sure you tell me because I shall then know that I have not the whole of Cowpers poems. *That* and the cat in the drawer and some others are in a third volume published last year.[5] Emma Sneyd read the snake and cat to me last night—as well as you could Ma'am and to my mind that is saying a good deal. Pray dont indulge yourself in *gabble*-reading. I hear from Fanny you read Evelina[6] that way to her and I am very angry. It will become a habit and spoil your *power* of reading.

Now I will give you a bit of nonsense to take the bitter taste of this advice out of your memory. Mrs. Crewe was sister[7] to Mrs. Greville. A lady heard the two sisters thus greet one another when they met at breakfast with soft sentimental looks.

Mrs. G—. How do?
Mrs. C—. Not well.
Mrs. G—. What mat . . (short for matter).
Mrs. C—. Dont know.
Mrs. G—. (squeezing up eyes and mouth) Um! Um!
Mrs. C—. (doing ditto and echoing) Um! Um!

[1] *The Confidante* provided the first idea for ME's *Helen* (1834).
[2] *The Borough*, Letters XIX (The Parish Clerk), and XXIII (Prisons).
[3] See above, p. xxxiv.
[4] *The Borough*, Letter XXIV, l. 6.
[5] First published in the supplement (1806) to Hayley's *Life and Posthumous Writings of William Cowper*. The edition to which ME refers is vol. iii, *Posthumous Poems of Cowper* (1815). The other poem is 'The Retired Cat'.
[6] The Edgeworths much enjoyed Fanny Burney's novels and ME quite commonly used her characters to describe people: cf. p. 45 n. 3.
[7] Sister-in-law.

Which morning salutation do you prefer? This or—How stand the affections today? Is all well within?

One more bit of nonsense—*not* for Pakenham. You have heard Mrs. Wheeler mother to tall Mr. Wheeler you met at Black Castle. Once she was young and once she was little and at that time Mrs. Sneyd was present one day when her mother called to her 'Harriet what have you in your mouth? Come here and tell me how many things you have swallowed.' Harriet then about 6 years old a very gentle pretty behaved young lady came and stood before her mother with her hands before her and in a voice of confession answered to her mothers reiterated question of 'How many things in your life have you swallowed?' 'A shell—a blue bead—a stud—a doll's eye—and another—Ma'am.' How impossible it is to preserve the delightful spirit of nonsense in carrying it from conversation to writing. I have felt this conviction 1 million times and yet I so much wish you all to hear whatever diverts us at the moment that I cannot help trying at it . . . Believe me most sincerely your affectionate friend Maria E. . . .

To Mrs. Edgeworth

Byrkley Lodge, 8 February 1819

Dearest mother . . . [after discussion of plans] Hunter will know nothing of us *till* I write. He has nothing to say to me at present. We have finished reading my fathers part of the MS. aloud to the Sneyds. They have suggested a few emendations about the time of the *Scarborough trip*—Mrs. E. Edgeworth's marriage[1] &c. It is now *all* to their satisfaction and I rejoice exceedingly that I have read it to them. Honora and Fanny have assisted in giving the last correction. It will be fit for the press now I think and so I shall send it to Hunters nailed up to await for further orders. The Sneyds think it highly entertaining and interesting but better for private than public reading. The ques-

[1] *Memoirs of RLE,* I, Chap. XVI. RLE and Elizabeth Sneyd with their families both paid a visit to Scarborough before their marriage. Because of malicious gossip RLE was at great pains to make it clear (RLE to his sister Mrs. Ruxton, 26 January 1781) that Elizabeth Sneyd was always carefully chaperoned.

tion what has the public to do with this must or at least may occur. If they were to chuse they would wish it *not* to be published. So should we all I believe but I have no power I think *not* to publish.[1] The result of all I hear and all I think and feel is that we should be in no haste to publish. I am much inclined to make my part as short as possible for I have no *entertaining* events nor have any *great* actions or great inventions to lay before the public. To interest it must be short. Not one word of this did I mean to say to you at this moment my dearest mother because unless the MS. were before you you cannot judge for me but I was run away with by the old habit of talking to you of whatever my mind is most full of at the instant . . .

Mrs. Sneyd took me with her today to Blithfield Lord Bagots—to return Lady Dartmouth's visit. She is a charming woman—appears most amiable taking care of all those grandchildren of hers—Lord Bagot very melancholy gentlemanlike and interesting—The house a fine old cloistered house with painted glass and galleries and in every hall staircase and gallery coats of arms wherever you turn your eyes and family pictures—back to the father of the favorite Devereux[2] and a full length of Popes Lord Bolingbroke[3] . . . Our visit today though delightful in every other respect was *uncomfortable* to me because Honora and Fanny were not with me. Mrs. Sneyd and Emma both thought and so did I indeed that it would scarcely be proper for them to go as in the message sent Miss E had been the only person named and Lord Bagot's spirits in fact seemed hardly equal to the meeting with Mrs. Sneyd. It is the first time he has seen her since his wife's death. He took both her hands and was as near bursting into tears as ever man was. I marched off to the pictures and he got through it and was very obliging to me and shewed me all over his house and gave me a most sweet bunch of Daphne Indi*cum* or *ca* but still I felt as if I had left 2 pieces of myself behind me and I could not enjoy myself thoroughly. I have some hopes they will invite us all there for a day. I believe I am

[1] RLE had exacted a death-bed promise from ME that she would publish the Memoirs.

[2] Walter Devereux (d. 1576), 1st Earl of Essex, father of Queen Elizabeth's favourite, Robert Devereux.

[3] Lord Bagot's mother was daughter to the 2nd Viscount Bolingbroke, nephew of the Jacobite Viscount Bolingbroke who was Pope's patron and friend.

spoilt. I am sure I am tired and therefore will be your affectionate M E . . .

To Mrs. Edgeworth

Tetsworth 12 Miles from Oxford, Friday [4 March 1819]†

My dearest mother . . . On Tuesday morning 11 oclock left dear happy luxurious warm Byrkley Lodge after spending there —Honora and I 4 months—Fanny 6 weeks. More kindness and more I will not say *uniform* kindness, but kindness encreasing with accelerated velocity never was shewn to guests friends or relations and mixed with the gratitude we feel for this and most agreeably supporting it is the encreased esteem and love for each individual from knowing their characters more intimately . . . But I beg your pardon I am detaining you all this time from our history.

Arrived Lichfield in hard rain. Good Mrs. and Miss Greaves after we had swallowed luncheon set about pressing us as hard as possible to stay all night—such a day!—But I was stout in refusal. I could not put off Lady Elizabeth Whitbread and Mrs. Moilliet a second time. Heaven blessed my decision and the skies cleared up and we praised ourselves and each other handsomely for it and arrived in the nick of teatime at Mrs. Moilliets—Smethwick—after having called at the Royal Hotel Birmingham and found another kind letter from her pressing us not to stop there. We were all much pleased with our reception and with Mr. as well as Mrs. Moilliet and her 5 children—Emily a pretty face—fine person but unfashioned *Coolure-shoulders.*[1] When I saw the way of going on in this family—mode of life—mercantile and literary and domestic—such a contrast in some respects to all Byrkley Lodge, Sudbury and Trentham I determined that if it could be managed we would stay a day more than we had *laid out* that Fanny might see it. They pressed eagerly and I asked 12 hours to consider and in the night contrived it—no matter how—but so as to be in time for our appointment at Oxford. So it was settled that we should stay

[1] A reference to the family of Admiral Sir T. Pakenham who lived at Coolure.

Wednesday and sleep Wednesday night instead of setting off at 3 as at first intended and go by day break on Thursday.

I rejoice that we stayed. Fanny saw and heard much to the purpose. Breakfast early—Mr. Moilliet then took us to his foundry. Of this I will talk to Harriet and Pakenham anon. Fanny independently of all the mechanical pleasures she had in the sight—heard much to our purpose in Mr. Moilliets conversation in the carriage as he went with us (his chaise very roomy held 4). He is intelligent without pretension and becoming quite at his ease amused *me* more by original anecdotes from real life and observations of his own than I could have been amused by any commonplace literary amateur or fine gentleman. In him Fanny had a fair specimen of what a mercantile husband may make himself working hard too at his vocation all the time.[1] Some of the entertaining anecdotes I will recollect hereafter for *general use* of the *family*. At present for *you* I must mention that he gave me a most interesting account of Mr. and Mrs. Blair. After spending at the rate of ten thousand a year in high London society he died almost ruined leaving his widow scarce £400 a year. She now writes novels if not for bread for butter. He gamed desperately and constantly almost every night—till late every morn at Brooks and lost immensely temper grew bad beyond description—so abstracted in manner and such a gaming calculator that often in company he used in the midst of other conversation to repeat unconsciously aloud his calculations of chance at Hazard. When nearly ruined wanted to gain a prize in the matrimonial lottery for his son a fine figure of a youth then at Glasgow. N.B. He was obliged to send his sons from home and keep them always away from him because he could not let them see the life he led. The heiress Mr. Blair wanted for his son was Miss De Vismes. Mr. and Mrs. Blair insisted and tutored him but in vain. The young man was independent in principle and *chuff* in manner and tho he might have liked her if it had not been a manoeuvre resisted and tho the proposal was made for him made himself so disagreeable to Miss De Vismes that she refused him. He went to Wales and consoled himself with marrying a Welch farmers daughter without 2d. and not presentable. His father and mother of course never would see

[1] See above, p. 142.

her or him and the father dying soon after left him only some thousands of snow and forest in Canada—supposed to have been won at play—but so little worth winning that the young couple forced to go there to live at all can scarce live—very bare biting! The second son is now at Birmingham struggling up in the world through some inferior mercantile situation. But all this is only what might be expected from what we knew and heard of Mr. and Mrs. Blair but I was really surprised to hear that the prudent Mr. Keir had been always ruled and led into almost desperate imprudences by this man—attached to him in early youth Scotchman to Scotchman and perhaps from some early obligation continuing to be swayed by him thro' life tho their characters habits and modes of life were so different and tho he detested and knew so well the danger of a gamesters character. They were partners you know. Whenever Mr. Blair had a bad run at play he drained the partnership of thousands to pay debts of honor—Then pretended to all the world that he was impoverished by the works at Birmingham which he was near destroying. Nevertheless tho Keir knew all this he was led by his speculating partner into taking against his judgment a large tract of colliery[1]—would have made him bankrupt had he not when near the brink of all we hate taken hearty resolution to separate from Mr. Blair in this concern—did so—and saved just enough to live and die upon—no more. (My dear mother with all his brilliant imagination and inventive genius how prudent my father was in the conduct of affairs.)

I would not go to see poor Mr. Keir for by Mr. Moilliet's description I found it could only give him and me unavailing pain—quite childish—merely alive—carried from bed and back only to eat and drink—paralytic stroke.

Mr. Busk Blair's son in law was as great a gamester as Mr. Blair. Once he won £30,000 by a bit of gambling insurance on 2 missing East India ships. The ships re-appeared. The underwriters were obliged to pay him but it was suspected that he had some private intelligence—in short that there was some foul play. He never could shew his face at Lloyds afterwards—has

[1] *c.* 1794, Tividale Colliery (*Life and Correspondence of the Late James Keir* by Amelia Moilliet, ed. A. Blair (1859), 133). It is stated (p. 137) that Dr. Blair with his brother carried on the colliery some years after Keir's death.

now lost all since—and in a poor way. What must have been this gamesters feeling while the £30,000 bet was pending and how comfortable to be the wife of such a man! Fanny listened and moralised charmingly on all this with her eyes as intelligent as you know them to be when she listens to what interests her.

Then Mr. Moilliet told us an anecdote of Madame la Comtesse de Rumford and her husband—apropos to my anecdote of 'Ce n'est qu'une legere peine' &c. The charming count one day in a fit of ill humor went to the porter and forbid him to let into his house any of Madame La Comtesses and Lavoisiers[1] old friends—all the society which you and I saw at her house. They had all been invited to supper Berthollet among them. The old porter all disconsolate went to tell the countess the order he had received. 'Well—you must obey your masters orders. You must not let them into the house but I will go down to your porters lodge and as each carriage comes you will let them know what has happened and that I am there to receive them.' They all came and by two or three at a time went into the porters lodge and spent the evening with her—their carriages lining the street all night. So much for a well chosen literary Count and Countess match! Mr. Moilliet gave us an account of Italian Counts who spent some days with him at the time the Emperor &c were in England[2]—Four Gentlemen of Verona—*one* very well informed. Mr. [Moilliet] has promised me letters to them if ever we should go abroad. He and Mrs. Moilliet go next year to Geneva for some months. He has purchased a delightful house on the banks of the lake which formerly belonged to some I forget which of the Bonaparte princes or princesses. Mrs. Moilliet and he in the most earnest manner invited me if I should go to Geneva to make this house our home till I should find one more agreeable—'*More room than they can want*' &c. 'But perhaps I may have a sister or 2 with me.' 'Bring them Bring them—most welcome.' 'And if Mrs. E should come—' 'Oh' said Mrs. Moilliet coloring suddenly all over 'You *know* how happy *that* would make me. Let me write to you my dear Miss E as soon as we get there and tell you all about the expences of

[1] The Countess Rumford was the widow of the chemist Lavoisier.
[2] In 1814.

travelling and carriage and all you want to know.' How *can* people be so kind!

We went to see dear old Mr. Watt—84 and in perfect possession of eyes ears, and all his comprehensive understanding and warm heart—his eye as penetrating as ever. He lives in a house as neat and comfortable as possible. Poor *Entray* is almost crippled with the rheumatism and is blind of an eye but as good natured and hospitable as ever. They were both heartily glad to see us and on every account I rejoice we went. It was so due to my fathers old friend. So many recollections painful and pleasurable crowded and pressed upon my heart during this half hour I had much ado to talk but I *did* and so did he—forgeries on bank notes[1]—no way he can invent of avoiding such but by an inspecting clerk and office in every country town. Talked over committee report—paper-marks—vain—Tilloch[2]—I have no great opinion of his abilities—Bramah[3]—yes—he is a clever man—But set down this for truth—no man is so ingenious but what another can be found equally ingenious—What one can invent another can detect and imitate. I mentioned my fathers scheme of employing first rate engravers—*above* imitation. But there are 500 now in England and Scotland—first rate and equal as far as any talents they could shew in the compass of a Bank note. Talked of chimney sweeper bill[4]—Many flues can*not* be swept by machines—explanation too long.

Watt is at this moment himself the best Encyclopaedia extant. I dare not attempt to tell you half he said. It would be a

[1] Sir J. Mackintosh in Apr. 1818 moved in the House of Commons for information on the enormous increase in banknote forgeries. In May he successfully moved for the appointment of a Commission of Inquiry. The question was related to the agitation for a reduction in the use of paper currency.

[2] Alexander Tilloch (1759–1825) invented and patented the process of stereotyping. In 1790 he laid before the government a mode of printing banknotes which would make impossible the forgeries prevalent at that time. He made a renewed attempt to get it accepted in 1797. In 1810 Augustus Applegarth's process was officially adopted and in 1820 Tilloch claimed in a petition to Parliament that the former's process was virtually his own.

[3] Joseph Bramah patented the Bramah lock in 1784.

[4] The Chimney Sweeper Regulation Bill had its third reading in the House of Commons on 22 Feb. It prohibited the apprenticing of boys under 14 to chimney sweeps. When the Bill went to the House of Lords, Lord Auckland said 60 out of 61 House of Commons chimneys had been swept by machine. Lord Lauderdale said climbing boys were like calomel and went into every nook and cranny. The Bill was thrown out by the Lords.

volume. I looked at him with admiration not unmixed with envy—84! Mrs. Watt has promised me a good engraving of his head. Chantrey has made a beautiful I mean an admirable *bust*[1] of him for Mr. Moilliet. Chantrey and Canova are now making two rival busts of Washington. Chantrey is said to have Nollekens bust of Dr. Darwin[2] from which Fanny *shall* finish her sketch from the cast.

Wednesday Evening. (I must hop, skip and jump as I can from subject to subject) Mr. and Mrs. Moilliet took us in the evening to a lecture on poetry by Campbell who has been invited by a *philosophical* society[3] of Birmingham gentlemen to give lectures on poetry. They give tickets to their friends—quite select—Mr. *Corrie* not *Currie*[4]—one of the heads of this society was *proud* to introduce us—Excellent lecture room well lighted with *gas* spouting from U tubes at the bottom of the gallery surrounding the room—the *pit* filled with *ladies* and *gentlemen* not so *genteel* but much more attentive than Davy's Dublin audience.[5] Lecture good enough—Latin poetry and Greek—from Pindar and Sappho down to Lucan Horace Ovid—Seneca. Mr. Campbell introduced to me after lecture—asked very kindly for Sneyd—many compliments. Fanny and Ho I believe think as I do that he is clever and agreeable and *modest*—query—a leetle of le fat modeste[6] but *dont* say so for I had not 5 minutes time to judge and with my quantum of judgment you know that is not sufficient. Mr. Corrie drank tea after lecture at Mr. Moilliets—very agreeable—benevolent countenance most agreeable voice—*fat* benevolent countenance. I am sure you guessed it lean. We particularly liked his enthusiasm for Mr. Watt. He gave a history of his inventions and gave instances of Watts superiority

[1] This bust is earlier than any of the statues or busts of Watt listed in Gunnis, *Dictionary of British Sculptors* [1953]. The bust of Washington is not listed.

[2] This bust of Dr. Darwin is not listed in Gunnis, op. cit. Another unlisted one is illustrated in *Memoirs of RLE* (2nd ed. 1821), ii, facing p. 242.

[3] The Birmingham Philosophical Institution was founded in 1800: J. A. Langford, *A Century of Birmingham Life* (1868).

[4] ME is probably wishing to distinguish John Corrie from James Currie, F.R.S., the well-known Liverpool physician. ME had an Irish connection called James Corry of Shantonagh, Co. Monaghan. He was the prototype of King Corny in ME's *Ormond*.

[5] The Edgeworths heard Davy lecture in Dublin in 1810.

[6] A man who, though he does not push himself, yet fancies himself a little as a man about town.

both in invention and magnanimity when in competition with others. I note for Fannys future explanation for you—Steam engine—*crank*—double piston &c. Dr. Corrie *saw* Fanny understood all he said but I was vexed with her for not saying more herself because when I led to subjects on purpose for her she left me to *talk all* and plunge on—getting in and out as *I could*—or as I could not. I have now given her and Honora my sacred word that if they do not talk hereafter I will become silent—not say one syllable.

Mr. and Mrs. Moilliet notwithstanding these sins of silence like them altogether so much that they have pressed us exceedingly to come again for some days on our return—Mr. and Mrs. Watt ditto ditto—almost with tears in his eyes and I was ashamed to see that venerable man standing bareheaded at his door in the cold to do us the last honors till the carriage drove away. (I beg your pardon for going backwards and forwards in my hurry skurry.)

At Stratford we saw Shakespears house. I find Fanny is just telling you this so I forbear. At Shipton we did not see Mother Shipton. At Blenheim—Fanny has told you *all that* and I have left Oxford to her discretion. Their pens have been scribbling a l'envie l'une de l'autre while I have been writing this so I hope and trust you have all the history of our two days.

What I chiefly wanted to tell you was that they have I think been spent *usefully* for Fanny as well as agreeably. Under the head *useful* I put her being gallanted all day about Oxford by Mr. Rothwell and Mr. Vernon young gentlemen of such different sorts. After luncheon–dinner I finished at Oxford signing and sealing a letter to Mrs. Sneyd which Mr. Vernon took to enclose to Lord Vernon—was obliged to go to some engagement—pressed us to summon him on our return—Such a pleasure and honor &c.

Mr. Rothwell stayed delighted—transported to the last gasp and begged and entreated we would permit him to attend us on our return so that I thought he never would let the chaise door be shut or let polite and finely dressed Madame Dupuis's head push itself in to do the parting civilities of her Hotel—among other things to apologise for not offering me a print of a Dutch school which I had admired . . .

To Mrs. Edgeworth, [9 March 1819]

We drove on pleasantly, warmly apron'd with 2 frieze cloaks and one cushioning my back twelve miles to Tetsworth—excellent inn—not usually a sleeping place—therefore perhaps the people more civil and attentive—excellent bedchamber 2 spacious beds—comfortable quiet parlor—(Woodstock adventure—drunken man Fanny promises to tell)—We are writing so comfortably—I at my desk with a table to myself and the most comfortable little black stuffed armchair! Fanny and Ho at their desk and table near the fire—We must have 2 pair of snuffers! Yes *my lady*—directly. So now my lady—good night—for I am tired a little just enough to pity the civillest and prettiest of Swiss looking housemaids who is sitting up for us and who says in answer to my 'We shall come to bed soon' 'Oh dear *my lady* we bees no ways particular in this house about time o' going to bed. Pray my lady dont hurry yourself.' How much do you think I shall have to pay tomorrow morning for having swallowed *my Lady* ninety nine times this night . . . Your heartily obliged and affectionate Maria E. . . .

To Mrs. Edgeworth

Grove House, Kensington Gore, Tuesday morning
half after 8, [9 March 1819]†

My dearest mother . . . I cannot tell you *how* kind Lady Elizabeth Whitbread is. We are with every convenience and luxury as if we were at home. She never comes out of her room till between 12 and one. Indeed she seldom wishes to see any body till dinner so all the morning without unkindness to her or losing her company are ours. She has put her coach—coachman—footman and horses entirely at my command every day while we stay and she has done this in such a manner that I feel the kindness without the burden of obligation. 'You will oblige me by using my horses. I never go out myself. They want exercise. There are 4 of them—so can be used by turns—every day. Write your orders every night and give them to the coachman who shall come up to you regularly.' And he has done so and the most agreeable of coachmen he is—Like Lady like man. Are we not better qualified than any people in the world to contradict all Madame de Stael says about the impossibility of getting into the London petites boites fermees? When once you are in there is nothing in [the][1] world that kindness *can* do that is not done [ ]. I only feel in constant surprise at the [ ] shewn us! I feel overwhelmed by it. I hope [ ] not to be spoiled by it. In our circumstances and [ ] it is more valuable even than our friends *can* guess.

We stopped at High Wycombe 2 hours to see Lord Carringtons beautiful house and place—an old monastery modernised with excellent taste—gothic not gloomy—heard he was expected every hour—left a letter for him on his table—Received a letter from him yesterday—With one from Madame Gautier in my next packet.

Sunday. Lady Elizabeth Whitbread invited to meet us at dinner Mr. and Mrs. Le Fevre her son and daughter—good—Lady Hannah Ellice her sister and Mr. Ellice—M P—he a good talker—she is quite plain enough in face not plain enough in manner—Mr. and Mrs. Holland—son of the architect who has had sense to go into business—has made a large fortune. He is as agreeable *clever* and conversible man as ever I saw—She a most amiable and *agreeable* woman—intent upon 9 children as you are but like you not spoiled for society by her being an excellent mother. She is a charming as well as excellent woman. Que de vertues vous me faites aimer! After this you may guess she is a great admirer of Early Lessons Moral Tales Parents Assistant &c—But not one fulsome compliment—Proofs of their having been of use delightfully brought home to me—*Harry and Lucy* particularly talked of . . . Adieu. ME.

To Miss Charlotte and Miss Mary Sneyd

Grove House, Kensington Gore, Wednesday,
[? 10th March 1819]

With your own pen which I find the greatest convenience to me I write to you my dear kind aunts . . .

Monday dinner. Mr. and Mrs. Le Fevre Mr. R. Talbot—Mr. S. Whitbread—good but too meek looking youth—Mrs.

[1] MS. torn.

Nisbet—Mrs. Brownrigg could not come because a relation of hers died—Miss Dashwood—a friend of Anna's. Miss Dashwood is handsome and fashionable without pretension and with charming manners and countenance—plays well and draws—pleasant evening again.

Tuesday. Lady Grey—Lady Elizabeth's mother a fine straight-backed thin dried benevolent smiling eyed looking woman whom I like much—She is so fond of her family!—Lady Hannah Ellice again—Still I cannot swallow her but she is very civil—I *suspect* she is silly—Mr. Battye—much esteemed neighbor of Lady E. Whitbread's—I suppose I shall like him when I know him—very good—Evening dullish.

Fanny wore her green silk and it looked beautiful. All the fashionable trimmings are of that rolled sort of flounces. Lady E. Whitbread has one a Spanish flounce she says—so pretty and easily made that I will send pattern in my next. The hems tell Millward are run with packthread which Lady E. Whitbread says is used because stiffer and sits better than bobbin. I wore one day Emma's turban and another day brown and white net. Both days I looked lovely I am confident. We called on Miss Brooke. The bonnets were very pretty and elegant but far too large both in crown and leaf. She was very civil and will make them exactly to our tastes.

Mrs. Roberts too was very civil. Sitting with her I found an elegant lady with nice bonnet and long shawl held prettily *over the opposite arm* and she stood up and stood back a little as I came in. 'Pray dont let me disturb . . .' 'Ansell—Ma'am—I believe you know her' said Mrs. R—. I did not indeed. She was so exquisitely accoutred . . . Adieu ever affectionately M E

To Mrs. Ruxton

Grove House, Kensington Gore,
Friday, [? 12] March 1819

My dearest aunt, Your commissions Sophys and Margarets shall all be executed with pleasure and to the best of my capacity. I hope you will not be disappointed or angry with me if I should send this letter half finished or with only half a page written for I am in such a hurry skurry from morning till night that I can scarcely command 10 minutes. But I know you will think a little better than none.

We arrived here on Saturday last—found Lady Elizabeth Whitbread more kind and more agreeable than ever. Her kindness to us is indeed unbounded and would quite overwhelm me but for the delicate and polite manner in which she confers favors—more as if she received than conferred them. Her house, her servants her carriage, her horses are not only entirely at my disposal but really more useful to me at present or more used by me than by herself . . . One of her footmen is Irish—Queens County—the Butler Scotch from the Highlands—both excellent specimens of their country, I never saw better servants. Brian the Irishman usually goes with us. Lady E. Whitbread insists upon it because 'You know he is used to London and your good old man is not besides the stones shake his old bones too much.' When he stays at home he helps the servants here. Once when we were going only to Chelsea to Chantreys I insisted upon not taking her footman and she had the goodnatured consideration to go down to the door to desire the coachman would take care always to have George Bristow on the box lest the shaking should be too much &c. I mention these little things because they will best give you an idea of her kindness. She never has and I think never will recover her spirits. Romilly's death and the manner of it shocked her much. She makes however great efforts to be chearful . . .

Mr. Talbot is often here—L'ami de la maison and very much ours—Lady Grey the mother a fine amiable old lady—Lady Hannah Ellice Lady Elizabeths sister not so agreeable person mind or manners as herself.—Mr. Ellice very good humored and agreeable—Mr. and Mrs. Le Fevre son in law and daughter very agreeable good and happy—little to live on now but will have a little trifle of fourteen thousand a year when old Shaw le Fevre dies. My dear aunt I am more and more convinced that happiness depends on what is in the head and heart more than what is in the purse or the bank or on the back or in the stomach. There must be *enough* in the stomach but the sauce is not of much consequence.

By the by Lady E. Whitbread's cook is said to be the best in England Royalties excepted—lived with her as she says in the days of her prosperity and has followed her here. Often she has taken fine judges of good dishes down stairs to shew that her cook is not a man cook but a woman cook which seemed to those Judges incredible. This woman has had her children 2 daughters grown up in Lady E. Whitbread's service and says she can never leave her Lady. All her servants are attached to her in the same manner. I am just going to see some orange dressed by her in a particular way which I shall study for Molly Coffey and you for I know you will like them . . .

The first part of the MS. is in Hunters hands—well corrected and going to press. I shall correct the proofs. This will [take] two or three months. By that time I hope the second volume will be ready. I shall bring it back with me and you will be so kind as to read it all over again for me. [end missing]

To Mrs. Edgeworth

Kensington Gore, Tuesday, 16 March, half after 7, morning

Dearest mother . . . As far as we have gone the object of her [Fanny's] journey to London has been accomplished more fully than my most sanguine wishes could have hoped both as to persons and variety of life she has seen and as to the effect it has upon her mind. We have been for about 2 hours one morning with Lord and Lady Stafford—another morning ditto with Lady Lansdowne—pressing invitations to return. We have breakfasted with Miss Fanshawes—met Lord Glenbervie, whom we much liked and who liked us and will come to pay respects &c —Lady Charlotte Lindsay we are going to this morning—not in Town till today. We have been two evenings at Mr. Wilberforce's (next door)—met numbers of *Interestings*—Sir Alexander Johnstone—Bishop of Gloucester—Mr. Buxton—Mr. Parnell. I have not time to name more.

We have breakfasted twice with Mrs. Marcet—once private once public—with Dr. Holland Mr. Whishaw Mr. Mallet Captain Beaufort Mr. Lestock Wilson and Lady Young (and I dont know who the devil she is). We have dined at Miss Wilsons with Sneyd and Harriette—little Francis and old deaf Farington. We are now going to breakfast with the Hopes—Tomorrow with the Duchess of Wellington. Lady Harrowby I called on—in bed with a cold—most civil message by her own man—will wait upon us at Kensington entreats to see more &c—Miss Berrys stopped our carriage in the street and was near run over and in French transports &c—and we are to go there. All this I detail to shew you that one part of the object has been and can be accomplished for Fanny to any extent we please. I have adhered and shall adhere to my resolution not to accept of any dinners or evening invitations save only going in the evening or to dinner with Lady E. Whitbread to her own mother and sister and Mr. Wilberforce and a Mr. Battye her neighbors here which could not in propriety be refused. She goes nowhere else . . . Your truly affectionate M E

To Mrs. Ruxton

Kensington Gore, 24 March 1819

My dearest aunt, I have a moment to write to you and I will not lose it . . . Now I will as well as I can name the parties and families we have seen at their own houses and at these breakfasts and luncheons we have heard more conversation and seen more character and more of the interior of houses and minds than we could have done in any other way.

. . . The Miss Fanshawe's—breakfast—Lord Glenbervie there very agreeable—much French and Italian literature—beautiful drawings—full of *genius* (if there be any such thing allowed by Practical Education![1]). The Miss Berrys—very different—more dashing and fashionable Bel esprits—French ton—French gestures but not well bred low French voices—'Moi je dis' in every tone. We saw quite enough to know that we wished to see no more . . . Three breakfasts at dear excellent

[1] *Practical Education* (1798) by RLE and ME. 'In every family, you know, there is some standing subject of argument—Mrs. Edgeworth holds that hereditary propensities form the different characters of her children—I hold, that education either purposed or accidental produces all the differences of character . . .': RLE to Dumont, n.d. 1812 (MS. in Bibliothèque Publique et Universitaire, Geneva).

Mrs. Marcets . . . Third breakfast—Mr. Mill British India chief figurante—But he is not the least of a figurante nor a show man but a person of excellent sense and benevolence speaking fluent sense and giving information for pleasure of all his hearers not for his own glory N.B—not rich! *and* married!

Mr. Wilberforce's—2 evening parties—one saintly the other worldly—one stupid the other entertaining. At the last Sir Alexander Johnstone Mr. Buxton—Bishop of Gloucester Lord Harrowbys sister—Governor Farquhar Governor of the Mauritius—I never heard one word he said nor do I believe he said any one worth hearing. Mr. Buxton very plain sense and admirable facts about Newgate and Spitalfield weavers and all that. One fact I was very sorry to learn from him that Mrs. Fry that angel-woman is very ill.

Mr. and Mrs. Hope—breakfast—quite alone as we requested. Mr. Hope shewed the house[1] to H and F while I sat with Mrs. Hope. She is much altered in person but people say she is now recovered much in comparison with what she was some months ago. They were as kind as possible to us. We go to them next monday to stay at their house till the 1st or 2nd of April.

Duchess of Wellingtons St Patricks day—by appointment. Nothing could be more like Kitty Pakenham—former youth and beauty only excepted. There was a plate of shamrocks on the table. She presented a bunch of shamrocks to me as she came forward to meet me and pressing my hand as she gave it to me said in a low voice and with her sweet smile 'Vous en etes digne'. Colonel Percy was in the room with her when we first went in. She stood talking to him till he went away—Then drawing her own chair and mine closer together said 'How glad one feels to be relieved from the constraint of a third person's company when one has any thing interesting to hear from our friends.' She then asked individually for all her Irish friends. I shewed her what was said in my fathers life and by me of Lord Longford and shewed the drawing of his head[2] and asked if the family would be pleased or not by the inserting these. She spoke very kindly—said it must do her father's memory honor—could not but please every Pakenham &c. Something occurred about

[1] In Duchess St. See below, pp. 189, 191.

[2] Engraved as frontispiece to vol. ii of *Memoirs of RLE.*

a Bramahs silver pen which I shewed her and which my aunt Charlotte had given me. She went to her inner room and brought out a little box of remarkable good pens belonging to this pen-case and as I was looking at these she put her hand on mine 'Keep this for my sake.' She was obliging in directing her conversation easily to my sisters as well as to myself.

She gave an account of her ceremonial visit to the Duchesse d'Angouleme and of her first visit from Madame de Stael in Paris. She had purposely avoided being acquainted with Madame de Stael in England—not knowing how she might be received in Paris by the Bourbon when the duchess was to be embassadress. She found that Madame de Stael was well received and that consequently she must be received at the Duke of Wellingtons. She arrived and walking up in full assembly to the Duchess with *fire* of indignation flashing in her eyes, standing firmly with her feet asunder after her manner 'Eh Madame la Duchesse vous ne vouliez pas donc faire ma connoissance en Angleterre.' 'Non Madame je ne le voulais pas.' 'Eh Comment Madame! Eh Pourquoi donc?' 'C'est que je vous craign*ais* Madame!' 'Vous me craign*ez* Madame la Duchesse!' 'Non Madame je ne vous crains plus.' Madame de Stael threw her arms round her 'Ah je vous adore'.

I must end abruptly—more tomorrow if possible—affectionately yours Maria E (No I have one instant more)

While we were with the Duchess of Wellington a jeweller's man came with some bracelets. We saw that one was a shell like your Roman shell cameos of the Duke of Wellington's head of which she was correcting the profile. The most sentimental stage effect French lady could not have managed better than this which the plain truth brought out for the Duchess. She shewed us pictures of her sons and Fanny sketched from their pictures while we sat with her.

We saw in the hall or rather in the curve of the stair case Canova's gigantic statue of *Apollo*-Bonaparte which was sent from France you know to the Regent and which the Prince gave to the Duke of Wellington. It is ten feet high. I could not judge of it in the place in which it is cooped up. When he has a palace in the country I hope he will contrive a place large enough for this great man who now looks shockingly ill placed. We did not see the Duke himself at Apsley House. This we much regretted. Sunday—Lady Harrowby's by invitation to a morning party which she fixed on this day because she politely said Lord Harrowby much desired to make our acquaintance and this was his only holiday. We went at ½ after 3 stayed till five—Company —Mr. Ellis a young man just come into parliament from whom great things are expected. He is to be Lord I forget-who— Clever but bites his fingers from vexation when he is not talking. Mr. Wilmot—clever and a man of the world—Mr. Frere the celebrated—Lord Harrowby—most agreeable in conversation!—The most agreeable man I have seen—Lady Harrowby as Madame de Stael described her 'bien spirituelle'[1] and *very* polite—Lady Mary Ryder and Lady Ebrington. I dont like Mr. Frere much—not equal in conversation to his writing as far as I have heard yet.

Folding doors thrown open, 'The Duke of . . .' I did not hear the name nor guess it was the Duke of Wellington. Post— letter must go

To Mrs. Edgeworth

[fragment 25 March 1819]†

. . . We hurried home sooner than we wished from this delightful family party to be at home to receive dear Lord Carrington who came yesterday while we were out and sent his servant with a note to me afterwards at 10 oclock at night to let me know . . . I will enclose his Lordships note to save time in a packet per Ward.

Friday 3 oclock

Lord Carrington has come and is gone and is as kind as ever. He is going out of Town to West Wycombe for 4 or 5 days— will the moment he returns come to Hampstead to see us— talked of Pakenham—will say more of Hertford College &c when we meet again. I must say no more now for Mrs. Edward Bouverie is come to hear me and I must go and talk of what I

[1] Madame de Stael, *Considérations sur la révolution française*, Pt. 6, vi.

am not thinking. Indeed I cannot even if I had time tell you any of the thousand entertaining things I have seen I am so engrossed to stupefaction by one subject[1] when I write to you . . . Our luncheon at Lord and Lady Harrowbys delightful—saw the Duke of Wellington—like him—but very old quite a ploughed face of a war worn hero—simple manners . . .

To Mrs. Edgeworth

31 Harley Street, 30 March 1819

My dearest mother, Your calculations were so admirably just that your letter was put into our hands five minutes after we had arrived at Mrs. Hopes just when we had run up to our *Attics* to take off our pelisses and unpack before we saw Mrs. Hope or any body. Most happy we were to devour it in our snugs.

Lady E. Whitbread's kindness to us went on encreasing to the very last. Five minutes before we went away she took me into her own room and begged that when we have completely finished all our visits and all that we want to do in Town and in short when we are on our road homewards we should come to her on our way and repose with her 3 or 4 quiet days . . .

Mrs. Hope's house will shew her [Fanny] a brilliant panorama. For the first time Mrs. Hope had an evening party last night. At dinner we had Miss C Fanshawe Mr. Henry Hope Mr. Cockerell (too fine)—Mr. Moore son of the archbishop of Canterbury fine too but with excellent conversation—Mr. Hammersley well informed—Mr. W. Hamilton under secretary of state—very agreeable and unaffected—In the evening Lady Clare—Lady Charlotte Lindsay—Mrs. Burrowes Mrs. Hope's sister—Lord Glenbervie—Miss Fanshawe and several other figures whose names I cannot recollect. Fanny and Ho looked very pretty. F in white gauze—pink gauze handkerchief—Ho—Scotch muslin—very pretty little roses in hair. Mrs. Hope paid *me* many compliments about Fanny's beauty and I kept saying she had not pretensions to *beauty* &c. She asked most kindly for you.

[1] Fanny's love affair.

Mr. H. Philip Hope's brother has given him his fine collection of Flemish pictures. The pictures are now piled seven deep in the gallery or passage leading to our bedchamber with their faces to the wall. Mr. Hope has built a gallery on purpose for them.[1]

This day Lord and Lady Darnley Lord and Lady Jersey and I forget who and there is to be a *small* party in the evening. I am glad Fan will see all this. I have promised to come for an hour every day to Harley Street to let her make her own comparisons. All I can do is to do nothing at all in some situations as Colbert[2] found the most difficult thing in the world . . . Yours affectionately Maria E

To Mrs. Edgeworth

T. W. Carr Esqre., Frognell, Hampstead,[3]
Friday morning, 1 April 1819

My dearest mother, Here we are this delicious spring day in the midst of spring delights and in the midst of the far greater delights of a family happy as our own once was and united as they were and are and I hope ever will be—Thanks to you—*mother-in law of four families*—a higher title to respect than mother of any Fatima Sultan or Emperor that ever existed.

How people can be so very kind to us as they are I cannot conceive . . . the Hopes were so very good in their way that we were happy there and in the midst of their magnificence quite domesticated. Then coming here afterwards was delightful. After all, what is comfortable in a house and home is far preferable to the utmost grandeur and magnificence. By candlelight, splendidly lighted and filled with Dukes and Duchesses &c &c that house of Mr. Hope's is festive and *fit* for *gala*-nights, but by day the size and gilding of the rooms and the company look of all the furniture and the want of little ordinary tables that you can use without scruple prevent the feeling of enjoyment such as *we* have been used to. When I one day said to Mr. Hope 'I am

[1] Designed by himself.
[2] Jean Baptiste Colbert (1619–83), minister of finance to Louis XIV.
[3] The Carrs lived at Maryon Hall, at the top of Frognel Lane.

really afraid to put my writing desk down on these beautiful inlaid tables', he answered 'Write on the *wood* of that table if you please and I shall be glad of it.' Yet still there was a feeling that prevented *comfort*. The moment we came here we felt at *home* completely and mixed with the every day habits of the family. I never saw a family that would suit better with our own. I long for you and all my sisters and Lovell to know them as we do. Some time or other I hope this will be . . .

Monday morning [4 April] . . .

I forgot to tell you that we had seen Lord Carrington—very kind but much older in appearance and much depressed in spirits. He says he will come and see us here or will manage somehow that we shall meet. I wish it might be at High Wycombe in our way homewards. I have seen Hunter lately. Have agreed to give him the whole of the MS. in September. He is to send me over the proof sheets. That operation will retard the publication but it is in my opinion quite necessary. He means to have it out by Xmas. The first volume is now going to press! Thank you and Lovell for Mr. Days picture.[1] Say when it sets out. Direct it and Lord Longford's to 31 Harley Street.

Fanny is so nursed and so loved by all this family that you would be delighted with them as I am. So far from being any trouble to them I am sure it is a pleasure to them to do all they do for her and they will like her all the better for the kindness they shew her. Mrs. Carr is the most kindhearted motherly creature I have seen since I came to England. How fortunate we were to come here just at the moment we did. We have a delightful airy bedchamber with chearful bow window—large bed for Fanny and me—a room adjoining for Honora and a little dressing room—with a double door and tiny antiroom that shuts out all noise. As Mrs. Carr says I am sure these 3 rooms were intended from the Creation for the 3 Edgeworths they fit and suit them so exactly.

Mr. Carr! Oh mother I *almost* envy these dear good girls the happiness of the affection they have for their father. If you could see them all from the eldest to the youngest running to the gate to meet him as he rides home on his white horse! He is *one* of

[1] To be engraved as an illustration to the *Memoirs of RLE*. The picture is by Wright of Derby and is now in the National Portrait Gallery.

the very happiest men I ever saw—of the happiest temper—working hard all day usefully and honorably and coming home every evening to such a happy cultivated united family. When he sits down to dinner in the midst of his children he says he throws aside every care for the remainder of the day and enjoys himself. He is passionately fond of drawing and music and one daughter draws admirably and another plays and sings admirably—and all their accomplishments are for *him* and for their own family. They are really happy people. Certainly Fanny has had the advantage of seeing a greater variety of the insides of families of all ranks than could have been expected—even by my sanguine imagination . . . God bless you. Maria E

To Sophy Ruxton

Duchess Street, 2 April[1] 1819

My dearest friend, . . . I left off abruptly in my last to my aunt just as the folding doors at Lord Harrowbys were thrown open and the Duke of Wellington was announced in such an unintelligible manner that I did not know what Duke it was nor did I know till I got into the carriage who it was. He looks so old and wrinkled I never should have known him from likeness to bust or picture—His manner very agreeable perfectly simple and dignified. He said only a few words but listened to some literary conversation that was going on as if he felt amused laughing once heartily. It was lucky for me that I did not know who he was for the very fear of falling on dangerous subjects about husbands and wives in various novels we discussed would have inevitably brought me into some scrape had I known who he was. On the contrary I talked on quite at my ease.

Put me in mind to tell some circumstances Lord Harrowby told me about Adele de Senange[2] (Perhaps I told it to my aunt

[1] This letter, though clearly thus dated, should precede the previous one. For a description of Mrs. Hope's house, see D. Watkin, *Thomas Hope, 1769–1831, and the Neo-Classical Idea.*

[2] *Adèle de Senange* (1797) by Madame de Souza.

in my last)—also—Lord Harrowbys conversation about two expressions of Madame de Staels 'On depose fleur a fleur la couronne de la vie' and 'Le silence est l'antichambre de la mort.'[1]

Mr. Hookham Frere was the most stupid person in company. I thought I was the only person who formed this opinion and was ashamed to tell it to anybody: but Lady Harrowby afterwards told me she had made the same observation and that all in the room thought so. I have since breakfasted with Mr. Frere twice at Lord Glenbervie and at Miss Fanshawe's with the most agreeable people of various sorts and have never heard any thing from him worth listening to. I dare not enter further into histories of breakfasts &c lest I should not have time to tell of the essential things but I will keep our book of engagements which will serve as a little text book hereafter for sofa and fireside conversations . . .

We came to the Hopes four days ago. She is indeed much altered in appearance but the same in kindness of heart and her mind much improved in literary cultivation and by travelling. Mr. Hope himself has in his whole appearance marks of having suffered much. The contrast between their depression of spirits and the magnificence of every thing about them is striking and speaks volumes of moral philosophy at a glance to the observer. They are very fond of one another. Put me in mind to tell you the history Mrs. Hope gave me of their illness and the death of the child and the behaviour of an Irish maid.

They were even more kind than I expected in their manner of receiving us all. One large gilt drawing room opening to the staircase and with access to the statue and picture galleries Mrs. Hope gave us for the reception of whatever friends and visitors we chuse to see whom we may take into her room or not as we like. Her carriage and horses which she uses only for one hours airing in the park she leaves at every other hour of the day entirely at our disposal and one of her footmen to walk with us or do our behests. Did you ever hear of people so privileged by kind friends—in London?

[1] The expression as given to ME by Dumont (14 Apr. 1813) was 'La solitude est l'antichambre de la mort'.

Mrs. Hope had never since her coming to Town had a large dinner party till we came to her but she assembled all the people she thought we might like to see—one day Miss Fanshawe—another day the Duke and Duchess of Bedford—Lord and Lady Jersey—Lord Palmerston—Lord and Lady Darnley—Mr. Ellis Lord Clifden's son—very clever and very conceited. Lady Darnley was very obliging and kind to me—just as she was when I saw her before. Lady Jersey is peculiarly agreeable and was particularly obliging to us. For example she sent me three tickets for the French play which is now one of the objects of London curiosity and competition. She also told me she would put down our names and give me some tickets for Almacks. Of the 5 Patronesses she is supposed to rule. I declined with all possible acknowledgements her offer about Almacks but accepted the tickets for the French play. In the evening Lady Grantham—Lord and Lady King—Lady Harrowby—Lady Ebrington—Lord and Lady Lansdowne—Lady Clare and daughter—Lady Charlotte Lindsay—Lord Glenbervie—and many more whom I cannot stay to name. The Duchess of Bedford talked much to me and agreeably of her travels—Italy—Germany—Spain—Portugal &c Poor Mrs. Hope was so exhausted by the effort of seeing all these people that she could not sleep and looked wretchedly all the next day—no one but her own sister and niece and Captain Beaufort whom Mr. Hope was so good as to ask to dinner . . . Next day multitudes of morning visitors—Lady Grantham and Lady Jersey half an hour separate visits entertained us much . . . Adieu. Love. M E

To Mrs. Edgeworth

Deep Dene,[1] Saturday, 17 April 1819

Deep *Dene*
Dene a saxon word meaning a deep rift
in a wood—in short a deep dingle

My dearest mother, Your wish that we should be at Deep Dene is accomplished. We are at last at this beautiful place in this sweet valley of Dorking. Not as we had last year hoped to

[1] Mrs. Hope's house near Dorking.

be, with the great and good Sir Samuel Romilly but still we are with hospitable and kind people and in the midst of all the luxuries of life and all that gilding and painting, and bronzing of Art, can do within, and all that Nature can do with hill and vale, dingle and bushy wood to make the owners and their guests happy.

The first evening of our arrival we were so late that even in driving thro' the vale of Dorking we were in an agony that prevented our enjoyment. We were cross because we were late. The Carrs who are enthusiasts about the beauties of the vale of Dorking and who know nothing of the Hopes but that he has built a great new brick house and pulled down some old house in Chirt park which they loved had spoken with sufficient indignation of the Manufactory looking brick edifice which they say has set the valley on fire.[1] At first sight the offices and the house all irregularly joined with archways and cupolas and strangeness of red brick certainly did strike us as frightful in the midst of a most beautiful country. Our friend the housekeeper and several footmen standing at the arched doorway watching in the dusk for our arrival, and the first words in answer to mine of 'Is it dinner time?' 'Yes Ma'am. Dinner has been waiting this hour' increased my uncomfortable feelings. Fanny was so much tired that we determined she should not go to dinner especially as we heard that Conversation Sharp and some other gentlemen were here. I had taken it for granted that the Hopes dined at the same hour in Town and country. But instead of 7 they dine at 6 in the country and various operations and leave takings and a visit to Lord—I mean to Lady Carrington had altogether detained us too late in Town. Fanny's health and the pity and interest which it and she excited stood us in good stead. We dressed in the utmost hurry skurry in less than five minutes I am sure made our appearance in the drawing room where luckily the circle were standing and sitting by dim firelight and our guilty faces could scarcely be seen. From the midst two

[1] Chart or Chert Park, next door to The Deepdene, had been sold by the heirs of Sir C. Talbot to Thomas Hope, who demolished it. Chert Park was in fact a nineteenth-century house designed by Ashpitel. The Deepdene was later stuccoed. It had been bought by Hope in 1806 and was enlarged by him, probably to his own designs, though he was assisted by W. Atkinson between 1819 and 1826. For a description see D. Watkin, op. cit.

black and white figures whom I knew to be Mr. and Mrs. Hope each with hand extended came to meet us and with one comfortable pressure of each hand set the mind at ease. I descried by the wood fire light the wooden cut of Mr. Sharp's face and was re-introduced to a Mr. *Harness* whom you may remember tho' I do not. He told me he was introduced to us *first* at Lydia White's just after we had been presented to the (Qy.) Duchess of Sussex.[1] He is an agreeable man and Mr. Sharp was what they call (and I hate the expression) *in great force* that day and there was an admirable dinner of all manner of well disguised French dishes and creams and soufflés and ices and more than would have sufficed for the dinner of the first bon vivant in Town was sent by the good natured Mr. Hope to Fanny. As soon as I could steal away after dinner I got to her and found her as pale as a turnep wrapped in my shawl. After having swallowed a little jelly she went to bed—a most comfortable French mattress—Canopy bed—large enough for four such as she and I—three rooms opening into one another—small but superbly furnished. I was cross even with the fine furniture that night and regretted the dear Carrs and the home comforts we found there.

I was shockingly afraid that Fanny was going to be ill again *here*. She had but little sleep in the night and in the morning a new misery! Honora wakened with one of her sad sick headaches —Impossible that either of them could think of getting up to breakfast. But there was one comfort. Mr. and Mrs. Hope breakfast in their own room. Only Miss Burrowes (Mrs. Hopes niece) and Mr. Harness were at the breakfast table. This whole first day was uncomfortable as you may guess. But this day all is well and bright and happy. Honora and Fanny are both refitted and we have had charming walks and drives. Fanny first was taken out in a carriage and then had a little walk with Mr. Hope and me—a beautiful walk through *the* deep dene!—Larch and young beech just come out?[2] and grass as green and fresh as Erin's—birds singing—lambs feeding and soft April air everything to delight Fanny going out for the first walk after her illness. She fixed on a beautiful place for a seat which Mr. Hope says he will have there and will call Fanny's seat. Nothing

[1] In 1813.

[2] Question-mark thus in MS.

can be more courteously kind than Mr. and Mrs. Hope are to us. I am very glad to see that her looks have improved much within this last fortnight and her spirits are better but she has too little to do too many real good fine things and too much time to think over painful recollections. Her living children are both fine boys and they will in time I hope reanimate her.

Mr. Hope keeps up in my mind the opinion I early formed—not of his taste, for I think his taste is the worst part of his mind, but of his information and general powers of conversation. In a very long tete a tete walk I had with him he gave me a history of the progress of architecture so perfectly clear that it might have been written down as he spoke it and your dear father and Louisa would have admired it and Leslie Foster with all his memory and all his accuracy could have found no fault. The most *entertaining* part of the conversation however was on persons not things. You may judge of the degree of our intimacy when I tell you that Mr. Hope related to me the whole history of his love courtship and marriage and moreover of Miss Berrys courtship of him—disappointment—anger—and quarrel with Mrs. Hope[1]—All of which I must reserve for future fireside conversations. One detached anecdote however I am afraid of forgetting and it is too good to forget.

When Mr. Hope was a young man and Captain in the Marylebone volunteers he was at a city dinner at his Colonels. A young lady sister to the lady of the house sat beside him at dinner. He was shy and she was shy and not a word passed between them during the first course but towards the end of the second the young lady as it is supposed feeling it incumbent upon her to do the honors of her sisters house and to say some thing to the young stranger and recollecting that he was just returned from his travels and that he had been at Constantinople she hummed several times and at last the first sound of her voice he heard in this question 'Pray Sir how many concubines has the Grand Seignior?' Mr. Hope was so entertaining during this walk that it was as much as I could do to enjoy the beauties of Nature. But so beautiful a walk and with such a variety of beauty I never had in my life and my companion judiciously refrained from pointing out beauties or forcing admiration from me. He

[1] See D. Watkin, op. cit., 17–18.

gently turned or stopped when we came to any delightful point of view but that was all and after a long walk one day he took Fanny and me again over the part which I had liked best to shew it to her. Nothing can be more obliging and kind than he is to us. I dare not attempt any description of grounds or country. All I can say is that I hope you will some time see them for yourself and that my present pleasure is incomplete for want of your sharing it my dearest mother and friend. I long also to have my aunt Ruxton with me but one cannot have everything—Tiresome old trueism which meets one at every turn of life.

This house is in its present condition scarcely handsome in its external appearance. The stable at the bottom of the hill looks like a vast square brick manufactory. The house like some of the views in *Athenian Stuart*[1] of Turkish buildings grotesque and confused among trees in no one particular taste and besides flaring in red brick instead of stone or marble. Mr. Hope assures me that many churches in Lombardy in particular that famous church in Milan Santa Maria delle Grazie is of red brick. I am sorry for it and I am glad that he intends next year to stucco this house and to take off the reproach from himself of having 'set the valley on fire'.

This house is magnificently furnished but to my taste much too fine for a country house even putting the idea of comfort out of the question. There is too much Egyptian ornament—Egyptian hieroglyphic figures bronze and gilt but all hideous. In one room called the Egyptian room there is a bed made exactly after the model of Denon's Egyptian bed[2]—a sofa bed broad enough for two alderman embossed gold hieroglyphic *frights* all pointing with their hands distorted backwards at an Osiris or a long armed monster of some sort who sits after their fashion on her hams and heels and hath the likeness of a globe of gold on her lappetted, scaly lappetted head. In another room there is a

[1] James Stuart with Nicholas Revett was the author of *Antiquities of Athens* (1762). Supplementary volumes by various hands had appeared in 1789, 1795, and 1816.

[2] See Denon, *Voyage dans la Haute et Basse Egypte* (1802). For Thomas Hope's taste in furniture see *Household Furniture and Interior Decoration executed from designs by Thomas Hope* (1807). Honora E commented that Deepdene 'with all the most costly furniture' was 'without those means of comfort which most English houses are so remarkable for'.

really curious collection of Raphaels designs of ornaments for the Vatican—from Titus's baths—something like those at Lord Sunderlins. How could Raphaels genius turn to such conceits—for instance branches of trees with groups of singing birds mocking an owl! I should never finish or should make a description fit for an auctioneer if I went through all these rooms. The French furniture is rich and beautiful mahogany veneered more exquisitely and shewing in better taste the veins and knots of the wood than any English workmanship I ever saw but all with clumsy keys as you saw in Paris. In every passage and hall there are collections of frightful monsters in bronze or stone or plaister. One bronze *genius* as I am told he is, about my own height with outstretched long arm offends me most, because I am obliged to come across him ten times a day in passing to my own door. I could with pleasure knock him down and break him in pieces. (Private. The first night I came here the impudent monster kept me a quarter of an hour prisoner in the water closet because I mistook his shadow for the shadow of a real man standing near the door. Do you wonder I owe him a grudge?) There are sundry mechanical impossibilities too in some of the statues which hurt my mechanical feelings for instance a resigned female Cariatides of white stucco whose head in eternal pillory supports a heavy staircase while her feet stand on a globe so small that it could never support her and it seems always slipping from under her—also a slice of a bronze candelabra figure in the dining room with arms painfully holding 12 candle branches heavier and larger than herself and without a resting place for her poor feet—on the contrary with a cruel gold basket hung on her ancles! But most I feel for a classical figure never so used before to my knowledge—The slave taking the thorn out of his foot—a cast in bronze on a pedestal but the pedestal so small that the leg on which the thorny foot is crossed has no support but sticks out in mid air—An eternally painful impossibility that hurts my eyes whenever I go into the dining room. There are some beautiful things however—for instance two casts of Canova's heads of Perseus and Paris and a Psyche of Thorwaldsen's. By the by that Danish stone cutter has jilted the highborn Scotchwoman—the Miss McKenzie who fell in love with him. He found that her fortune was not equal to his expectations and he has set off for

Iceland—One way of curing a lady's love. We have had no company here but two or three gentlemen Mr. Harness—agreeable and open hearted—Mr. Moore son of the late Archbishop of Canterbury clever but too much of the Poco curante for me—but not for the fashion—squinting a little and with a mouth that opens crookedly and lips that express scorn but a cela pres very agreeable and high bred and fond of his own comforts as Lambeth could make him! Of Mr. Sharp I need say nothing. You know him and his magic lantern of good things. Some new figures on the slides—Miss Burrowes Mrs. Hopes niece has been the only *femul* we have seen tho Lady Rothes and others called but we escaped from them. Miss Burrowes has been well-*mastered* and has travelled and all that but is but an insipid personnage with a flat back and well curled hair. She can *tell* a little about Florence but all her words and movements are so measured that I long to shake her to see if I could shake the affectation out of her and to satisfy myself whether there is or is not any thing else within her. She always moves with her toe pointed down on the carpet and as if she was winning her way between brittle glass or precious china and moving, or standing or sitting she seems evermore as if she had the fear of the five positions[1] before her eyes. But poor thing! as Mrs. Candor[2] would say, Who knows but she thinks it her duty and the whole duty of woman? But Mr. Hope really likes her and says that though a spoiled child she is not the least selfish . . .

Sunday morning . . .

Farewell Mr. Hope calls me to walk. G. Bristow in full feather with a new coat. Mrs. Hogan the housekeeper calls him 'that old gentleman of yours who is always walking about the grounds.' Tell Molly—Love to Kitty—*Hate* to all other inquiring friends . . . affectionately yours Maria E.

½ after 5 oclock. Just returned from a most beautiful walk with Mr. Hope. I have used the word *Beautiful* in so many different tones of admiration within this last hour that I am afraid I have almost worn it out so I will let it rest as I am instructed to let

[1] In dancing.

[2] The scandalmonger in Sheridan's *School for Scandal*.

the Galvanic battery[1] Miss Sebright gave me, rest whenever it is tired that it may recover its power to act.

Pray tell Sophy Ruxton all about Lord Carrington and our intention of going to High Wycombe the 1st of May. She says she is surprised that I do not mention Lord Carrington. Bless her I have not time to mention half the people and things I ought to mention. I could not write to her this moment unless you were to cut me in bits and give me two heads and 2 right hands. When I can only write to one you dearest mother have the first claim of affection duty and gratitude—Lucky and pleasant when all those three go together. I never can thank you enough for lending me Fanny. You shall soon have her back again I hope the better in health and in happiness for her journey. She has just come in from her poney ride and liked it. But here I was interrupted by a dreadful disaster—Mrs. Hope came softly stealing into the the little room where we were all three writing and in her hand she held a superb Malachite necklace and cross with gold chains! Oh mother I admired a piece of malachite in a marble table the other day and Mr. Hope explained to me that there is only one mine of it in the world in Russia. And Mrs. Hope has given me this necklace! And I could not refuse her her lips trembled so and she was in such agitation about it.

Fanny is well. She has ridden out every day on a nice little poney with Henry Hope on a ditto and a servant on a prancing chestnut like Wat Tyler. I would not let Mr. Harness, who much desired it, ride with them instead of the servant on said prancing horse because I am told he is a bad rider and I should have been in an agony the whole time beside the real danger. Yesterday we went in the carriage and Fanny rode to see Wotton Mr. Evelyns most beautiful place—Woods worthy of Sylvia indeed![2] The distance from Deep Dene about four miles. Fanny rode there and back without fatigue. The whole ride delightful through lane and village with every variety of landscape and banks rich and gay (better than rich and rare) with primroses,

[1] An apparatus for the production of electricity by chemical means. It was at this date merely a scientific toy.

[2] John Evelyn, *Sylva* (1664). Wotton was famous for the landscape gardens laid out by Evelyn in 1643–52, the earliest attempt to make a genuine Italian garden in England. The house was even in ME's day a great mixture of styles from 1640 on.

violets orchises in profusion—White thorns and fruit trees in full blossom—neat cottages and old English country houses of all sizes from noble to simple. The house at Wotton is not pretty but up and down old fashioned and interesting from being Wotton with all its traditions. We sent up to ask permission to see the library and an old thin stupid wizzen looking Mr. Evelyn received us with goodnatured awkwardness and told us we were welcome to see whatever we pleased but he knew nothing about his ancestors or their pictures by which he was surrounded. All he could tell us was that there was a portrait of Mr. Evelyn with his book in his hand and he *did* also know a portrait of Tillotson. The library is not nearly so large as Edgeworthstown library nor so pleasant—More like Brianstown—but filled with choice old books all growing damp. The oaf said 'Aye here are more books than I shall ever read Im sure and there are some up there that never were down I dare say since they were put up.' He turned out some old prints before us and old plans 'Since you are curious to see such things.' He was very civil and we were very ungrateful for thinking him insufferably stupid.

Mr. Harness is as far from stupid as possible. I like both Mr. Hs all three *H*s very much—Hope—Harness and Hitchings. Mr. Harness is one of the most natural characters I ever saw and Mr. Hitchings an excellent clergyman. Both appear the more amiable for liking each other as they do.

I must go out—Mrs. Hope waiting. Adieu. We have been very happy here. Tomorrow by tea time at Grove House. Ever affectionately your scrawler Maria E.

To Mrs. Edgeworth

Grove House, Kensington Gore, Tuesday, 26 April 1819

Dearest mother, Here we are again with this kind friend Lady Elizabeth Whitbread who met us with open arms and open heart at the head of the stairs when we returned and made us feel immediately at home again in her house and as if we had never separated from her. Everything in our rooms prepared in perfect comfort for us—The low arm chair at the fire, the footstool—the writing table turned to the right way for the light for me. Oh my dear mother politeness in the manner of doing kindness, as you and aunt Ruxton so well know adds incalculably to the value of the favors conferred.

Fanny who is scribbling to you says she has told you what a dreary drive we had from Deep Dene to Kensington and how completely we were prevented from enjoying the sight of Richmond by rain-fog. I came round by Richmond on purpose because my aunt Ruxton was so fond of it and I wanted to see and to shew it to my companions. Fanny had seen it and had her own recollections! But we have had so few little disappointments of this sort during our journies that we have no right to complain . . . [end missing]

To Mrs. Edgeworth

Grove House, Kensington Gore, 30 April 1819

I suppose your mind is by this time quite at ease about Fanny's health: if it be not it may be so my dearest mother for she rode 9 miles yesterday and was not the least tired and not only in my opinion but in that of all who see her she looks and is better than she has been since she came to Town. If admiration and admirers could preserve health she certainly would be in rude health. What do you think of her having been taken notice of by the Persian Ambassador yesterday as she was riding in the park with Mr. S. Whitbread—True upon my veracity! I have Mr. Whitbreads word for it not contradicted by her own very modest suggestion that it was the poney which his Persian Highness noticed. N.B. She has a new brown habit which fits to admiration. Seriously as she was cantering in the park they saw approaching the Persian embassador in his black turban and scarlet flowing robes and with a very long bushy black beard mounted on a beautiful horse, attended by two Persians and a great number of English gentlemen—of the first distinction no doubt. The embassador was walking his horse quite slowly and all the others did the same. Fanny and Mr. Whitbread pulled up their canterers and walked them slowly to have a full view of men and turbans. His Persian Excellency then did himself the honor to point to Fanny with his stick saying at the same time some words with emphasis to the gentlemen with him. These words have been interpreted (that is humbly supposed to signify) that she is far fairer than his far famed Circassian—whom by the way his Excellency it is said is willing to give to whoever will have her, since she has been seen by the eyes of men and consequently has lost all value in his eyes!

Mr. Whitbread who has become quite Fanny's gentleman in waiting attends every evening to know when and how and where she would be pleased to do him the honor to ride with him the next day. (I am sure Fanny is a fine example if any were wanting of the truth that gentlemen always run after ladies who will not run after them.) Besides riding in Hyde Park yesterday they went for me to Alpha cottages in the Regents park in No. 2 of which Mr. Heaphy resides. Fanny carried a message to him about Charlotte's drawing of the Irish dance which he has undertaken to have well engraved for me. Mrs. Stewart has sent me the original drawing so we have every possible means of having it done as well as it can be done. I am at this moment in expectation every minute of Heaphy who is to breakfast here. Wilkie is now in the breakfast room. He has undertaken to get the Knave and the Slave engraved for me. These are the only two I will have done.[1]

Honora is riding out this deliciously fine morning with Mr. Whitbread. I entreated her to do so and Fanny's and my joint persuasions seemed to join with her own inclinations. She has been out since half after eight and it is now near ten. She has gone the same ride which Fanny took a few days ago through pretty lanes &c and with a *moving termination* in prospect—to see steam engine and saw machinery of *Brunel's* Battersea[2] and the method of making moiré metallique.[3]

My last scribble to you I think ended at the moment when I was going with little Francis to Lord Greys. Lady Elizabeth Whitbread did not like to go with us; the associations she says

[1] Charlotte E's drawing was engraved by W. Cox, and *The Knave and the slave* (also by Charlotte) by G. Lewis (*Memoirs of RLE* (2nd ed. 1821), ii).

[2] Brunel's saw-mills were at Battersea (see above, p. 65).

[3] Or fer blanc moiré, 'a variegated or clouded appearance like watered silk, imparted to metals for ornament' (*O.E.D.*). In Apr. 1822 Harriet Edgeworth wrote of visiting a Mr. Barton at the Mint who made steel buttons in imitation of mother of pearl.

with former times are so painful in that house and with her brother *there* that she cannot bear it. She said 'I know you will do your business better without me. I could not command myself, or you would see me struggling painfully and *you* would feel for me I know and attention would be distracted. In short I beg you will go without me.' Were we not right to obey? She warned us that with Lady Grey as well as with Lord Grey it is essential to be very punctual—Neither too soon or too late. Dear Jack *her* that is *our* excellent coachman was there to a moment. As we passed through the hall and found the two footmen at different landing places on the stairs ready to announce us we saw the hand of the clock pointing precisely to *one*. Lady Grey received us most cordially. Lord Grey with his most encouraging and benevolent smile entered directly into conversation—took little Francis by the hand sent for the sons of his age to introduce him to. Francis spoke and looked so like a gentleman and gentlewomans son and like a boy of sense and honesty and courage that I am sure Lord Grey was pleased with him. His eyes said so. The only little thing that gave me a *squangy* feeling was that Francis at every question of Lord Grey's repeated *What!* before he answered. I never told him of it at the time but laughed about it with Lady Grey afterwards who politely told me how often she had felt the same sort of vexations about her own children just at the moment when she wanted them to be perfect.

Lord Grey told us an excellent story of a boy Sir Charles Moncks son at school with his son who ran away from school because his father sent him back to school one holiday. The boy 9 years old went off with two shillings in his pocket travelled 120 miles was overtaken by his father and police officers . . . but I have not time to tell it *well* now. I must only *memorandum* that at first setting off he paid a debt of sixpence out of his two shillings to a pastry cook. This and other anecdotes which Lord Grey told us I mention to prove that he was not so reserved as he is said to be in general. Lady E. Whitbread says it was wonderful! and an incontestible proof of his liking us. He asked Francis many questions about his school affairs and was very kind to him. We kept Francis at Lady E. Whitbread's this night. *I* invented and we all three *executed* sleeping three in a bed that

F might sleep in Honora's little bed. Mr. Whitbread being at home his bed could not be had and the measles are at Mr. Battye's. Our bed was an unusual size five foot nine! So we slept better all of us than we had done for a week before and were as happy as possible particularly when we imagined you my dear mother looking down upon us and scolding us. The reason I kept Francis was because we had engaged to breakfast next morning with Lord Carrington and I wished irresistibly wished to take him there. It is the only time I have ever kept him beyond the due hours. I rejoice that I did so. Lord Carrington spoke as if *I* had done *him* a particular favor by bringing him. All the family hailed him at once as if they were perfectly acquainted with him from Lord Carrington's description—Frank—this is Frank—dear little Frank! Lady Carrington is so much improved by her travels and liked Frank Fanny Honora and to the best of my belief myself so much that I quite love her . . . Affectionately your M E.

To Mrs. Edgeworth

High Wycombe Abbey,[1] Tuesday, 4 May 1819

My dearest Mother, You always calculate so well that your letters hit their mark exactly at the predicted time and place. The evening we arrived at this delicious place your delicious letters were put into my hand at the tea table in the library. Thanks a thousand thanks for all your kindness to myself. Stale! How can such kindness ever be stale. To Fanny your expressions of approbation and affection are delightful. If she wanted cordials she could have none equal to these but in fact she is quite well mind and body, quite free from *ennui* and every other mental malady. She rode the first stage and it was 16 miles *sixteen!* not the least tired—went the rest of the way in the open carriage.

We found Sneyd and Harriette here: they had arrived a quarter of an hour before us and Lord Carrington and two Miss Smiths the eldest and Miss Georgiana Smith who came down

[1] Lord Carrington's house.

on purpose to receive us and who had arrived a few hours before us. We met in the library (45 feet long) the most agreeable room I ever was in opening into a conservatory which I formerly described to you but which now appeared to me infinitely more beautiful than when I first saw it because it was full of roses and flowers of every hue in full bloom.

This house is by far the most agreeable and finished and furnished in the best taste of any of the fine houses we have seen and the place is most beautiful. But—for there is no pleasure in this life without a *but* Honora has caught cold (not in the open carriage she avers and I believe it was coming on before). She had a crick in her neck and this morning lay in bed *wisely* and is now up and much better sitting with me and Harriette in a most comfortable sitting room (scarlet cloth and black furniture—Large Wyatt window[1] plate glass—tables most comfortable). This room Lord Carrington brought me into this morning and said 'I beg you to consider this room as your own while you are here. I made it for my own writing room.' Then he opened a beauteous escritoire 'Lock up your papers here.'

I should never finish if I detailed the instances of his kindness and politeness. The most pleasing to me are those which he shews to *dear little Frank* as he calls him. This morning he asked me to drive through the grounds with him in his cabriolet while the rest of the party came in a baruche. Seeing me look back at Francis he offered to make room for him between us and took him up and talked to him most agreeably about little Pakenham —lions—elephants &c told him a story similar to that my grandfather records of Lady Edgeworth's presence of mind about the candle—*gunpowder* and barrel of black salt.[2] We had a charming drive and all that was wanting to my happiness was to have had you my dearest mother and Lovell and all of you here. *Only* 5 of my family are here you know. It is surprisingly agreeable to

[1] Similar to a Venetian or Palladian window, without the semi-circular head in the central portion.

[2] *Memoirs of RLE* (2nd ed. 1821), i. 12–13. RLE took the story from his father's MS. Black Book of Edgeworthstown. See H. J. and H. E. Butler, *The Black Book of Edgeworthstown* (1927), 3–6: the maid had unwittingly left the candle in the attic in a barrel of gunpowder which she thought was black salt. Lady Edgeworth went upstairs and took it out before any damage was done.

see so many well known faces of my own in every cloister *pale* in this abbey . . . affectionately yours Maria Edgeworth

Lest I should forget it I must tell you that Wyatt[1] who was to have altered this Abbey for Lord Carrington according to his own fancy and according to his own scale of expense began by bringing him in a bill for the sash frames of the library and two or three other rooms—sash frames of oak and beech—gothic, total £1048. At the same rate of going the whole house would have cost a hundred thousand pounds. Therefore Lord Carrington stopped his hand and checked his pride—formed a plan of his own brought down to his scale from Wyatts and instead of ending as some improvers do by living in a jail now enjoys his delightful Abbey . . .

To Mrs. Edgeworth

7 May 1819

Of all the houses and places I have seen Deep Dene, Norbury, Wotton, Wimbledon Trentham, Bowood, West Wycombe and Dropmore,[2] I should if the choice were offered to me and a fairy waiting this moment in her car for my answer, chuse High Wycombe Abbey not for magnificence, but for comfort good taste and beauty—take house and grounds together.

We have within these last 8 months received so much *kindness* that we are become quite connoisseurs in that article both as to substance and mode. No one in both has exceeded Lord Carrington. The usual Edgeworth terms for going to friends houses were far exceeded by those he gave. Not only house and carriage and servants at our service but he actually went down to the country nearly thirty miles, in the height of the London season and took two of his daughters with him and three or four servants on purpose to receive us—invited not less than five of our family to fill his house—which house and everything in it and about it from the moment we entered till we quitted it was devoted to our use and pleasure.

Lord Carringtons kindness to little Francis was unceasing.

[1] Wycombe Abbey was reconstructed by James Wyatt *c.* 1804.

[2] No record survives of the visits to the Locks' house, Norbury Park, Surrey, or to Lord Grenville's house, Dropmore, Bucks.

And I must say that no boy could behave better or do more credit to his education. Lord Carrington indulged me in always inviting him (much to the inconvenience of his own driving) to sit between us in the gig. I wish you had heard all Francis's conversations. He is an excellent exemplification of my father's principle that nothing is ever lost that is well learned and that feeding the mind with knowledge of all sorts is the way to have good conversation. His memory has indeed been admirably cultivated. Not a fact he has read or heard but he uses it in its right place and season. We were talking of cruelty to animals. The best fact produced was his—that some anatomist had been so cruel to dissect a hedgehog alive to shew how tenacious of life this animal is. The hedgehog never sent forth any sound of complaint during the operation. We were talking afterwards of fine horses. Francis repeated the two descriptions of horses which he learnt with Fanny—Dryden's Virgil and Pope's Homer—one beginning 'The fiery courser when he hears from far'[1]—The other beginning [blank in MS.][2]—asked which we preferred and gave his reasons for his preference of Homers. When we were talking of Mr. Pitt and I asked Lord Carrington if he knew Dr. Darwins compliment to him in the Botanic garden

> Hear him ye senates hear this truth sublime
> He who allows oppression shares the crime.[3]

Francis knew and helped me out with the 'twinkling gem from beauty's ear'. When we had been some time silent in a dull part of the road Francis started this question 'Maria! which would you rather—not be able to hear—or not be able to speak—would you rather be deaf or dumb?' It was a very entertaining subject to us all. Lord Carrington talked more and brought out more stores of anecdote and literature this morning than I ever heard from him. He was quite delighted and animated by the pleasure he took in this boy. Oh my dear mother how often I wished for you. But I assure you Francis did not know how much we admired him. Lord Carrington repeated for him the verses from Oxford and Cambridge upon the King's sending

[1] Dryden, *The Georgics translated from Virgil*, Book III, ll. 130 ff.

[2] Probably Pope, *Homer's Iliad*, Book VI, ll. 562 ff. 'The wanton courser thus, with reins unbound . . .'

[3] Erasmus Darwin, *Botanic Garden*, Pt. II, Canto III, ll. 387–8.

troops to Oxford and *books* to Cambridge.[1] Speaking of extempore wit he told us the reply lately made by a Swiss to a Frenchman. The Frenchman insulted the Swiss soldier with 'Point d'argent —Point de Suisse. Vous Suisses vous vous battez toujours pour de l'argent, nous autres François c'est pur l'honneur que nous nous battons.' 'Oui on se battent toujours pour ce qu'on manque.' (I believe for *battez* and *battons* you should read combattez and combattons &c but I have not time to make it right. You must put it in good.)

At Lord Le Despensers former place West Wycombe there is in the rock upon which the house is built a cave of great extent in which he and his strange profligate absurd Medmenham Abbey set held their orgies and where at great expense he made a representation of the infernal regions—the river styx—Charon's boat &c The Styx is collected from rivulets in the rocks and is let down or kept up just as company come or do not come! Here he had Pluto and all the infernal deities. In the house are preserved portraits of him and various *ladies* in the habits they wore at these orgies! Strange folly of profligacy![2] To this I am sure Mr. Cobbe might say What bad taste! . . . Once more Yours affectionately Maria E.

[1] 'The King, observing with judicious eyes
The state of both his universities,
To Oxford sent a troop of horse, and why?
That learned body wanted loyalty:
To Cambridge books, as very well discerning
How much that loyal body wanted learning.'

Joseph Trapp, *On George I's Donation of the Bishop of Ely's Library to Cambridge University*.

'The King to Oxford sent a troop of horse,
For Tories own no argument but force.
With equal skill to Cambridge books he sent,
For Whigs admit no force but argument.'

Sir William Browne, *Reply to Trapp's Epigram. Nichols' Literary Anecdotes* (1812), III. 330.

[2] The activities of Sir Francis Dashwood, later Lord le Despenser, and his friends (the Hell Fire Club) were probably much magnified by gossip. They met chiefly at Medmenham Abbey which was rented by Sir Francis and there is no real evidence that they used the caves at W. Wycombe. A list of the group is given in *Passages from the Diary of Mrs. Philip Lybbe Powys*, ed. Emily J. Climenson (1899), 381. What has been supposed to be an account of the Medmenham Abbey set is given in the eighteenth-century novel *Chrysal, or the Adventures of a Guinea* (1771).

To Mrs. Edgeworth

Byrkley Lodge, Friday morning, 14 May 1819

My dearest mother . . . We spent 3 days at Mrs. Moilliet's very agreeably. We went one day to see Hagley and the Leasowes (Shenstone's)[1]—Honora Emily Moilliet and Susan Moilliet in Mrs. Moilliet's chaise. Mrs. Moilliet, Mademoiselle Bernard the governess and myself in our open carriage and Theodore with George in the seat behind—Fanny on a nice little Welch poney of Mrs. Galton's Mr. Moilliet riding along with her. She rode about 20 mile that day so you may conclude she is pretty strong . . . Mrs. Moilliet was most affectionate in her whole manner and conduct to us. She is very fond of you and was exceedingly interested in all we told her of Lovell's late conduct.[2] Honora had sent my aunts your letter giving an account of the Sheriff and jail business but Mrs. Moilliet is to have it. We sent it to her today. Her children are fine fat chubby slow creatures who would all put me out of patience except the eldest Emily who tho too slow is very pretty and interesting and genteel and *simple* and classical in appearance—like an antique figure on a vase. Mrs. Moilliet herself is fatter even than when you saw her—quite a heavy mass in person—much older in appearance than her age . . . [signature cut out]

To Honora Edgeworth

Holyhead, arrived here 3 P.M. Tuesday, [2nd June 1819]†

Alas my dear Honora the boxes and small portmanteau trunk

[1] The home of the poet William Shenstone (1714–63) in Worcestershire. The grounds were a famous example of landscape gardening.

[2] 'Lovell (my eldest brother) has set an excellent example in this part of the country this year as Sheriff: by doing all that was formerly done by military force, by the civil power only—he walked himself with constables, without soldiers to conduct the prisoners through an immense crowd in the town of Longford to and from the jail—and when he as sheriff executed the dreadful duty of attending the executions of the condemned, he attended without any of the military. There was perfect tranquillity and perfect silence—very unusual in such cases in Ireland—ten or twelve thousand people assembled . . .' (ME to Dumont, 29 July 1819 (MS. in Bibliotheque Universitaire et Publique, Geneva)).

sent by Miss Greaves from Lichfield have not arrived. We cannot therefore send your black things nor have we without the portmanteau trunk any trunk or box in which we could put your goods from the carriage-large trunk which, sent by *dear* Jack has arrived safely. After conning over your list of wants in Fanny's possession we have decided that it is best not to send you any thing. The wants do not appear urgent and the expense of buying a box, or the hazard of sending them in a parcel added to the certain expense of said parcel altogether decide me against it . . . I will direct Harriet Beaufort to open the box which contains the mourning and take yours thereout as soon as it arrives in Dublin and she shall keep it there ready to be sent over to you if you should through any public mourning be put to your last gasp for want of it . . .

Nothing new however can I find to tell you from Knutsford. Mrs. Mary Powys tell my aunts is exactly the same as ever

'The objects altered but the *fuss* the same.'[1]

How she can find so many things to fuss and discomfit herself about every hour and minute of the day is quite surprising and still more astonishing it is that it has not yet worn her out or worn a wrinkle the more in her forehead or an ounce of flesh off her bones. There she is at 75 well-struck with her body so well cushioned with fat that throw her which way you will, out of a three pair of stairs window if you please and I would engage fall which way she would she could not break a bone so well cushioned are they. Then her mind! as active as wideawake as susceptible as at 15 and her senses so acute! So much too acute for her own comfort or the peace of her neighbors that some other of my friends who deplore decaying sight or hearing may really be consoled as suffering the least evil of the two. She convinces me that excess of irritability is worse than defect of excitability —for the bystanders. Apropos to dinner, Apropos to breakfast, apropos to everything she sees she finds something to fret or rather to fuss about. One morning when she came to breakfast she had not been in the room half a minute before her Lynx eye espied a spot of ink not larger than a minnikin pins head upon

[1] 'The object altered, the desire the same': Matthew Prior, *Henry & Emma*, . 579.

a plate across the table. 'Whats that Ma'am I see there! Something or other very extraordinary upon that plate—Jane Jane. That plate—this plate is not clean Jane!' &c Jane her maid is an absolute angel in temper and will certainly have a high place among angels. When I found how little our good friend has been altered in the daily, minutely habits I quite rejoiced my dear Honora that my aunts did not put my bright scheme of coming to Knutsford into execution. How infinitely happier they are in the forest at quiet Byrkley Lodge and with you my dear. Mrs. Mary Powys is as well known and understood at Knutsford by all the Hollands and their connexions as by any of us and what is surprising she is fully and justly estimated, her great and good qualities as well as her petty foibles and fussings and except at the moments when the little blisters torment the patient beyond all patience she is really loved and respected. She has wonderful energy and benevolence and a warmth of heart that has lasted without cooling one degree from youth till 75. The morning we went away there was she up in her dressing gown at ½ past 5 and at our door before we were dressed to wish us one more good b'ye. We never displeased her once in any thing large or small and we blessed our stars at the end of every day! and could hardly believe it when it was well over! She was certainly gratified by visit—liked Fanny very much—was quite tender towards her—paid her the greatest compliment she could pay her 'I think Ma'am Miss Fanny has a likeness to the first Honora[1] . . . she certainly has.' I did not answer she certainly has *not*. On many other occasions she said she was an *Edgeworth*. So she is and *I am glad of it*. Upon the whole including all my fears and all together I rejoice much that I paid this visit and I leave my fathers oldest friend now living satisfied with me. Nothing could be more kind and affectionate than the Hollands. Mr. Holland grew so fond of Fanny he could hardly bear to part with her. Miss Mary Holland gains very much upon acquaintance. Lucy is a good natured goose.

We dined with Mr. C Cholmondeley and met a man who has a passion for seeing men hanged—cant stay away from an execution and yet is a soft goodnatured youth. Saw many good

[1] Daughter (d. 1790) of RLE and his second wife Honora Sneyd. Like her mother she died of tuberculosis.

prints of Florence gallery—British Ditto—Who'd have thought it—and the Simplon in a China model—very paltry.

We walked in the rows at Chester to 3 booksellers to try to get Lord John Russells speech and Ricardo on bullion[1]—in vain—bought a lilac ribbon—called at the post office—no letter from Honora—called at Bangor post office—Ditto. We crossed Conway ferry luckily when it did not rain. Fanny liked it—Sketched it. A man in a blue callimanco[2] sur tout galloped down the bank just as our boat was putting off. The boatman staid for him with all signs of reverence—a Welch Mr. Tuite in manner tho not in dress or beauty—Mr. Lloyd the master 'I am sorry to tell you ladies you are under my command—But I am at yours.' I asked him to pay for us. He did most courteously saying he blushed to be obliged to take our money. It was a long days journey 88 miles to Bangor Ferry—quite light enough though raining—a *latent* moon. Arrived near eleven—all in bed and great knocking to rouse the sleepy heads—George helpless as at Joanna Baillie's gate—waiting till somebody should come to do something for him. 'I never see such a place as this for an inn. There's nobody at all coming nor stirring.' But we got in at last and two night capped Welch maids gave us at last a good bed and a lemon and hot water and much Welch and English mixed and we slept well through all the noise the wind could make under door and over window. I forgot to tell you that I was afraid of being robbed half the stage between Conway and Bangor ferry by a man in a pink plush waistcoat who would run after the carriage and who seemed in Welch mysterious confederacy with the driver who never would go out of a certain pace and got off and walked with this man. It proved however only a confederacy about a draught of ale. All's well that ends well and we laughed at our fears when they were over. I would have been horribly sorry to have been robbed of 40 good pounds . . . And now give my love to my dear aunts and good bye. I ought to have been writing 6 other letters while I have written this for my own diversion and yours. Maria E.

[1] D. Ricardo, *The High Price of Bullion, a proof of the depreciation of Bank Notes* (1810). Lord John's speech is perhaps that given on 18 May in support of Tierney's motion for a Committee on the state of the nation, a general censure of ministers.

[2] A glossy woollen stuff, twilled and chequered in the warp so that the checks appear on one side only (*O.E.D.*).

1820–1822

EMBOLDENED by the success of her English visit in 1818–19, when Maria had finished preparing her father's Memoirs for the press she set off with her half-sisters Fanny and Harriet to visit France and Switzerland. In April 1820 on their outward journey through England, though they did a little sight-seeing, they paid no visits, but on their return in December they went to Clifton to see their sister Emmeline King and stayed at Bowood and Easton Grey before going back to Ireland in February 1821. Seven months later, in October, the three set out again for England on another round of visits and to spend a season in London. Their main purpose was to make a pleasurable excursion, but, just as in 1818 Maria had taken her sister Honora as companion partly in order to give her wider opportunities of finding a husband than were available in the Edgeworthstown neighbourhood, so she now wished to do the same for the younger pair. They returned to Ireland early in June 1822. Both the visit to the Continent and this later English visit were paid for with £2,000 from the profits of Maria's books, in particular *Harrington* and *Ormond* (1817). These last two books had been written in great haste in order that her father might be able to see them in print before he died and she had determined never to spend on herself 'one farthing of the income of that Harrington and Ormond dreadfully earned money'.[1]

To Honora Edgeworth

Mrs. Watt's, Heathfield, April 1820[2]

I was much surprised at finding that the postillion who drove us from Wolverhampton could neither tell himself, nor learn from anyone up the road, along the heath, at the turnpike, or even in the very suburbs of Birmingham, the way to Mr. Watt's!

[1] ME to Mrs. E, 13 Oct. 1818. Hunter had paid £1,150 for the copyright.
[2] MS. missing. Printed from *Mem.* ii. 48–50.

HARRIET EDGEWORTH

From a skiagram ($\frac{1}{3}$ original size)

I was as much surprised as we were at Paris in searching for Madame de Genlis;[1] so we went to Mr. Moilliet's, and stowed ourselves next day into their travelling landau, as large as our own old, old delightful coach, and came here.

Oh, my dear Honora, how melancholy to see places the same —persons, and such persons gone! Mrs. Watt, in deep mourning, coming forward to meet us alone in that gay trellice, the same books on his table, his picture, his bust, his image everywhere, HIMSELF nowhere upon this earth. Mrs. Watt has, in that poor little shattered frame, a prodigiously strong mind; indeed she could not have been so loved by such a man for such a length of time if she had not superior qualities. She was more kind than I can express, receiving Fanny and Harriet as if they had been of her own family.

Mr. James Watt, Mr. Tuffin, and the Moilliets dined here. Mr. Tuffin told us of a premium left by a London citizen of the name of So for the best epitaph on his name—

'As *So* lived, so did *So* die,
So, so! did he so? *So* let him lie.'

The following, which Mr. Watt avers to be on a real tombstone in a churchyard in Birmingham, even Irish confusion of head and heart could hardly surpass:—

'Oh, Death, how couldst thou be so unkind,
For to take her, and to leave me behind?
To have taken both, or to have left neither,
Would have been better for the survivor.'

Emulous of this, Mr. Tuffin tried to match it by an inscription on a board set up by a London shoemaker:—

'Such are these cruel taxing times of yore,
Which our forefathers never knew before.'

In the morning I fell to penning this letter, as we were engaged to breakfast at Mr. James Watt's, at Aston Hall. You remember the fine old brick palace? *Our* Lady Holte affronted the lady of Sir Lister Holte, and hence it was left away from her.[2]

[1] *Mem.* i. 161–9. The Edgeworths visited Madame de Genlis in 1803.

[2] Sir Lister Holte left Aston Hall, Warwickshire, to Heneage Legge, nephew of his first wife, instead of to his brother Sir Charles. It was built 1618–35 for Sir Thomas Holte.

Mr. Watt has fitted up half of it so as to make it superbly comfortable: fine hall, breakfast room, Flemish pictures, Boulton and Watt at either end. After breakfast, at which was Mr. Priestley, an American, son of Dr. Priestley, we went over all the habitable and uninhabitable parts of the house: the banqueting room, with a most costly frightful ceiling, and a chimney piece carved up to the cornice with monsters, one with a nose covered with scales, one with a human face on a tarantula's body. Varieties of little staircases, and a garret gallery called Dick's haunted gallery; a blocked up room called the King's room; then a modern dressing-room, with fine tables of Bullock's[1] making, one of wood from Brazil—Zebra wood—and no more to be had of it for love or money.

But come on to the great gallery, longer than that at Sudbury, —about one hundred and thirty-six feet long,—and at the furthest end we came to a sort of oriel, separated from the gallery only by an arch, and there the white marble bust of the great Mr. Watt struck me almost breathless. What everybody went on saying I do not know, but my own thoughts, as I looked down the closing lines of this superb gallery, now in a half ruined state, were very melancholy, on life and death, family pride, and the pride of wealth, and the pride of genius, all so perishable.

To Lucy Edgeworth

17 April 1820

My dear Lucy,

This *short-bread* perhaps you will not like but you must taste it and make all the tea table round your bed or Crampton-frame[2] taste it. It was given to me by Miss McGregor Mrs. Watts sister—a true and worthy McGregor as ever was born—and it was made at Glasgow by two young men who are called the philosophical bakers. Their business is baking—their pleasure is

[1] George Bullock (d. 1815) was a producer of English buhl furniture. He started his career in Liverpool.

[2] Lucy Edgeworth had a spinal complaint. Mr. (later Sir Philip) Crampton was the surgeon and an old family friend.

science. Their business followed with great punctuality enables them between times to follow their pleasure and it is their pleasure to make excellent thermometers and barometers which have introduced them to the notice of all the men of scientific note in Glasgow and Edinburgh.

Times as Miss McGregor observed are much improved since the drinking club used to meet in Glasgow at which a man drank himself to death at one sitting and when one of the company observed 'Mr. Lindsay I think is looking very grim' another answered 'Grim! why maun he has been dead this half hour—but I would not break up good company by noticing it to you'. When one of this good company was between 60 and 70 and a good aunt said to him 'It is time for you now to take up and live a soberer life for you are growing into years'. The other replied 'In years womann! Why when Methusalem was my age he hadna yet got on his first briggens (breeches).'

I am afraid this wont make you laugh without the help of Miss McGregors true Scotch pronounciation and look but give me credit dear Lucy for the wish to amuse you. Eat shortbread but not short allowance. Give me the great pleasure of hearing that you are not in pain and believe me very affectionately yours Maria E

To Dr. Beaufort

Maidenhead Bridge, Half after 9—
Wednesday night, 19 April 1820

Mr dear Dr. Beaufort—I have wished for you so often within these three last days that I cannot number the times sometimes for your own sake that you might have the pleasure of seeing what peculiarly suits your taste, sometimes that you might sympathise in the pleasure Fanny and Harriet have felt but more frequently have I wished for you my dear friend to give us the advantage of your taste and information in that peculiarly kind and polite manner in which 'you teach as though you taught us not'. Continually have I regretted, especially in seeing *architectural sights*, that I had not your knowledge on these subjects for my own sake and for the sake of my sisters. How much we have seen without knowing or being able to profit by all we have seen within these 3 days you will guess when I name Aston-Hall—Kenilworth Castle—Warwick Castle and Oxford!

Aston Hall a fine old brick mansion built in a quadrangle in King Charles 1st time with *balls* from Cromwells soldiers in its thick walls has lately passed from the Holte family and its entailed possessors into the hands of its present tenant Mr. Watt son of the great steam engine Watt. He has shut up half of this immense mansion including *the kings-room*, the *banqueting* room —'Dick's haunted garret gallery' &c. A great gallery of 136 feet long remains also unfurnished; that part of the house which Mr. Watt has furnished has been fitted up with good sense and more taste than could have been expected. He has such an unassuming amiable simplicity of character and such pious enthusiastic admiration of his father and gratitude to him for the wealth which his genius earned that we were exceedingly interested for him. This made me wish the more for you my dear Doctor that one who like him could and would have profited by your hints and experience in architecture and convenient arrangement and furniture might have had this advantage.

Yesterday leaving Mrs. Moilliets near Birmingham after an early 7 oclock breakfast we proceeded to Wroxall Abbey[1]—Miss Wren having requested me to call upon her namesake and relations there and having given me a letter of introduction. Mr. Wren is a well informed gentlemanlike man who reminded Fanny and me of Mr. William Beaufort though his eyes and complexion are dark—Mrs. Wren a comely portly active Rubens wife looking lady with a Hans Holbein sort of headress meant I believe for a Scotch bonnet of black velvet with an immense plume of feathers. They received us most kindly—shewed us all that they had done and intended to do to the Abbey—all the little dens of nuns cells, now servants rooms and cloisters and refectory now offices and chapel and turrets and stairs without end. One part of this abbey was built in King Stephens time. Mr. Wren appears to have considerable information on architecture and antiquities and here I often wished for you to

[1] In Warwickshire. It had been bought by Sir Christopher Wren in 1713. The main part of the building was Elizabethan, though some of the nunnery remained. The house was pulled down in the 1860s.

confirm me in my opinion that all he had done was well done and I know you and Louisa would have delighted in the books of architectural prints and collections of Sir Christoper Wrens which he spread before my unworthy eyes—And much about gothic and Saxon arches and different kinds and dates of gothic so reminded me of you that I felt absolutely at home and comfortable and I almost took root in an hours time in Mr. Wrens' library. We were obliged however to up-root ourselves in an hour or two and leaving a promise most politely pressed from us to return if we could this way we proceeded to Kenilworth Castle on our road to Warwick.

And there we viewed the remains of this vast palace-Castle—Caesars tower—Lancasters building—Elizabeths *dressing room*—Leicesters great banqueting room and the tilt yard where to pleasure her gracious majesty Leicester expended so many thousands upon thousands—where all was once mask and revelry, and now all silence and ruin!

Even with the assistance of a good book on the antiquities of Warwickshire with which Mr. Wren had provided us and with a plan and manual which an old woman thrust into my hand at Kenilworth we could not well make out the plan of the whole fabric—And at every arch and every window and moulding marking different styles how I did wish for you my dear Sir who would have made us understand ten times better than we did all that we saw and would have literally put tongues in stones.

Warwick-Castle was new to Fanny as well as to Harriet. They were both delighted with it. It struck me I think more this second time of seeing it than it did the first. We spent an hour and half there and I hope I shall see it again when we return. It is altogether the most beautiful thing I ever saw. And in the hall and in the armoury, and in going through the pictures and at the keep, and on the terrace and at the Warwick vase[1] and every where we wished for you and for all you could have told us. Fanny and Harriet had at least the next best thing to a *good guide*, one who left them to exercise without interruption their own taste and observation. I dare not begin to dilate or I should not sleep this night but I may just note that some of the pictures

[1] A very large marble vase of the fourth century B.C. It was found at Hadrian's Villa at Tivoli and presented by Sir William Hamilton to the Earl of Warwick.

we liked the best were *Ignatius Loyola!*—Duke d'Alva Gondemar—and—Circe—Ganymede and the Muse of painting by Guido. I mention these because I daresay you and Louisa remember them all. The vase is beautiful!

But I must get on to Oxford. I had written to Mr. Russell brother of Mr. Russell of the Charter house—found an answer at the Roebuck—exceedingly regretted absence on a college progress &c. but had deputed a young friend—travelled well informed gentleman—Mr. Biddulph to shew us Oxford. Mr. Biddulph came—very gentlemanlike—very agreeable. He shewed us as much and *no more* than we could well see in three hours—the rest we are to see on our return. We saw the schools, the theatre,[1] the Bodleian library, Kings [*sic ?* Queen's] College chapel—New College—Christchurch and Maudlin. In Maudlin chapel the altar piece our saviour bearing the cross (by some Spanish painter name unknown)[2] struck us particularly. H and F liked much Sir Joshua Reynolds and Jarvis's window,[3] *seen through the opening in the organ*[4]—And in New College chapel we admired Westmacott's sculptured white marble altar piece—Our saviour taken down from the cross—most beautiful![5] The Bodleian library with all its pictures and portraits delighted Harriet.

I did not think it possible that after having seen Oxford and Warwick with my father and with all the recollections of this I could ever again have felt so much pleasure in revisiting these places but I have felt great pleasure in shewing them to my dear sisters and feel with gratitude to Providence the wonderful power he has of creating new interests in the mind from our affections even springing from what we have lost forever . . .

Excuse abrupt ending—very late but better late than never.

affectionately your grateful Maria Edgeworth

[1] The buildings round the Schools Quadrangle, under the Bodleian Library, and the Sheldonian Theatre.

[2] *The Bearing of the Cross* by Francesco Ribalta (*c.* 1570–1620).

[3] In New College. It dates from 1778–85 and was executed by Thomas Jarvis from designs by Reynolds.

[4] This organ screen was put up in 1789–94. It was designed by James Wyatt and had a Gothic opening in the middle to give a view of the Reynolds window. The screen was replaced by a new one in Sir G. Scott's restoration of 1877–81.

[5] Richard Westmacott's altar is almost the only survival today from the Wyatt restoration.

To Mrs. Edgeworth

Sittingbourne, 20 April 1820.

. . . Nothing has happened worthy of note this day but that we have had a delightful journey—Fanny and Harriet almost all day in the Baruche seat. Harriet was charmed with the views at Richmond—Chatham Gravesend etc.—In Kent the hedges and horse chesnuts and many others quite out in green leaf and the gardens!—one continued garden I may say for many miles from Richmond beautiful! The fruit trees in white blossom seemed as if Nature had used her best powder puff during the night. As Fanny quoted from Denham it was

'A shower of blossoms and a wild of flowers.'[1]

As we passed some of these gardens I recollected your wish for carnation seed and I watched every face in every garden by the roadside till I saw one to my mind—A man hard at work in his own garden a very pretty flower garden all gay with almond flowers jonquils &c. I stopped the driver and *motioned* to the man—liked his countenance and after some previous questions asked if he could let me have good carnation seed. 'Oh yes and welcome—but rooted plants would be better.' So I made him whip out of the ground in a trice 50 rooted years old carnations of various sorts—names too tedious to mention—to say the truth I had not time to hear them. I divided them in two parcels and packed them in the carriage and send this night 25 to Sophy Ruxton and 25 to you dear mother. I hope they will reach you alive and if they prosper and you like any of them pray call them by the names of your 3 daughters F H and Maria. . . .

Yours affect. Maria E

To Mrs. Edgeworth

York Hotel, Dover, 21 April 1820.

. . . As I have *detailed* to Dr. Beaufort all our proceedings and as Fanny is now writing to Honora I will not go back to those

[1] 'A snow of blossoms and a wild of flowers' (Tickell, *Kensington Gardens* (1722), p. 4).

Oxford past-times further than to say that I rejoice that dear Harriet has secured so much of Oxford and we will see more with Russell or Biddulph on our return. I have now seen Oxford so often that I begin to be really acquainted with the principal objects. The picture of Duns Scotus in the Bodleian library (by Spagnoletta) never struck me before but I daresay you remember how fine it is. He made a vow you know that he would fast till he had copied the bible. The portrait is taken or supposed to be taken when he is copying the last chapter of revelations and wasted to a skeleton. It is very fine. It is at the end of that gallery where the *wings* of great copies of the cartoons stand out from the wall. It hangs in a corner opposite the window. Another curious picture had also quite escaped my attention till this time of seeing—Annibale Caracci's picture of himself his wife and mother and family in a butchers shop and in the character of a butcher and family. This picture he is said to have drawn on purpose to mortify the pride of his mother—a worthy and *pious* motive.[1]

Mr. Biddulph, when we were looking at the theatre where all the princes Emperor and potentates assembled at Oxford told us that he was present when the Prince Regent entered.[2] There was dead silence as he stepped over the threshold—then loud applause—for him—But on another occasion (as Mr. Biddulph told us) Lord Grenville the moment he took his seat in his velvet chair as Chancellor was assailed with loud hisses and groans.[3] Mr. Biddulph said he admired the dignity with which Lord Grenville behaved and the dignity and presence of mind with which the bishop of Peterborough (Parsons) rose and said in Latin 'Either this disturbance must instantly cease or I instantly must dismiss you from this assembly'. Dead silence instantly ensued. I omitted to mention this to your father *because* it was exactly what I had resolved to tell him.

[1] The picture of Duns Scotus hung in the University Picture Gallery, in what is now the Upper Reading Room of the Bodleian Library. Carracci's famous picture was and is at Christ Church. The 'wings of cartoons' are probably the copies by Cooke of the Raphael cartoons at Hampton Court, given to the university by John, Duke of Marlborough.

[2] The Prince Regent brought the allied sovereigns on a state visit to Oxford in 1814.

[3] Lord Grenville was not a popular Chancellor because he refused to support the university in its opposition to Catholic Emancipation.

To Mrs. Edgeworth, 21 April 1820

Canterbury

9 o'clock—breakfast—and excellent in a light bow window room—A very sensible civil master in this inn—The King's head. He says that many travellers who go to see the cathedral here on their way to the continent tell him on their return from abroad that they have not seen anything in France that ever struck them so much.

returned from Cathedral

We have spent an hour and a half at the cathedral walking above about and underneath. We were happy in being accompanied only by a discreet guide who never spoke till spoken to and said no more than just the thing he ought. I think my dear mother that we did not see this cathedral when we were here together? I was never so much struck by the sight of any cathedral. I prefer it to Gloucester—Lichfield and *York* as well as I remember it. The mixture of Norman and Saxon and Gothic architecture in the parts of the edifice as they were built at different times the lower part being saxon arches and the upper Norman little disproportioned pillars and capital of no *proper* orders may perhaps hurt the eye of a connoisseur architect but even these things on my ignorant mind encreased I think the *aweful* effect by marking the length of *time*, the lapse of generations which had been employed in raising this edifice and which had passed away even before it was finished—parts of it as old as Alfred—then added to by monarch after monarch. The idea of such successive numbers of human creatures of all degrees and all variety of views and interests so differing in opinions yet joining in the same religious *sentiment* and the same work completed not till after centuries and lasting century after century produces an effect of *moral* sublime on the mind which is I think beyond what can be raised by the mere view of regular orders of architecture. You recollect I daresay that here Thomas a Becket first reigned in all his proud prelacy and then was murdered and we saw the shrine at which he took refuge in vain and saw the *fresh stones* placed in the stead of those which stained with his holy blood were conveyed to the pope at Rome. And then we saw the chapel where Henry the 2d was scourged for this murder. And in the subterranean part of the church we afterwards saw the chapel called the chapel *of our Lady of the undercroft* where there was a virgin Mary in silver and a richly dight shrine canopied with precious sparkling gifts of the penitent or *humbled* Henry before which shrine he was forced to come to do penance. This shrine and all this vast subterranean part of the church was lighted up when the princes and Emperor came to see it in 1814 and it struck them our guide said more than any other part of the church. Here is also in this souterrain a French chapel for the refugees.[1]

How all these things and ideas meeting in one spot hurry the mind backwards and forwards in history with marvellous effect. Every thing seen in this cathedral conspiring to impress the idea of the perishable nature of human grandeur! and human talent. My old friend the Black prince's tomb is in this place—He stretched at his full length in crumbling stone and the very coat of mail he wore at the battle of Cressy with the fleur de lys still visible on it—his glove and helmet all hanging over his effigy. While we were looking at these tombs of departed men and monarchs all laid low and at these high arches raised by the hands of the dead the solemn sound of the organ had a fine effect. Service was over but one lone chorister had stayed to practice with his master.

As we were leaving the Cathedral Harriet called me back to look at an inscription the exact words of which I cannot remember but the sense is as follows and I am sure it will strike you as it struck me with the resemblance to what we have heard my father express.

'No monument of earthly stones
'Shall raised be o'er my decaying bones.
'Sons now unthought of shall hereafter say
'T'is here . . . T'is somewhere here that Barclay lay.
'There is no need that words exalt our name
'For our good deeds alone preserve our fame'[2]

. . . ME . . .

[1] The west end of the crypt was called the French church and had been granted to the Huguenot refugees by Queen Elizabeth. By 1820 their diminished numbers caused them to use a part of the crypt which had previously been a vestry.

[2] Epitaph of Robert Berkeley, ? by Henry King (1592–1669), Bishop of Chichester, who married his daughter Anne. ME's memory of the verses is not wholly accurate.

To Honora Edgeworth

Bowood Park, Wednesday, 20 December 1820

I write to you sitting in the Bow (or beau or bay) window of the room with yellow furniture and black stars into which we were first shewn by Lady Lansdowne the day of our arrival at Bowood my dear Honora. And Fanny and Harriet are actually beside me here and it is not a dream! and my project my wishes my hopes of having them here are accomplished and more than gratified as far as they are concerned. Oh my dear Honora how everything here reminds me of you, I can scarcely believe that you are not with me and yet I must believe it and can only wish and wish and wish—impossibilities . . .

Lady Lansdowne's reception of us was most cordial and for her wondrous warm. We arrived just at 5 oclock—dusk—up to our rooms—red breeches footman lighting us up and lighting our 6 wax lights informed us 'My lady was just come in from a long walk and *gone to change herself'*—But we found her quite unchanged. Before we had unpacked the needful from our imperials (which by the by are very comfortable) and while we were without shoes and half undressed up came Lady Lansdowne herself only half dressed with a shawl thrown over her. 'I could not let you be so long in the house without coming up to see you' and holding outstretched her arms she took me in and kissed me and then received Fanny and Harriet in the kindest manner. She says Harriet is very little altered in face. They both look very well and were mighty well dressed at dinner yesterday—White merinos trimmed with white satin Ma'am—Just on a par with others there. The people here are Mr. and Mrs. Ord and son—an Eton youth—agreeable—she Lady Oxford's sister—as Lady Lansdowne says a great contrast in mind—very amiable—Lady E Fielding—more affected than at Paris and full of dress and Venetian bracelets &c—Captain Fielding her husband very gentlemanlike and agreeable—Mr. Hallam—not so contradictory as of yore—The two Mr. Vernon and Granville Smiths—whom you remember with Mrs. Og—Mr. Fazakerley—very clever—Miss Vernon and Miss Fox best of all. Alas they stayed only yesterday—went off at 6 this morning. They introduced F and H specially to Miss Fox their niece—Lady Hollands daughter—very handsome—modest—agreeable—*not come out* yet. Besides these are two girls of 9 or 10 daughters of Lady E Fielding and today all the Romilly sons are expected and Mr. Whishaw tomorrow—Lord Kerry just come from school much improved. Lord Lansdowne your dear Lord L. I have not mentioned because I have not seen him. He was engaged to an Agricultural meeting and dinner at Bath—returns today.

Our man servant whose name is *Raines* suits the day which is *rain rain* rain. Moreover and what is more to the purpose he suits us—24 shillings a week and expenses back—Lucky to get him—ready dressed Ma'am—good blue coat—and surtout—hat —watch—umbrella all complete—from a gentleman's and lady's family that day—good character—very respectable and respectful and exact in obeying orders—comes to our door 3 times a day for *commands.* You know how necessary this is here where one might be murdered and buried before any body could *answer the bell* . . .

Now as to Rosamond[1]—Thank you my dear is the beginning and end. I think the pricked map upon the whole better out and have seen the proof sheets and left it out and repaired and beautified the print gallery so that you will walk in it with more satisfaction I trust. For the reasons your Judicious-ship gives I had determined before I received yours against inserting a packing up quarrel. The proof sheets come to me regularly. Those now before me end with Betty Hands epistle So you see we are near a close . . .

Yr. ever
Maria E

To Honora Edgeworth

Easton Grey,[2] 26 December 1820

My dear Honora I intended this frank for my mother but by mistake Mr. Ricardo turned it into Miss E and I was obliged to write to you. So you see you are not or ought not to be in the least obliged to me for this epistle—And why I asked for a

[1] *Rosamond: A Sequel* (1821). The pricked map was a plan of the streets of London to be made by Rosamond for blind Kate.

[2] Gloucestershire, Thomas Smith's house.

frank at all I cannot tell except for the honor and glory of having a frank from David Ricardo. He has been here one whole day and a quarter of another and encountered a desperately cold wind in a gig merely to have the pleasure of spending said day with us. Now this is what I call paying one a compliment in earnest and very grateful we are for it especially as he was exceedingly agreeable which makes gratitude exceeding easy. This house is delightful—in a beautiful situation—with river—old trees—fine swells and vallies and soft verdure even at this time of the year so that 'What must it be in summer time!' continually occurs. The house, convenient, comfortable, perfectly neat, without the teizing precision of order—the library-drawing-room furnished with good sense—delightful armchairs low sofas—stools, plenty of moveable tables—books on tables and in open book-cases and in short all that speaks the habits and affords the means of agreeable occupation. In short Easton Grey might be cited as a happy model of what an English country gentleman's house is or ought to be—perfectly well-finished well furnished well warmed well appointed in every respect and a striking contrast to French chateaux—the establishment in all its parts in excellent proportion. Mrs. Smiths easy unaffected well bred kind manners and Mr. Smiths literary and sensible conversation make their house one of the most agreeable I ever saw.

Last night he read to us from a book of manuscript treasures two admirable letters of Mackintosh written when he was in India and addressed to Mr. Whishaw. One was on his project of writing a history of England and described the qualifications necessary for an historian and in the description gave proof of his possessing them. Mr. Smith also shewed us some little unpublished poems of Lord Byrons and some notes of his in a copy of Scotch Bards and Reviewers which do him honor and which Harriet has copied into our book so that you shall all see them —in time.

Mrs. Smith has given me a book which belonged to my dear Mrs. Chandler. It is a collection of poems and letters of Mr. and Mrs. Days and of Mr. T Lowndes's which Mr. T L published it seems some years ago and which nobody ever heard of.[1]

[1] *Select Miscellaneous Productions of Mrs. Day and Thos. Day Esq. in verse and prose: also some pieces of poetry by T. Lowndes* (1805).

Mrs. Smith could hardly have chosen a more judicious or acceptable present for me.

But I see that the present pleasures of Easton Grey have made me forget to finish for you the account of our Bowood visit. I think I named all the people who were in the house and mentioned that the first evening *we* (at the sofa table under Callcott's picture of unloading the vessel in the Thames) played at letters and words spelling and then at Why—when and where at which we had much diversion—Mr. Hallam and Mr. Fazakerley playing with humour and good humour. Some of the words were—Bat—Eye—Canvas. Harriet made a good answer about the Bat—vampire bat and a national trait of mine. Finding an *eye* in a potato raised much laughter—*either* with me or at me. Apropos to *either*—one evening there was a discussion about the propriety of the use and pronounciation of various words and Mr. Hallam who seems to be considered as good authority (especially by himself) ruled that *either* should be pronounced *ither* and neither—*nither*—But what I was not prepared for followed. It was decided and the decision was supported by reference to Johnsons dictionary and by his examples from Shakespear and Bacon and Milton that *either* and *neither* may be used when speaking of three or of an indefinite number as well as of *two* things—to which I thought and I suppose you all think it should be restricted. Lord Lansdowne said he felt much relieved by this discovery and decision as he had often been tempted so to use these words and had refrained from the fear of grammar going against him.

At Bowood there was this time a happy mixture of literature and playful conversation sense and nonsense. One evening while Lord Lansdowne was talking to me on the nice little sofa by the fire very seriously of Mr. Windham's life and death and of a journal which he wrote to cure himself of indecision of character—Enter suddenly with a great burst of noise from the breakfast room door, a tribe of gentlemen neighing and kicking like horses. You never saw a man look more surprised than Lord Lansdowne did—putting his glass up to his eye—and afterwards same performers on all fours grunting like pigs and then a company of ladies and gentlemen in dumb shew acting a country visit—ending with asking for a frank—curtsying—bowing and exit. All this was acting a charade composed of two syllables and a *tout*—*Neigh*—represented by the first company of neighing horses—*bor*—with poetic or charade license—*boar*—represented by the grunting pigs—and the *tout neighbor* by the country visit. Another charade was still more diverting:—first syllable—*I*—Enter 2 Mr. Smiths acting *to the life* egotists delighted with themselves—followed by Lord Lansdowne Mr. Fazakerley Mr. Hallam &c. ditto—some with their fore fingers on eyebrows denoting persons in deep thought occupied solely with themselves. Second syllable *doll*—Enter Lord Lansdowne Mr. Smiths—Mr. Hallam and Fazakerley—each with little dolls made of their pocket handkerchiefs nursing them and playing with them in a most laughable manner—then exeunt and re-enter all the gentlemen carrying and surrounding Mrs. Ord who was seated in an armchair which they bore with great ceremony to the middle of the room set down and then all kneeled round to worship the *idol*. Another—Li-bra-ry—Enter all the performers one after another—Lord Lansdowne Mr. Hallam Mr. Fazakerley—Smiths—Mrs. Ord Lady E Fielding &c—the foremost telling the next and so on in dumb show something that excited surprise and incredulity denoted by uplifted eyes, shakes of heads &c—exeunt—*Lie* = Li. Re enter—braying like asses—bra—Exeunt asses. Re enter—all in succession—lame of one leg and making contorsions to represent *awry* or *wry* = to *ry*—Exeunt contorsionists. Re enter—my *tout*—people arranging a number of books for *Library*.

Perhaps this will all be very dull in the sober reading but I assure you it produced much laughter in the acting.

I was very glad that poor Miss de Lally was asked *Down* this evening—for my sake as Lady Lansdowne told me as this was our last evening. Nothing has changed in her mode of life. She has been in the drawing room but 4 times since we were there 18 months ago. Except at one time when Lady Lansdowne was alone, when Lord Lansdowne was in town and then Lady Lansdowne had her in her own room in the evening to read to her. She is however determined as we advised to stay—Mem. anecdotes for future of a letter Duchess of Buccleugh wrote about it.

Lord Lansdowne evidently cannot bear Miss de Lally. In all *other* respects I think him perfect and his conversation delightful.

He *liked* F and H—Lady Lansdowne warmer than she was in her manner to them than they expected. The long melancholy black eyed housemaid (I am ashamed to skip so suddenly from my Lady to the housemaid) but I was about to tell you that this housemaid was very glad to see me and inquired most kindly for you and shewed me with gratitude the tea tongs which I sent her—Our little German [MS. torn] Lady Lansdownes own maid *Marc* was [? as attentive] and as unaffected as ever and used to come to see what she could do for us. Once she curled Fannys hair and always admired their dress—to my satisfaction . . . Among the unprinted little poems which Mr. Smith has of Lord Byrons is a droll fragment of an epistle to his friend Hobhouse—entitled—Dear Hobby—on his democratic connexion

'And when amongst your friends you speak
my boy Hobby
How is't that you contrive to keep your
watch within your fobby'[1]

I will bring you the whole fragment . . .

Tuesday Evening [late Dec. 1820]

We have seen Badminton—pleasant drive because Mrs. Smith is always easy and agreeable in carriage or in room always the same. The French emigrants must have been exceedingly surprised by the sight of the country houses in England—not only of the nobility but of the gentry and not only of the first class of gentry but of all the subordinate classes. The size and magnificence of the great country houses and the comfort and finish of the others strike me continually.

The park at Badminton however though magnificent as to size—16 miles in circuit—is melancholy—an avenue two miles long—The house a large and dreary looking pile but the library delightful and a drawing room 50 feet long and in good proportion is an admirable room—small conservatories added to drawing-room and library make them both chearful. How this luxury of conservatories added to rooms and opening into them

[1] This is a slightly inaccurate version of a lampoon written by Byron in 1820 when Hobhouse was standing for Westminster with the radical Sir Francis Burdett (*Murray's Magazine*, Mar. 1887, and S. Smiles, *A Publisher and his Friends. Memoir and Correspondence of John Murray* (1891), i. 417–18).

has become general—enlivening old thickwalled mansions as well as new built boxes. At Badminton there is as at Trentham a chapel or village church into which a gallery in the house opens and a very handsome seat on high as at Trentham for the family. In this seat is the great curiosity of Badminton—Raphael's first sketch in chalk of the transfiguration that is of all the figures in the lower group. Tell my mother who will recollect the picture. It is wonderfully fine—The woman kneeling and the boy possessed by the devil and the man holding him and the man on the left hand side are admirable. Forgive me for noting these down—because this will recall them to my mind hereafter at home. There are several good pictures at Badminton though it is not a professed collection—4 Guidos—the 4 apostles Matthew Mark Luke and John—a Salvator Rosa and a holy family by Leonardo da Vinci which the woman who shewed the pictures told us was by *Vincy* Ma'am. There is in the drawing room a cabinet[1] brought from Italy by the 3d Duke of Beaufort as said shew-woman always carefully told us—a beautiful sarcophagus of white marble with figures in relievo bold and various colored marbles of which he had intended to build a temple but he died and the marbles remained unused for I dont know how many years. Lately the present Duke has ornamented with them the very prettiest bath my eyes ever beheld. In our climate it is fortunate for the marbles that they are under cover.

I fear I have been talking like an old catalogue—So now you shall leave Badminton. We were not frozen in going over this vast house for the whole is sufficiently heated from stoves below and hot air holes. Memm. In boring for something or other they came to a spring under the arch on which the great drawing room rests and there is now beneath it a well of pure water!

In driving away we eat cold beef with keen delight and saw with admiration a herd of red deer the finest it is said in England. Some of them were really as large as cows—Much larger than those we saw at Spy park.[2] Mrs. Smith ordered the postillion to drive up to them and they looked beautiful some standing at bay with their great eyes fixed and branching horns erect—some trotting away with their dappled young ones after them.

How shall I ever find room or time to tell you of roman

[1] Still at Badminton. [2] In Wiltshire.

pavements—roman rooms and a roman town found near this place?[1]—Much better worth than all I have been penning but I must put off all these till we meet.

For nonsense I have always time—A gentleman who was vexed at not being invited to Trentham wrote the following distich

'Tis a wonder that mongst all his punishments Bentham
'Never hit upon passing a fortnight at Trentham'

[no signature]

To Mrs. Edgeworth

18 January 1821

I write now in the most scribble haste about a maid for my aunts. I fell to work the very instant I read your postscript in Honora's received yesterday. Luckily a most excellent servant is now in our power—sister to the housekeeper who lived with Mr. Keir through all his illness—her character known and tried. I have this moment seen her. She has lived as housekeeper with a gentleman in this neighborhood but is not above putting her hand to anything—can preserve and pickle &c if required—Oh yes Ma'am would sweep and clean. She has lived also as ladys maid—her age about thirty—not pretty but good countenance—can mantua-make and do all sorts of work—is very neat but not fine in appearance—agreeable voice and no mincing manners—would undertake to do my aunts bedchamber and dressing room constantly and would overlook or look over the other house-maid. More I did not ask as I thought I could not gain it and it would be a pity to lose such a trustworthy and every way desirable person for a trifle.

But—the wages are as I fear you will think enormous—Sixteen guineas. I would rather subscribe 2 guineas towards these wages myself my dear mother than lose her for your comfort and my Aunts and so pray let that be without mentioning it to any body and name 14 guineas which is what Mrs. Moilliet gives. This woman is to provide tea and sugar for herself and no more about it. You will be so kind to write instantly and say whether

[1] Cirencester. Many mosaic floors had already been discovered there by this date. I am indebted for this information to Mrs. E. M. Clifford.

you will have her or not. Direct your answer to me here and if I am gone to William Mrs. Moilliet shall open the letter and write as we have agreed to this maid to tell her the ultimatum and to tell her if she is to come to meet me here and I will bring her over on the baruche seat which will save expense—and I can send her down from Dublin. I would not on any account take her round with me by Black Castle because I think it would incommode my aunt and she might think Maria was grown fine.

I once thought this woman might do for cook and housekeeper as she cooks well *all but made dishes* but she would not undertake it as she could not stand the fire. Moreover I presume she would not be a sufficiently good cook for you—But as housekeeper when you are absent or busy would I think be very useful without interfering with her duty to my aunts. *Trustworthy is worth almost any price* . . . Rosamond is out. Ever affecy yours Maria E

To Mrs. Edgeworth

Mr. Moilliet's Counting house,
Monday morning, 29 January 1821

Why does Maria write so often from Mr. Moilliets Counting house? Is she in love with one of the clerks? Thank you my good friends guess again. No you want to get on to something else—very likely—but you must first go through this preface which like most prefaces is nothing to the purpose. I write from Mr. Moilliet's counting house so often because all the letters come to the counting house two hours before we can get them at Smethwick Grove and I always like to see what the post brings me from Ireland and elsewhere before I write to you. This morning as we could not have the carriage so early we viz Harriet and I trudged off with Mr. Moilliet and John Moilliet—cold morning at first, delightful afterwards—all the better for the two miles and a half walk and rewarded moreover richly by finding Honora's letter of the 25th on the counter waiting for us—Dear kind Honora like Miss Belinda Portman always good, always kind always considerate.[1] Your letter saves me much

[1] The heroine of *Belinda* (1801), ME's first novel with an English setting.

suspense and delighted me by approving of all we have done and of all we are to do . . .

We shall leave this place G.W. God willing and H.W. (housemaid willing) on Thursday morning next. We shall reach Holyhead on Saturday night unless we break our carriage or our necks, which as we did not do in Swisserland I trust we shall not do on the fine English and finer Welsh roads— . . .

You perceive my good friends that I am in such high flying spirits at the prospect of coming home to you that I cannot get on straight forward with my business but must stop and stoop to crack every foolish joke that comes in my way . . . Now my dear mother I will now go rationally to business and write on the chapter of servants . . .

Chapter of Servants

If I were to begin with all the inventions and inquiries and dubitations I have had on this chapter and go on through the history of all the servants I have thought of—seen—and heard of this chapter would be a volume and perhaps a volume that would never end. Therefore leaving all that has been thought and said I shall go straight to what I have *done*—done bravely—I hope not rashly. I have actually engaged a cook and housekeeper in one. Nay start not dear mother—I had engaged her before I received your last letter saying that you could and would do without one and after I had read your letter I did not and do not repent of what I have done. She is not Sir John Wrottesleys cook. She is engaged by Mrs. Moilliet. She had an old father who could not consent to Ireland. My cook or rather your cook is between 40 and 50. She has lived eight years in the family of a Mr. Digby whom Mr. Moilliet knows well to be a very particular man about servants and good dinners—A lawyer used to entertain the *judges*—foreman of the quarter Sessions. She married went into business—her husband died—So much for her history. You see she is free from incumbrances in the first place—of a fit age neither to flirt nor drink she has a perfectly sober steady appearance—a remarkably honest countenance and when you hear her speak a good temper'd countenance but not good humored at first sight—So little that I feared to engage her on the score of temper. 'Why yes Ma'am you are right I do confess I am of a hasty temper but there it is soon over with me and with a reasonable lady I think I should never give offence.' 'The lady you are going to is perfectly reasonable and kind to her servants but she would never bear an improper answer from the best cook in the world.' Her answers and countenance thro' all this examination convinced me and Mrs. Moilliet that you would like her. Mrs. Moilliet has known her from childhood. She is daughter to a housemaid who lived with her father at Hill Top an excellent person. I do love to have servants who come of honest parentage and have been long known by some of our friends.

If I am not much mistaken this woman is a person capable of being attached trustworthy and able to supply to you in some degree the loss of our excellent Mrs. Billamore. She loves command over the servants—that she told me and she loves to be trusted. She said no master or mistress should ever find her extravagant but she did hope for the credit of the family that when a good dinner is to be given she shall not be stinted. She bakes good bread—pastry—confectionary pickles—preserves. She hopes the linen and grocery will be in her care as she has always been used to it. She is by no means fine but she has been always used to sleep in a room by herself and would prefer one never so small to sleeping in the room with other maids. I hope this can be arranged as I found it a starting off point and I could not conclude the agreement without it. Her wages with Mr. Digby were thirty guineas a year but that was several years ago. Wages have lowered since but twenty four guineas is the lowest she could take. In short I have engaged her at your own price my dear mother. You shall have her for twenty guineas and you must let me subscribe the other 4 to your annual comfort and the good of the family. It is really too hard upon you and quite unfit that you should have the cares of a housekeeper upon your hands and upon your mind—made God knows and my father knew for better things. He never would have permitted it nor will I by the blessing if I can help it and by the blessing of his generosity to me I can—without the slightest inconvenience. But sentiment apart, for sentiment and business never agree well—I have engaged to pay her expenses to Edgeworthstown and she engages that [if] she leaves you within a twelvemonth giving warning through her fault she is to pay her own expenses back but if she stays a twelvemonth and you afterwards chuse to part with her without any ill conduct flagrant on her part then you pay half her expenses back. I have warned her of every thing that I foresaw could be disagreeable at first setting out so she has nothing to discover—that she must dine with all the servants and never dream of a second table—that her housekeepers room is dark and not very convenient—that she will have turf fires instead of coal. She hopes the lady will allow her a few days time therefore to learn the difference and get her hand in. I send her per coach from Birmingham to Holyhead there to wait for us at Spensers but I trust she will not have more than an hour or two to wait.

So ends the chapter of the cook

Now for the ladys maid—Before your letter came and from the moment I had decided upon this cook and housekeeper I gave up Mary Collins the ladys maid of whom I spoke to you because she had too high qualifications and required too high wages and as she had been used to live as housekeeper—the two housekeepers would be too much for one house and all her superior qualities would be worse than superfluous would lead to rivalship of rule—misrule and contentions among the gods and godesses of the lower regions. It was besides as absurd to pay for her extra qualities as to pay for her knowing how to paint like Guido if she happened to be so wonderfully accomplished. As to scrubbing floors and cleaning grates—Oh my dear Ma'am when I saw her appear before me in a riding habit better or full as good as Fanny's and Harriet's and very like Honora's how could I propose such a thing and my aunts would never have been at ease with so respectable a personage—so there's an end of Mary Collins and her 16 good guineas per annum safe and sound.

But if there is an end of dear Mary Collins is there a beginning of a cheap and good somebody else. Ah there's the rub—cheap and good seldom or never go together. However depend upon it I am doing the impossible—and I will trample hard with my Sutton thick soaled boots upon all the prickles of the impossibilities and flatten them womanfully. Several people are now looking out for a good humored, healthy—steady phanix of a *housemaid*—for that's my word now who *can* sew and will clean and scrub 2 rooms and help make beds &c &c and run up and downstairs 100 times a day *wait upon my aunts well or unwell* . . . Postscript—A Surprise!

Yes an advertised surprise seldom answers and yet I think you cannot fail to feel some little surprise when you hear that Mr. and Mrs. Moilliet have determined to send their son James to Lovells school. Lovell is actually to bring him back with him to Ireland. He is to board as the other boarding boys do but of all this Lovell will of course write to *advise* you or to advise with you . . . I was the original proposer of this scheme—but I pointed out strongly all the disadvantages and told Mrs. Moilliet that I would not send a son or brother to any school where there was not more superintendance out of school hours and where the boys at best were of such an inferior class. All this I said *before* Lovell the morning he breakfasted with us . . . I only pray Heaven that he may not learn more vulgarity than Latin and more Irish than English. Of the Irish *brogue* Mr. Moilliet has more than a due horror. . . . [no signature]

To Honora Edgeworth

29 January 1821

Your conscious thrill of guilt diverted us all excessively and we enjoyed your remorse. I hereby send you a plenary pardon but remember as Fanny says you are bound to like the present preface best and I am afraid youll find that a hard matter because it is four times as long. The chances are then four to one against its being as neat though perhaps it may be more appropriate. That is all my hope. I suppose it is with you by this time. Hunter writes me word the sale has hitherto fully answered his expectations sixteen hundred in a few days. He had not he said heard any opinions because no one at the time he wrote had had time to read. Luckily Rosamond poor little creature had a fortnights start of the Queen[1]—To pray or not to pray for Whom is all the question at present all over England.

[1] Queen Caroline returned to England in the summer of 1820. Immediately afterwards a bill was promoted for divorcing her from the king but this was

I find mean time that you have had a sore ear and a whitlow. Sympathy My dear Ma'am. I have had a boil or a bile (v Johnson) behind my ear and Harriet a Whitlow—Good in everything! our delays have given time for these plaguing things to get well before our journey. You are sensible that poultices and dressing wounds on a winters journey would not have been over and above pleasant . . . Your ever affec Maria E

To Mrs. Edgeworth

Holyhead, Monday 3 oclock [22 October 1821]†

Monday! you exclaim dear friends but why not sunday?

Because in one word my dear friends I was a goose and slept at Merrion Street at the Hotel d'Amitié[1] because it was so very comfortable instead of coming to the hotel at Howth on Saturday night as I ought to have done. Of consequence, tho up at ½ past 5 oclock and exerted ourselves to the best of our ability *we* were just five minutes too late and our carriage would have required half an hour to put it on board. We had the mortification to see the Meteor glide off from the pier on which we stood and quick as Lightening it had gone a mile while we turned our horses heads and drove to the Hotel at Howth. I see I see Louisa's look of bitter scorn! I hear I hear Aunt Mary's gentle 'What a pity!'

We made the best however of our bad job—eat a good breakfast—walked to Lord Howth's—saw his old place—quite a *Bacon's garden*[2]—beech hedges 9 feet high intersecting kitchen and pretence to flower garden—allies of green grass and meander of gravel walk and stagnant pools &c—saw the aristocratic old castle disgraced by Plebeian whitewash—saw the room and stunted bed with high head in which King William slept—his

abandoned in November, though her reputation had been seriously damaged by the proceedings. Her name was omitted from the Prayer Book and she was excluded from the Coronation.

[1] 31 Merrion St., Dublin, the home of Mrs. Edgeworth's aunt, Miss Waller. Matthew Boulton, RLE's Lunar Society friend, had called his house at Handsworth *l'hotel d'Amitié*.

[2] Bacon's *Essays* (1625), No. XLVI, Of Gardens.

legs must have been half out of bed or he must have had the shortest ever seen—Saw the picture of Granawhule[1] (ill spelled) who ran away with the infant of the family because they gave her nothing and returned it only after a world of difficulty on condition the gates of the castle should never be shut till after 9 at night to gentle or simple. Saw! more than I can say but did not see the family tho I made known that the uncle of the Miss Edgeworths who were with me was married to the Bishop of Cork's daughter.[2] Dined—Soup soals cutlets apple pie—Slept well—2d chambermaid on shewing us to rooms afraid of mistaking what first had intended about best bedchamber said 'Are *you* Ma'am the *ladies* who *disappointed* the packet this morning?' Too eloquent and polite to say who was disappointed.

The Lightening—the packet in which we sailed this morning has turned into the Sovereign since his Majesty was in it[3]—Captain Steevens—very polite—fine voice—and Steevens beat time for he brought us in 6 hours and ¼. Fanny and H now very well—both very sick—I not so bad as usual as you may guess by *this*. I did not know a soul or body in the packet nor see any worth seeing. I staid in chaise—lay at *full length* tell my dear aunts most comfortably.

Met at Spencers a Mrs. Leicester or Lester [Lyster] one of whose daughters is married to Mr. Smythe of Barbavilla—whose other daughter has married a fine looking Frenchman. She is here just returned from Paris and looking with withered artificial flowers like a caricature of une Anglaise . . . Your ever affec. Maria E

[1] Graine Ui Maille, or Grace O'Malley (1530?–1600?), finding the gates of Howth Castle shut at dinner time, seized the young heir who was at nurse in a nearby cottage and only restored the child on the express stipulation that the gates should be thrown open when the family went to dinner, a practice which was still being observed in the early 1820s.

[2] The Revd. William Beaufort married Emma, daughter of Hon. Thomas St. Lawrence, Bishop of Cork and 2nd son of 1st Earl of Howth.

[3] George IV visited Ireland in August and September. He landed at Howth from the *Lightning* on 12 Aug.

To Mrs. Edgeworth

Cernioge, Tuesday, 23 October 1821

My dearest mother—We have had a most delightful day. After sleeping well at Gwyndu we were in the carriage and *off* before the clock had finished striking six. In an interval of showers—a bright gleam of sunshine—passed Bangor ferry and breakfasted nobly. Mr. Jackson the old old man who was some years ago all pear-shaped stomach and stupid has wonderfully shrunk and revived and is walking and alert and civil and his fishy eyes brightened with pleasure on hearing of his friend Mr. Lovell E. Fine old waiter—a match in age and civility for the master and a fine old dog—Twig—a match for both and as saucy as Foster[1] for Mrs. Twig would not eat toast unless buttered forsooth! . . .

On to Mrs. Worthingtons—Excellent motherly woman—The Mrs. Brinkley of the slate quarries—Her first questions about you and William won my heart—her manner was so kind and she seemed so to have seen into you both by the penetration of the heart which is full as quick as that of the head (if there be any difference). She and her son were delighted to hear that William is in good health. He said he never saw any young man so zealous for information. Poor young Worthington himself is rather peeky-weakee. He has a sore throat and a diamond pin to keep all snug up about his throat and *thick* inch proof cork soled shoes. I guess his mother *tends* him a wee bit too much. I fear she will lose him if she do not take less care.

There is a fate against my ever seeing Mr. Worthington Senr. Do you remember our crossing England scenting him to Liverpool and not finding him there at last?[2] Nothing could be kinder than Mrs. Worthington. She furnished us each with a pair of Devonshire clogs that fitted each as if made for us and then as her poor son was disappointed by his sore throat of the pleasure he had intended of shewing us every thing himself he gave us a note to a Mr. Williams at slate quarries and good dear Mrs. Worthington herself in her white gown and worked borders trampoozled out with us thro' the splish splash to all the yards and with her master of the works shewed us the saw mills and the mill for grinding flint etc. for china-works.

[1] ME's spaniel.   [2] See above, p. 4.

Waiving the description of these it being much too late at night to write sense I must skip to the cakes and sweet wine no —sweet beer with which Mrs. Worthington regaled us on our return to the house. This beverage was delightful yet Mrs. Worthington assures me it is only sugar and water and wort. She is to give me the receipt and I am to give it to you. I presume fermentation is to be added. The Worthingtons are one of a numerous class in England who enjoy in profusion all the physical and most of the intellectual pleasures of life without any of the shew of either—neither caring for fame on a large or a small scale and doing good from pure benevolence—satisfied with the feeling without thinking even of thanks. Lest Fannys feet should be wet at the Slate quarries about which she saw I was anxious she begged me to carry the Devonshire clogs with me and send them back by the postillion and so I did and great comforts they were. She put into the carriage after us cakes of all sorts and sizes—Some of which looked so pretty that I named them the *Taste and try* buns and others *Flat and not flats*. We eat them with a *God bless Mrs. Worthington* after two hours exertion of legs, eyes, ears, and *admiration* most fatiguing of all at the Slate quarries—Glaciers of slates! I will not say a word of these however because I wish Harriet to write her own fresh account of her own impressions. I feel that she was even more pleased than I expected she would be and I rejoice that this first *sight* which I had promised myself the delight of shewing her is *secure*. Come what will she has seen the slate quarries.

This days drive through Wales has been charming—a few showers but always at the best time for us—not a drop in the slate quarries nor when we were passing through beautiful parts. I have at different times of my life seen Wales at all seasons of the year and after all I prefer the autumn view of it. The withering red brown fern is a great addition of beauty on the white and grey rocks and often so resembles the tint of autumn on beach trees that you cannot at a distance tell ferns on the mountains from young plantations touched by autumn colour. There had been rain and enough to fill and froth all the mountain rills and streams.

But I have no more time for the picturesque. I must tell you of our manservant whom I forgot to mention I believe in my last. Mr. Jacob engaged William Gaynor the man who had lived with Sir Richard St. George. I enclose Mr. Jacob's letter to me by which you will see that he has secured with great precision all that I required about *riding* &c. *Gaynor* for so we call him—not William—is a very respectable looking servant about Richard Ruxton's size and not unlike him as Richard observed the moment he saw him—But much uglier—Richard Ruxton with a turn up nose and with his face squeezed closer together from chin to forehead—red hair and fair—and at first looking scared but that was only from the superabundant awe with which Mr. Jacob had inspired him of *me*—even little me. This is fast wearing off—I hope not too fast for I mean to make salutary use of it. He has very good respectable clothes—watch—cane—and I have added umbrella. Memm. He dropped his cane once from the baruche seat and he went back (while we waited) a quarter of a mile—found it—but I told him if he dropped it again we could not wait again. 'Very well Ma'am. Certainly Ma'am.' He is very respectful—speaks well—not at all a brogue'oneer. 'I *shall* Ma'am' is his strongest mark of Irish servant. He is not *too* clever but very attentive and *biddable* and useful in travelling. In short hitherto he seems all we wish for in a servant . . .

Good night. We have just dined at this delightful inn at Cernioge where you and Fanny slept in 1818. The inn I am sure you remember is kept by two sisters—each with sweet good humored countenances—most active obliging people—One married Mrs. Weaver—and Mr. Weaver brings in the head dish. The sister is a great favorite of Lovells and smiled most graciously when I mentioned him and said we were his sisters. I think the most discontented of travellers old growling Smollett[1] himself if he could come from the grave in a fit of the gout could not be discontented at this inn or at least with the people of this inn—A cut glass jug as bright as any I ever saw on the first tables in the land, with water sparkling from the well such as an anchorite who I suppose is an epicure in water, could not find fault with. F—H and I have just determined that if ever we are reduced to earn our bread we will keep an inn—like this.

[1] In the person of Matthew Bramble in *Humphrey Clinker* (1771), as well as in his own *Travels in France and Italy* (1766).

Lest you should think that all the little sense I had is gone to nonsense I must tell you that during part of this day we have been very wise. When there came ugly bits of road Harriet read Humboldt 5 vol narrative—and I was charmed with it and enjoyed it the more from the reflexion that Lucy can share this pleasure with us. She has Humboldt I hope. If not pray get it for her. The account of the venemous flies which *mount guard* at different hours of the day is most curious.[1] Humboldt is the Shakespear of travellers—as much superior in genius to other travellers as Shakespear to other poets. He seems to have at once a *vue d'oiseau* of one half of the world and a perfect knowledge of the other half so as to bring together from all parts of the earth and from all times observations on the largest scale from which he draws the most ingenious and useful conclusions. I will write to Madame Gautier to ask her to beg Humboldt to send me *portraits* of each of the insects that appear on the banks of the Oronooko at the different hours of the day and night—by which the natives mark the hours. It will make a fine contrast to the watch of Flora . . . Yours affectionately Maria E

To Honora Edgeworth

Drawing room, Smethwick Grove,
Thursday Evening, 25 October 1821

Here we are my dear Honora once more at the dear hospitable Moilliets, in the same drawing room where we sat together in 1819—on the same sofa with the *little* table before me—the furniture as clean as bright as if just new—every object animate and inanimate so much the same that it seems as if all the intervening time and events had been a dream from which we have just wakened!

Emily making tea at the same well furnished tea board with her slow motions and careful nearsighted beautiful eyes picking

[1] *Personal Narrative of Travels to the Equinoctial Regions of the New Continent during the years 1799–1804* by A. de Humboldt and A. Bonpland, trans. H. M. Williams (1821), v, chap. xxiv. For the Watch of Flora, below, see Erasmus Darwin, *The Botanic Garden*, Pt. II, Canto II, n. to ll. 165 et seq.: 'flowers which close and open their petals at certain hours of the day; and thus constitute what Linnaeus calls the Horologe, or Watch of Flora' (4th ed. (1799), 89–90).

her way among the cups and saucers, and getting through the arduous task of teamaker at her snails pace in a miraculous manner. The *stork's* own *beker*[1] turned silver coffee pot I am sure you remember. I am happy to tell you that it is as bright as ever and not a cup or saucer different—no alteration except in Emilys hair—much for the worse curled like Fannys but it does not suit her. She must go back to her antient Herculaneum vase looking figure. She has one of the few faces that become the parted hair fashion.

Mr. Moilliet is now showing Harriet a plan which he and Mrs. Moilliet have made out of Heldersham [? Hilderston] Hall their new place. It belonged to a Colonel Hamilton whose English wife is related to the De Salis's. He expected his father would leave him a large fortune and on speculation bought an estate to suit and raised many thousands on this estate to pay for it but the father dying left him but a very small fortune and he is obliged to get rid of the large estate as fast as possible. Mr. and Mrs. Moilliet say that Mrs. Hamilton is so amiable and the Colonel so frank that they are excessively sorry to take this excellent house from them though in fact they do them a great service. Colonel Hamilton had the place but a twelvemonth and loses £5000 by it . . .

The drive last night from 6 till nine through the *land of flames*[2] was most sublime. I cannot decide which struck Harriet most this or the slate quarry. The *blast* which we heard and felt when we were in the dark subterranean passage of that Welch giants causeway was most sublime! But I will say nothing about it.

We have just seen John Bristow. Mr. Moilliet sent to let him know we were come and this evening his day's work first finished he appeared in the Smethwick schoolroom. His first appearance is wonderfully altered by a wig—same color as his whiskers yet still it makes a great change. He looks younger—more healthy—fatter—more stumpy and Englishified—sobered—steadied into a man of business—more than I thought possible *formalised* into

[1] Probably a narrow vase-shaped vessel such as the stork used for the meal to which he invited the fox.

[2] See ME's *Harry and Lucy Concluded* (1825), ii. 158–62. The visual character of the description in the book is most unusual for ME. The Giants Causeway is on the north coast of Co. Antrim.

the Birmingham-man-machine sort. He has quite lost his petit air evaporé et effaré. The motions of his neck are stiff in his cravat and his *slow and sure*[1] in their expression—his arms quite still by his sides—So much for first appearance. But in talking to him and talking to us by degrees the Irishman wakened within him and came through the English outward case hardening—lighted in his eyes—and John Bristow was himself again—all but throwing off his wig. He was delighted to hear of Williams health. 'There never was a more grateful gentleman to me in this world nor a kinder. I was ashamed to think how good he was to me *slaving* himself to shew me everything in London. I hope the spire stands well Ma'am—and Mr. Huttons clock.[2] Oh Ma'am how glad I am.' . . .

Tell Lucy that by not arriving yesterday we have missed seeing a man who would have furnished me with materials for making her laugh—a French man who has been 17 years learning to play on the flute and cannot play and who has been ten years learning to speak English from phrase books and yet told Mrs. Moilliet that he had a letter to Lord Porcelain to whom his mothers aunt was somehow happily related. By Lord Porcelain he meant the Duke of Portland. He left this place determined above all things to see the residence of Lord *Malbrouk*. Mrs. Moilliet slowly endeavoured to set him right and to put the song out of his head which had unluckily got possession of his imagination but nothing could turn Malbrouk back again into the Duke of Marlborough. He quoted the song with the authority of an antiquarian as an old legend. Blenheim, Mr. Moilliet told him was the name of the Duke's house. 'Ah oui yes. Blenheim that is the *inn* I know.' Good night . . .

Yr. ever affec M E

[1] Thus in manuscript.

[2] The spire of Edgeworthstown church was constructed on the ground on a cast iron frame and hoisted into place in 1811. It and the clock in Edgeworthstown House were both designed by RLE.

To Mrs. Edgeworth

Wycombe Abbey, Tuesday morning, 30 October 1821

Fanny p'on honor is very well—
self ditto—Harriet not worth
mentioning.

We spent two days instead of one at Smethwick because our seeing the Moilliets at Hildersham Hall in Spring seems uncertain. Nothing could be kinder than they were to us and they speak with so much gratitude and affection of you and Lovell that even if they did not like us as they do to an extraordinary degree we could not help loving them and feeling quite at home with them. Nevertheless as dearest friends must part we parted from them Saturday last had a delightful journey to Woodstock —went not to the same inn which you and I went to Honora, where the drunken youths tumbled downstairs but to the Bear— and such a civil Bear! that I intend hereafter always to say as civil as a bear—But the first words I heard were 'You cannot see Blenheim tomorrow Ma'am because it is sunday'. Now one of my chief objects was that Harriet should see Blenheim which she had expressed a particular wish to see. F and I had only a glimpse of the pictures when half dark the last time we were there.

Imagine our disappointment! But I set to work with a note to Mrs. Fellowes the housekeeper and the result was that if we could see it before church time the next day she would shew it and we might drive all through the grounds. Joy! Up between 6 and 7—Coffee and bread butter a la Francaise in our own room—Left our own loaded carriage—Mr. *Master of the Bear* furnished us with an elegant chariot—nice easy baruche seat for F and H—delicious morning—just enough of the autumn tint upon the woods—drove for an hour and a half through the magnificent park stopping at every fine point of view. I was delighted by the satisfaction expressed by my dear companions and the only interruption to the pleasure of this morning was the regret I felt that my dear Honora had not enjoyed the same. She had the tooth ache when she was at Blenheim and besides I was an idiot then and had not thought of *driving* through these grounds. I had fancied by walking we could see enough—quite impossible.

At ¼ past *nine* the hour appointed for seeing the house we were at the door and civil Mrs. Fellowes was at her post in the hall. She let us enjoy the sight of the pictures saying no more than just the thing she ought and I will endeavor in that to follow her good example. F and H will tell you that they were pleased and you may be sure I was happy—not the least tired though admiration of all sorts and particularly admiration of pictures is in general very tiresome when it lasts above an hour.

At—Oxford—by twelve o'clock—Letter from Lord Carrington most punctual of men waiting for us at the Roe-buck—happy to see us 29th time appointed &c—But no letter from Mr. Russell—sent the porter with a note to him. There is a fate against our ever seeing him—answer—Mr. Russell is gone to see his brother at the Charterhouse. Porter trudged again with 2 notes—One to Tom Beddoes—not at Oxford—not *come up* this term—Another note to Mr. Biddulph—He most civil and alert of College Cicerones arrived almost as soon as the porter returned with his '*very happy*'.

Tell Honora that this time I did not call Mr. Biddulph Mr. *Shepherd*. He walked us about to all those College Halls and beautiful College gardens which we had not seen before—Balliol and University gardens—beautiful—At Corpus Christi fine altar piece—rested at Mr. Biddulph's most comfortable rooms—saw plans of Repton and Wyatt for improvement of Maudlin—Wyatts beautiful gothic but requiring £100,000 to execute.[1]

All Oxford is now in a ferment about the Review of Classical Education in the last Quarterly. It is written by Sandford the new Professor of Greek at Glasgow and the passage about malignant dullness is said to be meant for Copleston who was his friend—Copleston wrote advice to a young reviewer &c[2]

[1] James Wyatt's designs were made 1791–5. Humphrey Repton's designs are dated 1801. For an account of both projects, see T. S. R. Boase, 'An Oxford College and the Gothic Revival', *Jnl. of the Warburg and Courtauld Institutes,* xviii (1955).

[2] The article is in the *Edinburgh Review,* xxv (July 1821). It is a review of Andrew Dalzel's *Lectures on the Ancient Greeks* (1821). 'malignant dulness' is on p. 304. Copleston's *Advice to a Young Reviewer* (1807) was a parody of the style of criticism in early numbers of the *Edinburgh Review* and he later had a prolonged controversy about Oxford education with this periodical.

Mr. Biddulph is a fellow of Maudlin. The life of a fellow of a college he says he has liked for 3 or 4 years then got tired of it and hated for 4 or 5 and absented himself. He observes that men shut up in colleges are apt to grow stiff in all their opinions and this *uncontradicted* life is dangerous. Memm. He confirmed former information that between 2 and 3 hundred pounds support a gentleman and not a farthing less at Oxford. The Colleges are now so full that a young mans name must be written down 3 or 4 years before he can hope to get in—Christ church the tip top. Balliol and University are those where there are the best tutors. At *Merton* almost all *fellows*—None but gentleman commoners at Maudlin. Pembroke—Worcester and Christchurch have *exhibitions* for Charterhouse boys—to be had by those who are on the foundation or can make out founders-kin or who happen to be the only Charterhouse boy at any of these colleges. Tom Beddoes went to Pembroke—because he was the only Charterhouse boy there is likely to have the Exhibition worth about £80 a year. I huddle together all I could learn from Mr. Biddulph. It may be useful some time to our dear F. *Moral* his name must be written down at some College or other soon.

Meantime we went to Maudlin chapel—Evening service—4 o clock—going in from broad daylight—fine expect [*sic*] Chapel lighted with many candles—dim light through brown saints in the windows—Chaunting of the service good—anthems very fine—two of the finest voices I ever heard—young boy—Organ fine—Pergolesi's hymn to the virgin—F and H liked it much. Perhaps Louisa and Sophy were singing it at nearly the same time.

Mr. Biddulph dined with us—Excellent dinner—tell Honora very unlike the shabby lagging luncheon which put us to shame when Messrs. Vernon and Rothwell were with us—Exceedingly well served with the exception of one slight error of precedence —roast before boiled—Oh shameful chance—a roast loin of veal pushed in before delicate boiled chicken—But all the rest stewed eels in particular worthy of the first epicure-fellow in England—All for 5 shillings a head—Wine 7/6. The whole expense of luncheon and dinner and a day in short at Oxford at Roe Buck was within 2 guineas—very different from the Star—My stars! how different.

At parting Mr. Biddulph told me he intends to visit Ireland next summer and I gave him a *particular* not a general invitation to Edgeworthstown. I am sure you and L will like him.

Drove off in fine style—lamps lighted—without and within our carriage—for you must know I have bought a *beautiful* little lamp which Mr. Moilliet had made on purpose for me for the inside of our carriage. It fastens on a staple in the bar between the front windows. We can read by its light. When not upon duty in the carriage it is a very ornamental and convenient hand lamp and it cost—I will not tell you what. Tell my aunts that not a pin or peg stirred in the carriage during this journey. Most comfortable and luxurious it is. Thank *them* for this most delightful *convenience*. Our servant is just what we all like—respectable—alert and obedient.

During our illuminated drive from Oxford to Tetsworth Harriet repeated to us the game at ombre canto of the Rape of the Lock.[1] Thank you for two such travelling companions as no other woman I will venture to say ever had before. Good tea at Tetsworth and after tea Fanny sung to me Moore's Minstrel boy.[2] So finished one of the most agreeable days I ever spent—full but not o'erflowing with various sorts of pleasure. Two good bedchambers opening into each other—White dimity beds—fit for a king as Pakenham said of the bed at Kinnegad. Indulged ourselves till nine o clock instead of rising between 5 and 6 as we had risen on our journey. Breakfasted like ladies at 10—staid till two reading books in the *Royal Oak* inn library—'Coelebs'[3] —Harriet—'Sentimental journey' Fanny. Resolved that I would arrive quite rested and fresh at Wycombe and only just in time to dress for dinner. I whiled away the hours writing the lines enclosed on 'The travellers lamp'[4] and between this and Coelebs and Sentimental journey we amused ourselves by watching at our gazabo window the arrival and departure of 10 or 12 stage coaches—any one of which outside and in would have been a study and a fortune to Wilkie. Besides this there was the rubbing down of a horse in a new fashion—with a beesom. At first we thought the horse would have been affronted—

[1] Canto III. [2] *Irish Melodies* (1807–34).

[3] Hannah More, *Coelebs in Search of a Wife* (1809).

[4] The manuscript of this does not seem to have survived.

No—quite agreeable—The dried flakes of yellow mud first beesomed off—then brushing under stomach raised such a dust that in the dust they raised man and horse were lost.

Arrived just in dressing time at Wycombe—Honora you remember the beautiful library—Lady Carrington alone stretched full length on chaise longue left hand fire opposite corridore and conservatory—She in white satin—Very gracious but rather poorly. Lord Carrington soon appeared very kind very chearful —much better than when in Paris—*Agh!*[1] at Deal and Miss Georgiana Smith obliged to go to her yesterday staid for us 3 days—Miss Smith (eldest of forms) here Miss Emily and Miss [blank in MS.] . . .

H and F wore black gauze yesterday and will today—nobody here. Ever yours most affectionately Maria Edgeworth

This was written absolutely in the dark.

When I say we shall leave Wycombe Abbey Wednesday sennight I ought to add provided we do not some of us or all of us break our limbs or our necks on these horribly slippery beautiful floors and stairs. Honora knows how difficult it was in her time to *stand* it—worse now. The carpets on our bedchambers and dressing rooms skate about and we upon them just as the mat on the ice at Kilbixey door on the famous skating day.

Private—for Mrs. E and Honora

Paragraph of domestic news from the High Wycombe Journal

We observe with much satisfaction the elegant morning and evening toilette of two Irish *Elegantes* now at Wycombe Abbey—

Morning costume—1st morning—grey silk
Evening—black gauze

2d morning white French worked cambric muslin
Evening—White muslin over satin

3d morning—Colored muslins—much worn here
Evening—White Merinos—much admired

Mornings Ditto—white gowns and tabbinets—and Evenings afterwards a happy alternation of lace gowns—Merino—and muslin

[1] Harriet, Mrs. Crewe, one of Lord Carrington's daughters; 'Agh' was ME's nickname for her.

As the Miss Smiths have all lately been at Paris they have fine remains of their Parisian toilettes and Fanny and Harriet at all times looked as well dressed as they did—in my opinion better—the materials and make better and no flowers or [ ][1] frippery. In short I am sure you would have been pleased if you had seen them. People tell me they are very pretty and I am very modest about them depend upon it.

To Mrs. Ruxton

Wycombe-Abbey, 2 November 1821

My dearest Aunt

The most agreeable thing we have heard since we left *home*, and our second home Black Castle has been Sophy's account of your continuing well. We are heartily grateful to her for sending us this assurance. Without it we could not enjoy any of the pleasures by which the kindness of benevolent Lord Carrington surrounds us. I will go on with our history from the time of our arrival here as I am sure you have heard from Edgeworthstown of all our prosperous journey—our seeing Blenheim and our happy day at Oxford.

In the first place you who sympathise with all my feelings even about people whom you have never seen will rejoice to hear that Lord Carrington seems to me in much better health than when I saw him a year ago; and his sight is not nearly so much affected as I had apprehended. Last night he read by candlelight a manuscript of Walter Scott's verses on Pitt,[2] and did not seem to find more difficulty in making them out than I should. It is impossible to be kinder than he is to us. Indeed I feel ashamed of all that he does for us. Every person of his acquaintance whose company he thought could be agreeable to us he wrote to invite to meet us . . .

We have had Mr. Wilberforce for several days and I cannot tell you how glad I am that I have seen him again and that I have had opportunity of hearing his delightful conversation and of seeing the extent and variety of his abilities. He is not at all

[1] Word illegible in manuscript.

[2] *Marmion, a Tale of Flodden Field* (1808), Introduction to 1st Canto.

anxious to shew himself off: he converses—he does not merely talk. His thoughts are wakened and set agoing by conversation and you see the *thoughts* living as they rise. They flow in such abundance and from so many sources that they often cross one another. He leaves many things half said and sometimes a *reporter* would be quite at a loss. What he says could not be taken down. Often it is only thinking-aloud—an idea suggested and left—a quotation pointed to by a word and then turned away from as too trite. As he literally seems to speak *all* his thoughts as they occur, he produces what strikes him on both sides of any question. This often puzzles his hearers but to me this is a proof of candor and sincerity and it is both amusing and instructive to see him thus *balancing* accounts aloud. He is very lively—full of odd contortions—no matter. He is full of anecdote of all the great political and literary characters of Pitt and Fox's time. Tho the friend of Pitt he speaks of Fox with indulgence and an affection. Indeed Mr. Wilberforces *indulgent* and benevolent temper has struck me particularly. At first I apprehended that he would be much too good for me and that I should be quite too bad for him—No such thing. He made no pretension to superior sanctity or strictness—never led or turned the conversation that way—never made any side blows or probings and in the course of an hour I was quite at ease with him and I parted from him this morning much regretting that he could not stay another day. He now lives near the Hopes in Surrey and has given us a most pressing invitation to his house.

Besides Mr. Wilberforce we have had Mr. Manning (Member for Oxford) a gentlemanlike person who has travelled and lived in the world and that's all I know of him. His son a young man of two or three and twenty was with him—very unaffected and agreeable. They live in Surrey near the Hopes so that we shall probably meet again. Mr. Abel Smith another agreeable young man nephew of Lord Carrington has also been here and Mr. Hales an old batchelor—diplomatist—who twelve years ago was envoy to Sweden—afterwards to Denmark and I believe chargé d'affaires at some other courts. Since that time he has been living *to* himself and *for* himself as I should guess—Very slow and (perhaps) sure—a dry and dried man. However he told me the wittiest name I have ever heard given to Bonaparte which he says he intends to have engraved on the pedestal of his bust *Jupiter-Scapin*[1]—does not this name contain a volume?—All the sublime and ridiculous of his character in two words. This name was given to him by one who knew him well—his former friend *De Pradt* who wrote the account of the Austrian campaign and Austrian court.

Yesterday arrived Count and Countess Ludolf. He is embassador from Naples—a very agreeable man—not more of a diplomatist than is quite becoming—Volto sciolto[2]—not literary but travelled—knowing so much of the world and such numbers of celebrated people, and mixed up with so many curious circumstances that he does not want *books* for conversation. He was *of* the Empress Catherine's famous journey to the Crimea and saw the wooden villages and canvas painted houses prepared as Tooke describes[3]—Speaks English well and can talk about all common things—'Blaack-cattle *poultry yard*—you call this—and pigstye.' During our walk this morning he was very agreeable by the simple power of turning his mind to every passing object and being ready to be pleased. He knew Mr. Hope formerly at Constantinople—says Anastasius[4] is the best picture he ever saw of the manners and the country it depicts. Countess Ludolf is a grecian lady—from the Corfu—but nothing Grecian about her—more like a little Frenchwoman—with pretty artificial flowers in her cap—talking a vast deal but saying nothing.

We went one morning to see Lady Young step daughter I believe to *your* Lady Young (Miss Talbot)—A pleasing woman. She and her husband live very near Wycombe Abbey in a delightful situation. One of the prettiest villages I ever saw is near their gate—a *natural* village[5]—not one of those forced villages made by impatient aristocratic benevolence. . . .

You would never guess the anecdote in my fathers own life which Mr. Wilberforce mentioned to me as having struck him

[1] Scapin, a servant in Molière's *Les Fourberies de Scapin*, was an audacious and resourceful liar. The nickname was also used by Greville of Lord Brougham (*The Greville Diary*, ed. Wilson (1927), i. 477). De Pradt's book was *Antidote au Congrès de Rastadt* (1798).

[2] A frank, open, and ingenuous exterior: Chesterfield, *Letters to his son*, 19 Oct. 1748.

[3] W. Tooke, *Life of Catherine II, Empress of Russia* (3rd ed. 1799), iii. 164.

[4] T. Hope, *Anastasius* (1819).

[5] ? North Dean.

particularly: The two lovers who shot themselves together at Lyons.[1] In fiction as he observed this would not have struck him at all but when certain of its being truth it made a great impression. Mr. Wilberforce spoke with much respect and tenderness to my feelings of my father and of that book. He said but very little that could be called compliment, but whatever he did say or *imply* was delicately done. I am the more anxious my dearest aunt to convey to you my present impressions of Mr. Wilberforce because I am conscious that if I described him to you before it must have been in a different manner. I had *seen* him it is true but I had not *heard* him. He was then excessively tired—quite worn out. I thought he was not willing to express his mind when he was really not able—Uncharitable wretch that I was. . . . Good b'ye—My dearest aunt

To Lucy Edgeworth

Wycombe Abbey, Sunday, 4 November 1821

My dear Lucy . . . We are reading Madame de Staels dix ans d'exil[2] with delight. Tho' there may be too much egotism yet it is extremely interesting and tho' she repeats too often and uses too many words yet there are so many brilliant passages and things which no one but herself could have thought or said that it will last as long as the memory of Bonaparte lasts on earth. Pray get it and read it—not the plays or poetry which make up the last volume. Why will *friends* publish all the trash they can scrape together of celebrated people? Even Fanny is angry with M. de Stael for this want of judgment. Mr. Hales my dry diplomatist tells me that the Swedish minister assured him that Madame de Stael provoked Bonaparte by intriguing to get Bernadotte on the throne of France and that letters of hers on this subject were intercepted. You will not care much about this, but you may tell it to some of your visitants who will in due time be as full of Madame de Staels dix ans d'exil as I am at this moment.

[1] *Memoirs of RLE*, chap. xii. The two lovers lived as well as they could while their money lasted and when it was all spent killed themselves.

[2] *Dix années d'exil* (1818), ed. Auguste Louis de Stael Holstein and the Duc de Broglie.

Here is an old distich which my dry diplomatist came out with yesterday at dinner on the ancestor of Hampden. The remains of the Hampden estate are in this neighborhood and as we were speaking of our wish to see the place in which the patriot lived Mr. Hales observed that it is curious that the spirit of dislike to kings had run in the blood of the Hampdens some centuries before Charles' time. They lost 3 manors in this county, forfeit for having struck the black prince.

'*Tring, Wing and Ivangoe*
'Old Hampden did forego
'For striking the black prince a blow.'[1]

. . . . . .

Besides two spacious bedchambers and a dressing room munificent Lord Carrington would insist upon our having a sitting room to ourselves and we have one that is delightful—windows down to the ground and prospect, park—woods and river so pretty that I can scarcely mind what I am saying to you.

Bob[2] came home yesterday—25 years older since I saw him last—much *worn* out—but Fanny will not allow it. His cousin John Smith who is also here I much prefer.

Yesterday arrived a Mr. Hay—a finish man—very well informed about Mummies and Egypt &c—talks well and as if he lived with all the learned and all the fashionable in London. When I have found out clearly who he is if you wish to know I will tell you more of all that I have heard him say. His account of the unrolling of a mummy which he lately saw in London was most entertaining. All the folds of the thinnest linen which were unwound were laid more smoothly and dextrously as the best London surgeons declared than they can now apply bandages. They stood in amazement. The skin was tough the flesh perfect —the face quite preserved except the bridge of the nose which had fallen. Count Ludolf who has been a fine painter in his day, says he has used mummy pitch or whatever it is in which

[1] A version of a fourth line runs 'And glad to escape so'. This ancient rhyme, which provided Scott with the title of *Ivanhoe*, records an apocryphal incident, said to have taken place during a game of tennis at Hampden House. The Hampdens never held the manors of Tring, Wing, and Ivinghoe (*Victoria County History of Bucks*. iii. 380).

[2] Lord Carrington's only son, Hon. Robert John Smith. He visited Edgworthstown in 1813.

mummies are preserved as a fine brown paint—like bister—'only bitter to the taste when one suck one brush.' . . . Adieu my very dear Lucy we long to hear again of you Your affectionate Maria Edgeworth . . .

To Mrs. Edgeworth

Gatcombe Park[1], 9 November 1821

My dearest mother, We arrived here Wednesday evening to tea as I told you we should but an hour and half later than we ought to have been because under the fear of being too early we had idled an hour after breakfast at Oxford and we did not know how hilly the road would be. But no matter—fine moonlight night—arrived at Gatcombe about half after nine. At the gate the first operation was to lock the wheel. We went down, down, down a hill—not knowing how it was to end or when or where the house would appear—that it was a beautiful place was clear however by moonlight. We passed a kind of embattled circular wall very romantic at first view (but it was only a wall that masked the stables or kennel). A dog began to bark loud and incessantly but we came within view of an excellent house—Hall with lamp and lights very chearful—servants all ready on the steps—Mr. Ricardo happy to see us—beautiful hall—pillars—flowers but just seen in passing—into a most comfortable sitting room—family party—books open on the table.

Mrs. Ricardo is a large fat woman with brilliant black eyes and benevolent countenance—rather vulgar in voice and manner but not nearly so much as I had expected. She is *manieré* but only as if it were a manner learnt—no pretension—no affectation no thought about self. She has such cordial openhearted benevolence that I should feel not only *mean* but treacherous if I ridiculed or criticised her. 'My daughter in law Mrs. Osborne Ricardo Miss Edgeworth'—a beautiful tall figure and fine face—fair and profusion of light hair like what Harriet Beaufort's was. Mrs. Osborne Ricardo has a most modest countenance and is not bashful or awkward. Mr. Ricardo Junr.—Jewish countenance but good

[1] Ricardo's house in Gloucestershire.

—two younger daughters Mary about fifteen handsome and a child of ten, *Bertha*—beautiful.

Tea and coffee—table covered with silver tray and silver urn and coffee pot, with all manner of good things—No reproaches for being late—Comfortable bedchambers and we were left to ourselves to rest . . .

It was a very fine day—all chearful—and a delightfully pleasant house with downhill and uphill wooded views from the windows of every room in front of the house—Rides and drives proposed. I *asked to see* a cloth manufactory in the neighborhood. Mrs. O. Ricardo offered Fanny her horse. Mr. O. Ricardo rode with her. Mr. Ricardo drove me in his most safe and comfortable phaeton—Harriet and Mrs. Osborne Ricardo in a seat behind. The back of the phaeton was so low that we were all one company—The horses pretty and strong and moreover quiet so that tho' we drove up and down hills almost perpendicular and along a sort of *Rodborough Semplon* I was not in the least alarmed. Mr. Ricardo is laughed at as they tell me for his driving yet I preferred it to *dashing* driving. Sydney Smith who was lately on a visit here said that 'a new Surgeon has set up in Minchinhampton since Mr. Ricardo has taken to driving'. We had delightful conversation both on deep and shallow subjects. Mr. Ricardo with a very composed manner has a continual life of mind and starts perpetually new game in conversation.

Nothing can be more different than the style of conversation at Gatcombe park and at Wycombe-Abbey. There is much more *life* here and much more warmth and affection among the young people. This makes amend for want of manner—loud voices &c. It is really useful to the mind whether young or old to have such different modes of life, such different characters and manners, such different materials for happiness brought into contrast and comparison. The Miss Smiths (now it is over) would tire me to death if I were forced to live with them. They have no conversation—no animation. Lady Carrington sits on a sofa all day long or drives or walks out just for health and is always poorly—Very like Lady Bertram in *Mansfield park*—and the conversation of the house is like all those novels—like *Emma* in particular.[1] One of the Miss Smiths is a perfect walking red book—

[1] Despite this slightly pejorative remark ME was very fond of Jane Austen's novels.

knows all the fashionable marriages—births and deaths and who is to inherit titles and fortunes and the young ladies who are *fine* without being well bred sit with books in their hands without reading them all day or walk in and out of the library, perfectly well dressed morning and evening and one wonders how it can be worth their while to live on this way always—And one wonders how it can be worth their while to drop out of their mouths so many questions about people for whom they don't seem to care in the least. They know every body at home and abroad and are proud to tell you so but they can tell you nothing worth hearing about any body. I should be extinguished if I lived with them long and I felt that I was as stupid and more stupid than themselves when I was sitting opposite to them. I did not know how much I wanted better conversation and more warmth of character till I came here.[1]

But I must get to Rodborough to the cloth manufactory. You will pity me perhaps for being in an open carriage on the 9th of November but you may spare your pity. I will tell you how I was wrapped up. 1st my grey cloth gown—2ly. furred pelisse—3d. red shawl 4thly a large fur tippet of Mrs. Ricardo's so long so broad that I could have been wound round with it and covered from head to foot and I am sure that if I had been thrown out of the carriage I should not have felt it (the fall) through this soft elastic cushion. I should have rolled down the hill like a ball. Besides all these coverings I have enumerated I had a great box coat across my knees. In short I was as warm as a dormouse.

Harriet is writing to Pakenham the account of the cloth manufactory so I will say nothing of that except that the proprietor Mr. Stevens explained it admirably well; and that besides the pleasure of seeing it which was great, I had the still greater pleasure of Harriet and Fanny's enjoying it exceedingly. Fanny had a delightful ride of about 7 miles there and back through a beautiful country and excellent roads. Rodborough I think is the prettiest country town I ever saw and country about it is well wooded.

On our return we found Mr. and Mrs. Austen and their children and Mr. and Mrs. Smith of Easton Grey. Mrs. Austen is

[1] ME felt this so strongly that she included a general comment of this kind in *Harry and Lucy Concluded* (1825), iv. 128.

a daughter of Mr. Ricardo's—handsome—lively—clever and with a high toned harsh voice. She is accomplished—plays and sings *joyously*—Something of the sort of person that Miss McCausland[1] is or might have been if she had had a large fortune, indulgent parents and her full swing in life—*Slap dash* manners —pride of independance and sincerity—going into the spirit of contradiction and '*I like my humor well brave boys*'. Her whole character is in the *bravura* style. Yet through the whole of this character, which naturally is not agreeable to me there is a strength of affection for her husband and children and her brothers and sisters and father and mother, and a firm, high sense of duty which I cannot help admiring and loving. Even her humor would *on a pinch* submit to her sense of duty. Her husband is a cloth manufacturer of distinguished character in the country—older than she is and in ill health. She is devoted to him. A beautiful creature a sister of hers who died a year or two ago married Mr. Austen's brother. Neither of these matches were agreeable to Mr. and Mrs. Ricardo but they let their children do as they pleased. The fault of the whole family seems to me to be *wilfulness* and independant spirit gone too far or gone wrong and often mixed with a froward temper.

Mr. Ricardo is too mild and systematical to correct these defects but they all live well together and love each other dearly and they are all happy and though it may not be according to our *fashion* that does not signify. The mind becomes more enlarged and liberal from seeing great variety of modes of being happy and good. F and H have settled that Mr. Montenero[2] was like Mr. Ricardo in countenance but that he was taller and rather more gentlemanlike—More benevolent and mild he could not be. Mr. Montenero had not half Mr. Ricardos talents. I never argued or discussed a question with any person who argues more fairly or less for victory and more for *truth*. He gives full thought to every argument brought against him and seems not to be on any side of any question for one instant longer than the conviction of his mind is on that side. It seems quite indifferent to him whether *you* find the truth or *he* find it provided it be found. One gets at something by conversing with him. One

[1] An Irish acquaintance from Navan.
[2] The father of the Jewish heroine in ME's *Harrington* (1817).

learns either that one is wrong or right and the understanding is improved without the temper being ever tried in the discussion.

He has an excellent library and there are books in every sitting room—Wonderfully good eating and horses and carriages! —and affection and openness and hospitality among all the individuals of this large family. They all seem to understand and like Harriet and Fanny very much. Mrs. Ricardo in particular likes them for *tho'* she is neither polished nor literary she has great penetration and a very warm heart. But I must come to an end of this letter for we are going out to see her school. She has 130 children and takes as much pains as Lovell. N B has been horribly cheated and disappointed by one angel of a girl who finished by stealing a ring and a five pound note &c. But she is like Lovell too benevolent and too believing to be stopped in her course by such things. I envy her.

We shall go to Easton Grey—perhaps wednesday perhaps Thursday. Notwithstanding all the praises I have in all sincerity poured forth and from which you might think me in love with all these people yet I should not like to live with them. You know my aunt Ruxton said 'Maria dislikes vulgarity more than vice.' I think I have learned that absolute insipidity and the affectation of the *stillness* of fashion are *more* insupportable than vulgarity—but I would rather be without both these defects. One great use of travelling is to make one if *possible* better satisfied with home . . .

November 10th

I have seen Mr. and Mrs. Ricardo's schools and like both boys and girls schools much. They are not however at all equal to Lovells. The chief thing that struck me was that the school rooms were comfortably warmed—No flogging allowed.

Yesterday evening a Mr. and Miss Strachey dined here for the first time they had been at Gatcombe. They have lately bought a place in this neighborhood. They are nephew and niece of the Mr. Strachey whom my aunts knew at Lady Holte's. He was at Madras for many years—secretary. He is a pleasing sensible very shy *bronzed* gentleman—she perfectly a gentlewoman with something of the Sneyd appearance and manner—

at least I fancied so—a nice small pretty shaped head like Honora's—something delightfully gentlewomanlike in her voice and mode of speaking. I had a great deal of conversation with her about Lady Holte whom she perfectly remembered to have seen and Mr. and Mrs. Bracebridge and all their affairs—and Mrs. Nisbet and a Miss Harriet Sneyd whom Mrs. Nisbet took care of and of whom I know nothing but I dare say my aunts know a great deal. She is gone to India now with her brother. There was a great deal of agreeable conversation last night. Mr. Ricardo and Mr. Smith[1] suit each other delightfully. You know that the wit of conversation flies off and is not to be brought back again. However one or two scraps I recollect—an English bull of Lord Camdens—He put the following advertisement in the papers

> Owing to the distress of the times Lord Camden will not shoot himself or any of his tenants before the 4th of October next.

Mr. Cripps the member for Gloucester (I believe) speaks broad Gloucestershire dialect and some one in parliament observed that Mr. Cripps was a perfect representative for he spoke not only the sentiments but the *language* of his constituents.

Much conversation about cases of conscience. Query. Whether W Scott was right to *deny* his novels. It was decided by all the wise and virtuous that the wrong of the lie fell upon those who forced him to tell it by that [*sic*] unjustifiable questions. Paley of course quoted[2] &c. Then came the Effie Deans[3] question and afterwards much about smuggling—Lady smugglers. Lord Carrington says that all ladies are born smugglers. Lord Carrington told me that some years ago when Lady Carrington was on the coast of Devonshire and he at Deal-Castle she wrote him word that there had been a wreck on the coast and that her butler had *got* a pipe of wine for £36—that it was safe in her cellar. Now said Lord Carrington I said to myself here I am in the

[1] Thomas Smith of Easton Grey.

[2] W. Paley, *The Principles of Moral and Political Philosophy* (1785), chap. xv. Paley distinguishes falsehoods which are not lies, including answers to questions 'where the person you speak to has no right to know the truth, where little or no inconvenience results from the want of confidence'.

[3] See *The Heart of Midlothian* (1818). Jeanie Deans refused to tell a lie to save the life of her sister, condemned to be hanged for the murder of her child.

kings service *can* I permit such a thing—no. He wrote directly to the proper Excise officer and gave them notice that in Lady Carrington's cellar at such a place there was a pipe of wine which had not paid the duties. By the same post he wrote to Lady Carrington to tell her but he did not know that the offence of taking the goods from the wreck was a *felony*. As pale as death the butler came to Lady Carrington and said 'I must fly for it my Lady—to America.' They were all thrown into the greatest consternation. What did they do? At last they staved the wine and when the officers came nothing was to be found. Lord Carrington of course lost his *£36*—and saved his honor. Much discussion upon this story. Mrs. Ricardo said Lord Carrington might have done better by writing to order that the owners should be apprized that he had the wine was ready to pay a fair price for it and the duties.

Goodby my dearest mother. I live in hopes of a letter from you in half an hour. Fanny quite well today. Depend upon the exact truth always from your grateful M E

To Lucy Edgeworth

Gatcombe Park, 12 November 1821

My dear Lucy . . . We are perfectly happy here—delightful house and place for walking—riding—driving. Fanny has a horse always at her command—I—a phaeton—safe horses and Mr. Ricardo to converse with. He is altogether one of the most agreeable persons as well as the best informed and most clever I ever knew. My own pleasure is *infinitely* encreased by seeing that Fanny and Harriet are so much liked and so very happy here.

In the evenings in the intervals of good conversation we have all sorts of merry plays: *'Why—When and Where'*—our words were *Jack—Bar—Belle. Caste Plum* the *best.* Another evening Mr. Ricardo and Mr. Smith danced jigs but we were gone to bed before the jigging began and Miss Mary Ricardo objected to her fathers *doing it again* for us. I liked her reasons and never pressed for his doing it. She said it is all very well in our own family but I dont think it suits papa &c.

We acted *words*—charades last night—

Pillion. Excellent—M. F. H. little dear pretty Bertha—and Mr. Smith the best hand and head at these diversions imaginable. First we entered swallowing pills with great choking—Pill—next on all fours roaring lions—Fanny and Harriet roaring devouring lions much clapped—Next as to my tout—Enter Bertha riding on Mr. Smiths back *pillion*

Coxcomb Mr. Smith. Mr. Ricardo—F—H—and M crowing. Ditto—ditto ditto combing hair Mr. Ricardo solus—strutting coxcomb very droll

Sinecure Not a good one

Monkey—very good Mr. Ricardo and Mr. Smith—as *monks* with colored silk handkerchiefs cowls—a laughable solemn procession Re enter with *keys* My tout Mr Ricardo—monkey

Fortune-tellers—the best Fanny—Fortune—unluckily we forgot to blind her and she had not a *good* wheel and she had only my leather bag for her purse but nevertheless she made a beautiful graceful Fortune and scattered her riches with an air that charmed the world—2d scene—Mr. Smith and H—*tellers* of the house—the *ayes* have it Fanny—Maria—H—*Fortune tellers—much approved* Love sick—Bertha with a bow made by Mr. Smith in an instant with switch and red tape and a long feathered pen—Bertha was properly blind and made an irresistible cupid—She entered and shot—and all the company fell—*sick*—H—Mr. Smith and Maria all very sick—3d Fanny—a love sick young lady—Maria her duenna—scolding and pitying and nursing her with a smelling bottle size of mine of cut glass—The whole much applauded—Mr. Ricardo only wished *she* had looked at him.

Post—yrs. affec Maria E

To Mrs. Edgeworth

Gatcombe Park, 14 November 1821

Our last day here and we are very sorry for it even though we are going to Easton Grey to the Smiths whom we like much. But every day we have been here we have more and more liked the place, the mode of living the family all together and

Mr. Ricardo in particular. I cannot help regretting that my father did not know him and that he did not know my father. They would have so admired and delighted in each other though they are as different as slow and quick, gentle—and warm tempered. In all their ways of thinking they would have suited. Yesterday Mr. Ricardo so put me in mind of him by saying that if any body offered him for himself or any of his children such an encrease of fortune as should take them out of their rank of life he would not accept of it. There would be a necessity for living according to new habits and spending according to the expectations of others instead of according to his own taste &c. At the same time he allowed that if he had been born Lord Lansdowne or any nobleman of great possessions he might have been as happy as he is now.

You know we have often observed that *my* first impressions—perhaps all people's first thoughts of strangers require to be corrected by second thoughts. So it has happened about Mrs. Austen. She has much more *merit* in her good spirits than I could guess at first. She nurses a sick boy who will die I fear after all of water on the brain and she nurses her sickly husband and yet is always the same chearful creature—the life of her family.

I mentioned Mrs. *Osborne* Ricardo the son's wife—for Osborne read—*Osman*—not Osmond—I am quite right this time depend upon it. When Mr. Ricardo Senr. was paying his court to Mrs. Ricardo some of their friends not approving of their attachment they corresponded for some time under ye feigned names of Osman and Jesse[1] and they afterwards agreed that they would call their eldest son *Osman*. Would you have guessed Honora that this slow political Economy-man was so romantic?

Mrs. Ricardo has still the remains of beauty and is good nature itself. She is an excellent mistress of house and servants—keeping all tight and right and building and planting and trudging about—now to the new conservatory and now to her gold and silver pheasants who feed sumptuously every day upon all the eggs (chopped) that are not eaten at breakfast. The pheasants inhabit grey-painted pens or houses all down the steep

[1] Osman is the sultan who loved and married a Christian slave in Voltaire's *Zaire*, translated by Aaron Hill (1736). Jesse is presumably Jessica from *The Merchant of Venice*.

slope that goes from the front windows of the house to the water. But I must not let these gold and silver pheasants for whom I have not the slightest regard carry me away from what I was going to say about Mrs. Osman Ricardo whom I quite love and I defy any body to be in the house with her three days without doing ditto. Harriet (Mrs. Osman Ricardo is Harriet too) is very fond of her. She is a charming creature! *Almost* as fine a figure as Mrs. Dallas—not quite—with a fair face—profusion of hair and a most winning countenance and manner—very desirous to improve herself and an understanding the extent and excellence of which I did not at first estimate. She was a Miss Mallory—an antient *Norman* family of Warwickshire—knew the Bracebridges. Happening to name somebody of the name of Waller[1] whom she had known at Bath where she lived before she was married I found out not only that she was acquainted with Jane and Belinda Waller and their mother and Major and Mrs. Waller but that she is related to them—*Cousins* and if cousins to the Wallers *connected* with *us*—that is with F and H and if with them with me surely. You cannot think how pleased she seemed and how politely Mr. Ricardo rejoiced in being able to say *Cousin Harriet* and cousin Fanny. Indeed this family and ours would suit remarkably well. I am sorry there is no son of an age to make into a brother-in-law. There is only a young-cur—Mortimer now at Eton—But for our brothers if they were so inclined here are still two unmarried sisters—one of eleven the other perhaps 17—both very handsome Mary and Bertha—Bertha beautiful! This family agree so well and we feel that they love each other so sincerely that it encreases incalculably the pleasure of being with them. Mr. Ricardo when we were walking on before the rest the other day said to me 'What a fortunate thing it was for us that Osman chose such a woman for his wife. She was quite a stranger to us. She might have broke up all our happiness but on the contrary she has joined us together more than ever and at once she became part of the family and made my girls love her as their sister—even little Bertha! as you see.' Her manner to her father in law is really so perfect that I do not wonder he doats upon her—so respectful and yet so affectionate.

[1] Mrs. Edgeworth's mother was a Waller of Allenstown.

They have another married daughter Mrs. Clutterbuck who I hear is quite an angel and has children better managed than ever angels children were if angels ever had children. Mr. Ricardo says she is not nearly so lively as Mrs. Austen but has more softness. We shall see for as I go through Bath I will call upon her. How happy they are in having their married son and two daughters within reach at agreeable distances—Mr. and Mrs. Osman Ricardo at *Bromesbarrow* Ledbury Herefordshire—30 miles distance and a most beautiful place—Mrs. Austen 14 miles off—Mrs. Clutterbuck 27.

Mr. Ricardo began to tell me a part of his history when we were out walking the other day through a charming wood. 'We were 15 children. My father gave me but little education. He thought reading writing and arithmetic sufficient because he doomed me to be nothing but a man of business. He sent me at eleven to Amsterdam to learn Dutch, French Spanish but I was so unhappy at being separated from my brothers and sisters and family that I learned nothing in two years but Dutch which I could not help learning.' Then . . . Oh there came some interruption from a fine prospect that broke upon us and I was very sorry—people came up and there was no resuming.

He told me another time that Mr. *Mill* the Mr. Mill whom you remember fighting with Mrs. Barbauld and Wakefield about education[1] was the person who encouraged him to educate himself and pursue his studies after he had made a fortune. He doats upon Mr. Mill—says he never could find a blemish in him—But dont you pity me for having his story interrupted before he came to the point of his conversion. N B—I have hitherto escaped saying anything about jews—not even *as rich as a jew* has ever passed my lips but I live in fear that I shall not get out of the house without stumbling upon some thing belonging to jews.

Mrs. Ricardo was a *quaker* and is now remarkably fond of Coquelicot color and red flowers and gaudy floss silk and chenille

[1] Mill was living at Newington Green near Mrs. Barbauld in 1813 and the meeting probably took place when the Edgeworths visited her between 13 and 19 June in that year, as recorded in *Henry Crabb Robinson on Books and their Writers*, ed. E. J. Morley (1938), i. 128. If Mill, Wakefield, and Mrs. Barbauld and RLE all talked together on education the visit must have lasted longer than the quarter hour sourly reported by Crabb Robinson.

borders worked on black for she wears nothing but black—and splendid white blonde—her figure is not as unlike your Mrs. Theresa Tattle[1] as I could wish it to be but her face very pretty —The Lady Fingall style of face only with bright little Jewish black eyes however a quaker came by them.

I told Lucy in my last abruptly finished note that we spent one or two evenings acting words. Since that Mr. Smith and all of us acted the following

Pilgrim—Psyche—Spursheim Falstaff—Fire Eater—Conundrum.

Pilgrims—by Mr. Smith and Mr. Ricardo Mrs. Osman Ricardo and Mary—Mr. Ricardo and Mr. Smith in box coats with girdles and with *cockle-shells* made of paper (fanned) and pinned over the capes—eyebrows *corked*—admirable figures—dresses for ladies and gentlemen prepared by Mrs. Smith—nice woman.

Psyche—Mr. Smith and Ricardo 1st *sighs* 2d [illegible] *keys*—dress prepared by the governess Miss Lancy who is very clever I believe but somehow we do not like her—disagreeable voice and pert. Nevertheless her silver paper wings and butterfly for Bertha were beautiful and Bertha was a charming little Psyche. She was to have danced a little ballet but she was so timid she could not and we liked her all the better. She conquered her shyness so far as to go into the room dressed as Psyche and danced a few steps but ran out again red as a peony and we found her on the sofa in the anteroom ready to cry and pulling off her wings. Miss Lancy wanted to have her on the stage again but we protected her against this cruelty and she loves us—

Spursheim[2]—Harriet and I did this—Enter with *spurs*—Enter teaching Harriet to *hem*—Enter M—as Spursheim—dressed in coat and turban with face corked—skull of dog in hand—felt *heads*—created good diversion.

Fire Eater—Harriet and I acted—1st—looking up the chimney—alarm of fire. Mr. Ricardo said we alarmed him so well that he was going to call for assistance. 2ly. I was an epicure and Harriet set dinner before me—eating you know always

[1] A character in ME's story 'The Mimic' (*The Parent's Assistant*). Mrs. Edgeworth's drawing is the frontispiece to the 1800 illustrated edition of the book.

[2] Kaspar Spurzheim (1776–1832), German phrenologist.

succeeds on or off the stage. 31y Harriet performed to admiration as Fire eater—I held lamp (like Harriet Beaufort's candlestick) and lighted *spills* which she seemed to devour—only burnt her lip a *leetle*.

Falstaff—Mr. Ricardo and Smith 1—Enter and *fell*—very well 2—Re-enter with staffs—3 Falstaff—Mr. Smith excellent.

Conundrum—Mr. Smith and Ricardo—partners—I came in with draft to be signed—21y Mrs. Osman Ricardo—a beautiful nun in white and black beads and veil Harriet in black and veil very pretty—Maria a drummer—White hat and feathers and band box for drum—strangely beat and bungled but creating much mirth. Then re enter Cos—nuns and—drum and stood in a row—thunders of applause.

It is very pleasant to do such things for those who enjoy them so much. You have no idea how easily grave Mr. Ricardo is amused. He delights so in Mr. Smiths acting that he cannot help laughing and forgetting his own part when he is acting with him. I hope this will divert Lucy.

The Smiths went home yesterday. We spent yesterday evening making a parallelogram into a square you know the puzzle and Bertha and Mary and Mrs. Osman Ricardo had the 3 5 and 8 gallon vessel[1]—and after nonsense came sense. Mr. Ricardo and we had an excellent argument about misers and spendthrifts—which are most advantageous to a nation. I say spendthrift he says miser—too long to write . . .

Thursday morning—the ash trees still with green leaves—many in full leaf . . .

The *physique* here is excellent. I never was in a more *comfortably* splendid house 110 feet of rooms opening into each other in front all perfectly well warmed so that you never want to go to the fire but may sit to read or write in any part of them and with doors open for the hall which lies between the two drawing rooms and the dining room and study is as warm as the sitting

[1] The 3, 5, and 8 gallon puzzle was invented by the French mathematician Simeon Poisson. The problem was to divide an 8 gallon vessel of liquid into equal halves with the assistance only of a 3 gallon and a 5 gallon vessel (*The World of Mathematics*, ed. J. R. Newman (1956), 2419). Another version of this problem is how to finish with one gallon in each of the smaller vessels (H. E. Dudeney, *The Canterbury Puzzles* (1907), No. 6) (I am indebted to Mr. H. R. Calvert of the Science Museum for the last reference).

rooms—with good fire-stove and turkey carpet. The 4 globes of gold fish who live in the 4 corners of that hall are happier than goldfish ever were since the days of the King of the black Islands.[1] In this house all the luxuries that riches can give without the ostentation. As marks of the comfort of the establishment I may mention that the fires have always been lighted long enough before you come down in the morning to warm all the rooms and the breakfast has all the sun that can be had every day in the year. Paper—pens ink wax and wax candles in abundance. Excellent servants—3 in handsome drab and crimson—one out of livery—The housekeeper and ladys maid phoenixes . . .

In the house with such a wise man as Mr. Ricardo you might expect to hear of wise books and new books but I cannot tell you of any. We have been looking at old ones and perhaps this is a proof of our preeminent wisdom. Harriet is much entertained with Gibbons letters.[2] I think his life and letters would entertain Lucy. I have a mind to send them to her. Shall I? When I go to Mr. Smiths which we do at 3 oclock this day, I will enquire about new books for you.

Sydney Smith says that if a man was to go to the opera house and cry 'Mr. *Smith's wanted*' half the house would get up and if he cried 'Mr. *John* Smith is wanted' half those who got up would sit down. Not a scrap more wit—sense or nonsense at present from Yr. Affectionate Maria E

Hunter wrote me word yesterday that he had sent *Frank*[3] as far as O to Edgeworthstown. What has become of it? I have not seen or heard a sentence of it and no sign of its arrival or departure in Honoras journal. I suppose it is like Gilpins hat and wig on the road or stolen by the stealers of jewels.

[1] In the Arabian Nights.

[2] *Miscellaneous Works of E. G*[*ibbon*] *with Memoirs of his Life and Writings; composed by himself; illustrated from his Letters, with occasional Notes and Narrative by John, Lord Sheffield* (1797, new ed. 1814).

[3] *Frank: A Sequel to Frank in Early Lessons* was published in 1822. This refers to the proofs.

To Sophy Ruxton

Easton Grey, 18 November 1821

My dear Sophy . . . We are very happy here. Mr. and Mrs. Smith are most agreeable conversible connected by friendship with most of the literary people whom we know and with many whom we do not know—for instance Hobhouse—Burdett &c. Sydney Smith and his wife have very lately been on a visit here and at Gatcombe. We were unlucky not to meet them. They had here also lately Mr. Macdonald who is one of the clever agreeable diners-out of London and they expect a Mr. Warburton a young man who unites genius—learning—fortune and all that is delightful *but* he is so unpunctual and so difficult *to have and to hold* that I daresay he will not come or come the day after we are gone.

We have had a Mr. and Mrs. Holford M P here one day. He is a great friend of Lord Liverpools. I mean Lord Liverpool is a great friend of his and Lady Liverpool was a most intimate friend of Mrs. Holford's. She is Irish—was Miss [blank in MS.]. He has written on prisons and is at the head of the London penitentiary and Sydney Smith who wrote the review in the last Edinburgh on prison discipline has according to his fashion first patted his friend Holford on the back and then cut him up with infinite spirit and humor and no attention to the cries of truth.[1] Mr. Holford's connexion with Lord Londonderry he alludes to as if Mr. Holford were a sycophant flattering for patronage for some nephew or son. Nothing *can* be more false. Mr. Holford is a man of large fortune who uses it for benevolent purposes and wants no patronage for any creature. . . . [end missing]

[1] G. P. Holford's *Thoughts on the Criminal Prisons of this Country* was reviewed in *Edinburgh Review*, xxxv (1821), 286 et seq. Sydney Smith, the author of the review, speaks of Holford's good sense 'preceded by the usual nonsense about "the tide of blasphemy and sedition"'.

To Mrs. Edgeworth

Easton Grey, 22 November 1821

My dearest mother—Mr. Smith's name is Tom. I am sorry I forgot to tell this till it can be of little or no use to you as we leave this delightful Tom the day after tomorrow. A very happy week we have spent here. Mr. and Mrs. Smith are such amiable well informed people and suit so nicely and their house and way of living is so entirely what I like! Though they have had for their intimate friends most of the literary people of London &c Sydney Smith—Horners—Tennant Wollaston Whishaw Romilly &c were in the habit of visiting them frequently yet they do not disdain their country neighbors but keep up a kind intercourse with them like yourself. Mrs. Smith gives dinners and parties in which there is every thing that is proper and nothing for parade. She is beloved by all her neighbours as well as by all her friends . . . Yesterday was a full cup of pleasure and satisfaction from morning till night. To begin with—Before breakfast—between 8 and 9 Mrs. Smith knocked at our door (while I was writing to Francis E. in reply to a nice letter of his about some books which he wishes to have in lieu of Western Isles[1]) 'Mr. Ricardo is come! Has ridden 9 miles to breakfast with us!' Joy—down went pen and Maria—Delightful conversation at breakfast—all laughing and openhearted—mixed with placid deep philosophy now and then from Ricardo and playful humor from Smith—Fanny and Harriet taking most agreeable shares. Mr. Ricardo apropos to Kings visit to Ireland[2] spoke of Smiths[3] theory of the inclination which people feel to sympathise with persons in high rank—rich and prosperous—why and how is this compatible with *envy* of riches—of the envy felt for those who rise to a rank or fortune to which they were not born. He spoke beautifully and *nobly* on this subject—on the faults and unhappiness of each party—and he has avoided all these faults. No one envies—all admire him.

[1] Perhaps Johnson's *Journey to the Western Islands of Scotland* (1775) or J. Macculloch, *A Description of the Western Islands of Scotland* (1819).

[2] See above, p. 239, n. 3.

[3] Adam Smith, *The Theory of Moral Sentiments* (1759), Section 4, chap. II, 'Of the origin of ambition and of the distinction of ranks', 108–28, esp. 113.

After breakfast he and Mr. Smith were obliged to go off to Tetbury—meeting about saving bank. We 4 ladies with a stool in a roomy chaise, not in the least crowded set out to see Charlton—Malmesbury Abbey and Lady Catherine Bisset. I perched upon the stool in the corner sat most comfortably listening all the way to Harriet who read a most diverting little poem (not new but excellent)—Advice to Julia[1] by Mr. Luttrell. If you have not seen it or cannot get it in Dublin tell me and I will send it per Ward leaving off the cover. It would perhaps be objected to by starch people because Julia is like all Julias no better than she should be. Mr. Wilberforce when he was last here stole it out of the library under his arm when he was going to bed and confessed next morning it had diverted him exceedingly and he thought it full of wit and talent. It would as he justly observed be much better and indeed *perfect* in its way if the *mistress* had been a wife and if one third of the poem had been left out. There are some parts in what Mr. Cobbe would justly call *bad taste—moral* and figurative. But pray get it nevertheless for the kept mistress will do no harm to any creature at Edgeworthstown I will answer for them.

Charlton is the seat—as your bone[2] of genealogy or Britton's beauties of England[3] must have long since informed you—of Lord Suffolk. It was built by Sir J. Jones and the outside of it does him honor—a magnificent pile of building with *cannon* chimnies—the whole in good taste—outside—But inside—gloomy small rooms. One wonders what has become of the space which the outside promised. One good dining room and a small drawing room all that are what the spoiled moderns would call habitable in the house and except their pigeonholes of bed-chambers these were all the rooms the *family* ever had to live in. There is to be a magnificent hall which will be superb when 10 or 20 thousand pounds have been spent upon it. At present it is *cat and clay*[4]

[1] Henry Luttrell, *Advice to Julia, a Letter in Rhyme* (1820).

[2] i.e. bump, 'one of the prominences on the cranium associated by phrenologists with special faculties' (*O.E.D.*).

[3] J. Britton, *The Beauties of England and Wales*, xv (1814), 623–5. The architect is unknown but was not Inigo Jones, as ME and Britton suggest. The unfinished part was by Matthew Brettingham.

[4] Straw and clay worked together into largish rolls and laid between wooden posts in constructing mud walls.

with a finely stuccoed dome as like the old London Pantheon[1] as it can stare.

The pictures at Charlton I leave to Fanny's journal—observing only that we had luckily light enough tho the 21st November to see them—Some very fine but there were two frightful Domenichinos landscape and figures and a reputed Titian which I would sell tomorrow to finish and furnish the house. For the Domenichinos he has been offered £9000. All the dark passages that lead to nothing at Charlton are hung with faded full lengths of ancestors in stiff skirts and strange silks and there is a gallery something like the gallery at Sudbury tell Ho—only not nearly so handsome—hung with faded Lords and ladies looking proud or pretty all in vain—many of Charles naughty beauties—among others the famous Dairy maid looking like a duchess.[2] One of the white faced grand aunts of the Suffolk family looked as Harriet said as if she had literally cried her eyes *out*. Upon enquiry from the woman who shewed us the house she said 'One of the young gentleman Ma'am Master James ran his stick into that eye and put it out.' There is a hole in the canvas in lieu of the eye which has the oddest effect imaginable. The gallery was the play place of the children.

I forgot to mention in the right place, the library—a full length of the late Lord Suffolk by Sir T Lawrence which is literally a nine years wonder for he was 9 years painting it. Lawrence who was usually paid half price the first sitting began a picture 12 years ago of Sir H Davy and he was so dilatory that Sir Humphry out of patience sent to desire he would return his money or finish the picture. Lawrence returned him his money with interest compound interest calculated thereon and made up to the day. How the quarrel was afterwards made up I cannot tell but it was for you know he has lately finished a capital full length of Sir Humphry Davy.

But nothing of what I am telling you is what I want to tell you—After being in admiration of pictures and pigeonholes of

[1] The first Pantheon, on the south side of Oxford St., was built in 1772 and 'dedicated to the nocturnal revels of the British nobility', but it was later turned into a theatre. Burnt in 1792, it was rebuilt without its dome. ME must have seen it as a schoolgirl.

[2] According to Britton, op. cit., among the pictures was a Lely of Charles II and a portrait of 'his mistress Lady Mary Davis', said to have been a native of Charlton.

your dear *thick-walled* rooms till we were as cold as Christmas not to say as cold as death we once more were packed 4 into our warm box and drove off to pay our visit to the Lady Catherine Bisset daughter of the late sister of the present Lord. How do you picture her Ladyship and her house to yourself? She is as unlike the Lady Catherine in Pride and Prejudice as you can conceive. In person she is a little like Marianne Fox or an ugly likeness of one of Murillos Madonas—sedate—mild—slow—the most unpretending lady of quality I ever saw. The blood of all the Howards appears only in *habitual* good breeding. Oh how unlike all that is put on for company-effect! She lives in a cottage or rather a very small house at the end of the park at Charlton. That park is the most flat stupid expanse of park I ever beheld. It makes one yawn to look at it. The house which Lady Catherine inhabits is something like Mr. Bradfords former house in Collon—with a garden at the back—the rooms rather larger and far more genteelly and comfortably furnished. The contrast between this and the magnificent *great* house was striking. I never saw any one appear more happy than she does. She has no children of her own but has the care of two nice little girls of her brothers—he and his wife are in Italy—Little Lady Mary-Rose (I am glad it is not Rose-mary) and Lady Frances.

Now for the romantic part of her story which I kept for bonne bouche. It was a love match—12 years in despair for old Lord Suffolk would not hear of it. Mr. Bisset tho the most agreeable man in the world was too gay—it must not be. Lady Catherine dutifully submitted—pined and drooped. At last Lord Suffolk fearing she would droop to death gave his consent but the daughter was too delicate to accept such a reluctant consent. Mr. Bisset meantime went to Ceylon spent 12 years—returned—first news he heard on setting his foot on English ground was that old Lord Suffolk at past eighty had breathed his last. So must I—Post—Mr. Smith lighting candle I must leave you in the dark till the day after tomorrow. ever affec M E

To Mrs. Edgeworth

22 November 1821

I left off when Mr. Bisset had just set his foot on English ground and Lord Suffolk was breathing his last—he breathed it —and in due time afterwards Lady Catherine Howard became Lady Catherine Bisset and ever since has lived in a cottage on love most happily. Mr. Bisset I have never yet seen. He was snatched away from home by some duty just as we came here but he spends tomorrow here with Lady C. He is brother to Mr. Jephsons friend Bisset and I *can* have no doubt of his being a very *sensible* man *because* he has in two notes expressed the most becoming desire to be acquainted with us.

After we had been five minutes in the room with Lady Catherine yesterday she watched an opportunity when nobody was looking or hearing and laying her hand upon my arm and squeezing it most affectionately looked up in my face with the sort of expression Mrs. Leslie Foster had when *her heart was in it*. 'Do you know I have been half my life trying to be your good French governess?[1] I love her.'

I should tell you that Lady Catherine with her two little nieces had been to see us the day before this and Fanny had won Lady Mary Rose's heart partly by means of some Madeira and Portuguese little figures from the chimney piece which she ranged on the table for her amusement and partly by the aid of a *Phizgig* which Fanny plays to admiration. And what is a Phizgig? If you don't know you must wait till we send you one. Mean time—Fanny having won Lady Mary Roses heart her little pretty Ladyship and her little ugly Ladyship sister came running into the room in their straw bonnets and various images of wood were produced representing Cingalese peasants and nobles—hewers of wood and drawers of water and merchants and military men with turbans or caps after their fashion all made of wood peculiar to Ceylon as light as pith—varnished and painted curious figures about the height of Lucys china fidler which used to stand on my chimney piece. All these were made entertaining by the anecdotes and comments of a certain Captain Fenwick an olive colored man from India who was at Lady Catherines and

[1] *The Good French Governess*, a story in ME's *Moral Tales* (1801).

who had been years at Ceylon—whether a navy or an army Captain is yet in dispute with us. You may be sure F and H liked him because they decide he must be a *Navy* captain.[1]

I just forgot to tell you the two things best worth mentioning indeed the only things worth mentioning about these Ceylon curiosities. One of the figures which is represented climbing a tree has a rope fastened round his two ancles with length of rope enough between the ancles to embrace with the feet half the stem of the tree. This assists in climbing. Sometimes another cord of twisted grass is put around the waist and tree and tied *looseish* so as to leave the climber space enough to push it up as he climbs—his arms are then at liberty and with the aid of these pulls and ties he climbs with astonishing rapidity as Captain Fenwick says. Lady Catherine shewed us one of the elastic ivory bottles used in Ceylon for sprinkling the guests with rose water—a signal to let them know that the visit may be ended as soon as they please. These bottles are made of the finest sort of ivory—scraped thin. This was shaped like a small florence flask[2]—cut into a pentagon of quite smooth sides. On pressing the ivory bottle in your hands you feel that it gives way and is quite elastic. Its neck is long and as small as the neck of an ivory [? pounce] bottle which used to stand on the library table ages ago. Holes at the top and through these holes spouts rose water when the bottle is pressed. If you dont understand it it is my fault not yours and never mind it—or any of my faults if you please.

On our way home after this visit we reflected sagely in the carriage upon Lady Catherine and Love in a cottage[3] and the essentials and non essentials of happiness. Our succession of visits at Wycombe Abbey—Gatcombe—Easton Grey afforded materials for comparison. One reflexion has been *forced* upon me—that much happiness is compatible with much want of polish of manner—provided that there is real good nature and good temper and provided the unpolished people have no desire to mix with the polished people.

[1] Because their uncle Francis Beaufort was a naval captain.

[2] A flask used to contain Florence oil (olive oil), bulbous with a long narrow neck and a straw or plaited grass cover (*O.E.D.*).

[3] 'Love and a cottage! Eh, Fanny! Eh, give me indifference and a coach and six!': Colman, *The Clandestine Marriage* (1766), I. ii.

We stopped to see Malmesbury Abbey. I never saw any reality so like its picture. The engraving of Malmesbury Abbey in Britton is perfect representation.[1] Give my love to Louisa and tell her that many mixed pleasing and painful recollections of the time when she first shewed me those 'Beauties of England' came into my mind when I saw this Abbey. I wished that she had been in my place who deserves so much better to see such beautiful specimens of Architecture and who could have told F and H so many useful or curious circumstances. This Abbey is beautifully placed. Its front looks down a hill and has a great command of distant country. The height of the arch which was the center arch of the Abbey is sublime! The Cross is so like the engraving that except the children playing beneath its porch you seem to see nothing but what you had seen before in the print.

As it was late and cold*ish* by the time we had admired sufficiently the outside of the Abbey and as the red streaks in the sky seen behind the ruins gave the signal that the sun was setting and as Fanny had still some *propensity* to cold in her *head* and *feet* we determined not to go into the Abbey to see old tombs. We drove *home*.

When I was speaking of Lord Suffolks family I forgot to tell you about the marriage of the present Lord. When he was Lord Andover a Miss Dutton was at Charlton where all went on I guess much as at Delvile Castle[2]—Very formal—very silent—Miss Dutton very amiable excessively timid. One day after dinner Lord Andover in the presence of Lord and Lady Suffolk and speaking *out loud* said 'Miss Dutton I see from the way in which things are conducted here that I shall never be permitted to have the opportunity of speaking to you alone unless you now be so good to walk with me into the library and give me leave to have half an hours conversation with you.' To the inexpressible astonishment of Lord and Lady Suffolk and of all the formalists present Miss Dutton rose. Lord Andover handed her out and when he handed her in again and announced his intended marriage. She made an incomparable wife and daughter in law. The old couple grew excessively fond of her. She lived 9 years at Charlton with them. The elder brother of the present Lord

[1] J. Britton, op. cit., plate facing p. 601.
[2] In Fanny Burney's *Cecilia* (1782).

Suffolk was the Lord Andover who was killed by a gun going off as he crossed a ditch out shooting. There was an old old dowager Lady Andover whose picture I think I saw at Mr. John Sneyd's and who was either his relation friend or connexion.[1] Honora or my Aunts can make this out for you. I am not clear about it.

Today (Thursday) we went to see a Mr. and Mrs. Sheppard who live at a beautiful place called the Ridge. I would not for five guineas attempt to describe it to you. I can only with Frank[2] say most beautiful Mamma! By the by a sheet of Frank came to me straight today. Hunter says it is of so much consequence to him to get it printed and out by Xmas that he begs not to send proofs to E Town which would delay it three months. He is setting other presses at work he says to finish it quickly. I have sent him word that he may do as he pleases. I think this but just to him though I am very unwilling to give up your corrections and Honoras. Tell Ho that in the last sheet she sent me we cut out the child coming behind Franks horse. F and H hated it and they say she will rejoice it is out. Why did she not cut it out?

Hunter says he has received only to page 217 of the 3d volume and he asks if this is all the Ms. or not. Please to tell me for I don't know. I write tomorrow to say with what lines the Ms. ends (thats all I know). Friday 23rd November. If any more Ms. remains at Edgeworthstown (which is very unlikely) please send it to Hunter in a Freeling frank. Did you ever observe that Mr. Freeling never dates his franks? And do you know that there are but 3 people in the empire who are so privileged that they may frank without date. Freeling is one—Bloomfield is 2d—and Sidmouth 3d of this privileged order.[3] This fact was told me yesterday by Mr. Sheppard a sort of English Mr. Whitney who worked hard to bring into conversation that he had that very morning had a letter from Lord Sidmouth and who finished with great condescension by asking Mrs. Smith to accept of the cover franked by his Lordships own hand which she might like to keep

[1] Mary, daughter of Heneage, Earl of Aylesford and wife of William, Lord Andover. There was a connection with the Sneyds of Keele through Lord Bagot.

[2] ME's *Frank: A Sequel*. The first two vols. were printed by Charles Wood, Poppin's Court, Fleet St., and the third by J. McCreery, Took's Court, Chancery Lane.

[3] Mr. Freeling was Secretary to the Post Office, Sir Benjamin Bloomfield Keeper of the Privy Purse, and Lord Sidmouth at this time Home Secretary.

among her *autographs.* You may guess at his whole style of conversation by this said to me 'I think Ma'am the wind this morning is what I call rather inimical to conversation!'

His daughter draws beautifully—as well as you do—and has given me some of her sketches *and* has a nice little *atelier* at the end of a delicious conservatory that joins *her* to the dining room, drawing room and library—a fine, and rich carpeted suite of rooms at one end of which Mr. Sheppard stood with just self complacency pointing out to me in Mr. Whitneys own fair-day subdued tone of modesty the beauty of the coup d'oeil. People understand the comfort of the inside of houses better now than in Inigo Jones time and Vanbrughs days—Lie heavy on them earth.[1]

Farewell—Mr. Ricardo is just come to breakfast and all his family. I must put on my shoes. Yours affecy. Maria E . . . Can you recollect whether in the Louvre in 1802 we saw *Le Raboteur* —the holy family in the carpenters shop—a small picture which was on the left hand side as you walked up the gallery—Joseph at a carpenters bench drawing up a cord to mark a line—Our Saviour leaning on the end of the bench and the Virgin Mary sitting at work. The contrast between vulgar business thought and divine expression is beautiful. At Charlton there is what they assure you is the original Raboteur by A. Carracci. The late Lord Suffolk bought it for £300 and has been offered £3000. I would sell it with the Domenichinos to furnish the house but Mr. Fox would despise me as a vile upholsterer.

Mrs. Estcourt a lady in this neighborhood whom I was to have seen is sister to who do you think—to Lord Sidmouth. I am sorry that contretemps prevented our meeting!

A Whizgig for Pakenham in my next—

Mrs. Smith sends her love to you and loves Harriet who as she says is very like you.

[1] Satirical epitaph by Dr. Evans on Sir John Vanbrugh the architect:

> Under this stone, Reader, survey
> Dead Sir John Vanbrugh's house of clay:
> Lie heavy on him, Earth, for he
> Laid many a heavy load on thee!

To Mrs. Ruxton

Bowood Park, 26 November 1821

My dearest Aunt, We were fortunate enough to find Lord and Lady Lansdowne just returned from their tour—two days before I wrote to offer to spend a day or two here on our way to Portsmouth. They *looked* at the Pyrenees but could not go into Spain for the yellow fever rages on the borders and a cordon is drawn which prevents travellers who might be disposed to brave the danger of the fever. The troops do not leave them any praise for prudence because they have no choice—they fire directly if any attempt is made to cross the cordon. Lady Lansdowne would quite satisfy you by her love of the Italian women and her dislike of the French. She read Mrs. Marcet's letter to me, which you saw and she assures me that her favorable picture of the society at Florence is not exaggerated. I asked her if she thought that anything *appeared* in Italian society at Florence or Rome which would be likely to hurt a young Englishwoman. 'All I can tell you is', said she 'that I never had anything said to me or before me during the whole time that I was in Italy that made me blush. I know others have but I cannot help thinking that it must be partly their own fault.'

We found the first day we came to Bowood which was the day before yesterday Miss Vernon and *Miss Fox* Lord Hollands sister—and Miss Fox Lord Hollands daughter—no other company except Mr. Ogden the widower of the beautiful and extraordinary lady whom we met here two years ago. He seems to have recovered from his loss and is much more conversible and agreeable than he could appear to common acquaintance when absorbed by her perfections &c. He has a great deal of cool, grave gentlemanly humour with which he has just been amusing us with an account of a visit he paid yesterday to Bowles the poet—His musical sheep bells and his susceptibility to criticism and his credulity—and his history of his loves Mr. Ogden made very diverting. Bowles in the simplicity of his egotism wrote to Murray to desire that he would watch everybody who came into his shop to see whether they read the article in the Edinburgh Review that treats of his controversy with Byron and Gilchrist and begged that whenever any body was seen to take up that review Murray would pop his pamphlet by way of antidote into his hand.[1] Concieve Murray receiving and laughing over this letter in the midst of his room filled with the bel esprits of the day. The history of his loves and of his telling them to Mr. Ogden and another gentleman with Mrs. Bowles sitting by I must keep for your fireside or for a walk with you to the Weir.

Miss Vernon (aunt) and Miss Fox (niece) are both very agreeable though in very different ways and Miss Fox the young lady is beautiful timid and charming . . . [end missing]

To Mrs. Edgeworth

Bowood Park, Tuesday, 27 November 1821

My dearest mother and dear friends . . . Fanny and Harriet might never have another such good opportunity of seeing together Lord and Lady Bathurst Lady Georgiana Bathurst—Lord Apsley—Lord and Lady Morley Major Colebrooke who all arrived yesterday to dinner—Besides Miss Vernon the two Miss Foxes and Mr. Ogden! Lady Boringdon you know has turned into Lady Morley and you recollect Lady Boringdon at the Duke of Devonshire's breakfast at Chiswick? You remember Lady Bessboroughs speech just before she introduced me 'If you can get over her voice and her manner you will find her very amusing'.

She is very clever—and very entertaining—One of those who say everything that comes into their head. The last thing I can recollect that made me laugh was her manner of answering Lady Bathurst who told her in her most delicately polite manner that an end of her frill was unpinned (Scene All sitting out in the sunshine in the portico—you know Honora). 'Which would become me best do you think (appealing to all the company)—to pin or not to pin it. I think rather *not to pin*. It looks less soignée

[1] In 1806 Bowles published an edition of Pope with a very hostile introduction on his poetic principles. Byron and others were involved in a long controversy with Bowles over this. Exactly which of Bowles's several pamphlets is here involved is not clear, but it was probably *A Vindication . . . from some charges . . . in the Quarterly Review* (2nd ed. 1821). Bowles thought Octavius Gilchrist was the author of some uncomplimentary remarks about him in a review of Spence's *Anecdotes* in the *Quarterly* (not *Edinburgh*) *Review*, vol. xxiii (1820), No. XLVI.

but then I may lose the frill.' I asked if the wanting or the having a pin could decide the question. 'Oh no, I have a pin and what you wont believe a pincushion.' Out it came from behind to the astonishment and uplifted hands of Lady Georgiana and politely expressed surprise of Lady Bathurst—the flattest [illegible] of a pincushion that could hold only one pin abreast. 'And I dont doubt but if my frill's to be sewed I could find needles somewhere sticking about me.' The conversation skipped to swallowing pins and needles. I told story of Lady Somebodys swallowing paper of needles—feared it would not be believed that they came out—she survived. Lady Morley—'O I believe it for I can tell you something more extraordinary which you would not believe. I know a lady who swallowed sixteen hundred larch trees! She did upon my honor to strengthen her, and they did strengthen her timbers.' Much amazement and laughing that is smiling from Lady Bathursts Chesterfieldian-ly[1] educated mouth. 'The thing was thus—My friend Lady So and So had been ordered Iceland Moss and thought she had been taking it a fortnight when one day her brother said to his man "Whats become of the packet of seedling larch that was to come?" "My Lord—My lady eat them. They was mistaken for Iceland moss and the cook boiled 'em into broth and they are finished."'

Next Lady Morley told of a Marriage in high life—Miss Vernon daughter to the Archbishop of York the Miss Vernon who has lost a leg to Mr. Acheboom I believe or some such sounding name which she said could not be decently pronounced. Then she went off into what you would not like and she was stopped by Lady Lansdownes not encouraging. Thats enough for the present of Lady Morley—just a sample.

Honora knows Lady Bathurst and Lady Georgiana so I need not describe but I must observe that Lady Georgiana Bathurst is more solidly and sensibly dressed and more agreeable than when I saw her before—Lord Bathurst like my uncle Edward Sneyd—very gentlemanlike. Lady Bathurst told me last night a new cluster—constellation of anecdotes of *the* Duchess.[2] I dare

[1] I could heartily wish that you may often be seen to smile, but never heard to laugh: Chesterfield, *Letters to his son*, 9 Mar. 1748.

[2] Of Wellington.

not begin to tell them because they would never end and I must only *memorandum.*

Flowers in balcony—*snubbing* Lady Bathurst about
Not answering Duke at dinner

What the devil's the meaning of all this Kitty—You did me injustice . . . I hope everybody loves me as well as I love myself. Yours affec. Maria E

To Mrs. Edgeworth

Mall,[1] Clifton, 3 December 1821

. . . And now having scribbled all that is absolutely necessary and I hope satisfied you on the points on which you would all be most craving I may go back to where I left off in my last from Bowood. The additional day which we spent there was exceedingly agreeable. All the new people opened more and more towards us and Fanny and Harriet (in their white merino gowns) seemed to give universal satisfaction.

Lady Morley was amazingly entertaining. She is one of the very best mimics I ever saw not excepting my own sister Anna or my cousin Sir Charles V[illegible].[2] We will give you at secondhand some time or other *her* Lady Cholmondely and her conversation on *coincidencies*—the tone exactly like my own idea of Lady Clonbrony[3]—lisp and all to perfection. Lady Morley behaves admirably to her husband. She seems to me to have a right good heart for she ended by falling in love with us and gave us pressing invitation to her house in Devonshire whenever we can come—good for Fannys health &c. Though we shall never go there yet I own it gratifies me to feel that all who see them wish to see more of *them* as well as of Mrs. authoress.

Mr. Crabbe the poet spent this last day at Bowood—An amiable old chalky looking thin man—simple in his manners—I think rather *too simple.* Lady Lansdowne who has good penetration said to me 'I am not quite sure that *all* Crabbe's *naiveté* is

[1] At the home of ME's sister Emmeline King.

[2] ? Sir Charles Vernon (1766–1835), Chamberlain to the Lord Lieutenant of Ireland.

[3] In ME's *The Absentee, Tales of Fashionable Life,* v–vi (1812).

quite natural. I think he sees it pleases and so carries it a little further than is natural.' He praised Mrs. Leadbeater much to me and I shall write about that to Mrs. O Beirne by and by.[1]

The day we left Bowood we did various commissions at Bath with Miss Wilkinson and others too tedious to mention—Harriet and Fannys muslin gowns to be fresh made up for Bathursts &c—Then to Widcombe House to dine. Widcombe House is the house in which Squire Western lived—Nothing remarkable in it but a fine old dark mahogany staircase and a large lobby at landing place leading to bedchambers something like the lobby at Allens Town[2]—Bedchambers excellent—sitting rooms low and small—At least so they appeared to us after Bowood—And the whole change of scenery decoration manners and conversation very amusing and edifying. Mrs. Clutterbuck is a beautiful woman—Italian face and figure—devoted to her husband—children and *father*—who doats upon her and shews his judgment by thus doating. Mrs. Clutterbuck's children are charming—like your pictures of children. Fanny has sketched little Kate as she sat on the carpet in the midst of her playthings by the firelight when we first came in. These children are admirably well managed. Mr. Clutterbuck is a gentleman and goodnatured and thats all. He has been in the Blues but does not look like it . . . Goodby affecy Maria E

To Mrs. Edgeworth

Cirencester Park,[3] 5 December 1821

Our picture day at Leigh Court[4] surpassed our expectations—Poussins famous land storm—St. John by Domenichino and the most striking divine head of our saviour by Leonardo da Vinci with many others too tantalizing to mention . . .

[1] Mrs. Leadbeater was the author of *Cottage Dialogues among the Irish Peasantry* (1811), to which ME wrote a preface and notes. Mrs. O' Beirne, the wife of the Bishop of Meath, had introduced the two authoresses.

[2] The seat of Mrs. Edgeworth's cousin, the Revd. M. H. Noble Waller.

[3] Lord Bathurst's seat.

[4] A classical house near Bristol built by T. Hopper for P. J. Miles in 1814. It had a famous collection of pictures, dispersed in the 1880s.

To Mrs. Edgeworth, 5 December 1821

Left Clifton at eleven striking—arrived at Lord Bathursts just to a shade in right time—exactly at the dusk firelight hour when all are separating to dress.

This antient house with modern furniture and arrangement of luxuries and *comfortable* luxuries is delightful. We have two rooms opening into each other. F and H sleep in two little beds size of Lucys under one large four posted canopy—very pretty and comfortable made so that they can be wheeled out and large bed put in the place occasionally—Mine a French bed with old chintz. I am now writing in a delightful arm chair—high backed antiquity—modern cushions with moveable side cushions with cushion elbows lying on the lowest of low arms, so that there is just comfortable room to sit down in a place between cushions in which one niches snugly—so snugly that when Harriet sat down she thought she was so happy she would never get up again. Think what a luxurious chair that must be which so affected her Stoic philosophy. God help me have I wasted ten lines upon a chair! (Memm. a ledge round 3 sides of a flat light writing table very convenient—things carry on it without danger of falling. I have felt that within these five minutes.)

Miss Wilkinsons blanching and remaking of Fanny and Harriets muslin gowns answered perfectly—Tulle all freshly *crimped* beautiful over white satin. My dear mother I wish you could have seen how well they looked. I dont mean only the gowns.

The company at dinner were—Lord and Lady Bathurst Lady Georgiana Lady Emily—Lord Apsley Mr. William Bathurst Lady Georgiana Lennox—Major Colebrooke—Mr. Fortescue —Lord Fortescue's son whom we met at Paris at Lady de Ros and fancied was the gentleman going to marry Lady Frederica Murray because he looked so like a lover. I wish he were a lover of any of my friends—he is so very agreeable melancholy and gentlemanlike but Cupids will be done we cant *manage* any of these things and it would perhaps be worse for us if we could. So Henry Pakenham is going to be married and to an heiress. *That* I should have guessed—and what becomes of his love for death! . . .

The conversation though not so literary as at Bowood goes on remarkably well here. Lady Bathurst is perfectly well bred and *easy*—much more easy in manner than Lady Lansdowne—Lord Apsley as far as I see very agreeable and fond of Georgy and Emily and playful with them. Lady Georgiana is very agreeable in her own house—very goodnatured to F and H—Lady G Lennox—in ill health—very gentlewomanlike—thats all I know of her yet—A striking difference between the *ease of motion*—manner—conversation of these high born fashionables compared with those whom we saw at Wycombe Abbey—But comparisons are odorus and ungrateful too so I make none but eyes will see and ears will hear and tongues will talk and pens will scribble.

The Duchess of Beauforts French governess published in 1817 *Valoe*[1] a book which threw all high bred London into confusion. It is called [blank in MS.] Everybody who is any body is in it in feigned names—The picture of their persons and manners and character—All supposed to file off one after another before the hero (the Duke of Devonshire) for his choice. Lord Apsley who has a finely bound copy with a manuscript index of proper names lent it me this morning and I have read 2 Lady Pagets—*Rosa*—Lady G Bathurst (admirably done) and some others. Almost every likeness is flattered they say but little faults are found and little anecdotes told which vex amazingly. For instance Lady Catherine Melville formerly Osborne has all the virtues under the sun 'Mais un certain raideur qui desole tous ceux qui s'interessent a son succès. Elle danserait a merveille si elle pouvait oublier de se *redresser* en commencant'—No wit but little tittle tattle truths. They say all the governesses of her acquaintance supplied her with their observations and anecdotes. She has displeased every body trying to flatter almost every body. She has left the Duchess of Somerset [? Beaufort] and God help her and —myself for I have but ¼ to dress—at the last gasp Yours affecy. Maria E You cant buy the book if you would give your eyes for it—all bought up by the Duchess of Beaufort—but I will try to *beg* a copy.

It is after dinner—Coffee time and I have run up to my room to add a line or two. Fanny had a pleasant ride this morning with Lord Bathurst Mr. Fortescue Major Colebrooke and Mr. William Bathurst. She was the only lady because Lady Emily was unwell. The gentlemen returned unanimously charmed with

[1] *Valoe*, Conte by H. de C— (1817). Lady Bathurst eventually lent a copy to ME.

her manner of riding and she with her ride. Harriet and I mean time had been taken out by Lady Bathurst and Lady Georgiana in what they call their boat-baruche (from its boat shape)—a carriage like an Irish jingle with a [illegible] on one side. We had a delightful drive through this magnificent park. At the meeting of nine avenues in a star in the middle the view was *superbe*. The woods are seven miles in extent—'Who plants like Bathurst'[1] &c. We saw Cottswold wild and 'Saperton's fair Dale'[2]—a beautiful dale it is. We saw Pope's seat. The canal[3] here goes two mile underground in a tunnel which has lasted many years. There *will* some time be a tunnel between Holyhead and Ireland.[4] We passed by this morning in our drive a house in this park in which Swift Addison Pope and Prior *had like* to have been destroyed. They had all dined there and had just gone out when the roof fell in.

News from the best authority—perhaps it will be in the newspaper before it reaches you—Lord Wellesley is to be Lord Lieutenant of Ireland and Mr. Goulburn a most agreeable man formerly Lord Bathursts Secretary to be Secretary in Ireland.

Breakfast! *twice summoned*—Fanny quite well p'on honor 6th November [December]

To Mrs. Edgeworth

Mrs. Clutterbuck's, Bath, 7 December 1821

When I was here last I asked Colonel Johnson who had been at Calcutta whether he had ever happened to see an officer of the name of Macan and I told him of the present of pebbles[5] and Cowry shell necklace. Mr. Clutterbuck overhearing me said that he knew of a gentleman of the name now at Bath and he invited him to meet us yesterday at dinner. This gentleman proved to

[1] Pope, *Moral Essays*, iv. l. 178.

[2] Pope, *Imitations of Horace*, Bk. II, Ep. II, l. 257.

[3] The Thames and Severn Canal, for whose construction an Act of Parliament was passed in 1783.

[4] RLE had a project for a tunnel across the Menai Straits: Schofield, *The Lunar Society of Birmingham* (1965), 412.

[5] In 1813 Mr. Macan had sent ME 'a present of a set of Indian Moccoes': *Mem.* i. 296.

be the elder brother of my unknown friend. He tells me that if his brother had not died on his last passage from India he would certainly have come to see us. He was a most benevolent man and made himself adored at Armagh where their estate lies. But it was not my purpose in writing this note to give his panegyric but to tell you that he says 'If a writership were offered to me for my son or ten thousand pounds I would take the writership and thank you'. He says there is no danger for health if a young man does not drink. He is healthy himself. Much hurried Ever yr M E

Now I step into the carriage (our dear home) and we shall read Humphrey Clinker till we reach Salisbury by *firelight* and dine with Dr. and Mrs. Fowler . . .

To M. Pakenham Edgeworth

7 December 1821

My dear Pakenham—A few nights ago in a crowd of people I heard one lady tell a fact which I wished that you could hear.

An English Captain Thompson whose name and history you may perhaps have met with in your 'Winter Evenings'[1] went some years ago to New Zealand and when he was taking leave of the Zealanders one of their chiefs consented to accompany him to England to see London the wonders of which Captain Thompson described to him in a most tempting manner. But when the poor Zealander arrived in London Captain Thompson instead of taking him to see any thing for his own amusement or leaving him at liberty to walk about and divert himself shut him up and made a show of him by which he made a great deal of money. When public curiosity was satisfied and Thompson could make no more money of shewing the Zealander he carried him back to his own country on his next voyage there. During the voyage he further insulted his prisoner by making him cook for him which is thought by the Zealanders a great indignity and once he gave him a blow. The Zealander kept his resentment concealed till he arrived in his own country and then told his countrymen how he had been treated. They were so enraged at it, that

[1] Maria Hack, *Winter Evenings* (1818), does not refer to Capt. Thompson's story.

they seized Captain Thompson and his whole crew and killed and eat every one of them excepting one old woman and a boy who as the Zealander told his companions had used him well during the voyage.

In vengeance for the murder and the devouring of Captain Thompson and his crew another party of savages who were friends to the English went to war with these Zealanders conquered them in some skirmish, then it was their turn to kill and eat. They cut off the head of the Zealander who eat Captain Thompson embalmed it in some way of their own and sent it to England by a Captain Roe or Row brother to the lady who told me the story. It is now in his possession. It looks as if it had been tanned—The inside of the head taken out—The lips drawn up so as to shew the teeth—The whole face so perfectly preserved that it hardly looked as if it was dead.[1]

We met at Lord Bathursts, a Major Colebrooke who was very entertaining. He and Lady Bathurst mentioned some curious instances of the stupid exactness of the Chinese in imitating whatever is bespoken from them. Lady Bathurst sent to China one of a fine set of China dishes to have a set made by it. The dish she sent had a crack through the middle of it and in every one of the new dishes made by this pattern the crack was carefully imitated. Major Colebrooke knew a gentleman who sent a glove to China as a pattern bespeaking ten dozen of the same. The glove he sent was a left hand glove and he received ten dozen left handed gloves. He had forgotten to say *pairs of gloves*. . . .

Breakfast is ready therefore I am in a hurry to be Your very affectionate sister Maria Edgeworth

[1] The 'fact' which ME heard and passed on to Pakenham bears all the appearance of history in the process of becoming legend and combines at least two unrelated incidents. The New Zealand chief taken to England and mistreated was probably Ruatara of the Bay of Islands who volunteered as a sailor on the *Santa Anna* commanded by a man called Moody. The chief's experiences in London were described by Samuel Marsden (*Letters and Journal*, ed. J. R. Elder (1932), 64). On this story has been grafted an account of the *Boyd* massacre which occurred at Whangaroa, north of the Bay of Islands, in Dec. 1809 while Ruatara was returning from England. Marsden's version of the incident (ibid., 87) was that during a voyage from Sydney to Whangaroa Captain Thompson of the *Boyd* punished and insulted a chief, Tara, who retaliated on his arrival by engineering the massacre. I am indebted for this note to Dr. E. H. McCormick.

To Mrs. Edgeworth

George inn, Winchester,
Wednesday Evening, 12 December 1821

I have seen, heard, felt so much within these 5 last days my dearest mother that I hardly know how to tell it all—But I will endeavor to go on in the John Trot regular course from the place where I left off. We arrived at Dr. Fowlers by firelight just as we had projected. The house is in the suburbs of Salisbury —quite out of the Town—a very good comfortable house with library and dining room opening into each other. They live in the library—open shelves—mixture of half bound and bound books. All look as if they were read or appealed to continually. The *look* of the tables and of every thing in the room shewed at once what sort of people lived in it. We were received with such kindness that we felt at home directly. Mrs. Fowler is a little like Lady Lansdowne in face and has a much prettier figure. She has not an agreeable voice. She speaks through her nose and in a gruffish short way too like the Sackville Hamiltons.[1] But except this she is delightful—steel to the backbone—truth and activity and kindness personnified. As to Dr. Fowler he is a most amiable, simple hearted, benevolent creature with very polite manners—highly cultivated understanding—mixed literature and anecdotes and science—and hobby horses—Geology his present favorite hobby horse and for enjoyment of this he is happily situated near Stone Henge and the barrows and old Sarum &c. Little boys and men come to him at breakfast and dinner and supper with specimens of stones which they have found for him and he jumps up and runs to these with delight. Then his patients send for him every hour and leave him but just time enough to be the happiest man in the world. I think I never saw a happier. Next to his stones—or before them in his favor—I cannot tell which nor can he for the soul of him, come three huge cats (as large as the Persian cat) and a great black dog. Luckily husband and wife agree in doating on these cats and this dog. Never did I behold cats so spoiled. They walk on the damask breakfast cloth with their dirty paws leaving footsteps and Mrs. Fowler

[1] The eldest son of Sackville Hamilton (d. 1818), chief secretary to Ireland, married Caroline Pakenham, ME's friend.

only says 'It is quite clean dirt'. And when at last Mrs. Puss began to drink the cream and Mrs. Fowler gave her a slight box on the ear to send her off the table Dr. Fowler half turned from his drawer of specimens in which he was rummaging for some pretty specimens to give us and exclaimed 'Ann I hope that was not my cat'. Someone called this house the paradise of cats.

One night when he took us into his Sanctum Sanctorum to shew us his collection of fossils in pushed the great black dog—leaping first upon master and then upon mistress and backwards and forwards through a small room to the imminent peril of the precious fossils. And Dr. Fowler was divided so between his love of them and of the dog and his wish to get him out of the room and his incapability of turning him out! There never was any thing like it but my aunt Mary. Foster[1] came one night when my Aunt Charlotte was asleep and she wanted to hinder him from barking and stopped him with her hand and pocket handkerchief. She would doat as we do on Dr. Fowler. He is more like your dear father than any one I ever saw. He continually put us in mind of him. He is so generous that I wonder he has any thing left to give and he is generous even of the hobby-horses. He has given us quite a collection of specimens. Whenever he saw a remarkably pretty or curious stone in looking over his drawers he put it aside for us. 'You must have *that*. I have another' or 'I can get another.'

Fortunately for us he was not called away from home to any distance while we were at his house—only to Lord Radnors and others in the neighborhood. He was always at home for a wonder as Mrs. Fowler says breakfast dinner and tea. His whole time taken up in doing good or kindness to his fellow creatures and in enjoying literature and conversation for which he has always leisure. He obviously takes extreme pleasure in literary conversation and his pleasure is in the ideas and not in the display —The same activity of mind in obtaining knowledge which we have so loved and admired. On every subject when a doubt is started he goes to his books snatches up the candle and away to the very spot in the bookcase where the book wanted is to be found—and such an excellent memory! And never too much said

[1] ME's spaniel.

on any subject. We were never tired of listening to him because he listens to others.

From the moment we came till we left them Mr. and Mrs. Fowler were contriving or executing something for our amusement or information. The first day we went to see Stone-Henge. You have prints of it either in the Philosophical Transactions or some travels. Pray look at these. We did so before we went and read an account of the fall of some of these giant stones which happened a few years ago. My first impression on seeing them was disappointment. They did not look nearly so large nor take up so much space on the ground as I had expected. But the longer I looked the larger they appeared. They seemed to grow in my imagination as I compared them with other objects. At first there was no object of comparison but ourselves for they stand in a vast plain. A curricle drove up and it looked like a scollop shell. I enter not into the disputes and theories which abound concerning the origin and use of this Stone-Henge. Most votes are in favor of its being a Druid's temple. Dr. Fowler and i think it was a monument erected in commemoration of the victory which Henges obtained over Vortigern and of the killing which he made of his enemies. The stones which look like gigantic tomb stones are of three or more different sorts and all different from any stone found in the neighborhood. How they were brought here none can guess. On the bottom of the stones which have fallen we could see by the discoloring how far they had been originally sunk in the ground and this was wondrous little compared with the height—not above 3 feet and their whole height suppose 18. Good bye Stone Henge. I have not room or time for more of you. We staid till near sunset and the Post horses were sadly tired dragging us over the hilly wet grass for there was no regular road. One of the horses had the asthma and humane Mrs. Fowler must needs have us out at every *montant* to save the wheezing brute. Fanny did not catch cold. N.B. Our Devonshire clogs were of sovereign good. We were to have seen Wilton in returning from Stone Henge but Lo it was too dark to see a picture!

I should tell you that Wilton is never shewn when the family are at home but Lady Pembroke had graciously expressed to Mrs. Fowler when she asked permission before our arrival that she would like to see us and would herself shew us every thing at Wilton. We saw her and a most unaffected amiable person she appears—not at all handsome I think but F and H say very handsome. You know she is the daughter of the great Woronzow and that her brother is the famous General Micheli Woronzow. Her jewels are said to be the most splendid in Europe but like Cornelia[1] her jewels are her children—Beautiful children!—from the infant in arms to Lady Elizabeth Herbert eleven years old in every gradation of childish beauty. In the room in which Lady Pembroke was sitting there is a group of cupids by Rubens and we thought she might have her children painted to match it. This day we saw and thought of nothing at Wilton but the mother and her children. *Another fair and good and wise as she* has arisen before Time threw his dart.[2] The lamps were lighted in the great gallery before we had finished our morning visit, and as we walked through it to leave the house we had delightful glimpses of what we were to see the next day. The gallery looked beautiful and the statues sublime by this lamplight.

Next day Dr. Fowler and Mrs. Fowler went with us to Wilton and we spent three or four hours in going over the whole. Of the statues and marbles in the great gallery I will say nothing lest I should say too much. The double-cube room[3] built by Inigo Jones is beautiful but upon the whole I far prefer Warwick Castle. Wilton is a mixture of Grecian and Gothic.[4] It is not a whole. Lady Pembrokes own dressing room to which she took us to rest after luncheon (partridges) was a very snug happy looking room. The pictures of her father and brother were there. Lord Pembroke was not at home. Dr. Fowler says he is a charming man and we hope to be charmed with him in London. She said most politely that she hoped to see us in London—that she could not think of inviting us to her house in her *widowed state*.

[1] The mother of the Gracchi and daughter of Scipio Africanus.

[2] 'Death! ere thou hadst slain another
Fair and learn'd, and good as she,
Time shall throw a dart at thee.'
William Browne, *Epitaph on the Countess of Pembroke* (1591–1643).

[3] This refers to its dimensions.

[4] The Gothic detail at Wilton was largely the work of James Wyatt at the beginning of the nineteenth century. The 'Grecian' part was the famous south front built in the early seventeenth century to the designs of De Caus and Inigo Jones.

It was surprising and very agreeable to see so perfectly simple a person in the midst of so much magnificence and with so many causes to be proud so free from pride—Her happiness seeming to be quite independant of these external circumstances. I could never have guessed by her manner or language or accent that she was not English. Indeed she has lived in England since she was four years old.

Next day we went to *Longford*—Yes to Longford—Longford Castle—Lord Radnor's—The oddest castle upon the face of the earth. Lord Radnor after travelling far and near resolved that he would build a castle in his own way. I enclose you the plan which Dr. Fowler drew of it for me last night. The first old castle was a triangle and he has built a new castle round it so that at present the light of heaven can hardly enter the inhabited house. It *is* to be blest with seven towers when finished but finished it will never be in this mans frail life and his son who hates it says he will throw it down.[1] Lord Radnor had a fancy to have this castle on an eminence and he has thrown away thousands and thousands and thousands in shovelling away the earth and *letting down* trees from high places to lower to make a slope which is scarcely seen. A laborer said of him that he troubled the face of the earth. This is like he *bothered* the earth[2] but not so good. If this Lord Radnor had [not] been as immensely rich as he is or was mankind might never have seen how far obstinacy can carry a weak man.

While we were looking at his superb gallery of pictures he came into the gallery and spoke to us—a shambling figure in gaiters appended in the oddest way to breeches that looked too short. His face looked all flabby muscles—weakness trying to look strong—with a *glimmer* of sense and good nature too in his eyes. But poor man he has fits of complete loss of memory. Dr. Fowler found him the other day with half a dozen letters which

[1] In 1796 James Wyatt had made designs for additional towers and his work was carried on by D. A. Alexander 1807–17. It was never finished. The old triangular castle built in the sixteenth century in the form of an emblem of the Trinity is still embedded in the newer work. ME underrated Lord Radnor who was an enlightened local magnate and connoisseur of pictures (*Complete Peerage*, x. 718–19; *Victoria County History of Wiltshire*, v. 220–1).

[2] Cf. ME's glossary to M. Leadbeater, *Cottage Dialogues* (1811), 275: an Irish labourer speaking of an agricultural experimentalist says 'Troth, the *jantleman* has *bothered* the land'.

he had just written and he could not recollect one word he said that was in them if he was to be shot for it! But to leave Lord Radnor for what is much better worth speaking of—his pictures. I never yet saw any private collection in which there were so few bad and so many fine pictures. Fanny and Harriet were delighted. They will tell you in their journals what pleased them most and I will not tire you with repetition.

Dr. Fisher Bishop of Salisbury came in with his daughter and company while we were in the gallery at Longford—pas grande chose—very civil and Mrs. Fisher is the civillest of the civil—something like Miss White Miss Godby's governess cut shorter—dress and all. We went to the palace and you think I suppose that I have forgotten the Cathedral. No nor can I ever forget it while I live. It far surpassed my expectations. I wished a thousand times that Louisa had been in my place. It surpasses Canterbury in unity of architecture. Dr. Fowler tells us that it is the fourth highest building in the world 1st the great Pyramid—St. Peters—Strasburg—and Salisbury. I suppose Louisa knows this. Give my love to her and to your mother.

Dr. Fowler told me of a Mr. Douglas's family who were left in straitened circumstances. Their friends proposed publishing to his son to publish by subscription his fathers works for the purpose of making a provision for the widow and children. This being understood the subscription filled in a short time and ten thousand pounds were subscribed and paid. All but 3 persons have paid—Lord Lansdowne so many copies as amounted to 100 guineas and so on. All this Dr. Fowler mentioned to shew how benevolent subscriptions fill quickly in England. In Ireland I fear the money would not be *paid*. What do you think of it? It occurred to me directly for Dr. Beaufort's work[1] . . . Love to my aunts Mary and Charlotte. Your very sleepy and affectionate Maria Edgeworth.

[1] At the time of his death Dr. Beaufort was preparing an improved edition of the Memoir which accompanied his *Map of Ireland* (1792).

To Honora Edgeworth

Deepdene, Wednesday, 19 December 1821

My dear Honora . . . I have only a moment to condense our history. I wrote to Mrs. O Beirne from Winchester and Fanny to Aunt Ruxton so you know I take it for granted all up to the last day at Winchester. We arrived here on Saturday—good time for unpacking—*up* to our rooms—not the splendid apartments *we* had but much more comfortable attics—2 rooms divided only by passage. Company the first day—Lady Mary Bennet—Lady Tankerville's daughter—eternal Miss Burrowes as much a doll, as well dressed a doll as ever—with her foot ready for *chassé glissade* or contredans-forward as the case may require—Mr. Alny the new tutor (forward and silly) the Prince Cariati—a Neopolitan a banished man who had been a favorite of the king and expressly chosen by him to be embassador in England (Private—He is in figure and motions a shocking caricature, black likeness of Lovell or of what Lovell was when he first came from France—very long skirted coat which he holds up often by tucking one hand under inside the bottom of the waist behind in a manner indescribable by my pen but conceivable by your imagination). He is good humored and plays all kinds of French *petits jeux* and describes and directs them with vast emphasis and is delighted about nothing and thats all. Lady Mary Bennet is very amiable and took to us *quietly* from the first hour. *She* was not in Madeira at the time Henry was there and she had only heard he was in ill health.

Mrs. Hope has recovered her beauty that is as far as it can be recovered when the bloom of youth is gone—which even rouge cannot supply. She and Mr. Hope are as kind to us as ever. They asked quite affectionately after you. So did Henry who is as much a simple good boy as if he had never been at Eton. Little Johnny in the jaundice—Mrs. Hogan excellent Mrs. Hogan grown much older but in all other respects the same and next to our own dear Mrs. Billamore the most active and attached person in her station I ever saw. But why waste my time on housekeepers when I ought to tell you of the Duke and Duchess of St. Albans son Lord Burford and daughters the Ladies Maria and Caroline Beauclerk who arrived here on Monday and Lady Westmeath and Mr. Lock (son of the famous *painter*). Mr. Smith arrived—author of rejected addresses. These all came by appointment to go to a certain annual ball at Dorking of which Mr. Hope is one of the stewards. A Dorking ball may not sound grand but I assure you this was very genteel. Fanny and Harriet in their Paris white gauze—Mrs. Hogan who dresses Mrs. Hope's head always so beautifully at my request dressed Fannys and she *built* it most firmly and ornamented it in perfect taste—a tress added to her own and plaited with puffs of her own hair in its centre and pomegranates and white flowers happily mixed and *well fastened* into the tress—Her gold and pearl comb in front of the tress—All together lovely. It was next to Mrs. Hopes the best dressed in the room—allowed by all.

The Lady St. Albans are both beautiful—in the style of Vandyke beauties of King Charles time—very young 22 and 18—Lord Burford very handsome same style black head—but quite unanimated and stupid. At first we thought him pompous but I now do him the justice to believe that the only reason nothing comes out is because there is nothing in and the only reason he never moves one hand from his breast is because he does not know where upon earth else to place it (Not satyrical indeed Ma'am only diversion). Mr. Lock is tall as his sisters in the dancing print—beau comme le jour with a curly head like Harriets—manners very elegant but not fine—quite fit to win a heart and I think he is winning very fast the heart of Lady Caroline—But to return to my muttons.

Fanny danced a great deal and well with nobility and gentry named in her journal—*Country dance* first or as the French fashionable name terms it—*Les Colonnes*—Quadrilles—Polonaises (merely walking round). Waltzes were danced but F did not waltz. They ended with Sir Roger de Coverley at six oclock morning. Harriet danced in this last and in two quadrilles—very well quite well enough. We met at this ball Mr. Greenough and Mr. Angerstein Sneyds friend who travelled with them and Mountain in Swisserland—very agreeable. Met also Mrs. Hibbart of the beautiful cottage—Lady Rothes step mother to the Lady R who married the gardener—and her two daughters. Lady E Leslie you remember was going to be married when we were here last but at the moment when all was to conclude the mother broke it off for want of something in the settlements. The lover was sent to travel to Russia to kick his heels till Lady Rothes should die but he died first—not before he had sent over beautiful fur tippets and amethysts to Lady E Leslie. She wore weeds for him some months and now wears the fur tippet and amethysts and danced in a flandangering way at the ball to the amusement of all unfeeling spectators.

Mr. Smith the rejected addresses man is excessively entertaining. He sings humorous songs of his own composition inimitably—See Fannys journal for their names. He has a continual play of wit and drollery and at the ball was the delight of Lady Westmeath Mrs. Hope and all the Chaperons of our party. He *sung* for us *Quadrilles*[1] while they were dancing.

Mr. Angerstein was right glad that Mrs. Hope asked him to the Deepdene. He came home with us on Monday was here yesterday and is but just gone. Yesterday none up till eleven. Evening spent in playing at *the ring*—a ring on a string held in a circle by a circle and passed from hand to hand while fool in the middle seeks it and challenges any suspected hand. Many other petits jeux in which the Prince directed and delighted—Very good things for a large party. Alas Mr. Smith went away yesterday and Mr. Hope could not appear he had such a headache. This morning petits jeux again. Even the moment breakfast was over went to the *hall of the marble table* and there played at *petits paquets* (not time to describe) a great deal of running and laughing among pretty men and pretty maids . . .

I wrote the preface[2] which I send you yesterday. Harriet copied it this morning before breakfast. I will not send the original to Hunter (unless he requires it) till I hear from you. Pray my dear Honora send me your opinion and corrections and my mothers and Aunt Marys as soon as you can . . . Ever most affectionately your friend Maria E

I forgot to mention a Mr. Sneyd I met at the ball—not of Keele—a *gentleman* and a clergyman's son—I know no more.

The result of all I have felt since I came here is that I rejoice F and H have had an opportunity of seeing so much good

[1] Perhaps Moore's poem 'Country Dance and Quadrille', *Poetical Works* (1881 edn.), 579. I can find no poem of this name by Smith.

[2] To *Frank: A Sequel*.

company at so little expense of trouble. They see and are seen more thus in a party in a house in the country than in a season in London.

As I stood in a window with Mr. Hope this morning looking at a ring of company playing at French blind mans buff we both agreed in observing that we had never seen more beauty male and female collected in one circle of 12 persons. Out of 12 there were only two ugly—Prince Cariati and Henry Hope.

Mrs. Hogan who stands before me at this moment thanks you with all her heart for your Thady.[1] She has just announced to us that 'Prince Chemdelle [Cimitelli]† and another name which I am ashamed to say I can never *twist out* is come to dine here today' 'Prince Lolkoiski perhaps' 'Yes the very thing Ma'am—and two others.'

Mr. Smith told Fanny that he had intended to put me into the rejected addresses[2]—had actually written part of it in the character of an Irish laborer but as he told me it was so flat that he could make nothing of it. He threw it aside.

Steel buckles and ornaments in silk and velvet bonnets very fashionable—No long ends to sashes at your peril—Steel buckles to belts in the morning gold in the Evening preferred to sashes.

Tell my mother that I did talk to Lady Bathurst about Kitty Hamilton and she told me that as Kitty Hamilton grew up she was not a favorite with the duke of Wellington and she and Lady G Bathurst spoke of her as an awkward looking girl not at all entertaining or agreeable.

As a specimen of Mr. Smiths good choice in quotation take a *tory simile* by *Moore* which Smith gave me

> 'As bees on flowrets lighting cease to hum
> 'So settling upon Places Whigs grow dumb.'[3]

[1] A drawing of the old steward in *Castle Rackrent*.

[2] *Rejected Addresses* (1812).

[3] A slightly inaccurate quotation from *Corruption and Intolerance: Two Poems: Addressed to an Englishman by an Irishman* (1808).

To Miss Charlotte Sneyd

Frognel,[1] Xmas day 1821

My dear Aunt Charlotte, For how many years your affection and kindness have been a constant and essential part of my happiness I will not say but every returning Christmas day brings to my recollection the feeling of your soft kind hand upon my cheek when you advised little Maria not to do some foolish thing which she was just going to do. That was during the holidays which I spent with you at Lichfield. How those early days come back mixed with great pain and great pleasure to the mind—but after all as Johnson said so strongly because he felt so strongly no friendships of later date, no acquaintance however agreeable can give us pleasure equal to those early associations which are woven into our existence[2] . . .

I hope this will find you well enough to be able to hear her [Mrs. Edgeworth] read to you Walter Scotts new novel.[3] I send the 1st volume, which nobody here has yet seen. Tho there have appeared extracts in the Literary Gazette[4] no one whom I have seen has yet read the book. Those extracts must have been made before the book was published. We would not forestal our pleasure by reading them. I hope the book may amuse you. It is the surest means I can think of adding to your Christmas sociability. Not Christmas pye or goose pye, nor Sir Roger de Coverley in all his glory, can unite in pleasure every Christmas party so surely as a new novel of Scotts—that inexhaustible genius. The 2d and 3d volumes I will send by Mr. Ward through Crewe that I may not exhaust Mr. Mangin's patience.

We shall have a copy for ourselves today or tomorrow. Mr. Carr is going to buy it and he will read it to us. We are particularly glad to be now in this family and at this quiet place, where we may do just as we please and live as if we were at home . . . Mr. and Mrs. Carr are kind and warmhearted as ever—Mrs. Lushington quite as agreeable as she was when we saw her here two years ago. I am sure Admiral Pakenham would like her

[1] The house of T. W. Carr.

[2] Boswell, *Life of Samuel Johnson* (Everyman's Library ed.), i. 182.

[3] *The Pirate* (1821).

[4] *The Literary Gazette, and Journal of Belles Lettres, Arts, Sciences etc.* (London, 1817–58).

now. She looks however as if she had gone through a great deal. She is much thinner than Fanny. She seems quite happy and as a wife very agreeably happy. We have as yet seen but little of Dr. Lushington because he is much engaged by business in London but all I have seen I like better than I expected.

Many of the accounts which we saw in the papers of what he said and did the morning of the queens funeral procession were false. Till they returned to England they never saw these or knew what had been reported as to his sayings. '*Touch it at your peril*' was false. There is a form of words which as Executor he was bound to go through. *That* he said and no more. As to the unlucky time for the marriage, Mrs. Carr has explained to me how circumstances made it really impossible that it should be otherwise.[1] It would be too long to explain it to you in writing so you must wait till we meet for details. They have taken a house in Great George Street Westminster . . .

We saw Joanna Baillie and her sister yesterday—as kind and agreeable as ever. Tell Honora that they send their love to her and Mrs. Hope often said 'What a *nice* person Honora is'. . . . Believe me my dear Aunt Charlotte Your affectionate niece Maria Edgeworth

To Mrs. Edgeworth

[no date, no address—franked 29th December 1821]

My dear Mrs. E, . . . We are most completely comfortable and happy here with these hearty friends. Francis is now on the sofa reading together the murder of Mrs. Stout—supposed to be murdered by an ancester of Lord Cowpers family. This is a famous state trial which used as Mr. Spencer told us to puzzle the judgment of the great C J Fox. Mr. Spencer met C J F at Lord Cowpers and used to hear him talk about [it]. He never could make up his mind whether Mrs. Stout was murdered by Cowpers ancestor or not. After going over it again and again he

[1] Dr. Lushington married Sarah Carr on 8 Aug. The Queen had died on the previous day. Both Lushingtons followed the coffin to Brunswick where the Queen was buried. There had been differences between Ministers and the executors over the Queen's desire that the name plate with her royal title should be fixed on the coffin and over the route of the funeral procession.

one day at dinner put down his knife and fork and striking his forehead vowed he never would look at that cursed trial again it puzzled him so but in spite of his vow he was at the book again that evening. Pray be at it if you can borrow 13th volume State Trials in Octavo. The year of the trial is 1699—Title—Trial of Spencer Cowper and others for the murder of Mrs. Sarah Stout.[1]

a propos—I forgot to tell you when I was at Mr. Clutterbucks this curious fact. Mr. Clutterbuck being well acquainted with the disposition of one of his friends to delay till *tomorrow* said to him laughing one night 'You are just the fellow to get a reprieve for a man and put off giving it till the man was hanged'. 'By G—' cried his friend starting up 'Youve hit it. I have a reprieve for a man in my pocket this minute.' That instant he ran to horse and if he had not galloped hard would have been too late—just reached the place of execution.

We read—I mean we heard read by Mr. Carr who reads admirably—half the first volume of the Pirate—stopped at the chapter ending with the description of the witch *Norna of Fitful head*. We were much pleased and interested especially with the beautiful description of Mordants education and employments—the sea monsters &c—most poetical—in Scotts master style—The description of the two sisters excellent—The miser *Baby* diverting—The manner in which by scarcely perceptible touches he wakens the readers interest for his hero admirable—unequalled by all but Shakespear—The satire upon modern agriculturists in the character of Yellowly excellent. *But* I fear the repetition of his Meg Merriless. We shall see and we may well trust to this wonderful genius who can raise an interest even on the barren rocks of Zetland. Aladdin's magician is nothing to him. He could only raise palaces at will but the mighty master

[1] Spencer Cowper (1669–1728), brother of 1st Lord Cowper. He and three other lawyers were accused at Hertford of murdering Sarah Stout, a Quaker girl whom they had visited one evening on business. Her body had been found floating in the river the following morning. There was no direct evidence and they were acquitted and no further proceedings were allowed as the prosecution was held to be malicious: the local Tories wished to convict a member of an eminent Whig family and the Quakers to defend one of their body from the imputation of suicide. Cowper later became a judge. Both then and since the case aroused much published argument. ME refers to W. Cobbett's *Complete Collection of State Trials*, 33 vols. (1809–26).

Scott can transport us in five minutes to the most remote desart corner of earth—aye and keep us there and make us wish to stay there among beings of his own creation raised by his wand—breathing—living—speaking—interesting us even to the forgetfulness of all objects around us—to the exclusion of all the other joys or cares of life—Even made me forget that it was time for Fanny to go to bed but she did go at 11.

Last night we were all seated in this manner as happy as possible[1] listening to Mr. Carr reading the Pirate. Shew this ground plan to Honora who knows the room and she will insense you.

Thanks to the printing press—the mail coach and the steam packet gifts beyond the gifts of fairies we can all see and hear what each other are doing and do and read the same things nearly at the same time. [no signature]

To Sophy Ruxton

Frognel, 3 January 1822

My dear Sophy, I reproach myself for having written as I fear I did yesterday a most stupid letter to my dear Aunt . . . I believe I left off abruptly when I had mentioned the Pirate[2] which I hope you have and are reading to my aunt. The characters of the two sisters are beautiful. The idea of Brenda's not believing in supernatural agency and yet being afraid and her sister Minna not being afraid tho she believes in Norna's power is new and natural and ingenious. This idea was Joanna Baillie's. The picture of the sisters sleeping and the lacing scene is excellent and there are not only passages of beautiful picturesque description but many more deep philosophical reflexions upon the human mind and the causes of human happiness than in any of his other works. The satire upon agriculturists imported from one country to another and who set to work to improve the land and the habits of the people without being acquainted with the

[1] Plan given here—with commentary on characters in their places. See p. 304.

[2] ME to Mrs. Ruxton, 2 Jan. 1822: '. . . I think you will not like the winding up of the story The Pirate and upon the whole you will rank it as inferior to Waverley and Kenilworth—but superior to the Abbot and the Monastery. . . .'

circumstances of either is excellent. I am sure my uncle will like this and laugh with Magnus Troil. It is wonderful how genius can make even barren Zetland fertile in novelty. Norna of the

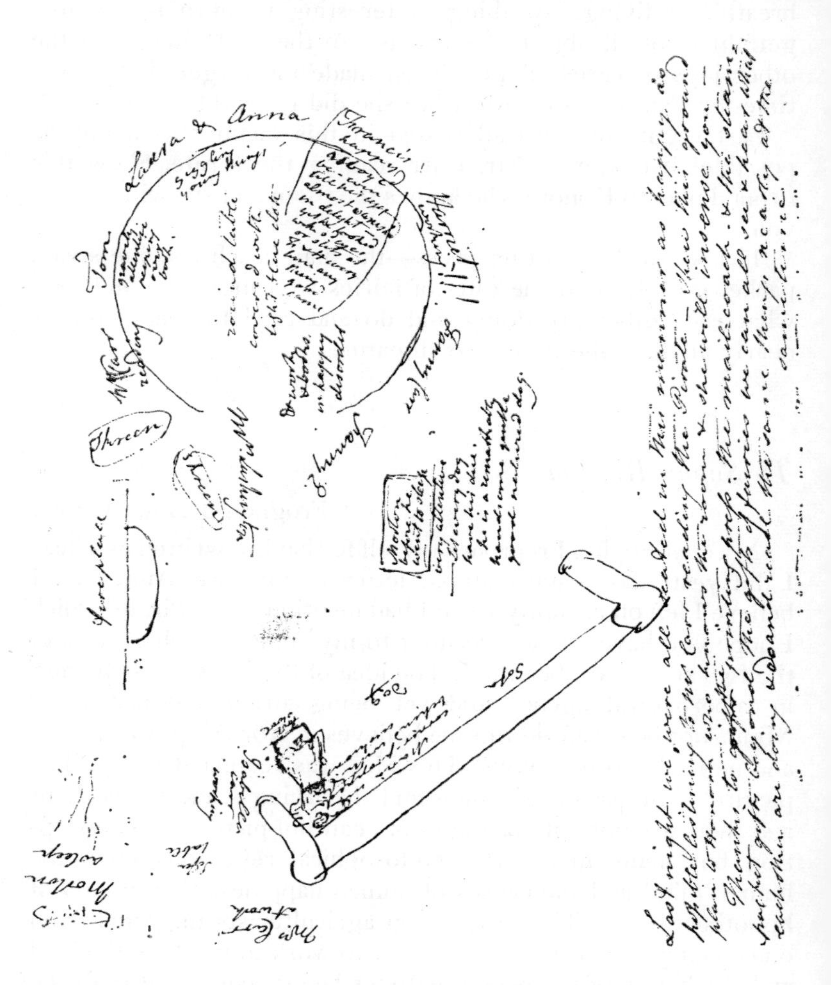

fitful head is quite new—not the least resemblance to Meg Merriless or any of his other hags though I am sure that common readers will all say this is a repetition of himself. I wish I could hear what you all say as you read on. The pleasure of

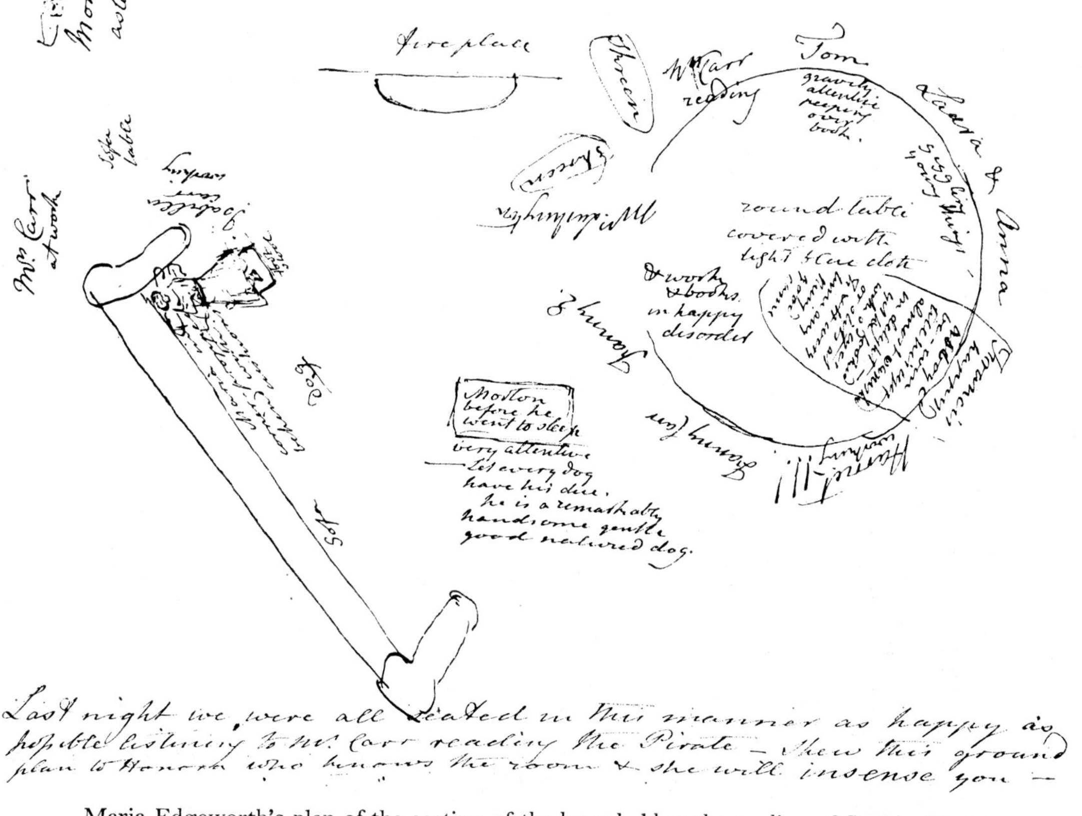

Maria Edgeworth's plan of the seating of the household at the reading of Scott's *Pirate*

reading such books is infinitely increased by reading them with friends who take a strong interest in them. I think I see my aunt laying down the book to tell you what she thinks of particular passages. Pray my dear Sophy remember for me whatever she most likes or dislikes.

I have written to Edgeworths Town to desire that letters should be sent to you and I hope Honora will send you a scrawl of a ground plan I drew of the manner in which we were all seated the first night Mr. Carr began to read the Pirate to us. Taking it for granted that you have or will soon have said ground plan before you I must observe that I did not sit long bolstered up in state on the sofa as I have represented myself but surrendered it to Mrs. Lushington and Fanny who lay at full length feet to feet the next night and Morton did not go to sleep. He was very much ashamed of having slept this first night. Both Morton and Tom are very amiable young men. Tom is clever—both are handsome—Tom dark—like an Italian portrait—Morton fair—light hair and quick coloring with every emotion. He has such a high sense of honor and chivalrous sentiments, and delicacy of taste with regard to the characters and manners and dress of women and such a strong feeling of what is due to our sex from his that I should say there was quite the making of a hero of a novel in Morton Carr. But Alas he is in sober reality to be a special pleader and cannot afford to be a hero for many years to come. I wish you had seen him the other day when a cruel anonymous letter was sent to his sister Mrs. Lushington on whom by the by he doats. He is as warmly fond of her as Richard at his age (20) was of you. New years day was Mr. and Mrs. Carr's wedding day and it was kept as it always is in the family with family rejoicings. Dr. Holland has dined here every new years day for the last six years and he dined here and so did Miss Mulso another intimate friend of this family a niece of Mrs. Chapones was also of the party and Joanna Baillie and her sister. These with Mr. Carrs whole family and ourselves made 20 at dinner. Little Francis I believe I told you has been here ever since we came. There was much diversion after dinner, Mr. Carr gave many family toasts which we stood up to drink 3 times 3—6 times 6 and 9 times 9. Some were so affectionate that they made the tears roll down the cheeks of his children. They are a most united amiable family. In the evening all the family had a merry dance in which Joanna Baillie and her sister joined. And about half an hour before we went to bed, as it had been previously agreed upon we all at a signal given ran up to our rooms to dress in different characters for a sort of Masquerade. We did not know what characters different people would appear in but we had decided upon our own. Fanny was to be a nun. She was dressed in a white muslin veil and drapery over her black gown in a minute and I fell to decking Harriet who was to be a pert travelled young lady just returned from Paris at the height of the fashion. She was an excellent figure—crowned with feathers of all colors to an amazing height with a golden diadem and profusion of artificial flowers—a nosegay of vast size—rose colored gauze dress with a border of roses—scarlet sash and a waist of peaked length—And ringlets of dark hair and dark eyebrows which so completely altered her that no creature guessed who she was. Mrs. Carr at last knew her as she said by her likeness to her mother. Harriet supported her character with great spirit and with such an ease of motion so unincumbered by her finery that instead of looking like a vulgar fine lady as had been intended she looked like a real fine lady overdressed by some mistake. Everybody said she was quite handsome.

I was an Irish nurse in a red cloak &c come all the way from Killogensawce to look for my two *childer* that left me last year to go to foreign parts and was I heerd at Mistress Carrs. Little Francis was Triptolemus in the Pirate—an excellent figure. Mrs. Carr was *Baby* (Miss Yellowly in the Pirate)—Mr. Carr a jew with an enormous nose and beard. Miss Isabella Carr was an old lady in an old fashioned dress with Laura Carr her daughter in powder and a court dress—Mrs. Lushington their maid—Anna Carr a French troubadour—singing delightfully—speaking French perfectly—William Carr the youngest son—a half pay officer who as it was justly said looked as if he had been the king of the coffee-house for the last ten years—Tom—a famous black beggar in London called Billy Waters—with a wooden leg and a guitar. (His wooden leg he said was so painful to him that he never would have put it on if he had known how much he was to endure. He now and then set it upon other people's feet and they suffered too.) Morton was Meg Merriless—Dr. Lushington a housemaid Betty Brush—Miss Mulso an English ballad singer —*Mr. Burrell* I forgot to mention as one of the established friends privileged to be here on new years day—he was a Spanish gentleman—Don Pedro Velasquez Tordesillas—very good ruff and hat and feathers but much wanting a sword when insulted by the black who trod on his toes. In the scuffle of dressing for which only ten minutes were allowed no sword could be found for the Spaniard.

The Miss Baillies did not stay for the masquerade which I was sorry for but they were not told of it. It had been kept a dead secret. From the quickness of preparation and our all being a family party this little masquerade went off very well and was very diverting to the persons concerned. . . . Your affec Maria E

To Harriet Beaufort

Frognel, Hampstead, 5 January 1822

My dear Harriet . . . Captain Beaufort dined here yesterday. Mrs. Carr is very fond of him and all the family seem to know his value. I was sorry that instead of Dr. Holland, an uncle and aunt and cousin dined here who did not add much to the pleasures of conversation. There was a very sensible well informed lawyer Mr. Rolfe who has written an admired political-economy pamphlet[1] and who converses remarkably well, but I fear that Mr. Holland, after we ladies left the room got into some legal or mercantile discussion with Mr. Carr which prevented Mr. Rolfe and your brother from talking and shewing themselves to each other . . . Mr. Rolfe has lately seen and questioned one of the men from new South-Wales—I should say an *Australian*—So they chuse to be called. He gives a horrid description of the natives who seem by his account but a step removed from beasts. When a whale is thrown upon the coast, they run down to feast upon it and eat to such excess that they can scarce move then rub themselves all over with the fat and in that greasy swollen helpless condition lie down on the shores to sleep like so many sloths.

[1] I cannot identify this.

As I have not time for easy transitions skip if you please from the Sloths and the Australians to Dr. Wollaston and the Royal Society. Mr. Rolfe was present one day when all the London scientific men were present Arago, Biot, Kater and all the grandees and just to prove how few people even of the best informed have their knowledge ready or can use it when suddenly called upon he went round to each and asked 'What o'clock is it now by sidereal time?'[1] One repeated the words *'Sidereal time!'* Another answered 'I can tell you when I go home.' Another—I forget what. But not one could answer directly. I think if William had been there he would have answered rightly.

This morning we have had a visit from one of Dr. Wollaston's greatest admirers Miss Sebright—daughter of Sir J. Sebright—the lady who gave me that smallest galvanic battery which went into her flattened thimble as I believe you saw. . . . Mrs. Marcet brought Miss Sebright here and was so good as to spend two hours here this morning. Oh how unlike most morning visits when one longs to see the hand put upon the bell to ring for the carriage—that is what one most fears with Mrs Marcet. I never knew any woman except Mrs. E— who had so much *accurate* information and who can give it out in narration so clearly, so much for the pleasure and benefit of others without the least ostentation or mock humility. What she knows she knows without fear or hesitation and stops and tells you she knows no more whenever she is not certain. As Mrs. Carr with her characteristic love of integrity observed Mrs. Marcet never goes one point beyond what she can vouch for truth and never practises any of the little arts of professed conversationalists to hide the *bounds* of the knowledge or to excite sensation and surprise.

You saw her letter to me about the schools at Florence. She told us many other curious facts relative to the state of Florence. The grand Duke of Tuscany[2] brother to the Emperor of Austria she describes as a very amiable man—not of great ability but of a liberal and even magnanimous character—willing to give his

[1] The period between the departure and return of a meridian to a star is a sidereal day. Sidereal time is based on the movement(s) of (a) star(s). ME was probably wrong in supposing that her brother could have answered the question off hand.

[2] Ferdinand III of Habsburg.

people as much liberty as his brother of Austria will let him. He encourages men of literature and science. One of the literary men told Dr. Marcet that lately the Emperor sent to the Duke a list of 200 persons in Florence whom he *advised* him to *suspect* and in short to arrest as disaffected. The Duke read over the list and tore it instantly down the middle exclaiming 'Tell my brother of Austria that there is not one person named here who would not shed his blood to serve me.'

Mr. Carr after joining with all of us in admiring this trait worthy of the Romans in their best days observed that in time such people must make themselves free. Mrs. Marcet thinks so too. Pray get General Pepe's pamphlet[1] or I will get it and send it to you if I can.

'When I wish to know the state of any country' said Mr. Carr 'The three first or most important questions I would ask are "What is the state of education? What degree of liberty of the press is allowed? And how is justice administered?"'

After having answered nearly according to the letter you read the question relative to education, Mrs. Marcet as to the liberty of the press *permitted* by the Grand duke in Florence stated that there is a bookseller there a Genevese who keeps a sort of coffee-house, where many English newspapers are openly read daily—and Italian and French papers—Galignani[2] and others. When the Austrian troops at the time of the late revolution came to Florence the Austrian officers used to go to this coffee house delighted to read these papers, to them contraband and quite new. They learned from [them] they said where they were going and what they were doing and to do. At this critical moment the Swiss master of the coffee-house library threw the Italian papers from Naples containing the patriot proclamations into a drawer and did not produce them to the Austrians lest he should be informed against and ordered to shut up his house; but he knew the Austrian officers were so delighted with the English and French [papers] that they would keep his counsel and their own. There was a certain Lord Dillon at Florence

[1] Gulielmo Pepe, *A Narrative of the Political and Military Events that took place at Naples in 1820 and 1821* (London, 1821).

[2] *Galignani's Messenger*, a paper founded in 1814. It had a large circulation among Englishmen on the Continent.

about this time who used to frequent this library and to flame away in the most *patriotic* revolutionary style against the Austrian government. The Master of the house went up to him one day and begged of him to restrain his liberty of speech for a few days till the Austrians should have left Florence 'for if you do not Sir my house will be shut up—I expect the order every hour'. Lord Dillon complied. The house was not shut up. This proves a degree of liberty permitted by the Duke at Florence beyond what I had any idea of.

Mr. Carr next asked about the administration of justice. 'I am ashamed to tell you' said Mrs. Marcet 'that I do not know exactly how that is. I do not know how the judges are appointed or paid or how justice is administered.' We admired her as much for confessing what she did not know as for telling us all she did. I only wish I could tell you 1/100th part of it.

I have this moment recollected that when I was telling you of the Australians I omitted the very thing which I most wanted to mention—An instance of the folly of endeavoring to govern these three quarter savages by the laws of civilised England. They had been used to pillage the English and one day when a number of them had assembled for this purpose the English magistrate attended by military went down among them with intention to *read the riot act* and then fire upon the mob; the wretched natives on first sight of the military scrambled up into the trees and there sat clinging and jabbering like monkeys while the magistrate read 'In the name of our Sovereign Lord King George &c' and the moment they had on their side *jabbered* over the riot act they fired on the *rebels* in the trees and killed them as if they had really been fair game! A Scotch gentleman who heard this anecdote told us that in Edinburgh a humourist friend of his being disturbed night after night by cats caterwauling on the leads of his neighbors house got up one night went out read the riot act to them and then fired. I have only to remark that he ought to have read the riot act nine times to the cats for each of their nine lives.

If you chance to meet the Solicitor General[1] pray tell him what I heard an eminent English lawyer say yesterday that law books have so encreased of late that it is absolutely necessary

[1] Charles Kendal Bushe.

for a lawyers library to have a *thousand* volumes to begin with and twenty five guineas a year must be spent at least upon it to keep it up to the current of modern practice. God help, as the gentleman said, poor young lawyers who scarcely can make 25 Guineas per Annum. We dined yesterday with the gentleman who told me this—Mr. Richardson an intimate friend of Walter Scotts—Jeffrey and all that Scotch Constellation. He has given me a box made of wood 700 years old—made of the old cupola of Westminster hall. We were to have had Mr. Bell the celebrated anatomist at this dinner but he was not able to come. We had only his pretty genteel and well informed wife who was pleased with my telling her the truth that I had read nearly 20 years ago her husbands eloquent preface to his Anatomy[1] and that the impression is as fresh in my memory as if I had just read it that impression was so strong. It left on my mind a horror of ignorance rushing in where knowledge fears to tread. I think my dear Harriet you read it at the same time when my father recommended it to me. How long afterwards we have felt the advantage of all he recommended! There is in this recollection a feeling of mixed pleasure and pain which I would not part with for anything upon earth.

I met yesterday at dinner the author of Barry Cornwalls poems[2]—Mr. Procter a lawyer—the most pitiable object ever beheld. He has been struck either with what he calls a coup de soleil or insanity . . .

I enclose for the amusement of your convalescent a song which Mr. Smith (Rejected addresses) sung for us at the Deepdene 'Quadrilling'. Another of his has been in the newspapers but I hope what I send you has not yet been published. I have not time to say more except that Mrs. Lushington is now as agreeable as we first thought Sarah Carr and has shewn since we have been here a degree of strength of mind and self command about a duel[3] in which her husband had nearly been doomed which was worthy of Mrs. Honora E herself! Dr. Lushington has been

[1] C. Bell, *The Anatomy of Expression* (1806), *A New Idea of the Anatomy of the Brain* (1811).

[2] Barry Cornwall, *Dramatic Scenes* (1819), *Marcian Colonna* (1820), *A Sicilian Story* (1821).

[3] Dr. Lushington challenged a Mr. Blacket, who had jilted his sister. A long letter (13 Jan. 1822) about it to Mrs. Edgeworth is omitted.

much misrepresented in the newspapers. He is an amiable private character and has many friends strongly attached to him. As to his politics I have nothing to do with them. I only hope and believe he will make his wife happy. On her journey home from Brunswick by the Rhine she took 90 sketches—beautiful . . . Ever affectionately yr. ever hurried Maria E.

To Mrs. Edgeworth

Frognel, 7 January 1822

. . . This is our last day at Frognel! We are very sorry to leave these excellent kind friends, this happy united family who have such a constant flow of spirits, conversation and occupation . . .

Mrs. Marcet has quite won the hearts and heads of all this family but I will say no more of her if I can help it. I wrote a long account to Harriet Beaufort yesterday of her morning visit and conversation here. Mrs. Carr is most anxious to cultivate her acquaintance especially for Mrs. Lushington who is to live in Town. We have the delight of feeling that we now as formerly draw together our mutual friends who are best suited to each other. Mrs. Carr almost afraid asked Mrs. Marcet without ceremony to dine here in a family party next day. She frankly said she should like it of all things. She came yesterday and a delightful evening we had. The part of the conversation which most concerned me and all I have now time to repeat concerned Writerships and boys educated for India. Mrs. Marcet told me that Mrs. Prinsep the mother of her sister in law has 6 sons now in India and prospering there—two merchants—two underwriters an engineer and an essayer at the mint. Mr. Prinsep from the time he destined his boys for India turned his mind to educate them for it. Hearing that war was over and military engineers likely to be out of employ he made his son attend to civil engineering—made him go out with a surveyor &c. In consequence he was employed as a civil Engineer the moment he got to India. Mr. Prinsep heard that an essayer of coins might be wanted. He gave £500 to the Essayer at the mint in London to instruct his 2d son. The consequence is that he is now Essayer of coins in India. The others went through regular education at

Hertford College.[1] In consequence of the improved education and regulations for the Company's servants in India the whole system manners and morals have changed and as Mrs. Marcet assures me there are no young better informed better principled or better conducted than those who now go out as Writers to India. With the danger to their morals much of the danger for their health has decreased. The 6 youths I mentioned are examples of this. They are all in good health and speak without any horror of the climate. When I go to Hertford you may be sure I will keep my eyes and ears open for all that may concern Pakenham . . .

You justly guess that Mrs. Marcets present house could not admit of her lodging us but she will undertake to find apartments for us so near to her that we shall have the advantage I first proposed to myself in coming to Town of being with her almost constantly. She *wishes* it and loves us. All the rest you know follows. I have money enough and cannot bestow it better than in making this month or 6 weeks in London (the last probably I shall ever be there) perfectly comfortable to my dear sisters. Therefore we shall have as good apartments as can be had and very good I hear are to be had for 5 or 6 guineas a week.

Our carriage has been looked over by Mr. Carrs experienced coachman; he pronounces it quite equal to the Scotch journey[2] and will take it into his yard and take care of it while we are in Town. We shall have a good job coach which will hold friends . . .

I shall so arrange and *limit* our goings out with the assistance of judicious Mrs. Marcet that Fannys health shall not suffer by over excitement. I am not strong enough myself either to like going out in the evenings after we have seen sights in the mornings. This I shall insist upon. We shall keep out of the fine whirl of London and yet I trust see all worth seeing. I shall put all the sense and resolution I have in requisition to accomplish these points. I know they are difficult but I trust much to myself when I have so great an object before my eyes as justifying your

[1] Hertford College (East India College) was founded in 1806 for the education of the servants of the East India Co. It was at first situated in Hertford Castle but moved almost immediately to new buildings at Haileybury, two miles to the south-east of the town.

[2] ME had intended after leaving London to go to Scotland to see Walter Scott, but because of the latter's other engagements she abandoned the idea.

confidence my dear mother and doing as my father would expect from his daughter Maria.

I have just corrected the proof sheets of the Preface to Frank.[1] Mr. Carr has read and approves it. By his counsel I have strengthened the passage I had inserted about mistaken ideas of manliness.

I do not agree in general with your low opinion of the Pirate.

Tom Carr took little Francis to the play last night[2]—Hamlet —by Young—admirable—Pantomime new—very entertaining —Mother Bunch—The yellow dwarf on a yellow cat—beautiful view of the gold mines—being the palace of the king of the gold mines the rival of the yellow dwarf in the affections of a beauty daughter of the Queen of the ruby-nose. The arches of gold and long perspective of the gold mines with reflexion on the stream flowing beneath was I am told truly enchanting. Besides this yellow dwarf pantomime there was a pantomimic representation of Johnny Gilpin on his horse which by the by was curiously patched. He galloped across the stage and leaped over a five barred gate. In short Francis was delighted with his nights diversion and I hope Pakenham will be amused with the description of it and you will be pleased with Tom Carrs good nature in taking Francis. They are all 3 very amiable young men excessively fond of their father mother and sisters and not fancying it *manly* to affect the contrary . . .

Pray as soon as you and Lovell can make up your minds let me know whether Pakenham is to come to the Charterhouse this spring and what time exactly. I wish to be provided with this knowledge before I go to see Mr. Russell. Sydney Smith to frighten a little boy who was going to school or perhaps to laugh him out of his fears told him that at his school the boys were flogged with *three-usher* power—as good as what he said of a man's eating with a 3-parson power. Great danger of drowning in England unless a frost make all solid again. . . . I must now go and pack up for change of dwellings. Ever affectionately yours Maria E . . .

[1] *Frank: A Sequel.*

[2] At Theatre Royal, Covent Garden. 'Harlequin and Mother Bunch or the Yellow Dwarf, a new Pantomime', opened 26 Dec. 1821. *Hamlet* with Mr. Young and Miss M. Tree opened on 4 Jan. 1822.

To Mrs. Edgeworth

Mrs. Baillie's, Hampstead,
Tuesday Evening, 8 January 1822

My dear Mother—Fanny's cold is much better. She has been with me in town today in good Mrs. Carrs coach which is as hospitable as her house. We went to a certain Mrs. Ducks one of those necessary animals called dressmakers. Fanny went to try on a comfortable warm blue cloth pelisse which fits her well and looks well—trimmed with broad black velvet after the fashion of Lady G Bathursts. Harriet has a cloth gown to match it and a pelerine to wear with it— *or/and* her black velvet spencer *will* go over it in sharp frost—So I hope they are both handsomely provided against cold. Bought for Fanny also a pair of outside furred shoes—price 13/6—but better bestowed than a guinea fee to a physician.

After *fitting* at Mrs. Ducks which was performed in all the elegant luxury of a fashionable dressmaker in a room with an excellent fire Mrs. Carr set us down at our Town *home* Mrs. Marcets while she went to do various commissions for her daughter in the city and then to ultimate George St Westminster No. 2 to see Mrs. Lushington in her new house in which she has been but one day and is in all the horrors of settling.

Mean time Mrs. Marcet not being at home we went upstairs took possession of the drawing room sat down the pictures of comfort—Maria in a low arm chair—Fanny on sofa—read Mill on Political Economy[1] and she Prinseps political history of India[2] till Miss Marcet and Dr. Marcet appeared—*delighted* to see us —talked with the Doctor and admired some beautiful drawings of Miss Marcets—views in Swisserland and Italy—till Mrs. Marcet returned with her benevolent face always full of welcome for us—Luncheon—She would toast a bit of bread for toast and water for Fanny. It should be a thick lump mind and the instant it is soused into the glass of water the glass should be covered. I suppose you who know all things know this but I ignoramus as I am never am five minutes in Mrs. Marcet's company without

[1] James Mill, *Elements of Political Economy* (1821).

[2] H. T. Prinsep, *A History of the Political and Military Transactions in India during The Administration of the Marquess of Hastings*, ed. C. R. Prinsep (1820).

learning something new of the arts of life. She can give one entertaining titbits of scandal too—a whole history this morning of Madame Chenevix and Sir John Sebrights sayings and doings about her marriage—But I have no time to repeat scandal . . . [no signature]

To Lucy Edgeworth

Miss Baillie's, Hampstead, 12 January 1822[1]

I have been four days resolving to get up half an hour earlier that I might have time to tell you, my dear Lucy, the history of a cat of Joanna and Agnes Baillie's.

You may, perhaps, have heard the name of a celebrated Mr. Brodie, who wrote on poisons, and whose papers on this subject are to be found in the Transactions of the Royal Society, and reviewed in the Edinburgh Review, in 1811.[2] He brought some of the Woorara poison, with which the natives poison their arrows and destroy their victims. It was his theory that this poison destroys by affecting the nervous system only, and that after a certain time its effects on the nerves would cease as the effects of intoxicating liquors cease, and that the patient might recover, if the lungs could be kept in play, if respiration were not suspended during the trance or partial death in which the patient lies. To prove the truth of this by experiment he fell to work upon a cat; he pricked the cat with the point of a lancet dipped in woorara. It was some minutes before the animal became convulsed, and then it lay, to all appearance, dead. Mr. Brodie applied a tube to its mouth, and blew air into it from time to time; after lying some hours apparently lifeless, it recovered, shook itself, and went about its own affairs as usual. This was tried several times, much to the satisfaction of the philosophical spectators, but not quite to the satisfaction of poor puss, who grew very thin and looked so wretched that Doctor Baillie's son, then a boy, took compassion on this poor subject of experiment, and begged Mr. Brodie would let him carry off the cat. With or

[1] Manuscript missing; printed from *Mem.* ii. 165–7.

[2] *Philosophical Transactions* (1811), Pt. I, reviewed in *Edinburgh Review,* xviii (Aug. 1811), 370.

without consent, he did carry her off, and brought her to his aunts, Joanna and Agnes Baillie. Then puss's prosperous days began. Agnes made a soft bed for her in her own room, and by night and day she was the happiest of cats; she was called Woorara, which in time shortened to Woory. I wish I could wind up Woory's history by assuring you that she was the most attached and grateful of cats, but truth forbids. A few weeks after her arrival at Hampstead she marched off and never was heard of more. It is supposed that she took to evil courses: tasted the blood and bones of her neighbours' chickens, and fell at last a sacrifice to the vengeance of a cookmaid.

After this cat's departure Agnes took to heart a kitten, who was very fond of her. This kitten, the first night she slept in her room, on wakening in the morning looked up from the hearth at Agnes, who was lying awake, but with her eyes half shut, and marked all puss's motions; after looking some instants, puss jumped up on the bed, crept softly forward and put her paw, with its glove on, upon one of Miss Baillie's eyelids and pushed it gently up; Miss Baillie looked at her fixedly, and puss, as if satisfied that her eyes were *there* and safe, went back to her station on the hearth and never troubled herself more about the matter.

To finish this chapter of cats. I saw yesterday at a lady's house in Hampstead, a real Persian cat, brought over by a Navy Captain, her brother. It has long hair like a dog, and a tail like a terrier's, only with longer hair. It is the most gentle depressed-looking creature I ever saw; it seems to have the mal du pays, and moreover, had the cholic the morning I saw it, and Agnes Baillie had a spoonful of castor oil poured out for it, but it ran away.

Joanna quoted to me the other day an excellent proverb applied to health: 'Let well alone'. If the Italian valetudinarian had done this his epitaph would not have arrived at the 'sto qui'.[1]

[1] The full epitaph is 'Stavo ben, ma per star meglio, sto qui'. It is quoted by Dryden in *Dedication to the Aeneis* (*Essays*, ed. Ker (New York, 1961), ii. 169) and was applied to a man 'who, being in good health, lodged himself in a physician's house, and was overpersuaded by his landlord to take physic (of which he died)'. It is also quoted by Addison in *Spectator*, No. 25. It is not possible to convey the full play on words, but the phrase means 'I was well, but through trying to be better, I am here'.

Captain Beaufort tells me that they have found out that the wool under the buffalo's long hair is finer than the material of which Cashmere shawls are made, and they are going to manufacture shawls of buffalo's wool, which are to shame and silence the looms of Cashmere. Would my mother choose to wait for one of these?

Francis, Harriet and I went a few nights ago to see a little play at Mr. Frere's; but I hear that Harriet has just written an account of it to you. This is the first note I have addressed to you these six weeks, but believe me that, whether directed to you or not, to amuse you is my first object in all my letters.

To Mrs. Edgeworth

Hampstead, Tuesday morning, 8 oclock,
14 January 1822

We are come to our last morning at this hospitable house. Most affectionate hospitality has been shewn to us by these two excellent sisters and with such good sense and good taste that we have been in every respect as luxuriously comfortable in their small house and with their small means as we have been with the grandest people in the land with £40,000 per annum at their disposal. I part with Agnes and Joanna Baillie confirmed in my opinion that the one is the most amiable literary woman I ever beheld and the other one of the best informed and most useful. At 64 Agnes Baillie is as active mind and body as a woman of 20 and Joanna in spite of many literary disappointments is the most candid and generously indulgent to all her rivals and the most affectionate to her friends. Both these sisters have nursed Fanny with the utmost tenderness and have never for one minute oppressed her with the *too much care* . . .

I rejoice that Mr. Bushe is Chief Justice. Mrs. Bushe sent me through Anne Nangle a most kind message alluding to our Patronage *second sight*.[1] An hour after I had read your letter arrived the gentleman who franks this letter and with whom as

[1] Charles Kendal Bushe was the original for the lord chief justice in ME's novel *Patronage* (1814).

your daughters inform me you have been in love this 8 years. So have I and his conversation last night has sunk me over head and shoulders. He is one of the most sensible quiet well bred conversers I ever heard—quite unlike the *professed* agreeable men. Mrs. Abercromby who was to have come with him had such a cold she could not come out—was not that comfortable? It was curious that he began with giving us an account of all Lord Wellesley has been doing in Ireland—how he jockied and jostled Downes and Saurin out to make way for Bushe. He certainly shewed great cleverness in duncing old Downes and making him resign when he had resolved not to do it till Saurin pleased and then telling Saurin that Downes had resigned and by that means throwing Saurin into a fit of ill humour in which he plump refused to accept the Chief Justice-ship—a refusal which Lord Wellesley took au pied de la lettre and bowed him out. I must own much as I rejoice in Bushe's promotion and much as I dislike Saurin for his intolerance[1] I think he has been ill used.

Mr. Abercromby tells me that all is quieting and will be quieted in Ireland. His means of information are good and I hope he is right. He entertained us for 3 hours with anecdotes of Fox and Mrs. Fox with whom he was very intimate and with accounts of Lord Grenville with whom he has lately been staying at Dropmore. He says that when he first went there and heard there was no company in the house he was frightened almost out of his wits at the thoughts of a tete a tete with silent Lord Grenville but to his astonishment he found him tete a tete the most communicative talkative of men. He had only to ask him whatever he pleased and set him agoing and on he went delightfully —like the Primate.[2] People mistake and those who can venture to talk to him freely please him and conquer his constitutional bashfulness. Mr. Abercromby says he is the most goodnatured man he ever was with. At breakfast he has 3 or 4 Spaniels always jumping upon him whom he feeds with fingers and keeps down as well as he can protecting from the newspaper which he is reading all the time. Of these spaniels for want of children he is doatingly fond. He is remarkably fond of children.

[1] Saurin was ultra-Protestant.

[2] Hon. William Stuart, Archbishop of Armagh.

Mr. Abercromby saw him with two little boys sons of a friend and all morning he was diverting them in the library looking for entertaining books and prints for them—such a new idea of Lord Grenville. I must see him again—and see him at Dropmore—safest to begin with a little aversion! He has cut out of public business. He has some tendency to ossification in his head which occasions dreadful headaches.

Mr. Abercrombys account of Charles Fox confirmed all we have heard of his domestic amiability. Mrs. Fox he says was of all women he ever knew the most destitute of any thing like intellectual taste—a mere good sort of housekeeper devoted to him. 'If any body else had been put there and as good to him Fox would have gone on with her and liked her.' He had a vast deal of Mr. Transfer[1] about him!—liking what he was used to and too good natured to object or change. *Trotter* was put about him by Mrs. Fox. All Fox's friends disliked him: he was a mean fellow of no abilities and has been a constant drain to Mrs. Fox since C J's death—Impossible to supply his extravagance &c . . .
Your ever affectionate Maria E

To Mrs. Edgeworth

Beechwood Park,[2] Wednesday, 16 January 1822

My dear mother After a pleasant drive on a sunshining day arrived here yesterday just in good time for dressing for dinner. Sir John Sebright who had galloped past us as we left St. Albans and who had taken a good stare into the carriage, met us at his park gate to welcome us with the most gracious countenance that his eyebrows would permit. A very fine park it is with magnificently large beech trees which well deserve to give their name to the place. The house is a fine looking house—was a convent in the days of Edward the 6th—part of the building of that time still in being but all so modernised that this is only *to say*. The library with books on all sides on open shelves is very handsome and comfortable—40 feet long opening from a carpetted hall and seeing into a little snuggery at the farthest end

[1] J. Moore, *Zeluco* (1786), ii, chaps. lvi–lix. The simile is not very apt.
[2] Sir J. Sebright's house in Herts.

in which there was a blazing fire formed a goodly view on a cold day to travellers on their first entrance. At a large fireplace in the middle of the library Mrs. Marcet was standing with Miss Sebrights. We rejoiced to make sure of her—and from some dusky corner of the room the form and countenance of Dr. Wollaston next became visible—another good point gained—He kindly recognised Fanny—Mrs. Somerville—the famous learned Mrs. Somerville—nothing learned or famous in her appearance—little slight-made—about the size of Mrs. Barbauld and a flattering likeness of what Mrs. Barbauld in her best and most youthful days might have been—only she has no *set* smile or prim look—no *mimps* with her mouth—fair and fair hair with pinkish Scotch color in her cheeks—eyes grey—small round intelligent smiling eyes uncommonly close together—Very pleasing countenance—remarkably soft voice though speaking with a strong Scotch pronunciation—yet it is a well bred Scotch not like the Baillies. She was dressed in geranium colored Chinese crape. She is timid not disqualifyingly timid but naturally modest with a degree of self possession through it which prevents her appearing in the least awkward and gives her all the advantage of her understanding at the same time that it adds a prepossessing charm to her manner and takes off all dread of her superior scientific learning. In talking to her we forget that La Place said she was the only woman in England who could understand and who could *correct* his works. She puts me in mind of Harriet Beaufort more than of any one I ever saw. In the course of last night and during a walk this morning I have become perfectly at ease with her. Indeed our mutual friends Mrs. Marcet Dr. Holland and Mrs. Baillies had prepared the way for our liking each other. Mrs. Somerville and Mrs. Marcet have undertaken to find me a first floor in some house half way between their houses in Harley St. and Hanover Square and they have invited us to come to them at all hours begging that we may drop in morning or evening so as to rest and make a home of their homes. Now as Dr. Wollaston and Dr. Holland and Mr. Warburton and Kater and all the best scientific and literary society in London drop into these two houses daily this privilege I consider as most valuable. Dr. Somerville though not equal to his wife yet is in my opinion more agreeable than Dr. Marcet though not so pretty a man. He is round red Scotch faced and Scotch accented—has been in America—Italy—France and knows people and things well.

Of the 4 Miss Sebrights I know nothing yet but that the eldest monopolizes Dr. Wollaston as much as she can and that he looks as if he had rather that she should not quite swallow him but also as if he had no objection that people should see she is inclined to do so. She has a prodigiously wide mouth and goes very close to him but still I think he will not let her swallow him.

A truce to nonsense—I am now coming to sense. Fanny caught no cold during her journey here, nor in the more severe trial of crossing a quarter of a mile of blasting cold passage in this house from library to dining room and bed rooms besides sitting out a long dinner in a dining room large as Sir G. Fetherstones. As Dr. Holland much insisted on Fanny's eating the best part of her dinner at luncheon we had hot luncheon mutton steaks poached eggs &c at St. Albans so we defied the waiting for dinner. In the evening came a Mr. and Mrs. Protheroe, country neighbors who might be Mr. and Mrs. Bothero for anything I know of them for F— H— Mrs. Somerville and I were sitting on the opposite sofa all night and Dr. Wollaston sitting before us talking most agreeably and giving us a clear account of the improvement of refining sugar[1] which Mr. Howard who established his patent for the same just before his death has left five thousand a year to his children[2]—a good reward for one invention!—for an improvement in a common process. Observe it is on an article of universal consumption. You expect perhaps that I am going to explain it to you. Tout au contraire. I am going to quite another subject and I leave this for Fanny's clearer head. . . .[3]

We sat round the breakfast table and lingering round the fire in the breakfast room this morning till half after one o'clock—Dr. Wollaston—Mrs. Marcet—Sir John Sebright—Mrs. Somerville and Dr. Somerville too conversing most agreeably. Sir

[1] ME gives a description of this process in *Harry and Lucy Concluded* (1825), ii. 245–54. By means of an air pump the sugar was boiled in a vacuum. This required 100 degrees less heat.

[2] ME's grammatical carelessness.

[3] A long and trivial anecdote about Mr. Chenevix is here omitted.

John Sebright is certainly a clever man and entertaining when he does not talk *all*. Mrs. Marcet says he is afraid of me and that this keeps him agreeable. I am glad of it. He has not yet got to talking above 2/3ds. His eyebrows are prodigious natural curiosities—color—size and projection . . .

Our bedchamber in which I am now writing is about the size of the largest bedchamber at Sonna[1]—same style of room but papered with old Chinese paper with birds of all sorts and sizes with green and purple necks stretching up and down from boughs and flowers and stems of trees such as nature never saw and the beaks of the birds are hopelessly wide open catching at dragonflies and at butterflies of enormous size and trying to reach berries and flowers which they can never reach. It is just a paper to drive a feverish person distracted—yellow damask curtains and yellow damask bed exactly like our old yellow damask which seems to have had its day and its night too all over the world.

Fanny and Harriets blue cloth pelisse and gown trimmed with black velvet look pretty and are comfortable. In the evening their new ruby Italian gauzes trimmed with satin are pretty and becoming. Yesterday evening five ladies out of eight at dinner were in the same color. Yr affecy. Maria E

To Sophy Ruxton

Beechwood Park, 17 January 1822

My dear friend—Often when I have not time to write a regular letter I hear scraps of things in conversation which I know would entertain my dear Aunt and I long to tell them to her. This moment for instance I have heard an anecdote of Walter Scott which proves beyond a doubt—if any doubt remained—that he is the author of the novels attributed to him. You know that he edited the family Memoirs of Lord Somerville.[2] In the manuscript copy of these Memoirs, which were put into his hands to prepare them for the press there are passages marked by his

[1] The home of the Tuite family in Co. Westmeath.

[2] *Memorie of the Somervilles; being the History of the Baronial House of Somerville*, by James, 11th Baron Somerville, ed. W. Scott (1815).

pencil to be omitted. Among these passages are some from which he took the idea of the Lady Margaret's perpetual reference to the famous breakfast which his Majesty did her the honor to take with her.[1] The ancestor of the Somerville family continually refers to the *dejeuner* (spelled in the old Scotch French des*j*euner) which his Majesty was pleased to take at his humble place &c. Also for another corroborating proof the scenery described in describing the salmon fishery in Guy Mannering is precisely the scene near Melrose.[2] These particulars have just been told to me by Dr. Somerville a near relation of Lord Somerville's and an intimate friend of Walter Scotts. He has promised that I shall see the Ms. with the passages marked to be left out by Scotts pencil and thus reserved for his own use. By how many small coincidencies which oddly meet and which seem to have no original connexion with each other the truth is discovered. Whether about a novel or a murder the truth will out.

We have spent two days pleasantly here and *though* it is a very cold straggling large house with endless passages and a hall door to the north blowing through them Fanny has not caught any cold—Thanks to good warm shawls carefully put on and put off at proper moments. We have had here Dr. Wollaston—Dr. and Mrs. Somerville—Mr. Giles and a Mr. Franks—besides our own dear friend Mrs. Marcet . . .

You may perhaps see in the papers an advertisement of a family of Laplanders with their household furniture who and *which* are to be seen in London. But besides these who are to be seen for money, Dr. Wollaston tells me that there are two young Lapland ladies who have come over to gratify their curiosity with the sight of London. He is acquainted with them. From the intercourse with Norway—with English merchants there and English Captains of vessels they have learnt a smattering of English so that they can express themselves sufficiently to let us know what impressions are made on them by the wonders of London. We are to see them. Mrs. Somerville will invite them some evening to her house and we are to meet them. As an example of their mode of speaking English they were asked by Dr. Wollaston if they had been at the play one night. '*Yes I see the play. My sister escaped.*' I wish you had heard Sir J Sebrights

[1] In *Old Mortality* (1816). [2] *Guy Mannering* (1815), chap. xxvi.

description of his mode of breaking horses and taming hawks. Sir J Sebright is very entertaining—quite a new character—But here I must stop . . . Your ever affec friend Maria E

To Mrs. Edgeworth

Mardoaks,[1] 19 January 1822

. . .[2] Sir John Sebright is one of the most entertaining characters I ever saw. He is very clever—very vain—very odd—full of fancies and paradoxes and with abilities to defend them all. He has not as much natural wit as Admiral Pakenham but he has a much greater variety and range of acquirement in literature and science—an excellent chemist—mineralogist—horseman—huntsman—breeder of horses and dogs and pigeons whom he breeds and educates on philosophical principles. An essay on the teaching of dogs which he published in his huntsmans name and gave to me yesterday is as philosophical an essay as Bentham with Dumonts help could have written on Rewards and punishments[3] and a lecture he gave me at breakfast on breaking horses and throwing a horse on his haunches was worthy of the first lecturer in Christendom. His maxim is that no violence should ever be used to animals—that all we need do is to teach by gentle degrees the language of signs which tells them what we want them to do. 'Now suppose' turning to Fanny 'you were my horse—I want you to do so and so.' Half the company, including 2 of his daughters, were sneering and suppressing smiles while he was lecturing with great ability upon horsemanship. But alas notwithstanding his philosophical tenderness principles about dogs and horses I am afraid he has been violent with his children. He has treated his daughters like dogs perhaps and his dogs like children. Certainly they all look under abject awe of him and scarcely speak above their breath when he is within hearing. They have all dogs faces—dogs mouths. I think the

[1] Sir J. Mackintosh's house near Hertford.

[2] A long piece of scandal about the marriage of Mr. Chenevix is here omitted.

[3] E. Dumont, *Théorie des peines et des recompenses, par J. Bentham, redigée en français d'après les manuscrits* . . . (1811). ME wrote a long incomplete review of this in *Philanthropist*, vii (1819) and *Inquirer*, i (1822).

Pophar[1] would be struck with horror if he were set down in the midst of these girls. Miss Sebright is the least disagreeable. There does not seem to be any communication between the sisters. They do not seem to live happily together and in the midst of luxuries and fine house and park this perception chills their guests. It was such a contrast to the Carrs.

Sir John however amused me incessantly. He is quite a new character—strong head and warm heart and oddity enough for ten. He explained to me what is meant by being *in the fancy*—pigeon fanciers—rabbit fanciers &c. He shewed us his pigeons—*one* which he would not sell for a hundred guineas. He took it up in his hand as he spoke and shewed me its pretty little white head but I could not see the difference between it and one not worth 10 shillings. The pouting pigeons who have *goitres* as Mrs. Marcet said are frightful. They put their heads behind these bags of wind and strut about as if proud of difformity. We saw four Antwerp carrier pigeons. One of these Sir John told us went from Tower Hill to Antwerp in six hours.

I am ashamed to see that I have wasted 5 pages on pigeons and scandal . . . One morning he [Wollaston] spoke of dreams in an entertaining manner and told us that he was much pleased with his own ingenuity once in a dream. He dreamed that he wished to weigh himself but suddenly he fell and then was hurried forward on the ground till he came to a spot where he found that the power of gravity ceased to act—Still he was to weigh himself and how was this to be done when gravity ceased to act? He bethought himself of a spring steelyard and with the joy of successful invention wakened. Sir John Sebright however would not allow Wollaston to be proud of himself for this. He insisted that it would have occurred to himself in a dream or to any common man acquainted with a steelyard and with the principle of gravity. We argued this point for ¼ of an hour and each went away as usual of his or her original opinion . . . We called at Hatfield in our way here—sent in my card to Lady Salisbury—went over the house—a fine pile of old house and a fine bronze statue of King James in one drawing room[2] and many faded pictures—Burleigh and Cecil and Leicester and Elizabeth—Curious

[1] ? a reference to ME's spaniel Foster, but the name is quite clearly written.
[2] This stands over the mantelpiece. It is painted to look like bronze.

many but very few good. A Mr. Giles who had spent some days with us at Beechwood and who had left us but an hour before had reached Hatfield before us. He is one of the tame men of the house—Came to us while we were in the great gallery (146 feet long) and told us that Lady Salisbury wished very much . . . honor &c. So we went into the library where she was sitting. Do you remember meeting her at Lady Darnley's? And did not she look like an old harridan with a face of wrinkled white chalk? That was my recollection of her—But no such thing—She is a little lively good humored darkish faced looking woman—very alert and active! What do you think of her foxhunting tho past seventy? She had been expected to hunt this day at Beechwood—true as I am alive! An old groom goes out with her—rides a hunter a little better than her own—rides on always a little before her to shew her where she may go—turns to her every now and then and says 'Come on. Why the d—l don't you leap?' or 'You must not go there. Why the d—l do you go there?' &c. This was told us by Mr. Franks who often hunts with her. He and Mr. Giles and all the young men declare that she is more lively and good humored out hunting than any of them and they say she is very popular and deserves to be so in the County—civil to everybody—'an excellent heart'. (Excellent hearts I observe come in at the end of every thing and are cheaply given nowadays.)

At Hatfield there is a ball and a public day once a week. Lady Salisbury was mighty civil to us and talked of her Emily (Lady Westmeaths) having met us at the Deepdene and talked of Ireland and her being an Irishwoman—daughter of Lord Hillsborough—had been in the County of Longford in her way to Hillsborough. Her daughter Lady Georgiana Wellesley came in—not handsome but I like her countenance better than Lady Westmeaths.

We had intended to stop and eat Luncheon at Hertford about 3 o clock but when we got there not a room to be had all occupied by young gentlemen returning to College—*So* I ordered a cold chicken into the chaise and we soon dispatched its wings and breast and Gaynor profited by its carcase (Mem. Gaynor goes on well). We arrived here in our usual happy time—firelight—an hour before dinner—But Sir James Mackintosh must not come in at the fag end of a letter. I will now tell you only that we have been most cordially received both by him and Lady Mackintosh—that this house is pretty the library comfortable—the hall and staircase beautiful and the whole house filled with books. His library is immense—8000 volumes at least. Our rooms open into each other—warm and comfortable . . .

As I have told you so much scandal in this shameless letter I must end with one anecdote to the honor of poor human nature. Mr. Wilberforce you know sold his house at Kensington Gore. The purchaser was a Mr. Mortlock a Chinaman the keeper of a China shop I should say in Oxford St. When the purchase money—ten thousand pounds—was paid and the deeds executed Mr. Mortlock waited upon Mr. Wilberforce and said 'This house suits you Mr. Wilberforce so well in every respect that I am sure your only motive for parting with it must be to raise the money. Therefore permit me to return these title deeds. Accept of this testimony of esteem due to your public character and talents.' Wilberforce did not accept this handsome offer. I think I would have accepted it if I had been him would not you? [end missing]

To Mrs. Edgeworth

Mr. Malthus's house close to Hertford College,[1]
Wednesday, 23 January 1822

To begin with that which is uppermost in my mind and of the greatest consequence. I have asked all your questions my dear mother about the preparatory school for Pakenham. Mr. Malthus and Dr. Batten who is the principal of Hertford College know nothing of that school at Woodford of which you sent me the advertisement. This in the first place is against it but as they both candidly observed 'the school *may* be very well conducted though it has not yet made itself known to us'. But without hesitation Mr. Malthus and Dr. Batten declared that they should prefer having a boy sent to them from the Charter-House to having him from any lesser preparatory school—especially from any which promised peculiarly to prepare them for Hertford College or for India.

[1] Hertford College (East India College) was founded in 1806 for the education of the servants of the East India Co. It was at first situated in Hertford Castle but moved almost immediately to new buildings at Haileybury, two miles to the south-east of the town.

We wish, they say, to have boys from any of the great public schools prepared only by being well taught in general made good grammarians, good scholars, good arithmeticians and in short prepared as young men who are going to Oxford or Cambridge without any bias or attempt at preparation for the particular destination to India. We would rather that the boy should not know that he was intended for India till he comes to us. All that we have to teach him will be easily super-added to what he has learned if the foundation of classical education be good. We have found that wherever attempts have been made to prepare for Hertford by giving smatterings of Persian grammar Sanscrit &c this has always done harm. Time has been uselessly devoted to this while the essential foundation of classical and mathematical knowledge have been neglected and the pupils have been made conceited and fancy that they have learned much when they have both neglected what they ought to have learned and have to learn over again what they have been ill taught. 'I always distrust' said Mr. Malthus 'any school which promises to teach a number of things in a shorter time or cheaper than others.' To this there may be exceptions, but these can be established only by time and by the success of the scholars after they have left the school.

The main point is clear that Batten—Malthus and all the masters of Hertford College desire to have boys from any great school rather than from any *preparatory school for Hertford-College*. They have a high opinion of the Charter-House from Charter-House boys who have been sent here and from seeing that at Oxford and Cambridge they have distinguished themselves. When I mentioned that Francis had been and is at the Charter-House they said that Pakenham's having a brother there was a great additional advantage and that in their minds there can be no doubt that it would be best to send him there. They inquired at what boarding house Francis is, and when they heard he was at Mr. Watkinsons they said 'So much the better, he is the most attentive to the boys.'

They do not wish to have pupils sent to Hertford till the age of sixteen. This is the sum of all I could learn yesterday when Dr. Batten the principal and Mr. Le Bas the mathematical professor dined here. I have penned it down while fresh in my head the first thing I have done this morning. We are just going out to walk over the college but my seeing the building will not much add I think to this information. If I glean anything more you shall have it.

Do you remember a Cornish friend of Davy's who supped with him the night of the Opera supper when Lady Darnley and the Russian Prince God-knows-who[1] and the Sneyds supped there and do you recollect Davy's saying that this Cornish friend was a very clever man and being anxious to do him honor and to be kind? This Cornish friend was *Mr.* and is Doctor Batten and now at the head of Hertford College. He does not however look more genteel now than he did then. He talks dreadfully loud with a strong Cornish accent and he talks almost incessantly, with a mixture of pedantry and affectation—pedantic sentiment. He is very full of himself and of his wife who is a very pretty woman done over with pink ribbons and scarlet trimmings. But tho' Dr. Batten looks and talks like the self opinionated provincialists of the Bristol school[2] *d'ailleurs* he is a very clever man and I guess a goodnatured. He had with him a rosy-cheeked happy-looking open faced son of nine years old whom we liked much and whose countenance and manner gave the best evidence possible in favor of his father and mother. Besides this son's evidence I judged Dr. Batten was good natured from seeing him much disturbed in the enjoyment of his dinner by thinking of a youth whom he had just been examining and who could not *pass*. At the close of the evening I saw Batten go to Le Bas and hold him by the button and they laid their two black heads together to consider what could be done about this 'poor fellow'. Le Bas is as deaf as a post but that is no matter because he is professor of mathematics and deals only demonstration. He has a very good natured intelligent countenance but he retired to a corner of the tea table and sat apart after the fashion of my uncle Ruxton. I hope to get something out of him tonight or tomorrow night. I intend to put my mouth into his ear and it shall not be my fault if I do not get something out for

[1] See above, p. 66.

[2] ME presumably refers here to the circle of men connected with her late brother-in-law, Dr. Beddoes, at the Pneumatic Institution. She paid long visits to Bristol in 1791–3 and 1799.

your service. Suppose I was to ask him as I used to ask the children *before* blowing into their ears 'Will you give me leave to blow your brains out—pray do!' I am told Le Bas has a great taste for humor and that he laughed heartily yesterday at some odd bit of nonsense of mine which caught his ear and broke at once the mournful gravity of his countenance. He has very fine eyes and I dare say a tongue.

Mr. Malthus speaks more snuffly through his nose and slower than formerly or perhaps the immediate contrast to Mackintosh's fluent eloquence, and brilliant quickness of wit and reason makes it appear more striking to me and intolerable. But why should I say intolerable? He is a most amiable man—of strict truth, perfect integrity and rational benevolence as all who know him declare—and this is the man whom party represents as a bloodthirsty monster—An Ogre![1] Cobbett began one of his papers lately with these words 'I have hated many men but I *never* hated any man as much as I hate Malthus.' I own in the midst of my love and admiration and *gratitude* to Mr. Malthus who is as kind as kind can be to me and mine I *do* wish that hair lip were away and that he could speak more like a human creature for if I were a child and had heard of his being an Ogre I should run away if he were to come near me and begin to speak. As to personal beauty F H and I agree that we would sooner *take up* with Mr. Hope. 'Nobody asked you Ma'am say they.'

Fanny as you may guess by my being up to nonsense-point is free from cough and sleeps and eats and I think I may say is well. She had some rides while at Mardoaks with little Mackintosh—Robert a very intelligent boy of 15. Give me leave to present him to you if I have not done so before. He is very little of his age—not above half a head taller than Francis—handsomer than his father but very like him. He listens to his fathers conversation with a delight which proves him worthy to be the son of

[1] Malthus in his *Essay on Population* (1798, revised and expanded, 1802 and 1817) argued that population expanded much faster than the means of subsistence and that the parish allowances given to the poor dangerously encouraged them to have larger families. He favoured the gradual abolition of relief. The poor rates at this period pressed very heavily on landowners and farmers and his very clearly written book had an immense influence which can be seen even in the reports made to the poor law commissioners in 1833 by the parish officers (mostly small farmers). The effect of his theories as crudely interpreted by Cobbett and the overseers was inhumane.

such a father and promises future excellence better than the best thing he could say at his age. His father last Session took him to the House of Commons to hear a debate and next morning lugged him up out of his sleep and sent him off to Holland House to give Lady Holland an account of the debate which I am told he did to admiration. I hope they won't give him too much praise *early*. They say he is an idle little dog and if they pay before he labors for it why should he work? But to go back to his riding with Fanny. Sir James Mackintosh lent her his own poney—a dull jogtrot animal but she had two pleasant rides thereon and thanks him for lending. It was more than Sir John Sebright would do for her. Though he had a capitally-broke horse for his daughter he would never let Fanny get upon it. He pretended he should be afraid and afraid to ask his daughter to lend it—*nonsense* when he knows he is as arbitrary as the grand-turk. As Mr. Carr says if he bid his daughters *lie down* he should expect to see the Miss Sebrights fall flat at their long lengths sprawling motionless crouching like spaniels. This stroke of vengeance was justly due for his refusing me a horse for Fanny but now I forgive him and will never say no more about it and it is only to you—you know.

Sir James Mackintosh held a fine metaphysical theory yesterday, that there is no pleasure in satisfied vengeance—that it is only relief from pain—the pain of the malevolent wish. It is *necessary* to make this out in order to prove to moral satisfaction that no pleasure is ever connected with or consequent upon the indulgence of malevolent feelings. I *hope* it is true. It deserves to be true. Mackintosh is much improved in the art of conversation since we saw him. Mixing more with the polished world and being engaged in great affairs and with great men and great women has perfected him in the use and management of his wonderful natural powers and vast accumulated treasures of knowledge. His memory now appears to work less, his eloquence is more easy, his wit more brilliant—his anecdotes more happily introduced. The whole is brought into better compass and proportion and he has the high-bred touch and go of the man of the world as well as the classical high and deep advantages of the scholar and the orator. Altogether his conversation is the most delightful I ever heard. It is superior to Dumonts in imagination and eloquence and almost equal in wit. In Dumonts mind and conversation wit and reason are kept separate but in Mackintoshs they are mixed and he uses both in argument—knowing the exact force and value of each—never attempting to pass wit for logic. He forges each link of the chain of demonstration and then sends the electric spark of wit through it.

The French may well exclaim in speaking of Mackintosh *Quelle Abondance!* Harriet counted the number of new things he told us yesterday at breakfast or at least before we quitted the breakfast room and how many do you think they were—*twelve.* It would be vain to attempt to record them in this letter. Besides taken out of their places in conversation they would only have the bad effect of a jest book. One however you shall have for a specimen. At Berlin at a time when all the different embassadors of Europe were assembled there, just when Bonaparte was in the height of his power Madame de Stael who was invited to dine with them came into the sallon [*sic*] a few minutes before dinner. She saw a picture of Bonaparte over the chimney piece and she addressed it in these words

Mortel!
Qui que tu soit voici ton maitre
Il l'est, le fut, ou le *doit* etre.[1]

Thats one. Now for another as Mr. Ward would say. Racine's son after his fathers death took to making verses and his mother alarmed at his following the perilous trade requested his fathers friend Boileau to *speak* to him. Boileau accordingly sent for him into his closet and when the youth appeared thus in a stern voice addressed him 'Jeune homme! Comment osez vous faire des vers avec le nom que vous portez?'

I know I am spoiling what I am repeating and doing Mackintosh an injustice in thus picking out plums. The pudding was exquisite believe me. Fanny and Harriet say that Mackintosh has far surpassed their expectations. The two new literary persons Fanny most wished to see in coming to England were Ricardo and Mackintosh. She has seen them in the best possible manner in their own families and at leisure to be not only wise

[1] Inscribed by Voltaire on a statue of Cupid which stood in his apartment at Cirey.

and good but agreeable. Harriet and she have *heard* more of their conversation and have had more opportunity of shewing themselves to these great men than they could in any other way have had during a whole season in London. Think how happy I feel in seeing them quite satisfied even if we have nothing more this season. Sir James and Lady Mackintosh seemed to like them much and I and they delight in Miss Mackintosh. She is one of the best informed and most unaffected girls I ever saw—not handsome nor ugly—with a sweet voice and admirable conversation—not *ugly* blue but every shade of beautiful and becoming color. Lady Mackintosh is much the same as when you saw her odd clever and good natured with something of Mrs. M. Powys's fidgettiness and a blazing red face. If she die of an apoplexy I hope that some of my young friends may have the refusal of Sir James.

We have just walked to see Hertford College.[1] I have not time for nice transitions. One facade of about two hundred feet is handsome on the design of the temple of Neptune—three Ionic porticos and pediments one in the middle and one towards each end—dwelling house windows between—an ugly square of buildings within—good ground for exercise—library and hall good and all the apartments I am told excellent.

There are eight professors—two for classical literature—three Oriental languages—one law and one political Economy and one Mathematics. The pupils stay two years. Mr. Malthus would advise three but India directors and parents are too impatient. A vast deal he says has been usually accomplished in these two years. They have sent out from thirty to forty [to] India each year since they have been established and they have been established seventeen years. So this may account for the improvement in East Indian conduct and society.

Good bye God bless you. Our dear Fanny has written these last lines for me whilst I have been resting myself. It is within a quarter of an hour of dinner and we are neither of us dressed. We shall be at Kensington Gore on Saturday to dinner.

I open this letter after dinner to add the essential information about the expense of Hertford College. There is no hurry to be sure but it may be useful to have all that is to be known about

[1] The buildings were designed by William Wilkins and built 1808–9.

it in one letter. The whole expense of tuition and board and washing is one hundred guineas. Besides this each boy must have an allowance for clothes and pocket money. The College rule or request to parents is that only 5 guineas shall be given the first year and 8 guineas the next. Clothes require from 30 to 40. This makes the whole expense about 150 guineas per annum. [No signature]

To Mrs. Edgeworth

Sunday morning, 27 January 1822

As if awakening after a long dream I find myself sitting exactly in the same corner on the same chair at the same table in the same bedroom where Fanny and Honora and I were three years ago! Three years is it possible?

Lady Elizabeth Whitbread looks better than she did when we left her though she is much thinner. Upon the whole her spirits and the state of her mind altogether appear to me to be more composed. Her kindness and the winning dignity of her manners just the same as ever. We arrived in good time though we did stop a quarter of an hour at Dr. Hollands. We were shewn up to the drawing room-library—Skreen and everything in the room tell Honora exactly the same as the day we left it even to the angle at which the footstools stood before the arm chairs when the room was dressed for dinner—hearth swept—candles just lighting—but no living creature visible except the new man-servant who lighted the candles. After a few minutes silent pause Mrs. Holloway the housekeeper whom Honora may remember as the dragon in spectacles appeared at the end of the skreen behind the sofa. She is not nearly so much like a dragon as form-erly—much paler moreover—very respectable and respectful and glad to see us 'But Miss Grant Ma'am I am sorry to say is not here. She has been absent a fortnight with Mrs. Nisbet and my Lady has been to Town to see Lady Grey and is lying down, I hope asleep.'

We determined to go to our bedrooms but while we were waiting till the imperials &c should be carried up Lady Elizabeth appeared peeping softly from behind the end of the skreen with her bonnet and pelisse on just as she had returned from her mother and with smiles and tears struggling in her affectionate countenance she pressed me in her arms then held them out to *Fanny* pronouncing Fanny in the soft tone which Honora knows and can make you hear. 'And this is Harriet! I must have her in my arms too! But I miss my *antient*. I miss dear Honora.' Then she sat down in Miss Grants armchair and told us that Julia she hoped would be here on monday—that she had written to tell her we should be here before her. Next she spoke of little Francis and of you—Then of her mother, who is very ill—fading away. She goes to her every day either to spend the morning or the evening.

At dinner Harriet carved in Miss Grant's place and Fanny sat in Honora's place opposite to me—Very foolish to mention these things but I fancied Honora might like to *see us*. During dinner a new poodle dog Jubal was let into the room—very like Lion, only younger and handsomer—milk white silken curls all over except the poor shorn half that is sacrificed to poodle-fashion. Jubal is the son of Lion—Lady E. Whitbread who exerted herself to be chearful at dinner told us that one of the little Battye girls said to the other 'Do you know that Lady Elizabeth Whitbread has a new dog—Lion has *hatched* a new dog?' 'Oh my dear *hatched*' answered the sister '*laid* you mean.' I hope this will make Aunt C and M and your mother and Lucy smile. Give my love to them all whether it makes them smile or not. Old Lion made his entrée soon after his son. He is become quite gentle tell Honora and does not scratch at one's legs. I think he feels bound now to *behave* and set his son and heir a good example.

After dinner Lady E. Whitbread shewed us a miniature picture which Mrs. Battye has done of her and another of Mr. Battye. Mr. Battye's is beautifully painted and she has turned him into a fine Spanish looking gentleman with a cloak over one shoulder. Lady E. Whitbread is not nearly so well. It is like her air and attitude (half length—arm leaning on the arm of her chair and hand hanging very like her attitude) but the expression of the countenance is wanting and the mismanagement of the shade makes the face look as if it wanted washing. Lady E Whitbread —kind soul—was sorry we could not like it—on Mrs. Battye's account because she is now taking miniature likenesses to earn money for her family. Lawrence said he admired it which is of rather more consequence than our liking it. Mr. Battye is gone off—where do you guess Honora? To live with Lord Bute—who doats on him and his only complaint is that Lord Bute will not let him have time enough to himself he is so fond of his company. Lord Bute moreover gives him something for his company per annum—I do not know how much. But poor man he was glad to accept of this *situation*. He pined and wasted almost to a shadow Lady Elizabeth says because he could do nothing for the support of himself or his children and he saw his wife working her fingers almost off all day. Eleven children to support! I did not understand that they were so poor when we were here before. All this for Honora my dear mother it cannot interest you.[1] . . . But to return to our own *muttons*—I was wakened this morning by Lady Elizabeth's own maid who tell Honora I am beginning to fall in love with. Her cap is flattened and she seems to have quite laid aside her conceit. 'Ma'am my Lady wants to know if you would like to have the young gentleman today Master Francis (bounce I was up) and she wants to know if you could send your man for him.' Kind creature!—is not she? Fanny wrote to her uncle and Harriet to the Carrs while I dressed. Honora knows how we used to go on—she and Fanny writing notes for Lazybones while Lazybones was dressing. Lady E. Whitbread breakfasted with us at ½ past nine. She went to her own church and afterwards to her mother—Harriet and I to Kensington—Battye's pew. Fanny we left at home for the good of her body and Lady E. Whitbread for the good of her soul left that wicked Cain[2] with her.

On our return from Church Fanny was alone standing by the fire looking very grave. We had expected to find F with her. 'Here is a note from Uncle Francis for you Maria.' Much mortified I took it. 'So Francis is not come how is this?' The little rogue jumped up from behind the sofa and was delighted to surprise us. F H and he went out to walk by particular desire round the lawn here and I came to my room to scribble this. But not

[1] A long passage on the unsuitable marriage of Lady Elizabeth's elder son is here omitted.

[2] *Cain: A Mystery*, a tragedy published by Byron in 1821.

one word have I yet said of the only thing I intended to say when I resolved to write. I said to myself it shall be only 3 or 4 lines just to say the needful.

Francis tells me that Mr. Russell is anxious to know whether Pakenham is to come to the Charter House this year—after the midsummer holydays? Or when? Mr. Russell has asked these questions repeatedly as I knew he would and I beg to be provided with an answer before I go to see him. As Pakenham's name has been written it is necessary that Mr. Russell should know on account of keeping or giving up a place. Mr. Watkinsons boarding house which, as I think I told you, Malthus, Batten, Le Bas and all the profesors at Hertford unanimously declared they knew to be the best at the Charter house has had such a run upon it lately that Mr. Russell was obliged to limit the number to a hundred. Some boy or boys are going away—some at Easter and one or two at Midsummer. One of these places must either be kept for Pakenham or not. You my dear guardians must be so good as to let me know your decision. . . .

Fanny was so charmed with Sir James Mackintosh that the night before we left Mr. Malthus's she talked of him in her sleep. He had spent the evening with us and conversed delightfully. In the middle of the night I heard Fanny exclaim 'How tantalizing!' I waited to hear what and after another minute she added 'To be within arrows-shot and not to hear!' Then another time she said 'There never was anything so delightful.' . . . [signature missing: half a page torn off]

To Mrs. Ruxton

Grove House, Kensington Gore, 1 February 1822

This mild spring weather which calls forth primroses and rose leaves in abundance delights me my dearest Aunt because it calls you out too. I have heard of your having walked as far as the Sallow garden and I hope you will do the same the day you recieve this if it should be tempting sunshine. I know how good it is for you to be out in the open air even if it be only to walk round the house or to the sheltered garden or to the Weirs indented brim. How I love it! . . .

We have seen since we came here only Mr. and Mrs. Le Fevre and Lady Hannah Ellice, Lady Elizabeth's sister (very unlike her)—an affected lisping, chalk-faced flimsily dressed dawdle. Her husband Mr. Edward Ellice is a jovial *parliamentary good fellow*, who sticks to his party and considers a *rat* the most despicable animal in nature. He diverted us at dinner with a description of the way of tormenting rats at Brook's by calling to them perpetually to take care of their tails. Mr. Ellice is a *thick and thin* friend of Lord Byron's and defends him and all his works against his wife and all the world. He *would* read passages of Don Juan to us and to tell you the truth the best of us and Lady Elizabeth herself could not help laughing. Lady Hannah turned her face almost off her shoulder and picked the embroidered corner almost out of her pocket handkerchief and she did *not* laugh. Mr. Ellice asked kindly after the Bishop of Meath and all his family with whom he is or was well acquainted.

When I said that we had seen only Lady E. Whitbread's own family I made a mistake. We have seen *Dr*. Russell who was so kind to ride here from the Charter-House yesterday on purpose to see us. He looks as little like a *Dr*. or a schoolmaster as can be concieved. His only fault I think is looking too young and too good natured as Francis says for a schoolmaster. He gives us the most gratifying account of Francis—The very tone of voice in which he pronounces his name shews that he likes him . . .

I have not seen Mr. Talbot nor has Lady E. Whitbread seen him lately—More of this when we meet. Did you ever hear a Navy *slang* phrase '*I was not born tomorrow*'—when persons mean to praise themselves for their penetration—equivalent to the French phrase 'Je ne suis pas d'hier.'

Could you conceive that a rejected suitor of Lady E. Whitbread's a man of twenty thousand per Annum and of old family could make use of such a vulgar expression as this 'When I come to see your Ladyship you know I have always my *sitting breeches* on.' I saw this in a letter she received from the gentleman yesterday. He declares she is the woman he loves above all others tho he has been married these 15 years—but a romantic history of his romantic attachment lost all its effect on my mind by these *sitting breeches* and with you the same it would have been I am sure . . . [end missing]

To Mrs. Ruxton

[*c.* 4 February 1822]

[beginning missing] . . . Several persons have shewn me that they were very much interested in that book[1] and I am gratified by perceiving that it has made my father's character known to many who had not before been acquainted with it such as it really was—for instance Lady Elizabeth Whitbread in particular. She said 'I wish I had known him as well as I know him now, and I should have had much more courage in talking to him. I should not have been afraid of him.' . . .

At breakfast this morning I was reminding Mr. Ricardo of his having begun to tell me some anecdotes of his early life during a walk we took in a wood of Gatcombe park when we were interrupted by a beautiful view which burst upon us at an opening through the trees. I told him that I had always regretted this interruption and hated the prospect to which I had been obliged 'How beautiful!' He was diverted and has promised me that I shall lose nothing by that prospect for that he will tell me his whole history—some day. I wish that day were come. Speaking of the little incidents which make an impression in childhood and through life he told me that he could never forget a circumstance that happened to him when he was nine years old about a pair of shoes. He was in Holland at the time at the Hague; he saw in a shop window a pair of shoes with an edging of fur to which he took a fancy and he entreated that they might be bought for him. It was represented to him that he did not see exactly what sort of shoes they were and that they would not suit him. He persisted and they were bought upon condition that he should wear them. He found that they had wooden soles and these made such a clatter upon the pavement that every body turned to look at him as he walked and instead of the fur shoes proving a gratification to his vanity they became a daily mortification. He would have given anything to have got rid of them but he had no others and he says none but himself can conceive the pains he took to slide in walking so as to prevent the noise of his wooden soles from making disgraceful clatter. This story of the furred wooden shoes is like some of Franklin's

[1] *Memoirs of RLE.*

apologue stories of his youth—of the whistle—and the new cap[1] &c—and perhaps for this reason it particularly [pleased] Mr. Ricardo's American guest Mr. Ralston.

Mr. Ralston told us that every English book of celebrity is reprinted in America with wonderful celerity. For instance on the twenty ninth day after one of Walter Scott's novels was published in London it was republished in Philadelphia and sold at a third less than the London price—a guinea instead of a guinea and half.

Speaking of the population of America England and China Mr. Ricardo told us what perhaps my uncle knows but it was new to me that the population of England within the last 15 years has in spite of war &c increased near 2 millions. From 9 millions it has become Eleven millions. America is twenty one million. Mr. Ralston had a relation who lived for sometime at Canton and who told him that the number of people who live on the water on the yellow river is above 80 thousand. I mention these facts for my dear uncle. I know they will interest him . . .

I am very glad my dear aunt that you like the preface of little Frank but I much fear that his engineer and his scientific dialogues will tire you. Skip and go over to the 3d volume. If a second copy should come to you, as I have sent two and if you should not desire to keep both will you give the second copy to Mrs. O Beirne with my love and respects.

We have this last week seen all Callcott's principal pictures, and those by Mulready, an Irish artist: one of a messenger playing truant; the enraged mistress, and the faces of the boys he is playing with, and the little child he had the care of asleep, all tell their story well; but none of these come near the exquisite humour and ingenuity of Hogarth. I have the face of that imbecile, round-eyed, half drunk friend of ours in the corner of the Election Dinner[2] now before me, and I can never think of it without laughing.

We have seen Sir Thomas Lawrence's magnificent picture of the King in his coronation robes, which is to be sent to the Pope. He flatters with great skill, choosing every creature's best. An

[1] 'The Whistle: a true story written to his nephew', *Works of the Late Benjamin Franklin* (Dublin, 1793), 167; 'On Luxury, Idleness and Industry' (from a letter to Benjamin Vaughan, Esq., written in 1784), ibid., 231. Cf. also ME's own story of 'Rosamund and the Purple Jar' (*Parent's Assistant*, 1795; transferred to *Early Lessons*, 1801).

[2] In Hogarth's series of Election engravings.

admirable picture of Walter Scott; ditto ditto of Lady Jersey and Lady Conyngham. Lord Anglesey came in while we were with Sir Thomas: he is no longer handsome, but a model for the 'nice conduct' of a wooden leg. It was within an inch of running through Walter Scott's picture, which was on the floor leaning on the wall; but, by a skilful sidelong manoevre, he bowed out of its way. His grey hair looks much better than his Majesty's flaxen wig—bad taste.[1]

To Mrs. Edgeworth

Kensington Gore, Wednesday morning, 6 February 1822

. . . To return to Colonel Talbot whom I named in my last. He is just cast in the same mould as all the other Talbots I have ever seen but he is stouter, his face has been browned by hardships and *scorched* by the reflexion from the American snows—His manner of speaking slow but not too slow—only slow enough to be quite calmly distinct—and when relating wonders and dangers to give you at once the certainty of truth and the belief in his fortitude and intrepid presence of mind. He related to us all you have heard of the first visit he received from a European friend after he had been a considerable time in his lake Erie settlement where he had built for himself a *Loghouse* but was obliged to be servant of all work to himself. He appeared that day in 3 characters to his European friend—First as a ploughman in his carter's frock. He was leading his Horse at plough when he saw the extraordinary sight of an English Officer on horseback approaching. 'Friend can you tell me if a Colonel Talbot lives near here?' 'Yes Sir' and he pointed the way to the house and while his friend, without recognising him in his carter's frock, rode on the long way that he had pointed out, to the log house Colonel Talbot untackled (I would not say unharnessed) his horses, turned them into the wood and ran by a short cut to the house—Whipped off his frock—washed hands and face, and appeared in his log drawing room as Colonel Talbot agreeably surprised to see his European friend. 'As I have no regular servants here you must permit my absence now and then

[1] The manuscript of the last two paragraphs of this letter is missing. They are printed from *Mem.* ii. 175.

today and take things as you find them.' Off he ran when his friend sat down to write a letter and throwing aside the gentleman's coat, cooked the dinner brought it in, set it on the table as his own butler—and then exit butler—Re-enter as Colonel Talbot—conversed with his friend on all their acquaintances in Europe and on the state of his own affairs—at night he desired he would leave his boots and coat outside of his door—Got up at five—kneaded the bread and put it into the oven to be ready for breakfast—brushed the coat—blackened the boots and shoes, and had breakfast and hot rolls ready for his guest. All this you and I have heard before from Sophy Ruxton or Mr. Strickland but it is a satisfaction to hear it confirmed by the person's own words. Colonel Talbot gave us an account of an attack of the Indians some years ago upon Fort-Talbot. It was during the war in 14 or 15. They were on the borders of the lake and the Indians hated them as English settlers and resolved to get possession of Colonel Talbot and carry him off. One day as he was looking out of his log house drawing room window he saw an Indian coming towards the house—thought it was a messenger at first from some officer, called to his servant to go out to him and went on writing a letter but his servant stood petrified looking out of the window. 'What is the matter?' 'The Indians! They are coming!' Colonel Talbot looked again and saw them coming two or three advanced before the rest. One opened the door and walked in. Colonel Talbot with perfect composure as he represented himself wellcomed him and gave him something to drink. Another followed. With the same calmness and hospitality he received him asking innocently what they came for and pretending to concieve them friends. He would go out and wellcome the rest of the party. He saw them at a little distance on one side of the house—walked leisurely round making signs of wellcome and unconcernedly examining the posts of his veranda which had been hurt by the cattle till edging on and on by degrees till he had turned the corner of the house and was hid from their view he jumped into a deep ravine behind the house where he knew he could run without being seen and ran off with all speed to the woods—wandered till night—got into a tree heard the party in search of him come to the foot of the tree and talk and depart in search of him—escaped. The Indians not being able to find him went off. On his return to his house he found they had carried off every individual thing. He had nothing left but his Russia duck jacket and trowzers in which he had run off. They had set fire to the house but one good natured Indian returned to tell him where the concealed fire was and warned him in time to put it out. He gives me an idea of the most cool courage imaginable. I could not help looking at him as if he were Robinson Crusoe come to life again and continuing stories from his own book.

He has now a very comfortable house—or palace I should say for he's not only Lord of all he surveys but actually king. He governs by the English laws. He sends all his acts or laws to be ratified by English Government. He went out originally with 4 followers. He has now twelve thousand subjects—native Americans—English—Welsh—Scotch—Irish and Dutch. Of all these the Highlanders and Irish are the most difficult he says to manage—the most difficult to satisfy—the most craving—The Irish the most disorderly in their habits and most enraged when the *Yankies* have anything given to them. This opinion of the Europeans that the natives were of a race so inferior to themselves and not entitled to have any of the comforts of life proved most troublesome to King Talbot who finds it still very difficult to adjust the claims and jealousies of his subjects. But the settlement has upon the whole prospered beyond his most sanguine hopes. They manufacture all the clothes they wear. They have one good town—Fort Talbot. He has a regular post who brings him letters and newspapers from New York every friday.

We asked him about steam boats. He thinks highly of them for American rivers. There are 100 steam vessels from New York to Philadelphia and others constantly going from N to S-America. They are of immense size. He was astonished by the smallness of our steam packets—was afraid to venture in one from Liverpool and with reason. He was near being lost in it. He says that in the American steam vessels they have means of taking up the machinery when the water becomes rough and the vessels are all rigged and provided with sails like any other vessels when they chuse to take to their sails. This should be done with *all* our steam vessels for if the machinery is broken by storm or accident there is no resource in these unrigged vessels—nothing but Paddy's old dependance on good luck!

Do you recollect the American Mrs. Griffiths writing to tell me that a nephew of hers a Mr. Ralston would come to see us. He was in Dublin—inquired—found that Miss E was not at home and to my extreme disappointment concluded that none of the family were at Edgeworths Town and did not go down to see Lovells school which he had a great desire and I a greater that he should have seen. He found us out here and Lady Elizabeth Whitbread who takes every creature in of every kind, who interests us desired me to invite him to breakfast yesterday. I was in some anxiety for his first appearance lest he should be an American unlicked cub. Quite the contrary—a very gentlemanlike—pale soft voiced—modest—yet properly confident young man—travelled all over Germany Italy Swisserland. He was in Swisserland last year just after us—had his letter of introduction for me in his pocket half over the world. How lucky that we met at last! He is going to Spain in a few days—had made all his preparations but upon my giving him a note of introduction to Mackintosh with a draft on him for five minutes conversation and notes to some other celebrated people, he like a sensible man determined to delay his journey on purpose to see them. Lady E. Whitbread has been so kind to ask him to dine here today and commissioned me to invite whoever I pleased to meet him. First we wrote to your brother but he could not come—then to Dr. Holland—most unfortunately he was engaged to Holland House but in his note to me Dr. Holland says 'I have seen Mr. Ralston several times and have been greatly pleased with his ingenuousness acquirements and agreeable manners.' He Mr. Ralston is immensely rich. His father and mother are grand and what is rather better most benevolent, people in Philadelphia. They have established there an Orphans Asylum—a widows asylum and I dont know how many other asylums . . .

But I forgot to finish the sentence about the invitation to dinner. My third invitation was to Mr. Callcott the painter with whom we became acquainted a few days ago and who is a very gentlemanlike well informed and most obliging man. He has promised us his tickets for the sight of the Exhibition before it is opened and has been more civil than I can tell you about preparing the way for F and Hs seeing pictures of Lord Liverpools —Sir J Swinburnes &c. *So* I was glad to have this opportunity of asking him and *he* breaks an engagement to dine with the Academy to accept of Lady E. Whitbread's. More of Callcott in my next but now I must put on my bonnet to go to Lady Greys. She is the most touching sight! And Lady E. Whitbread's affection and respect for her! She has desired to see Fanny and Harriet this day. Adieu dearest mother—love to your dear mother—Maria E

at Mr. Cartwrights dentist

I invented that I could bring pen ink letter in my bag and continue it here while Mr. Cartwright should be cleaning F and H's teeth. There is a little stump which was left in Fanny's mouth which was left by the last operator and which Cartwright says must come out. While I was writing this presto!—it is out. He is as unlike Waite as possible!—a most quiet apparently slow—really quick man. He is now cleaning Harriets teeth—no drawing necessary—require a great deal of brushing and *frequent*. This is the burthen of every dentists song—All depends on health Mr. Cartwright says—chiefly or rather first on the health of the child from 4 to 5 or 3 to 4. But this being quite in the preterpluperfect tense for all we love till Fanny and Harriet have little ones I will leave it there and go back to Colonel Talbot. He is quite a Talbot.

But I can tell you no more now—I have stopped at Lady Greys in my way home to seal and send. I hear there is a letter for us at Kensington.

To Mrs. Edgeworth

Saturday morning, 9 February 1822

My dear mother . . . Sam is in disgrace till he clears himself for his name is not in todays paper in the Minority against the insurrection act.[1] His mother is with reason enraged that he should absent himself from such a debate—and not to be *here* either! We must hear what he has to say for himself tomorrow. Mrs. Lock was one of the manoeuvring mothers who wanted to draw him in for her daughter and I could tell you a story about

[1] This Act dealt with measures for the control of agitation in Ireland. It provided for the temporary suspension of Habeas Corpus.

partridges which would divert you but have not time. Luckily he got safe out of that snare. Before I forget it I must tell you a better name than even the dead dandy for Rogers—Callcott told me yesterday—*Mr. Von Dug-up*. I will in my next send you a letter from Madame Gautier. I have been to see Lady Bathurst, 5 days have elapsed and she has not yet returned my visit.

'*Just as Mr. Taylor pleases*'—Sir H V Tempest when a poorish man married Angelo Taylors daughter.[1] A Taylor was a pompous man and wrote to Mr. Tempest to hint that he could not conveniently receive him at his country seat to which Sir H V Tempest replied in a laconic letter containing only these words '*Just as Mr. Taylor pleases*'. Presently a large fortune and title were left to Sir H V Tempest and then Mr. Taylor wrote to invite him most cordially and to tell him there was room for his horses dogs and everything. Sir H V Tempest answered as before with only these words '*Just as Mr. Taylor pleases*'. This has become a saying with Lady E. Whitbread and we adopt it. Pray do the same if you like it—as I do. affect yr M E

To Mrs. Edgeworth

Kensington Gore, Monday, 11 February 1822

Questions that desire an answer . . . Will you inquire for Wilkie what is put on the caps of the Inniskellen 6th Dragoons. He wants to mark one of the figures in the picture of the Chelsea pensioners for an Irishman—the man is in his undress—has a woolen cap and gaiters. Tell me anything in the dress or person that would mark it for an Irishman. If you know of any Dragoon that would be better than the Inniskillen tell me and describe particulars . . .

Now my dear mother having cleared away the business I will go on to my pleasure which is to pen down as fast as possible all I can recollect that is amusing for home.

Mr. Ralston is the hero of the present hour. Lady E. Whitbread has become so fond of him that though she does not quite

[1] Sir H. V. Tempest was the *brother*-in-law, not the son-in-law of Michael Angelo Taylor, M.P. The latter married his sister Frances Anne. Tempest succeeded in 1794 to the estates of his uncle, John Tempest.

say she wishes heaven had made her such a man yet she has more than once declared her wish that heaven had made many such men for her young friends and more for the example and shame of the London loungers. Her strong liking and strong indignations often put me in mind of my Aunt Ruxton and I love her all the better. 'I declare I cannot bear those fine puppy-men' said she. 'Yesterday when I was walking to Hertford St. to see my mother one of them was strutting before me with his great coat gathered behind *nicely* gathered like a woman's between button and button and I am sure he thought as much of his dress as the prettiest girl of 16 in London. I could not bear to see him —I really could not. I had a great mind to go up to him and say "For shame! Are you not ashamed of yourself? You a man! and an Englishman!"'

But to return to Mr. Ralston—he has won his way by being quite unaffected—yet attentive sufficiently in his appearance to mark respect to others—His manners timid yet not shy. What he knows he tells with coloring modesty as if supposing that others know a great deal more yet always ready to relate what they desire to hear—clear in his facts whether anecdotes or scientific facts. The more I see of him the more grievously I regret that he did not go down to Edgeworthstown and see Lovells school and all of you in my profane opinion still better worth his seeing. He speaks with warm gratitude of the hospitality with which he was treated in Dublin and likes the Irish better than any people he ever was among. He thinks Dublin the most beautiful of cities and in short was so charmed with it that he had a great mind to have spent the winter there. He staid 3 weeks there when he had intended to have staid only 3 days. Yet from all I could gather he had not fallen into or risen into the best company in Dublin. The person who had shewn him the most kindness he said was Hamilton Rowan and he spoke of having been often at Lady Morgan's whom he thought very entertaining and according to his indulgent manner of seeing handsome all but &c. Hamilton Rowan he says made himself independant and respectable in America during his banishment; he established a bleach green and lived by his own exertions. One day at Lady Morgans, a lady who had travelled in America and who had been received there with great kindness began to talk of her travels without knowing that Mr. Ralston was present. She asserted that all the ladies in America young and old took snuff. Well that was let to pass but she went on to assert that *all* the ladies in America chewed tobacco and smoked. Even Mrs. Patterson Jerome Bonaparte's wife she would not except. Mr. Ralston's blood boiled with indignation he says. How she 'scaped receiving the lie direct in her teeth I marvel; but the instant she left the room the slander was execrated. You may guess how much with this American warmth of feeling for his country he admires Mackintoshs concluding pages of the Review of Stewart.[1]

The conversation at dinner yesterday chanced to turn upon Bonaparte. Mr. Ralston told us an anecdote which he heard from a lady to whom it was related by one of the party concerned—Madame Lavalette. She and Josephine and two other favorite ladies of Josephine's court once in Bonaparte's absence amused themselves in her chamber with cooking in secret some vulgar dish which Josephine used to have in her low state and which she was ashamed ever to ask for as Empress. While they were thus like naughty children cooking their mess in secret they suddenly heard the Emperors voice and his step coming quick towards the door. Josephine ran to lock it. He thundered—kicked—would have the door broken up that instant if he were not let in. They scuttled about in dismay. One would have thrown the soup or whatever it was out of the window but the window could not be opened—another throwing the ladle under the bed and all hiding plates and dishes however and wherever they could. Napoleon burst in the instant the key turned—all their hidings were vain he must know the truth—and the truth was told him and when he found that only a vulgar dish instead of a vulgar man was at the bottom of the business he burst out laughing—told them they need not have been so much frightened or have taken such pains to hide their utensils for that he would sit down along with them and partake of their fare. Accordingly soup ladle—dishes, plates reappeared and the Emperor sat down and eat along with them but I should think their appetite for the frolic had been frightened.

I forgot to tell you that Wilkie dined here yesterday to meet

[1] *Edinburgh Review*, xxxvi (1821–2), review of Dugald Stewart's *A General View of the Progress of Metaphysical, Ethical and Political Science* (Pt. I, 1815; Pt. II, 1821).

Mr. Ralston—and Wilkie opened out wonderfully to the surprise of Lady Elizabeth and of all present excepting myself. I was delighted but not at all surprised for I have always maintained that there is a good deal in him if he could but get it out. Pray my dear Mrs. Honora do me the justice to recollect how I used to battle with you about him when you were out of patience with his dryness and his slowness. When I do bear with a slow person I surely ought to have it remembered to my credit. Now Honora see Wilkie after dinner with his con*sid*ering look on—with his circumspect eyes, and his round but *not* unthinking face. After a pause at the close of the last anecdote he began in his slow voice and Scotch accent uttering with difficulty as if he were speaking a foreign language, supplying his want of fluency with his constant hack phrase you *know* and working with his hands in the air before him and on the table as if he was feeling for the words he wanted.

'Bonaparte you know sent a *box*—you know—to Lady Holland you know—and Lady Holland sent for me to ask you see about having it engraved you know so I saw it and heard all about it you know.'[1] I will not teize you my dear Honora any more with poor Wilkie's manner but give you his matter. The box is about this size[2]—the top one onyx—the ground chocolate color—the lights white—beautifully worked in relievo figures. Within Lady Holland found a card—a French playing card—the 6 of diamonds which had been cut just to fit the box and on taking this out she found written with his own hand on the plain side of the card these words 'L'Empereur Napoleon a Miladi Holland—pour lui temoigner sa reconnaissance et son estime'. Bertrand brought this box to England. When all his goods were visited at the English custom house on landing he mentioned this box and the custom house officer put it into his hands declaring it should not pay any duty. Bertrand had Bonapartes orders to deliver it into Lady Hollands own hands. He wrote to tell her so. A day was appointed and it was as Lady Holland says most affecting to see the emotion of Bertrand in delivering it. He told her that about a fortnight before his death Bonaparte sent the surgeon with whom he had been consulting to order that all the

[1] See Earl of Ilchester, *Chronicles of Holland House* (1937), 15–16.
[2] Diagram given.

trinkets and curious things he possessed should be brought and placed before him. He looked them all over and after considering carefully fixed upon this box which he thought Lady Holland would like better than any thing else. He desired Bertrand would tell her after he was dead that the only circumstance to which when dying he could look back to during his imprisonment at St Helena without feelings of pain was her kindness. These words he desired Bertrand would exactly repeat to her—The only pleasure he had had had been in unpacking the boxes which she sent him. He always assembled those about him whom he most liked and made it quite an hour of pleasure. As Wilkie said 'It must have been an affecting sight I do think.' I suggested to him that it might make a good picture—of historic and domestic interest—the figures and circumstances being of sufficient notoriety and interest.

Wilkie mentioned another anecdote—I fear I shall not have time to finish it but I will begin. Lady Holland used to ask her friends if they liked to send Bonaparte any trifle in these packages. Lady Something Spencer who chanced to be present when one box was preparing sent him Coxes life of the Duke of Marlborough beautifully bound. He was much pleased with it. After having chosen the Pope's snuff box for Lady Holland he the same night recollected this book—sent for it and said that it was the history of *un brave*—that he would send it to *des braves*—he would make it a present to the regiment to whom his friend the surgeon belonged—then stationed at St. Helena. 'Tell them un brave sends it to them.' He took a pen and wrote in the first page 'L'Empereur Napoleon'—I forget the words but the sense was a present from un brave a des braves—worthy of them. Sir Hudson Lowe heard of it. The surgeon was obliged to shew it to him and the moment he saw the words L'Empereur Napoleon he said it should not be given—it could not be accepted because the English do not acknowledge him to be emperor. If he had written *Bonaparte* he should not have objected. He kept the book. When the surgeon returned next day to Napoleon the first words he said were 'How did they receive the book? What did they say?' The surgeon was silent. Bonaparte turned away. 'I see how it is. I understand it.' The officers wrote home to England to remonstrate and insist upon having the book—as a legacy—or a death bed gift. How it will end I know not. . . . affec M E

Tuesday, 12 February 1822

Like a child who keeps the plums of his pudding for the last but who is so tedious in getting through the beginning that his plate is taken away before he gets to his plums, *so* I often put off what I think the plum of my letter till '*The post Ma'am!*' hurries it off without the best part.

In my hurried conclusion yesterday I forgot to tell you the best part of Mr. Ralston's conversation. He has lately become acquainted with the discoveries of Mr. Parkins the American who has tried experiments in the compressibility of water the results of which have astonished all the Scientific world. Instead of water being as it was formerly believed almost incompressible Mr. Parkins demonstrates it to be compressible to a degree which I hardly dare state in figures lest I should make a liar or at least a blunderer of myself but I believe one twenty-eighth. He obtained the necessary compression and demonstrated its effect by plunging a bottle a perfect cylinder filled with water in the sea with a rod attached to its nicely fitted cork which then acted as a piston. The piston was forced into the bottle a certain depth when under a given pressure and this could be measured by its rod. When the bottle was raised again the piston rose till when taken out of the sea it was in the neck of the bottle and the bottle was full of water as in its first state—recovered if I may say so from its compression.[1]

Wollaston as Mr. Ralston affirms has verified and warrants the truth of these experiments. They have not yet been published and the author of course wishes to have the producing them to the public therefore my dear mother you will not send them through Mrs. Tuite to Mr. Chevenix. The most wonderful part appeared to me so incredible that I cannot help thinking Mr. Ralston mistakes. He said that under a great degree of compression *water turns to a gas*. Keep this for your own chamber wonder till I have inquired further from Wollaston. These new

[1] Perkins published his experiments in *Philosophical Transactions*, lx (1820), which cannot yet have reached Edgeworthstown. His discovery had a particular importance both in the evolution of the theory of matter and of geological theory.

discoveries it is expected must change all the systems of geologists—all the theories of earthquakes and all the old theories of the formation of the earth—So you or any of your friends who have any of these things lodged in their heads must give them *notice to quit* immediately—at furthest at the next meeting of the Royal Society. If any resistance be made I will get for Harriet Beaufort and Sophy Ruxton's use a regular notice to quit signed by

Sirhumphrydavy

When we were talking the other day to Mr. Talbot of this diverting direction of the letter to Sir Humphry Davy he mentioned that he had received safely a letter that had been directed to him only Robert Talbot London. He inquired how it was possible that the post office could have made him out. He was told that the post office in difficult cases assemble the letter carriers and ask round 'Have you a Talbot in your walk? Take this letter and try it.' So round them all day after day till the person is found or reported not in *London*. Excuse the way in which I tell you these things without order or apropos.

Apropos to excuses I must give you one of a school boys. (I hope it is not in Joe Miller.[1] Whether it be or not Lady E. Whitbread told it to Francis last saturday.) The schoolboy was called up to be flogged for having staid out too late. To excuse himself he said the Archbishop of Canterbury had invited him to dinner—Well but why were you not back before evening prayers—Because Sir the Archbishop pressed me to stay to take a row with him as far as Putney. Imagine the Archbishop rowing in his long sleeves! Francis laughed till he rolled—but very likely this joke like most jests sent to a distance will fall flat.

Mr. Ricardo has just called—Twitch goes the letter . . . [no signature]

[A letter of 18 February to Mrs. Edgeworth is here omitted. It deals in detail with the suicide of Mr. Gordon who had married Samuel Whitbread's sister, and the effect of the news on Lady Elizabeth.]

[1] John Mottley, *Joe Miller's Jests* (1739). The name is taken from the humorous actor Joseph Miller. There were many later editions with supplementary material.

To Mrs. Edgeworth

20 February 1822

. . . The Member for Middlesex is beginning to hold up his head again in his own family. It can now be seen over the skreen as formerly. Lady E. Whitbread is pretty well.

Miss Mackintosh breakfasted here this morning. Harriet with Gaynor behind her walked halfway to Holland House to meet her; while I lay in bed till my usual time and then heard Fanny read Ricardo and Peel's speeches[1] while I was dressing—Oh luxury! Miss Mackintosh is a very nice girl but her mother was foolish for presenting her and her sister at Court last year. None of the Opposition mothers but herself presented their daughters. Her rank did not require it and her fortune required the contrary. If I had time I could tell a good story about her puce colored train and a consultation about turning it into a pelisse. Lady Mackintosh spent so much last year that she cannot come to Town this season. Sir James came after breakfast—Much beautified by having had a cold having taken calomel and rest and having had his hair cut. He is without exception the most agreeable talker I ever heard talk. Fanny is over head and shoulders in love with him—much more danger of her carrying him off than of her being carried off to America.

I enclose Mr. Ralstons note. The handwriting is horribly ungentlemanlike and ought to be a warning to all who write like cats and flourish like schoolmasters—But the style sentiments—feelings I am sure you will like. Return the note to me because I must shew it to Hunter on account of a passage about reprinting in America which may be useful to him.

Nothing decisive was done yesterday about taking lodgings. The house I went to look at was taken before I reached Town and Mrs. Taddy said she had been ill used and was angry for my sake about it but I am quite as well pleased to be without it and not to take a house or any part from Mrs. Bull whom I cannot abide first because she told a lie and behaved shabbily about this

[1] Ricardo's and Peel's speeches of 18 Feb. 1822 were made on a motion for a Committee on the Agricultural Distress. They dealt with the relation of agricultural distress to fiscal measures for the reduction in the supply of paper currency and a return to cash payments (*Parliamentary Debates*, vi, cols. 479–86, 491–8).

house and next because she flattered me in such a nauseous manner about my improved complexion that I could have shut the door flat on her nose with pleasure. She is the widow of Mr. Bull our old landlord. Perhaps you may remember—No great matter if you don't. I have another set of good apartments in view in Holles Street which street Lady Lansdowne and all the friends who are so kind to interest themselves for us say they 'Approve'.

Lady Lansdowne was here yesterday while I was in Town house hunting. She heard that F and H were at home and got out and sat with them a quarter of an hour and was very agreeable and very eager in her hopes to see more and a great deal of us. Lady Bathurst has been here and Lady Georgiana and Lady Bathurst has satisfactorily accounted for her delay and was most particularly intimate and gracious and wished us much to come to a select party on friday—very agreeable people—Countess Lieven &c &c whom she was sure we should like. But we declined because these are our last days with Lady E Whitbread. Besides it is best not to run down Lady Bathursts throat. Let her run down ours if she pleases and then we shall be on sure ground.

You are welcome to the lemonade-Syrop. I have sent my aunt another bottle. So to end with a bonne bouche of wit which came from the lips of Sir James Mackintosh this morning—You know that Lord Buckingham is made a Duke and that one of his family titles is Birmingham. Sir James says 'We have been used to have a *Sheffield* Duke of Buckingham, but now we have a Birmingham Duke.'[1] . . .

I wish I could send you Lord Morleys history of his son. It is ridiculous beyond all contradiction. It is a thin quarto hot pressed and gilt edges and green binding and superfine elegance—ending with an anecdote about his Lordship calling the close-stool *The bookseller* because the outside had false books—So witty so playful so interesting. If it were a burlesque on biography what more could be done? However it is not *published*—only printed and given to particular friends. What a treat it

[1] John Sheffield was the last Duke of Buckingham of the 3rd creation. Birmingham or Brummagem means counterfeit, sham. Birmingham made brassware as Sheffield made plate. Birmingham was not one of the new Duke's titles.

would be to reviewers—Lady Bathurst told me they were in fits of laughter reading it.

I do not know that there is any truth in the report of Lady Georgianas intended marriage with Lord Liverpool. I should rather think *not* because when we were at Cirencester Lady Bathurst read aloud after dinner a passage from a letter from London joking with *Georgy* upon the subject. 'So I hear Lady Georgiana is to be our prime minister.' 'I understand that' said Lady Bathurst 'Just a way of asking us whether it is to be so or not.' Now Lady Bathurst is too worldly wise to put it about I think if the thing were really going on. I went to Lord Liverpools a few days ago. He was in deep mourning and the hatchments still up on his house—his notepaper half an inch black border. If he were courting surely the black border would diminish and the hatchments be taken down. I wish it may prove true—for I like both parties and think it would be remarkably well suited . . . [end missing owing to torn edge of paper] . . .

To Mrs. Edgeworth

Grove House, Sunday, 24 February 1822

This letter shall according to the law of hotch-potch, for I have nothing but trash to give you my dear mother and no time to bring it out in decent order.

Of a hundred female heads that we meet in the park or the streets, 75 of those who are fit to be seen are crowned with black bonnets silk or leghorn or velvet and the remaining twenty five wear beaver bonnet-hats which you may call drab or dove color according as your fancy inclines to drabs or doves. Said bonnets black and beaver have colored or white linings according to the taste of the wearers—pink most general—All black velvet inside and out most genteel exactly like those of your own daughters but only the young and fresh colored can stand this black and all black. Till within this last fortnight I have never worn anything but the black silk bonnet which you my dear mother toiled so hard and so successfully to make for me. I should have been bareheaded long since but for you. It has lately been drenched with rain and is now fit only to be a servant of all work. I love it still even in its degraded state but as fine ladies might not have the same charity for it I have bought another—black velvet—with a new plume—white satin lining and plaited border of figured blonde—which altogether makes me look as lovely—as *possible.* My sage-colored French velours simulé pelisse and Fanny and Harriets purple ditto are quite the thing for carriage visits and F and H's blue cloth and my grey for walking—our 3 tabbinets also good in their season. Their ruby imperial nets have done for all dinners here. So much for all the dress we have *yet* wanted. Did we ever tell you that Agnes Baillie sums up the characters of all of whom she highly approves with these words spoken in a most awfully emphatic tone

'And she drasses rema-rk-able well.'

Yesterday the LeFevre's dined here and a Mr. Pearce—a natural son of the famous Mr. Hares—nothing very agreeable or remarkable neverthemore—Though he has been in Syria and at Mount Lebanon and Constantinople and has known Lady Hester Stanhope and Captain Beaufort and all that should make him interesting. I hear that he was very entertaining when he first came home but it has worn off and faded and little now remains but an indolent tone of voice and manner which seems to have been learnt from the turks and hot climate. He so admired the Turks when first he returned that he had ¾ of a mind to go back and live among them. He remembered that Captain Beaufort was a fine fellow—a very clever man—believed he was then about some survey but he never read Karamania—had not heard of it.

He told me that a certain Dr. Meryon [was] some time ago commissioned by Lady Hester Stanhope to send her out to Mount Lebanon some Swiss waiting maids. The Doctor took or sent out the maids but in a short time there was the *devil to pay*—such work between them and the Turks!—that Lady Hester was in as great haste to get rid of them as she had been to obtain them. To one she was forced to give £20 to another £30—to another £40 to get rid of them. Doctor Meryon had to conduct this negotiation and to convoy the maids back *agen.* Do you not think he had enough to do?

Yesterday Captain Beaufort and his unburnt boy walked here to see us and then walked with Harriet and I to Lady Listowel's, ci-devant Lady Ennismores who has a splendid *villa* within half a quarter of a mile of Grove House with a beautiful conservatory at the end of a range of three or four rooms hung with pictures some good some bad. I think that you or Aunt Ruxton reproached me with not having gone to see this lady and her house the last time I was at Kensington Gore so I was determined to do it this time and contrived you see to manage it on our last day but one. She was excessively civil—all in her stiff held-up-head way. She looks just the same as she did at Kilkenny[1] sitting beside Mrs. G. Bushe in her frogged-spencer—the only difference that she now wears a frogged crimson silk gown and is a countess and many days older. My Lord is a little bilious crumpaty but better than I expected. He can talk and loves his conservatory and his pictures but does not know much of either and she is as stupid as possible about them. She never knew the name or properties of any one plant in her magnificent conservatory and even with the help of catalogue ground plan cards of her rooms she never could make out the names of her own pictures and their masters. It was always 'Lord Listowel whats this and whos that?'

I am sure she is one of those helpless statue women who have won hearts upon the principle of lady Lucy Barry who never mended a pen for herself 'because the men always like to be asked to do it for one'. Francis and his boy liked the *sights* and the walk. Lord Listowel has two curious pictures done by an Irish boy or man of the name of Grogan or Grogham—of Cork—who never had any instruction. One of these is of an Irish wake. There is a great deal of original humor and invention in it—of the Wilkie or better still of the Hogarth style . . .

Yesterday we went to see Mrs. Moutray at Mr. Sumners most comfortable and superb house. Aye that's something like living in Town if you please. I hear from some who pretend to know him that Mr. Sumner is odd tempered and disagreeable but from all I heard from Mrs. Moutray I should think he must be one of the best natured of good friends. Mrs. Moutray had expressed a wish to see the poor Queens[2] pictures and goods which are now a show previous to the sale. Mr. Sumner who is

[1] At the theatricals in 1810 (*Mem.* i. 237).

[2] Queen Caroline died on 9 Aug. 1821.

the busiest of parliament men nevertheless recollected this wish bought a 5 shilling catalogue bid her put on her bonnet and took her there. Mrs. Moutray says it is a melancholy sight—All the Queens dress—even her stays laid out—and tarnished finery to be purchased by the lowest of the low. There is a full length picture of her when young and happy—another where she is standing screwing up a harp with one hand and playing with her little daughter with the other. Mrs. Moutray says this is a beautiful picture of Opie's or Lawrences—I forget which. We will see it. Mrs. Moutray looks better than she did and seems to be enjoying herself or at least with her usual amiable temper and good sense trying to taste all of happiness that she can find in this world with the help of kind friends. She has been to Belzonis tomb[1] and says it is well worth while. We shall go there with Captain Beaufort next saturday and take our Francis—also to see the Laplanders who lodge next door . . .

To Mrs. Edgeworth

26 February 1822

My dearest Mother, I have this moment taken *a house* No. 8 Holles Street—from this day—at 6½ guineas per week for a month said by all the wise ones to be cheap—a pleasant house —Lady Lansdowne advised Holles St. We shall go there after luncheon time friday 1st March—No more time Maria E

I have engaged a ladys maid thro' Mrs. Marcet—2½ Guineas for 6 weeks and a *thorough* maid for cooking and brooming 1 shilling per day. Mrs. Taddy who is very knowing approves all my doings. I hope you will. I have a bed and nice room for our dear little Francis.

To Mrs. Edgeworth

Holles St., No. 8, Sunday, 4 March 1822

It was in No. 10 we were in 1813—My dearest mother! But now I am here with your daughters else how miserable I should feel myself and how lonely in this world of pleasure. You see

[1] Alabaster sarcophagus of Seti I discovered by G. B. Belzoni in 1817 and bought by Sir John Soane for his museum in Lincoln's Inn Fields.

that some way or other you and yours are essential to my happiness—to the remainder of my happiness—And a prodigiously great remainder it is considering what has been taken away.

This No. 8 belonging to Mr. and Mrs. Tyerman is a much more comfortable house than No. 10—better furnished and with plenty of presses—drawers—wardrobes—pegs for ourselves—good kitchen pantry—attics—Two drawing rooms with folding doors—small but pretty with sofa in one Chaise long in the other—blue—*blue* new glazed calico furniture very like Mrs. Whitneys—a small *boudoir* (English closet) at the end of the back drawing room with scarlet moreen curtains new green cloth on floor which looks as *paradisaical* as a lodging house boudoir can possibly be expected to appear. We have a nice little attic for our Francis. Our bedchambers opening into one another are perfectly comfortable and a little room over the boudoir and within Harriets bedchamber serves for a gownery. I have had cloak pegs put all round it and it has an ample deal wardrobe so that we can *hang up* instead of folding up in a hurry.

Mrs. Taddy has given me a footstool—Lady E. Whitbread has lent us a teachest with an impenetrable lock—so you see we are very comfortable and I know this is the most agreeable thing I can tell you.

We have an excellent maid Margaret Bolton recommended by Mrs. Marcet and a very decent old asthmatic body for thorough-going bed maker and cook. Her name is—very difficult and romantic—Elizabeth Vennelock. But the essential point is that she mashes and browns potatoes for luncheon so well that Miss Dennel[1] would be charmed with them and she roasts fowls and makes mutton steaks as well as the first *she* or *he* in the land as far as we 3 know to the contrary. We shall I presume seldom dine at home but always lunch and hot lunch—and people drop in. Therefore the cooks luncheon-skill is not only of use but credit to us.

We have taken this house from the 26th for a month at six guineas and a half per week. We pay 13/6 moreover for linen. We pay Margaret Bolton 2 guineas per month—Elizabeth Vennelock—1 shilling per day—M. Bolton 12 shillings board wages—E V—ditto—Gaynor 14 shillings ditto. They provide

[1] A character in Fanny Burney's *Camilla*.

tea sugar all for themselves. I have taken the best advice in all economical points from Mrs. Taddy Mrs. Marcet Mrs. Somerville and they have been kinder in all household minutiae of counsel that I could have concieved possible. I hope you will approve.

I forgot to say that we have an excellent job landau—roomy as heart could wish and quite *iligant* coachman horses and *all*—for one pound per day including coachman. Mr. Carr got this for us. Our own carriage under his coachmans care 3/6 per week standing. It will do for all our journey if we go to Scotland. Harriet pays all the house account bills and I without further trouble shall put down in my book H Acct. so much. You understand the comfort this will be to me. We shall try one week how the cook manages leaving it to her to provide our little luncheons and if Mrs. Somerville my *grand-juge* says it is not extravagant I shall go on leaving cook to save M E all thought of what we are to eat. Harriet keeps the engagement book and I only ask her whether each new one crosses an old one or not before I say yes. Fanny reads and writes as I *beg* or *dictate* all answers. You see that my eyes—head—hands—stomach are trebled and the best that can be had (thanks to you) for love or money.

You need not be afraid that we should have damped Lady Bathurst or Lansdowne by our first refusal—Tout au contraire. Lloyd the bookseller is one of the persons who send out visiting tickets when the number passes the powers of footmen. I sent out yesterday by his means above 50 cards as Lady Bathurst &c advised simply to say where we are. The *sending* instead of taking such visiting tickets is a great saving of time—servants and horses. Numbers of return cards and invitations pour in rapidly.

Fanny and Harriet were at a little dance at Mrs. LeFevre's on saturday last. She is the mother in law of our Mrs. LeFevre. They looked very pretty and danced 5 or 6 quadrilles with good partners—which will be mentioned in their journals no doubt. We dined yesterday en famille with the Carrs—Francis E and all—kind friends!—delightful singing and playing (I wish Louisa had been there) in the evening—Morton charming (I wish he were rich enough to marry and live)—No company but a

Mr. Rolfe—Chancery lawyer—young—clever—gentlemanlike and all this I think Mrs. Carr thinks and I have a notion he will do for Fanny Carr. I took him this morning with us to breakfast at Mr. Ricardos where we have general invitation to take who we will—delightful morning. Went to Mrs. Weddells afterwards—delightful. Snapped off Maria E

To Mrs. Ruxton

Holles Street, 9 March 1822

My dearest Aunt . . . We were last monday at a select *early* party at Mrs. Hope's. We went from a party at Mrs. Blakes where we had spent an hour and a half with Mrs. Marcet—Mrs. Somerville—Dr. Wollaston and others of their society and arriving at Duchess St. about eleven found in the great drawing room only Mr. and Mrs. Hope—Lord Gower and Miss Burrowes who had dined there. We were glad to have some minutes conversation with Lord Gower who is very agreeable. The tide flowed in about ten minutes and it was high tide in a quarter of an hour but this party was very select—*only* about a hundred. The newspapers would tell you the duchess of Richmond and daughters—Lady Lansdowne and sister Lady Charlotte Lemon (whom I saw for the first time and hope it will not be the last) —Lady Londonderry Lady Salisbury—Lady Gwydyr—Lady Morley Lady Louisa Lambton &c &c.

Seeing the panorama of passing figures was amusing for an hour but to me the most entertaining five minutes were the last when the rooms emptying half a dozen of the elect gathered round Mrs. Hopes sofa and talked over those who had passed away. Mrs. Hope called me to sit between her and Lady Gwydyr on the sofa, so that I could hear all—Lady Londonderry standing behind the sofa intending to move on to the door every instant but detained by Lady Morley who stood in front attracting irresistibly with the combined powers of mimickry and scandal —Fanny and Harriet sitting on a *bed of roses* (Ottoman) with Mrs. Hopes niece, at a little distance but not within hearing, because the scandal-mongers closed close, and spoke low. The prime object was a certain Mrs. Bohem [Boehm] I am not sure I spell her name rightly though a few years ago all London knew it well as she was a famous masquerade giver, and every one went to her fine parties. Now *they are ruined* and everybody laughs at them. She had appeared this night and walked through these rooms, an object of ridicule to those for whose applause she had sacrificed her fortune. 'Mark how the world its veterans rewards.'[1] If Lady Gwydyr and Lady Morley do not belye her she must however be a strange person. Lady Morley mimicked her manner of going up close to the king one night at the Pavillion at Brighton and running over the sticks of her fan, whisper to his Majesty 'Sir you look so very handsome tonight I should *so like* to kiss you.' Then said Lady Morley the King turned of course and did kiss her audibly—audibly—so that it could be heard from afar. Is it credible? And yet these ladies protest that they saw and heard it. Moreover Lady Gwydyr added that one night at supper lately the king speaking of Mrs. Bohem and former times said 'I don't tell you that I was ever in love with her, but there was a time when she was d---nably in love with me.' What manners! If the kings bag had been opened I think it would have matched the Queens.[2]

Mr. Hope's new gallery of Flemish pictures given to him by his brother is beautifully arranged and most of the pictures excellent but I am not going to plague you with a catalogue.

We have several *established* pleasant breakfasting houses where we have general invitations to go whenever we please and to bring with us one or two gentlemen whenever we please —writing a note by 2d. post the day before to say how many. These delightful family breakfasts are at Grove-house (Lady E. Whitbread's)—at Mr. and Mrs. LeFevres (Lady E. Whitbread's daughter and son in law)—At Dr. and Mrs. Marcets and at Mr. and Mrs. Ricardo's. At these breakfasts we see people more and more agreeably than at any other time. All who have any sense themselves or any taste for sense in others are ambitious of knowing Mr. Ricardo and his kind permission to me to bring who I please to breakfast with him has put it in my power to oblige several especially our young American friend

[1] 'See how the world its veterans rewards.' (Pope, *Moral Essays*, Ep. II, l. 243.)

[2] A reference to the scandalous evidence produced in the House of Lords on the introduction of a bill to deprive Queen Caroline of her royal title and dissolve her marriage to the king, July–Nov. 1820.

Mr. Ralston and young John LeFevre (brother of the gentleman who is married to Lady E. Whitbread's daughter)—a reading man and a dancing man and much approved by F and H though I think he looks like a face cut in charcoal and 100 years old. But above all others I have had the greatest pleasure in Francis Beauforts going to Mr. Ricardos with us. They enjoy each others conversation so much. It has now become high fashion with blue ladies to talk political economy. There is a certain Lady Mary Shepherd who makes a great jabbering on this subject while others who have more sense like Mrs. Marcet hold their tongues and listen. A gentleman answered very well the other day that he would be of the famous Political economy club whenever he could find two members of it that agree on any one point. Mean time fine ladies now require that their daughters governesses should teach political economy. 'Pray Ma'am' said a fine Mamma to one who came to offer herself as governess 'Do you teach political economy?' The governess who thought she had provided herself well with French Italian Music drawing, dancing, &c was quite astounded by this unexpected requisition she hesitatingly answered 'No Ma'am I cannot say I teach political economy, but I would if you think proper try to learn it.' 'Oh dear no Ma'am. If you don't teach it you wont do for me.'

Another style of governess is now the *ultra* French.[1] A gentleman told me he met a Madame de Tilly a high born ultra who reduced in fortune came to London as governess in a family of distinction. She and another lady governess of the Orleans party or of the liberaux I forget which met and come to high words, till all was calmed by the timely display of a ball dress trimmed with roses alternately red and white—a trimming which is called *Garniture aux prejugés vaincus.* This I think should have been worn by those who formerly invented *bals aux victimes.*[2]

But to go back to our breakfasts at Mr. Ricardos—*After* the last at which Captain Beaufort was with us we saw—what do you think? Oliver Cromwells head—not his picture—not his

[1] Right-wing supporters of Louis XVIII and the elder branch of the French royal family.

[2] The condition of admittance to these balls was that every *dame* and every *cavalier* should lately have had a near relative guillotined.

bust—nothing of stone or marble or plaister of Paris, but his real head, which is now in the possession of Mr. Ricardo's brother in law (Mr. Wilkinson).[1] He told us a story of an hour long explaining how it came into his possession. This head as he well observed is the only head upon record which has after death been subject to the extremes of honor and infamy—It having been first embalmed and laid in satin state—Then dragged out of the coffin at the restoration—chopped from the body and stuck upon a pole before Westminster hall, where it stood twenty five years till one stormy night the pole broke and down fell the head at the centinels feet who stumbled over it in the dark twice thinking it a stone, then cursed and picked it up and found it was a head. Its travels and adventures from the centinel through several hands would be too long to tell. It came in short into the Russell family and to one who was poor and in debt and who yet loved this head so dearly that he never would sell it to Coxe of the Museum till Coxe got him deep in his debt arrested and threw him into jail. Then and not till the last extremity he gave it up for liberty. Mr. Wilkinson its present possessor doats upon it. A frightful skull it is—covered with its parched yellow skin like any other mummy and with its chesnut hair eyebrows and beard in glorious preservation. The head is still fastened to the inestimable broken bit of the original pole—all black and happily worm eaten. By this bit of pole Mr. and Mrs. Ricardo and family by turns held up the head opposite the window while we stood in the recessed window and the happy possessor lectured upon it compasses in hand. There is not at first view it must be owned any great likeness to picture or bust of Cromwell but upon examination the proofs are satisfactory and agree perfectly with historic description. The nose is flattened as it should be when the body was laid on its face to have the head chopped off. There is a cut of the axe (as it should be) in the wrong place where the bungling executioner gave it before he could get it off. One ear has been torn off as it should be and the plaister of Paris cast which was taken from Cromwells face after death, being now produced all the measures of jaws and forehead agreed wonderfully and the likeness grew

[1] See K. Pearson and G. M. Morant, 'The Portraiture of Oliver Cromwell with special reference to the Wilkinson head', *Biometrika*, xxvi (1935), esp. pp. 24–6.

upon us every instant as we made proper allowances for want of flesh-muscles—eyes &c. To complete Mr. Wilkinson's felicity there is the mark of a famous wart of Olivers just above the left eyebrow, on the skull precisely as in the cast. But then Captain Beaufort objected or was not quite convinced that the whole face was not half an inch too short. Poor Mr. Wilkinson's hand trembled so that I thought he never would have fixed either point of the compasses and he did brandish them about so afterwards when he was exemplifying that I expected they would have been in Fanny's eyes or my own and I backed and pulled back. Mrs. Ricardo *gave her staff to whom she listed*—she could not bear the weight of Old Noll thro' this whole trial. Mr. Ricardo gave up too when a bit of cotton wool was dragged from the nostrils ('Oh I *cannot* stand the cotton wool.') He delivered over the staff and went to the fire to comfort himself dragging up the skirts of his coat as men do in troubles great.

I was glad Captain Beaufort let the poor Mr. Wilkinson off easy about the length of face and we all joined in a chorus of conviction. He went off with his head and staff the happiest of connoisseurs. Moreover I suggested that for future convenience of shewing he might have it fixed under a glass case—the broken staff to fit into a tube as candle in candlestick. How much time and paper it takes to tell anything in writing! (Excuse tiresomeness! inevitable when I have not time to make things properly short)

I will just *note* down what we did yesterday—breakfasted at Dr. and Mrs. Somervilles at ten—Anecdotes of Walter Scotts quickness and skill in working up every fact he gleans in conversation and even every good expression. Clerk and Thomson are two friends of his who have helped him to much in antiquarian lore and in humourous expression. Clerk is an odd long armed figure. Once when he was stirring the punch before supper he saw Scott and Thomson laugh. 'I know you are laughing at me —I know I look like the red lion on a sign post predominating over a bowl of punch.' This appears word for word in Waverley.[1] The first volume of the Abbot or Monastery was printed

[1] *Waverley* (1814), chap. viii, last para.: '. . . a huge bear, carved in stone, predominated over a large stone basin, into which he disgorged the water.' See Lockhart, *Life of Scott* (1893 edn.), 59.

when one day Clerk went to Scott with an old musty record he had rummaged out, of some Monastery's accounts in which in the bill of daily fare appeared what do you think Scott? Why oatmeal porridge I suppose or broth or *broz*—No such thing—stewed Almonds. In the next volume Scotts monks were feasted on stewed Almonds[1] and Thomson meeting Clerk exclaimed 'How this Walter Scott finds out everything. I thought I had the stewed Almonds a secret snug to myself. How did he get at it?' 'I told it to him' answered Clerk. If any proofs were wanting who could doubt after this of Scotts being the author of those novels.

But to go on with our day—Mrs. Somerville went into her painting room and F and H sat by an hour while she was going on with a view of Paestum about as large a picture as your Colosseum. I mean time was taken by Dr. Somerville up to the children's school room. 'You will see we follow as far as possible Prac Ed!'[2] The children I am sure do credit to it—especially in happiness and happy tempers. Left Mrs. Somerville at one oclock after settling that we would take her to breakfast with Lady E. Whitbread on thursday and on to Callcotts at Kensington—to Wilkie's to see their pictures now preparing for Exhibition—Chelsea pensioners Wilkie—Seizure of Smugglers—Callcott.

From Mrs. Somerville's went by appointment to Lansdowne House. Lady Lansdowne is most kind and quite affectionate to F and H. She had fire and warm air in their superb new statue saloon[3] on purpose for them. The room is 110 feet long—suppose 40 broad—semicircle at each end where the principal statues stand—windows on one side—high up as in Dr. Beaufort's Collon study—large and good light. The roof is truncated with a dome at each end and glazed windows at the finishing of the truncated part. Behind these windows on the roof at the outside the lamps are placed on gala nights when the whole is to be lighted. Will this be intelligible? I fear not.[4] The niches are all hung with crimson cloth which shews off the statues—beautiful—The ceiling gilt roses—no trumpery ornaments—much better

[1] *The Monastery* (1820), chap. xxiv and Note M.

[2] *Practical Education* (1798).

[3] This gallery had been re-modelled to the designs of G. Dance, jr., between 1816 and 1819.

[4] Sketch plan given here.

taste than our dear Hopes—beautiful statue of Cupid and Psyche and one little head of a frightful Greek antient Venus with which Mr. Knight is in love and about which as Lady Lansdowne says he says long things which he does not understand.

Mrs. Kennedy Romilly's daughter entered towards the end of our visit—invited to meet us and we liked her very much—not handsome but very pleasing manners. Enter Mrs. Nicoll lately married—Lady Lansdowne's niece—daughter of Lady M Talbot and the passionate father—very pleasing. 'Let me make my niece known to you. I like that you should know all I love' said Lady Lansdowne. She finished by asking me to dine there on tuesday 19th and sisters in evening and we all go to her *early* party tomorrow night.

After leaving Lady Lansdownes went to Captain Beaufort for him and Mrs. Beaufort and Francis—intended to have taken his 2 boys, but they had colds. So we 6 went together to see Belzonis tomb[1]—the model first and afterwards the tomb as large as life and painted in proper colors as represented in the book. It is a very striking spectacle but I cannot describe it. The book has done this as well as it is possible to give the idea by description.

Next door to the tomb is another striking sight which we went to—The laplanders. At the end of a vast room you see within a railed space their 2 huts. Between the huts sat the little Lapland man about my size in his fur jacket and cap at work intently but stupidly on making a wooden spoon pricking holes as in your Norway box (Sophy). The wife was more intelligent—a child of five years old—very quick and lively little grey eyes sallow complexion—not unlike Irish cabineers when pinched a little with hunger. The child is learning its English alphabet—can count 8 and learns with ease. In the middle of the apartment is a pen in which are 5 reindeer about the size of asses with longer necks very gentle and ravenously eager for moss of which there is a provision in a basket at the entrance of the room. Each person is allowed to take some and to feed the reindeer who stretch and snatch for it eagerly. This moss which they love as their own has been fortunately for them found in great quantities on Bagshot heath.

[1] See above, p. 359 n.

Went home and dined at home because we wished to have little Francis and two of his schoolfellows Mr. *china* Barrows sons. Mr. Harness a very agreeable man whom we knew first at Mr. Hopes undertook for us to take them to *Tom and Jerry*[1] an entertainment which is said to be High and low life in London fitter for boys and gentlemen than ladies. Lady Lansdowne had given us her box for the Opera. We went to the Opera. Mr. Harness joined us there after he had in a most good-natured manner secured the diversion for the boys and despatched them home to bed. Bed we reached ourselves by one o clock. Tom and Jerry was stupid I hear—Our Opera La Gazza ladra was delightful—the old story of the magpye—the ballet Pandore[2] . . . In the next box to us sat a great and fat heiress Miss Greatheed (and her head is very large). She is going to be married to a Mr. Percy whom as the story goes she has been in love with ever since she was six years old—More shame for her! The substance is all on her side the family on his. This pair have been called *Quantity* and *Quality*—or better still—*Flesh and Blood*—Almost as good as if of Irish invention.

We went one night to the House of Commons—to the Ventilator. Mr. S. Whitbread took us there. There is a garret the whole size of the room or Chapel below—Kitcats[3] of gothic chapel windows stopped up appear on each side above the floor—the roof beams &c as in a garret—one lantern with one farthing candle and one tin candlestick all the light in said garret but ample room. From what Lady Harrowby formerly told me I thought we were to be squeezed into a hole. In the middle of the garret appears what seems a sentry box of boards the height of a common deal board—old chairs round it for us to stand upon

[1] A dramatization of Pierce Egan's highly successful *Life in London: or, The day and night scenes of Jerry Hawthorn, esq. and his elegant friend Corinthian Tom* . . . (1820). There were several stage versions of which the two most popular, by W. T. Moncrieff and by Egan himself, ran at the Adelphi (93 nights) and at Sadlers Wells.

[2] At the King's Theatre. The opera is by Rossini. Between the acts there was a 'Divertissement, called VILLAGEOIS, and after the opera the ballet of PANDORE.'

[3] A kitcat is a less than half-length portrait, so called after a series of portraits of members hung in the dining room of the Kitcat Club, *c.* 1700. The unreformed House of Commons met in the medieval St. Stephen's Chapel. There was no Ladies' Gallery and the only way in which ladies could see or hear debates was by peering through the Ventilator in the flat ceiling which had been inserted below the vault *c.* 1707. A sketch of the attic with the Ventilator is to be found in M. Hastings, *Parliament House* (1950), 133.

—we got up—peeped over the top of the boards—saw the large chandelier blazing with lights immediately below—a grating of ironwork across from which it hangs veiled the light so that we could look down and below we saw half the Speakers table with the mace lying on it and papers and two figures of clerks could be had at the farther end by peeping hard but no eye could see the Speaker or his chair. His voice and terrible note of *order* was soon heard. On each side of the table we could see part of the treasury bench and the opposition members in their places. The tops of the heads—profiles and gestures we could see perfectly. It was not in itself a very interesting debate—On the Knightsbridge affair[1] and on the salt tax[2]—But it was entertaining to us because we were curious to see and hear the principal speakers on each side. We heard Lord Londonderry—Mr. Peel—Mr. Vansittart—and on the other side—Denman—Brougham and Bennet—and several hesitating country gentlemen who seemed to be speaking to please their constituents only. Sir John Sebright was far the best country gentleman speaker. He was as much at his ease as at Beechwood in his own drawing room! Mr. Brougham we thought the best speaker we heard—Mr. Peel next—Mr. Vansittart the best language and most correct English tho there is little in what he says. The Speaker I am told has made this observation on Vansittart that he never makes a mistake in grammar. Lord Londonderry[3] makes the most extraordinary blunders and Malapropisms. Mr. Denman speaks

[1] On 28 Feb. Alderman Wood, a strong supporter of the Queen, submitted a motion on the Knightsbridge riots of 26 Aug. 1821. The occasion for the riots was the funeral procession of two men who had been shot by guardsmen in the disturbances over the Queen's funeral procession. The funeral procession of the two men was ill-advisedly arranged to pass Knightsbridge barracks where a tumult arose. The military authorities (supported by the government) and the Sheriff of Middlesex disputed the facts of what happened and the policy which should have been pursued (*Parliamentary Debates*, vi, cols. 801–37).

[2] John Calcraft moved the repeal of the duties on salt. This was part of a general move for a reduction of taxation after the Napoleonic wars (ibid., col. 837).

[3] Fanny Edgeworth commented on Lord Londonderry, 'His manner not at all the dignified nonchalante manner it is described to be. He was I believe really in a passion at so much opposition his action is incessant and monotonous slapping the table most violently—then stepping back to his seat to find a new sentence generally leaving the last unfinished.' She said of Brougham that 'he was the only speaker I heard who made you quite forget to feel anxious about how he should get on—he seemed more perfectly at his ease and master of his subject than any of them—I liked his action too.'

well—Mr. Bennet very ill. He stammers painfully and is impatient with himself and others. Upon the whole the speaking and the interest of the scene far surpassed our expectations. We felt proud to mark the vast difference between the English House of Commons and the French Chambre des deputés.

Nevertheless there are disturbances in Suffolk and Lord Londonderry was obliged to get up from dinner to order troops to be sent there. Before he had swallowed two mouthfuls he rose after reading his despatches.

Now it is darkening and I must go to dress to dine at [ ][1] with Dr. and Mrs. Lushington. Yours affecy. Maria E

To Mrs. Edgeworth

8 Holles St., [Saturday, 16 March 1822]

. . . Yesterday I engaged to take this house for another month (or 4 weeks) from the 26th of March at which our present *take* finishes up to the 23rd of April. I could not get it at the same rate because as the season advances rates you know advance and if I had waited another fortnight the price would probably have doubled at least so Mrs. Tyerman assures me—that she could then get 13 guineas a week for it. I have closed with her after an hours jabbering for 8 guineas a week. I hope you will approve my dear mother. I thought that without hurrying ourselves to sickness against which you wisely warned me, I could not get all that is to be seen and done in London into less compass of time. Heaven grant!—then I may feel I have done for the best . . .

Mrs. Weddell's praise of both F and H was what went to my heart and must go to yours. I wish their father could have heard it . . . 'Ma'am they are always ready to converse and speak the best sense in the best language and they never come too forward or keep too backward in company. Ma'am they have been what I call perfectly well educated.' . . . 'In my time Ma'am' continued Mrs. Weddell 'We lived with our parents when we were children and my father I remember took pains to make us speak well—I mean distinctly and in good English but now young ladies are shut up with French maids and French governesses

[1] MS. torn.

till they come out and half the young ladies I see cannot speak their own language or speak in such an indistinct manner that *I* cannot hear or comprehend them. And they are so bashful at first and so confident afterwards! I have no pleasure in their conversation. They have learned everything I suppose but I learn nothing from them.'

I found this dear accomplished old lady and Mr. Prince Hoare sitting together when I came in pronouncing F and H's panegyric. She painted (copied) last year in her 72d year a beautiful crayon portrait of Lady Dundas—lying down every half hour to rest. What a difference between the use and abuse of accomplishments!

Your brother Francis is agreeable and kind to us beyond description. He lets us take him where we will into society. He spent a morning with us at Mr. Ricardos and Mrs. Weddells—dined at Mrs. Weddells with Lady Louisa Stuart (Primates sister)—Mr. Bigge of Botany Bay—Mr. Stanley of Knutsford and many others. In the evening Sir Willoughby Gordon and Lady Gordon—very entertaining accounts of America and Bigges drawings.

I will begin at the beginning of yesterday (Friday) and tell you all we did that day. We got up in the morning and put on
2 1
our shoes and *stockings* after the manner of Harry and Lucy[1] and our pelisses which were not invented in their time and we breakfasted—not on apples—but on green tea—much better in my humble opinion than green apples. N B our green tea is of superfine quality given to Mrs. Taddy by a friend at the India House and given to us by Mrs. Taddy—So no more of that. We went straight to Newgate by appointment[2] the moment we had swallowed the said tea. The private door of the jailor opened and at sight of our tickets the great doors and little doors and thick doors and doors of all sorts unbolted and unlocked and in

[1] See ME's *Early Lessons* (1800). The episode referred to is in the first part of 'Harry and Lucy' and was written by Mrs. Honora Edgeworth and printed but not published in *Practical Education* (anon. 1780).

[2] Mrs. Fry's note to ME made an appointment for the 15th at 10.30, 'the day that we do not generally admit company . . . I shall be more at liberty to pay you that attention that my heart would dictate for I can assure thee I feel as a *mother* one of those who are under *much obligation* to thee for the assistance thou hast given us in the education of our children.'

we went and on through dreary but clean passages till we came to a room where rows of empty benches fronted us a table before them on which a large bible lay chairs before the table for Mrs. Fry and her sisters—chairs and benches on each side for company auditors. Several ladies and a gentleman arrived and took their places in silence. We knowing no better had seated ourselves on one of the front empty benches. Enter Mrs. Fry in drab colored silk cloak and plain borderless quaker cap—a most benevolent countenance—a Guido Madona face—calm—benign —'I must make an inquiry—Is Maria Edgeworth here and where?' I went forward and shewed her where my sisters were sitting. She told me that the benches were for the convicts and bid us come and sit beside her. Her first smile as she looked upon me I never can forget. The prisoners came in and in an orderly manner ranged themselves on the benches—All quite clean—faces caps—hair—hands. On a very low bench in front which I thought had been for the feet little children placed themselves and were *settled* by their mothers. These children seemed to be from 5 to 6 or 7 years old—All as clean as if they had been at Lovells boys school—or at Harriets girls school. Mrs. Fry told me that almost all the women I here saw about 30 were under sentence of transportation but though under this sentence many would probably be reprieved. Some few were only under sentence of fine and imprisonment. One who did not appear was under sentence of death. She was ill. Frequently women are so affected by that sentence as to become ill and absolutely unable to attend Mrs. Fry. The others attend regularly and voluntarily while she reads prayers or the scriptures to them.

She opened the bible and read in the most sweetly solemn sedate voice I ever heard—slowly and distinctly without any thing in the manner that could distract attention from the matter. Sometimes she paused to explain which she did with great judgment. In addressing the Convicts she often said *We*—*We* have felt—*We* are convinced &c.

They were very attentive—unaffectedly interested I thought in all she said and touched by her manner. There was nothing *put on* in their countenances nor any appearance of hypocrisy. I studied their countenances carefully but I could not see any which without knowing to whom they belonged I should have decided was *bad*. Yet Mrs. Fry assured me that all these women had been of the very worst sort—all confined for transportable offences. She confirmed what we have read and heard from others that it was by their love of their children that she first obtained influence over these abandoned poor women. When she first took notice of one or two of their fine children the mothers said that if she could but save their children from the misery they had gone through in vice, they would do anything she bid them and when they saw the change made in their children by her schooling they begged to attend themselves. I could not have concieved that the love of their children could have remained so strong in hearts from which every feeling of virtue has so long been dead. The Vicar of Wakefield's sermon in prison[1] is it seems founded on a deep and true knowledge of human nature. The spark of good is often smothered never wholly extinguished.

Mrs. Fry often says a prayer extempore but this day she was quite silent while she covered her face with her hand for some minutes. They were perfectly silent with their eyes fixed upon her impatient to hear her not to go. When she said '*You may go*' they all went away *slowly*. The little children sat quite still the whole time. When one leaned the mother behind set her upright. Mrs. Fry told us that the dividing the women into classes has been of the greatest advantage and putting them under the care of Monitors. There is some little pecuniary advantage attached to the office of monitor which makes them emulous to obtain it. We went through the female wards with Mrs. Fry and saw the women at various works—knitting—rug-making &c. They have done a great quantity of needlework some of it most neatly executed and some very ingenious. When I expressed my foolish wonder at this Mrs. Fry's sister (who by the bye appears to me as sensible and active as herself) replied 'We have to do recollect Ma'am not with fools but with rogues.' The profit of their industry is all theirs. The actual good done by employing these people and keeping them tolerably happy during this period of imprisonment is great and there is hope that many when they are set at liberty will continue their orderly and industrious habits. This must as some of them said depend upon whether they get employment when they

[1] Chap. xxix.

are out of jail: Mrs. Fry is raising a subscription from all visitors to apply to this purpose—*How*—Heaven knows. At all events she has effected much good and far from being disappointed when I saw her and all she has done I was delighted.[1] There was only one being among all those upon whom she has tried to make salutary impression upon whom she could make none—An old jewess. She is so depraved and so odiously dirty that she cannot be purified body or mind. Wash her and put clean clothes on her and she tears them and dirties them and swarms with vermin again in 24 hours. She is a nuisance which they cannot remove either. We saw her in the kitchen where they were served with broth—a horrible spectacle she was which haunted me the whole day and night afterwards. One eye had been put out and closed up and the other glared with malignant passion. I asked if she was not happier than before Mrs. Fry came to Newgate. She made no direct answer but said 'It is hard to be happy in a prison. If you were to taste *that* broth you'd find it is nothing but dishwater.' I did taste it and found it very good broth—full as good as the diet of a jail ought to be. The most striking thing to me was the effect of employment—the seeing that even under sentence of transportation these people went on working and that they are so much happier for this hourly exertion and hope of small remuneration—Small motive—certain and constant produce astonishing effects.

When I was to subscribe—Oh misery! I had forgotten my purse. Not one of us 3 had one farthing. I applied to a lady with a pleasing countenance who trusted me and lent me a sovereign. She was the daughter of Lady *Eve*! Mrs. Fry has asked us to come and see her at her own house and will give me tickets which are rather difficult now to obtain for Captain Beaufort Alicia and Mr. L. Wilson. Your brother is anxious to see Mrs. Fry.

I told Mrs. Fry what Harriet had done in her own little school and if I am not mistaken she was pleased with Harriet. I spoke of Lovells school to her and I hope when he comes to England again he will see her. She is prepared to like him and his doings.

We emerged again from the thick dark silent walls of Newgate to the bustling city and thence to the elegant part of the

[1] In a letter of 15 Mar. Fanny Edgeworth commented '. . . They did not shew the sort of affectionate admiration towards her [Mrs. Fry] that I had expected. . . .

Town and before we had time to arrange our ideas and while the mild quaker face and voice wonderful resolution and successful exertions of this admirable woman was still in our mind morning visitors flowed in and common life again went on.

Three or 4 of this mornings visitors were very agreeable—Sir Humphry Davy—Major Colebrooke—Lord Radstock and Mrs. Scott. You ask who Mrs. Scott is. I can only tell you that she is sister to Lady I dont know-who—that she is Mrs. Scott of *Dane's fort*[1] *which* and whom I am sure we described in some of our letters from Lord Carringtons. Major Colebrooke has just married but—The bell man! . . . Yr. affecy. Maria E

To Louisa Beaufort

8 Holles Street, 23 March 1822

. . . We have made him [Captain Beaufort] and Mrs. Beaufort acquainted with your friend Mrs. Napier and her husband. They all drove out together with us a few days ago to see a fine blow of Camelia-Japonica. I proposed this because I think people get much better acquainted when they have some object in common and are not to sit looking at each other with nothing to say. Our excursion was very pleasant—fine day—landau open—Camelias beautiful. A few days afterwards we appointed to meet again at the British Museum and at this meeting all parties seemed to increase in liking for each other—So I hope it will do well. At the Museum the keeper of the insects who is author of a book called (I believe) The Entomologists companion shewed us several of the insects with which dialogues on Entomology[2] have happily made me acquainted—The Termites—and the lion ant with his ingenious case for his eggs—and the solitary bee—the mathematical bee.

We dined at Mr. Hopes a few days ago and a most delightfully pleasant dinner it was—much pleasanter than at Lansdowne

The jailor also said when Maria asked him if a great change had not been created since Mrs. Fry had come there—Some change Ma'am certainly in some respects—but not of any great dependence.'

[1] Danesfield, nr. Marlow.

[2] *Dialogues of Entomology* (1819) was by Louisa Beaufort. I cannot identify the other book.

House or at any other place at which I have dined in London. First and foremost we all three dined there and there was a happy intermixture of gentlemen—a gentleman for every lady and one to spare. I sat between Mr. James Smith (rejected addresses—very entertaining. He was at the head of the table) and Mr. Bankes the great traveller—Next to him Miss Burrowes—Mr. Moore (late Archbishop Canterburys son) Mrs. Nicholson Stewart Lady Davy's half sister—Mr. Harness—Miss Fanny E. at foot of table Mr. Hope—on his left hand Mrs. Damer—Mr. Stewart—Miss Harriet E Dr. Holland—Mr. P. Knight—Mrs. Hope. Mr. Bankes was exceedingly entertaining though he did not say a word about his travels. I did not think it would be polite to lead to the subject as he avoided it but I hope to see him again and his collection of fine drawings &c.

At Lansdowne House at dinner only i was invited. There were too many men! Yes really too many! All black heads down the sides of the table—no ladies but Lady Lansdowne and her sister Lady C Lemon and myself. And though all the men were very clever it did not do. A little mixture of female nonsense is useful *alloy* to make the solid work well. Mr. Baillie the traveller was of this party. He has been in Nubia and Asia Minor and all over the world but he thinks too much of himself and his beauty. I hope to see his beautiful drawings hereafter. All the wiseacres are now settling that all we have remaining of Egyptian architecture is quite modern. Tell me if you have any questions (architectural) to ask and put them in form for you know I am as ignorant as a dolt on this subject. . . . Ever your affectionate Maria Edgeworth . . .

To Mrs. Edgeworth

8 Holles St., 1 April 1822

It seems to me an age since I have written to you my dearest mother. I believe the bell-man twitched my last letter out of my hands in the middle of something about Mrs. Fry and Newgate but what it was I cannot recollect. I only remember that we ended that day with Lydia White and that the contrast between her and Mrs. Fry in every point of appearance and reality, external and internal struck me strongly—Her bead hat crowned with feathers her haggard face—rouged and dying!—her life hanging by a thread over the brink of the grave and she turning and clinging to the gay world!—that world which is forsaking and laughing at her.[1]

Ever so many morning visitors *and* a visit of our own to Shoe lane steam printing press and to Lansdowne House afterwards to be introduced to Lady Harriet Frampton, altogether have run away with my morning so that I literally have only time to say Fanny is well—has been out riding this morning . . . [no signature]

To Mrs. Edgeworth

8 Holles Street, 3 April 1822

Dearest mother . . . Now I may go on to *nonsense*—Geo-bo-doi! F and H went to that grand exclusive paradise of fashion Almacks. (Observe that the present Duchess of Rutland who had been a few months away from Town and had offended the lady patronesses by not visiting them could not at her utmost need get a ticket from any one of them and was kept out to her amazing mortification. This may give you some idea of the importance attached to admission to Almacks.) Kind Mrs. Hope got tickets for us from Lady Gwydyr and Lady Cowper. The patronesses can only give tickets to those they *personally know*. On that plea they avoided the Duchess of Rutland's application. She had not visited them. 'They did not really know her Grace.' Now Lady Cowper swallowed a camel for me because she did not really know me. I had met but had never been introduced to her till I saw her at Almacks.

[1] Lydia White herself observed 'Were I to present myself as I naturally am, without any of these artificial adornments, instead of being a source of pleasure, and perhaps of amusement, to my friends, I should plunge them into the profoundest melancholy' (L'Estrange, *Life of Harness* (1871), 160). ME's own final verdict was 'Of all the people who ever sold themselves to the world I never knew one who was so well paid as Lydia White nor anyone but her who did not sooner or later repent of their bargain—But she had strength of mind never to expect more than the world can give and the world in return behaved to the last remarkably well to her' (ME to Basil Hall, 25 Apr. 1827).

F and Harriet were beautifully dressed. A long story about a wedding dress that cost 20 pounds and that I got for 3 guineas and a half I must pass over because it would cost me a page. Suffice it that said dress made in Paris of silk *pattinet* gauze or something like it was trimmed at bottom with two flounces and two rows of vine leaves and bunches worked in white chenille and glass beads with foil inside imitating steel—The body with 3 festoons of ditto in front—sleeves beautifully worked to match —and steel bugle belt. I *bouldly* invented and executed the cutting out one stripe of the trimming and one flounce to trim a fellow dress for Harriet. The gap was filled up with plain pattinet gauze and two folds of white satin over the joinings and this bobbery of Fannys gown made a complete trimming of a ditto dress for Harriet. Body and sleeves were made *nearly* to match and bugle belt. The whole was performed by our incomparable maid who tho horrified at my first suggestion came into it with wonderful obedience and executed it with admirable celerity. The two dresses cost F and H only £2–17 apiece.

Their heads were dressed by Lady Lansdowne's hair dresser (Trichot)—beautifully—But I must confess this was an extravagance of mine. Lady Lansdowne did not know that this man charges 10s. a dressing. Well I cant help it. They looked very pretty. Mrs. Hope sent Harriet a wreath of her own of French roses. They were put on sideways and she looked like a gentlewoman-bacchante who did not care about her dress and was the more engaging. Fannys hair was perfectly well dressed in large curls with additional I would not say false hair at the back raised in your old sort of bows on the crown with geranium colored hyacinths hanging on one side. The result was that their appearance and manners were universally admired as I have heard from 100 meeting sources and *believe*. Fanny was said by many to be if not the prettiest the most elegant looking young woman in the room—and certainly elegance, birth and fortune were there assembled as the newspapers would truly say. Henry Wellesley a most fashionable fine-one asked F to waltze with him but she most properly declined and he most provokingly did not ask her for the quadrille tho I purposely added she *only* dances quadrilles she never waltzes. Alas! she did not dance at all.

Towards the close of the evening Captain Waldegrave (who never dances for which I hope he will be punished here or hereafter) came to me with Mr. Bootle Wilbraham who has alternately called himself Wilbraham Bootle and Bootle Wilbraham till nobody knows how to call him to please him—No matter for me. He came up to say he was at our service and our most devoted humble servant to shew us the Millbank penitentiary whenever we pleased. He is a grand man and presently returned with a grander—the grandest in the room. Who do you think? The Marquis of Londonderry—who *by his own account* had been dying for some time with impatience to be introduced to us—talked much of Castle Rackrent &c and of Ireland. *Of course* I thought his manner and voice very agreeable. He is much fatter and much less solemn than when we saw him in Irish House of Commons. He introduced us to jolly fat Lady Londonderry who was vastly gracious and invited us to one of the 4 grand parties which she gives every season *and* it surprised me very much to percieve the rapidity with which a ministers having talked to a person for a few minutes spread through the room. Everybody I met afterwards that night and the next day *observed* to me that they had seen Lord Londonderry talking to me for a great while &c!

We had a crowded party at Lady Londonderry's but they had no elbows. Lady Selkirk has just come in—stops me—yrs. M E

To Mrs. Edgeworth

4 April 1822

I recollect that I left off yesterday in the midst of a well bred crowd at Lady Londonderry's[1]—Her Marchioness-ship standing at her drawing room door all in scarlet for three hours receiving the world with smiles and how it happened that her fat legs did not sink under her I cannot tell. My chief feeling while we won our way from room to room nodding to heads or touching hands

[1] Most of the Edgeworths' political acquaintances were, like themselves, firm Whigs and Harriet Edgeworth commented to Harriet Beaufort 'You may imagine what a reversion of blood took place in our Whiggish bodies on entering this Tory mansion.'

as we passed was regret that F and H wore their steel trimmed gowns of which the beautiful vine leaves at the bottom were wasted except at one moment of entrance when each person was indeed completely seen and passed in review by all the nice judging many. Their vine leaves however were in no ways impaired and they had done signal service this day at a dinner at Lady Swinburnes and afterwards at a concert at Mrs. Haldimands (from which we had departed at eleven *just in time* for Lady Londonderry).

The chief I may say the only satisfaction we had at Lady Londonderrys, besides the prodigious satisfaction of feeling ourselves at such a height of fashion &c was in meeting Mr. Bankes and Lady Charlotte and Mr. Lemon behind the door of one of the rooms and proceeding in the tide along with them into an inner sanctuary in which we had cool air and a sight of the great Sevre china vase which was presented by the King of France to Lord Londonderry at the signing of the peace—much agreeable conversation from this travelled Bankes. We heard from Lady C Lemon that her entertaining sister Lady Harriet Frampton had just arrived and when I expressed our wish to become acquainted with her Mr. Bankes exclaimed 'She is so eager to know you that she would willingly have come to you in worsted stockings just as she alighted from her travelling carriage with sandwiches in one pocket and letters and gloves stuffing out the other.'

Enter Mr. and Mrs. Hope. Mr. Hope characteristically curious in vases turned me round to a famous malachite vase which was given by the Emperor of Russia to Lord Londonderry—upon a pedestal high as my little table. There is another vase a present of [blank in MS.] to Lord Londonderry so you see his Lordship has a congress of vases. 'En digère t'il mieux?' He was at the house of Commons and did not return home while we were there that is, till half after one. Many! many! dinners and evening parties have rolled over one another and are swept out of my memory by the tide of the last fortnight . . . I will go on to a dinner at Miss White's. We have dined with her twice—once a dinner of Lords and ladies—among them Lord and Lady Listowel and Lord and Lady Bective. The next dinner was much more agreeable—Mr. Henry Fox Lady Hollands lame legitimate son between whom and young Mr. Ord I sat—Fanny between Mr. Milman (the martyr of Antioch) and Sir H. Davy the martyr of matrimony[1]—Harriet between Dr. Holland and young Ord—Mr. Moore (Canterbury) and old-ish Ord completed this select dinner. In the evening the principal personages were Lord James Stuart and Mrs. Siddons and her daughter. Mrs. Siddons from whom I never heard till this evening anything worth listening to in conversation was exceedingly entertaining. She told anecdotes of the stage—or her own times—went through all the characters in Shakespear plays which she had acted—told which she liked best and why—Cordelia—Constance and Queen Catherine. She was vexed that people in general think she can *only* succeed in Lady Macbeth. She likes Belvidera and Jane Shore[2]—repeated some passages from Jane Shore beautifully—Ended by asking us to a private evening at her house where only Miss White and ourselves and Henry Fox and two or 3 more transcendental men are to be presented to see and hear her—next Saturday.

I am glad you think we lead a tolerably rational life and to keep up our characters as reasonable women I must tell you that we have dined with Kater without *any* company at dinner except one French lady and a delightful day we passed there with their fine children (to whom I told the 3—5 and 8 gallon vessel puzzle with great effect)—Wollaston and Dr. and Mrs. Somerville's in the evening. Dr. Wollaston shewed us a percussion gun lock—without flint—let off with chlorid of silver.[3]

I should have put the morning before the evening by rights and ought to have told you that we went to Steam printing press[4] and to Lansdowne House but Harriet at this moment

[1] Sir Humphry and his wife were known to disagree. Milman wrote *The Martyr of Antioch* (1822).

[2] Belvidera is the heroine of Otway's *Venice Preserved* (1682). *Jane Shore* is a play by Nicholas Rowe first performed in 1714. Jane Shore was one of Mrs. Siddons's favourite parts.

[3] This should be silver fulminate, a substance whose composition was unknown. Wollaston would probably not have referred to it as chloride of silver. I am indebted to the Science Museum for this information.

[4] Despite her earlier reference to Shoe Lane (p. 378), it seems likely that ME here refers to Robert Bensley's Steam Printing Press in Bolt Court, Fleet St. Bensley's printing works had been burnt down in 1819 but was shortly after rebuilt (C. H. Timperley, *Encyclopaedia of Literary and Typographical Anecdote* (1842), 856–7, 871).

tells me she has given you an account of all this. We have become intimate with Wollaston and Kater and Mr. Warburton and Dr. and Mrs. Somerville and they and Mrs. Marcet form the most agreeable as well as scientific society in London. We have been to Greenwich Observatory. Dr. Wollaston and Mr. Kater went in the carriage with us and we had their delightful conversation all the way there and back again. You remember Mr. and Mrs. Pond? His nose has grown prodigiously large and purple *but* I liked him much for the candor and modesty with which he spoke of the parallax dispute[1] between him and Dr. Brinkley—of whom he and *all* the scientific men here speak with the highest reverence. Pond only holds to the negative—that he has never been able to see what Brinkley has seen but he does not pretend to deny that Brinkley may be right. He shewed us all the instruments and Warburton and Wollaston assisted in explaining them to us. Kater and Wollaston are fully aware of Fannys scientific abilities. This is very gratifying and adds much to my pleasure in their society. We went yesterday with Lord Radstock to the Millbank Penitentiary[2] where by appointment we were met by Mr. Wilbraham Bootle. We had the pleasure of taking with us Alicia and Captain Beaufort who much desired to see the Penitentiary. The building is a hexagon round a large court. It is the cleanest prison I ever beheld. Capital punishments are here commuted for 10 years imprisonment—Others in proportion. The principle is solitary confinement for the worst offenders—Solitary confinement in *darkness* first—then tried at work in solitary cells. By industry and good behaviour they may earn the privilege of working in company with a companion or

[1] Brinkley believed himself to have discovered relatively large parallaxes for four of the brightest stars (i.e. they appeared to subtend different angles from different positions). Pond disputed this and the controversy between the two astronomers, which lasted from 1810 to 1824, was at the time inconclusive, though Pond is now known to have been right (A. M. Clerke, *History of Astronomy during the 19th century* (1902), 33).

[2] Though ME's comments on the Penitentiary read harshly to us today, she belonged to the most advanced school of penal theorists of her time and the conditions in the Penitentiary compared very favourably with those elsewhere. It was the largest prison in England, built in 1812 as a modified version of Bentham's Panopticon, six pentagonal buildings radiating from a circle containing the governor's house. 4,000 to 5,000 prisoners passed through it annually. For a description of the horrors of eighteenth-century prison life, see *English Prisons under Local Government* by S. and B. Webb (1922).

two—a taskmistress and master to each ward—male and female separate of course. They work in their cells at various trades shoemaking tayloring weaving. A portion of their earnings 1½d. in every shilling is kept for a fund for each on leaving the prison. One man who had lately left the penitentiary had £17 accumulated in this way. There are many young offenders in this prison —as young as from 16 to 12. The Governors say they are horrid plagues *as* they are not allowed to flog them and these young ones are not afraid in the dark holes. It is a curious fact that the young are little influenced by the dark confinement. The men and the oldish men are much afraid of it—Another curious fact —Those who work much with their arms at the mills are free from Scrofula—those who work with their feet at the treddle mills are subject to it. The disease most common in this prison is scrofula.

Adieu I must here break off because Mrs. Primate Stuart has come in—made a sitting and left me no time for more—The Primate has recovered and has set out for Winchester with his son this day to see some haunts of his youth—takes a trip to Bath returns in a few days and I hope we shall see him. Affecy. yours Maria Edgeworth

To Mrs. Edgeworth

8 Holles Street, 6 April 1822

I left off yesterday in the Millbank penitentiary but what more I was going to say about it I cannot recollect. So my dear mother you must go without that wisdom. All that I now know is that I saw a woman who is under sentence of death for having poisoned her sister. She appeared to me to be insane and I think will end by doing herself or others some mischief. It is said that it is a frequent attempt of the prisoners to sham madness in order to get themselves sent to Bedlam from which they can get out when *cured* but from the Penitentiary there is no chance of escape. One woman deceived all the medical people, clergyman jailor and turnkeys was removed to Bedlam as incurably mad and from Bedlam made her escape.

Another of the criminals I saw was a girl of about 18 who had been educated at Miss Hesketh's school and had been just to service in a friend's family. She was in love with a footman who was turned away. The old housekeeper refused the girl permission to go out the night this man was turned away and straight the girl went into the housekeeper's room to look in some drawer of hers for a letter there she saw money—took it—and put a coal in the drawer to set fire to the house. For this she was committed tried convicted and would have been hanged but for Sir Thomas Hesketh's intercession who had her sent to the penitentiary where you know the punishment of death is commuted for 10 year imprisonment. Would you not think that virtue and feeling were extinct in this girls heart? No—The task mistress of her ward told us when we visited her cell where we found her making a shirt in company with two other women that she had earned by her constant good behaviour since she came to prison the privilege of working in company. She was intent upon shewing Mrs. and Miss Wilbraham's the clean work of the shirt which she had made. One of the Miss Wilbrahams turned back after all the other visitors had left this cell (except myself) and said to the girl 'I think I saw you once when I was with Miss Hesketh at her school?' The girl blushed and her face gave way at once and she burst into an agony of tears, turning away without being able to answer one word. After I left the cell I turned back and peeped in again that I might ascertain whether this was acting or natural. It was natural for when she did not know I was looking at her she was crying as if her heart would break.

I am nevertheless sorry she has taken up so much of my paper. Solitary confinement answers all the purposes of taming and reformation which had been expected from it. Women and young women are said to be much more violent at first confinement than any men. One girl of 16 was as Mr. Holford told me the most ungovernable creature he ever saw. She tore to atoms 3 suits of clothes as fast as they were put on. She said she *would* go to Botany Bay or as she expressed it she would *volunteer for the ship.*[1] She would do something she swore to make the Governors

[1] 'Deportation to Australia had lost all its terrors. To be deported was simply to emigrate at the expense of the Government to a better climate, and emigration

send her to Botany Bay. At last they convinced her that she could not get her punishment of imprisonment changed and darkness and solitary confinement tamed her so that now she is quite docile.

Through the long passages you look as you pass through wooden perpendicular rails into each cell and see the prisoners each in their narrow cell at work—some at the silent needle others at the whirring shuttle and loom. There are outer doors to each cell which are usually shut, except when visitors pass and the prisoners are not allowed to talk from cell to cell. If they did they would be heard by the taskmasters and mistresses—Thro' panes of glass in the rooms of each of these they can see what is done in each of their wards. It is all on the Panopticon[1] principle. At first it was found difficult to combine the discipline of good conduct with the industry of artificers but the clergyman assured me that this is now pretty well accomplished. At first the task-masters and mistresses to favor the industrious who earned most and to get forward the manufactures of the prison concealed their instances of misbehaviour but this has been detected and rectified. Mr. Bennett the clergyman a very reverend apostolical looking person has obtained great influence over the prisoners. He says the most reprobate never insult him. He has been often sent for at 11 o clock at night by prisoners who wish to confess to him and consult him. He shewed us many mss. volumes of his journals which I longed to read. They must contain much interesting history of human nature.

But perhaps you would rather go on to our individual history. Yesterday we breakfasted with Mrs. Somerville (and I put on for her a blue crape turban to shew her how one of Fannys was put on with which she had fallen in love). We then went to the museum—spent two hours there and then we went home and Mrs. Stewart came in and cut short my letter and morning. We dined at Mrs. Hughan's (formerly Miss Milligan's Joanna Baillie's niece)—Excellent house full of flowers and shrubs and luxuries—Select party dinner early for Sir William Pepys who

was becoming increasingly popular with the working class' (E. Halévy, *History of the English People in the Nineteenth Century* (Paperback, 1961), ii. 108).

[1] 'Bentham's name for a proposed form of prison of circular shape having cells built round a central "well", whence warders could at all times see the prisoners' (*O.E.D.*).

is eighty two and a most agreeable lively polite old gentleman who tells delightful anecdotes of Mrs. Montagu Sir Joshua Reynolds, Burke and Dr. Johnson with whom he lived in former days. Once Mrs. Montagu seeing a shy awkward man coming into the room whispered to Sir William 'There is a poor man who would give one of his hands to know what to do with the other.'

In the evening came various people too tedious to mention—But many were not tedious—The Baillies and a Miss Jardine grand-daughter of Bruce the traveller and niece of a certain Mr. Jardine whose travels in Spain[1] you may have read. We carried Sir William Pepys off with us at half after nine o clock and when we had been gone about half an hour Mr. Pepys son to Sir W Pepys a *young* man between 40 and 50 put up his glass to his eye and spying about for his uncle [*sic*] discovered that he was gone and could not concieve how or where. He went all about the room inquiring. Miss Milligan informed him that Miss E had carried him off—But where to? Nobody knew. His own carriage had been ordered at eleven and arrived and Mr. Pepys unknowing what was to become of him or what had become of his uncle got into it and was brought by private orders to the coachman to Mrs. Somerville's door. We had been commissioned by the Somervilles and the Katers to bring him there to hear Mrs. Kater sing and play Handels music of which he is passionately fond. There was no party—only Somervilles Katers and Wollaston happy together. Mr. and Mrs. Kater really sing divinely. I never heard any voice so touching as Mrs. Katers. She gives the utmost effect that musical expression and voice can give to poetry. Every syllable of the songs she sings is heard and she has perfect expression without affectation. She sung '*The cypress wreath*' the music of which Mr. Kater has arranged and has promised to Fanny and '*Tears such as tender fathers shed*' which Louisa sings. She sung another beautiful song said to be written by the naughty Lady Vane whose history is in Mrs. Pilkington's Memoirs.[2] This is in my opinion superior to Sappho's far famed

[1] Alexander Jardine, *Letters from Barbary, France, Spain, Portugal etc. by an English Officer* (1788).

[2] Frances Anne, Viscountess Vane (1713–88) was the source and probably the writer of 'The Memoirs of a Lady of Quality' which form the very long chap. lxxxviii of Smollett's *Peregrine Pickle* (1751). She does not appear either in

ode.[1] Here are some scraps of it which are all that I can recollect

'Too late for redress and too soon for my ease
'I saw thee I loved thee, and wished I could please . . .[2]
'I fancied your eyes read the language of mine
'And saw my loves image reflected in thine. . . .[2]
'But awaked from my dream to my sorrow I find
'That words were but civil which once I thought kind.
'I'll break this gay bauble my fancy has drest
'I'll drive this tormentor this love from my breast.'

How my aunt Ruxton would like Mrs. Katers singing! especially of this song! It was worth while to bring Sir W. Pepys to hear her singing he really admires and enjoys it so much. So does Wollaston who sits mute as a mouse and still as the statue of a philosopher charmed while she is singing. He has a great deal of feeling. Mrs. Somerville has been almost worn out with her last months London life and is going into the country for a week to refit. We love her more and more. She is so like in character and gentleness and modesty to Harriet Beaufort. We go on Monday being Easter Monday to the Deepdene and spend Monday and tuesday with those dear kind Hopes and return on Wednesday. The Lansdownes are asked there but unluckily they do not go on the same days that we shall be there. Besides the real pleasure of going to the Hopes we rejoice that they invited us again because this proves that they are not tired of us.

I forgot to tell you that Lady Elizabeth Belgrave as pretty and winning as ever came to see us. Lady Stafford came and also sent various messages and yesterday morning for the 3 time I called at her door and was told by a pimple faced red blotched door *holder* that her Ladyship was not at home but after he had turned the card to another form out of livery, he thought better of it and came forth to the carriage door saying 'My lady is at home to *you* Ma'am'. So out we jumped and up we went and Harriet for the first time saw the gallery &c. Lady Stafford was very gra-

the *Memoirs* of Letitia Pilkington (1748) or Mary Pilkington (1804). This is an extreme instance of ME's muddles over names.

[1] Only one complete ode by the Greek poetess has survived. It does not resemble these verses.

[2] ME's dots.

cious and very entertaining with fresh observations from Paris and much humor. She imitated the old Duc Des Cars voice and manner so that I could have sworn he was in the room saying as he does in his courtier tone of the old crippled king 'Ce n'est pas qu'il ne peut pas marcher mais qu'il ne veut pas.' She says she is sure there is some peculiar charm in the sound of the clinking of their own swords in walking up and down the gallery at the Thuilleries which the old stupid ones delight in as they walk up and down at this same pace for hours every day. Lady Stafford says that she met with much grateful attention from the royal family and from any she had formerly [*sic*] but they could not give her entertainments because they had not the means. The Comte d'Artois apologised—he has no separate dinner—always dined with the king and *very sorry for it*. Lady Stafford asked us all three to dinner but unluckily the day she asked we are engaged to Mr. Morritt. So she is to ask again after our return from the Deepdene. She asked very politely for Honora and was very attentive to Fanny. This morning we breakfasted at *nine* with the Katers who you see are the reigning favorites. God bless you. I am not dressed and the carriage with Mrs. LeFevre in it has just come to take us to dine at Grove House. Fanny well. Yr. ever M E

To Mrs. Ruxton

London, Holles Street, 10 April 1822

My dearest aunt, . . . We have lately been much in the scientific society in London which is excellent and which meets in the most easy and agreeable manner—Mr. Pond—Astronomer royal at Mrs. Marcets Mrs. Somervilles—Lady Elphinstone's (sister to a scientific Mr. Warburton) at Mrs. Blakes and at Mr. and Mrs. Katers. With Sir Humphry Davy's grand Academical Conversaziones you know we can have nothing to do as no ladies are admitted. It happens that many of the wives of the scientific men and several of the scientific ladies themselves are remarkably agreeable, have taste and talents for painting and music *and* for good conversation. Mrs. Kater has the most delightful voice and manner of singing I ever heard. She and her husband sing and accompany each other and are always ready to relieve conversation by music—never to interrupt it. But I must restrain myself on this topic—I must not give you a duplicate of a panegyric which I lately wrote on Mrs. Kater and Mrs. Somerville addressed either to you or my mother.

Even geology which I thought never could interest me has become interesting by the manner in which Mr. Warburton has spoken of it. Mr. Warburton is a young man of fortune—benevolence—pleasing manners—agreeable conversation—excessive shyness—and something incomprehensible about him. He vanishes from time to time from London and Country society and no one not even his favorite sister Lady Elphinstone can tell where he is or anything about him till it be his pleasure to re-appear.

Mr. Bankes the traveller is a man who would entertain you much tho' he made Lord Lansdownes head ache by talking as Lady Lansdowne says too much—not too much for me becaase all he tells is interesting and he speaks from fullness of head and heart and from the honest warm wish that others should share in his enjoyment.

The great variety of society in London and the solidity of the sense and information to be gathered from conversation strike me as far superior to Parisian society. We know at least 5 or 6 different and totally independent sets—of scientific—literary—political—travelled—*artist* society and fine and fashionable—of various shades. You will know from our last letters home that we have been to Almacks and to Lady Londonderry's—very entertaining—Mais a quoi cela mene t'il—à—*nothing*. But *something* always remains from sensible society and often more even than information—friendship. We have certainly added some friends in this line to our store. It gives me very great pleasure to see Fanny and Harriet appreciated as they are and still more to see how steady their heads are in the choice of what is best for their future happiness.

Among the sets of different company which I just now enumerated I forgot to mention the *theatrical blues*. Through Lydia White we have become more acquainted with Mrs. Siddons than I ever expected to be. Tho' she cannot vary her solemn voice she is entertaining when she speaks of stage anecdote. She gave us an account of her first acting of Lady Macbeth and of her resolving to play in a new manner the scene in which Lady Macbeth walks in her sleep.[1] Contrary to the precedent of Mrs. Pritchard and to all the traditions she resolved to *set the candle down* on the table before she began to wash her hands and to say 'Out out vile spot!' Sheridan knocked violently at her dressing room door during the 5 minutes which she had desired to have entirely to herself to compose her spirits before the play began. He burst in and prophecied that she would ruin herself for ever if she persisted in this resolution of setting down the candle. Her reply to him was almost comic by the solemnity with which she spoke it as if the fate of the universe had depended upon it. She persisted however in her determination—succeeded—was applauded and Sheridan begged her pardon. She described well the awe she felt and the power of the excitement given to her by the sight of Burke—Fox Sheridan—Sir Joshua Reynolds &c in the pit. Johnson never saw her in the theatre.

Mrs. Siddons invited us to a private reading party at her own house—made for our little selves—Present—Only her daughter a very pretty young lady—a Mrs. Wilkinson her companion and proneuse—Dr. Burney—Dr. Holland—Lydia White Mr. Harness and ourselves. She read one of her finest parts and that best suited to a private room—Queen Catherine. She was dressed so as to do well for the two parts she was to perform this night of gentlewoman and Queen—in black velvet and a black velvet cap and feathers. She sat the whole time. She did not as I had seen her before at a reading partly spoil the effect by half reading half acting[2]—standing up and looking from time to time through *hand* spectacles to her prompters book. *That* I could not bear. She now sat upon a raised cushion on a sofa with a large Shakespear and in reading Queen Catherines part which she had by heart she seldom required the help of glasses. She recited it incomparably well—the changes of her countenance were striking. From her first burst of indignation when she objects to the Cardinal as her judge to her last expiring scene was all perfectly natural and so touching that we could give no applause but tears. During the scenes of the Queens trial and farewell to her

[1] See J. Boaden, *Memoirs of Mrs. Siddons* (1827), ii. 145.

[2] 'Formerly she recited' written above.

attendants and to the king it was impossible not to recollect the late Queen of England and to consider how different our feelings for her would have been had she preserved the dignity of injured innocence—even in manner.

Mrs. Siddons is beautiful at this moment. Some who had seen her act Queen Catherine on the stage assured me that her acting had this night a much greater effect upon them in this part in a private room because they were near enough to see the changes of her countenance and to hear the pathos of half suppressed voice. Someone observed that in the farewell dying scene her very pillow seemed sick. She spoke afterwards of the different parts which she had liked or disliked to act. Lady Macbeth she liked but seemed hurt that some people think it her best character. She preferred Cordelia and Isabella in The fatal marriage.[1] She piques herself upon tenderness—in which I hear she never excelled. Mr. Wilbraham Bootle and Mr. Morritt told me that in her best days her Belvidera[2] tender scenes were mawkish—her grief always excellent—her indignation *admirable*. She disliked to act the Grecian daughter and Calista.[3] When she mentioned the characters and parts of the scenes which she found easy or difficult it was curious to observe that the feelings of the actress and the sentiments and reasons of the best critics meet. Whatever was not natural or inconsistent with the main part of the character she found that she never could act well. Acting in this way becomes the test of natural character and of consistency.

Mrs. Siddons has a handsome daughter whom she brings into society. She does not appear to have any of her mothers talent. Mrs. Siddons tells comic anecdotes sometimes but in such a sepulchral voice that it gives the effect of tragic-comedy. Charles Kemble was once trying to teach Braham to say some English sentence necessary in one of his parts in which the word *enthusiasm* was to be pronounced but he never could get him to pronounce it any way but *entousy-mousy*. Mrs. Siddons has carried me farther than I intended. I must return to our own history.

[1] Southerne's *The Fatal Marriage, or The Innocent Adultery* (1694), revived by Garrick as *Isabella, or the Fatal Marriage* (1757).

[2] In Otway's *Venice Preserved* (1682).

[3] Mrs. Siddons played Euphrasia in Murphy's tragedy, *The Grecian Daughter* (1772). Calista is the heroine of Rowe's *The Fair Penitent* (1703).

To Mrs. Ruxton, 10 April 1822

We have been at the Deep dene for three days. I hear that if any fine people have the misfortune not to be able to go out of Town in Easter week they close their front window shutters and live in their back rooms to make believe that they are out. I am glad Mr. and Mrs. Hope saved us from disgrace. Seriously I am very glad that they are not tired of us and that they shew more desire to have our company now than at first. Nothing can be kinder than they are to Fanny and Harriet as well as to myself.

The company at the Deepdene were—Mr. C. Moore—Mr. Harness—Mr. Philip Henry Hope Mr. and Miss Burrowes—Lord Fincastle—son of Lord Dunmore—Lady Clare and Lady Isabella Fitzgibbon and Lord Archibald Hamilton. Lady Clare is a painted—made up—vulgar thorough going woman of the world—her voice—brogue—turn of expression crossness and economical and bantering sayings are so like our dear cousin Mrs. Fox of Foxhall that when I shut my eyes I could have believed she was speaking. Her Ladyship pressed me to visit her in Ireland but I never desire to see her again. Her daughter Lady Isabella is a gentle pleasing girl—handsome—with a Roman nose. Her mother much to her discomfiture just when she was going away sent her upstairs to take off her beau-cap and put on her other cap '*for* under your bonnet you know. I always put my beau cap in my bag and keep a bonnet cap which I just put on my head after breakfast when I am going but young people never think of these things Miss Edgeworth and the consequence is Isabella always tells me always when we are going anywhere "Mamma my caps are all dirty. I have not one I declare fit to be seen."' Is not this in the spirit of Mrs. Fox?

The Deep dene is beautiful at this time of year—The hawthorn hedges—the tender green of the larch and sycamore in full leaf. We had a delightful walk one morning—Mr. Hope all the time conversing very agreeably and telling me anecdotes—fresh from life.

You know that Sir Harry Englefield is dead and that we are interested in this on account of our friends the Stricklands. Mr. Strickland his executor has come over to London. I told Mr. Hope this and mentioned that Sir Harry has left Petersham his house near Richmond to his niece Mrs. Strickland. This led to Mr. Hope to speak of Sir Harry Englefield's character and affairs. You [know] he has been a rival man of taste and collector of Etruscan vases and besides many of Mr. Hopes [? Sir H. Englefield's] intimate acquaintance were also of Mr. Hopes society. Of this number was the family of Spencers I mean William Spencers—The Mr. Spencer who wrote

> 'I staid too long forgive the crime
> Unheeded falls the foot of time
> That only treads on flowers' &c

This man is famous for conversational wit and *professionally* the enlivener of every dinner and every party to which he was invited. Delighted with this flowery life he paid no attention to the conduct of his wife or to the education or morals of his daughter. You know the scandalous end of the daughter—her seduction by a married man with all the *public* consequences and her absolute banishment from England did affect the fathers spirits for some time. She married abroad in Italy or Germany some soi-disant Count who said he was delighted to be connected with the great Duke of Marlboroughs family and upon the strength of this took the wife for better or worse and made no inquiries. His settlement upon her in English money amounts to seventeen pounds per annum. She is now said to be living in some obscure lodging in London. No one sees her—But this disgrace is not all. Mr. Spencers wife is as bad as his daughter as Sir Harry Englefield is said to have known too well. But this is not all. Both husband and wife lived with Sir Harry in Town and country latterly. But this is not all. Avarice on the ladies part and shabby begging tricking avarice was joined to all her other faults. But this is not all—her own son a spiteful shrewd elf of fifteen one day reproached his mother with her mean and interested habits before Mr. and Mrs. Hope. Mr. Hope described the scene to me which he says would have been comic if it had not been too shocking and too disgusting. Mrs. Spencer began by talking in raptures of a certain remarkably fine ruby ring which Sir Harry Englefield wore. 'Mamma' said her son in an ironical tone 'Could you not get it from him you who get so many things from him. Could you not get this?' 'And if I did' cried the mother coloring with anger and outraged beyond her prudence 'And if I did Sir it should not be for *you.*' Can you concieve anything more horrible than mother son daughter and father. Yet he is to this hour one of the gayest and most agreeable men at London dinners. We met him the last time we were at the Deepdene and he was repeating bon mots and poetry and among other poetry repeated

> 'Who would touch the tainted posies
> 'Which on every breast are worn?
> 'Who could pluck the spotless roses
> 'From their never touched thorn?'

Some other lines like Ariostos rose trodden under foot[1] I recollect his repeating which were so dreadfully applicable that all felt it round the table but himself and all eyes were cast down. He is wretched however except just at the moment he is wound up for company. He never appeared in the morning never till dinner and then wound up by opium! What different gaiety from what we have been used to dearest Aunt—And what different sorrows!

Before I finished this letter, one from my mother brought that sad account of my excellent aunt Charlotte's death—I cannot add more at this moment except that we are going this instant to Lady E Whitbreads who most kindly receives us till we can hear again from home. Your ever affectionate and grateful niece Maria Edgeworth

To Mrs. Edgeworth

8 Holles Street, Saturday morning,
[20 April 1822]†
Just returned and unpacked from Grove House

Here we are dear mother once more settled again in our comfortable house in Holles Street . . . Just returned from water color pictures—Some of Prouts of Mayence Metz &c and old Towns abroad in perspective beautiful—all like Chester—met *there*, not at Chester, Lord Grey—Lady Stafford—The Swinburnes and Wilkie Mulready Lord Radstock Miss Waldegraves and various others with whom we had agreeable conversation.

[1] See above, p. 162 n. 2.

Lady Stafford has more ready and good 5-minute conversation than anybody I know. She says the French have lost all their national recollections. In travelling through France she asked for various famous places in history of which they had lost all memory. As good be Americans who have no traditions. Little F went with us and in looking at a picture of the inside of some rooms at the Charter House met Lord Grey who recognised him agreeably. Carriage at the door and I have not begun to dress. Maria E

To Mrs. Edgeworth

8 Holles Street, 24 April 1822

My dearest mother and all of you my dear friends most especially dear Aunt Mary . . . I have only a moment for amusing topics—Take an abridgement. Since we came to Town we have done as follows—went on saturday to water color exhibition—Mrs. Frys at Plashet in the evening—beautiful place—happy unpolished family—eldest daughter too pert and talkative—her husband lisps and has an instinct for finding birds nests. She is delightful at home or at Newgate. Sunday—took little Francis with us to Captain Katers. He has promised to teach him all he can and that is a monstrous deal if F will come whenever he has an hours leisure to his house—luckily very near Manchester St. Captain Kater shewed us experiments on polarisation of light—beautiful. I look upon the friendship formed with Captain Kater as a permanent family blessing. I read him a passage in your letter which gratified him justly. Paid a visit afterwards to Lady Derby—full as agreeable as when we saw her but half as fat and twice as old—asked most kindly for you and received your daughters with gracious grace—met there Lady Mansfield and her Lady daughters. I like Lady Derby for talking of John Kemble without being ashamed of former profession. Dined at Ricardos—vulgar relations—Jewish Basevis—But he is always sufficient pleasure. Monday—Went with Mr. Cohen and Mr. Cockerell to St. Pauls. Mr. Cockerell[1] remembered former times

[1] Cockerell wrote of this encounter in his diary (22 Apr. 1822) '. . . Went with Miss Edgeworth to St. Pauls. Miss E went thro' this as a duty. She yawned

with Fanny and you—apologised for impossibility of visiting Edgeworthstown—was very agreeable and shewed us all his renovations in St. Pauls which are done in excellent taste—Beautiful building!

Dined at Miss Whites with Mr. Luttrell Mr. Hallam Mr. Sharp and Mr. and Mrs. Stewart Nicholson (Lady Davy's half sister)—Most agreeable conversation—dinner—none more agreeable than Lydia White. Poor creature how she *can* go through it I cannot imagine. It is dreadful to look at her. In the evening—the Miss Stables Anna's friend and a hideous dressed out deformed sister—desperately fond of me. Met this night for the first time Lady Cunliffe and Mrs. Cunliffe (Miss Crewe)—very agreeable and tho not regularly handsome very pleasing in countenance and person. Dr. Holland here for an extraordinary length of sitting—The Katers too who go wherever we go and we must believe that it is as they say for the pleasure of meeting us.

Lady Listowel tall fine figure with a grand daughter almost as tall, Lord Ennismore and a doltish son in law (very unlike any of yours) in various waistcoats one as red as a robin redbreast. This youth was quite *new*. I believe it was his first appearance on this or any other stage. After a prelude of changing legs he moved opposite to Fanny and stuck there almost all night like a fascinated statue with his hand not daring to move even into his own bosom at the entrance of which it was held as if by a spell.

Tuesday—we spent a happy hour at the Museum with Raphaels prints—paid visits—one to a Mrs. Barker who has a wonderful memory and told me heaps about the prints I had been seeing and all the painters in the world *and* gave me the sweetest rose I ever smelled in London (the Lady Greys not excepted). We dined at Mrs. Marcets with only herself and

frequently or suppressed a yawn—took great pains to convince me of her perception of the beauties of St. Pauls—her manner flattering, not sincere, an eulogium uncalled for of Mr. Hope—the youngest intelligentish and interested in St. Pauls—the other pretty and aware of it. . . .' I am indebted to Mrs. Crichton for permission to print this extract. It perhaps illustrates Harriet Edgeworth's comment of how 'unhinged' ME was by people unsuited to her. She had no visual taste and was apt in aesthetic matters either to echo the views of those who were with her or to speak in the phrases of the textbooks of the picturesque. For an earlier comment of ME on Cockerell see above, p. 188.

children—Then to an *at home* at Ricardos merely for 10 minutes to see the famous Mr. Hume. Dont like him much—Attacks all things and persons—never listens—has no judgment. Went to Mrs. Sothebys—great crowd with court headdresses—from morning drawing room and opera—Katers and Wollaston here —snug talk [end missing]

To Mrs. Edgeworth

Friday, 3 May 1822

My dearest mother—I rejoice that you are all satisfied with our determination and I do think it has been for the best.

Since Harriet last wrote we have been to Harrow to hear the speeches in Latin Greek and English of the first class of boys—our future orators. It was a very interesting scene attended by many ladies, as well as gentlemen—mostly friends of the scholars. Two of the English speeches were from Henry the 4 and 5 about the crown tried on—Another from Cato[1] and Alexanders feast[2]—Well repeated and very difficult you will allow. The situation of the school at Harrow is beautiful—the lawn laid out with great taste—The master Dr. Butler a very well informed and agreeable man with a picturesque head. One of the boys answered to some one who said 'I like Dr. Butler. He is very agreeable' 'You would not say so if you knew him as well as I do.' We had a very *elegant* collation and I sat beside a very agreeable thin old nobleman of the old school Lord Clarendon.

Captain Kater in many points of character understanding and temper reminds me of my father. I think you would like him much and that you will find he will make a valuable friend for William. If we did nothing more by our prolonged residence in London I am satisfied that our cultivating further our friendship with this family will be of essential advantage. We spend as much time as we can with them.

There is not danger my dearest mother that we should feel it difficult to quit the society we are in. We long to bring home to you and to my dear Aunt Mary and Honora and Lucy all the

[1] *Cato,* a tragedy by Addison (1713).

[2] *Alexander's Feast* by Dryden (1697).

means of amusement we have collected for them. This is the object to which we continually are looking forward . . . Bellman Maria E . . .

To Mrs. Edgeworth

11 May 1822

My dearest mother . . . The sudden death of the Primate and all the horrible circumstances attending it have incapacitated me from writing to you more at this moment. I send the beginning of a play-play letter[1] to you which fell from my hands when I heard this. Mrs. Stuart gave the medicine! Harriet knew I should be so shocked at it that she did not tell this last circumstance to me for 2 days. This morning we breakfasted with Dr. Holland to meet Sydney Smith and in the course of his merry witty conversation out came suddenly in laughing at the bishop baiting in the house of Lords, the name of the Primate and the facts were then related to me by Dr. Holland. All you have seen in the newspaper is exact but I believe the newspapers did not mention the most striking fact that when dying and struggling under the power of opium he called for a pencil and wrote these words for comfort to his wife 'I could not have lived long my love at all events.' One of his daughters has never spoken since. Her danger has roused Mrs. Stuart. I shall send to his sister Lady Louisa Stuart whenever I *can* to inquire what becomes of the wretched Mrs. Stuart. How dreadful that people must live on! Yr ever affec Maria E

To Mrs. Edgeworth

Holles Street, 20 May 1822

My dearest mother, I have been as it seems to me an age without writing to you, but I have been unable literally to find a minute when I could write. Perhaps it is all for the best. We shall have more to tell when we come home and shall not be like empty bags.

[1] Perhaps the letter printed below as of 30 May.

I enclose a note just received from Lady Louisa Stuart the Primates sister. It is most touching—especially the account of the feelings of his parishioners. I believe I told you in my last every circumstance I knew or that is known concerning this dreadful affair. It is dreadfully astonishing that the mistake about the medicine should have happened. All her life before she had been remarkably careful about medicines—an excellent nurse accustomed to attend the sick and specially cautious about the Primate but he had asked for his draught twice before it came, and in her hurry she snatched it from the servants hand poured it out and gave it without looking at the label. The bottle was fully labelled as the apothecary has since gone about shewing everybody. Who can blame him for he would have lost his practice and the bread of his children if he had not proved this. Poor Mrs. Stuart! I cannot concieve misery so great as hers and yet she must go on living. Compared with this my dearest aunt Mary how much lighter is your affliction—how different grief unmixed with self-reproach of any kind—the grief that is on the contrary mitigated and soothed by the consciousness of having done everything that the most tender active affection could invent for the beloved lost friend—supported yet more by the delightful certainty that this was felt by that friend to the last moment of life . . .

Our history is full of hurryful nothings—paying and receiving visits in the mornings and going out to dinners and parties in the evenings. Our intimacy with the Katers has led to much music. We have been to the Antient Music twice—a thing unprecedented—the difficulty of obtaining tickets for non subscribers is so great. We have been to the Caledonian ball of which you will perhaps see an account in the papers (Harriet at this moment tells me that she has written a description of it to Pakenham). We have been also to a very pleasant dance and musical party happily alternating at Mrs. Shaw LeFevre's where Fanny and H had good partners and were much admired.

There is to be an Irish ball on the 30th and Lady Lansdowne has pressed us much to go and offered us tickets but observe the tickets cost 2 guineas apiece this is like bringing you in free at an election. But it is a charity ball and charity covers a multitude of follies as well as of sins. I have subscribed ten pounds (apropos) to the Irish poor subscription. I hope you will approve. Spring Rice whom I very much like tells me that he has been touched to the heart by the generous eagerness with which the English merchants and many of the city people whose names will ever be unknown to fame have contributed to this fund for the relief of the Irish. A very large sum is already at his disposal and he has wisely considered that if this money be not judiciously applied it will do more harm than good. He has done me the honor to consult me about his plan of which I enclose you a copy . . .

We dined lately with Mrs. Lushington to meet Lady Byron—alone—result—I dont like her—cold—and dull and flat-dog looking face.

Lord Darnley and Lady have been amazingly civil—dinner there and all manner of attention. Greenough has been most kind—admirable collection of fossils on which he has two mornings lectured us—taking out all his 1000 drawers—ending with such *collations* too—ices &c. Bellman yr ever affecy M E

To Mrs. Edgeworth

28 May 1822

My dearest mother—In the hurried life we have led for some weeks past and among the great variety of illustrious and foolish people whom we have seen pass in rapid panoramas before us, some remain fixed forever in the memory and some few touch the heart. While the impression on both is still warm I must tell you of this mornings breakfast. We have just breakfasted with Spring-Rice our Irish patriot who has all the characteristic excellencies of his nation, without as far as I can see any of those counterbalancing defects with which our countrymen are reproached. He has genius without imprudence and generosity without extravagance. So much and enough for Spring Rice. His wife—his *Lady* I should say, is the daughter of Lord Limerick, the Lady Theodosia Rice. She is a *crumpetee* in figure—more like the idea I formed of Julietta the deformed yet pleasing heroine of Mr. Parnell's *able*, silly novel.[1] Lady Theodosia is not taller

[1] W. Parnell, *Maurice and Berghetta; or the Priest of Rahery. A Tale* (1819).

than I am and has a decided hump but her countenance though it bears the characteristic look of a deformed person has none of that odious look of pretension or false gaiety which is too often seen in the faces of those whom nature has *disgraced.* Lady Theodosia has a most humble yet placid resigned and amiable, I had almost said winning countenance. I may indeed quite say *winning*—for she has won and kept the heart of one of the most distinguished men in the British parliament. He treats her with a mixture of respect and affection which is quite touching. She has 4 or 5 pretty curly haired children such as you or Sir Joshua Reynolds would paint. She presided at the luxurious breakfast provided for us, helped us all without seeming to do anything and then breakfasted on her own invalid breakfast as she called it, a glass of Seltzer-water and milk!

The company at this *home*-breakfast were all intimate friends either domestic or political. They were his own sister Lady Hunt—a charming woman but I must not dilate on her charms—Mr. Grant our late Secretary—with sense and goodness—feeling and indolence in his face—Mr. Randolph the American patriot—who is in figure like a painters mannikin more than a man—very tall and thin and as if a stick across the shoulders instead of shoulders stretched out his coat and waistcoat. He looks as if he could not stand without leaning, his feet being always close together and turned in. He leans just as a mannikin leans and is ready to fall or stick in whatever attitude you put him. His yellowish hair is tied tight behind with a black ribbon, but not pigtailed it flows from the ribbon like old Steels with a curl at the end—mixed brown and grey—his face crinkled like a peach stone but all pliable muscle moving with every sensation of a feeling soul and lively imagination—quick dark eyes with an indefinable American expression of acquired habitual sedateness, in despite of nature—His tone of voice quaker-mild and repressed, yet in this voice he speaks thoughts that breathe and words that burn. He is one of the most eloquent men I have ever heard speak and there is a novelty in his American view of things, in his new world of allusions to art and nature which is highly interesting.

Besides the pleasure we should naturally have taken in his conversation I own we have been doubly pleased by his gratifying attention to ourselves and my dearest mother still more by the manner in which he distinguished your Francis. We asked leave to bring him to this breakfast and mixed with *men* he did not attempt to appear a man but was content to appear to be what he is the most promising and natural and well informed boy I ever saw. He took an opportunity when breakfast was ending to go round to the elbow of the sofa on which Mr. Randolph was leaning and he asked him to be so good to tell him where the quotation from Shakespear is to be found which he had made at the meeting of the African institution where he had heard him speak a few days ago. Mr. Randolph was pleased with the question. Spring Rice took down Shakespear but it had not our verbal index. No memory not even Mr. Randolphs own could make out whence the quotation came. Mr. Randolph asked Francis to walk home with him that he might find it in his own index. Francis went with him. Mr. Randolph shewed him all his books and some remembrances of a little nephew of his of whom he had been very fond. He ended by giving him a little Dictionaire de la fable in which he had written his name and noted that it is a gift from J. Randolph . . .

And now it is all over and that this dream of London life is over I can look back to it without regret at quitting it and with the most perfect satisfaction at the enjoyment we have tasted. My two companions have had as they assure me, more satisfaction, more amusement more information than they had expected and I have had infinitely more pleasure than I had expected in seeing them pleased and please. Even more in their own country than abroad I am sure they have been appreciated. This is a solid satisfaction—will be a source of pleasure to me to *you* to them through life. Whether they ever return to London or not I am sure they will always be remembered with esteem I may say with affection by the first persons in the best society of England —the first in virtue—in literature—in science—in manners . . . [half a page cut off]

Thursday

Dear Mother I have just received your two admirable letters about Ireland—have carried your copy of Mrs. Stricklands letter and your own account of your neighborhood to Mr. Spring Rice —have also copied a page about the Archbishop of Tuam &c for

Rice and he is now gone with same in his pocket (and many thanks) to a meeting of the Committee who are settling how to dispose of the subscriptions for Ireland . . . Yr. ever the same—Maria E

To Mrs. Edgeworth

[30 May 1822]

Dear Mother *This is an old scrap* begun a month ago and found at the bottom of my writing desk this day May 30th

What do you think our bill for meat last week came to?—4 people *always*—*sometimes* 6 at hot luncheon to be sure—the bill was 1 shilling. Now I know you will think this should be £1 not 1 *shilling* but I tell you in so many letters as plain as I can write *one shilling*. Now you know the real way to grow rich—to live in lodgings in London, see the whole Town and give hot luncheons. Ours are much admired moreover and the best part of them is that I hope that they will make you and the breakfast table laugh—Of eggs—apple pies—custards &c I say nothing nor of a beef and pigeon pie that had stood over from the preceding week.

Since writing this our luncheons have become rather more expensive. We have given most elegant repasts as I shall have the honor of describing to you soon when we are all together nonsense-ing round Lucys sofa [no conclusion]

To Mrs. Edgeworth

3 June 1822

My dearest mother—a few lines ever so short ever so hurried are better than none to put you out of doubt as to our past and future proceedings.

We gave up our house paid our bills—left London and went to Frognel on Saturday. Delicious Frognel—hay making—profusion of flowers—Rhododendrons as fine as 4 of mine in one flowering down to the grass—All friends with open arms on steps in Veranda ready to receive us—2 days spent there—a large party of Sothebys and Lord knows who first day including a Mrs. [? Tuite]—put by for future description—Second day Wollaston Holland—Miss Holland &c—Wollaston particularly pleased with Harriet who sat beside him at dinner and to whom he talked unusually veiling for her the terrors of his beak and lightning of his eye.[1] He gathered a large Rhododendron and put it in her sash—all the rest of the young ladies having one in their heads.

Today I have brought my sisters to Town with Mrs. Carr and Misses to a Prison discipline meeting where they hope to hear Mackintosh speak. I could not stay left them have done worlds of business meantime—including having sat a great half hour with Lady Harrowby and Lord Sandon to whom I went to ask them to promise young John Moilliets admission as soon as possible to Balliol or Oriel—all places bespoke for 2 years but if any of the claimants die or change their minds Lord Sandon through Peel promises that he will get Moilliet in—a point his father and mother much desire. I have seen her this morning and parted she loving me I hope better than ever . . . Yours ever affec Maria E

To Mrs. Edgeworth

12 June 1822

My dearest mother. We have accomplished much to our satisfaction our long intended journey to Portsmouth. On tuesday last at 9 o'clock in the morning we found ourselves in our own dear carriage at your brothers door. He and Francis seated themselves on the baruche-seat—we three precious souls within —imperials—heavy trunk and poor heavy Gaynor (who has no fault upon earth by the by except being heavy) left behind—No luggage but our two chaise seats—carpet bag—dressing boxes, writing boxes and small portmanteau trunk stowed in boot for the two Francis's gear. *So* the horses made nothing of us five little creatures nor did either horse or man ever think of taking 4 horses at any stage on the Portsmouth road tho we had been

[1] Gray, *The Progress of Poesy* (1759), i. 24.

warned that it was the most impertinent and extravagant road in England. But that was in piping days of war. Peace has starved the inn keepers into better tune. The weather on our journey it must be owned was bronzing and melting hot but Francis Beaufort would insist upon being melted and bronzed for us and during the heat of the day he and Harriet or he and Francis E sat on the baruche seat—He in a stoical style disdaining to use a parasol tho why it should be more unmanly to use a parasol than a parapluie when the times require it I cannot for the sense of me understand. When much enforced he and Harriet and Fanny too declare it is too much trouble to hold a parasol. I believe you too are of the same *Stoico-sybaritical* sect so I will waive the subject and get on to Portsmouth where we arrived on Wednesday to breakfast—Fountain inn—Letters sent to Lady and Sir James Lyon—Lady Grey and Captain Loring. Captain Loring appeared first in reply to Mrs. O Beirnes letter of introduction—a short fattish man in naval uniform—cocked hat gold bound—a more good natured face never yet belonged even to the navy. He is at the head of the naval college here. After inquiring into our plans he immediately set about to forward them. Mrs. Loring having just produced a new creature into the world was good for nothing of course for our purposes but Captain Loring took us in his carriage directly to her—a good natured motherly Scotchwoman. Proceeded to Lady Greys—the wife of the General. She is Commissioner I believe behind the scenes a good deal even when he is at home. Now in his absence she was all in all. She is a Saint[1] you know —looks a little peevish—like a saint who would make others pay for having mortified herself. However she was very civil to us therefore I will not be such a sinner as to be ungrateful. Tell Pakenham that we saw in her beautiful and thick-walled cool house a pretty little museum in a passage room between two drawing rooms—stored with all the offerings of sea captains and seafaring friends from all parts of land and sea—Badgers and seals and sword fish and tyger skins and claws and skeletons of bird beast fish. The most curious things or at least those which stand uppermost in my head were two balls found in the stomachs of a calf and a lama. Honora I am sure recollects the ball

[1] An Evangelical.

of this sort which we saw at [blank in MS.] but this calf ball was considerably larger—the size of our largest nine pin bowl. That found in the lamas stomach was without any exaggeration as large as Pakenham's head! It was as black and smooth on the outside as ebony but a crack shewed that this outer coat was as thin as paper and that the inside was a conglomeration of hair and I know not what—something like the incrustation at the bottom of a tea kettle. These balls you know Ladies and gentle-*man* are formed by the animals trick of licking hair off his neighbors coat—But I have not time to stay longer in this tiny-oval passage room museum.

Lady Grey ordered all the works and dockyard &c to be open to us and told us the government [boat] should be at our command whenever we pleased. We pleased to go out upon the water this first morning directly and to leave the block machinery till the workmen should be prepared for us—rowed out—and saw with your kind brother everything to the best advantage—1st The kings yatch in which he went to Ireland—gilt elegance—2ly The Nelson—just finished but uncommissioned a first rate man of war 120 guns. Francis took us all over her from the deck to the hold and shewed where the different works of war and peace go on and how the ship is *cleared for action* and where the men stand at their guns in the dread hour of battle. As no one was on board this we had only space and silence. 3ly—We went on board the Albion a guardship—a 74—to see a ship alive. One of the officers—a silly-ish midshipman walked with us to shew all and we saw the extremely good arrangements for keeping everything large and small in order—from the sailors hammocks each numbered and placed in fresh air on the sides of the vessel on deck, down to the Armoury in which every gunlock, cartridge nail screw peg were arranged in bright order on the walls and beams in quaint devices—stars and triangles &c—so that you could see at one view and lay your hand upon whatever may be wanted. Even the brass headed nails made G R. It is but fair to indulge the fancy when it contributes to so good a principle as order.[1] In time of service how many lives would be lost if proper places were not made and kept for every thing that is wanting.

[1] See ME's *Harry and Lucy Concluded* (1825), iii. 59–61.

I cannot get away fast enough from each recollection all was so interesting. As we rowed away from the Albion Francis pointed out to us the Phaeton. We begged to go on board her. He said not worth while but we put it to the vote—out voted him and much to our satisfaction went all over the Phaeton. What feelings he must have had on standing again on her deck. He shewed us his midshipmans birth—Then his Lieutenants cabin—the last a comfortable pigeon hole enough. Between decks in the Phaeton we saw the men at dinner with their wives—An admirable scene for Wilkie.

Rowed home again—And now for the block machinery[1] you will all say. But it is impossible to describe this in a letter of moderate or immoderate size. I will say only that the ingenuity and successful performance of the whole far surpassed my expectations—much as these had been raised. Francis—your Francis was delighted. Machinery when perfect appears to act with the happy certainty of instinct and the foresight of reason combined. Private. My dear mother I wish we had seen Portsmouth when we were all together in 1813. I cannot tell you how much my pleasure was embittered by your not being with me.

The next day we went to the dock yards and Francis Beaufort shewed his dear nieces and nephew a man of war in every state of existence—from the first skeleton when only the vast ribs (like those of a dead horse or what we may imagine of a dead mammouth) arch from the backbone—Then a ship with her decks in and another completely finished. He shewed us Sir R Seppings improvements in ship building[2]—cross braces and iron shoulders—which I just note here to be explained and expatiated upon at leisure hereafter. Of a ship of teak-wood F and H will tell you. I was too much tired to go on board this and wisely sat in the shade the while. One thing I gathered however that teak wood is valuable in ships because it is not subject to dry rot.

After going through the birth rise and progress of the building of a man of war and after having seen how a vessel is propped up when the bottom is to be repaired or to preserve the bottom

[1] See ME's *Harry and Lucy Concluded* (1825), iv. 235–7.

[2] A method of diagonally bracing and trussing the frame timbers of ships to avoid the tendency of the head and stern to drop. This system was adopted by the Admiralty in 1815.

in dry dock and after having heard described an improved method of doing the same—And after having seen a crane land boards on a cart more neatly than any man could do it we left the dock yard and took *barge* for the Isle of Wight. A charming day Ma'am—only melting hot—but on the water you wont find it so—always a cool breeze on the sea—Very true indeed—A very pleasant row across of about ¾ of an hour—Landed at Ryde—dinner—never to be despised by travellers—still less by voyagers—2 dishes of fine strawberries—Surinam size—many with two points which we fancy peculiar to the Isle of Wight. I am ashamed to mention such a trifle but cannot help it now. We did not bring our carriage to the Isle of Wight but travelled in a sociable of the Island—exactly like a Swiss sociable or Irish jingle—viz a four post bed on wheels with curtains tied to posts.

Drove on to Steep hill through at first rather a stupidish flat *County-of-Longford-looking country*—the best part like the road to Clonfin or Hugh Kelly. Little Francis asked what he was to admire in the Isle of Wight? 'Is this your Isle of Wight?' He took the new Arabian tales and presently his uncle struggled to get them out of his hands. 'You can read them at any time.' 'But why should I not read when there's nothing to see.' 'Well take your own way and live the longer my boy.' Accordingly Francis held fast to *Maugraby*—till the spiced honeysuckles in the hedges wafted such sweets as we passed that he could not help looking up and Captain Beaufort jumped out and gathered a handful for Fanny. Soon after it was not necessary to jump out to gather them for the lanes were so narrow that the hedges touched the carriage and the flowers were just under the hand. Presently the beauties of the Isle of Wight began to appear—Something like Swisserland—Something like Wales—Yet different enough to make us rejoice that we had come to this Island which Mr. Sharp would call a gem of the ocean.

Steep Hill well named is very pretty—with a Welch-ish inn—nice freshly mown lawn soldier making hay—too large he for the lawn. He ran good naturedly to look for Francis E who had jumped out of the carriage on sight of Steep hill—a very steep green hill by the road side he would run up it and we were some time at the inn before he was visible—but found! found! found!

And we drove on to Shanklin another of the famous beautiful points. Such ascending and descending without intervention of horizontality! very picturesque! But how the horses did it I cannot concieve. Observe these were the horses with which we had been travelling all morning for such is the fashion of the Island. You take horses and sociable and the Felicity-hunter goes on with the same as far as he can or they can. The famous Chine at Shanklin is something like the Dingle at the Hills[1] magnified by the king of the giants best magnifier at least 100 fold. Walks and steps practised on each side by the Samuel Essington[2] of the place who let off for us at the end of all things a very respectable waterfall—not to be despised even by travelled ladies whose noses ought to have turned up after having seen the Riesbach and all the *bachs* in Lauterbrunn and Grindelwald &c &c &c.

Returned late in the cool of the evening or night to our inn at Steep hill. The two Francis's uncle and nephew had a rare game of romps by the way. Whenever we came to a steep ascent Uncle Francis summoned nephew to get out and walk but he lazy dog would scramble into the carriage again whenever he could escape from his uncles hand or eye and over the back scrambled he and Uncle after him and caught and dragged him out—then walked a bit—then escaped again while uncle was gathering a red Virginia creeper leaf for F. In scrambled little Francis by the coach box but caught by his uncle while sprawling on his stomach on coach box—half in carriage—hauled out after clinging like a monkey. You may guess by this how happy uncle Francis was on this journey. It was the most gratifying thing possible to me to see him so happy and all of them! The pleasures of this journey 100000000 times surpassed my hopes. Pray tell dear aunt Mary this who lives in the happiness of her friends. She was so kindly anxious that we should go to Portsmouth. Pray tell her how well it has answered.

We slept at Steep hill. Next morning went to see Carisbrook Castle—very fine old ruin—with fine recollections—saw the room (that is F and H did) where Charles was confined[3]—saw the famous well I dont know how many feet deep—A lamp let down it—beautiful circle of light—threw water down into the

[1] On the Edgeworth estate in Co. Longford.

[2] See above, p. 72.

[3] In 1647.

well—length of time before the sound was heard at the bottom gave a sublime idea of the depth. Gave up seeing the Needles which would have taken another day and we were assured by the best authority and are determined to believe are not worth the trouble of going to see. A pleasant drive to the place where we again took boat for Portsmouth—roughish—but Captain Beaufort gave us great credit—we were not sick—landed at ½ past six—were to dine at 7 with Sir James and Lady Lyon—Stupid dinner—tired us more than all our journey—but they were very good natured and we saw two beautiful books of prints—One of Guercino's—the other of various masters. But I was stretched on the sofa asleep before the 2d vol came. Sir James Lyon you know is the queens lion[1]—a very fair faced good natured tall man—bashful—*as* but not *like* Mr. Knox.

Left Portsmouth next morning—prosperous journey back towards Slough. But Oh my dear mother as Francis Beaufort was reading the newspaper at the pretty flowery lawned inn where we dined he came to the death of who do you think? Our dear Mr. Smith of Easton Grey—too true—He and Mrs. Smith were at Sir B Hobhouses near town. She had gone to a ball. He died of an apoplexy while she was away. On her return she was told he was unwell and was persuaded not to go in to disturb him till morning when the dreadful truth was disclosed. But a few months ago he was the gayest of the happy acting pantomimes with Mr. Ricardo and us and she the fondest happiest of wives. We went to the Ricardos to inquire about her the moment we got to Town. She is gone home with two of Sir B Hobhouses daughters with her and the Ricardos who had heard from them say she is better than they could have hoped. But in these first moments she is stunned and she will be worse afterwards. Poor poor creature! You will pity her—and here pause—I know you will.

We had been invited by young Mr. Herschel to go to Slough on our return. We did so. The Katers met us at the very bad inn at Slough. Sir W Herschel is in such a nervous, I fear almost imbecile state that he cannot see strangers and Lady Herschel is suffering with the gout. Mr. Herschel therefore could not ask us to his house but we dined there and spent all the day with him looking at telescopes and walking and driving. The great

[1] Sir James had commanded the 96th (Queen's) regiment, disbanded 1818.

telescope[1] which we saw you remember is there still but the supports are decaying as Lady Herschel observed with tears in her eyes. It is never used now. Mrs. Kater and Mr. Herschel walked through its forty feet long tube and we saw the machinery by which it had formerly been moved.

Drove to Windsor—At last accomplished my wish to see Windsor—the building and the terrace equal to my expectations—pictures very bad. At night the clouds having been so good natured as to disperse we went out a star-gazing—Mr. Herschel Jun having mounted 2 useable telescopes for us in the lawn—And we saw a double star[2]—a great curiosity I would have you know if you do not know it—and we saw a kind of shadowy blob with a circle of light round it. Nobody knows what it is—a star or no star—Much to be said about it by those who know how to say about it but I do not. But I know that Mr. Herschel appears to me one of the cleverest and most amiable young men I ever saw—Most amiable in his behaviour to his father and mother.

Captain and Mrs. Kater finished the evening with music and singing—Slept at our hot inn—those who could sleep—arrived at Kensington Gore about one o clock—called on Lady E Whitbread. Lady Hannah Ellice had arrived about half an hour before us as Miss Grant told us—So no room for us but Lady E Whitbread took our visit very kindly. She is very thin—mild and resigned. I wish it had happened that we could have been with her. We might have been some comfort because she loves us and had obliged us and it is always a comfort to see those we know feel grateful and sympathise with us. After kissing me for the last time her last words were to charge me to 'remember her love to dear Honora'. You know that Mrs. Nisbet's daughter has lost her husband Colonel Brownrigg—by apoplexy! Miss Grant has been dividing her time between that distressed family and Lady E Whitbread. She is really one of the best of human beings.

We found our house No. 8 occupied but our obliging landlady let us have her unoccupied No. 25 for two nights. Dined at uncle

[1] Sir William Herschel's 40-ft. telescope completed in 1789. Few nights were clear enough for its use and it was left to decay.

[2] Close stellar pairs believed to afford a sensitive test of the earth's motion.

Francis's—breakfasted at the Katers—took leave of them—packed—ordered horses for 6 o clock next morning—this morning to set out for Ireland . . .

I forgot to tell you that we walked over the fortifications at Portsmouth with your brother and your son Francis had such a good idea of them afterwards that the moment he got to the inn he drew the enclosed [plan of fortifications] His uncle shewed him the faults and explained to him the general principles of fortification. What happiness to have such an uncle Francis—No harm in having a brother Francis.

In the Isle of Wight as we were walking up a steep hill in a narrow lane Francis met two charterhouse boys! to our and his surprise and amusement . . . [no signature]

1830–1831

WHEN Maria Edgeworth left England in the middle of 1822 she intended to return and revisit her friends there in the not too distant future, but family finances prevented this. Though she was able to take her sisters Harriet and Sophy to Scotland in 1823,[1] her brother Lovell was falling behind with the payment of the family annuities and at the end of 1825 he was forced to reveal serious money troubles. In his will their father Richard Lovell Edgeworth had in fact charged his estate with rather more than it was able to bear.[2] Lovell Edgeworth had no talent for management and he spent more than he could afford on his school at Edgeworthstown. When he was a prisoner of war interned in France he had probably drowned his sorrows in drink and now like many an Irish country gentleman before him he had taken to conviviality to cover his sense of failure. He owed £25,000. The feeling of family loyalty was strong in the Edgeworths and, moreover, the incomes of almost the whole family depended on the Edgeworthstown estate. Maria pledged her own credit for the payment of her brother's debts and took over from him the management of his affairs. As agent for the estate she was ably supported by her stepmother and by her half-sister Honora, and the rest lent such sums as they were able to tide over the immediate difficulties, but it was Maria alone who had the force, courage, and skill to carry out what was a very intricate rescue operation.[3]

By 1830 the most acute financial troubles seemed over and Maria decided to pay a visit to London to her sister Fanny who at long last had married Lestock Wilson at the beginning of 1829. Maria's *Tales of Fashionable Life* and other similar stories

[1] See R. F. Butler, 'Maria Edgeworth and Sir Walter Scott: unpublished letters 1823', *Review of English Studies*, N.S. ix (1958); C. E. Colvin, 'A Visit to Abbotsford', *Review of English Literature*, v (1964).

[2] Appendix to MS. Black Book of Edgeworthstown (Irish State Paper Office).

[3] Ibid.; see also letters written by ME to CSE in 1826 (Edgeworth MSS.), giving details of financial transactions.

were written out of the experience of her father, her relations, and her friends, and from the scanty knowledge gleaned in a six weeks' visit to London in 1792. The letters so far printed are the record of her own direct experience of a fashionable world which she came to know well between 1813 and 1822. The letters of 1830–1 mostly describe a rather different social milieu. Though she inevitably continued to be lionized a little and her aristocratic acquaintance did not abandon her, she spent most of her time with her own family and with their more middle class, if not undistinguished, acquaintance. She settled Fanny into her new house in North Audley Street, she visited Sneyd Edgeworth at his new house in Kent, and she saw her youngest half-brother Pakenham off for his service in India. She led a life that was less feverishly exciting but it is clear that the semblance of settled family life which was now possible to her in London greatly enhanced her real pleasure there.

To Mrs. Edgeworth

Liverpool, Saturday, 16 October 1830.

My dearest mother

My head is so full that whichever way I turn it, even upside down if I could so turn it I believe not a drop would come out but I will try and even for a quarter of a drop your good natured avidity will be satisfied.

Francis wrote to grandmamma all that befell us up to our arrival at Rimroses hotel before breakfast yesterday and finding Fanny sitting in breakfast room reading Clarissa,[1] and tea not yet made. I did not think she looked well at first sight but after breakfast second thoughts pleased me better. She thinks that sea bathing has made up for the detriment of crossing the sea but she is not yet quite up to the point at which she stood at our parting with her. After an excellent breakfast—large window of room open and view of almost a fleet of sail vessels and steamers going out from Liverpool we walked to a Canal boat to carry us back to Liverpool 4 miles—pleasant—put me in mind of Bruges boat.[2]

[1] Fanny was of course re-reading Richardson's novel.

[2] On which ME had travelled on her journey to Paris in Oct. 1802 (*Mem.* i. 121).

Tiny steamboats ply here every 15 minutes—go and return to places on opposite shore—man and woman are perpetual motion engines. Arrived at Star and garter—found quarters eat luncheon—went out—saw the docks immense line of old docks and still more gigantic new docks. Saw an American New York packet—finely ornamented and fitted up with mahogany and gorgeous gilding—And next swarms of finely dressed American ladies looking at their future births. Went to see the Corporation rooms[1] of which the Liverpool people are so proud that it would be cruel not to have seen them—*Superbe!* 90 feet long ball room 45 feet broad 40 high—now I have done my duty—the dining rooms you may imagine—2400 people were squeezed together the other night and had not room to see each others dresses!—But all was delightful.

Next we walked (how Fanny did it I know not) and *walked* thro streets fine and coarse and then took a Liverpool *car* as a small coach drawn by one horse is called and deposited Fanny at our temporary home of Star and garter. She lay on sofa. I walked again with Francis Beaufort and daughter to the great Market[2] house here—length 550 feet 140 wide—3 different alleys for flesh—fish—vegetables cocoanuts fruits from all parts of the world—the order and contrivances for keeping order admirable. The groups of men women and children—most entertaining. Here a painter should study who wishes to become a Teniers or to excel in the Dutch school line.

After market house came back for Fanny—*drove* and *walked* to *Cemetery*[3]—new—of which I send you a proof print. The burial places are chiefly excavations in the rock. The place below is pretty at present—green grass and gravel walks and shrubs but in danger of becoming all spoiled by upright headstones against which we have been declaiming. Other faults and observations I have not time here to note excepting only that Captain Beaufort has so objected to *horses* entering with the hearses that I have no doubt the hint will be taken and that the coffins will be lowered

[1] The town hall, built to the designs of John Wood of Bath in 1749 at a cost of £30,000. Additions, designed by John Foster, the corporation surveyor, were made 1795–1820.

[2] St. John's Market was laid out by Foster in 1820–2.

[3] St. James's Cemetery, also laid out by Foster in the late 1820s in an exhausted stone quarry.

by machinery as he proposed and then borne by men. The church you do not see. The view is taken from the church—You see the clergyman's house. A number of little school boys were running leaping and laughing over the new laid grave stones and an old man reproving them and they flying for the same. Remember the Bewick of boys riding in fools caps on tombstones[1]—Human nature at different ages ever the same!

We may say with Mrs. Carr we saw a great deal this day! Good dinner—good tea—good newspaper—good sleep—good breakfast 9 o clock and punctual Liverpool people—2 gentlemen invited—arrived while water was running into teapot—Mr. Roundell—O—Mr. Hodgson—partner of Cropper—one of first houses in Liverpool—full of the railway—says we shall have a £20 dividend on each share next year! When I touch it I shall believe it. He—Hodgson—is a very sensible man—And I a very silly and unfortunate woman for the 1st thing I did at breakfast was to overturn a cup of coffee. Francis's quickness saved me from all disgrace and inconvenience and sat in the wet for me. . .

This morning we have been to see a sugar bakery[2]—by steam all heated—to avoid danger of fire. A dirtier hotter place never saw I.

Francis Beaufort is now folding up print and making up packet for the Scribbler. He Francis is going by the Manchester rail road to Manchester—Thence to Bedford—And very sorry very very I am to part from him. In a few minutes we shall be off. We are to go a certain distance on the rail road—Arrive at Knutsford this evening. That [is] all I know—and here I have lived quite *in the surface of my mind* many hours . . .

Love to my dear friends all

Ever affec

M E

coaches come

To Mrs. Edgeworth

Knutsford, [18 October, 1830]†

The moment a letter has gone out of my hands my understand-

[1] Bewick, *A History of British Birds*, ii, Water Birds (*Works of Thomas Bewick*, 1822), 310, tailpiece to article on 'The Tame Goose'.

[2] Probably in the neighbourhood of Dale St., where there had been sugar refineries since the time of Charles II.

ing comes to me and I recollect all I ought to have said. The chief reason why I sent you that print of the cemetery at Liverpool was that you might see the square plot in the centre which is allotted for the intended monument to be raised over poor Mr. Huskisson.[1] There he lies. They have given him the space of 20 ignoble graves. Lord Grenville was the person deputed to convey to Mrs. Huskisson the wishes of the Liverpool people to have him buried at Liverpool. She took a night to consider of it and her answer which was repeated to me by a gentleman who heard it, was most simple and beautiful—she sacrificed her private feelings as she thought it her duty to do for his honor. I hope she will never end like that disgrace to her sex Mrs. Heber.[2]

We were invited by Mr. Hodgson—whom I like much and who is something like Mr. Moilliet—to go on the Liverpool railway in the very carriage in which the Duke of Wellington went. We ascended the very step ladder off which Huskisson fell and we got into a fine crimson velvet canopied car in shape resembling a Swiss charabanc or our old caravan with a four post-bed covering our head—stiff gilt *carved* tassels to look like solid gold all round the top and a stiff edge which is to look like drapery and which tears bonnets and knocks heads. 4 of these cars similar in size and shape but not decorated like the Dukes were linked together on the rail way—the seats in the cars—benches covered with cloth—back to back. In front of the Dukes car was an empty space in the *poop* into which Mr. Hodgson had chairs brought for us—viz Fanny Lestock—Captain Beaufort and Sophy. Fortunately Francis was prevented from going in the common train of *railway cars* from Liverpool to Manchester by losing his place and Mr. Hodgson managed that he should come with us—No matter how.

Our carriage was sent on to meet us about 13 miles from Liverpool at a place called the *Viaduct*.[3] Red paper tickets were put into our hands on getting into the cars on which were printed *Trip to the viaduct*. One of these I intended to send you but a man came round and gathered them all in from us afterwards. Before

[1] Huskisson was killed at the opening of the Liverpool and Manchester Rly. on 15 Sept. 1830. He was buried in St. James's Cemetery on 24 Sept.

[2] Mrs. Heber's offence in ME's eyes was probably the publication of letters relating to private life in the *Life* of her husband Reginald Heber, Bishop of Calcutta (1830).

[3] The Sankey Viaduct.

our poop was a kind of Orchestra car for the musicians. They sounded horns and at a signal given off we flew. The swiftness of the motion could be percieved only by the apparently swift *receding* of the objects we passed and by the freshness of the breeze we created. We went under a tunnel in darkness for 300 yards and were glad to come safe to light again. F B was quite disappointed by not going at greater speed—the utmost rate being somewhat short of 20 miles an hour and the slowest when we were going *up* the inclined plane the rise of which was one in 96—was Thirteen miles and a quarter. The inclined plane is 2 mile and ¼ long and 2 mile and a quarter fall the other way. To make this a level road little as the inclination may seem would as Mr. Hodgson told us require a hundred thousand pounds. By and by I think they will do it.—We went the 13 miles from Liverpool to the Viaduct in 48 minutes—this was at the average rate of 16¼ miles an hour. When we passed the train of carriages coming from Manchester their speed being the same as ours the passing speed was above 30 miles an hour. The rapidity of this motion was so great that we could not distinguish a single feature in any face nor indeed a single face only a mass of people. The motion was so easy and every thing so secure and well arranged that no sentiment like fear occurred even to me—except when I was under the tunnel in darkness and that was only folly. They use Telegraph signals—flags white—red—and blue—for *all right—moderate speed—stop*. At night they use colored lights. I do not mean that they run during the whole night but they run after dark to accomplish the passage sometimes.

You are to comprehend that a regular communication goes on now by trains of cars on this railroad backwards and forwards to Liverpool and Manchester—two roads space (but little between) and beyond the sides. Independently of these regular trains the proprietors make use of these gala cars which they have fitted up for the Duke and the show of the opening and every day they go on with this '*Trip to the Viaduct*' with their red tickets—for whoever wishes to have a ride—five shillings apiece there and *back*. And every day for these 5 weeks every one of the 4 cars have been crammed full of Liverpool ladies and gentlemen all dressed as if for a fete. Even this makes money. Mr. Hodgsons head is full of a new railway from Liverpool to Birmingham and from Birmingham to London and he sees guineas continually rolling towards him. The brickfield land near Liverpool now brings in a rent of £25 per acre. Liverpool is wonderfully enlarged and we saw millions of bricks for future buildings. Our bogs appear to me much less ugly than these brickfields.

F B at last agreed that they are very prudent not to begin by going at great speed. They could go at 25 miles an hour but Mr. Hodgson wisely keeps it to 15. He says slow and sure—We are but in our infancy yet—we have much to arrange and improve. They have not yet begun to convey goods—only passengers. They wish to have the experience of a winter over Chat Moss before they begin to carry goods. Part of the road over which the rail road goes is as yet supported only by wooden posts. There are only two coaches now between Liverpool and Manchester. All the rest have been put down by this rail road already. What a change will be made by these rail roads! We saw the canal of the Sankey Navigation[1] running below us and pretty sail boats. Oh the sail boats have all the *beauty!*

I had much conversation with Mr. Hodgson on this question—what should a body do who has canal shares to great amount? If Aunt Mary wishes to hear the result I will write it—not else it would be too tiresome. I asked all the questions on purpose for her—Captain *Scoresby* came with us this Viaduct trip. He is now in the church and is settled at Liverpool—has the *Marine* church. He is very agreeable and told me how his father educated him to have presence of mind by perpetually making himself [*sic*] ask himself what should I do if I were placed in such and such a dangerous dilemma. Have not time to explain—hope those round the breakfast table *understand what I don't say*—

By some misunderstanding between Lestock and his nonpareil of a groom the carriage which was to have met us at the Viaduct where we stopped and got out of our triumphal crimson car went on to another Viaduct beyond Newton. We waited and waited and eat a dinner of bread and butter and cheese at a cottage Alehouse by the roadside and then after messengers had

[1] The Sankey Navigation Canal was built between 1755 and 1768 to connect the St. Helens coalfield to the Mersey near Warrington. It then ran west to Widnes. It was the earliest artificial waterway in England (as distinct from channels of rivers deepened and straightened).

gone back and forwards in vain set out and walked 2½ miles to Newton—found the carriage there—came on to Knutsford where we had purposed being at tea time—but our walkings and wanderings had not only brought the time to eight o clock but had brought us into no condition so that Nem con we determined to have tea and dinner in one at the inn and go to bed first writing a note to say we would call in the morning and spend some hours—leaving breakfast as you observe wisely in doubt—potted meat Ma'am at tea almost as good as you would have given me for luncheon. Lestock is so very attentive and kind that it is delightful to travel with him. As Fanny observes '*He really has a sort of good nature*' that makes him remember all one's little fancies. She was so much tired &c that the nights rest did not quite recover her and she was not able to get up in time for *breakfasting* at the Hollands. Mr. Holland came 4 times; twice before I came down at half after 8 and twice while we breakfasted to persuade me to go with him but it was all affectionate fidgetting. He was not the least affronted and has quite recovered from that bothered state in which he was at Edgeworthstown and is the dear good tame old father of the family *and* of Dr. Holland that he used to be. Susan whom I remember as the least of things is now five feet seven well measured and really a very fine girl. Lucy I like very much—she is very droll and very obliging. She desired to be most kindly remembered to Lucy and she and Mr. Holland were excessively sorry that she is unwell again. Pray *mention* her in your next and do not begrudge your words about her. One of the first inanimate objects that struck my eye in Mrs. Hollands newly furnished drawing room was a sort of pyramidal tin flower pot on the table beautifully filled with Dahlias mignonette and honeysuckle. This sort of flower pot struck my fancy so much that I inquired where it was made or could be got—In Knutsford—only—made by one man—then he must make me one and must contrive to have it sent over directly to Mrs. E. No sooner said than done. The little fairy who watches over my fancies was instantly about it. Miss Lucy Holland offered to bespeak the flower pot instantly. I paid for it—not beforehand for Miss L H is to keep the money till she has the flower pot—and—now here is my fairy's promptness—Arthur Holland the youngest son is to go over to Dublin next week and will carry it over for me to Merrion Street with my card of direction *to go to Edgeworthstown by Clyne.*[1] I have paid Arthur beforehand by a ticket of introduction to Merrion Street friends. He is going to spend 6 or 3 months in Dublin with a surgeon Mr. Hutton I think.

After spending the morning very pleasantly with the Hollands and fortifying ourselves with luncheon we proceeded on our journey—delightful evening—Impossible to have had pleasanter weather to enjoy rich clean looking England. I believe travelling opens the mind by forcing upon the attention in quick succession so many different views of different modes of life and interests as different from our usual course of thoughts as from each other—At Liverpool all full of rail ways and canals and the great bustle of a commercial sea port town—At Knutsford—all inland thoughts and views—Then burning coke and coal country and Staffordshire and its potteries—and on further Birmingham and all the world for Hardware.

I forgot to tell you that Fanny and I tried swift perpendicular motion as well as swift horizontal motion yesterday at Liverpool. When at the Sugar bakery we got on the platform on which the workmen are usually drawn up rapidly by the steam engine to save the time of going up their little odious dark and dirty innumerable flights of stairs. Up we went a darkish perpendicular tunnel and were landed safe at the top of the building! We wish that there was such a contrivance in every house for carrying up turf and people. I wish most for the turf—Fanny for the people. (Slept at Stone.)

We arrived at Hamstead Hall[2] this morning about ½ after one. It is a beautiful place and an excellent house. I regret and so does Mrs. Moilliet in particular that you my dear mother did not see it. They are the same kind good friends as ever—Mrs. Moilliet not the least altered—except for the better in her looks—Mr. Moilliet quite well—Emily as pretty as ever and amiable—Susan the cleverest and most active of the family wonderfully improved—and very fond of Lucy. James came home from Birmingham on a beautiful horse—and quite a great man now; his father talking of giving up all the banking business to him. He is as simple and good as you saw him and always full of loves for

[1] The carrier. [2] The Moilliet's new home near Handsworth.

you—all. We have been walking about this beautiful place all day. Fanny came in and rested. She is much better today. Mr. Moilliet cannot go to Sneyd now and will not purchase Bedgebury I am sure. He thinks it too large and expensive and he cannot purchase immediately and that must be bought now or never. He wants to settle both James and Theodore before he *buys* an estate for himself and retires to his snugs and he wisely says 'Better take time to look about me.'

Now I must stop and rest. I am writing at an unlawful time between dinner and tea—when all the good credulous world below think I am in the arms of Murphy . . .

I am my dear mother Ever affectionately yours

Maria Edgeworth

Beg Louisa will send Mr. Butler the name of the dictionary or works whatever they be which will give the explanation of Irish names of places. I forgot to make this request from Trim.

Monday—striking eight—

To Mrs. Edgeworth

At Welbeck Street[1] still—2 Nov. 1830

My dearest mother, . . .

By the by to change from grave to play—which I feel as natural and as necessary to me as my poor sister Anna did &c—From the wearing of wigs and morning borders—all the pathos of sublimity of grey hairs are almost at an end for parents, except in a few such respectable instances as yours—It must now be 'Her children have brought her *brown scratch* with sorrow to the grave.'[2]

I think I told you in my last that the Malthuses declined me because their journey to Town was fixed for the day after I proposed. They came here last Saturday—sat an hour and he spite of all that Nature did to make his uncouth mouth and

[1] The Wilson's house, which, before his marriage to Fanny, Lestock shared with others of his family.

[2] Mrs. Edgeworth wore her own grey hair, almost all covered by her cap, but ME wore a front and sidepieces of dark brown hair which appeared very conspicuously in front of her cap (see frontispiece). This was misleading; ME was fair and in her youth her hair, of which a lock survives, had been very light brown. She had blue eyes.

horrid voice forbid made us admire and love him—*us* means F.M.W. and M.E.—LPW being always in the city till 6 o clock as you know. He gets miraculously well now in the mornings and his kindness to me is beyond belief—So I will say nothing about it. We are to go to the Malthus's[1] in March—when more is to be done than March will hold. Your regrets about the fortnight you did not stay are so like you! Extinguish them with this certainty that if you had staid you would have vexed and disappointed Honora in particular and Aunt Mary very much.

Lestock took me last Sunday to the Zoological gardens.[2] Fanny was not able for the walk and most prudently (pray dont forget to admire her for it) staid on sofa, L and I went in coach and returned on foot. I was properly surprised by the new town that has been built in the Regents park[3]—and indignant at plaister statues and horrid useless *domes* and pediment crowded with mock sculpture figures which damp and smoke must destroy in a season or two. The Zoological gardens charmed me—very fine day. Francis Beaufort was there with Alicia and a party of *Carrs* of his own—nothing to our Carrs. I walked with Lestock and was very glad to have his quiet cicerone-ing. He never says *too much* and I have not time or spirits at this moment to say *enough.* Suffice it then that I was happy and much amused for that hour. The horrid *Harpy-eagle* (lately arrived) I think struck me most when it spread its dark wings and darted at the bars. Another fine eagle in a house of his own, all to himself in the middle of the garden was a fine dignified creature. Eagles and vultures struck my imagination most and I was charmed with the graceful demoiselle. I admired Fannys favorite tiger too—and the leopards—and the little Bengal bull—and the beautiful sleek grey little Brahmin cow—and the Lamas—and Kangaroo who jumped well for us and walked on his *3* legs—meaning his hind legs and his tail. What a strength of tail! The beavers would not come out. The otter fished for live fish thrown into his pool and bit off the head of one the instant caught and played

[1] The visit to Malthus did not take place.

[2] The Zoological Society had been founded in 1826 and the Zoological Gardens opened in 1828.

[3] John Nash's first plans for the development of the Crown estates in Marylebone (later known as Regent's Park) were made about 1811, but the terraces he designed were largely built 1821–30.

with it horridly as cat with mouse and granched it bones and blood till I was sick looking and yet could not move my eyes—like the girl looking at the murder thro the cranny in the wainscoat (in Munster tales[1]—Honora will remember).

We set out at 2 and were not home till ½ past 6—walk home by half daylight and at last quite lamplight very pleasant to me. Lestock shewed me the palace built by Martin's-blacking for his own residence[2]—and Greenoughs new house.[3] I walked altogether above 3 miles and was not more tired than was quite agreeable.

I long to go again with Fanny to pay a second visit to the birds and beasts. They were all before my eyes when I was going to sleep and the vultures scream in my ears and the feeling of the monkey pulling my bonnet and shaking it with all his might. I forgot to mention that to you—he got his paw into one of the velvet bows when I turned my back to look at the other side of his alley—much too narrow that Alley! It is to be reformed. I am sure you would have laughed if you had seen me. I was so surprised and Lestock and the other gentlemen so hastened to the rescue. I hope this will make Aunt Mary and Lucy laugh.

Pray—apropos to velvet bonnet—tell Evans and Aunt Mary that all Evan's packing, which she did so kindly for me, came quite safe as if it had never stirred a hair's breadth since it left my room—black velvet bonnet not a bit the worse for its journey and quite the thing—as far as I have seen. You infer I hope rightly from the above that my black trunk is in my possession (cost me only *14/1*—a deal box containing Sophy Beaufort's Leghorn bonnet arrived also and cost *11/1*—bulk not weight paid per steamer). Mrs. Alicia is very glad nevertheless to have the bonnet safe as she could not get another for a *guinea* in London. Your little packet of hair[4] in the crown of said hat came safe. Was it your own? I must have a bracelet of it.

[1] Gerald Griffin, *Tales of Munster Festivals* (1827).

[2] In Park Lane. It was designed by John Goldicutt. Day and Martin, Proprietors of Real Japan Blacking, had their business in High Holborn (*P.O. London Directory 1835*).

[3] Grove House, Regent's Park, designed for Greenough in 1823 by Decimus Burton.

[4] The packet of Mrs. Edgeworth's hair was for use in hair jewellery for MPE.

Lestock has this morning concluded bargain with Gap for horses 22 guineas a month—5 shillings additional if in country. This is our first day. They will be at the door anon.

Interrupted here most agreeably by the entrance of —Joanna Baillie—dear dear Joanna—Just the same kind simple creature—Most kind enquiries from her heart for Lucy. Some people always even in 5 minutes stay increase our good opinion of human nature—some our ill opinion. Joanna has just left the most agreeable impression by her last anecdote which hurried as I am I must tell. When Sir W. Scotts first difficulties came on every generous rich friend offered assistance, among others Dudley and Ward—now Lord—always gentleman. He immensely rich offered to engage for the *whole debt*—to pay by instalments! Sir W. Scott wrote a charming note of thanks and refusal which I am to see—or hear. Joanna says that Sir Walter behaved nobly in refusing every one of the numerous and pressing offers of assistance and worked on for himself. He is not yet quite clear.[1] Visitors still and ever swarm upon him and infest Abbotsford to his cost day and night . . . Yours Well and affectionately Maria E

Fanny is getting *better* but if I talked forever that is all I could say. She looks well.

To Mrs. Edgeworth

4 November 1830

Business[2]

Mrs. Dease's house—My disapproval of the man of figure Mr. Johnstone for a tenant arose *entirely* from Mr. Geoffrey's having given me his private opinion that he was *insufficient*—Even for a half years rent. He said with a jerk sideways of his head—contemptuous 'he would not in my place venture upon him'. I enclose a note to Mr. G—Read—seal—send—and hear what he says in reply. If the man of figure has actually *secured married* a woman with 11 thousand pounds fortune then he is a

[1] For a modern account of Scott's finances, see *Letters of Sir W. Scott 1787–1807*, ed. Grierson (1932), i, pp. lxxx–xcv.

[2] See above, p. 414.

substantial tenant and I make no objection to his standing in Mrs. Dease's shoes provided he takes the house for 20 years from the time he commences that we may not be plagued with flitting tenants. The rent to us is to be from his commencement the *raised rent See Rent book*. If Mr. Bond will take it I should prefer him—*on the same terms—Much prefer* him—because we have experience of the Bonds being *good pay* and of one of the Johnstones being bad pay—and a mans saying he hopes we shall find him a very different person from his brother is awkward at best.

Whatever you do, put it in writing and get Geoffrey to witness the paper.

You understand that Mrs. Dease is *bound* to us for two years and *cannot* let the house without written permission. I cannot understand the contradictory reports I have heard. Geoffrey assured me Mrs. D had no wish to let to Johnstone.

Next as to Quins agent Morgan letting No. 5 Mary Row (formerly Johnstone's) for seventeen guineas per Annum—agreed—if it be taken for *2 years*. I am willing to lower the rent thus from 18 Guineas to 17—as you percieve I do—(vide Rent book). Require that the tenant undertake all repairs and do not pay any repairs on the *new take*. Please to have the agreement made in writing and signed by Lovell if at home or Mr. Hinds and witnessed by Garrat Keegan.

Now for my own houses—

Notwithstanding Garrat Keegan's most weighty opinion and notwithstanding the conviction I have of his zeal for my particular interests in this matter I *demur* about Mrs. Ganly. She is the most *difficult* person to get rent from that I have had to deal with. I don't say this is her fault—but even if it be her misfortune—it must also be mine if I take up with her. Her *expectancies* of boarders are not realised. Her present boarders the McPeak's never are paid for regularly and her making them over to me as security would be a mockery of woe—And all her prodigious facility of words and airs of the head would only add to my discomfiture. She would leave me pennyless and talk me dead.

Notwithstanding all the above is my private view of the matter. I am willing to take further counsel. Can she find any one who will go security for her paying the rent—who will for instance join in a note for a years rent? If the boarders are security they would be good for others as well as for me. If they are not why should I take them?

Besides—next comes the question Can we let her present house immediately for the same rent she pays and without loss?—repairs &c? If not—for Lovells interest which I ought to consider before my own she should remain where she is. I am always averse to the perpetual flitting; that changing of houses by which the poor landlord always spills cash. It would be well to ask Geoffrey's and Mills private opinion. Both those gentlemen know as well as Mr. Harman was wont, how many eggs are in everyones pudding. My voice would be still for the gentlemen Engineers—if there be any reasonable hope of them—and for the catholic curate by the month[1]. . .

Fanny and I have just been to return dear Joanna Baillies visit—most cordial and kind both she and Agnes were—Agnes whom time cannot alter nor custom stale—she must be near 80 and she is the most lively entertaining person I have yet seen in London or its vicinity. Hampstead and London are now almost joined. Some of the plaister streets are really magnificent when one forgets that they are plaister—but there is ever some voice near which cries

> Must fall! must fall! must fall!—
> Must scale off—soon soon soon—See See See . . .

Ever affectionately yours with love to Aunt Mary particularly

Maria E

To Mrs. Edgeworth

Brandfold,[2] Wednesday, 17 November 1830

My dearest mother and all friends at home greeting. We are all here safe and well—and it is well to begin with telling you so, as the exaggerated reports we see in the E[nglish] papers of the

[1] For another aspect of ME's relations with tenants, see *Mem.* iii. 168–70 and M. C. Hurst, *Maria Edgeworth and the Public Scene* (1969).

[2] CSE's house near Goudhurst, Kent.

mobs and burnings in Kent may have reached you and may have twittered all your kind nerves.[1]

Sneyd has written and just read to me what he has written to Honora giving an exact excellent account of what has really happened in this parish and neighborhood and of all that immediately concerns him and us. I shall therefore add only my opinion of the part which he has taken. It will be most creditable to him—both what he said and what he did. Captain Kings manner expressed that strongly *on the field* and I am clear from all I heard said in London of the folly and danger of the Kentish gentlemen in having yielded to *mob*-demands that his steadiness will be justly approved and that his name and conduct will be distinguished. To say the truth the farmers and middle gentlemen have acted like cowards and fools hitherto—with few exceptions. I almost suspect they wish these disturbances to go on that *they* may in their turn have a plea for forcing the higher landlords and the aristocracy to pay all in lowering rents—and also in forcing the clergy to lower tithes. I have no doubt that something ought to be done and *must* be done but not by the *mob*. If any step be gained by *mob*—all is lost—for there is no saying to the mob any more than to the sea so far shalt thou go and no further.

If the ministry change as from this majority against them seems inevitable those who come in *must* see what they can do for reform and then all the grievances must come before Parliament in constitutional form. I think it is absolutely necessary. Otherwise there would be *risings* and revolution—for though it is easy to put down *one* mob in the beginning—as here—yet you cannot put down the sense of real distress if the perception the people have of what has been gained by them by combinations [*sic*]. There are too many *agitators* who keep this ever in their view. The great point which no one yet whom I have heard speak can decide is whether the majority of the army would or

[1] This was the beginning of the 'Captain Swing' agricultural riots in Nov. and Dec. 1830. Their origins lay in the general rural distress after the Napoleonic Wars, the high price of corn and the outbreak of revolution in France and Belgium. Rioting had begun in Kent at the end of Aug. with the destruction of threshing machines, but by the end of Oct. there were also disturbances over tithes, rents, and wages. Round Goudhurst, the next village to Brandfold, the trouble was at its height 9–15 Nov. The mob there was eventually dispersed on the 15th by a troop of dragoons with a magistrate from Cranbrook (E. J. Hobsbawn and G. Rudé, *Captain Swing* (1969), 98–113).

would not side with the people if it came—which Heaven forbid, to any great trial.

This instant Sneyd comes in and tells us that one of the ring-leaders of the Kentish mobs and one of the *burners* has been taken up by a Bow street runner who has long been after him and he is carried up to London. For the *present* all will be quiet here. Whether the quiet will continue I *doubt*. But I may enjoy the present and now go on to tell you something more agreeable.

I am charmed with this house and whole place. I am very glad you did not over praise it to me—it far surpasses my expectations. I arrived by coach at night—ten o'clock—in rain—and weary—but I revived immediately on entering the chearful hall. What a pretty staircase! And the library is such a delightfully habitable, comfortable home-feeling. I don't care for its being a low room—the bookcases and all the furniture look so handsome! The *altogether* at first sight by candle and lamp light and good fire light so pleasant. And my own bedchamber (which was yours I believe) is so comfortable. In the morning Ma'am my Venetian blind pulled up my eyes were charmed with the view from my window. The trees have not yet lost their leaves—the oaks keep their autumn foliage here so beautifully late—Sneyd says till after Christmas—View from the stair-case window rich—and when I went down to the library I cannot tell you how much I was charmed even with the fuschia-trellis looking paper—so gay and cottagy looking—*Dark!*—No no—I assure you the room is quite light enough for there is at the end opposite you as you enter a large-paned glass-door-window on the right hand side of the chimney place, from top to bottom of the room—opening to the bright sunny South on a beautiful green house full of geraniums, fuschia, chrysanthemums, and all manner of pretty things in full blow and looking as if they had been there always tho I am told they have been there only since yesterday. Have you or do you know the lovely little Fuschia Microfolia? It is now in my eye and I don't wish it out. Sneyd has drawn the green house for Honora so no more of that. The trellis is raised and arched high enough now and covered beautifully as your own with profuse flauntings of everblowing darlings and Jessamine green as summer—beautiful! Oh beautiful—and through the arches the grass sloping down soft and green as Irelands, and the knots of flowers Mrs. E has made with so much taste, hydrangeas and double stocks and American groundsel all making such a show. The rain has swelled the little river below so it looks quite broad and respectable winding silvery far and the banks rising beyond are so beautifully curved over with hedgerows and trees (I am afraid I shall wear out beautiful and beautifully but I cant help it. They will be honestly worn out at any rate) 'I like—and I like' everything I see! I like the hall and the chairs with the crest of the pelican and the stained glass and even the old man fiddling to the birds in their cage in the upper pane of the dining room bay window. I am afraid you will condemn me for Cockney taste in liking that window with its odd bits of paintings but I do and I cant help it. The dining room is large enough for all they want and is a most chearful breakfast room with sun shining on the close green grass—tiny lawn skirted—a waving skirt not a hedge—with evergreens, the laurestinus in profuse blow this November. I am not miserable about the roads not being changed tho the lawn is small to this front and the house too near the road—no great harm. Best keep money in both pockets and do it at some future time—good to have an object unaccomplished in store. In Mrs. E's own bedchamber—a south window with large panes has been opened and there is fine landscape—windmill and all seen from it. I like all they have done and think it was all necessary (especially the Commodité) and all well finished and painted—The new spare bedchamber—*too good*. As to the expense—Oh d—the expense. I know Sneyd will pay as he goes and therefore never can go too far. N B this house is insured—all but the greenhouse—the hay and our lives. I have been above about and underneath—the old kitchen makes an excellent housekeepers room or servants hall or whatever they please and the pantry laundry new kitchen. Dairy and servants rooms are most comfortable. There is great satisfaction to life above stairs in knowing that life below stairs is comfortable and has air and light and room enough sleeping or waking—and not only satisfaction but great selfish convenience for work *can* be well done *then* by the lower for the higher powers. Oh such want of comfort for servants as Lestock and Fanny found in the London houses with fine reception rooms—But let that be—no affair of mine.

The bits of red *Claude*[1] glass through which I see the shrubbery in one of these windows of the green house on my left hand as I sit at my own desk and a dear little table are very pretty—thanks to the bright sunshine too. The wetness of the soil and the want of gravel near are certainly disagreeable circumstances. Gravel comes to thirty shillings a load—worse than ourselves and 2.12.6 every load of lime—and lime necessary to kill worms in garden.

Harriette has this instant brought me a saucer full of ripe sweet strawberries from the garden. How good and ill are mixed in this life! We cannot have it all good. But I will stop and eat my well sugared strawberries and say no more of the price of lime that kills the worms that would have eaten (for aught I know) everything in the garden. Seriously the best comfort for all the expense to which Sneyd had gone is that the attorney who drew the papers and made the bargain says he should be glad to give him the price he paid for the whole and is very sorry he did not purchase the place—*And* adds that every thing Sneyd has done is just what he should have liked to have done himself if he had had the place so if ever he should wish or be forced to part with it there is a purchaser ready. But I should be very very sorry indeed that they should not have the long and full enjoyment of what they have done so well and what they enjoy so much. I never saw Sneyd so well and agreeable since the olden times when he was Sneedy Weedy—And Mrs. Edgeworth is so well bred and kind!—and converses so charmingly that I am inclined to exclaim 'Be ever thus'—and if her health permitted I think she would. It is quite astonishing how with such constant ill health she has thus lasted—So very little altered considering. Worn her face certainly is but not her figure and she is so perfectly gentlewomanlike—lady like and kind. Heaven send it may last my time and that I may do and say nothing wrong. I am quite at my ease and fearless and in some cases I believe the Duke of Wellington quite right in his saying 'There is no danger but fear'. It is a pity that did not occur to him about the city

[1] 'A somewhat convex dark or coloured hand mirror used to reduce the proportions of a landscape' but sometimes applied to coloured glasses through which a landscape is viewed 'to give the objects of nature a soft mellow tinge like the colouring of that master' (*O.E.D.*).

dinner but it is quite nonsense in earnest to suppose he was afraid.[1] He rides through the park where he knows mobbikins are waiting to hoot or hurra him every day—as Francis Beaufort *saw*—ce que vous appelez vu . . .

5 o clock Returned from drive—

Have only to add that all is settled here all safe—all well—And what the newspapers will tell—or will have told you by the time you read *this*—that the Duke of W. and Peel are out—But no one here knows who's *in* yet.[2]

I know I am ever yours affect.

17th Nov 1830 Maria E

To Fanny Wilson (*née* Edgeworth)

Brandfold, Thursday, 18 Nov. 1830

Alive and well my dearest and I hope you have not been anxious about me though I have not written as I ought to have done but there came such packets of business letters from home to be answered and so much to be done seen felt heard and understood here that truly I could not. The messenger for the post goes off at such an unconscionable hour too! Well well—can't be helped.

I take it for granted that in the community of letters between you and Lestock mine to him has reached you and I have only to add this to my story—That all is quiet now—But I must say that I think the gentlemen farmers have done very foolishly in their meeting at Cranbrook yesterday—where Sneyd was not. They agreed to raise the wages to 2/3—which was exactly what the mob demanded and had been crying for—so that after all it was just teaching them to cry again and only pretending that they would not give them what they wanted *while they were naughty*. 'There now! there now! Have done crying wipe your

[1] The king and his ministers were to have attended a civic banquet at the Guildhall on 9 Nov. but because of the prospect of hostile demonstrations the Cabinet cancelled the arrangements on 8 Nov. Greville reported that this decision aroused much ridicule and abuse (*Greville Memoirs: A Journal of the Reigns of King George IV and King William IV* (1875), ii. 54).

[2] The government was defeated on 15 Nov. on a motion on the civil list. The Duke of Wellington and his colleagues resigned on the next day.

eyes—and—There it is for you.' And what a fool the child must be if it does not roar again for the next thing it wants—no not *wants* but wishes for. And so it will be I feel almost sure with the people here but next time they will cry for tithes to be lowered.

This change of ministry however and the hopes of real parliamentary reform of abuses may however prevent the danger which from all I can gather spreads far and wide over England. The great English evil poor laws[1] *must* I think be abolished and some better mode of providing for the really helpless poor be adopted—which mode should not be so expensive in the execution and so *absurd* in the principle as the present perverted system which encourages idleness and fraud and improvidence in early marriages at the expense of industry honesty prudence and all the virtues by which a state can thrive. I like Peels speech[2] much very manly and really patriotic.

Not one word of this did I mean to say but when I begin to you my dear what is at the top and bottom of my mind must come out all at once in glorious disorder . . .

Your ever affectionate friend sister

Maria E

Lady Morgan[3] amuses Harriette and she thanks you for sending it.

The papers have not yet told us what Lestock used to tell us every day that

'Lord Grey is minister.'

We know from the papers that the Duke and Mr. Peel are out but who are in remains yet untold—unknown.[4]

N B I have just heard that heads of the mob said they had no fear of the soldiers—That they would have willingly shaken

[1] The high cost and the method of administration of the Poor Law had been subjects of concern at least since the economic distress after the Napoleonic Wars. Now the 'Captain Swing' riots (see p. 429 n. 1) were held to have been worst in parishes where labourers had become pauperized by the 'allowance' system (S. and B. Webb, *English Poor Law History* (1929), Pt. II: The Last Hundred Years, i. 1–46).

[2] On his resignation from office.

[3] *Book of the Boudoir* (1829), *France* (1830). Most of the permanent value of the latter book was due to her husband's assistance.

[4] The king sent for Lord Grey on 17 Nov. The latter's Cabinet arrangements were completed within the next two days.

hands with the muskets for they knew that the Military would have fired over their heads. In this they were mistaken for Capt King delayed to fire only because he was determined that if he did fire it should not be *in vain*. The soldiers to all appearance were staunch.

Thursday In the parish of Marden adjoining us every man has refused to be sworn in as special Constable. This is the worst thing I have. It looks decidedly to the future and to future mobs. Mr. Courtop the rich man who was dragged out of his carriage by the mob has not slept these 10 nights they say and is suspected of having written the letter on concession which is signed 'One of the great unpaid'.

Carpets too dear—pithy sentence

To Fanny Wilson

Brandfold, Goudhurst, 25 Nov. 1830

Dearest and best. Observe my modesty—I didn't say '*First & fairest*.' Thank you for note. Sneyd says I don't deserve it. He has been reproaching me a gorge deployée these 2 days for not having written to you but I tell him he does not understand us and that a note more or less can make no difference in our concert of the heart (worthy of Lady Morgan!). N B I have been exceedingly entertained by her last volume and I am sure you who judge for yourself and are above Captain Beauforts prejudices will be entertained and informed too by it. As to her vanities what matter? Every reader ought to have a thrashing and winnowing machine going in their own hands which should throw off the chaff and keep the grain. 'Life in India'[1] also has amused me exceedingly and I have great anticipation of pleasure from the thoughts of seeing Pakenham read it before me. The dear little dog, the dear little *Griffin* I should say but why you will never know till you read 'Life in India'. Thank you my dear for sending that book with me—Half an hour after I go up to my bedroom at night I sit delightfully reading it by a bright wood fire till the clock strikes eleven and hour and a half I read

[1] Mrs. Monkland, *Life in India; or, the English in Calcutta* (1828).

it in the morning before breakfast viz from 8 striking, till half after 9. I get up at 7-striking—out of bed *Mem* (and you will never know why I say '*Mem*' till you read 'Life in India').

Anne Kiernan the Irish housemaid here ministers more to my happiness than housemaids or any kind of maids usually do. She has such Irish heart about her—and not always in her mouth the only place some people's hearts ever are, but in her eyes and more far in all her doings. She thinks she never can do enough for me and fancies I have done so much for her but what it is I don't know. However I am very glad to come in for a share of the blessings falling due on your mothers head and Honoras. I am clear that if I would let her Anne Kiernan would lift me out of bed and sit me on her lap and dress me all the time saying 'Oh Miss Edgeworth dear! dont be thinking of my trouble it's a pleasure sure—and I can never do enough for any of the family. Its a pleasure. Oh if it wouldn't what would I be?' . . .

No more burnings here—and I have no doubt that all disturbances will cease when the example of firmness well-armed is seen. To be sure gentlemen must volunteer to defend their property, hearths and homes—or lose them . . .

I say nothing about new ministry and Lord John Russell[1] because this would be too vast a subject for a note but I assure you I read or hear read all the speeches and rejoice and reprobate as you do and especially rejoice in Mr. Stanleys appointment—and am ever yr M E

To Sophy Ruxton

[fragment] after breakfast—Thursday [? 29 Nov.]

. . . I find that I have omitted as usual to say what I was most intent on telling you and which I had kept for the last as bonne-bouche—that Pakenham is with us and has left the East India College with the greatest credit. He was at the head of the College—that is he had obtained more prizes and medals and

[1] Lord John Russell became Paymaster General. According to Greville (op. cit. ii. 70) he was to have had the War Office but his brother, the Marquis of Tavistock begged that the appointment might be changed because Lord John's health was unequal to it. Stanley was Secretary for Ireland.

character for good conduct than any other person in the College. We have heard also from various quarters, from Spring Rice downwards, and upwards, that both the masters and young men his companions speak of him in the highest terms. Mrs. Baillie told me that a lady who has a son at Haileybury and who did not know that Mrs. Baillie cared aught about the Edgeworths told her that her son had an excellent friend at College whose influence and good conduct had been of the greatest use and a great deal more too good or too long for repetition—and this friends name was Edgeworth. Mr. Malthus spoke of him to me in the highest terms. *By the by* Mr. Malthus is a *very sensible man and I like him much* and I hope you will laugh at me when you read this. I wish to make you smile dear Sophy at any rate.

Pakenham is allowed to stay till May before he goes—for ever—to India. He is waiting for an answer from home to settle his plans for s[ix] months—he dined at an East India Director Mr. Tuckers and a young college friend of his Maltby was to dine there but he was stopped an hour in Piccadilly by an immense crowd going up with an address to the king.[1] The mob was wondrous peaceable and well behaved as the newspapers truly state but nevertheless it seems dangerous that such numbers should assemble in these ticklish times and above all dangerous and surprising that without the government having any information of the probability of such an assemblage [*sic*].

This instant—a frank—sent from foreign office from Edgeworths Town enters and now my head is in the packet there and you must wait till it comes back to me.

I have not been able yet to touch Helen.[2] There she lies unpacked at the bottom of my trunk and much I fear will lie till I return to dear leisure at home. I am as happy here with Fanny as can be but my taste for London life is quite over—and the hurry. If I were once in the vortex would soon kill me. As it is I have as much as I can do—and *will* not have more. F will not be in her own house I think till new year. I have never seen more than the outside—upon honor never to look in. The situation is charming.

[1] An address of loyalty was presented to the king by the Trades of London on 8 Dec.

[2] ME's novel, published 1834.

I omitted when speaking of the present King of France to tell you an anecdote we heard from Mr. Jacob. He has—or had—a copy of a letter which the present King then Duke of Orleans[1] wrote to Pitt begging him to use his influence to get him the *sityation of King of Brazil!*—and at another period during Bonapartes times *he applied* to be made King of Spain and apologised for seeming to interfere with the claims of Bourbon relatives by a list of the wrongs his branch of the family had received from the other elder branches from time immemorial—Very like an Irish *belying* proceeding and—what odd strange adventures do happen to kings in these days—more wonderful than Voltaire's table d'hote dinner of Ex Kings.[2]

To Mrs. C. S. Edgeworth

69 Welbeck Street, 6 Dec. 1830

Il n'y a la que de *cervelle*[3] said Talleyrand when Bonaparte once in an affirmation of some sentiment struck his hand upon his *heart*. I am afraid my dear Harriette you may have begun to suspect the same of my heart since I have never yet written one word of thanks . . . Lestock was much interested in reading Mr. Millers statement of the mode of living, wages &c of the laborers in your part of Kent and all the facts are safe lodged in Lord Lansdowne's head along with the history of the mobbing burning &c and the lady who had the *bile on her liver* and complained of the parish soup for being too good. I spent a very pleasant morning at Lansdowne-house on Saturday and felt particularly obliged by their having made quite a private really select not London-select party for me of their own family and most intimate friends who as Lady Lansdowne said were all my old friends whom I had formerly known at Bowood or seen in Town frequently. There were only 22 people and of those 10 were their own family—Ld and Lady Lansdowne—Lady Louisa S—and Lord Henry Petty a very *pleasing boy* (a very rare animal)—Lady Theresa Strangways and Miss Fielding—two nieces of Lady Lansdownes (both pretty)—Mr. W. Strangways her brother—Lady E Fielding her sister—Sir William Lemon (her

[1] Louis Philippe.
[2] In Chap. 26 of *Candide*.
[3] See below, p. 497 n.

brother in law)—Miss Fox—(Lady L's cousin) Mr. and Mrs. *Kennedy* (Mrs. K you know is Romilly's daughter) Mr. William Romilly—wards of Lord Lansdowne—Mr. Whishaw—Mr. Fazakerly (a most agreeable man—both *habitués* of the family) —Lord John Russell—Lord Auckland—Sir J McDonald *from Skye*—Mr. Turner a bank director, *well* known to every body (but myself) for a famous pamphlet on the corn laws and Mr. Sharp—Conversation Sharp—an old stager—in my opinion quite worn out and all his stories staled by repetition—and you smell them coming—too plainly and too often. But he is a very good natured man and luckily I recollected him perfectly and remembered before he put me in mind (which his mouth was open to do) that 8 years ago he had introduced me to this very Mr. Turner who had shewn me the bank of England and the famous machine-*hand* which weighs the guineas without assistance from mortal touch. The conversation (barring Sharp) was extremely agreeable especially Lord Lansdowne's own part of it—he having a great deal of sub-drollery which few suspect and which he never lets out but to quite his particulars. He gave a comic account and laughed till he could not speak in giving it of a Monsr. Cottu—a man who wrote a famous book on English laws[1] and who is half pedant, half puppy and altogether turncoat and coward. I had met him at Bowood formerly at the time when he came over to collect from Scarlett and others materials for said book and when after going circuit with the Welsh judges he spent two days at Bowood criticising the dishes he had eaten of or *not* eaten at the Circuit dinners and curling his hair on his forehead at the glass. A fortnight before the *coup d'état* Cottu thinking the Royal side would prevail sent Lord Lansdowne a pamphlet the get of which was to recommend absolute power and a dictator in France. But Lo! the coup d'etat went the wrong way and never did man's consternation so completely bereave him of presence of mind. He had dined at some country house near Paris and walking home, all spruce in silk stockings &c he met his maid who brought him word of the risings of the people in Paris—told him she had heard in the crowd the cry of '*A la lanterne*'. No sooner had she articulated that sentence than Cottu

[1] *De l'administration de la justice criminelle en Angleterre* (1820). For ME's previous meeting with Cottu, see above, pp. 82–4.

turned about and fled. Without ever returning to Paris to see what had or might become of house or family, he set off for England and neither stinted nor staid till he reached London and in the dead of night drew M. de Vaudreuil's curtains and exclaimed 'Tout est perdu. Je viens des *massacres* de Paris'. But when Vaudreuil asked for explanations and facts not one word more could he say. Vaudreuil could not persuade him to go to bed and rest his perturbed spirit but out he went and made his way to Scarletts. Arrived just when the shutters were opening and the housemaid brooming—She seeing such a pale, woebegone, much besplashed, strange scared looking figure thought he was mad threw down her broom and was going to shut the door in his face but he pushed in caught her and to convince her (as Lord Lansdowne told it) that he was in his senses kissed her and finally persuaded her to go up and tell her master that a French gentleman fresh from Paris *must* see him directly. Scarlett took pity on him and *harboured* him for some days and when the newspapers at last quieted his apprehensions a little he thought the best thing he could do was to go '*ba'k ageen*' and see after his house and family . . . Command me always and believe me your affectionate sister Maria E

To Sophy Ruxton

[69] Welbeck Street, 8 Dec. 1830

My dearest Sophy . . .

The change of ministry has scarcely yet had time to make itself felt but much is hoped from the moderate beginning. Spring Rice came in the midst of this multiplicity of business and sat and talked for half an hour as if the budget were not weighing on his mind. The sum of all he said and I believe of all he thinks is that though it requires nice steering we shall get through—that the mobs will be put down by yeomanry and gentlemen volunteering to defend their own properties—that there will be no danger in Ireland from the AntiUnion party—*that* will die quietly. Government have already received adhesions from one prime opponent of the Union and it is thought that the rustling of a silk gown will have happy effect upon another.

Spring Rice far surpassed all I had expected from him in kind attention and cordiality of manner to me. During a first visit however I could not get in many questions to this Secretary of the Treasury about own little concerns which I had to ask—about tolls and customs and walls round fair greens &c. That must be for the next time. Lady Theodosia Rice is much younger and more agreeable every way—perhaps richer and happier—not always synonymous terms—But in hers they may because she had everything else in this world except health and wealth—and beauty. As she was lucky enough to have secured Love without having beauty—What need she care how plain she be? She has a very fine family—Eldest daughter now beginning her first Campaign—Eldest son a very fine pleasing and I hear very clever young man—educated by his father.

I spent a morning and an evening very agreeably at Lansdowne-house—She was quite cordial in her manner and he always the same. They invited me to come to drink tea with them in private—begged me to come as early as possible. I went at 9 and found I had been really expected at a quarter before 8—All her own family—and all the persons now living whom I had formerly known as their favorite private society and as she politely said my old friends at Bowood and at their house in Town . . . I was very glad to get away from him [Mr. Turner] to hear some agreeable conversation about Talleyrand. I hope I shall hear some of his wit some day from himself. Lord Lansdowne thinks him in the full possession of all his mental powers. Talleyrand amused himself with persuading Lord Aberdeen that he had survived his faculties and was become quite imbecile. They say that Charles the 10th is quite at his ease amusing himself and not troubling himself about the fate of Polignac or any of his ministers. There is great danger for them—But still I hope the French will not disgrace their revolution by spilling their blood. Talleyrand says he is now come to complete the restoration of the Bourbons. Lord Lansdowne has a good opinion of the present King of France. He mentioned an instance of his presence d'esprit. A mob in Paris surrounded him. 'Que desirez vous Messieurs?' 'Nous desirons Napoleon.' 'Eh bien! Allez donc le trouver.' The mob laughed cheered and dispersed applauding.

Next to the change of ministry and politics the next subjects of the day have been the election of the President of the Royal Society[1] and the expected trial of Mr. Long.[2] Mr. Herschel had I believe all the wishes in his favor of every man of science in the Royal Society even of those who from circumstances were forced to vote in favor of the Kings brother. Herschel has been happy in having had all the honor and escaping all the trouble. It would not have been a situation suited either to his fortune tastes or manner. Tho I am sure Captn. Beaufort would be indignant against me for saying so I am in my secret soul of opinion that it is best as it is. Tho the Duke of Sussex is not a man of science he may do the honors to men of science and fill the Presidents place more agreeably than a rival or a judge. How he is to get through his speeches or discourses to the Society annually is another affair but bought science I suppose may be as good as bought wit and if he reads well or can get by rote—alls well (I hope Margaret smiles). Poor Davies Gilbert to whom the place was in every way unsuited is well out of it. I hope he thinks so.

Mr. Jacob and his daughters drank tea here the day before yesterday. They made most grateful inquiries for you. The kindness and hospitality shewn them was not thrown away. Tiresome as he is and shrill as their voices are I quite liked them for their good feelings.

I have seen dear good Joanna Baillie several times—always the same—and the Carrs. It has been a great pleasure to me to feel myself so kindly received by those I liked best years ago in London. It is always gratifying to find old friends *the same* after long absence and interruption of communication but it has been particularly so to me now when not only the leaves of the pleasures of life fall naturally in its winter but when the great branches on whom happiness depended fall.

[1] Augustus Frederick, Duke of Sussex, the king's brother, was P.R.S. 1830–9. He succeeded the Edgeworths' old friend Davies Gilbert (Giddy).

[2] St. John Long, 'professor of the healing art', was arraigned for treating Mrs. Colin Campbell Lloyd with a dangerous lotion which produced a septic sore of which the patient died. Mrs. Lloyd was reported to suffer from 'globus hystericus' and the lotion was no doubt intended as a counter-irritant. St. John Long was acquitted (*Morning Chron.*, 21 Feb. 1831). It was not the first time he had been in trouble of this kind and he afterwards issued pamphlets in his defence (ibid. 6 Jan. and 21 Mar. 1831).

I have dined out but once—at Dr. Hollands—a very small party to meet Southey who scarcely spoke a word that I could hear and looked like a worn out Italian actor with very black eyebrows and a very grey-mop-head. A lawyer opposite to him Sir Edward Alderson *talking all* and in that very ill bred odious ton de barreau as if he was pleading in court against Brougham and making his point good across the table for the bare life—sometimes with knife and fork up and bit suspended between plate and mouth. Oh how I disliked him and his distended wild-beast looking eyes. But no matter for my fine feelings, he makes a mint of money and whenever he opes his mouth for or against a man down there comes handfuls of gold. I'm sorry I have wasted so many lines upon him.

Dr. Hollands children are very fine happy looking children and he does seem so to enjoy them. His little boy in reply to the common place *aggravating* question/observation put to children of 'Who loves you—nobody loves you in this world Im sure' replied 'Yes there is somebody—Papa loves me I know—Im sure'. And throwing himself on his back on *his aunt Mary's* lap he looked up at his father with such a sweet confident smile! The father was standing between Alderson and Southey—The one sure he had him by the ear and the other by the imagination but the child had him by the heart and looking over the lawyers gesticulating arm the father smiled and nodded at his boy and with an emphasis in which the whole soul spoke low but strong 'Yes I *do* love you'. Neither the lawyer nor the poet heard it—to the best of my opinion.

Here I was interrupted by the by whom [*sic*] I was very glad to be interrupted (and that is saying as much as I can)—Mr Creed—dear good friend! and most agreeable and radiant-looking with good will and not a day older than when I saw him 8 years ago. He is now happy too in the hopes of getting an employment that suits him—Secretary to a great rail road company—in *posse* but not in *Esse* as Mr. Alderson would say (Evil communication corrupts good manners). The canvas for this Secretaryship is going on and we hope to help him and for that purpose of course I had a letter to write. The letter was to Mr. Hope who sent me a most kind reply and will do what he can but that turns out to be 0. The Hopes are at the Deepdene.

When they come to Town after Xmas I will tell you more—that is if you care to know.

You know we talked over together my plan of living in London—keeping out of mere fine company grand parties &c. I shall find no difficulty but great comfort and advantage to F.L. and self in so doing. I have made all my friends understand this—and farther I am almost determined to refuse in future all dinners because I find I am invited alone to dinner and they in the evening and this is very uncomfortable to me—better go *all together evening*. Too besides the dinners would soon undo my health—want of rest after dinner I feel—&c—But Fanny to whom I have pleaded all this with perfect truth so objects to my making any positive general resolution lest I should lose something for which I would afterwards give my ears—that I submit to hold this resolve in abeyance and to refuse or accept *as it happens*—Just as Madame Gallatin said she went to court or not as it happens. NB—I dine at Lockharts on Saturday next.

Here the carriage came to the door—2-oclock—which ends all writing for 3 hours. Went to Lady E Whitbreads and to return Mrs. Callcott (formerly Graham)'s visit—she living at Kensington Gore near Lady E W. Lady Elizabeth is as kind as ever—very affectionate to Fanny and fond of Harriet and Honora just as of old. It is very agreeable to be with her—such a well bred manner of being kind too. She is struggling between her natural pride in her brother's ministerial appointment and natural affection which makes her justly fear for his health—He being one of the few who take the affairs of England closely to heart.

Mrs. Callcott was very glad to see me and entertaining too but there is something too bold and odd about her—Lestock says too much of the bold dragoon—nothing feminine or ladylike and all men dislike *that* intensely. Mr. Callcott however looks well and happy and thanks her for it—with eyes and with mouth and there's the essential for her and him. He is very kind and agreeable and has painted two or 3 beautiful pictures for this years exhibition. He most kindly remembered your little protégé—asked how he is going on and promised to do all he can for him whenever he comes over to London. If that should be while I am here—tant mieux.

To Mrs. Edgeworth, 10 December 1830

I am writing between 8 and 9 before breakfast and it is so very dark in a thick London fog that I can scarcely see what I write. I hope you will.

Adieu my dear Sophy . . .

Love to dear Richard Bess and Margaret

Ever affectionately yr

Maria Edgeworth

To Mrs. Edgeworth

10 Dec. 1830

My dear and best of agents, factotums and friends—Thank you —and now my houses are off my shoulders and 6 months hence I shall begin to feel for them in my pockets—where I hope to find about twelve pounds (be the same more or less) the heavier . . . Here Mr. Babbage came in and sat an hour and was so entertaining!—But still my hour is gone We can't have our hours and enjoy them too . . .

We 3 drank tea yesterday at Mrs. Baillies to meet Jo and Ag who have been there this week—Very agreeable evening—Nobody there but ourselves (Pak had a cold and would not go lay on a sofa reading at 69). Among other memorabile Joanna told me that a German prince asked Ada Lady Byron's daughter *whether she had her fathers genius.* Can you concieve any human being to be so stupid and illbred? Princes in general have habitually—instinctively the tact which preserves them from such blunders . . .

We, Fanny and I and Isabella Carr went yesterday (Lady Lansdowne having given me a universal permit) to Lansdowne house to see the Statues and pictures &c. The whole house has been new done up—beautifully and some new pictures and statues—One a sleeping nymph or Venus in white marble as naked as ever she was born and her hair as well and better curled than any hair dresser could curl it, having taken eternal buckle in Parian stone. Fanny would have it that this Venus or nymph was a Magdalen!!! and we had much laughing about it. Tell Honora that the black coated Italian (*Tuttuli*) who used to stand at the *urn* table at breakfast at Bowood is still to the good[1]—

[1] See above, pp. 92–3.

Only more pear-shaped than formerly and a little lame I suppose with gout. It was he who attended us through the apartments drew up blinds & &c. Very good fire in delightful Library—because my Lord not left Town.

Pakenham has just returned from seeing the dissection of a mummy. The membrane over the brain was perfect which nobody can account for. It never happened before I am told. I wish you would tell this to Crampton. I have not time. P says the whole operation and all he saw disappointed him notwithstanding the wondrous perfection of said membrane. The embalmers were cheats for they had not embalmed this mortal up to his quality and his price as noted by his garments and insignia. This man had been put into a great cauldron of Asphalte by which means it had been burnt and shrivelled up—Whereas the approved way for the aristocracy are embalmed in quite another way [*sic*]—wax spices &c as Louisa knows and scorns me probably at this instant for venturing to speak in a subject of which I know nothing. But of how few should I speak if I restricted myself to those of which I know something . . .

I must now break off abruptly

Ever yours well & affecy

Maria E

Mr. Creed thinks that those who have Canal shares had better hold them on for that the present panic[1] will by and by be over and people will find out that there is work enough for both railroads and canals of sorts which never can interfere with each other. I tell you all I hear said by Messrs les Experts—that is all I can do.

To Mrs. Edgeworth

13 Dec. 1830

It is incredible how often I send off a letter forgetting the principal thing I intended to say [in] it. My dear Mother I have never thanked you for that for which I am most grateful—for that which gave me a great deal of pleasure and which I shall

[1] Canal shares were not seriously affected by railway competition till the late 1840s. The bulk of the Edgeworths' capital was tied up in the Irish estate but they invested in new industrial development, e.g. in gas, railways, and docks.

prize and love as long as I live and leave to some one of your children to prize and love when I am no more—the bracelet of your dear own hair. I shall wear it for the first time on Fanny and Lestock's wedding day, and little Marianne's and M E's birthday. We are now I *believe* on the *eve* of getting into No. 1 North Audley Street. The painters are actually all out and their pots of paint are to follow them this morning. Furniture is all going in and we are to follow as soon as it has all settled itself in its proper places. I have never yet been in the house.

I verily believe that Mr. Ralston has run away with my black gown and is figuring in it on shipboard or elsewhere. I inquired for him in vain the other day at Millar the American booksellers. By the by you never sent me the other promised packet of American letters. Since I wrote last on Saturday per Spring Rice frank nothing new except dinner and evening that day at Lockharts—a very pleasant dinner of 10—first—a clever gentleman whose name I never compassed—2ly. Mr. and Mrs. Mansfield (lawyer he and rich and she clever and agreeable)—Sir Francis Freeling *useful*[1] and daughter pleasing—3dly—Lady Gifford widow of a great lawyer who grew from plain *Mr.* into *Lord* G. She is clever but not agreeable—piques herself upon sincerity under pretence of which she indulges her temper in saying *brusqueries* in which I could see no wit but much ill breeding. They say she is good natured in *deeds* but that never compensates for ill natured in words. Philpotts—bishop of Limerick[2] was the grandee of the dinner and certainly he eat and talked with 100 horse power. He was exceedingly entertaining and as I sat next him I had the best of it. Mr. Lockhart appeared very well in his own house tho Joanna Baillie tells me he does not please in London in general he is so silent and reserved. To me he was quite the contrary and Mrs. Lockhart whom I always loved I now love the more when I see her sweet natural character and manners in London. She does the honors of her own house in the most agreeable and winning manner—never thinking of herself—only of how she can make every one comfortable and happy. She gave me that engraving of Sir Walter Scott

[1] He franked many Edgeworth letters.

[2] A letter of her sister Fanny makes it clear that ME means Henry Philpotts, Bishop of Exeter.

which Harriet tried in vain to get for me in London—the same as Fanny's and Sophys. She took it out of the frame where it hung in her own bedchamber. 'Oh you must you must indeed take it. You know I have a picture of him below stairs—and I have the original. *You* must have this—Think only what a pleasure it is to me to have found out anything in which I could so please you'—said with such a persuasive sincere smile. So I took it and kissed her and I defy anybody who has either a heart or brains to help loving her. Her husband doats upon her. Poor little-John is now seemingly in good health but a sad sad sight in such contrast to what I last saw him at Chiefswood that I could hardly bear to look at him lest he or his father and mother should see what I felt. His breast bone sticks out and in short he is quite deformed. Mrs. Lockhart told a friend that she had been horribly shocked in seeing him again after a few weeks absence. She really had never before as she declared known that he was deformed. It had come on gradually and she had not perceived it. Her second boy is the finest creature I ever saw of his age and her little girl engaging like herself and with her fathers handsome eyes—all her children *natural* and unspoiled.

Fanny Lestock and Pakenham came in the evening and liked it. Mrs. Lockhart played on the harp and sung as I (poor ignorant as I am) thought delightfully because most feelingly ballads of which I could hear every word and understand—and her own figure at the harp and pretty hands and expressive unaffected countenance altogether were charming.

Lady Charlotte Bury who came in the evening and who sat opposite to Mrs. Lockhart while she played was in such contrast! —every way. She must have been a very fine perhaps beautiful woman with a fair complexion and bright color but on a very large bold scale and now the remains are melancholy not interesting. She dresses too young and is not well made-up—her own gray hair coming here and there into view between the false—too evidently false masses of brown. Her own hair is dragged up some way so that it gave me a pain at my temples to look at her. Her mouth once beautiful is now all fallen in and she is like a much-worn antique bust—Strong marks of the passions having passed over the countenance but '*L'amour a passé par la*' is not the first thing that occurs to one.

To go on with this never ending history of the party at Lockharts—Among other notables in the evening was Mr. Murray the bookseller whom I now for the first time saw face to face and a very ugly face he has and probably he said or thought the same of me. Still—I dont squint and I hope I don't look vulgar which in spite of all I had heard of Mr. Murrays being fine I think *he does*. He was very civil however—down to the ground to me—rather awkwardly puzzled tho' how to be *paying* his devoirs to two Lionesses at a time—Lady Charlotte Bury and Miss E. Of course I stood out of his way as much as I could but I did not fail to take him at his word when he offered his services at last to me and pinned him on the sofa where I made him sit down for the special purpose—engaged him to do whatever he can for the poor French translatress[1]—put her letter into his pocket at least made him put it there—and he is to breakfast here anon and give a definitive. He spoke handsomely to me of Bertha[2]—he *beginning* the subject which gratified my pride. I told him we were quite satisfied with his conduct. 'I fear I was a little *dilatory* but I hope I was right in the Essential point.' 'Quite satisfactory' replied I. I have not done justice to Lady C Bury's manner which is high-bred and quite easy. Her voice and conversation are both agreeable—unaffected—free from authorship pretension or pretension of any sort. We talked first about her daughter Lady G-Cummings kind attentions to my sisters and to me when I was ill at Forres[3]—then about the inundations which covered with sand the pleasure grounds.[4] Above ten thousand pounds worth of damage was suffered by Sir Gordon Cumming N B. Her Ladyship called him Gordon Cumming not Cumming Gordon—if wrong—the blame be hers.

My dear mother what do you think I have just done? Oh I hope I shall not repent—laid out fifteen guineas on—an Indian shawl. You know it will do me credit as long as I live and do somebody else service afterward which is better even than

[1] Possibly Louise Swanton Belloc who translated ME and many other well-known English authors.

[2] Harriet Beaufort's book, published by Murray. The BM Catalogue gives this anonymous work to Mrs. Marcet but it is quite clear from letters in the Edgeworth papers of Feb. 1830 that it was written by Mrs. Edgeworth's sister.

[3] ME was ill with 'erysipelas' at Forres in July 1823 (*Mem*. ii. 229–30).

[4] At Altyre, near Forres, seat of Sir William Gordon Cumming.

washing and wearing and making an underpetticoat afterwards. What color?—guess—guess my dear friends. All I hope is that you will like it.

Mrs. Lockhart and Mrs. Jacob came in while I was writing and Mr. J staid out of all conscience—So I cannot send this letter today—and perhaps it is all for the best, for I may hear from you tomorrow and answer some question of vital importance—

Tuesday Morning

Yesterday Evening at Mrs. Skinners—You know she is the keeper of a Menagerie for lions of all sorts and sizes &c. We were not at the feeding of the beasts (having refused). Those of note in the evening were—Sir George Staunton—grown very old and lean and chou-chouing in quick time in the oddest manner. I never saw anything so droll as his bows and I thought they would never cease at every fresh word I said on meeting him—Chou! chou!—as if he had been pulled by a string and brought up again by a spring to perpendicular then churning head and whole body up and down as you might push up and down a figure of old on spiral springs jumping up on opening a snuff box. Sir G however is very good natured and his visit to Edgeworthstown embalmed in his memory—fresh as ever—next to him Mr. Collier, Davidoffs Collier—fresh from Russia and with his recollections of Edgeworthstown also as fresh as ever within him. Davidoff he says feels sadly the difference between his own country and those which he has visited—No wonder. Concieve the despotism. For 3 weeks after the coup d'etat[1] no newspapers were permitted to be delivered in Petersburg. One at last was smuggled in by some English man and Lord Heytesbury sent to buy the favour of a sight of it. In time the news got out and circulated low in whispers. When it was known that all knew it the newspapers were released and out they came in numbers stale! When Mr. Collier went to see Davidoff at his country house he omitted to ask for a passport on leaving at Petersburg and it would take a page to recount all the difficulties into which this led him with the police—history of why he came to Petersburg and why he went and whither &c

[1] Polignac's decrees dissolving the Chamber in July 1830, followed by the flight of Charles X and the accession of Louis Philippe in early Aug.

&c &c and at last a petition to the Emperor. Oh John Bull if you did but know your bliss how blest you are! But—to go on with *Davidoff*—He has come into possession of his estate—It is the custom for the tenants on receiving the heir and master all simultaneously to kneel down and present him with salt and corn. Davidoff did all he could to prevent the kneeling but the habit of subjection and the love of national custom proved too strong for him and kneel they would and kneel they did one and all. Davidoff is to come into possession of another large property soon and in the mean time Collier says I shall have a letter from him soon. I saw a pretty stamped leather shoe which Mrs. Skinner has just received from him. She was very kind to him and really seems to have felt his merits.

A Mr. Swinton was the next I saw—(married to Mrs. Skinners sister)—a man who spent 30 years in India and was 30 years in making his fortune tho a *high officer* with all opportunities. He is uncle to *somebody* who at Calcutta will or may be of great use to Pakenham and for this reason Mrs. Skinner who really is deed-y-ly good natured specially invited Pakenham whom she zealously patronises to meet him.

A puppy—one of the greatest puppies I ever saw in England came in the way and prevented me for some time from getting out of the quiet India looking gentleman what I wanted but at last we got rid of the great puppy who was also a little poet writing charming little things in Annuals—v—*gems* in the Gem[1] &c. Then Pakenham leaning over the back of the sofa, and we having it comfortably to ourselves Mr. Swinton went to work to tell me all he could think of useful to Pakenham. Sum of all is—that on his arrival in Calcutta he must have there about £300 sterling which will set him up sufficiently and handsomely—not extravagantly—But if he has not that he would be obliged to borrow—at great disadvantage—would be cheated and would never for years afterwards be able to get from under the weight of debt. The necessary expenses are furniture for his house—a palanquin—a horse and thirteen servants indispensable—*8* of these palanquin bearers—*2* Khitmutgars Anglice—butlers—1 Musalgy—anglice—footman—1 Metre—Anglice—housemaid-man who does all the dirty work being of the lowest

[1] *The Gem, a literary annual*, ed. T. Hood (1829–32).

caste—1 Syce—Anglice—groom—Amount of yearly wages of all the thirteen about £84 sterling (Mr. Swinton said to P. 'Stick to the Revenue line. All the good things are there.') Mr. Swinton remarked that a civil officer as Pakenham is to be must have a more expensive establishment than a military because considered superior.

The chief advice he gave to P— was like what we have heard from all quarters to be very temperate both in eating and drinking—to avoid going out in the heat of the day—To resist every offer of money from the numbers who will offer to lend it—and to be very attentive to the ladies who are worshipped as idols in India in their evening assemblies. If a young man were to play London dandy or affect nonchalance in the service of the ladies there he would be lost in Society and considered as vulgar past redemption.

Mr. Creed has given us the lists and bills of his sons outfit by which we shall be able to calculate pretty nearly with the difference between civil and military, what will be necessary for P—. Lestock must look them over before I can send them to you. That cannot be I think before Sunday next—Lestocks only leisure day. Pakenham has taken 5 lessons (for 1 sovereign) at a riding house and feels himself the better for it and when he comes back he will take more. 'Come back! Why where is he going?' Oh Ma'am to Paris immediately. He sets out on Thursday next not sure yet whether from London by steam—or *by Dover*[1]. . .

Even in age Hope will stick to us—to me at least and may it I pray Heaven as long as I live.

M E

To Mrs. Edgeworth

n.d.

My dear Mother . . .

Mr. Marshall the poor pale dunced old man who visited us with Mr. Wordsworth came here yesterday with a very pleasing daughter full of gratitude for *my* kindness to him—meaning

[1] An account of the illness of an Edgeworthstown man, now a servant in London, is here omitted.

yours my dear for certainly I was too sick a wretch to do anything for him and was only upon sufferance myself lying like a log upon the sofa. Nevertheless he was charmed with his visit to E Town[1] *and* has done something particularly agreeable to Fanny—invited us to their box at the Opera some night. These Marshalls are rolling in wealth. Think of 2 fine country seats one at the lakes of Cumberland another in Yorkshire and fine house in town and box at the Opera! Well well *he* does not look like the spoiled child of Fortune and yet he is. Would you change your health for his wealth? You'd be a fool if you did.

Ever your impertinent and most affectionate and obliged

Maria Edgeworth

To Mrs. Edgeworth

[n.d.]

I hope this will reach you Jany. 1st 1831 anniversary of Fanny's wedding day and birthday of Marianne &c

Many happy returns of this day to you Dear mother—and grandmamma—and from all I see round me at this moment and from all I hear, feel, and understand you are more likely than any one I know to have every future return of this day happy—blest as you, beyond all I have ever known deserve to be, in your children, your own—and those you have made your own . . .

Monday last I went to Hampstead and the 5 days I spent with the good kind and very entertaining Joanna and Agnes were very happily spent though away from Fanny. More cannot be by mortal pen expressed. They are so much more amusing from being so different than they could be if each were ditto—ditto—and they have such variety of knowledge and *facts* the most rare of all things and they are so *true* that one is never in the condition one is all the time one is reading Lady Morgan's book[2]—alternately admiring and doubting and fearing to be taken in to believe what is all a sham. They are so genuine and warm hearted that if they had not an ounce of literature between them I should nevertheless love them o'er and oer. Too besides I am sure they love me and with poor little ME that goes I own a great

[1] In Sept. 1829. [2] See p. 434 n. 3.

way down into my heart. Out of my own spontaneity I remembered you and Honora very affectionately to them both even before I had received your letters ordering me so to do. They spoke so truly and kindly of you that they deserved all the love I gave them and Lucy's love too they richly merited by the interest they felt for her and then of Honora! I always knew they had liked her but I was not aware how much till the evidence came upon [sic] of their perfect recollection of everything about her and their distinguishing *estimation raisonée* of her character temper and understanding. They told me that they had more inquiries made after her by people who had seen her at their house than for any of my sisters—that to make sure which Miss E was meant they had asked some of the inquirers to describe—answer —'The tall thin elegant looking young lady with a high color and with such a remarkably lady-like manner.'

I saw various comers and goers, morning, dinner and evening visitors at Mrs. Baillies—Whole gangs of mighty rich well drassed remarkably well drassed Mrs. Nevin and Milligans in gangs—most of them nauseously affected—but for those who don't mind that very good people (whom I never desire to see again tho they all worshipped me *quantum suff*). I do not include in the above sweeping [? clausing] a certain Mrs. Hoare who is a perfectly unaffected *charming-good* woman with a sweet voice quite naturally sweet and composed manner. Sick people, of whom many have fallen to her lot, declare that her voice and *ways* are so delightful to them that when they have been used to her they cannot bear to be without her—that her voice medicines them to repose. Joanna Baillie seeing me over head and ears and eyes in love with her said 'I don't wonder at you, for she is just the *same sort* as your own Mrs. Edgeworth (only she is younger and fresher looking) and she has the same power of holding a whole family of people of different ages and humors, and tastes all together, round her, and generation after generation and the wee grandchildren are hanging on her now and she doting on them. Its one of the happiest sights to see. She's such a genuine soul.'

But Mr. Milligan the husband of Joanna's niece is the heaviest bore I ever saw! They say he is in danger of a determination of blood to his head—If so—I suppose it would be a sad thing.

Miss Aikin I saw one evening and one morning and got acquainted with her and thought her very entertaining; though she has some primnesses and *suavities* of manner now and then caught or imitated from Mrs. Barbauld and that odious way of softening the voice below natural and contradicting in the mildest of all possible slow obstinate ways when she is vexed in argument. But upon the whole she is more agreeable than Mrs. Barbauld. She is a merry soul and has humour and tells good stories and is not overgrand. Do you remember a Mr. Mallet we used to know in Dumonts time? He is married again to an agreeable woman and is very agreeable himself and though his white eyelashes and blême look do not promise sense, very sensible—told us many good anecdotes—of Dumont Mirabeau &c. Dumonts Memoirs of his times[1] which are (I dont know when) to appear relate chiefly to the French revolution and his acquaintance with Mirabeau. Mirabeau received immense sums from the Royal family as fees or douceurs in their cause and spent the money in luxuries and extravagance inconcievable. Of all this Dumont—who saw it—tells.

Madame du Cayla's Memoirs[2] he says are entertaining—*One chapter especially* which she has taken from Talleyrands Memoirs.[3] She heard Talleyrand read this chapter to the King and whether with or without Talleyrand's knowledge or consent Mr. Mallet could not tell me published it! Memoires de Fauche Borel[4] he also mentioned as a very curious book—not new—gives a true account of Pichegru and all that work if you have not had enough of it already.

Mr. Wordsworth wife, son and daughter are all at Hampstead at Mrs. Hoares. Poor woman I would not be in her case. I saw wife and daughter and think them terribly tiresome.

[1] *Souvenirs sur Mirabeau et sur les deux premières Assemblées Législatives* (London, 1832).

[2] There are no published memoirs of Madame du Cayla. ME perhaps refers to *Mémoires d'une femme de qualité sur Louis XVIII, sa cour et son règne* (1829). Anon. [compiled by MM. Étienne Léon de Lamothe-Langon, Damas-Hinard, Pierre Armand Malitourne and Maxime-Catherinet de Villemarest].

[3] Talleyrand's Memoirs were not published until 1891. *Album perdu* [attrib. H. Thaband de Latouche], published in 1829, is a book of anecdotes relating to Talleyrand.

[4] Louis de Fauche Borel, *Mémoires dans lesquels on trouvera des détails et des éclaircissements sur les principaux événements de la Révolution* (1829).

Mr. Wordsworth spent an evening at Joanna Baillie's—The last evening—Friday when Fanny and Lestock and Mr. Baillie dined there. Mr. W—says so much too much about everything.[1]

Miss Douglas has sent me a bust of Wordsworth a plaister cast size of Mr. Crampton's and ugly and much in my way. She moreover threatened sending me one of herself along with one of Sir Walter Scott. But I took up my pen and wrote my note praying that these might remain at Chantrey's till I send for them 'as they would run the hazard of being broken in moving from house to house'—a good come off says she. I have not time to dilate upon Miss Douglas but in short she is more rational than she was yet I rejoice that she has left London and that I shall see no more of her . . .

But instead of gossiping about other people's business it would be well if I could go on to my own. I wish I could ever in a letter say the thing I want to say but so much rubbish comes in my way!

On our return on friday night last from Hampstead Fanny and Lestock brought me home [to] their own-own house where I 'hadna been before' and they took me up to 'my own-own room' and I should be very sorry if I were told that I should 'never go there no more' for it is a most comfortable delightful *apartment* which many a peeress's daughter in this great crowded town might well envy me and would doubtless well envy me if they could see it . . .[2]

And now I have at last done with the house and I trust you think I have almost entitled myself to a recommendation as puffer to Christie or any more fashionable auctioneers—and

[1] Fanny reported to CSE (28 Dec. 1830): 'In the evening Dr. Baillie's daughter and her husband joined the party and Mr. Wordsworth and his daughter. He was placed beside me but I do not think he said anything very poetical or agreeable except that Edgeworthstown was the only place in Ireland (except one other) where he saw *groves*—which made it look so much more like an English place of some standing and respectability than other places—which were either quite bare or surrounded by great masses of plantation more for profit than ornament—and his description of the sound of the horses hoofs in some of the forests in France where you could hear the distant echoing through the still trees of the deadened tramp on the mossy yet hard ground formed by the long surface roots from the trees—but he is very tedious he repeats everything so often as to dunce one's understanding and totally destroy ones powers of attention.' Cf. *Memoirs of RLE* (2nd ed. 1821), i. 326–7 for improvements to the landscape at Edgeworthstown.

[2] A long description of Fanny's new house is here omitted.

equal almost to 'the remorseless old man' himself—as the now-Bishop of Lincoln[1] called poor Lord Sunderlin, the day he shewed and puffed Baron's Town to Lord Carrington and all of us—I! then dying of weariness and praying in vain for shortening the view of the premises . . .

She [Fanny] is much obliged to Harriet for the newspaper containing O Connell's strange eloquent nonsensical wicked speech.[2] Why cannot he let well alone. But I dare not touch upon the world of politics—too vast. All is quiet here at present and thats all I will say.

Mr. Creed came in while I was writing yesterday and prevented my finishing this letter but I was not at all angry at being so interrupted. He has been *unanimously* elected Secretary to the Company for the London and Birmingham railroad. Unanimously is very honorable because there were other candidates of merit but who all *vailed* to his superior merit and all their patrons did the same. The emolument is small provisionally—that is till the act of parliament empowering them to proceed has passed—then the annual pay to their Secretary will be *very considerable.* They are all sanguine—sure of getting the act through. Canal shareholders will make no doubt as much opposition as they can.

He is of opinion that my Aunt Mary and Honora, Trent and Mersey and Grand Trunk shareholders, should *not* at this moment be in haste to sell—though he would by all means advise them to decide to sell at the first favorable opportunity—and he who will now have means of judging will keep them in mind and give us timely notice. He means that there will be some revulsion for a short time probably in consequence of some check or disaster or overtrading on the expectations of these rail roads and then panic may lower them below real value and the share holders in canals may profit by a temporary rise and get out.

But I am wrong for telling all this—here. I should have kept it for my *business sheet* to which I will now go—shameful that I did not do *that* first.

[1] The Bishop of Lincoln was John Kaye (1783–1853), who had been tutor to Lord Carrington's son. The visit took place in 1813.

[2] Probably his speech of 26 Dec. in Dublin. O'Connell was at this time torn between his disapproval of Lord Anglesey's proclamation (see p. 461 n.) and his support of the Government over the Reform Bill.

To Mrs. Edgeworth, [*no date*]

Stopped here 5 oclock tuesday—We drove out this morning half way to Hampstead to look for . . . no matter what—Snow thick upon the road—thawing all day too—but snow still to the good—some inches—say 2.

Wednesday—Freezing again— . . .

And now good b'y dear mother
Ever affectionately & gratefully
Your own dear little
Maria E

Maria's *Apartment* Aspect *West*

The square room[1] is my sitting room. It is 12ft 8—10ft 10 and 10ft 2 high. The lesser room is my bedchamber—same height 7ft 5 by 10.10—Just such a little snug sleeping room as I like. The bed is in a recess—bed-stead made of iron to protect me from being eaten up[2]—curtains of white dimity which *I* like.

Both rooms are papered with the same patterned paper of which you have the pattern—raspberry cream color with stripes of darker shade and [? conscience] pattern wriggling through it. It looks much better up than you would imagine—Very like silk and elegant—The border a very small ribbon and staff—brown and green. Both rooms are carpeted throughout—with the same a new and beautiful carpet—the colors suiting the paper charmingly. If possible I will enclose a pattern of it for you.

The curtains of both rooms the same—warm full and handsome—The same which you (Mrs. E) had in your room at Russell place—cut to fit. The windows—2 in the sitting room—one in bedroom are all large and large paned so that the rooms are very light and chearful—looking out on garden *partly*.

You see there are fireplaces in both rooms and dear F and L wanted me to have fires constantly in both but this would be quite too much as I am never in the bedroom except when I am warm in bed under blankets gillore or when I am washing myself—when a body must be cold. I dress in the sitting room where dressing table and wardrobe are. I should hate running about from room to room in search of my *duds* So my Abiding place the sitting room has a constant good fire.

[1] Plan given.

[2] The joints of wooden bedsteads often harboured bed-bugs.

To Mrs. Edgeworth, [no date]

The table marked in the middle of the room is a nice Pembroke table like that in your dressing room only a thought smaller—a drawer *all through*—this table is on castors. Besides this Pembroke table there is a spider table you see—between the two chairs opposite the wardrobe. This spider darling is the very moral of Mrs. Beauforts dear old spider table at Collon.

My green-box—my constant delight stands in the corner by the fire and makes the best because lowest seat possible for putting on shoes and what should be mentioned first—stockings. The wardrobe I believe is an old acquaintance of yours—with bookcase with green silk curtains and glass above and wardrobe below—footstool—Nice mahogany wash hand stand in bedroom *and* every convenience which a pig could *not* want.[1]

To Mrs. Edgeworth

[fragment, n.d. 1831]

Mr. Vernon's a gentlemanlike young man with a spice of humor and that's all. We met them (as he reminded me) at Byrkley Lodge[2]—when he was almost a boy.

Dear natural, feminine obliging charming Mrs. Lockhart played on the harp and sung Scotch ballads to oblige the company tho she knew that she was encompassed round about with critical musicians and that she has no voice to speak of—But she has such delightful expression that to me who have no ear to speak of and who have I hope some heart, she is more interesting than the finest performer could be. Besides she looks so pretty when she is playing on the harp—Pretty perhaps is too much to say but she looks so full of what she is singing or saying as if without the affectation of inspiration she were really inspired excited by the true feeling of what she sings. She sang—tell Harriet—Rob Roy—Bonny house of Airlie—and *Up and Awa' lads*.

[1] A gentleman, who had floored a room with boards for one of his tenants, found the pig one day in sole possession of this room; and upon asking why the pig was allowed to have the best apartment in the house, was answered, 'Becaase, plase your honour, it has every convaniency a pig could want': Glossary by ME in Mrs. Leadbeater's *Cottage Dialogues* (1811), 310.

[2] See above, pp. 146–9.

We are to spend Wednesday evening with her and I am glad of it for I do love her. Not a word of truth in the report of Anne Scotts intended marriage with Mr. Russell. Mrs. Lockhart laughed at the idea—says Mr. R is an old friend and relation and Anne would as soon think of marrying her grandfather if she had one. . . .

We delay returning visits as much as possible that Fanny may get into her drawing rooms before people come trooping. It is awkward having them in here in our little private *confusion* and *snuggery*. The polishing up of the drawing room grates takes a world of time. Lord Pomfrets old rust had so eaten into the steel—and then hanging curtains—3 men are hammering over my head this minute in the library fitting in old bookcases in new places—Such a Buxton puzzle[1] as it [is]. Before breakfast this morning—Lestock and F were *at it* for half an hour and I standing by. There must be some new book cases made but the old will save a *deal*—of time too. This week will make a finish—it is hoped—of the library. But here is the carriage at the door and I must go out and return cards!—

(Returned for our course) Much better than carding—we were let in at Mrs. Lockharts and Mr. L came up and we had half an hours delightful conversation—in short hand—quick—and peals of laughter all round the fire! And in the midst of it I did Mrs. Napiers (secret) business with Lockhart about a review—effectually and as none I flatter myself could have done it but myself. Oh Vanity vanity! thy name is Edgeworth!—not *Maria*. Well well be that as it may it all ended in the very thing of all others to please me—An extempore invitation to dine with them at 6—to be at a twelfth cake drawing and children's Christmas revelling which is to last only till ½ after 8—Then to bed to beds all little *heads*.

The only drawback to my promised pleasure is that much I fear Lestock and Fanny cannot contrive to come before it is all over—To dinner impossible—for *he* cant be home till 6 or ½ after and I must be there for dinner 5 minutes before 6.

However I will hope that F and L may manage it for ½ an hour before the little merry ones are nightcapped. There is to be no

[1] Perhaps an interlocking puzzle of the Derbyshire spar from which obelisks, urns, and inlaid tables, etc., were manufactured at Buxton.

grown up creature except a Mrs. Terry widow of Terry the actor and a Mrs. Wilson a cousin of Mrs. Lockharts and mother of many chickens say 12—her 12 and Mrs. Lockharts 3 and Terry's 3 and thats all. The huge cake is given by whom do you guess? A person—a lady who gave it to Mrs. Lockhart when a child every year and now gives it to her Johnny. In Scotland in Mrs L's home originally it was quite a new thing and the diversion of drawing for King and Queen had all the charm of novelty added to the glories of Royalty. Mrs. Apreece then and Lady Davy now gives the cake. She is really a most good natured woman. *Still* I am glad we are to have the cake without the founder this evening. Lockhart said If you come you shall be Queen—Queen Dowager then it must be—No Queen-Mother! cried he—And laugh we did at the scandalum implicatum till the walls resounded (Pray dont tell Louisa this). No more nonsense at present.

Fanny read to me in the carriage Mr. Stanleys letter upon the proclamation of Lord Anglesey[1]—We made all the observations upon its good intentions and its unlimited dangers which appeared in the paragraph of observations on said letter in same page—which paragraph we of course thought excellent—v. Morning Chronicle of 3d inst—which you will get the day you get this letter. I think the calling out the Yeomanry a wise measure but the power undefined left in the hands of the magistrates and the exhortation to use it are a tempting to abuse that unless party spirit be dead within them it will be most dangerous —Unless in short they be angels instead of men—Angels would have feared to tread where fools will rush on.

No more politics this day—worse than nonsense—Harriet my own curlyheaded [illegible] of wit may see all my nonsense—County of Trim and all. Give my love to her and send me a *fresh* bit of hers in return

Ever yours M E

After luncheon—Went out again to return Lady Theodosia Rice's visit . . . Bought a Boa (not constrictor) since I last laid down my pen—And now must write as fast as pen can go to

[1] Of 25 Dec. 1830. It forbade the tradesmen of Dublin to assemble on the 27th at Phibsborough to march to present an address to O'Connell thanking him for his advocacy of Repeal.

Sophy Ruxton—You see the reason why I am your ever affec Maria E

To Mrs. Edgeworth

Wednesday Morning, 5 Jan. 1831

The royal party at Mrs. Lockharts was even more delightful than I had expected. The word of promise was kept to in the first place about the dinner party—only Mrs. Terry the actor's widow—and 2 cousins of Lockharts a Miss Wilson and brother—No relation to our Wilsons but it was so odd to hear their familiar names and see the figures answering to them quite strangers—rather pleasing but nothing remarkable—Mrs. Terry a genteel figure and has a 'mitigated' accent but Scotch throughout. Her boy is a Godson of Sir Walter Scotts and she told me various instances of Sir Walters good nature to him and to her. I made out in the course of the conversation that Mrs. Terry keeps a seminary or academy or whatever it is right to call it for young ladies.

Dinner [illegible]—family dinner—and Lockhart beside whom I sat very entertaining dropping out drolleries in his half unintelligible half mumbling *blurting* way and always most rank Scotch when most *indignant* and diverting in his anger against whatever crosses his fancy. 'That Philpotts is a very clever man as you say. In conversation I scarce ever met with one quicker—But—I wish he'd get reed of thot hypocreetical manner of his—if it pleased Gud.' Among other anecdotes Lockhart told me—The King has just sent for Chantrey and bespoken a monument for Mrs. Jordan—to be put up where she died near Paris! As it will not be in this country—Very well. And at the same time the King has very properly refused the urgent entreaties of the Fitz Clarences's[1] to make them peers. The Captain Fitz was in such a passion when refused that he tore his commission before his Royal father's face—To no purpose.

Wilkie you know had the honor of making a portrait of his late Majesty a little while before his death. He told Lockhart it

[1] A statue of Mrs. Jordan by Chantrey is in the possession of the Earl of Munster (Gunnis, *Dictionary of British Sculptors* [1953]). She was buried at St. Cloud. Her children by William IV were called Fitzclarence.

was the most difficult and melancholy business for there the man was wasting away frightfully day after day and the King tho he was well enough to look at when dressed up in robes and hung about with orders and ribbons and set up to be seen across the room yet when Wilkie was to go close and get the light upon him to copy him it was he says 'parfaitly frightful—a'w'fu'ly. And then it took 3 hours to get him into those clothes!—to lace up all the bulgings and excrescencies!—The horrid ideot of a Dandy of 60—and what do you think his last coat cost? A blue silk coat it was charged by *Stultz*—six hundred pounds. The Duke of Wellington was in a tow'ring passion about it and swore it should not be pe'd but when he came to examine into it Stultz charged no more than he had a right to. For there he was at Windsor he and two of his men for 3 weeks or more residing o'purpose to try this coat on every succeeding day and cut it and coax it and fine draw it upon the old dying dandy and an alteration and fresh seaming at every sitting for the picture. Why when he was well even he always looked like a great sausage stuffed into the covering but what it must have been at the last—Think o'n't. The Duke agreed that Stultz had not overcharged—You know the most fashionable London tailor and his 2 men—Their time worth as much as a minister o' states and two secretaries.'

From this specimen you may guess how amusing Lockhart was—Many anecdotes of Byron and Campbell to boot. Campbell not only was intoxicated as was evident when he wrote that letter about Lady Byron[1] but is drunk every day or night of his life —and with gin—the wretch!—No matter where he goes—Lost! lost! lost! No pleasures of Hope or of Memory left for him —How melancholy and disgraceful to genius! As Lockhart observed, how little of the truth comes out to the world in all the lives written by professed biographers. 'Moore only gives you

[1] After the publication of Moore's *Life of Byron* (1830) Lady Byron, in order to defend her parents against any charge that they coerced her into the separation, printed privately *Remarks on Mr. Moore's Notices of Lord Byron's Life*. Moore, with her consent, had it bound up with his second volume. The *Remarks* caused an unreasonable outcry against Lady Byron and Campbell wrote an injudicious defence of her in *New Monthly Magazine*, xxviii (1830), 377–82; see also E. C. Mayne, *Life of Lady Byron* (1929), 319–20 and C. Redding, *Literary Reminiscences and Memoirs of Thomas Campbell* (1860), ii. 204–12. Campbell's *Pleasures of Hope* came out in 1799, probably partly inspired by S. Rogers, *Pleasures of Memory* (1792).

slightly to understand that Lord Byron had in his life made somewhat too free with his constitution and therefore a slight illness overset him. But Moore knew as well as I do the truth that he for the last years of his life drank brandy to such excess that not only he never went sober to bed but it often required two stout fellows to drag him by force away from the bottle and to break bottle and glass before they could get him off—else he would have finished himself in some fit sooner even than he did. He never got up till 12 or one oclock and then he was to dose himself with soda water, and plunge into the water and go out rowing if he could just to try to get his body and mind round again after the last nights debauch.' 'But how could he write as he did during the last years?' 'Why if you look at Don Juan the last cantos—much of it is sad stuff much what might be expected from a man in that state. When he was just excited enough and not too much there came some splendid lines—last rays of genius but debased and disgraced! Oh its melancholy to think of!' I was glad to hear this from Lockhart and hope he will take warning—since a man does not die 'much bolder by brandy'. The surgeon who opened Lord Byron after death declared that his liver was all gone and that the brain &c he should have thought belonged to a worn out old man of 66 or 70 instead of to [a] young man of 36 or 38! I asked if Lockhart believed that he had really expressed affection for his wife or child in his last moments or if he had shewn any religious feeling. 'I don't know —hard to say. I should rather think all those last words were more delirium than anything else.' His man Fletcher made a keen observation upon him and Lady Byron, 'It is strange that my lady was the *only* woman who could never manage my Lord.'[1] Even the lowest of his female companions for the time being had absolute power over him and could make him do good or ill as they pleased but Lady Byron *never*. (If half or all I have told you is in the newspaper—please excuse. I have not read it.)

Lockhart tells me that he has some of the proof sheets[2] that

[1] Moore, *Life of Byron* (1830), ii. 223.

[2] Moore recorded in his journal (17 and 21 Dec. 1829 (*Memoirs, Journal and Correspondence*, ed. Lord J. Russell (1853), v. 99, 102) (the cancellation at proof stage of verses in a poem to Lady Jersey which reflected on the king, but there is no reference to cancellation at this stage of Byron's sneers at his wife, nor does Mrs. Langley Moore (*The Late Lord Byron* (1961)) with full access to Murray's archives

were cancelled between Murray and Moore who put their wise heads together about the life as it was going through the press —So to make it consistent they cut out all the parts of the letters that sneered at Lady Byron. For instance I have a capital letter and little poem of Lord Byron's about a Derby charity ball of which her Ladyship was patroness—the refrain of which is

'What matter what comes of sins sinner and all
While my lady the Saint has her charity ball.'[1]

I hope Lockhart will shew me these cancelled pages and yet it is an idle gossiping curiosity unworthy of M E except just for the literary and biographical curiosity of knowing how these things are cooked up for the public and how vain it is to expect to get at truth in biography any more than in history.

So now I will go on to my delightful young innocent Christmas party. After dinner Mrs. Lockhart got up and arranged the round table in the corner of the room on which stood the magnificent iced plumb-cake. There were to be 12 children—impossible to have room for chairs for all round the table. The King and Queen it was settled should alone be invited to the honors of the sitting. But Lockhart in a low voice and with a parental look of great statue-feeling said 'Johnny! There must my dear Sophia you know be a chair for Johnny—at the bottom —yes—here—all's right now.'

Lockhart filled out for us bumpers of Frontignac or some sweet wine and then filled up the bottle with the pure element as he said to make it fit for the children 'who would take anything they had out of a wine glass'. Then corked it up and set it in the midst—A nice desert arranged on our great table for their supper—and Enter first Miss Binning a young lady of 15 who was Johnny's particular friend and had been invited for the occasion by his particular desire to make crowns for the king and Queen—A very nice elegant *looking* Scotch girl slight figure and with all the innocence and simplicity of childhood, the more

make any such suggestion. Moore was 'very desirous to pass them [the events of the Byron separation] over in the manner least offensive to anyone and above all to you' (Ld. Holland to Lady Byron, 9 Mar. 1830, quoted in D. Langley Moore, op. cit., 319–20).

[1] *Poetical Works of Lord Byron* (Oxford Standard Authors, 1957 ed.), 108. Two verses were published in Moore, *Life of Byron* (1830), ii. 540.

striking from her wonderful growth (grand daughter of Doctor Monro and daughter of some Scotch grandee I forget who)—No matter—pleasing in her own right.

Then came from the top of the stairs peals of merry laughter and in came the revel rout—The king and queen with their gilt paper admirable crowns on their heads and little coronation robes. The Queen was the youngest child of Mrs. Lockharts—like a dear little fairy—and the King to match—only a few years older and looking as if he thought himself of years of discretion —*All* the others in various ways pleasing looking children and the girls prettily dressed in white muslin and muslin of varieties of color. If you fancy what pleases your eye thats enough—plenty of ringlets of glossy hair—fair and brown none black—and laughing blue eyes and silky fair complexions. All now look at the tickets they have drawn for their 12th night characters and read them out. One is Lady Georgiana *Marigold*—fair as the driven snow—and much delighted at being a *Marigold*. It's a little *matter* as Falstaff notes that will make a youngster laugh that has never known the heartache.[1]

After laughing and eating as much cake &c &c &c as could well be compassed the revel rout ran up stairs again to the drawing room where open space and verge enough had been made for hunt the slipper—and down all popped in a merry circle—of which you may see the likeness or something like in Rogers pleasures of Memory.[2] When this hunting had lasted till huntsmen and hunted had enough—then came dancing quadrilles &c and as the little and large dancers were all Scotch I need not say how good it was. Mrs. Lockhart in an interlude took me upstairs to her own and her childrens rooms and shewed me how nicely everything is arranged for comfort and happiness. In her childrens sitting room or nursery as she called it there was a great Chinese lantern which somebody had brought them from China and all the room hung with Christmas garlands like one of Sneyds or Francis's doing—3 cages of birds all special favorites quietly asleep heads under wings in the midst of the revelry and noise enough to wake the dead. The only bird that had been turned out was the great parrot of whose biting strangers Mrs.

[1] This is not Falstaff but I have not been able to identify it.
[2] Published 1792.

Lockhart had been afraid. (You recollect Lady Raffles says the beak of the parrot was what alone the children feared who feared not the young bear or tiger.[1]) The parrot was turned into Mrs. Lockharts bedchamber also a wooden horse. In short like some other mothers rooms hers was made a refuge for all outcasts and lost stray things. Mrs. Lockhart is really a delightful creature—the more loveable the closer one comes to her—and in London! How very kind of her to invite me to this quite family party! If she had invented forever she could not have found what would please me more.

But everything must have an end (even this letter). The carriage came for me. I had been living in hopes that Fanny and L would have come in it this evening but Lestock came home late and had business and could not so—it was all over for me and I had an appointment at 9 to go to Lady Theodosia Rice's—where by rights I ought to have dined. Went—All very agreeable there—but so different—like changes in a dream. Still this was a family party to which Spring Rice had most kindly engaged me—Only her own sister and 3 gentlemen. Her sisters name may be found by looking in the Almanack. I have never had time to look and my ear caught only Lady Cecilia—when we were introduced to each other.

Much talk of politics and Mr. O Connell. *S R* (not Sophy Ruxton) says O C is a most distressed man—executions &c and that money is at the bottom of his agitations—that he expects 50 thousand pounds from this collection now making. Government are resolved to let him get it and glad that the people should see and feel that he taxes them—At the moment when he *has* pocketted this—they mean to—XXXXX. My stars! I hope this will excite great wonderment.

My great object through all the quantity I heard and said was to find a moment to speak of Mr. Strickland to the Secretary of Treasury. . . .[2]

Here I was interrupted by a loud knock: Mrs. Carr and Miss I Carr. They were quite surprised by the grand outside of No. 1 and much pleased with the inside though it does not correspond with the outside hopes of magnitude—being much after the

[1] *Memoir of Sir T. S. Raffles* (1830) by Lady Raffles.
[2] A long piece about patronage is here omitted.

fashion of Edgeworthstown house in *respect of* putting the largest front foremost. No sooner had the Carrs said their says and gone their ways than knock! knock! Knock! again

'Captain and Mrs. Basil Hall'

She is more pleasing in appearance and manner than I expected—Nothing either particularly elegant or the contrary but certainly no airs or pretension. He is less on the fret and the fidget than formerly and tho inconveniently for his own and other peoples comfort full of himself yet not so much quite as his confidential letters to me led me to expect. He talked in a frightful manner of putting down some opinion I gave contrary to his in a journal—publishing it! Oh what a pest of society such a journalist—with his journal hanging over one's head so that a poor creature cannot talk nonsense and laugh in freedom—Publicity—versus—Intimacy—Celebrity—versus—Confidence—Fame—versus Friendship. Bad exchanges . . . [end missing]

To Mrs. Edgeworth

1 North Audley Street, Thursday, 6 Jan. 1831

Yes my most kind friend and mother of Fanny I was perfectly *well* and as perfectly happy as any creature in this world could be on my birthday and her wedding . . . You will see by the little sheets I have directed to Honora in this cover that we have gone out some days this week and last but upon the whole we have enjoyed wonderful quiet in London and Evenings at home even as if we were at real home. This room (under the library) being at the back of the house hears none of the rolling of carriages and double thunderings—double-double toil and troubling. Here we sit and study sometimes and nobody a bit the wiser for it (for *study* sometimes read talk and laugh generally—and Lestock laughs as much as any of us—I did not say as loud). Fanny usually reads aloud. She is now reading the Water-Witch[1]—only ½ thro 1st vol—Too soon for such a slow and prudent person as I am to speak an opinion. Lestock sometimes [reads] and he reads exceedingly well—that is with sense

[1] *The Water Witch; or the skimmer of the seas. A tale*. By the author of *The Borderers*, etc. [J. F. Cooper] (1830).

and no whine or tone or monotonous cadence and he thinks so much of what he hears read and criticises so well—not as a mere literary critic appealing to authorities or sticking to the *Traditions* but what is to me infinitely more profitable and agreeable besides the variety as a man new to literature but old to the world and to right sense and feeling.

I have a delightful little table—oval with 2 leaves which I can let up or down as I choose to spread or diminish my space—2 feet 6 from one tip of the wing to the other by 7 ft 6—in middle utmost breadth of oval—Very steady Honora—no castors but so light that I can lift it and desk on it easily and quickly—a drawer all through and all to myself. And here I sit with a skreen at my back by the side of the fire and here I can scribble away and hear the scribble scribble and squeak squeak of my own pen or to give the better measure of 'Silence was pleased'[1] I could hear the tick tick of a watch. I had no conception that I could live so quietly and comfortably at home in London.

We are making the most of the *emptiness of the world* at present all who are properly called the World being out of Town at this season, and others have leisure left them to be happy—synonymous often I believe with being happy . . .

This letter was interrupted by morning visits—Aunt Alicia—full of a new house in Baker Street—an excellent house which I hope she will decide Francis to purchase. She wants however to find a house with equal conveniences and with the further convenience of being *near* the London University[2] for her sons. But this is out of all probability and she had better take the goods the Gods provide her and not disgust Good-luck by wanting to have it Good luck & *Co.* After she had sat half an hour see-sawing Alicia went away and I to Miss Gerrard about white blonde gauze sleeves, without which there is little possibility of living—decently.

Then again to my letter but scarcely had I taken up my pen and breathed when other morning visitors entered—The Miss Jacobs whom I wished up Jacobs ladder. But I was wrong for they proved quite entertaining—Especially one you never saw

[1] *Paradise Lost*, iv, l. 604.

[2] University College, London, at first called London University, was founded in 1826. It was and is in Gower St.

who has been about 3 or 4 years ago in Germany Poland &c &c. They told us heaps of things and good things. They knew a certain old Princess Czartorinska in Poland who was the most amusing collector and arranger of curiosities I ever heard of—national souvenirs of all sorts. She had one pavillion aux grands hommes with Shakespears chair *real* bought at Stratford upon Avon—beside Rousseaus Chair &c—Then another for Prussian relics; she was well acquaint' with Frederick the Great but did not love him a bit. What Pole could? Had his pen—the very pen (sworn to) with which he signed the partition of Poland. No more curiosities at present. The Poles detest Russians of course but not the Emperor so much as Constantine. He seems to be half brute and half fool. His delight is when strangers come to Warsaw English especially to have them brought before him and to make horrid faces to frighten them. The Jacobs escaped this because he was not there at the time and all the Warsaw people congratulated them. The people at the custom house begged of Mr. Jacob as a particular favor to be permitted to look at his daughters. They had seen Englishmen—but never had seen an English lady. They marvelled unquenchably at the ladies having travelled so far and to their country—for what? The Polish common people in Warsaw were dressed in long robes like jews and their long lank hair parted on forehead hangs down over their shoulders. The Poles rich and poor are abominably dirty—I mean all those (with Czartorinska exceptions) who came under the cognizance of Miss Jacobs senses . . .

I have only 5 minutes to make up this letter with all its multifarious contents and multitudinous covers

So—affecy. yours M E

To Mrs. Edgeworth

15 Jan. 1831

My dearest Mother

My foot is almost afoot again—and in every other respect I am perfect and perfectly yours—to question—or command or commission—or scold—but above all to love—M E

I have become acquainted with Dr. Fitton and like him much tho he is like Dr. Brewster a little fond of being in hot water—

and touchy. I advise Honora to get as soon as she can a volume just published of Lardners Encyclopaedia[1]—What *number* of *vol* no mortal can say—But this volume is by Herschel. The title is 'Discourse on the study of natural philosophy' price *6sh. worth any money*. I first borrowed then bought—Adieu—Spring Rice tells me that O Connell wants to be Lord Viscount Dinivane?[2] (or whatever his strange place is called)—More likely wants to be King of Ireland. He really looks to it they say. Much I fear Lord Anglesey is not a match for him. Doctor Holland who came in just as I was finishing my last words about Herschel sat ¾ of an hour and his remark is that O Connell sets his astucity in law against Lord Anglesey and the whole power of government. Whoever first loses temper will lose the game. I fear that will be Lord Anglesey. The proclamations it is supposed are all written in England. Ministry are frightened at the renewal of Burnings here. They do very wrong to *pardon* after the Judge's sentences—to pardon those not recommended by them to mercy.[3] Dr. Holland had just seen Justice Alderson one of those judges who was much displeased by it. He and the others had sat up all night to discuss with the greatest care which had any claim to be recommended to mercy—Then for ministry to get the popularity by this false mercy and to throw the odium of severity upon their own judges and to weaken the power of law by increasing the chance and hope of escape is . . . doing business no how.

finis—

[1] *Preliminary Discourse on the Study of Natural Philosophy* (*Lardner's Cabinet Encyclopaedia*, vol. xiv, 1830).

[2] Darrynane. Spring Rice's comment is unjust. (Cf. also the comment on p. 467.) O'Connell's 'astucity in law' was employed in the organization of successive anti-Union societies under different names, each in their turn suppressed by Government proclamation.

[3] The first rioters sentenced at East Kent Quarter Sessions had been given only three days imprisonment but when the rioting continued with more violence and spread to other counties in November and December punishments inflicted at later trials were much harsher, too harsh in the opinion of some people (e.g. *Morning Chron*. 22 Jan. 1831). The severity of the sentences varied according to locality but in the whole country 19 were hanged, mostly for arson, 644 jailed, and 481 transported. 233 out of 252 sentenced to hanging were reprieved (E. J. Hobsbawm and G. Rudé, *Captain Swing* (1969), 253–63). ME probably refers here to the reprieves. Irish experience had led both her and her father to set a high value on law and order.

To Mrs. Edgeworth

1 North Audley Street, Thursday morning,
20 Jan. 1831

My dear mother . . .

Meanwhile I write this 'certificate of existence'—moreover an affidavit of my being afoot again. After being poulticed night and morning for 4 days and nights by no hands but those of Fairly-fair and Kindly-kind, the swelling has now quite gone down except one spot about the size of a small pigeons egg and the pain is all gone and nought remains but a delightful blue-black! giving unspeakably satisfactory evidence of how very *bad* it *must have been*. I have now only a bandage to support weakness of relaxed muscle and tender consciences of friends—can go down stairs now without putting right foot foremost always like a child—And wear a black satin shoe like another! Last night at a dance at Mrs. Elliotts—Miss Lucy—where Mrs. E and many inquiring friends hoped Miss Lucy was well and that she had not suffered by the pleasure she gave and received in London with sundry pretty things about 'Simplicity—charming!—Sweet girl! &c &c.'

Then came simpering up an 'Et moi-aussi-Mademoiselle-face!' of a little weather proof Colonel who claimed introduction to me as having been my sister Miss Lucy Edgeworths chaperon, at the Ancient Music. I did not tell him what Fanny told me that my sister Miss Lucy thought he a great bore but I said with the sweetest smile the sweetest things—about gratitude—and delight and good nature—in London twice as good as elsewhere—and the *last* was true!—much to say of a compliment any where. Mr. Charles Elliott—eldest son whom Lucy never had the supreme happiness of seeing or hearing kept me in talk or in listening half the night with Norway *fiords* and forests and glaciers and boors and with Moscow and the Kremlin and the Hymalaya mountains! for he had been everywhere and seen everything—Leopard hunts in India and all—and told me a new circumstance of the often described Leopard hunts, that they separate the leopard at last from the prey when it is necessary to preserve it or its skin from being mangled by piercing it to the heart that the blood spouts copiously and then holding a bowl of blood to tiger he turns to drink the irresistible temptation and they seize his loosened prey.

Mr. C Elliott is a tall thin goodnatured coxcombical spoiled child of 30 whose father and mother having not been able to conceal from him that they think him the 8th wonder of the world have at last brought him to acquiesce in their opinion. Saw some good waltzing *though* as I have just read in Lord Byrons letters '*The English never waltzed well and never will.*' Saw also that *graceless* romping galopade!—which I would willingly banish to the servants hall as poor country-dances were to the kitchen.

Good music I believe—But I own I was talking and *hearing* most of the night (in another room) with Mr. Edmonstone who is like a very clever good natured quick eyed grey little baboon. My leading questions to him were all Indian for Pakenhams sake. Sir T Munro's letters[1] aided me delightfully and Sir Stamford Raffles[2] in getting into Mr. Edmonstone's good graces and helped him in getting over his excessive shyness which a world and two worlds of practice Indian and European have not been able to conquer. But with one jump over his reserve when we got alone in a corner, he fell to work and told me all I wanted —1st that my brother Mr. Pakenham is a charming youth. Only think of that! the word was charming I will swear—'A youth of great talents and acquirements who will do honor to himself and his friends.' 'And how much money do you think he will want besides his outfit when he gets to India—first setting out?' 'Why—about—let me see—3000 rupees—say £300.' 'Oh!hh! I thought—a friend told me—one hundred pounds would do.' Quick turned grey monkey's intelligent eyes upon me and he answered 'Don't believe it—he would be in debt—and would never get out of it—never. Don't try it—try £200—the least that can do if he is to appear like other people—and you would put him below his equals—cruel for a young man—and such a one. I can judge—I've two sons there.' 'But your sons—their style &c' 'Well! well!—no no. They cost me 4 and 5—but I tell you 2 hundred is the least—try that.'

Before I left the affair of my foot and poultices I ought to have noted that Lady Hunter Basil Halls mother in law gave Fanny

[1] G. R. Gleig, *Life of Major General Sir Thomas Munro, Bart., K.C.B.* (1830).
[2] See p. 467 n. 1.

on the spur of the occasion the best receipt for a poultice that ever was (probatum est). She had it from her mother who had it from her maid who I am clear had it from lackey necessity the old mother of invention—Bran boiled and stirred with a tallow candle till the said tallow candle melts and is all stirred away—To be put on warm but not very hot—It keeps warm and moist all night and never gets hard agen . . .

Now sign seal and deliver—for the bare life Ever yr M E

To Mrs. Edgeworth

1 North Audley Street
Saturday morng. 22 Jan. 1831

. . . Indeed we are a happy family! I may throw myself back in my chair and say like Lord Wellesley when half seas over—and '*happy*' is better than '*wonderful*' or glorious. I forget which Lord Wellesley said of his own. I left off at the Duchess of Wellington. I had resolved I believe you know not to take any notice of her Grace this time, as she took no notice of me last time I was in London but when I heard she was seriously ill my heart softened towards her and I had determined to write to ask if she wished to see me. 100 of the little London remoras delayed and stopped me—and fortunately—I almost always find cause to rejoice instead of deploring when I have delayed to execute an intention so that I must conclude my fault is precipitation not procrastination—the very day I had had my pen in my hand to write to her and had been called upon to write some other letter much to my annoyance—much to my delight a few hours afterwards came a little pencil note from the Duchess, begging me to come to Apsley house if I wished to give pleasure to an early friend who could never forget the kindness she had received at Edgeworthstown (If I can find the note you shall have it in her own better words). I was *in* or under my sprained foot at the time and had not been able to put it to the ground but I resolved (as she said '*the sooner the better*') to go next day at the hour appointed 3 oclock. I found it quite easy (with motive) to trample on impossibilities especially with the help of Fanny's arm to lean upon and time enough for right-foot foremost-ing down stairs like a child just learning to walk and clinging to the banisters. There was no going up stairs at Apsley House for the Duke has had apartments on the ground floor appropriated—a whole suite to the Duchess's use that now she is ill she may not have the difficulty of going up and down. So leaning on Fanny's arm I had only to go through a long passage which led to something—a magnificent—not from its size height length or breadth magnificent but from its contents—the presents of cities—kingdoms and sovereigns. In the midst, on a narrow, high mattrassed sofa like Lucys all white—and paler than ever Lucy was paler than marble—more delicate than life lay—as if laid out a corpse the Duchess of Wellington. Always little and delicate looking she now looked a miniature figure of herself in waxwork. As I entered I heard her voice before I saw her; before I could distinguish her features among the borders of her cap—only saw the place where her head lay, on the huge raised pillow. The head moved the head only and the sweet voice of Kitty Pakenham exclaimed 'Oh Miss E you are the truest of the true—the kindest of the kind'—and a delicate little death like white hand stretched itself out to me before I could reach the couch and when I got there I could not speak—not a syllable. I dared not trust my voice but she with most perfect composure—more than composure, cheerfulness of tone and look went on speaking—I don't know what she said just then—tho' it was something about Fanny. As she spoke, all the Kitty Pakenham expression appeared in that little shrunk face and the color of life the eloquent blood very faint color—spoke—and the smile of former times and the teeth—pearly no more—[but ?] still and ladylike—tho much larger in proportion appeared. And she raised herself more and more on her elbow as she spoke and spoke with more and more animation—in charming language and with that peculiar grace, and elegance of kindness—recollected so much of past times of my father most particularly whose affection she convinced me had touched her deeply and whose admiration I more than ever felt had been deserved.

Opposite to her couch, there was a deep glass case such as is seen in museums—the whole side of the room—in 3 compartments—middle projecting. At the back of the middle hung the gold *shield* in imitation of the shield of Achilles, with all the

Duke of Wellingtons victories embossed on the margin and in the centre the Duke and his staff on horseback—the groupe surrounded with blazing rays. This magnificent present you know was from the City of London. In the compartments on either side were the great candelabras belonging to the massive plateau given by Portugal (which you know cannot be lifted without machinery)—The figures multitudinous and ornaments belonging to this plateau lying on their backs in another glass case filling half the opposite side of the room. At either end in deep glass cases from top to bottom ranged the services of Dresden china and of German presented by the Emperor of Austria and King of Prussia—On each of the plates some medallion of great man or some allusion to great victories.

While I looked at these the Duchess raising herself quite up exclaimed with weak voiced strong souled enthusiasm 'All tributes to merit—there is the value! and pure! pure!—no corruption—ever *suspected* even. Even of the Duke of Marlborough that could not be said so truly.' The fresh untired enthusiasm she feels for his character—for her own still youthful imagination of her hero—after all she has gone through is quite wonderful! most touching. There she is fading away—living to the last still feeding when she can feed on nothing else on his glories on the perfume of his incense as fairies live on perfumes of less intellectual kind. When I left her it was with anxious desire to see her again. She begged that I would and as often as I could. She says she always dines between 2 and 3 and an hour after dinner lies down. I now understood—but scarcely knew how to believe that she did not always lie in this outstretched way.

She had heard that I was in London from Lord Downes (*ci devant Sir Ulysses Burgh* you know) and he had heard of me from the Countess de Salis. Fanny and I went to an evening party at her (fine) house 2 days after we had been at Apsley house. Met Lord and Lady Downes. He is with all the Burgh manner and vivacity and intelligence of eye—agreeable and a fine soldier. The Duchess spoke most highly of him—the Duke's opinion of him and his attachment to the Duke &c. Lady Downes is a Miss Burleigh style of woman in her looks tho' handsomer but something peculiarly Irish—vulgar—smiling—*company-vivacious*—affected but I dare say very good natured. She was I am told a great Carlow heiress. I dare say you know more about it than I do so I need no more labor that point. She explained to me that the Duchess of Wellington is not in such a hopeless state as I thought—that she gets up and sits up and is not confined as I fancied to that sofa—can walk as well as I can perhaps better at present—goes to dinner at least to dinner table tout comme un autre. Her physicians in short do not give up hope or do not allow that they despair. Her disease is not an inward cancer as I had been told but an inward rupture caused by violent coughing. But notwithstanding what friends and physicians say my own impression is that she cannot be much longer for this world. I hope she will not outlive the pleasure she now feels, I am assured in the Duke's returning kindness. I hope she will not last too long and tire out that easily tired pity of his. As to Love however of kin—it is out of the question now and that must be some security as it were for what remains to do.

He was not in Town at the time of my vis. He is now and some day I hope he may chance to come in while I am sitting with her. One quarter of an hour in company with them would tell me more—even one look would say more to my satisfaction than volumes of reports—on dits.

I took Pakenham with me yesterday morning to Apsley house—went in first and asked permission to present Pakenham E Sir E Pakenham's godson. With tears in her eyes she replied 'Oh do do yes yes.' She received him most kindly and among other things offered to introduce him to that *Fritz* who has at last turned out admirably and is now a judge at Madras. She said the Duke when he was asked the other day what education was best for an officer replied 'Such as you would give to a clergyman—I mean to the most highly cultivated *gentleman*. Officers now want all the knowledge (*classical* inclusive) which can be acquired.' Strong—from the Duke of Wellington in confirmation of my fathers principles in Professional Education.

I asked that P. might be permitted to see the gallery—Spanish pictures &c. The Duchess rang for the show woman and Fanny went with P and I remained with Duchess. As Fanny will tell you the gallery is *superbe* but few pictures are yet up and she is indignant at their letting the gigantic statue of Napoleon remain as heretofore cooped up in that nook of the staircase.

But I have no more time for indignation. I must leave Mr. and Mrs. Hope for another day because this day is gone.

I can only tell you that I wrote yesterday to Sir James Mackintosh to beg half an hour from him to introduce P—that he might see before leaving these countries &c &c the man who as Lord Byron (v his letter)[1] says left the greatest impression upon his mind of all the London great genii. Miss Mackintosh answered that her father is leaving Town and had but yesterday evening to tea or this morning breakfast in his power begged me to chuse and all manner of Compliments. The carriage had been dismissed and coachman gone to his lodgings au bout du monde so tea yesterday was impossible but this morning Pakenham and I went to 9 oclock breakfast—quite in time—urn came in after us hissing 'all right'. Mackintosh was excessively agreeable and kind to P and invited him to come in the evening of Monday. We 3 *dine* with him on Monday. I hope you will rejoice in my assurance. I think it is your principle as it is mine that it is of great advantage to a young man to have early seen the celebrated of his own or rather of the passing day.

5 oclock—Returned from driving over half the '*West End*' and paying a ½ a Cwt of useless visits and have a few minutes before the bellman breaks my heart . . . And now I have done—

Ever yours affectionately
Maria Edgeworth

To Mrs. C. S. Edgeworth

1 North Audley Street, [30 January 1831]†

. . . We 3 had a very pleasant *little* dinner at Putney last week with Captain Basil Hall—Chantrey Mrs. Chantrey and a Mr. Stokes (by way of a clever man and a humorist) and Lady Hunter Mrs. Halls mother. Chantrey has a good honest indignant English soul with a broad open jolly English face that could not be mistaken in any part of the world . . . We have also spent an evening at Mr. Jacobs and his daughters met a Mr. Jones whom I liked

[1] Byron, *Letters and Journals*, ed. Prothero (1898), ii. 256, letter of Byron to Moore, 1 Sept. 1813, describing Mackintosh as 'that brightest of Northern constellations'.

and find he knows Sneyd and was with him about some house (Brasted). He regrets S and you did not settle there—I told him how comfortable you are and well pleased with your Brandfold —2 dinners and evenings at Captain Beauforts where we met various literary and scientific people and this as well I can recollect all—except 2 dinners at Dr. Hollands which I believe I registered in some former note. I sprained my foot in coming down the steps from Spring Rices last thursday and was poulticing and bandaging it for 3 days and confined to my room from which or indeed from sofa I could not stir . . .[1]

The Duke had a suite of apartments on the ground floor all prepared for her and went down to Stratfieldsay when he heard she was so ill and had her brought up. They say he is very kind now and that she says she is happier now than ever she was. The only ornament she wore was a gold clasped cameo of him over her snow white wrapping gown over her wasted wrist—On the little table beside her a picture—miniature of the Duke by a Spanish painter—like but a hard likeness—and two gold bracelets with cameo heads of her two sons which they had brought her from Rome. She spoke of the Duke with all the enthusiasm and affection with which I have ever heard her speak . . . [no signature]

To Honora Edgeworth

1 North Audley Street, 10 February 1831

My dear Honora

I am just come home after breakfasting with Sir James Mackintosh. Fanny was with me—double! double!! joy and pleasure but we both feel as (we suppose) dram drinkers do after swallowing their *mornings*. My hand and my mind are both unsteadied unfitted for business or sober thought after this intoxicating draught. Oh what it is to come within the radiance of genius[2] not only every object appears so radiant, so couleur de rose but

[1] An account of a visit to the Duchess of Wellington is here omitted. See above, p. 474.

[2] A quotation from a letter of her sister Anna, written on the death of Dr. Beddoes.

I feel myself so much encreased in powers, in range of mind, with a vue d'oiseau of all things raised above the dun dim fog and bustle and jostle of a common-place life. Oh what a difference—inconcievable till *repeatedly* felt and compared! How can any one like to live with their inferiors—prefer this to the delight of being raised up by a superior to bright regions of genius. The inward sense of having even this perception of excellence is a pleasure so far beyond what flattery *can* give. Flattery is like a bad perfume—Nauseous and overpowering after the first waft and hurtful as well as nauseous . . .

Sharp who was at Sir James M's at breakfast talked over O Gorman Mahon's speech.[1] The nickname parliamentary for him is Ogreman. He first wanted to challenge the Attorney General and then to challenge the Speaker—with the whole house at his back! The house resolved to hear him with the utmost patience and cold silence. *He* felt this but Hunt as Sir James Mackintosh observed had not been enough in gentlemens company even to feel this sort of *excommunication*. Hunt was quite abject in his tone and manner they say—down to the ground to *'the' Honorable house* as he *repeatedly* said. This expression of 'the honorable house' Mackintosh says has not been used these many years—quite out of date—and marked his ignorance. He was not bad or good enough to excite any attention not absurd enough for a good butt nor powerful enough for a demagogue parliament man so there is an end of him. O Gorman felt that he was *undone* when he had heard out and expressed this as he left the house. It is very good for such people to be under the peine forte et dure of good company. They never know what they are and what they are not till they have thus taken and given their measure in public.

Sir J. Mackintosh gave us an account of a most absurd Russian traveller *Turganoff* (to whom he has given the nickname of Turk-enough).[2] Last night at Mr. Hallams this man went up to Sir James M and told him that he was the bearer of the Duc de Broglie's best respects to him tho' continued he you are aware

[1] On 8 Feb. the O'Gorman Mahon made an intemperate anti-Union speech on a motion to produce the proclamations of the Lord Lieutenant.

[2] Alexander Ivanovich Turganiev (1784–1845), traveller; known to have been in England Dec. 1830 to June 1831. He was no relation of the novelist.

that you *are no great favorite* with the Duchesse de Broglie and Miss Randal because you have spoken rather too freely of Madame de Stael's writings. What could this oaf be thinking of? Sir James M you know wrote the highest eulogium[1] that ever was published of her works and was her most admiring and admired worshipper—and *Miss Randall* too! You know her history. As Sir James goodnaturedly said the poor man had mistaken me for somebody else and did not know what he was saying. Next he told Sir James M that a literary friend of his had informed him that Bacon wrote Latin so habitually that he could not write good English. My good Sir go back to your literary friend and tell him from me that Bacon wrote latin so little that all his *latin works* were translated for him from his own English and we English consider him as one of the masters of English style.[2] *Moral*—How careful people should be not to talk of what they do *not* understand to those who do! But 'Fools rush in where angels fear to tread'. When I quoted this line this morning (apropos to this Russian or to Hunt or O Gorman, I forget which) Sir James Mackintosh delighted with it exclaimed that it would make such a good caricature and 'let the fool have his fool's coat and bells too. They will make a figure in caricature' &c. One of Sir James M's happy arts of pleasing in conversation is that he takes up the ideas of others so kindly and dresses them to the best advantage. Il rèleve si bien But—double rap rap rap

'Sir John Swinburne and Miss Swinburne'—come to me upon Miss Chawners business—(Lady Farnhams protegée—Cartoon paper)

Adieu my dear Honora—
Ever affecy yours M E

After visit ended

Sir J Swinburne says that Miss Chawner won't do at all—that young artists of merit are now copying miniatures on ivory at 5 shillings apiece—and even real original paintings selling for next to nothing—People all fearing to lose what they have

[1] *Edinburgh Review*, xlii (Feb. 1813).

[2] Bacon wrote fluent Latin, not in a very classical style. He employed translators, including Herbert and Hobbes, from absence of time probably, not talent.

of property and life instead of thinking of purchasing from artists.

Private

N.B. I was undone yesterday by a long interesting talk I had yesterday with Mr. Whishaw by appointment about the passage against Sir S Romilly in Byrons letters[1] accusing him of taking a *retainer* and then turning to the other side. I have not time to explain.

. . . [no signature]

To Mrs. Edgeworth

11 February 1831

My dear mother

You must have seen in the papers the death of Mr. Hope and I am sure it shocked you but it was scarcely possible that it could strike you so much as it did me—I who had seen him but a few days before, I who had been rallying him upon his being a hypochondriac—I who had been laughing at him along with Mrs. Hope for being as I thought merely in the cold fit after having been in a hot fit of enthusiasm while finishing his book![2] He knew too well poor man what we did not know. I believe I had not even time to describe to you the impression that visit made to him. I had actually forced Mrs. Hope to go up and say that he must see me—that an old friend who had such a regard for him and for whom I knew he had a sincere regard must be admitted to see him even en robe de chambre. He sent me word that if I could bear to see a poor sick man in his night cap he begged I would come. So I did and followed Mrs. Hope through all the magnificent apartments and then up to their attics and through and through room after room till I got into his retreat

[1] In 1816 Romilly had won for Byron an injunction in a case of a spurious publication. Byron contended that Romilly had a general retainer from him and was therefore debarred from acting for Lady Byron over the separation (Byron, *Letters and Journals*, ed. Prothero (1901), iv. 19, 268, 275, 316, 319, 480).

[2] 'Essay on the Origin and Prospects of Man.' It was suppressed by his executors because of the latitudinarian views expressed in it.

and then a feeble voice from an arm chair 'Oh my dear Miss Edgeworth My kind friend to the last'. And I saw a figure sunk like La Harpe—in figured silk robe de chambre and night cap—death in his pallid sunk shrunk face.[1] A gleam of affectionate pleasure lighted it up for an instant and straight it sunk again. He asked most kindly for my two sisters—faultered at their married names but shewed he recollected them perfectly. 'Tell them I am glad they are happy.' The half finished picture of his 2d son was in the corner beside his arm chair as if to cheer his eyes. 'By an Irish artist (he politely said to me) of great talent.' When I rallied him at parting on his low spirits and said 'How much younger you are than I am!' &c 'No no' shaking his head 'not in mind—not in the powers of life. God bless you—Goodby.' I told him I would only say *au revoir*.

And that never came. I am glad I forced myself into his presence. It seemed to give him pleasure and I never should have forgiven myself if I had neglected to go to see him. I went again a week afterwards. The porter answered not at home. I insisted that my card should be sent up to *Mr.* Hopes room even if Mrs. Hope were not at home and wrote on it in pencil—after my name—an old friend who begs to see Mr. Hope for 5 minutes. His own man came out to say Mr. Hope was so ill that day he could not see any body. I knew the man could not have had time to go all the way up to his masters room and felt quite provoked but there was nothing more could be done—pulled up the glass and drove home. It was but the next day but one afterwards Fanny read his death in the papers. It was dreadfully sudden to us. What must it have been to Mrs. Hope! I am sure she had no idea of its coming so soon if at all.

I forgot to say—As I got up I told him laughing he was only ill of a plethora of happiness that he had everything this world could give &c and only wanted a little adversity. Yes said he I am happy. Blest with such a wife and such a son! He looked with most touching gratitude up to her and she drew back without speaking. I wish to record this while fresh and full in my mind. Oh I

[1] Jean Francois La Harpe, the French literary critic (1739–1803), whom the Edgeworths met in Paris the year before he died (*Mem.* i. 153; E. Inglis Jones, *The Great Maria* (1959), illustration facing p. 64). At the time when the Edgeworths knew him he was in serious trouble with the literary world for his acid *Correspondance littéraire* (1801).

cannot tell you the impression the whole scene left on my mind —the very day after the sight of the Duchess of Wellington.

Post—cant wait

for M E

I know 0 of Mrs. Hopes circumstances—have written to her you may be sure.

To Honora Edgeworth

19 February 1831

My dear Honora

First for business . . . Luckily I had *penned* this far safely down when in came 2 most entertaining gentlemen who have completely robbed us of our morning and we can't be angry with them for it—Mr. Sedgwick—deposed or resigned monarch of the geological society—and Mr. Whewell—Both Cambridge men—friends and charming both tho one is black ugly the other fair handsome most agreeable quick conversation shining playfully with science and literature—and free from all testiness and susceptibility of some of the scientific grandees—Vide Babbage par excellence.

I quite agree my dear Honora in all you say and feel about Moore's life of Lord Byron and about Byron's own letters. Lord Lansdowne beside whom I sat at delightful dinner last tuesday said in his low voice in his snugs to me just the same that you do that he could not help liking Lord Byron often in reading his letters—that his impulses were good and his natural dispositions generous as many of his actions and expressions proved even late in life. Lockhart told me (I forget whether I told you this before) that in the mass of Mss letters which he has seen Lord Byron had abused outrageously every friend he ever had in the world at some time or other—the Countess Guiccioli in the grossest terms. If *all* had been published the whole truth would have convinced the public that Lord B's opinion of Sir S Romilly or of anybody was not worth a straw. I like Lockharts review of the book in the quarterly[1] extremely—all but 2 re-

[1] *Quarterly Review* xliv (1831), 168. The paragraphs to which ME objected deal with Byron's attitude to religion.

marks at the end—on the sending for the witch and on the last words. The witch was either a caprice or done to make folk stare. The words were delirious evidently or not sufficient to ground any rational deduction upon or moral lament.

Well there is an end of that and an end of my day—Carriage at the door. I am glad Mrs. Beaufort is better and wish she was safe in Dublin.

Fanny was with me at a grand party at Lansdowne house. I will tell you the only thing that she will not tell you better—that she looked remarkably well and was *remarkably* well dressed —Geranium silk and hair (by hairdresser) becomingly dressed with Vandyke comb. There were two prettier women than herself in the room but not one more gentlewomanlike. Lady Lansdowne was very kind—especially in advising me not to sit (ever) on a cane chair with a velvet gown—Miss Fox delightful —I beside her on sopha—Lord King behind at our elbow most agreeable and some other gentleman whose name I am yet to learn delectable—about 200—all—all—select—except Lady Dudley Stuart and how she came there Heaven knows—I believe through Lady Holland—née Lucien Bonaparte's daughter—a divorcée or worse a *bigamist* and worse again ugly and *ill* dressed —wonderful for a Frenchwoman.

Fanny is well—So am I—Lestocks leg coming on and I am forced to be this inst. affec yr M E

To Honora Edgeworth

4 March 1831

. . . Fanny is soon to give a dinner and I shall delight in seeing the ice pails the glass bowl (Aunt Mary's wedding present) make their appearance. At a dinner yesterday at Mr. Lockharts I heard Lady Lyndhurst (of whom more hereafter) and Mr. Hay (Colonial Secretary and mighty fine man) and Mr. Rogers discussing the merits of iced wines—and Lady Lyndhurst quoted a cookery-book lately published by Lady Charlotte Bury (it is said) for quiet people, in which it is laid down as law that *your champagne* must be in ice an hour and ½ at least before dinner.

To Mrs. Edgeworth, 14 March 1831

. . . I have not time for any diverting matter except—I must say—(private for you and Mamma) that I never in my life was in a room with any lady that *flirted* so atrociously as Lady Lyndhurst. She is vulgar and bold and shews legs and arms &c beyond all that I could have concieved. Mr. Hay and her Ladyship sat at a round table in the inner drawing room making such love! I was the *only* lady except Mrs. Lockhart at the dinner. I felt awkwardish—but I must finish

Ever hurriedly yr
Maria Edgeworth

To Mrs. Edgeworth

Monday, 14 March 1831

My dear mother

. . . Did I tell you that the Duchess of Northumberland left her card and at last the other day we came to the actual sight and speech of the Marchioness of Wellesley. We were fortunately at home when she and Miss Caton called and with us was a person whom they were delighted to see and who was charmed to see Lady Wellesley—Sir John Malcolm. Success to myself! who had had the assurance to write to beg to see him the very instant I chanced to hear of his having landed and thanks Oh 1000 times more thanks to his own good nature in thus coming to see me when he had only come to Town for a few hours. Lady Wellesley and he talked most agreeably over former times in India and later times in Ireland and all that might have been formal in a first morning visit between people who met for the first time was thus taken off by this agreeable common uncommon acquaintance. Fanny came out of her retreat in the library (it was before her illness) and all was pleasant. Lady Wellesley is not nearly so tall and magnificent a looking person as I had expected but more delicate—not much taller than Honora—say 5ft—5—Very ladylike in her motions and manner—as unlike all we have seen or imagined of Americans—her face beautiful—ivory colour—fine eyes. Her manner is rather *too* English—too composed—compassé rather more than appears quite natural—as if studiously *formed* on English manner and as if she were steering diplomatically clear of all difficulties yet without having been born or bred long enough in a court to do it instinctively—not the perfection of art which is never to let the art be seen. People say too often she has a remarkably good manner. Perfectly good manners should never be remarkable. It should be felt not seen. By what she praised it was easy to see what she wished to be admired for herself. She praised the Queens manner for never letting her emotions get the better of her. She influences the king and influences everything of course but in the best way—'never lets temper interfere &c and never shews that she has any power. Never speaks on politics nor the king either in his private society'. This last Lady Wellesley answered to Sir J. Malcolm who in his Admiral Pakenham way blurted out (purposely) some indiscreet question.

The carriage is at the door and I must cut short.

Sir J Malcolm is as entertaining and delightful as his Persian sketches and as instructive as his Central India[1] . . . Ever yr M E always well

To Harriet Butler (née *Edgeworth*)

North Audley Street, Wednesday, 16 March 1831

My dear Harriet . . .

I think Mr. Strickland will go with me to Lady Lansdownes tonight where I must go for an hour or so—by particular desire—and I hope Mr. S will have an opportunity of putting his thoughts on the poor laws into Lord Lansdowne's ears in the midst of the party. Mr. Strickland is here of course you know (by instinct) on Denis Brownes election petition[2] business—hopes it will be finished and they cleared of all bribery in a few days and then he is off for Ireland and we shall make him carry parcels and rags to 31 Merrion Street.

All at Edgeworthstown seem to read the newspapers to Fannys hearts content and to make Save my country Heaven the

[1] Sir J. Malcolm, *Sketches in Persia* (1827), *A Political History of India* (1826).

[2] Probably a slip for Dominick Browne (1787–1860), who represented Co. Mayo in seven parliaments and was created Lord Oranmore in the peerage of Ireland in 1836. The Rt. Hon. Denis Browne (b. 1763) had died in 1828.

first thing in the day. The days are in truth hardly yet long enough to read all mens speeches in Parliament. I get the result into me from Fanny and read only the *notables*. Mr. Norths *was* as you say the best and plainest speech he ever made—and so esteemed—Macaulays reads better than it was spoken—Quite marred in the delivery and he does not *look* the orator well—a mean whitey looking man—of the Babbage sort but more forward–vivacity of air and yellow hair all any-how except the right way—not with the inspiration–electrico look of Spring Rice. But no matter for all this—in spite of his outside, his inside will get him on. He has far more power in him than Mr. North. Jeffrey's speech was thought too much like lecturing his class—he is much broken—body not mind.[1]

As soon as Fanny is equal to it I will try to kill her a la Lanterne[2] with Sir C Lemon's assistance who is doing his best to get us there. Pray for us that we may chuse a good night and that Fanny may survive it and my conscience be clear of reproach. I am now 63—bien sonné and have found very few pleasures in life worth bearing the reproaches of conscience—But others who have tried more may say (no—think) differently for anything I know to the contrary. I speak the truth but I am sure Lady Lyndhurst is of a very different way of thinking—Scandal by transition—when we meet more of this. I hope you are in merry pin my dear and that I am not contre-temps-ing you.

16 March

The last notables you will see in Fanny's journal (which is to be my text book hereafter) are Marchioness Wellesley and Sir John Malcolm who luckily met here and were delighted with each other and we with them both but not with Miss Caton who is ugly and broad faced and not genteel looking or moving—But clever no doubt—Lady Wellesley more pretty than handsome. But I have said about her to Mamma in my last and I know you

[1] This refers to speeches on the Reform Bill. North's speech of 7 Mar. was anti-Reform. Macaulay made the first of his Reform speeches on 2 Mar. and Jeffrey, the Lord Advocate, spoke on Scottish Reform on 4 and 9 Mar. Both Macaulay's and Jeffrey's speeches were almost immediately published as pamphlets.

[2] At the ventilator in the ceiling in the House of Commons, the only place where ladies were allowed to listen to the proceedings (see above, pp. 369–70).

hate repetitions and cannot hate hearing them more than I hate writing them. Besides my *second* impressions are never so true as my first tho they might be perhaps better corrected by cooled judgment. But for friends *folly* is often better than wisdom—better means more entertaining. I have cut Miss Douglas several times—quite short and since the last cutting she has never come up again.

The Mr. and Mrs. Kirkland who were so kindly received at Bloomfield have been here. Mr. McLane the American ambassador has left his card and I believe, if Fanny is tolerable I shall go to their next *levee* with Washington Irving. I shall be curious to see a *genuine* American party—you remember Gallatins dinner! Madame Gallatin might well be vulgar—no wonder—she was a backwoodswoman—married up to Gallatin before he rose in the world himself. He is reputed to be very cunning and merely to *act* frankness and roughness but I liked him and like him still in spite of them a'.

Whenever Mr. Butler is able to read again I recommend to him '*Jones on the distribution of Wealth*'[1] published at the expense of the University of Cambridge—He being a Cambridge man. I like his book and himself. He is something of the same sort of looking man as Doctor Butler (only very different). I met him at Doctor Fittons—who by the by I like also tho I dont think him a first rate—but I do think Jones first rate in Political Economy. Malthus does not think he has yet made out his positions but as his making out *his* would overturn some of Malthus's—we must hear both sides. There is much in Jones book about rents and interests of landlords and tenants being the same and short-sightedness of rackrent landlords which I know you and Mr. Butler will like will wish well got into the heads of Irish landlords. I had thought of putting some extracts on Cottier[2] system in the Irish papers but who can do any thing good in this *turmoil of London life*. N B—This is only a copy of my countenance. I am and have been very happy *if* Fanny were but well again.

I told you to get the loan of the [ ][3] vol of Sir W. Scotts new Edition of poems continuing introductions (new) to poems

[1] R. Jones, *An Essay on the Distribution of Wealth and on the Sources of Taxation, Pt. I, Rent* (1831).

[2] See *Memoirs of RLE*, ii. 24–5.

[3] Blank in manuscript.

and essay on ballads and ballad writing[1]—all entertaining and a model for egotists—which very few (Basil Hall not excepted) will be able to follow tho many will strive and be laughed at for their pains. Medical Statistics by Bisset Hawkins of Exeter Coll Oxford pubd. 1829 worth troubling your own (and) or Mr. Butlers eyes with.

Rogers who is not more yellow than ever nor more satirical for both are impossible had been very goodnatured to me (and verily he hath his reward—above). He told me last time we met a capital murder-story and has lent me an English translation of Manzoni Promessi Sposi which will save me much looking in dictionary—for I am not as you are fluent in Italian . . .

Ever yours affectionately my dear Harriet—And 'if you knew how I admire and love you!'

Poor Lady Massereene—

Maria Edgeworth

Paris's life of Sir Humphry[2] is both tiresome and interesting —the scientific part admirable done—much bookmaking and loads of words in other parts. He is very poor and must book-make for bread—met him at Dr. Lushingtons. I had a very pleasant dinner there. Mrs. Lushington is charming such a real good mother and wife. I wish her children were handsomer. They are very sensible and agreeable—got round me directly and told me stories of tigers and elephants and boy put me in mind of Maxwell[3] but Oh how different in face and voice. Mrs. Lushington told me that she has never given a dinner since that which we were at 8 years ago. She found it necessary for Dr. Lushington to dine at 4 oclock and to get up at 5 or 6 and she gave up all dinner parties *literally* and all evening parties and only saw her friends in the morning and in short lives only for her husband family and friends. Now methinks with all her accomplishments and powers of conversation to boot she is a better sort of good woman than the old kind of good woman without a head.

Lady Stafford ought to be hanged. She has never asked me to

[1] Three 10-volume editions of the poetical works of Scott (1821, 1823, and 1825) were all re-issued in 1830 with new introductory matter to each volume. A new volume was added including the plays.

[2] Davy. See below, p. 511.

[3] Maria's sister Sophy's son.

dinner—yet made a great flourish of trumpets about it and about it. Lady F Leveson Gower is mighty like Miss Geoffrey I mean like that kind of sharpish tartish looking person—handsomer withal and very clever I'm clear but I never should care if I never saw her again.

I will write to Sophy Ruxton soon but have not time today. Ask to see (if you have not seen) Whateleys Errors of the Romish church and Whateley on the difficulties of St. Paul.[1] Lady Lansdowne recommended these. I have not yet seen them. Dont smile at my *yet*. Dr. Holland recommends a slight poem of the day called '*the Giantess*'[2]

To Sophy Ruxton

[21 March 1831]

[no beginning]

. . . She [Fanny] has not been out any where with me this last week except two morning drives one in the park and the other to Little Holland House Kensington to see Miss Fox (the most agreeable woman I know) who was not at home but we had a very pleasant sunny drive back through lane and park for our pains—the young hawthorn fresh green coming out in the hedges—one Sycamore in leaf in the park and willows in tender green.

I was at Lansdowne House (per engagement) last Wednesday and took Mr. Strickland with me—a very large party—even those spacious rooms crowded. Among the *notables* who were new to me whom I *heard* as well as *saw*—were Lord and Lady Nugent. She was a great beauty and her beauty has come into fashion in a kind of second spring from the celebrity of Lawrence's picture of her and an engraving from it I think in one of the Annuals. He looks like a humorous Irishman and doats on Ireland after a short visit there but is not Irish and has not a foot of land there or anywhere else I believe—poor and married for love and seems still very glad of it. Lady Davy affirms that

[1] R. Whateley, *The Errors of Romanism traced to their Origins in Human Nature* (1830) and *Essays on some of the difficulties in the writings of St. Paul, and in other parts of the New Testament* (1828).

[2] See below, p. 509.

Lord Nugent wrote that imitation of Scott—the fire—in the Rejected addresses[1] and declares that he now acknowledges it to be his *but* from all I heard of his conversation I cannot believe it tho he is clever enough too in another way—a kind of offhand dashing cleverness. She is very ladylike and just such a wife as he ought to have. She came to see me the day after I met her at Lansdowne House and I shall be very glad to see more of them.

Besides the Nugents, I saw for the first time that night Achille Murat a Colonel (son of Murat) and Madame or as the Americans call her *Mrs.* Murat his wife. She is an American—a great niece of Washingtons (who had more nieces great and little than the Dun-cow had ribs)—is very pretty—simple—young and *foreign* looking—Something like Pamela—the daughter I mean of Lady Edward Fitzgerald. Tho' American she looks and speaks much more like a Frenchwoman or an Italian than English. Everybody who did not know her and especially Mons Turgenief a Russian asked me if that Lady was not French or Italian 'Ah c'est là une femme pour faire revolution!' But she seems to be thinking only of innocently amusing herself and acting tableaux with her chere Christine—Lady Dudley Stuart—daughter of Lucien Bonaparte sister of Madame [Wyse]. By the by I am sorry she is her dear friend for by her looks and by her history I guess she is no better than she should be—She having married Lord Dudley Stuart while her first husband a Dane was living. The Pope has granted a divorce *as well as he could* and people visit her and go to see her Tableaux. What will people not visit for amusement fashion and wealth in this great London!

Achille Murat is a little insignificant *black-Mr. White*[2]-looking-sort of man and wears spectacles to boot. It is difficult to believe him a son of two beautiful people! Such a dirty trick of Dame Nature! But they say he (Colonel Murat) has charms within—That he is very clever and noble souled. His dark eyes and whole face light up when he converses and he is very easy to converse with and well bred. They have lived in Florida and I heard him describing the climate to Mrs. Alexander Baring (herself an American) as the most delightful in the creation.

[1] *Rejected Addresses* (1812) by Horace and James Smith.

[2] Perhaps Henry White, later 1st Lord Annaly, M.P. for Co. Longford 1823–32.

To Sophy Ruxton, [*21 March 1831*]

Next came the Duchesse Dino niece of Talleyrand—little and ugly—plain I should say for nobody is acknowledged ugly nowadays (but myself)—and then came Talleyrand—like a corpse with his hair dressed *ailes de pigeon*—bien poudré. As Lord Lansdowne drolly said 'How much those ailes de pigeon have gone through! unchanged! How many revolutions they have seen—How many changes of their masters mind.' Talleyrand has less countenance than any man of talents I ever saw. He seems to think not only that La parole était donnée a l'homme pour deguiser sa pensee but that expression of countenance was given to him as a curse to betray his emotions. Therefore he has exerted all his abilities to conquer all expression and throw into his face '*true no meaning*' which puzzles more than wit. Wit I heard none and I have now settled the point—that he does not chuse to talk to me or to let me hear him talk. There were plenty of people to re-introduce me to him. You know I had seen him at Paris but he would never let me know therefore I might fairly say I did not know him and I determined to suffer a new introduction and see what would come of it. Sir James Mackintosh a favorite said to be of Talleyrands was near me and ready but I preferred Miss Fox because Lady Lansdowne had told me that he talks more at Lord Hollands than anywhere and Miss Fox had told me much of his wit and powers of entertaining let out in conversation. I took her arm and begged her to talk to him first for some time without naming me that I might *hear*. Accordingly she did so but I heard nothing but about Lord Hollands gout and what le chevalier Brodie[1] saw who is not a chevalier all the time. Talleyrand about whom there was a great crowd and a circle of about 2 feet religiously kept gave a scarcely perceptible squint at me over Miss Fox's shoulder and then looked on some farther off object and talked on mere commonplace and then to Sir J. Mackintosh commonplace hopes and fears and sentences as *unfinished* and as lack-lustre and unmeaning as any of our good friends the present Bishop of Meath's can be when he does not chuse to give any opinion. I touched Miss Fox's arm as much as to say 'Enough! my curiosity is satisfied' and she named 'un nom qui doit vous être bien connu

[1] Perhaps Sir Benjamin Brodie, the surgeon, who did not receive his title till 1834.

Monseigneur'. Monseigneur with a face neither denying nor assenting nor expressing any human sentiment looked at me with fishy eyes and bowed and I returned the reverence as well as I possibly could with equal no-meaning and a dead silence of a minute ensued. I determined to leave the onus of that silence upon him as in duty bound and in etiquette. Somebody I don't know came up and spoke and Talleyrand seemed released and there it ended. Miss Fox whispered to me 'We will make him sit down and then'. I looked towards a sofa. 'No no not there he would not relish the neighborhood of Madame Murat.' There was an ottoman beside us. 'Monseigneur ne veut-il pas s'asseoir?' 'Mille remerciments—*bien comme je suis*'. . . . Miss Fox walked off with me and in a few minutes Talleyrand retired. He was not ten minutes in the room—I suppose only came to enter an appearance from ambassadorial etiquette. He is very infirm—[? supported]—and his head down on his chest.

It was a very *starry* night. All the ambassadorial stars of Europe were there—brilliant—and the American Ambassador with none but 'the star which rose in America'—Mr. Mclane. He had been to see me. Unluckily I was not at home. I was now presented to Mrs. McLane by Madame Murat who had fallen in love with me as quickly as [I] did with her.

Mrs. McLane tell Harriet Butler is not like Madame Gallatin in the least—not at all vulgar—but quite a gentlewoman in appearance and manner—unpretending and nothing extraordinary though American. It is impossible exactly to describe how this appears—I think it is in the want of *natural* quiet in the manner and in a very high pitched voice. Mr. McLane I am told by Lockhart and others is a very clever man and I shall know whether I think so or not tonight when I shall go for the first time to their assembly. Mrs. McLane apologised for its being a sunday evening party by saying that it was for the sake of the convenience of many of their countrymen who were lodging in the city and concerned in business and who had no opportunity on weekdays of coming from such a distance to see their ambassador &c (Totally—if I care. I only asked for information sake.)[1] . . .

[1] Family phrase of unidentified origin.

To Sophy Ruxton, [*21 March 1831*]

Monday morning

I have said nothing of public affairs. I know no more probably less of them than you do for the nearer the scene of action the more *on dits* we hear and the less power we have of detecting which of them are true—The on dits of each party being diametrically opposite and equally confident.

On dit—on the ministerial side that they will avoid attempting to carry the reform bill through the House of Commons even the 2d reading they will not try—*since* they were in a minority on the timber duties.[1] Whether they will dissolve Parliament or resign is the question? They feel it they say a point of honor and patriotism not to resign—on the other hand—dissolving parliament will throw both Ireland and England into terrible commotion and it is much doubted whether the New parliament would be more favorable to them and *their* reform.

If they went out Peel would come in and it is said would bring in a moderate yet *real* reform bill giving representatives to large towns that want them and not allowing the £10 qualification.[2] It is said that 2 evils both bad horns of a dilemma are awaiting the present ministers and *or* their bill of reform. Either it will throw too much power (when it works) into the hands of the aristocracy—or into the hands of the democracy. In either case the middle classes will have to complain and do not now fail to begin loudly.

I must end instantly for the carriage is at the door to carry us to Lady E Whitbreads and I have not begun to dress.

[no signature]

[1] The proposal was to reduce the duties on the cheaper and better Baltic timber while leaving those on Canadian timber unchanged, thus lessening the degree of colonial protection. The debate was on 18 Mar.

[2] The first Reform Bill provided that all boroughs should have a uniform franchise, the vote being given to every householder who had occupied for at least six months previous to the annual revision of the register a house with a rental of at least £10. Previously the franchise had varied widely from borough to borough.

To Mrs. Edgeworth

Tuesday, 22 March 1831

My dear mother

. . . She [Fanny] went with me to the American embassadors on Sunday evening and did not suffer by it. It was a *very* early party beginning between 8 and 9 and we were home by a little after eleven—not above 20 people—All Americans—received on a sunday because many of them live at the worlds end in the city and cannot come to their embassadors away from their business on any other day. Mr. Ralston was there and looked quite gentlemanlike in the midst. The only entertaining people were Newton the American painter and Murat and his wife and Mr. and Mrs. McLane theirselves. Newton a tall thin man tall and thin as Wilkie and pale is infinitely more agreeable and has the best conversation and manners of any American I ever saw or heard. He has been living in England these 9 or 10 years and in the very best society both in London and in country houses of the first style—Bowood—Trentham—Cobham &c—And he has been rubbing all the time against all the best literary men. Rogers is his dear friend only affronted him one day by telling him of answering No *Sir* or yes *Madam*—'That is American now' said Rogers 'at any rate it is vulgar to Sir and Madam people. Moore does it but I never do.' Newton says that Rogers is jealous of *Moore* and never fails to give him sly cuts in this way and that he is always contrasting himself with Moore in point of good breeding &c and being his dear friend all the time. Oh the pitiful work!

Mrs. and Colonel Murat (as they write themselves on their cards) I have described in a letter I sent yesterday to Sophy Ruxton—also have told all I saw of Talleyrand and other worthies or notables at Lansdowne House on Wednesday—Therefore have only to add Sundays second view of Murat—liked him—very conversible and he talked of the most interesting subject Bonaparte. First I called him *Bonaparte*—to feel my way—Then Napoleon. In reply he said 'my uncle'. It was an odd feeling to know that we were talking to his real nephew—so near—the son of Caroline. I finished by calling Bonaparte

L'Empereur and perceived *that* gave pleasure and why not? This Achille Murat was so young that he could not have seen much of him but he certainly *liked* him and was anxious to prove to me that l'Empereur was capable of strong attachment—*Ah oui Dessaix!*—and several others—Il fallait souvent sacrifier ses sentimens a son *devoir*. 'In the case of Josephine no doubt' said I. 'She was strongly attached to him but Marie Louise was a heartless creature.' To my surprise Murat would not allow this—assured me I misjudged her—that she was as much attached to mon oncle as Josephine. 'Then why did she not abide by him in adversity? Why did she not follow his fortunes to St. Helena?' 'Oh impossible—under the power of Austria.' 'But there was an opportunity—at the very first—at the moment of the abdication before she was under the power of Austria when she might have gone with her husband or *to* him.' 'But then she was under the power of Joseph.' All Murat said did not convince me however. I reminded him of Marie Louise having taken the Duke of Wellingtons arm going in to the Opera box at Milan. 'Was that wife-like? Was that a proof of affection?' Murat shrugged and squeezed his hat and said that it really ne signifiait rien—that the Duke had dined with her and then offered her his arm—it could not well be refused &c &c. What surprised me was that *Murat* should apologise for her.

Murat settled one disputed point with me. The very day before a certain Lady Nugent (Sophy Ruxton can tell about her) had reproached me with having given to Talleyrand a saying which belongs to Bonaparte viz The famous speech about the emigrant nobles '*sans avoir rien appris ou rien oubliés*'. Murat exclaimed 'Ah C'était mon oncle qui a dit ça.' I told Murat another saying which he had never heard and which lies also in dispute between L'Empereur and Talleyrand. One of them asseverating to the other put his hand on his *heart*. The opponent exclaimed 'Ah il n'y a *là* que de cervelle.' Murat was delighted with this provided it was his uncle's observation to Talleyrand. Ah! he was sure it was l'empereur said *that*—so like him and so applicable to Talleyrand.[1] But I have no time or room for more of Murat.

[1] 'Il n'y a là que de cervelle' is generally attributed to Napoleon, of Talleyrand, but Chateaubriand said of Napoleon, 'La nature le forma sans entrailles.' The authorship of the epigram on the émigrés is also disputed.

Yesterday morning Mrs. Hofland came here and brought her son (whose name which puzzled me nearly to death is Hoole). He is curate to some parish in the city. A more agreeably liberally and judiciously benevolent human creature of any rank or any age did I never see or hear converse and he has a delightful voice and manner so free from egotism and from all exaggeration. In his parish are a vast number of poor Irish Catholics—They often send for him when dying as they cannot get a priest and his own account of his principles in treating them was most touching—perfectly *Christian*. I am sure I shall all my life be the better for knowing even what I know in one hour of this excellent man. And his mother so doats upon him. Worn out in body a shadow of a woman she sat with bright eyes of love fixed upon him drinking in every word sympathising in every feeling and enjoying an ecstasy of affection beyond all other human pleasures. By the by I am delighted that you like Ps Steam [? essay].

½ after 5—Just returned from seeing Mrs. Marcet—Just arrived and as good and kind as ever and better to look at than usual.

Both Mrs. Hofland and her son Hoole knew the Hopes and gave me great pleasure by what they said of them. Mr. Hope had applied to Mr. Hoole to ask him to be tutor to his son but Hoole though he knew it would be highly advantageous and that in every respect it would have been agreeable to him declined from believing it to be his duty as a clergyman to remain with the poor of his parish where he could be of most use and comfort.

Mr. Hope at the time he received this answer said however disappointed he was in not obtaining such a tutor for his son he must respect and love Mr. Hoole the more for it all his life. He asked if he could recommend any one. He recommended a Mr. Smith who has accepted and has lived with them ever since and thus kept up a constant and intimate connexion between Hopes and Hoflands. They say that both Mr. and Mrs. Hope were extremely charitable in the most judicious manner and the least ostentatious. They supplied this excellent curate with money continually and largely for his good purposes and the tutor Smith tells his friends that nothing could equal the kindness with which he was treated. He for some months past foresaw that Mr. Hope's health could not last and deplored it as if he had been a father. 'Oh Mr. Hope cannot remain with us long' he used to say after a silence with a deep sigh as if it had been the thought preying upon him. Mr. Hope had appeared better a few days after I last saw him—So much better that he went out on the leads of the house had his arm chair carried out there and sat to examine and direct what some workmen should do who were repairing the skylight or roof over the new picture gallery. Think of that being the cause of his death—Ruling passion still! He caught cold—felt very ill. Sir Henry Halford insisted contrary to the advice of 2 other physicians on his taking a dose of James's powder. The 2 other physicians said he had not strength to bear it. He died the day after swallowing that dose.

I cannot yet hear any thing distinct about Mrs. Hope's affairs but he made an eldest son they say—very rich—and no doubt Mrs. Hofland says that Mr. Hope provided for his wife for he 'from first to last adored her as well he might'. She is at the Deepdene—young Hope in London—Spoke the other day in parliament . . .

Carriage—door

Ever yr M E

To Harriet Butler

North Audley Street, 29 March 1831

To Dear little Harriet who will never grow old—

Old as I am, and imaginative as I am thought to be I have really always found that the pleasures I have expected would be great have been actually greater in the enjoyment than in the anticipation. (This is written you know in my 64th year.) The pleasure of being with Fanny has been far *far* greater than I had expected—the pleasures altogether, including the kindness of old friends and the civilities of acquaintance much greater than I had expected and still more enhanced than I had calculated by the *home* and the retired library easy chair morning retreat I enjoy here. But above all the long expected pleasure of our visit to Herschel had surpassed all my expectations raised as they were and warm from the fresh enthusiasm kindled by his last work. Mrs. Herschel who by the by is very pretty—*which does no harm*—is such a delightful person—so suited to him, with so much simplicity and so much sense—so fit to sympathise with him in all things, intellectual and *moral*—without any pretension or thought about herself—trying only—no not *trying* but making all her guests comfortable and happy without any apparent trying or effort or trouble (Just like *U* in that and still more like *U's mother*). Mrs. Herschel was extremely kind to Fanny whom she took-to particularly and Fanny to her and Mr. Herschel to Lestock. They invited F and L in the most cordial manner to come back again—'and again—and again. Any saturday you know you can run down to us and go up again Monday morning as early as you please in time for Mr. Wilson's business.' 'But' added Mrs. Herschel 'I shall not leave it to this general invitation but remind you of it continually.'

This is above all delightful to me! to feel that the seeds of so much happiness are sown and likely to grow and flourish when I am far away. Of all the people I have seen and of all the society I think the Herschels are the best worth cultivating and the most likely in every respect to suit Lestock and Fanny jointly and severally—in their ways of living too, so comfortable and well regulated and neither too much nor too little—all managed by a woman of sense and taste, for a man of sense who never *meddles nor makes* in the matter but takes it all as Heaven sends and his guardian angel. I really think she looks very like an angel as well as I can judge by the most approved pictures of angels—with fair . . . but not too fair hair glossy and curling and ever clean and shining with or without the aid of mortal brush and never out of curl which I take to be an angels peculiar privilege (and yours—except on particular occasions—when Mr. Butler was sick for instance I can concieve &c). She is very fair but not a sickly fairness remarkably the contrary. The clean and lively look of health and happiness and sweetness without mawkishness—dovelike eyes—pink shell color in the cheeks coming and going with every thought and feeling and none but genuine natural expression—Something in her look and manner that gives the certainty that she is both good tempered and yet of quick feelings—that she will be the same tomorrow as today and yet that she will never tire or be tiresome. Then she is so fond of her mother and her young brothers and her own family. She seems as if she was a ready-made for Fanny and I have an internal conviction that she will come to Edgeworths town and like us all—Next summer—But these are things still in the air—and there let them rest in all the beauty of aerial perspective with the light of Hope playing on them.

Thursday I went down to Slough all alone by myself in Fannys carriage and our job horses in grandeur. Lestock was not quite well and Fanny would not leave him and I am glad she did not for he was very so-so, reduced to an arm chair on friday —*only* the complaint now fashionable with Lady Stafford and others (The cholera morbus). But he got over it by proper taking in time and on Saturday was able to come down to Slough with Fanny—But I am not come to that yet.

The thursday of my arrival there was no company. Oh how I rejoiced! The evening was very delightfully spent in hearing and talking. I had made various pencil notes in my copy of *his* book to ask for explanations—for instance *double weighing*—and especially on polarisation of light and the difference between prismatic and periodical colors. Next morning he brought out his apparatus and shewed me the periodical colors which I had never seen and then explained all that is *known* and all that has been imagined about them—alternating theory and experiment beautifully and accurately—and so patient and kind and clear! How my father would have admired him. Not that he explains as well as my father—I never knew body who did—But next best—In one respect more agreeable to the infirmities of my mind in that he permits similies and allusions and nonsense to mix with sense in explanations in a most refreshing style. For instance in explaining to me Newton's theory of the fits of easy and difficult transmission of rays of light he supposed an hypochondriac patient who had taken it into his head that he could not go through a door with his right foot foremost. Whenever he chances to come to the door with that foot foremost he stops—and suppose two people walking arm in arm the 2d person with the contrary hypochondriacism viz that he cant go through left foot foremost both must stop and neither could get through till separated but then one could pass—by your leave.

This will be unintelligible to you as explanation because it refers to another theory about rays of light acquiring sides after what is called polarization and some of the rays passing and others being stopped in going through the interstices of various chrystals. I only give it you as a sample of his playful nonsense—wonderfully in contrast with his severe reasoning and philosophic exactness at other times. This illustration was followed soon afterwards by admirable remarks on the dangers of *allegoric* expressions in science and of that sort of nomenclature which takes for granted that we know in chemistry or in any other thing the *whole* properties and nature of the body in question—in short that we poor shortsighted elves have hunted Nature to her elemental forms.

Saturday towards six oclock I began to grow very anxious and fears flitted through my mind that Lestock would not be well enough to come and that Fanny would never appear and in these apprehensions good natured Mrs. Herschel sympathised. But as we stood at the window that looks on a distant turn of the London road I saw a carriage glass flash and an outline of a well known coachman's form and then the green chaise and all right—Lestock's tone in stepping out denying that any thing was the matter with him and Fanny wondrous sprank.

Unluckily there were to be 14 people at dinner and she had come without an adequate gown trading upon the take for granted that there would be nobody—but no matter—only my mother will color and fret for half a minute if it ever come to her ears which I leave to your discretion my dear.

Company—The Provost of Eton in his wig—a large fine presence of a Provost—Doctor Goodall a very pleasant man—just that—laid out to be facetious and learned—Mrs. Goodall—a good natured good sort of round body—Mrs. Hervey very pretty and gave me a *Jardinia* or whatever it should be pronounced and spelled a white sweet smelling flower with small shining green leaves—smelling like a cape jessamine or like a tuberose and looking like a small white Camelia—Much talking about it and smelling and handing it about and I know no more but that it died with me—A young No-great-matter—

son of Sir C Knowles—Mrs. Gwatkin and daughter and niece—Mrs. Gwatkin is one of Sir Joshua Reynolds's nieces—sister to Lady Thomond. She invited us to see a collection of her uncle's pictures which she has at her house a few miles from Mr. Herschels. She has been very pretty and tho deaf is very agreeable and good natured and tho not very clever has all the effect of being so having known and being able to tell well about so many celebrated people. She is enthusiastically and affectionately fond of her uncle, She was quite indignant at the doubts people have expressed about his writing his own discourses.[1] 'Burke or Johnson indeed! No such thing! I am evidence. I can answer for it he wrote them all himself. He used to employ me as his secretary. Often I have been in the room when he was composing walking up and down—sometimes stopping and writing a sentence on a scrap of paper and making me pin them on between what he had been dictating' &c &c.

I will not trouble you with the names of the other people—particularly as I forget them all but Mr. Mackintosh—medical I believe—from Bombay and remarkable for being the godfather of Herschels nice dear little child—a girl of 2 years old—as agreeable as if she were Sophy's own—happy and good humored as hers and not the least troublesome and Mrs. Herschel and Herschel doat upon her as Sophy and Barry do on theirs and as discreetly. The child is not the least spoiled and Mrs. Herschel is like Sophy in never making a rout about her child and in being able to attend to conversation while she is in the room and never to be in agonies about her little falls and perils—as fine a bump on her forehead one day as you could wish to see and no crying or pitying—to signify. This child with little blue knots on her shoulders and dressed for all the world like Miss Marianne sat at breakfast on one of papa's knees and the cat on the other and the child alternately fed papa and the cat and a prettier picture or reality I have seldom seen—I don't say never.

Sunday—went to church—Windsor chapel—Royal family—King—Queen—and little Prince George of Cambridge—each seen through the separate compartments of their *bay* windowed seat—up aloft—and some lady in waiting with them Miss Bagot

[1] Reynolds's lectures on the principles of art delivered to R.A. students 1769–90 and published 1778–97.

I *believe*—am certain very pretty. At such a distance all that I can only tell you the K looks like a gentleman which is to be seen I know not well how—but clearly—(by the gestures perhaps) whether you be near or far off. The service, what with chaunting and anthems and long sermon—was altogether unconscionably long and so much standing that I dreaded Fanny could not have stood it out. She wisely sat down behind backs. Three hours and more it lasted—The organ fine but the singing not nearly so fine I even could perceive and the wise ones say not so fine as at St Pauls. But here there were no professional singers which in theory I prefer because &c—you understand. The Provost did not preach. 'If I had' said he 'you should not have had so long a sermon.'

The tide flowed fast and strong to the door at which Royalty was expected to go out and various beadlefolk did what they could to keep a proper space for K and Q's Exeunt but in vain. I was one of the foremost and a man begged and prayed I would stand back and even twitched my sleeve but I was deaf and at last whispered 'I'm a poor stranger! and never mind me! I *must* have a sight of the King or Queen now or never.' So he smiled and let me stand and quite close I saw her in her black bonnet like any body else! Her picture had led me to expect something younger and handsomer!—and above all with more of an air and a grace and a shape and a face. I did not recognise in her the dignified Queen of Lady Wellesley's idolatry—but a good natured looking good sort of body.

Went—by particular desire—to Eton College to see the Provost and Mrs. Goodall and the pictures of all the celebrated men who have been educated at Eton and of many who have never been any way celebrated. Some of the portraits of the celebrated taken when very young are curious and interesting some from being like, others quite unlike what you would imagine from their after characters—Canning—Lord Grenville—Lord Wellesley—Whitbread—*Lord Carlisle* (*too* like Lady Elizabeth Belgrave Alas!) The Duke of Wellington (by Lawrence the last of his painting). There are about 60 of these portraits and I own that I should have judged that many of those who never distinguished themselves by any performance had the faces of children of promise. Among these was one over a door of a very promising youth. 'Who is that?' I expected some grand name. 'A Mr. Beaumont Ma'am'—famous only I believe for being refused by one of Lord Greys daughters (The very man with the two days old spinage between his teeth—one of the £200,000 Lady E. Grey refused on the North road). Well there is no telling a man's fortune by his face—at least by his picture. We saw the books of themes and poems that had been judged worth preserving—Cannings and Wellesleys much esteemed—But as they were latin and greek they were hebrew to me.

The library at Eton College is the most *comfortable* I ever was in—turkey carpetted—2 large rooms opening into one and perfectly warmed and plenty of tables large and small and light and sitting places—snug or social. Saw drawers full of prints and paintings of Titus's baths Herculaneum and many rare books from the first Romance in English down to the Original unique copy of the Royal history of Reynard the Fox—The table of contents of which is so exceedingly diverting that I would fain have copied it on the spot for you and good natured Mrs. and Miss Goodall began running different ways for pen ink and paper for me but meantime the Provost told me that a *copy* of the delight can be had for 1d at any stall probably. This is invaluable only from being oldest and the undoubted original with all its first faults! (N B—An anecdote about Lord Carlisle too long to tell now but good for hereafter—feet on fender or stool.) Good luncheon—including potted char—and a great spider chased by the Provost over the tablecloth and caught by me in a spoon—not killed—to my knowledge—ordered for transportation. The footman knows the rest.

Got *home* to Herschels while the sun yet shone and I having the day before begged the favor of him to repeat for Fanny and L the explanations and experiments on polarised light and periodical colors he had everything ready and most kindly went over it all again and in so different a manner that I had new enjoyment—besides the pleasure of seeing Fanny's pleasure &c. Mrs. Herschel afterwards told me that Mr. H said to her 'It is delightful to explain these things to Mrs. Wilson. She can understand *anything* with the *least possible* explanation.'

It was a fine moonlight night. He took us out to see Saturn and his belts and satellites and the moon and her volcanoes or whatever they be. The great instrument is not in use but he shewed me the great 4 feet mirror belonging to it in good preservation. He now uses the same instrument which you remember we saw—standing in the corner near the garden house —reflecting telescope—20 feet long—ladder up to the top stage where its eyepiece comes up. I thought Saturn and his belts looked very like what he used to do—only I was warned he seemed vastly nearer—so I suppose—The sight of the moon did surprise and charm me—very different that from any thing I had ever seen or imagined of the moon. I saw a large portion of a seemingly immense globe of something like *rough* ice resplendant with light and all over protuberances like those on the outside of an oister shell supposing it immensely magnified in Brobdigagian microscope—that lustrous mica look all over the protuberances—and a distinctly marked mountain-in-a-map in the middle—shaded off delicately as my pen and hand cannot represent—After all whether this be mountain or crater—far be it from me to determine but I saw just what you now see—barring the differ between black and white. I must remark to you that all the time we were seeing we were 18 feet aloft on a little stage of about 8 feet by 3 with a slight iron rod rail on three sides but quite open to fall in front and Lestock repeatedly warned me 'not to forget and step forward'. Herschel runs up and down the ladder like a *cat* (because I would not say a monkey)—I in Fannys old plaid and she wrapped against her will in my new cloak went up and down very lei-sure-ly—Lestock behind us guarding petticoats and placing foot—or telling where to place —and I'm a fool for telling you this—cant be helped—always was and will be so.

Next morning—Monday—as usual following sunday—Our visit Alas was to come to an end. Herschel was under engagement to be in Town by a certain hour. He offered to take Lestock in his gig which offer L accepted with pleasure as it would bring him to his point at his time and give us time to fulfil an engagement we had made to pleasure ourselves by a sight of the pictures of Sir Joshua Reynolds in the possession of his obliging niece Mrs. Gwatkin.

I am not going to bore you with a list of said pictures—only to tell you that there is one of Charles Fox done when he was

18. The face is quite faded away till it almost looks like an uncolored sketch and not the least like any other picture I have seen of the jolly moonfaced C F—But some resemblance to the boy of 13 in the print that I begged or forced from Lord Buchan. The original girl with the muff here and very pretty—The original also of the picture of a child with a cap on sitting on a bank with flowers in her lap—I believe called Simplicity.[1] Mrs. Gwatkin told us that the flowers were put in her lap in consequence of an absurd provoking observation made by some fool of a woman. The childs hands are placed on her lap back of the arms and wrists turned downwards and fingers interlaced—ends up—as you have often seen children sitting when sitting at ease and thinking about something or nothing. 'Oh how beautiful' said the lady connoisseur 'and how natural the dish of prawns the dear little thing has in her lap.' Sir Joshua threw flowers over the prawns. I hope this is not an old story to you. It was new to M E. In this collection there appeared many sad results of Sir Joshua Reynolds experiments on colours—a very fine copy made by him of Rembrandts own picture of himself—all but the face *so* black as to be unintelligible—the face *so* good as to encrease regret that it must go too and that it is almost gone.

There was the first picture Sir J Reynolds ever drew of himself when he was a boy and the last he ever drew. This invaluable last is all going—risen in great black cracks and masses of bladdery paint. He painted this niece Gwatkin 7 times at different ages 'But dont be vain my dear' said he 'I only use your head as I would that of any beggar as a good practice.'

She is very good humored and quite quite unaffected. Her husband is one of the thin dried old race of true hunter and shooter men and roast beef of old England-men a true patriot loyal King and Konstitution man—I ween. He was wondrous rich but has run through two large fortunes and is now scrubbing on upon a few thousands—be the same more or less. Good natured old soul—hunted out from his archives a letter of Hannah Mores for me which happened to be particularly interesting to me—On Garrick in the character of Hamlet.[2] I will ask for a

[1] This picture is now at Waddesdon Manor, Buckinghamshire.

[2] *Memoirs of the Life and Correspondence of Mrs. Hannah More*, ed. W. Roberts (1834), i. 88–9, letter of H. More to Mrs. Gwatkin, 12 May 1776. A fuller and

copy and in hopes of obtaining it for Francis and you will not maul it now by piecemeal recollections. It was good—giving at least a decided view of what Garrick concieved the unity of the character.

From metaphysical to physical—finished with a noble slice of 'the roast beef of old England that was fed Ma'am' said Mr. Gwatkin pausing *on the knife* 'by his present Majesty—God bless him!—and what is your opinion pray Miss Edgeworth may I ask of this reform bill—for or against Eh?—and what wine do you take?' I gave him my *opinion* in a bumper toast 'Reform without Revolution if possible' with which he was quite satisfied and drank it down *possibilit*y and all saying that it should be his toast.

Arrived at No. 1 in good time and good plight Fanny not tired. Lestock had a pleasant drive with Herschel and a pressing invitation to repeat his visit with which he was much pleased . . . I must now go and dress to figure at Lady Davys dinner. Fanny is at this moment immersed in an arm chair comfortably reading 2d vol of a new book *not yet published* of Basil Halls called 'Fragments of Voyages and travels including anecdotes of a naval life chiefly for the use of young persons'[1]—Chiefly anecdotes of his own life. Altogether the 2 first volumes are very entertaining and some of the scenes from life drawn with great life and spirit but much about patronage and ways of rising in the world which to say the best is very problematical in point of morality and I question whether in point of expediency he has done well to tell to the whole world the secrets of the promotion list. There is a chapter entitled *'The first step on the ladder of promotion'* To which I have written as a motto (he having been promoted by Wellesley Pole)

'Bless every man possessed of aught to give
Long may Long Tilney Wellesley Long Pole live.'[2]

Herschel repeated to me that whole very excellent *address*. . . .

Wednesday morning

. . . We had full opportunity yesterday of comparing the sort of pleasure we had at a London dinner and evening party with

more interesting letter to her sisters on the same subject is on pp. 85–7. See below, p. 585.

[1] B. Hall, *Fragments of voyages and travels* (1831).

[2] H. and J. Smith, op. cit. i, Loyal Effusion by W. T. F. [William Thomas Fitzgerald].

the Evenings at home at Herschels. The dinner party at Lady Davy's consisted of 8 *select*—of Lady Davy flanked by Lord Ashburnham—end of table 3 Rogers—right—4 Maria next him —5 Gally Knight—at foot—6 L. Wilson—beside him—7 Lord Mahon—8 Mrs. Wilson. Well sounding party—number right for table—and Davy's fine plate and good dinner and champagne and all sorts of wines. And yet it did not do well. Rogers was cross and Lady Davy marked it and was cross to him when he would not eat flesh and would not like her Virgin her Madonna del Sisto. Then Lord Mahon who was pert after his fashion vexed Rogers more and more and then his Lordship blundered about something and Rogers had him down and coolly and spitefully trampled on him and though they talked over all the beauties of art and nature all over the world afterwards yet still there was a leaven of malice that spoiled all—The *bad butter* you know. Lord Ashburnham was very agreeable and seemed above all the dirty work. He has been eleven years roaming the world but is not the least foreign-fangled—a true good Englishman at heart he seems—and in manner has that invaluable sincerity which the best practiced art cannot imitate. *Lady Davy's* writhing and hard working affectation looked so ugly beside him and worked so hard in vain. (Very good cherry-ice! was some comfort.)

Evening—Lord and Lady Nugent—Mrs. Gally Knight—Lady Anne and Mr. Wilbraham—Mrs. Marcet and her daughter Mrs. E Romilly and Mr. E Romilly. Mrs. G. Knight is not at all pretty and had a garden sticking upright on her head which would have made an angel look frightful. Mr. Gally Knight has written a stupid jeu d'esprit called '*The Giantess*' which Dr. Holland had puffed to us and had sent us the night before. I had read half and could read no more and all the time Gally Knight was near me I dreaded that something would come round to this giantess but luckily I escaped—the dwarf came off safe. Gally has been guilty only of printing not publishing. I always thought him and am now convinced he is a bore with a tongue too large for his mouth and a great taste for the arts withal and very good but les bonnes intentions ne font rien in conversation any more than in writing. Dear good agreeable ever-the same and never tiring Mrs. Marcet was the happiness of the evening to me but she came late and Lady Davy could not let well alone but just when Fanny and I had got into good talk with Lady Nugent about Talleyrand she came up and snatched Fanny away saying 2 sisters must not sit together. I daresay my mother remembers in days of yore old Mrs. Cliffords stopping in the middle of the room when she came in at Lady Davys and making a regular bargain with her to be let alone. 'Now Lady Davy place me where you will but let me alone afterwards.' Of all the backbiters *ever I seen* dead or alive Rogers is beyond compare the most venemous audacious and universal and at last it can hardly be called backbiting for he bites before the backs are turned. He was *at it* to me against Lady Davy when she was within a foot of us and his answer to me when I warned him that he must be heard 'And if I am! When I mention no names—I might be talking of the Queen of Sheba. There! there! did you see that? Her look and his (Lord Ashburnham's)—it will not be her fault if it does not come to something.' Then she came quite close and instantly Rogers's look and tone changed and he was all oily flattery—with a *taste* of persiflage for the saving of his credit for *satire and taste* with the bystanders. At the last dinner where I met Rogers he and Mr. Hay were more than flirting disgustingly with Lady Lyndhurst. This night he said to me 'We have never met since we were in company with that *terrible* woman.' 'Very terrible you seemed to think her when you were sitting beside her.' 'There I protest I told Hay as we were coming in that he *must* be victim that night. Oh what can a man do—a gentleman? He can't go away when the woman begins. He can't leave her to herself you know. Besides she can *hate* as well as love. Oh she is an underbred creature who is pushing herself forward and it wont do. The ladies can't bear this.'

I think I shall learn some good lessons for my next novel[1]—but reality is beyond fiction—too strong—would not be believed. The insincerity of this London life strikes me more than when I was younger. Perhaps I am more a stander by and am more *let behind the curtain* and have no objects of my own—for sisters and self. Besides it all appears to me now so little worth while! M E

[1] Cf. *Helen* (1834), I, chap. xiii, 284–7, where Horace Churchill speeds the parting guests and then tears their characters to shreds.

To Honora Edgeworth

[2 April]† 1831

My dear Honora—I send you Mr. Gally Knights Giantess. I being a dwarf can see nothing in her. I am in dread of meeting him again for when I saw him last at Callcotts (Exhibition of pictures) he announced to me that he had left on my table something that was to make me laugh or as Mrs. G Knight said 'perhaps cry—cry with one side of my face and laugh with the other'. But it neither made me laugh nor cry. I think it flat stupid—the true no meaning that puzzles more than wit. Tell me what you think.

I believe I told you that I have found much instruction and interest in Paris' life of Sir H Davy.[1] I wish Mrs. Tuite would bespeak it for me for the Society[2] *Octavo Edition* now advertised. Tell me if she says that somebody else has bespoken it already for if that is the case I will buy it in Octavo for myself. They say that Sir Humphry's brother is going to publish his life. I have not yet been able to learn in detail what Lady Davy thinks of Paris' life but I am sure in general she does not like it. Indeed the single word *'florid'* applied to her own way of expressing herself must have displeased her—especially as it is too true. Doctor Holland and the scientific people as far as I have heard are satisfied with the scientific part of the book. The part that I think interesting and well done is the history of the steps and progress and habits of Davy's mind in making his great discoveries. It will all serve my purpose if ever I write my long intended Essay on invention[3] . . .

Tell Sophy that poor Lady Charleville came yesterday to see me when Lestock and F had gone down (after church) to Woolwich to execute some business of L's. I had some tendency to headache and did not relish the E wind—so kept chimney corner. I was so afraid of letting Lady Charlevilles 2 tall men bring her up these narrow stairs that I came down to offer to sit in the

[1] J. A. Paris, *Life of Sir Humphry Davy* (1831). J. Davy published in 1836 *Memoirs of Sir Humphry Davy*, in 1839 *Collected Works of Sir H. Davy*, and in 1858 *Fragmentary Remains, Literary and Scientific, of Sir H. Davy*. See above, p. 490.

[2] An informal book club in the Edgeworthstown neighbourhood. It is mentioned by ME as early as 1809.

[3] This was never written.

carriage with her which the men not her Ladyship rejoiced at. She said laughing that she was not the least afraid of being carried up any stairs—her men were used to it &c. I pity her very much for the loss of that grandson who really loved her and for the horrid state in which Lord Charleville is. Her description of him however is so nauseous that my pity merged in disgust. After Easter if Lord Charleville is in fit condition to sit at table we are to dine there . . .

I had intended as you may see by the size of my first bit of paper only to have written a very *leetle* but I am my very dear Honora ever affectionately and ever talkatively yours Maria Edgeworth

To Honora Edgeworth

[fragment, n.d. 1831][1]

. . . Fanny and I dine tomorrow at Mr. and Mrs. Guillemards. She is in as good preservation as ever—looks as if she had been drying in sand ever since we saw her at Bath—and just as good natured soberly—discreetly as ever. She says her brother was delighted to have done with the Presidency of the Royal Society. He gave them all an excellent dinner at last and pleased all (who were at it) by his way of leave taking and his wish to leave all scientific and other dissensions where they should be left—in oblivion.

I admire your remarks on Babbages book[2] because exactly what I felt. Babbage was here yesterday—with wet shoes—an intolerable day it was snowing and sleeting. But wet shoes notwithstanding he sat an hour and was very entertaining in a way which you never would expect. He began to talk of Italy—was there about 4 years ago—met on a public walk Contessa Guiccioli and after an acquaintance of a few minutes she mentioned Lord Byron. Babbage said 'I am delighted to hear you pronounce *that* name and since you have pronounced it I hope it may not in future be interdicted to me in conversing with you for Lord Byron is a person about whom all must be interested.' Super-

[1] This fragment may belong two months earlier.

[2] *The Decline of Science in England* (1830). It was an attack on the Royal Society.

fluous delicacy Babbage's it seems for she went on talking of Lord Byron and of her own attachment and connexion with him without the least reserve. She said that she could trace the origin of 'her predisposition', of this *fatality* to her early childhood when she had formed a most ardent wish to be distinguished to have the love of some distinguished person. Curious notion of *fatality*! Pretty much like the history of Lady Davy's love for Sir Humphry—She fell in love with celebrity. Babbage did not think La Guiccioli handsome but she had a pretty figure and the remains of beauty. A month after Lord Byron had persuaded her in that atrocious manner to go off with him and break through all even Italian conventional decencies, Lord Byron said to Moore 'I wish you had come a month sooner. If you had I should not have run off with a red haired Italian.' I wonder what the lady would have thought if she had heard this. This is one of the behind the scene speeches which are really better for morality than anything that comes on the stage. Babbage told me this speech. He is not sure nor am I whether it is *published* or not. Everything is published nowadays. I hear that there is an excellent review of Moores life of Byron by Lockhart in the Quarterly.[1]

Mackintosh with whom I have again had a delightful breakfast told me that all Lord Byron says about Romillys having accepted a retaining fee first from Lord Byron and then turning over to the other side is false.[2] Mr. Whishaw has some letters that throw light on the subject. He is to shew them at Mrs. Carrs to a party tonight to which Fanny and I were much pressed to go . . .

I intended only to write a few lines to you my dear Honora but I always exceed when I write to those I am fond of especially when they are so safe—from the mania of publicity. Now I am going to the library to be dirty and happy—putting up the books. They are almost all up—on the shelves—but have still to be arranged. They are only now divided into subjects in their different bookcases—All helter skelter as to sizes and volumes. They quite fill the room. It will be a most comfortable library. Fanny is but *so so* but not bad. Now good by. Yours affectionately Maria Edgeworth

[1] See above, p. 484. [2] See above, p. 482.

To Mrs. Edgeworth

1 North Audley Street,
Tuesday morning, 11 April 1831

My dearest mother—*Business*—*Before going* to anything else let me empty my head of what I am dreadfully afraid of forgetting and because it is quite out of my line of business. Did you ever eat a salad made of sea cale? I did yesterday—on my way back to London at the Revd. R. Jones—and a better salad never did I taste—it having the double advantage of tasting as if lobster was in it and of turning to profit the last days of your sea-cale when the world's tired of it asparagus coming in and shoving it from the table. Receipt—Take your sea-cale and boil it and let it grow cold and cut it as you would celery. Dress it with oil and vinegar—putting more oil than you would to another salad. It may be mixed with beetroot or not according to taste. Don't tell what it is till the world has tasted and given their opinions and if one was fed with his or her eyes shut I don't doubt but judgment would be given that lobster (or *crab* as Mr. Jones said) is in it. I expect that you should bless me all the remainder of your life or at least of mine for this salad—provided always that you have never heard of it before which much it fears me you have. Pray say.

Though I was up at 6 yesterday and horses at door by 7 yet that eternally slow morning brusher and washerman Lestock was not down till half after 7 and we were not seated on the woolsack in the carriage till ¼ before 8—And then Oh such a day! such a day of sunshine and pleasantness, so much done, said, seen in it, that Mrs. Carr's long remembered day of days was nothing to it! Lestock went with us as far as Sevenoaks from which he was to proceed by coach as he had an appointment at 3 in London but the first London coach being as full and fuller in and outside as could be in a country where the laws (about coaches) are respected. We were very glad of it as we could have Lestock with us at Knole—sun shining delightfully and neither too hot nor too cold we happy three set out to see. It would have been better a month later but still the larch were beautiful in their tender green and the thorns ditto and the fine ancestral *oak* beech elm spoke for themselves—as to age and size imagination clothed them with leaves. I believe this was just the time of year when you and Lucy saw Knole (if you did see it when you were last in England and I hope this is not a dream of mine). Not to weary you with my transports—I will only say that I *never* did see any place, house included which altogether pleased me so much. There is so much good taste in keeping up this fine old mansion[1] in its dear old style. What inlaid floor of modern parquetry could give the sublime feeling one has in walking upon a floor that was laid before planes were invented with all the identical clumpy nails of King John's time? The pictures that first come uppermost in my memory this morning (after having slept a night upon them) are—*One of the Strozzi family* a young man who or by whom unknown—Sir Kenelm Digby! by Vandyke—And Vandyke's own picture by himself—his head *turned* (not *quite*) but half round looking at you and Lord Gower with him—in *armour—why* can't say—Kit Kat—several beautiful landscapes by great names but none clean and clear before my minds eye except one of Salvator Rosa's—which if you remember—well—If not—I wouldn't do so ill by you and myself as to attempt to describe it. There was a charming Cupid also by *somebody* and Mrs. Abington by Sir Joshua—also a French-coquettish looking little beauty with a mask by him which are both full before me at this instant. I am sensible that I ought to remember and much more admire sundry naked Venuses and *dark* landscapes by Poussin but I cannot help it—I did not. I was exceedingly entertained with portrait galleries of the old and newly celebrated. But it would be endless to particularise—all the originals or copies of Houbrakens—Hamilton The Chevalier de Grammont. Particularly however I was glad to see various of his beauties not so good in colors, I thought, as in black and white. Sir Walter Scotts black and white picture of King James[2] made the full length portrait of his unkingly Majesty 100 times more interesting than otherwise it could have been to me—Mean odd strange looking mortal—*He! divine!* And then King James's *silver room* as it is called. How it

[1] The seat of the Sackvilles, Earls and Dukes of Dorset. It was mostly built in the second half of the fifteenth and the first half of the sixteenth centuries by Archbishops Bourchier and Wareham, and remodelled by the 1st Earl of Dorset at the beginning of the seventeenth century. The best silver was that made for Frances Cranfield, Countess of Dorset in 1680.

[2] In *The Fortunes of Nigel* (1822).

was gilt by the genius of Romance!—all Heriot the silversmiths masterpieces ranged on toilette and India cabinet would have been but cups and boxes without the master magicians touch. All these ewers &c are kept brightly burnished as if new yesterday—kept in silver paper in a chest all winter—come out Lady day when the shew-months begin. Such a vile little looking glass! on the toilette—How luxury has in some articles increased while others have stood still and in others vanished quite away. In the silver room a bed as the show woman trumpetted forth of gold tissue which cost 8 thousand guineas new now in tarnished tatters not worth with Christies best puffing 8 thousand pence this day.

Well! we were obliged to leave Knole at last and to leave Lestock at 7oaks to take his chance of coach or no coach and on we went on in our own chaise to Brasted where lives, be it known to you, Mr. Jones the author of the new book, of which I have raved to Honora 'On the distribution of Wealth'.[1] On the strength of having passed one evening in his company at Dr. Fittons and of my having liked him and his book so much I had written from Sneyds to offer said Jones a visit from myself and sister—Graciously and eagerly accepted the day before we left Brandfold—as see by note enclosed.

Accordingly out of the straight road to Town (see map) we diverged (D— the expense) and after a beautiful Oh beautiful! every instant—drive we arrived in the pleasant village of Brasted and at the curate's house. 'What! only a curate!' you say. No more Ma'am but deserves to be an Archbishop at your service—and a most elegant and most elegantly lodged curate he is—as ever the village of Brasted or any other ever saw—Something in the style of Mr. Jephson's friend Bisset before he was a bishop only more like in face and portliness to Doctor Butler—and uttering so rapidly, with such crowds of ideas struggling for precedency as to keep one quite on the stretch not to miss any of the good things—and ½ of them I am sure I have forgotten—no matter—for if I had not I could not tell them in half a volume. 1 Note for futurity—History of fair haired heiress now living shut up at an old place called the Moate[2]—

[1] See p. 489, n. 1.

[2] Ightham Mote. Its oldest parts date back to the fourteenth century.

old as King John's time—into which moated residence though guarded by an inexorable old grandmother Mr. Jones and *Whewell* forced their way and actually saw the damsel and ran through the house one day when the grandmother dragon was out. Remember—for I am sure I shall forget that her name is Selby. *Mr*. Jones (not Tom nor William) had like a born gentleman as he is invited Dr. and Mrs. Fitton to meet us and prepared a luncheon comme il y en a peu, with a bottle at each corner of wine of every degree beginning with Hock of Bremen, undoubted! brought by our mutual friend Mr. Jacob and far too valuable for an ignoramus as me to swallow.

'Chevening! You are afraid you shall not have time to see Chantrey's monument. Oh but you must see it.' So kind Messrs. Jones and Fitton laid their heads together and ordered gig and pony carriage and let our horses rest—appointing to follow and meet &c—and away we drove Dr. Fitton Fanny and Mrs. Fitton who is very qu'ite and pleasing—pony carriage (I am exceedingly glad my dear Honora that Aunt Mary likes hers)—And Jones the reverend driving me and pouring into my ear all unworthy! historical, geographical and agricultural facts that would have been so well bestowed on you dear Mamma and Louisa.

Then trit trot and gallop a gallop—Oh fie grey horse! We came to a beautiful parky place where Dr. Fitton flourishes for the summer—drove through and saw his children who had wished to see the mother of Frank and Rosamond.[1] Down 3 boys came running from a woody bank where they were dirty and happy and all rosy faces and nothing fearing up to the side of the carriage—'Only my hands are too dirty to give you to shake.'

Then—all right—drive on—Through Mr. Mannings park[2] of which I fear he has less enjoyment than we had for he gave seventy thousand pounds for it and wants money now and will never get *that* for it, all beautiful as it is. We never troubled a high road nor a by road scarce all the way but just through one gentlemans park to another till we got to Chevening church-

[1] Hero and heroine of two sections of ME's *Early Lessons* (1801) and their sequels.

[2] Coombe Bank, nr. Sevenoaks. Farington (*Diary*, vii (1927), 210) says that he bought it for £40,000 from Lord Frederick Campbell and it was thought to be worth £52,000.

yard. The white marble monument of Lady Frederica Stanhope[1] is in the church. How I wish you had seen it and Harriet *particularly* as she knew and remembers well about Lady Frederica. Plain tho' she was in life she is beautiful in death and I should almost say graceful—Something in the expression of her countenance of exquisite tenderness—maternal tenderness—and repose—matronly repose and yet the freshness of youth in the rounded arm and delicate hand with the bent back tips of the fingers that presses—lightly affectionately presses the infant to her while it sleeps—and she dies—if dying it can be believed to be—so free from pain or apprehension—so sweet—so placid—so happy—one wishes to be her! The head half turned sinks into the pillow which without touching one can scarcely believe to be marble and the hair so naturally yet so gracefully disposed—not *dressed*—at the back of the head neck shoulder like Fannys—and the feet so delicate! just seen beyond the drapery so decently composed. The infant covered up under the mothers mantle we fancy could have been so covered only by a mothers care. The only fault I felt was—that the childs head is too large and not pretty—uncovered without hair—*Why* when the body was covered why leave the head bare—The slightest fold of the drapery—I longed to pull it over. I am afraid what everybody says must be true and everybody says that the monument is raised *too* high on its pedestal. The pedestal is large—black—on which is inscribed, her name and age and death and her own words quoted from some prayer of hers—what she had wished to *be*. The words are very simple and good and most touching! when we recollect the circumstances of her early death. They so suit the look of purity and tenderness in the figure lying there! One could almost fancy she was dreaming that wish. I never saw any statue that touched me so much—Far! Oh how far superior to that of the Princess Charlotte.[2]

This work of Chantrey's is less known than any of his others and for a reason most amiable in him. It was never publickly exhibited because the Stanhope family could not at that time bear to call attention to the circumstances that followed her death.

[1] The famous monument by Chantrey (1823). ME and her sisters had met Lady Frederica in Paris on their visit of 1820.

[2] In St. George's Chapel, Windsor. It is by M. C. Wyatt (1824).

You know that Lady Frederica Stanhopes husband shot himself —found one morning in a summer house at Caenwood. I am sure Harriet recollects and can tell you all about and I am sure she remembers our seeing her at Paris just when she was going to be married. There is—tell Harriet—a wonderful something of likeness in the face to her—but an angelical likeness—not vulgarly flattered but softened—spiritualised—exalted as if the *woman* had passed through the delightful best feelings of wife and mother and was ready to quit her earthly nature—just quitting it.

We staid too long looking at this monument and then Dr. Fitton good natured Irishman as he is had run to the rectory to ask Mrs. Austen the rector's lady permission to see her garden. Permission granted—there was nothing for it but to go and a beautiful little fairy spot we found it—embosomed in evergreens —the sun warm there as in July!—Suddenly—the whole about half the size of the garden at Collon and part of it had been an added gift from Lord Stanhope and looked as if from a quarry!! —All rocky stones interspersed with rock-flowers such as at Bloomfield and in the nursery there and a *little* arbor and a little stone basin in view under arch of green—water always flowing in and bubbling and babbling—all the perfection of prettiness and neatness on a small scale. On my saying that it would be just the place to sit and eat strawberries Mr. Austen said 'I could give you bushels of the finest you ever saw if you would come in their season and eat Chevening strawberries.' (But nevertheless I would rather eat Edgeworthstown strawberries with you my old and young dears.)

Left Chevening rectory and can never forget it and drove— Chevening park—*Though*—it is death by the law in general and makes Lord Stanhope mad to drive through the grounds unbidden—and for a particularly good reason—Because all who do so must see as they go that the public road should go *there*— while Lord Stanhope has got it turned—no matter how. You understand great men job in all countries and counties (The County of Longford always excepted). If I were not afraid that you would all be as sick as I have sometimes been of the word 'Beautiful'—I should say as I said in driving through Chevening park—Beautiful! beautiful Beautiful! From the terrace road on the side of a hill you in one part see the vale of Holmes's dale which ne'er was won and never shall lying in rich cottage garden comfort below you and you rejoice in the boast and prophesy of the old song. But not a word of truth in it—Never mind. Few people know though Mr. Jones does and told me something about a battle in the time of Hengist (better forgotten). Mr. Jones would delight you; he is so full of history and biography—has it all 'so quick' and yet so accurately (as far as I know always understood). He began with Hengist as I told—Mais je renonce a ca—and named all the English battles that had been won and lost in which from that time the men of Kent were always nonpareils—and all the fields of battle to be kenned from the place where we stopped to reconnoitre—And lo! and *high* I saw this spot and that spot and strained my eyes and imagination at the sounds and the *sights* (some of which I never saw)—Battle of Hastings—William the Conqueror and then in the days of John and the Edwards.

At the *battle of Tunbridge*[1]—look in whose time Lucy or some of yees—probably my mother has it at her fingers ends—the men of Kent drove back *the enemy* and won those privileges which they enjoy at this day—for instance have still the Saxon laws of gavelkind. Whoever dies without will in Kent—their property must be divided equally between the sons—and in cases of treason no attainder can corrupt the family blood. In plain English there is no confiscation of property for treason or felony. A man of Kent may be beheaded or hanged in comfort—his sons will not lose their estates or be a whit the worse for it. Why am I wasting my time and yours telling you this which I daresay you know better than I do—and moreover that the *Wealds* of Kent mean the *wilds*[2] according to Mr. Jones tho Doctors differ about that. Dr. Fitton in the pony carriage behind me was giving at the instant another derivation to Fanny from the German. Let that pass there are the Wealds or the Wilds as the

[1] ME here confuses two different incidents: the siege of Tonbridge in 1088 during the rebellion of Bishop Odo; and the probably apocryphal meeting of William the Conqueror after Hastings with the armed men of Kent at Swanscombe. The chronicler Thomas Sprott writing in the reign of Edward I, tells how the men of Kent laid down their arms in return for an undertaking by the Conqueror to allow them their ancient liberties.

[2] OE *weald* 'woodland' (Ekwall, *Dictionary of English Place Names* (1947).

case may be and the *Charts* (from the *charters*)[1] all in Mr. Jones' parish and there is a chapel built by Porteus of latter days[2] to civilize some of the yet wicked ones of the Wilds. And then my showman who says he is reputed a good showman shewed me the house and place where some say Oliver Cromwell but for certain his son in law Ireton lived[3] and which after long belonging to his descendants has just been bought by Perkins the brewer who is doing away with all the ancientry! of it.

'Then Miss E you see to the right the village of [blank in MS.] where Henry the 8th used to sleep when he came from London on his road to Hever Castle to court Anna Boleyn—2 days journey he was forced to make of it—and there is the spot farther farther, to the right—now that rich green field where King Harry used to stop and sound his horn that the country might gather to help drag himself and suite in their heavy vehicles out of the heavy sloughs in the road.' (Suppose his Majesty had in a dream one night seen a steam carriage going on a rail road or felt himself on one.) *Hever*—See the Beauties of England.[4] Louisa I believe has them. Alas it is now in the possession of a rich modern improver who *can* afford and is determined to spend twenty thousand pounds in *improving* it. Mr. Jones groaned and I groaned and you will echo groan for groan.

But now the sun warned us that we must be gone—for he was going and his red beams said Very late ladies! you'll be very late in Town—but that's no business of mine. I leave you to the gas lights! I know.

After the most pressing invitations to No. 1 North Audley—from Fanny to Mr. and *Mrs.* Jones on the one part and from Mr. Jones on the other part to Mr. and Mrs. Wilson and Miss E to come back to Chevening—and on Miss E's third part to Mr. Jones to visit Ireland to settle the distribution of Wealth there and the poor laws and to see Mr. E's school (which he protests

[1] OE *ceart* 'a rough common, overrun with gorse, broom, bracken' (ibid.).

[2] A chapel built at Idehill in 1806 by Beilby Porteus, then rector of the parish (Sundridge) and later Bishop of London.

[3] One of the daughters of Gen. Henry Ireton (1611–51) married Thomas Polhill of Otford, who briefly, and after Ireton's death, owned Chepstead Place.

[4] J. Britton, *Beauties of England and Wales*, viii (1808), 1314–16. The usual version of the story is that he wound his horn to signal his approach as he reached the top of the hill from which the towers of Hever could first be seen.

he much wishes) we parted company—and it was near 8 oclock when we got to London and from one end to the other I thought verily we should never get. It seemed never ending streets. I really thought they drew out like telescopes. Finely tired as you may guess we both were and there was Lestock waiting dinner and much more patiently than Job ever did—but then he had not such a wife—quite. He—Lestock not Job—is a delightful person to live with in the article of not being easily annoyed about *hours* and trifles of any kind—Many men—many virtues—at least among our dear brothers in law. God bless and a health to them all—this day shall be drank.

We got to bed after Dinner and tea which followed close on each others heels—and slept—I gloriously—3 double sleep—Fanny single—but better than I expected this morning—not quite worn out. We took post horses if you care to know how it was—from Sevenoaks and our own slept and followed at their leisure and they are very well thank you today.

Unlucky that this day when we should have been glad of an evening to our little selves had been appointed for a dinner—Captain and Mrs. Hall—Mr. and Mrs. Lockhart—Sir George Staunton—Captain Beaufort—Captain Wilson and Mr. Drummond—In the evening perhaps Lady Davy—certainly Miss Carrs and Mr. and Mrs. Kay and Achille Murat and Madame.

And now I must go and dress. I will keep this letter till to-morrow that Fanny may write and I hope tell you she is alive after this dinner—Yr meantime affec Maria E

To Mrs. Edgeworth

14 April 1831

My dear mother . . . Great fears that there will be an immediate dissolution—of Parliament.

Mrs. Lockhart is going to her father who cannot come to London. She must go poor creature by sea because her poor boy cannot bear travelling in a carriage can only bear water carriage. She suffers dreadfully at sea and is so sorry that her husband cannot go with her but he *cannot*. Business must be done and the Quarterly-review-Master has no sinecure—tho a very profitable place. She looks ill—worn-mind—But you cant help it and why draw on your sympathy who have so many drafts on it at sight . . . Ever yours in a whirl wind M E

Friday morning

This letter was yesterday left at home with a take for granted that I should be back from the launch time enough to seal and deliver. We were stopped so long by trains of carriages and triumphant draymens carts in the city that it was past post hour.

Well! there is good in everything. I have *now* time while Mrs. Sotheby is *jaw-jawing* in the drawing room to that poor victim Fanny whom I turned out of the library to receive her—I have now time—just returned bonnet on from shopping—I have now time—hand shaking with hurry to tell you that we had a most delightful day yesterday and that it has not killed Fanny who has not been shopping this morning more than just to one house to buy a gown.

The launch was of a 700 ton vessel—The Duke of Buccleugh . . .

To Mrs. C. S. Edgeworth

Friday, 15 April 1831

. . . My dear Harriette . . . Fanny is not the worse for her dinner and little party which Mrs. Murat inclusive went off well. I dined on Wednesday with the Hallams—Monstrous good dinner—Company—Mr. and Mrs. William Ord (nephew of Lady Oxford *Mr.* is I believe—with some of her cleverness) —Mr. Wilmot Horton—Mr. Sturges Bourne a sort of London Mr. Whitney—The Lord Advocate and Mrs. Jeffrey and two ladies mother and daughter whose names I never heard distinctly —and no great matter—Sir James Mackintosh who if he had no name or if nobody had ever heard his name I think one must have found out to be one of the best informed and most agreeable conversers extant. In the evening among others came a Miss Mans*feld* or *field* as the case may be who talked much to me of Mrs. King and is blind of an eye as well as I could see but it might be only a false light that led me to think so. If a mistake let it rest with you.

Notwithstanding there were so many clever people at this dinner 'Middle ages'[1] and all I think more good things went in than came out—Jeffrey is not of the *gas light* company. I much admire that gas light touch of Emmeline's.[2] Wilmot Horton is delighted at the thoughts of going to Ceylon but vexed beyond measure at the Age having said that he was going there as a pauper emigrant. How foolish people are to mind what is said—especially when it is said on purpose to vex . . .

Yesterday we went to East India Docks—Captain Wilson East India ship 1200 ton (Dunira—from Lord Melville's place)—also to see the launch of the Duke of Buccleugh—700 ton (if that conveys any idea to your mind—none to mine).

We were to have taken Madame Murat who very much wished to go with us but her colonel-husband had such a cold that he could not stir out and she staid to pity him. Pity of her! as Molly would say. We had a charming day and picked up my Mr. Ralston in Kings Arms leaning against a doorpost and carried him along with us—Lestock and he sticking on behind in Smiths place! Lestock is really excessively good-natured and so *manly* that he makes no fastidious difficulties ever.

The launch was a beautiful sight—breathless too—The moment when she goes, she goes! 'The young Duke of Buccleugh—there she goes' cried a woman beside me—Irish ten to one—or 100 to 1 Ireland has the credit of her. Most capital luncheon Captain Wilson gave us on board the Dunira—Such quantities of choicest Chinese sweetmeats—dry and wet—and no scruple in swallowing as much preserved ginger as ever throat and mouth could bear because the captains are not allowed to carry any of the sweetmeats ashore not even the remains of their sea stores, without paying their weight in gold almost in duties. Among the Chinese sweetmeats were oranges—young or shrunk or dwarf—not above the size of a small plum or large gooseberry—Delicious!—and in my opinion Ma'am the little oranges or lemons on hot house orange or lemon trees would preserve well in this way. Suggest this to Mrs. Morland in

[1] Hallam was the author of *The State of Europe during the Middle Ages* (1818).

[2] Cf. ME's *Helen* (1834), ii, Chap. ii. 31: 'London wit is like gas which lights at a touch, and at a touch can be extinguished.'

grateful return for her bouquet. *One* white Camelia lasted till we got to Town—the leaves of all the rest *shed* by the way.

Today I have bought a new gown—*dress* I mean—for who has a gown nowadays—and a new hat double [? Dunstable] Ma'am—lined with figured silk all the fashion Mem depend on it and now having been double diligent in my sense of the word I rejoice in *being done*—Oh what English they talk in London—and Enter Mrs. Malthus—Scene the drawing room—Exit Maria E from library—Yours ever affectionately whether with a *pin* or a pen yr ever M E

To Harriet Butler

Brandfold, 16 April 1831

My dear Harriet I begin shrewdly to suspect that I am fond, very fond of you for I find that even when I have Fanny and *all* with me still my mind turns to curly-head and I find my joys incomplete without you to share or you to tell them to. Yesterday I went to Tunbridge Wells with Fanny and Sneyd, saw the Pantiles and Mount Ephraim and the very spot where Sir Sedley Clarendel's horses took fright[1] and *longed* for you 'to come along and help see, and help talk'. The pantiles looked to me wondrous small and narrow and the roof over the row too low—sadly too low for the lofty fine heads. However the flagged outer walk is broad and handsome and I daresay when there is music playing and gay dresses walking about in the season that it is all very well. Altogether though the pantiles were too small for my preconcieved notion my imagination was not at all disappointed, but delighted with Tunbridge Wells—especially with Mount Ephraim and all the views of the neighboring country and the *furze covered* land—Never concieved *that*—something always which no description prepares for. Camilla present every where. What astonishing power a good author has to give local interest. I suppose no one man woman or child who can read ever goes to Tunbridge for the first time without thinking of Camilla.

[1] See F. Burney, *Camilla* (1796), iii. 178–9. Mrs. Arlbery's horses ran away on Mount Ephraim and Sir Sedley saved Camilla by stopping them for long enough for her to get down from the carriage.

The Tunbridge ware shops—very pretty but very dear (I did not ruin myself). Walked in the rain back from Mount-Ephraim, met *Dr. Mayo* who lent me his umbrella and went on in the rain himself. He has an excellent countenance. What associations rose round him! We went to call—*not* upon Mrs. Tighe because after her *flash in the pan* of fine speeches to me about coming to see me in London she and her coadjutor Mrs. Cuffe (Lord knows who she is) never came to see me—a step. So intending to mortify her sorely I went to see my old school-fellow Mrs. Blencowes son's wife but poetical justice was defeated for the lady was not at Tunbridge, not expected for an hour! That hour we could not possibly stay—for a most cogent reason—*fish* and company at home. Sneyd must get home with a dish of fish—to supply one which the vile Lamberhurst coach had carried on to—far be it from me to attempt to tell *where* but somewhere wrong. These things happen everywhere and always tell my mother as well as Honora on the day of *Judges-Salmon*[1] —very fine Ma'am. And we got it and ourselves home in time —and there were the Soles &c which had found their way Heaven knows how meanwhile from Lamberhurst.

Did you ever hear the Irish expression *double-diligent.* Sneyd had it from John Bristow—thus—'Sir tho' I calls upon you twice but I hope you won't think me *double-diligent*' (doing too much)—as we should have done had we called on Mrs. Tighe . . . and am your humble servant M E

To Mrs. Edgeworth

1 North Audley Street, Saturday, 30 April 1831

My dear mother . . . You must have been shocked by the death of the Duchess of Wellington which the newspapers must have told you but your shock cannot have equalled mine. Monday last—Fanny lying down to rest I drove to Apsley House by myself without the slightest suspicion that she was worse than when I had last seen her. When I saw the gate only just opened enough to let out the porters head and saw Smith parleying with

[1] Honora E had ordered salmon for a dinner for the judge at Longford assizes in 1830. The salmon did not arrive, nor, fortunately, did the judge.

him, nothing occurred to me but that the man doubted whether I was a person that ought to be admitted—So I put out my card—and Smith returning said '*Ma'am The Duchess of Wellington died on Saturday morning.*'

The good natured porter seeing that I was really as he said a friend went into the house at my request to ask if I could see her maid. And after some minutes the gates opened softly and I went into that melancholy house—that great silent hall—window shutters closed—not a creature to be seen or heard. One man servant appeared at last and as I moved towards that side of the house where I had formerly been 'Not that way Ma'am walk in here if you please' and then came in black that maid of whose attachment the Duchess the last time I saw her had spoken highly and *truly* as I now saw—by the first look and words 'Too true Ma'am. *She* is gone from us! Her Grace died on Saturday.' 'Was the Duke in Town?' 'Yes Ma'am—beside her.' Not a word more on that subject but I was glad to know that certain. Lord Charles arrived in time—not Lord Douro. The Duchess had remained nearly as I saw her on the sofa for a fortnight—then had been worse and had been confined to her bed some days but afterwards seemed much better—had been up again and in that room and on the sofa as well apparently as when we heard her conversing so calmly so charmingly. They had no apprehension of her danger nor had she herself as the maid told me till friday morning when she was seized with violent pain! (Cancer I believe it was)—and she continued in torture till she died on Saturday morning 'calm and resigned'. The poor maid could hardly speak. She went in and brought me a lock of her mistress's hair—silver grey—all but a few light brown that just recalled the beautiful Kitty Pakenham's formerly! So ended that sweet innocent—shall we say happy or unhappy life of hers? *Happy* I think—*through all*—in her good feelings and good conscience and warm affections—still loving on! Happy in her faith—her hope and her charity—Yes happier I am sure than those who injured her can ever have been or ever be. (Just as I had written so far before breakfast I asked Fanny whether she had told you of the Duchess of Wellington's death and when I found she had I was going to tear this but Fanny held my hand and insisted on my sending it.)

I drove away and then came back all the bustle of this living world which goes on let who will die or who will feel—and it must be so. I went to Whitehall place to return Mrs. Stanleys visit and there saw the Secretary for Ireland the youngest looking statesman I ever saw and he was in the midst of bustle of election thoughts and preparation for going to Ireland. 'We shall get into the Phoenix at last' said he. Phoenix! At first—my head not being very clear did not understand *Phoenix park*[1] but thought of Phoenix insurance office.

What a dreadful fire that in Harley Street! Lord Walsingham —Wretched man! All the newspapers said about his going to bed intoxicated was true and he had the habit of reading in bed and trying to do so in this state it is supposed set fire to the curtains. The butterman with whom Fanny deals told her cook that he had been much shocked by Lord Walsingham's death because he had seen him the very day before a few hours before in such a brutal passion. Lord Walsingham had sent for a cream cheese—there was not one to be had. When his servant told him so he doubting that the servant had told him truth went down to the shop himself and finding it was truth and that he could not have the *cheese* scolded and stormed and that was the last seen of him—till they heard next morning of his horrid death.

His Lordships body was not found for some days and then in such a state—the head and feet burned off. Lady Walsingham a poor nervous lady was so terrified when her servant opened her door (she did not sleep in Lord Walsingham's room) and told her the house was on fire that she immediately threw up the sash and jumped out of the window into the back yard. Why the servant did not hold her back by force I cannot concieve. She was dreadfully smashed. They lifted her up and put her into the coachman's bed and she died in a few hours.

I have not written to you this week past because all my leisure moments have been taken up in writing 2 folio sheets of Chinese light paper to dear Francis who had taken it into his wise head that I had taken something ill of him because I had not written these 2 months. If he knew how many notes about nothing I have to answer. And here are three authoress's books

[1] The official residence of the Lord Lieutenant of Ireland.

lying unread on the table before me and letters of thanks that must be penned—Mrs. S. C. Hall superb silk and morocco copy of Old and new Irish sketches[1] the 2d volume dedicated to Miss E with warmest sentiments &c Next a novel in 3 volumes Abroad & at Home[2] (which by the by was the title of the first sketch of Belinda). This Abroad & at Home is by Mrs. Eaton née Waldy v Rome in the 19th Cent—and there is a preface with much about Miss E in it which neither Miss E nor anybody else in this house has yet had time to read—But answered she must be—by and by. Then there is Geraldine Desmond[3]—time of Elizabeth—3 volumes and long preface and Miss E in it—and very learned notes which tho uncut I can see are long and learned—and it is a book of great pretension by Miss Crumpe who sent it me with a note and a card and it was impossible not to return her visit—which accordingly I did yesterday (after having breakfasted with Rogers). Luckily as I thought she was not at home and I felt clear off but at night found on the table in hall another note from Miss Crumpe—'could not leave to chance opportunity of seeing Miss E—regrets disappointment—will wait upon her at one on saturday'. So I must finish this letter to be ready for her.

The breakfast at Rogers's was very agreeable—only that he had not asked Fanny with me. His sister as young and old as ever and as goodnatured presided. Lord Normanby grown within the last month into Lord Mulgrave—Mr. Luttrell and Tommy Moore. Mr. Luttrell was in very good humor and very witty and pleasant. Mrs. Lockhart saw him in a very different pin one morning at breakfast at Rogers he came in late and *snapped* at every creature living and dead. Lord Mulgrave is a very handsome gentlemanlike fashionable person—black hair well curled and very like a picture—I think his own—which I have seen somewhere—or in a dream. He conversed well and told many anecdotes Foreign and domestic—especially of *Landor*—whose poems (new)[4] lay on the table (N B—His shaking a Florence judge by the ends of his cravat—in a fury—His

[1] Mrs. S. C. Hall, *Sketches of Irish Character* (1st ser. 1829, 2nd ser. 1831).

[2] Charlotte Eaton, *At Home and Abroad* (1831); *Vittoria Colonna; A Tale of Rome in the Nineteenth Century* (1827).

[3] Miss Crumpe, *Geraldine Desmond, or Ireland in the reign of Elizabeth. A historical romance* (1829).

[4] *Gebir, Count Julian and other poems* (1831).

fancying a Florence beauty in love with him—offering to be her Cicisbeo—and how received).

Friday

Fanny had a dinner at home yesterday and a very pleasant evening party and all went off delightfully—Dinner—Mrs. and Miss Holland—Mrs. and Mr. Horsley Palmer and eldest son—contemporary of Francis at Charterhouse—Mr. Whishaw—Mr. Chantrey and Sneyd and Pakenham and selves. Sneyd had arrived in the morning and was delighted to dine here. Chantrey and Horsley Palmer you might not guess had aught in common but they had—about the coinage—alloy of metals—in which I should never have guessed Chantrey was skilled. But he has been consulted much about the designs for coins and medals and learned all about the alloys of metals for himself. 5 different dies were made and broke for the last coinage before they got one that would stand. But I'm only telling you that the dinner was excellent and well attended by a professional Butler *added* to Smith and John—My aunt Mary's icepails much admired by Sneyd. Chantrey and Pakenham suited well and talked charmingly across Fanny at dinner. Chantrey is a fine jolly hearted being and he told me he sat for *Sancho* once to a painter who could not hit off a Sancho.

In the evening besides the diners came Mrs. Hofland and son—Mr. Willing (an American from Mr. Ralston—very agreeable and gentlemanlike)—Mr. Drummond—Mr. and Mrs. Guillemard—Miss Gilbert nice girl Mrs. Somerville and Mrs. Chantrey—Mrs. Horner and her daughter and William Carr. These people spreading through the two drawing rooms stood and sat well and were not the least crowded and there was a great variety of conversation and all seemed happy . . .

Oh it is impossible to give you an idea of the talking and hurry-flurry about elections at this moment.[1] You know quite as much as either party here I am sure how the elections will turn out. I forgot to tell you that I dined at Lansdowne house on tuesday—Mr. and *Mrs. Osman Ricardo*—just the same charming amiable person—Mr. Milne just the same—dry and opiniated and clever and wearisome—Mr. Lubbock Junr.—silent man—

[1] Parliament had been dissolved on 22 Apr.

clever I'm assured—Mr. Corbin—American very agreeable—Mr. Murray *not* the bookseller but from Scotland—and I found out tell Harriet that he can be very entertaining—sat beside him at Dinner.

The result of all I heard at Lansdowne house convinced me that *that* party are in great doubt how the elections will turn out but as far as I can *guess* it will be favorably for the *Bill* and the present Ministry. Even if the majority should be against them and Peel and Duke of Wellington should come in it is thought by all and said *now* by the Tory party that they must and would grant some kind of reform for instance members for Manchester and Birmingham. 'But save my Boroughs Heaven' would be their first and last. And if a few rotten ones were left to drop off, I am not sure whether it might not be best to let the rest alone.

I enclose 'a leaf from future history of England' which was given to me by Lord Mahon and is written by him not published. It was written for the end of the Article in new Quarterly on reform.[1] Lockhart as Murray the bookseller told me thought it too jocular for the present *serious* moment and had the pages taken out persuading Lord Mahon that in consequence of the Dissolution of Parliament it was necessary to make a new ending to the article. I think the rejected leaf very good except the hit which is a miss at Sydney Smith—and how foolish to make an enemy for *nothing* of such a man. Rogers at his breakfast settled that he and the company at breakfast would have done the same thing better—I doubt it . . .

'Talking of coincidencies' as Mr. Ward would say—The other day we went down to Gravesend you know to see the Minerva and Pakenham's birth. Mrs. Probyn after doing the first honors of our reception on deck came to me and said 'Here is a lady who says you met her mother and sister at Slough and begs to be made known to you.' Mrs. Lowther a sister of Mrs. Gwatkin Sir Joshua Reynolds niece—Very well—that was something of a coincidence that she and a young niece should be going out to join her husband in India in the Minerva with my brother at this time. But go on—after sitting beside me some time—she mentioned that her husband lives at *Meerut*—Collector. At the word *Meerut* Pakenham said to me 'That is the

[1] *Quarterly Review*, xliv (1831), no. lxxxviii, Art. viii, p. 554.

place where Harry Bohle is.' 'Mr. Bohle! Oh I know him very well' cried this sister of Sir Joshua Reynolds niece. 'Mr. Bohle I see often he is our factotum.' He lives about 40 miles from their country house. She says he is a very clever fellow—that everybody knows him.

She went down to the cabin soon afterwards to write a letter and she petitioned me to give her my autograph—a few lines a few sentences in her album. You know how I detest the Album and autograph nonsense but as she can be good to Pak I complied and she was so well pleased that she promised to send me a little sketch done by the hand of Sir Joshua Reynolds. If she remembers it how much I shall be obliged to her but I don't expect it—too much! too much! I shall be quite content if she is goodnatured to Pakenham on the voyage and after.

Fanny has told you about his 7 Haileybury companions and his birth and chum. I liked his chum Maltby very much and his cabin as well as I can like any cabin in ship. Fanny thinks she did not mention to you a Mr. Martin a wondrous rich East Indian who is going out in the Minerva to see his mother. He has a superb cabin fitted up with a gilt backed nice collection of books and luxurious low sofas all round &c &c and they say that Mr. Martin will make this cabin very agreeable during the voyage to his select parties. It chanced that I was looking over the library I said to somebody that I thought I could have added some entertaining books to his collection and I mentioned Captain Halls *new* book.[1] Some days afterwards came a note from Mrs. Skinner that most goodnatured of female Pidcocks[2] who is the kindest of lion hunters and lion shewwomen. Mr. Martin had been told she heard by somebody who had heard Miss E say that she could have recommended some books to Mr. Martin. In short she advised me to send him a list in my own handwriting (invaluable) and she was sure he would do I don't know how much for Pakenham on sea and land. So this morning at 7 I made a list and my note and I hope P may be the better of it—Little worth it was.

But here comes Mr. South—Mr. South I have never seen—Enter and stay he did!! and talk he did! Oh how much but much

[1] Basil Hall, *Travels in North America in the years 1827 and 1828* (1829).

[2] Pidcock was a well-known menagerie keeper.

more agreeably than I expected! And a great deal of heart he has I'm sure—for Robinson especially—*and* remarkably civil to me and I pushed Pakenham and his going to India forward and his wish to see everything worth seeing &c. So Mr. South has asked him to breakfast and see all things and we are to go there after P is gone—Oh melancholy words—next Sunday—luncheon.

Scarcely had I settled here at my little table in library window to pen and ink work again when '*Miss Crumpe Ma'am*' announced by Smith in his most aggravating tone. '*She is in the drawing room Ma'am.*' So out I went—a very handsome too magnificently dressed lady!—about 30—and a squeezed up poke bonnetted old mother that looks and speaks as if she never had been used to sit at good mens or womens tables. I recollected at sight that these were the people that Lockhart had described to me as having met at an odd dinner given by Campbell to which he had entrapped the Countess de Salis. Lockhart said that Campbell was over head in love with the young lady and that she drank too much Champagne and that the mother was 'like a body from the streets—Regent Street now!' But this was satirical exaggeration. Still there was something too like it. Miss Crumpe talked and talked—on admiration—of me and of herself—and a nervous fever she had had pending the fate and reviews of her novel and then all the 16 reviews there had been of it and how she could feel or remember much about them I could not from any nature or experience of my own concieve.

Then the mother asked me about a horrid trial of Luke Dillon[1] of which I had never heard and she was wonderful surprised. Both ladies are from Limerick or neighborhood and Cats I should guess. Be that as may they both began at once to tell me the whole story—'not seduction Miss Edgeworth' said the young lady 'but much worse'. And all the worse and all that could be told they a l'envie l'une de l'autre told with all details and in a way which you could not have told it to me alone or I to you they retold it. Fanny came in and sat and could not look. 'And the man is to be hung I hear.' 'But why did the young lady go into a house with him by the way to eat and drink?' 'She was

[1] See *Morning Chron.*, 19 Apr. 1831. Luke Dillon was tried for rape in the Commission Court, Dublin, found guilty and condemned to be hanged.

a Catholic and from Tipperary or Roscommon so it was no way strange to her.' All I can say is that Miss Crumpe may have every virtue and accomplishment but she wants the natural feeling of modesty and yet all she said was quite moral and high-sentimental—very strange mixture. And at last they went away and then it was luncheon time and now having finished *that* I must make up this packet because the carriage will be at the door in 2 minutes.

Fanny is much better and was not killed off by her two dinners. Lestock was pleased and as far as I could judge pleased. I am sure his wines did—Champagne and Sauterne and Hock—and Claret & co and Constantia and Noyau &c &c. And pray remember that I dont forget to tell you about a *chicken and maccaroni pye*—Savoury pye or by whatever name—Much approved by Conoscenti.

I forgot to tell you that our windows escaped unbroken the night of the illuminations.[1] Lestock had ordered that if the mob came half a dozen candles should be stuck up in drawing room windows. There they were prepared stuck in wine bottles. A *poor* but numerous mob came from Grosvenor Square pouring about 12 oclock and as they rushed I shouted Huzzas and Lights. The candles were lighted but none were put up in F's bedchamber nor in mine nor in my dressing room and the mob after poking sticks in at the windows of next door kitchen passed on shouting—Many women in straw bonnets and children running and shouting as they ran—an odious noise and I saw and heard no more after they died away at the end of the street. I went to bed and fast aslee-p—and heard next day—*all* you have seen in the papers. It is true that they began to break windows at Apsley House and were fired at by servants and stopped when policemen told them that the Duchess's corpse lay in the house. Crockford's—£60 worth of thick plate glass broke. *Can* no more yr ever M E

[1] On 27 Apr. after the prorogation of Parliament, there was a general illumination in honour of Reform. It was promoted by the Lord Mayor. A crowd of several thousand in the West End broke the windows of those who did not light up. These included the Dukes of Gloucester and Northumberland, Lord Londonderry, and Sir Robert Peel (*Morning Chron.*, 28 Apr. 1831).

To Harriet Butler

1 North Audley Street, ½ past 7,
Friday morning, 6 May 1831

A promise of a fine May day made by blue sky tho only seen between chimney tops through smoke and London fog

My dearest Harriet—Next to his mother my mind must naturally turn to you when it is full of Pakenham. He is not gone yet but he goes today—at 4 oclock must be in the boat that takes the passengers to the Minerva at Gravesend. Captain J. Wilson intended to have gone with him but was forced to go to Bath. Lestock will go and Sneyd. I am glad it is not pouring rain as it was yesterday when we were paying farewell visits with him. For some days past Fanny and Lestock and he have all been busy getting together his outfit and *presents* and it is all nearly accomplished to satisfaction all the various things from all quarters have met in time though not till between eleven and 12 last night did the last driblets come in. Something is yet to be done to the Mountain measuring barometer. There is air where no air should be in the tube but it is to be expelled we expect by that great magician-scientific Captain Beaufort to whom for this express purpose at midnight an adjuration to breakfast here was dispatched last night. Pakenham is much pleased with this barometer and with the thermometers which Sophy ordered for him. Your desk is delightful. Fanny took a world of pains in bespeaking and supervising it and it is perfect—The right slope—the hinges invisible outside—a tray that will hold *everything* you want and take out with everything in it and a place underneath it for everything [blank in MS.] want—inkstands that shut impervious to ink—insured by the snail wheel tightener—in the infallibility of which by the by I dont believe but Fanny does. My bag was once filled with ink by one of these Infallibles but I'm told it was my own fault for not screwing well. I hope so. Lucy's present of the case of instruments is very nice and will I am sure be very useful. Barry's telescope and Honora's are Lestock's admiration and Pakenham's delight. L and F M W—Pak were all looking at Saturn and his ring till past midnight. All the books ordered for him by various friends have come home bound to *fit the head* (I hope you not [*sic*] that [? my last] impertinent expression for fitting the gentleman's *fancy*). The only things I could think of for him were a set of tools *in* one handle—Multum in parvo—and a dressing-case—leather-roll-up which he preferred to a box and an atlas (not in the dressing case but of moderate size—about the size of Granpapas Memoir of map of Ireland).[1]

He is gloriously provided with letters. He can count sixteen for Calcutta—two for the cape and 4 for Madras and I dare say he has more than he can remember . . . I enclose the last good natured note we received with the last from Lady Hunter for Madras—Arbuthnot—Basil Hall's wife's mother—to his mother in law—that poor woman who squints so terribly and whose eyes were naturally as straight looking as yours till too much suffering, too much feeling brought this on in a single night! How wonderfully and fearfully we are made! and how little we know about it—especially how the mind acts upon the body and the *nerves*!—and that Mrs. Gordon with her thumb sticking up!—and that other mad body with her forefinger always up thinking she must never stir it because the world rests upon it! Well! Well!

Among the farewell visits yesterday was one to Mrs. Lushington. She was so glad to see us and so kind and polite to Pakenham—She looks forward she says to his patronage in India for her two boys; Dr. Lushington is determined to send them both to India for he says every path and place is so full in England that it is impossible to get on without jostling or being jostled to death working the life out all the time and well if the conscience not out first. Mrs. Charles Lushington (the overland traveller) who is a very agreeable real person will send letters for Pakenham which are to secure for him a comfortable home-family pou sto[2] at Calcutta. When Mrs. Lushington had talked our fill about Pakenham she went on to Politics of which every head in London is fuller than they can hold. Doctor Lushington was elected for Ilchester and Winchelsea. As his servant expressed it remarkably well—'Moy Master sits for two places.'

Lord Suffield who was present in the House of Lords described the scene[3] as more extraordinary than could be imagined

[1] Published in 1792 by the Revd. Daniel Augustus Beaufort.

[2] From the Greek ποῦ στῶ 'where I may stand', i.e. a basis of operations.

[3] At the dissolution of Parliament on 22 Apr.; cf. Greville, *Memoirs*, ii. 136–7.

or almost believed. Lord Londonderry was held down upon the Woolsack legs up kicking with feet and sprawling with clenched hands like a naughty child—Lord Salisbury with his knee on his stomach keeping him down and two other Lords—names unknown to me—holding or trying to hold arms and legs with all their might. He was really out of his senses and Lord Mansfield as bad bawling—screaming at the top of his voice even till the doors opened and the King appeared as his Lordship pronounced the word 'ruin'! *Ruin* did not seize the king however, nor was he affected by the uproar in the least. His Majesty walked calmly on. Lord Suffield said 'I kept my eyes upon him I looked at his knees—they did not tremble in the least—I am sure I could not have walked so firmly, I dont believe another man present *could* have been so calm. Lord Lansdowne was pale pale —livid.'

The King quietly took out his paper—felt for his spectacles—put them on composedly and read with firm voice. While he had been waiting in the outer room for a few minutes the Lord Chancellor had gone out to his Majesty and the King hearing the wonderful noise within asked Lord Brougham what the noise could be. 'Sir it is the Lords debating.' 'No no—listen . . . that cannot be the noise I mean. Whats *that*?' 'Lord Mansfield speaking Sir.' They say that nothing since Charles 1st and Cromwells time was ever like it. The greatest wonder is that the kings head stood it. The great pressure of the motive seemed to steady him . . .

The day before yesterday we did a prodigious deal. By appointment Mr. Drummond came at 10 oclock to accompany us to the Mint and to see the Double printing press.[1] With useless care we had obtained thro Lord Lansdowne from Lord Auckland the Master of the Mint an order to see it but Mr. Drummond brought us word that no machinery is working there at present worth seeing—Disappointment soon settled by Mr. Drummond's telling us that the duplicate of the London mint machinery improved and executed by the very workmen who made the London machinery is now at Calcutta where Pakenham can see it at his leisure. We proceeded to the double printing press. And saw everything from the casting the types to the drying the

[1] The double feeder power platen press produced by David Napier in 1830.

printed sheets—the spreading the ink first on the elastic roller of glue and then on the table over which the sheet of paper passes—the receiving the sheet withouten hands between the opening and closing mouths of double bands of tape carrying the paper swiftly round the rollers and pressing and printing and letting them out again in one minute and less—all done!—the thoughts embodied on paper for an hours reading in one minute and for thousands of minds!—more wonderful than any fable of fairy land.

We were about 2 hours at the printing establishment and then went to the India House. There was some difficulty—some stop of a few minutes on account of our having left our card of admittance behind us and Pakenham's card with a pencil message from me to Dr. Wilkins was sent up. While this was being done a superb mock majesty man in scarlet cloak and cocked hat bedizened with gold motioned our carriage away. 'Coachman! drive on—no carriage can stand ever before the India-house.' That's the rule. Mr. Drummond was quite indignant. 'What it must be to come here sueing to these grand people!' said he. N B I have fallen quite in love with Mr. Drummond. He is so gentlemanlike and unpretending and sensible and amiable. He and Herschel are the two scientific people I shall be the most sorry to part from—perhaps never to see again.

Dr. Wilkins came out of his den—his most comfortable den to receive us. You are aware that he is one of Pak's great friends and *fauterers*[1]—his Examiner in Oriental languages. He received us most graciously and instead of handing us over to his show-man in waiting laid down his book and his spectacles and came out to shew us everything himself. Poor dear old man I cannot think how his enthusiasm and good nature enabled him to go through the bodily fatigue for he was full 2 hours at it walking —standing—talking the whole time. My mother has seen it all I believe except perhaps the full length picture of Bonaparte which was in Wilkins own room—By *Bellini*—in his coronation robes crowned with laurel. It was bought at Montpellier— ordered by the municipal Department for their council room but before the picture was finished Bonaparte was dethroned—the picture left on the painters hands. Some English merchants

[1] Abettor, patron (*O.E.D.*).

heard of it—saw—liked—bought and gave it to East India Company. It is a very fine picture—But that is nothing to you as I cant make you see it by anything I can say—only whenever you come to London again remember to see.

The strangest of all the wonderful things we saw assembled in the India Museum was *a toy* brought from Tippoo Saib's palace[1]—his very toy and quite worthy of a despot—an English soldier large as life—in his uniform—hat—shoes and all—in wood painted and varnished—lying at full length a furious tiger standing over him—painted to the life—with a handle (invisible at a distance) in his ribs which handle when turned by the slave in waiting produced sounds like the growling of the tiger and the groans of the man. This was all to frighten the English with the notion that prisoners were all to be given over to be devoured by tigers.

I hope Lucy and my mother recollect this and I will not bore you with more. You may *concieve* how tired we were by the time we had admired everything that was to be admired—Chinese—Egyptian and Ceylonese and Pearls diamonds and rubies and at last came his greatest curiosity!—a piece of a Roman pavement—most curious!—which Dr. Wilkins miraculously found and saved in Leadenhall Street one day chancing to come out of the India house and spy down into the shore they were digging up.

As he was shewing us some medals he came to the prize medal for Sanscrit—East India College—very ingenious device his own and beautifully executed. If Mr. Butler longs for an impression let him write or write you (Imperative mood) directly and I will try to get it for him. Dr. Wilkins paid Pakenham a handsome compliment—blurting the words out of his mouth as he looked askance at him. 'Had not you this medal? Why not?' 'Because I did not learn Sanscrit.' 'Well all I know is you might have had this or anything else you pleased.' I should think few young men had ever left Haileybury with a higher character in every respect or more beloved or having excited more interest in the minds of the masters. This dear dry old man beckoned Pakenham back when we had taken leave and gone forth from his cabinet and said 'Now! don't you go out shooting sparrows—you young man, when you get to India—like other young men

[1] This toy is now in the Victoria and Albert Museum.

who ruin their health by that work—Mind—Dont.' Fanny was not killed by this days work but we were all so tired that we went to bed by common consent before 10 oclock . . .

I am now crab like going back upon our history. I think I mentioned to my mother a dinner to which dear good Lord Carrington invited us—an early dinner at 5 that we might all go with them to the play afterwards. Never were any ladies fine or coarse so rude and ill tempered as the ladies Stanhope and Granville Somerset and Crawkee idiot Miss Smith were to us at this dinner. No nothing you have ever seen of them could give you an idea of it. I cannot do justice to them in writing without the tones and looks and twists &c—which I hope to give you to the life some day. Lestock was in amazement and took it so coolly and well but poor Lord Carrington! He did suffer. How these modern Gonerills *can* be so cruel to him and trample upon him I cannot concieve but he looks better nevertheless than he did ten years ago and his eyes are not out—But much better—dear good old man—His young granddaughter Miss Gardner is the only decent kind well mannered of his relatives. She is pretty and pleasing and I hope a comfort to him. She shewed me the house after dinner and an amazing good house it is—if that would make people happy—or contented but nothing more true than that bad temper cant be well housed.

The play—Alfred the great[1] was the most lengthy stupid thing I ever saw—on the old burning the cakes story five long acts—and two screaming women going mad different ways and so awkwardly and both so ugly that one wished them all dead and carried off before their time. I could have lain down at the bottom of the box with fatigue—But the pleasure of seeing the *Diorama* between the play and the after-piece quite wakened and refreshed me—Views of Swisserland—continually moving on as if you were going in a carriage and saw them from the window passing—passing and wishing now and then to stop them—The Semplon! Fanny thought it beautiful and all who have been abroad and seen these views declare that we see almost as much as if we had been there.

[1] At the Theatre Royal, Drury Lane, *Alfred the Great or the Patriot King*, with Macready as Alfred. It was followed by the Diorama, designed and painted by Stanfield and an operatic drama in two acts called *The Legion of Honour*.

I never saw any sight at the theatre I thought so beautiful. Pakenham enjoyed it very much. The little entertainment afterwards amusing. I will just note for future *talk* that it is translated from French and quite *French*—that it represents 4 generations great grandfather of 102—grandfather seventy—his son 50—great grandson—all the ages excellently played—Farren the best representation of amiable caducity I ever beheld (not painful like Mathews of Macklin)—Dowton and Liston in the sons—each x—and a little drummer boy of 13 a little pickle—They call me le petit diable—exquisitely acted by Miss Poole. As well done as you my dear your own self at your Prissy-age could have done it. I enclose a playbill which if I had recollected it before I wrote the last lines would have saved you and me trouble . . . Ever yours affectionately Maria E

We go down to the Creeds on Monday.

I forgot to tell you the very thing I had first in my head when I thought first of writing to you but Pakenham has turned my head upside down.

A dinner last week at Lansdowne house—in the dusk just before dinner came in—who do you think—your own dear Mrs. Osman Ricardo and Mr. She is as charming and unaffected as ever and I then thought as pretty and fresh but as she said to me afterwards 'That was by firelight and by candle light.' When she came to see us in the morning next day I saw the traces of suffering and time. She was very affectionate to us and still more in her manner of speaking of you. She regrets exceedingly that she has not heard from you so long. I know you did not know *how* to write to her but you will write I am sure now because she so wishes it. She is in tolerable spirits. She says Mary is even beyond what I could have expected in point of character and understanding. She and Mrs. Ricardo will not be in Town before I go—I am sorry. Mrs. Osman Ricardo has but just arrived . . .

To Mrs. Edgeworth

1 North Audley Street, 7 May 1831

I wrote yesterday to Harriet Butler all about Pakenham up to the moment he left this house in company with Sneyd in a hackney coach to join Lestock in the city. Lestock most kindly arranged to accompany them to Gravesend.

Half an hour after we had parted from Pakenham, and before we had recovered sense came a great rap at the door. 'Will you see anybody Ma'am?' I was going to say 'Oh no—nobody' but it occurred to me it might be someone that we should afterwards break our hearts for refusing to see so I bid Smith ask the name. Behind him as I spoke Enter—Mrs. Lushington—with her face all red—'I have forced my way up forgive me—it is for Pakenham—Here, I hope I'm not too late. I've brought him *good* letters from Mrs. Charles Lushington to Mr. McClintock and Mr. Marley Accountant General. Comprehending instantly the value of the letters and our carriage being most luckily at the door into it Fanny and I got and drove as hard as we could down to the Dock . . . Fear great of missing them and the letters in the hurley burley of packages and packers and passengers and sailors and *orderers* and hackney coaches and coachmen and boatmen men women and children swarming and bawling. But at last Smith and Lestock appeared together—Whence or How Heaven to this instant only knows but the letters got into Pakenham's hand and—All right—he and Sneyd gone into the boat. We saw no more of them and so much the better for second leavetakings are only double sorrow . . .

He is as well off I think as any young Writer need to be. He has £50 left of his outfit and £200 besides—One of Aunt Mary's and the other of mine. Of this he carries out with him one hundred in bills besides ten pound in dollars and Lestock gives him letter of Credit in Calcutta for the remaining £150. Indeed I believe good Lestock made his letter of credit for £200 if P should need to go beyond his £150 but this I am almost sure he will not. His salary you know commences from the time he touches Indian ground. I forget what it is but you know that all agree it is sufficient to *keep on with*. All that is wanted by a young man is a couple of hundred to begin with. If he has not this he pays dearly—high interest and gets in debt. Pakenham is so prudent that his having money at command will be the greatest advantage to him . . . Yr ever M E

. . . I am going to read Destiny.[1] Mr. Brittaine would adore me if he knew how many grand people I have induced to delight

[1] Susan Ferrier, *Destiny* (1831).

themselves with his books especially the *last*[1] which upon the whole I think the most powerful. Few people have abilities enough and sufficient knowledge of the Irish to comprehend the full merit of this admirable book. Fanny is pretty well M E

To Mrs. Edgeworth

[fragment, ? 18 May 1831]

Thank you dearest mother for the history of the election which was exceedingly interesting and entertaining to us and I read it *even on* and understood it perfectly notwithstanding your disparagements of your narration—I saw no cart put before the horse. I like Lovells address to the tenants and am very glad that his tenants all adhered to him so well. Indeed he deserved it from them—a kinder landlord cannot be. I am particularly glad that I was clear out of the way and that Lovell must distinctly feel that their attachment thus handsomely shewn is to himself.[2] It is so difficult to tell what is best for these countries at present that I am sure I should not know whether to vote for or against *the bill and the whole bill and nothing but the bill* if a pistol were held to my brains this minute—Anything short of this decided for or against—any pause to say a word in favor of moderation is worse than rashness—*trimming*—and people have completely forgotten in the invidious metaphoric sense of the word Trimmer[3] the original plain meaning—ie He who trims a boat or moves his weight from side to side in a storm to keep the balance and prevent oversetting . . .

To Honora Edgeworth

19 May 1831

My dear Honora, . . . I thought I had written a quantity to you about Mrs. Lawrence. Well if I did not I now tell you that I went to see her the moment she came to Town—not at home.

[1] *Irish priests and Irish landlords* (1830).

[2] For a discussion of the Edgeworths and elections, see M. C. Hurst, *Maria Edgeworth and the Public Scene* (1969), esp. 57 ff. and 77 ff.

[3] Halifax's definition in his *Character of a Trimmer* (1688).

She returned my visit and I liked her—a fair fat—not genteel but kind looking kind hearted Liverpool rich lady who gave me a book of poems (which you shall see and read if you like—some of them are pretty). It was at her house (I'm sure I did tell you this) that Mr. Huskisson was on a visit at the time of his death—her husband is one of the leading railroad gentlemen. I believe she was satisfied with me for she gave me a most pressing invitation to spend as much time at her house as I possibly can when I go to Liverpool. I promised at least to spend one day and it may turn into two. She spoke very highly of Miss Sneyd and most affectionately of all the family. . . . M E

To Mrs. Edgeworth

1 North Audley Street, Monday, 23 May 1831

My dear mother . . . Tell me . . . (Pray do not forget) what you think I ought to give I mean what would be handsome to give to the servants here who have one and all been my most humble servants and devoted slaves—cooking luncheons Diurnal delicate viands and tender—dressing me eternally—eternally—running my errands perpetually and doing my business in the depths of the city and the uttermost bounds of Sloane Street—up early and out late. T'is unknown what a life I have led them and if ever I say a word about it to my own particular slave Eliza she replies 'Oh pray Ma'am don't mention it—do not think of it Ma'am. I'm sure its a pleasure.'

Perhaps you would wish to know how much I thought of giving—A guinea to each of the 4 servants—Cook—housemaid—Smith and John and 2 guineas to Eliza. But I really have not the least guess whether this is right so I beg you will tell me without being in the least afraid to tell me if I am not up to *handsome point*. . . . yr affec Maria E

To Honora Edgeworth

Friday morning, 27 May 1831

. . . I rejoice that I *had* written before yours of today came to settle that I would go to see and meet Mrs. Sneyd and Emma . . .

Goodby—I dined and spent a delightful evening with Lady E Whitbread yesterday She wished for you and sends true love to you. Met at dinner Mrs. Sam Whitbread a charming woman she is (and must be very charming when *I* think so)—Mr. Sam—exactly same as ever with head seen above skreen passaging in—The 3 Lady Harleys—Jane—Anne and Fanny (*Harleian miscellany* you know)[1]—amazingly clever two of them and superlative musicians vocal and instrumental—Major Keppel—son of Lord Albemarle and author of 'My personal narrative'[2] and some thing of a coxcomb—young—and in the gout. Remember I tell you a hobble I got into about carrying or not carrying him home at night . . . [no signature]

To Mrs. Edgeworth

Salden House,[3] 6 June 1831

Here we are dear Mother, Fanny and I in the greatest comfort and happiness that kindness and quiet and quiet ponies and good cream and plenty of everblowing roses flaunting in red clusters like your own Veranda can give. I cannot tell you but you can guess how happy I am—how happy we are with these dear good Carrs. Mrs. Carr is so fond of you too—and of Fanny *too* and all the young ones so take care of her and pud-dud her so lovingly! I am sure she will be the better for it and Lestock dear generous Lestock will be rewarded for advising her coming here with me. He will see a leetle more flesh on her bones I hope—yet one week cannot make much flesh . . . Before I go further I must tell you that my last days in London crowned the whole in all that was entertaining—amusing—curious—gratifying and delightful to head and heart (I am writing while Isabella Carr is reading *us* Destiny loud and very well she reads the Scotch). You may think that I cannot enter into details of the past at

[1] Harleian miscellany was the title of a selection of tracts from the library of Edward Harley, 2nd Earl of Oxford (1744–6), but the nickname was given to the children of Jane, wife of the 5th Earl of Oxford because of their mother's notorious infidelity to her husband.

[2] G. T. Keppel, *Personal Narrative of a Journey from India to England* (1825). *Narrative of a Journey across the Balkans* (1830).

[3] Near Winslow, Buckinghamshire.

present and I know that Fanny has noted down in her last to Honora and in her Journal the details of our last days in London and I will fill up viva voce when I get amongst you once more my own dear dears.

I must just note—Lady E Whitbread—4 Lady Harleys—Opera with Lady Guilford and daughters—Fuseli's cousin &c—Medea—Pasta—thrilling *shiver*—gliding sideways to her children and sudden retreat—Next night—French play—Leontine Fay in '*Une Faute*'[1]—the most admirable actress I ever saw and in the most touching piece. I could not listen to some comic thing which came afterwards—nor look at it. 3 young men—S. Whitbread—Major Keppel and Lord Mahon separately told me the impression made on them by this actress in this piece was such that they could not sleep afterwards! I had no trial how this would be with me because we went off from the playhouse to Sir James Souths to see the occultation[2] of Jupiter. That was indeed a sublime reality!—no wonder we were broad awake till 3 oclock.

Next morning to St. Paul's[3]—moral sublime—Rammohun Roy—I sat next him and saw his countenance all the time and heard all he said. Memm. Rammohun Roy—men of war—Why are the boys set above the girls Sermon by Bishop of Nova Scotia—quotation from Fisher—conclusion—stranger suggesting an improvement—shadows mountain—*setting* sun—dele *setting*—Judge Haliburton—between Fanny and me Shipley—Luncheon at the Bishops—Mrs. Wynne the Bishop (Copleston's) sister and her niece Miss [ ]—40 people—Lady Davy and little niece—goodnatured to her—Basil Hall—Bishop of Elphin and 3 daughters—Bishop of Landaff very polite to Lestock.

Came home took off Marabou and packed up. Miss Gerrard always obliging packed all finery for long sea and saved me all hurry and fatigue just as kind Evans saved me all packing trouble when I left home. Mr. Creed dined with us this our last day—delightful—Captain Beaufort in the morning at breakfast

[1] By J. S. Mayer, first performed in 1812. It was played at the King's Theatre on 31 May. *Une faute* was played at the Theatre Royal on 1 June, together with *Le Quaker et la danseuse* and *Les Premiers Amours*.

[2] Eclipse.

[3] To the service for the anniversary of the Charity Schools, held on 2 June (*Morning Chron.*, 3 June 1831).

—always kind and to me most affectionate. But now I come at the very last to what surprised touched and gratified me more than all the rest—Lestock actually wept when he took leave of me and pressed me to his generous noble heart as if I was his own sister—urging me to come back again. You will feel more than I can say for how many reasons and how exquisitely this touched and gratified me. All my own future happiness with Fanny depending so much on his loving me and so much of her pleasure in seeing me *ditto* and the certainty that every word and look of Lestocks means so much more than it says—so much more than common speeches and independently of all that concerned myself the real delight in a generous character

I can no more—Ever your affecy. Maria E

To Fanny Wilson

Hamstead Hall, Saturday morning, 11 June 1831

Here I am with my little desk on a little table something like my dear little table at No 1—in a window looking out on this pretty lawn. I am quite well and have a footstool under my feet and my body is as comfortable as it can be, and my mind, trying to be happy after parting with you my dearest . . . Thank you my dears for all your constant kindness and tenderness to me. Pray write to me for I really feel very *unked*[1] after leaving you tho I am not subject to low spirits and the friends by whom I am surrounded are most excellent kind people and I am up to the lips in all the comforts and luxuries of life, yet it is very different from you and that I cannot help feeling and knew I was to feel and to bear but did not think I should feel it so much.

Your sending John to open the gates was a very useful measure. 8 out of 14 were opened by him without disturbing my equanimity but I thought we never should have got through those that came after he was gone. I was convinced that Mrs. Carr would have come into possession of her legacy of the Indian box when the last of these gates flapped in the horses faces and they backed to the brink of ditch but some good natured body

[1] Solitary, forlorn, lonely (*O.E.D.*).

came up just in the nick of time, and Mrs. Carr had no further chance of her legacy.

Give my love to her when next you write and tell her this and that I faithfully remembered my promise to her in my dying moments—as I thought them—and I hope you are laughing my dears.

Well—after the trials of the gates were over new trials—not of nerves but of patience—Arrived at Stoney Stratford quite in time as the innkeeper told me for the coach which would be in at 12—So it was—but Lo! this was the *Independant Tallyho*—and my luggage and myself were turned back. 'This is not the coach in which your place is taken Ma'am.'—Very well—I went back to my lonely little parlor on being told I must wait another hour and made myself very comfortable finishing sewing the Honiton edge on my frill. The next Tallyho came in—Then I started up, sure that this was my coach. 'No Ma'am—there is one lady paid a sovereign in London but not your name—her name is Hall—But there is a place in this coach you may go if you please.'—But this was the *Patent* Tallyho and put up at quite a different place in Birmingham from either of those Lestock and Mr. Moilliet had named. Besides I should have lost my sovereign—So finding that a third Tallyho was expected in another hour and that this third of the name was exactly the name recorded in Lestocks letter I bravely refused to get into the *Patent* Tallyho, and stood resolved to wait the last event of things. Long long it seemed to wait but I finished my border and had not I great reason to be thankful for that as good Molly Maccauley would say (I wish I was half as good). At last 2 oclock struck and five minutes after the joyful sound of the horn—But what should become of me if this third and last Tallyho failed me! But—'All right Ma'am heres your name in the way-bill—Edgeworth paid £1—to pay £1 5.' So in I was hoisted and up went my bag and baggage—and—now you think and so thought I there was an end of my troubles—Vulgar gin-drinking man in coach with glazed eyes and hiccup but that did not trouble me—excepting nose—and I was thankful there was neither nurse nor child. A very decent half lady farmers wife silent woman sat in far corner and I wished she had been vis a vis and a very civil Birmingham man beside me who would save me the trouble which I did not want to be saved of carrying my China box—found out that he knew Mr. Moilliet and hoped he would take-care-of-me to the end of my journey and hand me safe over to James Moilliet.

Dinner—Farmers wife would not get out but *I* did and was the only femul—and tried to eat lamb that was anything but tender. Oh how unlike your tenderness and [ ].[1] But I was entertained with the sight of the dinner—Stewed ducks and cabbage which all the company of 8 men, I could not say gentlemen were so eager to be helped to that I would not interfere. Scarcely had we swallowed when hurried in again and we went on at a charming rate—10 miles an hour the whole way. The horses were changed every 5 miles. They make the horses run only ten miles a day at this rate, and each pair run only 5 miles and rest and are taken out again for another 5 miles afterwards in another coach. They say that coaches are passing almost every hour. Wonderful England! With all your industry and all your prosperity I hope you will not be revolutionised—especially in our time. Après nous le déluge.

Arrived at 8 oclock at the Swan in Birmingham but my caretaker had been previously deposited at his own shop door—a great pawnbrokers shop in Birmingham—So I was to do for myself. The moment the coach stopped as soon as I could make my little voice heard in the midst of the universal hubbub I inquired whether Mr. Moilliet or his carriage were at the inn—No—no such person or carriage. The office full of people and the inn yard jostling with people scrambling for their goods all in a few seconds ran off different ways and I was left alone under the arch standing between my black box and red bag. Sent for a porter instantly to the Lion's hotel and the Albion and all the hotels where *any* Tallyho put up—all in vain. One hostler knew his carriage and had seen it in the course of the day going down Bull street but that did me little good. Sent the porter to Moilliets Bank and to his office in New Hall Street. Returned—'Office shut—Bank shut'—And all Birmingham nature seemed shutting up and there was a death like stillness and a dread repose in the yard and as clear a space as before the Theatre François after play hour—and the fine-lady landlady twisting

[1] Word illegible in manuscript.

her hair and looking at herself in the glass like any French-woman said to me 'No resource Ma'am—No resource! We have done the unpossible! Better stay here tonight Ma'am. Better take a bed here Ma'am.'

'No thank you Ma'am, not a bed, but a chaise and pair if you please directly for Hamstead Hall.' It was by this time 9 oclock. I hope you think this was the best thing I could do? *Spanked* off —But when the driver was fairly out of Birmingham and all alone with me and my trunks on the road he stops and turns to me and says 'You know the way I hopes Ma'am to Hamstead Hall? for I does not rightly—never was there in my life!!!' Ass! thought I—What have you been doing all your life! But he was worse than an ass he was a mule—so obstinate that he would go on his own way without asking and I was forced to pop my head out at window to beg *his* way from every passenger at every turn and at last the obstinate man would drive me up a wrong and very narrow avenue though I assured him the white house he saw was not Hamstead Hall. 'Oh yes Ma'am but you'll find t'is. The last man told me it was that there white house and here it is Ma'am.'

Then off his box jumped he—leaving me and horses to our fate while he opened a pleasure-ground wicket and went in and knocked at the door—candles lighted within and out came a scared looking maid who La'-blessed-us and told us this was Mr. Lewis's and not Hamstead Hall—Bless your Soul. Happily she did know that Mr. Moilliets was farther on and I having now the vantage ground of my mule forced him to let me out for my own satisfaction while he turned the carriage. Lord knows how he did—he was a wonderful time about it. I mean while walked back down the lane and set the gate open. By and by he came up and put me in again and at last we actually did arrive at the real Hamstead Hall and the friendly faces of the Moilliets all appeared at the door as soon as it was unbarred and opened. Nothing could be warmer and kinder than their reception of me. They had all done tea ages ago and were preparing for bed—it being by this time near ten—But tea and all manner of good things were got for me and Mr. Moilliet and James fell to explanations. Mr. Moilliet had gone to meet me instead of James who had had a sore throat. I was glad—(not that he had a sore throat but that he was out of the scrape and no blame could rest on him poor fellow!) The short of it is—that Mr. Moilliet had never received my second letter telling him the name of the coach in which Lestock had taken my place and the name of the inn where it put up so he had gone to every place but the right and not being aware that there are 3 Tallyho's had given me up when the second came in and had as he says of himself been so excessively credulous as to believe the guard of the Independent Tallyho who assured him that I would not come on this day because there was a place for me in his coach and I would not take it.

I comforted Mr. Moilliet as well as I could and dispersed the tear in his eye and convinced him by my merry talking that I was not vexed or a bit the worse for the wear. Slept luxuriously and in one unbroken rest till 6 and am better than ever today . . .

By the by Mrs. Carr was quite wrong in her belief that places in the coach need be taken from London for Birmingham at this time of year for Mr. Moilliet assures me and my own eyes confirm his representation that inside places are always to be had because all who can go outside prefer outside and the insides continually are empty. No matter! I have *wasted* about £1 13 by this journey and must make it up by future economy. I never grudge anything but waste . . . and no more at present from your affectionate Maria E . . .

To Fanny Wilson

Hamstead Hall, Saturday, 18 June 1831

My dear Fanny . . . Mr. Moilliet has promised me that he or Emily will send and let you know as soon as they can after their arrival in Town. He thinks they will be where she usually is when in Town at Kirkham's Hotel in Lower Brook Street which will be conveniently near you. She will take her own carriage and will have horses so that she will not put you to any trouble or fatigue. She will come to you and will be much obliged to you I am sure if you will go with her to Mr. Haughton and to Mr. Chantrey. I have written a note of introduction for her and Mr. Moilliet to Chantrey that they may have it in case you should not be able to go but I hope you will for you will be a support and pleasure to her. I fear she is in weak health. I think I told you that she is going by the desire of her husbands family to bespeak a monument—a *tablet* from Chantrey. And to have her picture I *hope* done by Haughton for Mrs. Moilliet. She says she would rather her childs picture was taken and hopes she may be excused from sitting for her own but her father says he will have her picture and pray do whatever you can to persuade her to it.

Ask Mr. Moilliet to give you an account of our breakfast at Aston-Hall with Mr. Watt and of the extraordinary circumstances of our visit afterwards to Mrs. Watt. Mr. Watt appeared much better at his own house—wakened and revived and conversed and shewed that he has still much knowledge within him and taste for literature—But he has nobody with him to converse with and it is melancholy to see him in that great house alone with his riches! He has bought a great many really very fine pictures and Cabinets and china and all sorts of valuables and the house is magnificently furnished and the gardens shrubbery—park and wood are of great extent (I walked miles till I could no more!) and all is the utmost that wealth can do for happiness and how little it can do is the result of all my reflexions and feelings after seeing James Watt in possession of the grand object of all his own and his fathers ambition for him—without wife—or child or friend to sympathise with him—in solitary grandeur!—his body overfed and bloated—his head and heart perishing for want of sympathy. *That* never will be the case with me while I have you my dearest and your mother and Honora and Harriet and *many* more. Happy creature that I am at 63! Have not I reason to be as thankful at least as Molly Maccaulay?

your ever affectionate
Maria E

I will get John Bristows direction and send it you when I return. I have seen both the young ladies that have been thought of for James Moilliet and required to give my opinion of them. I did not like either of them. His mind is not fixed at all and nothing has been said or done to commit him. I think Laura Carr far preferable. Query? would it do? Mr. and Mrs. Moilliet liked the description much but interference in these things never does rightly or is right to do. If they meet James perhaps might like her, but not if pointed out to him and perhaps Laura would not like him—So there it is.

To Fanny Wilson

Catton Hall, Wednesday, 22 June 1831

My dear Fanny . . .

I will tell you all my short history since last I wrote. Came here on Saturday to dinner—good time—was not aware that Catton is so far from Lichfield as 8 miles—Lady Farnham's carriage was waiting for me at the Swan and I drove grandly in it to Mr. Striplings and got Aunt Mary's parcel and then to Mr. Pallmers at the Bank to deliver her note and get her will. Mr. Pallmer said he had not it—that it had been returned he believed to Mr. Lister but he would have search made. I said I would wait while search was made—So—the will was found and I have it safe.

Lady Farnham has been as kind as possible to me and she is so good that it is impossible not to like her and I do not repent spending two more days here 'tho certainly neither Miss Herbert or Miss Kenny are agreeable to me and I dont well know why.

. . . Among other people too numerous to mention who have dined here Mr. John Sneyd made his appearance. I thought he had been dead but I find that stroke of the palsy of which I heard only kilt[1] him—and encreased his stammering. I think he is nearly the same as ever he was 'à cela près' and no great matter after all! He says that his nephew's drawings of the Scroggin family[2] made him sick—they are such caricatures!—such monsters!!!

[1] 'Much hurt': *Castle Rackrent, Tales and Novels* (1833), i. 119 (Glossary). Cf. also *The Absentee, Tales of Fashionable Life, Tales and Novels* (1833), x. 51: 'the widow dropped down dead and there was a cry as for ten *berrings*. "Be qu'ite" says I, "she's only kilt for joy." '

[2] Perhaps the boxer Scroggins (John Palmer) who proved to the prize ring 'what KEAN has been to the boards of Drury-lane theatre' and who was known for his skill as a comic raconteur. 'He possesses more confidence in telling a story than many persons who have finished their educations at a University' (Egan, *Boxiana* (1818–24), ii. 216; iii. 367). I am indebted to Professor H. W. Donner for this

And his own drawings for Rackrent?[1]—He does not think your picture the least like—I've done with him.

Now I am coming to Byrkley Lodge—The beauty of the forest on the charming day I went there struck me much in contrast with the altered state of the inhabitants but I found them less altered in appearance than I had expected—Mrs. Sneyd wonderfully well—Emma the most changed—the most irrevocably changed I think—a look of such deep fixed worn sorrow—pale as marble and the lines of age and grief chisselled in. She certainly is most strongly attached to her father. I loved her better this day than ever I did in my life and pitied them both excessively—especially as they were as chearful in manner and conversation as they could possibly make themselves. To my surprize Mr. Sneyd who had refused as they told me to see some of the Boothbys and his near relations consented to see me as soon as he heard I was come—They neither of them pressing him to it as the physicians order that should never be. I expected to be shocked and to see him worn to a skeleton—No such thing. He is altered to be sure—in 8 years that must be but I was astonished to see so little alteration, either in face or hands. His legs Mrs. Sneyd says are dreadfully thin but they were covered by his dressing gown as he lay, on the sofa—or rather as he sat up for he quite sat up supported by cushions—and tho' there was the look of suffering and twinges of pain every now and then yet from time to time he smiled and enjoyed conversation. They went on talking to each other and to me. He was in an airy bedchamber which you never saw I believe with a pretty view from the windows and there is a nice little antichamber where they dine and sit when not with him. Mrs. Sneyd always at night lies upon a sofa in that room in her dressing gown ready to start up whenever he wants. She has gone through a great deal—3 years next September since he was taken ill. That abscess the breaking of which Dr. Darwin and Mr. Birch thought would be fatal has not killed him. It has been open some time and his pulse is now 72 and 74 some time. He eats with

reference. Other possible candidates are Goldsmith's poor author in *Citizen of the World*, Letter XXX and Giles Scroggens in the comic ballad *Giles Scroggens' Ghost*.

[1] See above, p. 141.

some appetite. The result of all I observed is that there is not any immediate danger and that there may be hope but Mrs. Sneyd does not think so nor Emma and they charged me not to excite hope that might lead to worse disappointment in Aunt Mary's mind. Therefore I only take the satisfaction of telling my hopes to you. This much good is certain for myself—that the sight of him and the meeting and the whole day was not nearly so painful for me as I had expected and as I am sure my dear you feared it would be for me. His and all their manners towards me were affectionate and I felt that they took kindly to my going there. I did as your mother bid me and let it rest without saying that I went there to please Aunt Mary.

The house at Byrkley Lodge is very much improved by the new dining room and bedchamber and dressing room &c over it—The Veranda in front of the new room beautiful—the grounds much improved—a rivulet spread quite into a river within view of the house—pretty deer!—distant views opened—hedges cleared away trees grown beautifully—and there lies the poor master—sighing when I said so—*Ah! I shall never be able to go out again*—his sigh expressed—But to avoid giving pain I think to his wife and daughter he only said in words 'I wonder when I shall *come about again*' and he tapped the back of the sofa with Aunt Marys motion of the hand and her gentleness of resigned look. When I talked of Aston Hall which in the Bracebridge time they knew so well and when I pitied Mr. Watt for his being alone in his grandeur there—he said 'I am happier—with all the affection shewn me.' His look to Mrs. Sneyd and Emma was very touching. It reminded me of Mr. Hopes—and yet how different the men. The elements of happiness and misery however in all minds are the same—one of my flat truisms. When we left the room Mrs. and Miss Sneyd told me the history of a quarrel with Mr. (Granby)[1] Lister which I disliked hearing. Money was at the bottom—as Dumont used to say it is at the bottom of almost all quarrels and almost all crimes—which I feel it very difficult to believe—even when conviction stares me in the face. By their account Mr. *Granby* was quite in the wrong—But *hear both sides.* I should be very sorry however to hear any more about it and will not inflict it on you.

[1] T. H. Lister, *Granby* (1826).

They asked very kindly for you—said little about Honora—*just enough* about Aunt Mary—shewed me her rooms and by common consent we were silent on those points . . .

Give my love to Lestock. I had almost forgotten what is the incessant subject of conversation here—The coins that have been found in vast quantities in the river Dove just below Tutbury. The silver *claw* of an old chest has also been found which seems to indicate that a chest full of these coins was thrown into the river in the time of the wars. One man found coins which he has sold I believe at 1s. a piece for £300. The contention for these coins at last became furious—men women and children being in the water up to their chins all day. Some have perished from overheating and overcooling themselves. At last when from scolding and struggling they came to fighting it was necessary to call in military assistance to quiet them and to protect the *treasure trove* for his Majesty. What they have already got he leaves with them but forbids their further *groping* on their own account. The price of coins has risen amazingly and the Coino-mania is spreading fast and far. I send a few of the most approved of the curiosities. You will find in the folio Rapin[1] all that can be made out about them in the head and tail pieces and notes to the reigns of Edward 1–2d and third—and engravings of the coins. If you my dear Fanny have no wish to keep the specimens and if Lestock has no wish to have them or if he (as most likely he will) pronounces all this to be '*cursed nonsense*' or '*d-d humbug*' —pray return the coins to me because I know Mr. Butler and others would think them treasures.—Understand tho' I am in too great a hurry to express myself so as to be understood that of all people I would rather you and Lestock should have them if you really like them.

Now Lady Farnham will bear it no longer so I must finish—Love me excessively, and believe me Ever yours affectionately

Maria Edgeworth . . .

[1] Paul de Rapin, *History of England* (1726–31).

To Honora Edgeworth

Hamstead Hall, 25 June 1831

My dear Honora . . .

These few last days, with all that I saw and felt at Byrkley Lodge, and at Lichfield Cathedral—terrace—palace[1]—The present and the past, and the thoughts of the future so many recollections of the dead and anxieties for the living, the things that remain and the persons that have passed away—altogether so crowded upon my mind that I really felt at last quite stupified and unable to feel or think and move. I was all such a strange confusion of pain and pleasure and wonder at the ceaseless miracle of life and death wonder at the strange certainty of much that *has been* of which there is no trace on earth but in our own minds that I really could not settle my thoughts and feelings sufficiently to write to you my dear Honora yesterday. I have slept well and recovered from this sort of dreamy state which lasted all the way I drove home by myself from Lichfield to this place.

Now for common sense—Saturday last I went to Catton and arrived by dinner time . . .

Sunday—ourselves only—Monday—Mr. and Mrs. Matthew Gisborne—very pleasing both. She is an East Indian daughter of the late Professor of Oriental languages at the College at Calcutta. She may do Pak some good by mentioning him in her next letters to her brother and sister and various relations of consequence who are still living there. I think she will for I asked it and she seemed to like me as much as I liked her, and had a sort of cordial East-Indian sincere manner. I can't say as much for the eldest Gisborne brother—very oracular and squinting—So no more about him. Mrs. Gisborne the mother who had been given over by all the physicians—(Stone—I believe or something that way) has made a wonderful recovery at 72 after having quite lost her memory and intellect. After being seized with convulsion fits which it was thought would have terminated her existence, she suddenly grew still and wakened as it were at once to life and reason—she said 'My mind is come back to me I feel it.' And after being unable to stir from her

[1] See below, pp. 558–9.

couch—being with her knees drawn up to her chin with the agony of pain, she at once stepped off her couch and Mr. Gisborne met her at the top of the stairs! Her amazement and joy they say was most touching . . .

On Monday—many more at dinner than I have named—2 youths sons of Mr. Holdworthy—Wentworth the eldest had been a Charter house companion of Francis and Pakenhams but I could get little out of him but blushes tho I am told there's much inside. Captain and Mrs. Probyn—I dont believe you know or care about them—he loud—very and good natured very and made me write in his pocket book with the worst skewer of a pen ever I touched the titles of some books which I mentioned with praise and the books were Honor Delany Hyacinth O Grady and Irish men and I[1]—Next to me at this dinner sat—who do you think Mr. John Sneyd . . . I dont think he has quite as much feeling as people thought and No. 1 is his Summum bonum.

I was much interested, *exceedingly* by all I saw both of Mrs. and Miss Sneyd and glad to feel my old affection for them along with that gratitude which I hope I never can cease to feel for Mrs. Sneyds kindness to me and Fanny. They inquired kindly for her and *her husband* and I said well of both—and true. We all parted with affectionate feelings for each other I believe and I am very glad I went there.

I forget what happened next day at Catton. Oh—a Mr. Brooke Tipperary—lady sister in law to Mrs. Webster came and a Miss Head—dreadful drawling brogues. Quite a character Mrs. Brooke is whom I will think and talk of hereafter.

Thursday—took leave of Catton—Miss [? Kenny] took Miss Head in baruche with me to Lichfield to have this opportunity of shewing her the cathedral. I would much rather have gone alone but one can't have everything one's own way. I forgot her and everybody with me when I got into the Cathedral and thought my own thoughts as I walked up the aisle—my fathers marriage to Miss Honora Sneyd!—and all that had passed in those times—Miss Seward and all—and her monument with Sir Walter Scotts lines on her—and Mr. Saville's with hers on him!

[1] George Brittaine, *Honour Delany* (? 1829); *Hyacinth O'Gara* (1828); *Irishmen and Irishwomen* (1830); or *Irish Priests and Irish Landlords* (1830).

—and Garrick and Johnson's busts!—And Chantrey's beautiful monument of the two sleeping children! Then I walked on that *Cathedral shady walk* where so many of those most dear to me have walked in the most interesting moments of their lives and recollected my fathers phaeton and *the* grey horses standing at that palace gate—The trees living still—and the walls the same as ever!

I went into the Palace and asked leave to look at the house—nobody being at home. Miss or Mrs. Woodhouse now the proprietor had walked out. Her maid said I was welcome and I just looked and saw the changes!—and went on the terrace behind the house, where I remembered *old old* Mrs. and Mr. Seward and Miss Seward in all her glory!—and recollected so many things my father in times long past told me had passed here!—and all this now only ideas—the present real people all so different and they all to pass away—Miss Kenny and Miss (Irish) Head had walked in with me and asked many questions about Miss Seward &c which shewed how completely forgotten or unknown she and all about it is now!

It was time to recollect that Miss Kenny must go home to dinner and that I must go on to Mrs. Moilliets so we went out of the Palace gates and drove off and I reached Hamstead Hall before I well knew where I was—16 good miles nevertheless. Mrs. Moilliet and Susan were most refreshingly glad to see me. They are most affectionate people and I *do* love them—slow though they be (I am not so bad as you think me—I can tolerate slowness when joined to such good natures).

The character of this place is repose—The look of the cattle—feeding!—feeding!—feeding!—slow moving or lying in groups—and all those still broad shadows! and the hum of the flies and the very motions of the branches and leaves of the trees as I look up at them all breathe repose—and I am very sorry Miss Stovin is coming to break it for I enjoy it much and shall not I am sure like her affectation and secondhand old battered fine-ladyism. But it can't be helped she has sent word she will come tomorrow if her cold will let her. I only hope it will not . . .

yours affectionately
Maria Edgeworth

To Mrs. Edgeworth

Hampstead Hall, 27 June 1831

My dear mother . . .

I have been to see a very fine collection of pictures at Birmingham—pictures by antient masters. Many noblemen in this and adjoining counties have sent their pictures and the Duke of Wellington some of his—like an honest gentleman as he is to fulfill a promise he made when dining at Birmingham—None of his *Spanish* pictures but these which he did lend are from among those taken from King Joseph.[1] To save further prosing I will enclose the catalogue—just as I marked it in pencil and always marked without looking till afterwards at the Masters name. Perhaps you may have seen some of the pictures in this catalogue at their own homes. Yes at Warwick Castle I am sure you have and will remember *Gondemar*. At all events it gives me satisfaction to think that you and Honora and Lucy will be looking over the names of the pictures I have been so delighted with. My eyes are much greater means of pleasure to me now in my age than ever they were in my youth—I suppose on the principle that we always feel the value of friends and of every thing most when near losing them.

Mr. Creed—apropos to friends—has arrived at last and drank tea here on Sunday and pleased Mrs. Moilliet even more than I expected. She says she feels there is the making of a friend in him. What a pleasure it is to be the connecting link between friends! He will I am sure become very intimate in this family and this house will be a pleasant home to him in his visits to Birmingham which must be frequent in consequence of his *being about to be* acting Secretary of Birmingham and London Rail road Company. Mr. Corrie is the resident Birmingham agent—Perhaps you recollect him—a literary agreeable elderly man. Mrs. Corrie won my heart *before* she spoke in the highest terms of 'Dialogues on Botany'[2]—and she spoke in the highest terms of that book before she knew the name of the author. I had the pleasure of informing her that it was written by Mrs. E's sister. Mrs. Corrie I ought to add is a famous

[1] Eldest brother of Napoleon and King of Naples and Spain.
[2] Published anonymously in 1819 by Harriet Beaufort.

philosophical botanist herself and a most engaging person. N B —I am told that a famous Botanist who has brought home dried plants from far countries in a better state of preservation than ever seen before says that he believes his success depended upon his having taken peculiar care to *dry* the paper before he put his plants between the leaves—he baked it in an oven. I note this to make sure of its being told by somebody to Pakenham.

A letter from Mr. Moilliet has come in while I was writing. When they took their little child (Philippa) with them to Chantrey's she stopped before the monument of the sleeping children (Lichfield children) and looked and looked—and then wanted the children to get up and at last burst out crying . . .

Miss Stovin has not been such a nuisance as I expected to me. Moreover she has given me a fish—a very odd fish which I shall bring home with me among the strange odd things I am bringing with me. Oh I should be so happy if Harriet as well as Sophy could be at Edgeworthstown when I come. Do you think Mr. Butler could let her accompany me if I went round by Trim for her. Pray ask. I must finish—yr ever Maria E . . .

To Fanny Wilson

Hamstead not Hampstead Hall
as Mr. Moilliet informs me,
2 July 1831

You judged well my dear Fanny (as you *almost always* do) in quieting poor Mr. Moilliets hurried mind by the assurance that there was no absolute necessity for my being at home by any particular day. I am the more glad that you did so because my mother has so kindly written to me such a full permission, such plenary indulgence for all my past present and future changes of plan that I should have been absolutely illnatured to have refused him time to accomplish his own and his daughters objects (as dear to them as mine are to me no doubt). I should have reproached myself bitterly if I had had any hand in hurrying him, for he has returned looking the ghost of himself. Such a woebegone figure as he was when I yesterday saw him coming up the stair case!—groaning and Oh dear-ing himself and bending under the load of half a dozen parcels! I hope you clearly see him coming up with the hope of being pitied and nursed at home and what do you think awaited him at the top of the stairs? I—with the news—(at which his eyes opened pale and wide) that every creature in the house (myself and Theodore excepted) were ill and much worse than himself of this influenza—Mrs. Moilliet in her bed!—just bled with leeches unable to speak or move—Susan just able to crawl—not out of her room—Mrs. Jones—Housekeeper, coachman, footman, gardener all! all! ill! in their several beds.

Susan was first taken ill about 4 days ago. She was quite delirious one night and fancied she was in Australia among the black fellows. Mrs. Moilliet was next seized and she was in dreadful pain in head and back and face so swelled and flushed and pulse so quick—and she is such a bad subject for fever! Fortunately there is a very good surgeon near Birmingham in whose medical advice this family have great confidence—Mr. Hudson. He was here soon and quieted my fears by the assurance that there was no danger 'but it must take its course' above and below stairs.

And in the midst of this *course* came company. Miss Stovin had just cleared out before Susan took to her bed. Then came a Mr. and Mrs. Shirley—he of high *Ferrers family* and an evangelical clergyman—*she* an heiress and evangelical too and a niece to Mrs. Waddington. They brought with them maid and child and some archdeacon and his lady were asked to meet them but luckily the archdeacon's wife had the influenza and they did not come. Mr. and Mrs. Shirley were to stay *some* days—no one knew how many. The day they first came to dinner Mrs. Moilliet was just able to appear and very ill able—The next morning only came down to shew she must go back to bed—James and Theodore extant *only*. Well well! we got through it and they had excellent dinner, ices and champagne and grapes and all the *creature-comforts* which these saints seem to me to relish as much as any of the sinners. They went to Birmingham and bought china and saw all manner of sights and then at night had *expoundings* and long prayers, and I was quite out of patience with Mr. Shirleys affected mode of reading and expounding but I kept my indignation to myself and nobody knew my countenance as you do—luckily. When he is not acting saint he is an agreeable worldly man full of anecdote and good natured and well bred and his wife tho Mrs. Waddingtons niece has not the least affectation—is only a little pettish and selfish and cross like an heiress who thought she had a right to be humored by a husband on whom she had bestowed her valuable self. (I never *let on* to Mrs. Shirley that I had heard from her aunt Waddington and her name was never pronounced—so the boat did not sink with me.) Mr. Hudson having pronounced this influenza to be infectious they submitted with a few '*how provoking*'s—and '*Very sorry indeed*'s never to see Mrs. Moilliet all the time they were in the house. Susan *Mrs.* Shirley saw for a few minutes the last evening as she was then able to get up and come out into her mothers dressing room. Mr. Shirley had a great mind that his little boy, who is really a fine little lump of a 3 year-old should have been passed before Susan's door that she might have the pleasure of a sight of his beauty but the mother pleaded against it Mr. Hudson and the childs being asleep. 'Too late! too late my dear!' A letter came making it indispensible that Mr. Shirley should meet some other saint at Ashby de la Zouche next day and at 6½ oclock next morning I heard the sound of their parting wheels and running to my window had the pleasure of seeing the back of their landau and all the backs of their heads driving away!—Mrs. Moilliet very very poorly still!—and Susan only just able to crawl about her mothers room—and the footman a Welchman sure he should die and repeating that he should not like to be buried in this country. 'Thummas—very bad indeed Ma'am, but he keeps it all to himself like and the gardener who druv Mr. and Mrs. Shirley in his place all about Birmingham yesterday is down today—in his bed—as bad as any.' The housemaid who said all this had a bad *cough* and very bad head, but she had a good heart as she told me and indeed as I saw for she weathered it all waiting upon everybody—along with good pretty Anne Mrs. Moilliets own maid who shews true attachment to her mistress and her *young missess.*

This day came powdering down the avenue a carriage with a lady who must see *Miss* Moilliet at least (who had never seen her in her life). She came from a distance was a friend of Mrs. Knights—had had the influenza very bad just recovered and must see Miss Moilliet. So up she went and she staid but ten minutes (Thank Heaven) and disappeared in her *fly*—and who was she?—a Miss Cave—daughter to Sir William Cave—nearly related to the Otway Cave's we knew. By a mistake of a few words in a grandfather's will the estate went away from Sir William to Otway and Sir W was left only with the Baronetage and a pittance. Mrs. Moilliet when she was hardly able to speak told me this as I was sitting by her bed, having as she said some confused recollection that we knew the Otway Caves at Paris.[1] How oddly these knowledges and anecdotes of people come out! I forgot to tell you that the Shirleys came out with a perfect knowledge of Edgeworthstown and our charming society Mr. E's school &c—Through whom or how do you think?—Through saint to saint—Mr. Hoare. His mother corresponds with Mrs. Shirley (ci-devant Waddington) and they knew all the history of his loves with Maria Keatinge tho not her name. Mrs. Hoare had often mentioned her sons unfortunate attachment 'to which she had and has no objection but that they had nothing to live upon'. This proves that Mr. Hoare was sincere in his love and had not been trifling with the girl of which Mr. Keatinge in his indignation accused him. I wish I could get them a living from some of these bishops who doat upon me—yet I doubt if they would ever give me any thing but a Chinese pincushion. I will put it to the proof if ever I have opportunity for poor black Maria's sake and her cream faced saint. Observe I am very liberal to saints—as I ought to be for their covering me with their wings and sparing me with their beaks.

Sunday morning—Mrs. Moilliet is much better—only both her eyes are closed up and a furious eresipelas in one cheek in consequence of the leech bites and Mr. Hudson says Its all right—and she is going on just as he could wish. N B—Mr. Hudson is not the least like Mr C. Long—he is a plain spoken clear thinking man without any of the verbosity or pomposity of his profession. He and I have struck up a friendship 3 hours after sight. He has lent me a medical journal in which there is a horrid account of this Cholera morbus which he verily believes is the plague—it having all the symptoms therof—excepting only as I observed to him that rather striking difference of there being no plague-boils in this disease to which observation he replies

[1] In 1820.

that the boils are not essential characteristics of the plague. I doubt. He doubts on another subject which it would be useful to put beyond doubt if possible. He doubts that Chlorine fumigations *destroy the principle of contagion* tho of use in purifying the air. Query—worth referring to the Hospitals to answer.

This day is bright with the reappearance of Suzy at the breakfast table and Mr. Moilliet without his hand upon his chest—and the gardener without 'his headache' and Thummas—good Thummas sends word he is able to drive again—Willing he was even when he could only sit not stand. He wanted to go for his master to Birmingham but James went and drove his father home in capital style. Mr. Moilliet thinks he shall be able to set out on Wednesday next and by that time I trust leech bites and eresipelas will have disappeared from Mrs. Moilliets poor face and that we shall leave her convalescent to Suzy's care and James's. Most affectionate creatures they all are—and I feel so much obliged to them for letting me be quite as one of themselves during this time—letting me be in their sick rooms and nurse them to the best of my little capacity—Speaking to me when they could speak with such endearing kindness and looking at me when they could look with such soft delightful affection. I assure you I have been very happy for there is no pleasure *much* greater than that of being loved and of feeling one is useful to those we love—and I really do love these good souls though they are in slow bodies. I am almost ashamed to feel how much *soft manners* and affection weigh with me even without superior abilities but it would not do for a length of time. I should pine for something more and higher or I should not be my father's daughter or—your sister.

Helen[1] has been going on in my head I assure you through all and several things I have seen here and several I have heard will turn to profit to her account—Especially some which Mr. Shirley told me when his saintly fit was not on—One Italian story about the devil stealing away *true* shame and putting *false* into a man's heart. I forgot whether I ever mentioned Miss Stovins visit—she spent 2 days here before the trouble. Indeed it is now believed she brought the influenza with her for she was sick in a sort of a way all the time she was here—fainting on a sofa—

[1] ME's last novel, published in 1834.

and the next dressed out in a great Berri which she told me 'had made wonderful fortune with all the gentlemen in London'. A better specimen in worse preservation have I seldom seen of a battered elegante and Helen shall certainly profit by her. I can easily efface the marks of the individual and draw the affected class of which she is the charmante—no interessante representative. I quite agree with Sir Walter Scott that mixing with all sorts of society is most beneficial to a writer and that materials are often found where least expected . . .

What noble use of his hundreds of thousands Dr. Bell has made. I congratulate uncle Francis who I am sure rejoices in this good to humanity and as if it were a personal good to himself and that he is more proud of it for human nature than he would condescend to be if he had done it himself. Thank you my dear Fanny for telling me of this and of Mr. Marsden's giving up his 1600 per Annum.[1] I love to hear these good things and I hope Rochefoucaulds ghost blushes for his maxims[2]—all witty as they be . . .

I have pleased Mr. Hudson by recommending to him Manzoni's Promessi Sposi—for the sake of the plague. James Moilliet had it (not the plague) and lent it (not the plague) to Mr. Hudson. He has read Maddens travels[3]—you recollect his account of his treatment of the plague. Hudson says it is nothing new—that stimulants brandy &c had often been tried at the height of the fever—that there is a critical moment when if administered they save but the hitting this is the difficulty. There is in Madden a description of a boy who had the plague which he says is the best description of the symptoms he ever read—except in Defoe[4]—'and what does it signify whether the adjuncts of the story be true or not for our medical purposes if the symptoms and medical history be exactly given.' This is the same as to the use of all moral fiction. If the feelings and the

[1] In 1831 Andrew Bell, the educationalist, gave £120,000 to trustees for the benefit of Scottish education. William Marsden (1754–1836), the orientalist, who had been secretary to the Admiralty 1804–7, surrendered to the state his life pension of £1,500 per annum.

[2] François, duc de la Rochefoucauld, *Réflexions ou sentences et maximes morales* (1665).

[3] R. R. Madden, *Travels in Turkey, Egypt, Nubia and Palestine* (1829).

[4] Defoe, *Journal of the Plague Year* (1722).

passions and their consequences be well described no matter for the rest.

I am quite well and not being the least afraid of catching this influenza I shall probably escape it. Every evening I have taken a delightful walk before tea with that good natured silent-one Theodore. The lanes about this place are delightful—full of dog-roses and singing birds and every figure we meet—old man old woman, boy or girl with pitcher—ass with faggots or plough-man plodding home—picturesque—and even the *pigs—Morlands.* Yesterday evening returning home by sunset we heard a boy playing a flute or flageolet in a wood on the other side of the water so agreeably all the while we were coming up the hill and seeing the light of the sunset on the trees. I have much more pleasure infinitely more in my old age in the sight of the beauties of nature than I ever had in youth. It seems as if I had come into the possession of the fortune of my senses late in life and like all people not used early to riches I suppose I am inclined to make a sort of *parvenu* boasting of them.

Please! Pray excuse!—and believe me ever affec
your own Maria Edgeworth . . .

To Fanny Wilson

Wavertree Hall
friday 8 July 1831

Lest you should not know where upon earth Wavertree hall is let me tell you that it is the seat of Mr. and Mrs. Lawrence near Liverpool and this is answer to the concluding Query in the letter I have just received from you from Post Office Liverpool.

I left Mrs. Moilliet in bed on Wednesday morning at ten oclock but quite convalescent and Susan better than ever and all the servants even the chickenhearted Welsh boy well—So there's an end of that evil. We posted away Mr. Moilliet and I inside chaise Theodore on box—posted I did not say spanked tho Mr. Moilliet is never satisfied when travelling unless he is spanking away. We had a very pleasant journey and nothing to complain and what is more did not complain of any thing. Somewhat in consequence of your remonstrance and more in consequence of my mothers and more in compliance with my own wishes I plagued and *battered* at Mr. Moilliet till I persuaded him (tear in eye) to go to Maer Hall with me though it delayed him half a day and he was in a terrible hurry—but there was no help for it so he consented. *Mr.* Jos Wedgewood was unluckily in London—that excepted all right—and much gratified were Mrs. Wedgewood and 2 sons and 4 daughters by our visit. An entertaining character dined there of whom I have time only to say that she was the daughter of Edwards the ci devant great bookseller and after being widow of I forget who at Bath is now the wife of that Mr. Butt who was curate at Trentham when we were there. She told many anecdotes of Lady Nelson which Alas! I cannot now tell you—as I used to pour out all my gatherings to you.

I am excessively ashamed and vexed to be obliged to confess to you that I have not seen the Hollands. Mr. Moilliet was in such a tremendous hurry that he *could* not have stopped longer than while we changed horses but the plain fact (which all but you who know me would deem incredible) is that I passed through Knutsford without knowing. When we were a mile out of the town Mr. Moilliet observed to me 'I believe we are in Cheshire'. 'Then if we are' quoth I 'remember that I *hope* you will let me call on the Hollands at Knutsford I have promised.' 'Oh my dear Miss E Knutsford we have just passed through it.'

Give my love to Dr. Holland and Miss Holland and what you can say for me I know not. Mr. Moilliet scarcely stopped to swallow food when we arrived at Birmingham and got on the Liverpool and Manchester railroad to go back per Manchester to Hamstead Hall. (He has a new place in Cambridgeshire in view—on sale in a few days—Mum)

Mrs. Lawrence's chaise had been waiting 2 hours for us—brought *us* meaning Theodore Adelaide here and here we found Mrs. Lawrence as glad to see us as poor woman she could possibly be when her youngest son has the quinsey—In consideration of which—Instead of staying till tomorrow as I had intended I shall go today—I shall sail at 5 this evening and expect to be in Dublin between 9 and ten tomorrow morning . . .

Yr. ever Maria E

Epilogue 1840–1844

WITH a base established with her sister Fanny at 1 North Audley Street, Maria Edgeworth naturally intended soon to revisit England. By 1833 she had reduced the total of her brother Lovell's known debts to £12,000, but he then found himself obliged to reveal that, contrary to a promise of complete openness over his affairs, he had incurred further liabilities of £3,000. This was too much for his eldest sister and for those of the family who had been living a very uncomfortable life with him at Edgeworthstown. They refused to stay in the same house with him, but Maria again undertook to pay his debts and to make him an allowance of £250 a year if he would sell his life interest in the estate to his next half-brother Sneyd and go and live elsewhere.[1] Though Lovell could have met his immediate debts by some legal chicanery and a sale to some outside person, he was not without feeling for his relations and his sister's arrangement offered him a secure if small income for the future. He accepted the proposals. Sneyd, whose health did not permit him to live at Edgeworthstown, ruefully raised the money to buy the estate he had expected to inherit and Maria was again left to carry the burden of management. Harriet Butler (*née* Edgeworth) wrote to her brother Pakenham in India:[2] 'You can easily imagine the relief the freedom, the excessive happiness of Edgeworthstown now that it is freed from that Incarnation of a Lie . . . now that there is no hypocritical acting that we dont know the hypocrisy that was hourly acted to us, now that there is not the feeling that your servants know more of what is done than you do, that there is not a gradual corruption of every human being about you. . . .' Maria herself never put it so strongly. In the account which she wrote for the benefit of Edgeworth descendants she

[1] Harriet Butler (*née* Edgeworth) to MPE, 1 Aug. 1833; ME's Appendix to MS. Black Book of Edgeworthstown (Irish State Paper Office); Edgeworth Papers, 1833, passim.

[2] Harriet Butler to MPE, 1 Aug. 1833.

speaks only of Lovell's financial incompetence, never mentions the discomforts of living in the house with a weak-willed drunkard, and minimizes her own efforts as estate agent.

Though matters gradually eased and she was able to hand over the agency in 1839 (when she was 71), the Edgeworths were never again in the comfortable financial circumstances of R. L. Edgeworth's lifetime and Maria had no money, and often no time, for English visiting. In 1840, however, she was free at last to go over to Fanny. She spent from December 1840 to April 1841 in England and she paid a last visit from November 1843 to April 1844.

To Mrs. Edgeworth

Hamstead Hall, Thursday, 2 December 1840

. . . Here I am! And thanks to dear Francis (Wind and Steam favoring) after the best possible passage from Ireland and the quickest, easiest most pleasant journey from Liverpool here. We left Harriet and Louisa and their pretty and beautifully furnished baby house on tuesday afternoon, after luncheon dinner, sailed *and* steamed in the Prince at about ½ past five and without the slightest sea suffering reached Liverpool after an eleven hours passage. How a woman can possibly get on and get her *trunks* and all her *objects* on landing without a man and a gentleman to help her I cannot guess! Having had both a gentleman and a brother I had my way made for me with all the ease imaginable at 5 oclock lamplight through all the hurly burly to the Angel inn and lay down on a black sofa and slept till breakfast time Francis having wisely decided not to hurry off by 6 oclock train but to wait and breakfast comfortably and to go off by 8 oclock train—per rail-way—and so we did and it was delightful in the first place to see the orderly manner in which all the people and their goods were stowed into that numerous train of carriages—The goods belonging to the passengers within each carriage being with them either withinside or without—not as formerly pele-mesle in one baggage carriage where people were to find their objects as they could or could not in the hurry of the last moments. I had even my green baize covered writing box &c

under my feet as comfortable as possible—as if we had been in your own carriage—only one man and one woman-lady-ish sort of person for the first 50 miles and 2 men I did not care what they were in addition afterwards. . . We arrived here between one and two, having come the whole 180 miles in about 5½ hours —at the rate of five and twenty miles an hour allowing for stoppages at stations and going up-hill &c. We often went at 30 miles an hour but the average would be 25 and tho I had fancied I should feel some alarm from the recollection of late accidents, I felt none. Indeed Mr. Creeds letter in the papers about the proportion of the numbers who have gone and the few accidents that have happened gave me a confidence-raisonée much strengthened by Francis's company and the sunshine without and within (I was no more tired last night than if I had only been to Longford and not so much) . . .

To Harriet Butler

1 North Audley St., 26 December 1840

. . . Mrs. Darwin (*you* know I am sure that she is the youngest daughter of Jos Wedgwood)—she is worthy of both father and mother—affectionate and unaffected and full of old times all young as she is—putting me in mind of the first time she ever saw me when she was about Charlottes[1] age and then of the second time when she was a young lady at Etruria[2] and saw me then provoked by her mother's having contrary to contract, invited a whole company to meet me when the written contract specified that there should be only her own family. Mrs. Darwin has her mother's radiantly cheerful countenance even now when she is confined from all London gaieties and from all gaiety except that of her own mind by close attendance upon her poor sick husband. You know that he says he was ill in consequence of the sea voyage[3]—that he was never a single day free from sea-suffering. But Dr. Holland tells us that the voyage was not the

[1] Charlotte Fox, Sophy Edgeworth's younger daughter.

[2] Etruria Hall, nr. Stoke on Trent, Josiah Wedgwood's house near his pottery of the same name.

[3] The voyage of H.M.S. *Beagle,* 1831–6.

cause, only the continuance of his suffering—for that before he went to sea he was subject to the same. His stomach rejects food continually; and the least agitation or excitation brings on the sickness directly so that he must be kept as quiet as it is possible and cannot see any body. . . I rejoice to have seen the hereditary good qualities and racy warmth of heart of this daughter of the Wedgwoods . . .

One evening Francis amused us by reading a copy of unpublished verses written by his friend Tennyson. Pray make him read them to you they are full of the best kind of humor and prove that the writer has power to write in any style he pleases and that he has a highly cultivated mind. I am sure you will be pleased with them. Think of Francis's good nature in making a copy of such a long poem of a brother authors. Few authors have the good nature to *copy* unless for the purpose of stealing —few are like him really clean free from all taint of envy and jealousy. Though you will see Francis so soon and would hear all that I have to say (his praise excepted) so much better from his own mouth yet I cannot help giving you a quartetto which he brought home after spending an evening with this friend of his who seems to be not at all upon *stilts* in his poetry and genius but to catch at every thing diverting—Quartetto—which Fanny says should be a motto to the Wonders of the Microscope

> The little fleas—you might not guess[1]
> Have little fleas that bite 'em
> These little fleas are bit by less
> And so—ad infinitum . . .

To Mrs. Edgeworth

1 North Audley St., 30 December 1840

. . . Yesterday you know was Tuesday and we were to dine at Dr. Hollands . . . The company were—in the drawing room when we arrived only Dr. Hollands lady and own daughter and step-ditto, a very nice young lady of 17 or so—and two brothers boy and man—and then came Doctor Hawtrey master of Eton and ci devant Spring Rice now Lord Monteagle—and Sir James

[1] Based on Swift, *On Poetry*, l. 337, but there are later versions.

Clark![1]—Sir John Campbell (Attorney General) and his wife Lady Stratheden and the Belgian minister and his lady Baron and Baroness Vander-Weyer—and that's all.

Sir John Campbell took me down to dinner and I was seated of course beside him and he was as dry as a stick and a Scotch stick and stone-silent till he had eaten a bit and drank a glass or more. Lestock was confoundedly ill seated between the Belgian minister who talked French so fast and so Dutch-ly that he could not make him out and Sir James Clark whom he had long ago made out and consequently never wished to hear or to speak to. Sir James was between him and me and nobody spoke one word to him during dinner nor even wined him. I got out of him during the bray of battle the names of every body present. Not one name when introduced had I been able to make out from Mrs. Hollands slithering pronunciation. When I found that the silent man on my right was attorney General and a Campbell straight I went to Scotland and Sir Walter and Sir Thomas Munro and Sir John Malcolm &c &c and then he opened at once and turned from his statu-quo into a man and lived and breathed and moved celestial breath—and presently we got to Inverness and Forres[2] and in broad Scotch quoted Shakespear How far to Fo-res—But you pronounce it right Ma'am no doubt Forres—and with a glass of Champagne he brightened and brightened and at last on on thro' my illness leading me to a good medical man who had been educated at St. Andrews we got to such a pitch that he burst forth loud that all the table might hear '*St. Andrews!* thats famous for breeding great men—I was bred there myself'—Half in jest you know—but quite in earnest enraptured with me (Q E D). Dr. Hawtrey and Dr. Holland in the mean while had a good deal of dinner agreeable skim milk conversation.—Skimming over Walpoles late and early letters[3] and Miss Berry—and Crokers-Johnson[4] and wishing that Bozzy and

[1] Sir James was unpopular because of his failure in diagnosis in the case of Lady Flora Hastings, lady of the bedchamber to the Duchess of Kent, who was suspected to be pregnant when in fact she was dying of cancer.

[2] ME had been seriously ill at Forres during her tour of Scotland in 1823.

[3] Two editions of Horace Walpole's collected letters were published in 1840.

[4] *Life of Samuel Johnson . . . by James Boswell, Esq. A New Edition, with numerous Additions and Notes*, by J. W. Croker (1831). It was reviewed scathingly by Macaulay in *Edinburgh Review*, liv (1831).

Croker had been kept separate to which I acceded with the *illustrating* speech of the Irishman to the waiter of 'I'd wish to have the harn and the butter separate'.[1] This set the senseless bottom of the table in a roar and Dr. Hawtrey falling back in his chair laughed delightfully—while the upper end were going on grandly Minister to brother Minister—but turned a quick eye at one upon the lower end when they heard the laugh. I must say that I liked Dr. Hawtreys laugh and thought it always sounded like 'the hearts laugh' like Mrs. Weddells so unusual at London dinners—But it may be only the perfection of art that hides itself. One thing is certain that the Doctors laugh is accompanied with a total forgetfulness of personal appearances an absolute abnegation of self in one respect. Whenever he laughs he shews a set of teeth black at the very gums betraying his age to be far more than the rest of the outward lively man would warrant any guesser to name.

The ladies—Mrs. Holland and myself excepted—scarcely articulated at dinner and since my pen has nothing else to say of them I had better say nothing but that Lady Stratheden with light blue een is a pretty Blonde and *in/with* a pretty blonde cap with a profusion of blonde curls parted on bare forehead—a happy Lady's Mag. contrast to the Brunette vis a vis or *sidelong* with large English-French eyes and Sevigné headdress of black velvet with Sevigné jewel in front and bushed out hair at ears and a sort of black velvet ears on which lay cushioned and displayed prodigious fine drops of pearls. My pen will not describe it. Can I turn the pen into pencil for the nonce[2]—Madame la Baronne VanderWeyer née Bates—daughter of *Bates* of the house of Baring—a great heiress—*riche Americaine* and thats all—except that at Coffee time she spooned out a fine compliment to Miss E about Frank and Rosamond &c &c on which she had always doated from her earliest childhood! she was sure. And then she turned to Mrs. Holland to say in languid tone with embroidered flag of abomination at nose what a horrid cold she had and apologised for coming out such a figure so muffled—and *nose* so—so—so—in short—a proof you see that I am quite—have given up all vanity. And is it true Lord Monteagle—fixing her eyes upon him whose electrified grey spare hairs in the

[1] 'harn' = (cow) hairs. [2] Sketch here.

off-skip were through black coats just visible now is it really true he is going to be married again? Very true—and to Miss Marshall sister to two young men one of whom married his daughter the maid of honor and the other of whom is about to marry his eldest sister. It has been humorously said thereupon that they have made a fine Rice pudding of it.

At tea time—table cloth on round table—*beau milieu de la chambre*—Nice young Miss Holland Doctors eldest making tea—Lords ladies men women and children standing sitting clustering round—and gay and grave conversation between and between. Spring Rice—I beg his Lordships pardon—Lord Monteagle seated himself in an armchair beside Miss Edgeworth who had on first entrance made him rather a drawback stand-off curtsey when he had offered his greetings to her as an old friend (for reasons best known to herself). But now he seemed determined there should be a thaw—and to breaking the ice he went to Mrs. Lestock Wilson and his concern &c—and then to Father Mathew—neutral ground—and that was happily gone over—and he was delighted to find I was so much of his opinion and Lord Lansdownes about father Mathew and he told me that Mathew is building one of the finest churches in Ireland in Cork or Limerick I forget which[1]—Then to Mr. Nicholls and the poor laws[2]—with Lord Monteagles bent down to the tea table-cloth (totally d—n me if I care) deferential waiting for Miss E's opinion of the System and the working. With a courage that would have surprised you but which Thank Heaven never fails me when I have an object that I believe to be good in view I spoke to my Lord Monteagle much more roundly tho with less deference to his knowledge than I should (with good reason) to Mr. Butler and in short—Dr. Hawtrey nodding approbation—ended with *all will depend* upon how you follow up this test of destitution. When your workhouses have shewn all they can do viz to *number* and provide for the absolutely helpless—all that in Ireland will ever go into them—Then it remains to supply

[1] In Cork.

[2] George Nicholls was responsible for the recommendations embodied in the Irish Poor Law of 1838 and he lived in Ireland 1838–42 to supervise its operation. Its basic principle was similar to that in the English act, i.e. that no relief should be given outside the workhouse. See also M. C. Hurst, *Maria Edgeworth and the Public Scene* (1969), 102–5.

employment and wages for the able bodied and willing to work and this can be done in some measure by Government lending money and trying again with more precaution what was tried with Mr. Nimmo and others. He pressed me to name name the employments—Making roads and footpaths and draining bogs &c[1]—'Good good' and when this ended—I must end abruptly or this will be too late a third day— . . .

To Harriet Butler

1 North Audley St., 10 January 1841

. . . Enter Lady Anna Maria Donkin the day before yesterday (by firelight—five oclock bien sonnée). 'Miss E I heard that you were so kind to recollect me' &c. Then on one side and the other proper speeches—'pleasure' and 'honor'—and armchair offered and refused. Then down she sat and to it she set talking talking! —and I must say *delightfully entertaining* she was—so much improved by age or marriage, or both together, that Fanny did not know her by your and my former description. Only a little *zest* of poignant satire appeared now and then—only curry-powder tasted in a well cooked curry . . . Lady Anna Maria turned to me (after a decent time) and told the main purpose of the visit —to beg the favor honor &c &c of my allowing a friend of hers —an American lady the American ambassadors lady Mrs. Stevenson to pay her respects to me—to worship me in fact— for she quite worshipped Miss E &c &c—And then—most cleverly she drew the uncommon character of this Mrs. Stevenson proving that she herself is uncommonly well worth seeing.

[1] The Elizabethan poor law had never been extended to Ireland, where there had been no system of parochial relief. In 1833, at much the same time as in England, a commission of inquiry was set up. It recommended the establishment of local boards to deal with the aged and infirm poor and, to employ the rest, the organization of public works, financed by government loans and by the rates. The government found the latter proposal unacceptable and Nicholls, an English poor law commissioner and the strictest of Malthusians (see above, p. 331) was sent over to Ireland to report. He recommended a system of workhouses within which relief of a severely limited kind should be given; no out-relief should be provided. His recommendations passed into law in 1837 (R. B. McDowell, *The Irish Administration 1801–1914* (1964), 175–7). Between 1809 and 1830 the engineer Nimmo had been employed in various public works, bog drainage, coastal surveying, road making, etc. RLE and his engineer son William had been his colleagues in some of these affairs.

She has been well educated by Mrs. Madison wife of President Madison—lived with her and had all *book* means of information and cultivation of judgment and taste and all that American Presidents society could give of knowledge of the world—But that being very little and not at all applicable to our European world or London life she is quite astray in many points yet well bred in the main—attention to other peoples feelings and knowing their rights and values—morally but not conventionally. Having lived many months of many years of her life in solitude her own imagination working powerfully over books and thoughts, she has a degree of romance and enthusiasm about her which might appear ridiculous or affected in her present situation but that it is so evidently *natural* that all make allowance for even her bursts of exclamations and tears of rapture about Shakespear and Milton and Miss E &c. I shall like very much to see her my own share out of the question . . .

Charles Scott came yesterday while I was writing—people do visit on a sunday and think it no sin. He came in saying 'Miss E I am afraid you will not know me?' 'Not know you! Oh certainly I do.' And so I did know face and voice but as to putting the name of the man to either! far was it from me. So looking I am afraid too conscious he something doubtful of me and shy of himself took the chair opposite me and crossed his legs. Fanny made laudable efforts to dint it into me—lead to Lockhart judiciously and he said Lockhart had told him he had had the pleasure of seeing Miss E. But still that great blockhead Miss E did not take it but searched about in her imagination and could not fancy the worn little oldish man forenent to be young Charles—the boy who put her into the carriage early in the morning at parting from Abbotsford. At length his wisely saying 'my nephew and niece and Lockhart' and something about 'Abbotsford and my father' did convince me and we went on in the most satisfactory and affectionate manner. However *aged* in appearance by these 9 years of official clerkship hard work his heart is as young and as simple and open and kind as ever and it was delightful to see and hear him so free from airs or habits of diplomacy coming out of diplomatists office and 9 years apprenticeship to the business. He talked in the most refreshingly free manner of all things and persons the moment I asked him how he liked his occupation and situation. He began with Canning whom he never saw but who was his fathers friend and procured him this situation you know. He spoke of him as a person universally regretted by all those who were *under* him and none were *above* him in their estimation either for talents or kindness of nature and manner—He always remembering to help and push or lift forward each in his turn; and if obliged to miss a turn or disappoint or refuse as oft a minister must never once offending. As to sincerity—perfect integrity or *wholeness* according to the primitive meaning of the word, of course I did not ask and probably young Scott never knew—Pass on—Sir—Mr. *But*ler—No remarks. He spoke next of Lord Aberdeen. He was slow but sure. He always sent the *minute* down to the clerks perfect and often without erasure blot or interlineation.

Lord Dudley and Ward was the next he mentioned and he praised him con amore for quickness and decision! 'Decision!' quoth I. 'Decision—certainly' said Scott. His minutes were always stiff and formal but decided and well written and himself —he was the pink of courtesy to all his underlings even and ever and the rose of kindness to all who deserved well of their office or of him. The smell of the rose certainly stuck to the vase he had used—the grateful remembrance in the heart of this true Scott so long as he lives (which I fear will not be long—But no croaking—What use Maria?).

Lord Palmerston the dominating star he does not worship. Bright he acknowledges him to be—the cleverest of them all as to absolute ability but insufferably unfeeling and disliked by all under him—Each under unbearable discord crying out against him as loud as they dare and cursing deep.

The *Duke*—of Wellington always understood—he named respectfully by himself—one by himself 'superior and alone'—of the fewest words but those few always straight to the point and doing the business to be done at once—in writing minutes or directions of any kind—short and full and *clear*—clear as any dunce could wish and such—so simple that almost any one would think 'I could have written that'—till he tried (Columbus and his egg forever!).[1] Scott surprised me by saying that he and

[1] When a Spanish nobleman suggested to Columbus that there had been nothing difficult about his discoveries, the latter asked the assembled company if any of

the Clerks found the Duke very kind and considerate in manner.

I forgot—and cannot now squeeze in at the right place—something about Lord Palmerston essential to giving you and Mr. Butler for whose amusement this is penned a full idea of his Lordship as pourtrayed by Scott the son of Scott. He is so reckless of the feelings and time of his Clerks and *Messengers* that he will send for a messenger say to go to Constantinople immediately and bid the clerks get ready dispatches and take a pen to make out the minute of their orders for Despatches But keeping them all—pens up—mouths open ears cocked waiting—he will lay down his pen and turn to the box of arrears of letters and set about looking them over and minuting for them—regardless of both Clerks in the office and messenger in the Antichamber cooling or kicking his poor heels—and when at length reminded of Messenger in waiting 'Oh too late for today. Let him be here tomorrow'—and tomorrow tomorrow—and tomorrow—fresh kicking heels—if not cooling temper the Messenger is doomed to endure and this sometimes for 10 days consecutively . . .

To Mrs. Edgeworth

[? 2 February 1841]

. . . Mr. Babbage white as tallow candle as ever was there at Mrs. Marcet's—not a bit more burnt out than he was 10 years ago but quite as odious to look at. *Touching!* how horrible that must be. He said graciously to me but forgot I had ever seen his magnum opus[1] till I reminded him of his own explanations. He gave me cards of admittance to his Wednesday and Saturdays soirees for which I thanked him sincerely but sincerely determined never to use for what should I do in that galere—in that arena of all the show beasts and their worshippers and feeders and bear leaders—Lady Morgan and all! and all quarrelling . . .

them could stand a hard boiled egg up on its end. After all had failed Columbus took an egg, cracked the bottom and stood it up. When the company cried out that anyone could have done this, Columbus said 'Certainly, but none of you thought of it.'

[1] ME probably refers to Babbage's calculating machine, the prototype of the computer.

To Mrs. Edgeworth

8 oclock, Sunday morning, 14 March 1841

. . . *after breakfast Sunday morning—continued in drawing room*

I am at Croydon or near Croydon—Heathfield Lodge—Croydon the seat of Gerald Ralston Esq. . . .

Met at a long table luxurious merchant dinner yesterday sundry people of whom you know nothing and would not care to know anything but one whom you know and like—Mr. Napier—who was very agreeable and appeared so charmingly well bred, among the Americans and Croydon-ers that 'It made his sense with double charms abound' and would have made even actual nonsense please by sound. Then there was a celebrated and solidly sensible man whom you know by reputation as the author of many distinguished articles in North American Review and author of that life of Washington[1] which I liked so much—Indeed the only life of Washington I ever saw that was not too long and too tiresome to read to the end (see 4 volumes now in the Library). The author of the readable life is Sparks. He is not at all equal in conversational powers to what you might expect from his writing. This may arise from his having more judgment than wit—or my decision may result from my having more wit than judgment. Howbeit I believe he had wit or judgment enough to be mightily pleased with my patience in listening to his slowness and he has promised to pay me with a present of a great American curiosity—Washington's private account book—Lithographed—with every penny or pound spent during his public life—to prove that he spent no more than just the thing he ought.

Besides Mr. Sparks at dinner here is another American Mr. Clisson a man of fortune and a benevolent enthusiast about Colonization—in Liberia[2]—of the Blacks—liberated slaves—free blacks of America equal sent thither and colony kept a going that is masters of schools &c &c paid by private subscriptions in America and elsewhere without any aid hitherto or control from Government *American* or *British*. I have read such opposite

[1] J. Sparks, *The Writings of George Washington with a life of the author* (1837).

[2] Founded in 1821 by the American Colonization Society. The name only dates from 1824.

accounts of Liberia that I know not what to believe *exactly* but at this very moment while I am writing Mr. Clisson is in his American tone saying 'All I can tell you Madam is that all the *best* people in America are for us and for Liberia and all the *worst* are against us.' This dictum may give you an idea of his style of converse. 'At the hazard of interrupting you Madam, Miss Edgeworth-in-your-writing, I must put into your hands a paper which I consider of some importance to Ireland America and West-Africa—Also my card and when you return to your own place if you find this paper likely to do as much good as I deem it calculated to do my card will instruct how to write to me and get 500 more copies sent you where you please to direct at a moments warning.' . . .

The hour before I set out came to see me a man fresh from Africa—A Scotchman by birth—a missionary by vocation—who had been 20 years abroad—almost all that time in Africa—sent out by the Missionary Society with £100 per Annum Salary to the Cape—to the Hottentots in the first place—and he converted many of them and taught them to sow and reap and the women to sew in the other way were taught by Mrs. Moffat an indefatigable body!—and mind. In return the hottentots taught Mr. Moffat on their part how to speak or how to *do* the *cluck* language. Mr. Moffat did the clucking for me. It is indescribable and inimitable. It is not so loud as a hen's cluck to her chickens but more quick and abrupt. I said Do that again—and again—and he did it but I could never catch it with ear or with eye at the right moment. 'How do ye do it?' 'I do not well know.' He *considered* with his *grave* apostolic, blackish yellow Africa-burnt face and then told me 'Tis done Madam by pressing my tongue quick withinside of my cheek and withdrawing it sudden.' And I tried but never did the Bourgeois gentilhomme or his servant maid make worse work of saying u-. So I begged him to go on with the conversion of the hottentots and having finished that he went further and further to a Land beyond the Hottentots country—called to the best of my spelling and pronunciation Betchuan—and there they spoke without clucking Betchuanese. He found that these people did not see God in clouds or hear him in the wind nor fear him in any way. In short they had no idea of either God or Devil. Now to the best of my recollection

I never heard before nor read of any nation or tribe civilized or savage that had not some notion of a God—a Spirit above or below or about them—of some *Influence* or *Fate* ruling their destiny—to be worshipped or propitiated some way or other—But positively Mr. Moffat asserted that he had ascertained the fact; after he had learned their language and won their confidence he questioned them closely—Did you never think of anything but what you *saw* in this world—never think of who made you or what was to happen or what become of you after death —No we never thought about it—Or—we thought it would be as with the dogs or any of our animals. With great difficulty he got the idea of a God into them—The notion of the immortality of the soul too much for them and at the assertion of the resurrection from the dead some laughed and others were terrified or angry. Moffat shewed me anecdotes he has printed in one of his Discourses giving anecdotes noted down at the time of his conversations with some of these people—very curious and interesting—one in particular with their chief in which after laughing and scoffing and scouting suddenly he grew angry and starting up exclaimed 'Do not tell me that the dead will arise—all! I have killed hundreds of enemies with this arm (brandishing his weapon) and if they are to rise again!'

I think it was well for Moffat that he 'scaped killing on the spot. However here he is—to fight the good fight another day. He has succeeded so far as to prevail on them to refrain from killing one another every day as they used to do and their wives especially. They had no laws or governing customs except as to chusing war chiefs and going to war but a man might stab or strangle his wife at pleasure and no more about it. I am not sure whether they eat their enemies but they now live in peace. One of them just before Moffat came away said to him 'We have been so long at peace I am afraid we shall forget how to fight' —This natural hankering instinct for War still remaining. He had taught them not only to sing psalms very decently but to print them in Betchuan lingo and he shewed me the little book he had wonderfully well got printed at his private Betchuan printing press. He is a perfectly honest enthusiast with an unconquerably laborious mind with a calm cool outside, fire burning within and every ray of light and heat directed to one point.

He wanted to print a translation of the Gospel in Betchuan by this press but Governor Napier Governor at the Cape (our Mr. Napiers brother—one of his many wonderful brothers whose names meet me everywhere) advised Moffat to have his bible printed in London and to return to England himself to superintend it. Perhaps he also thought this would be good for his health. Moffat declared to me 'Madam I felt this as a sentence of banishment. I had lived so long in Africa I felt it my home—my all upon earth. I had almost forgot to speak English! I dreaded almost to see and be among *all* white faces again.'

He speaks English well but like a foreigner and with slow difficulty—measured book language—not one colloquial expression—nothing vulgar but *odd.* When he stood up to go and a ray of light came upon his face that reminded me of the portrait of Ignatius Loyola at Warwick Castle I asked him if he had ever sat for his picture. 'Aye. Yes Madam. I am going this morning to the painter again to sit to finish a picture of me that has been ordered and they are to have an engraving taken from it—and I will send you *one* when it is done—to this house shall I?' Accepted you may be sure. I forget to mention that he had made in the beginning various compliments about my books for children which I savoured and swallowed eagerly, as compliments from Africa were quite new to me and unexpected. Pray tell Harriet this. She often longed for tribute from Africa for me. Now I may *cluck.*

Forest Lodge
Kent

. . . He [Captain Napier] is very conversible and clever and full of humor when he forgets himself in conversation as he did last night. He has been to all parts of the world I believe—Navy Captain—Loves Ireland and the Irish and even Irish tone and brogue when he met [them] far away in one of the Virgin Islands on the coast of America. 'One moonlight night I was walking home late' said Captain Napier 'and I met a party of poor Irishmen to whom my heart warmed when they begged a trifle from my honor and told their stories—all lies—very likely—I knew —but still—I could not help you know giving him a trifle. The fellow into whose hand I put it, thought it was a penny I believe but as he walked away he looked at it—started—and I heard him exclaim as he held out his hand to his companions "See here —By Jabers—It's a dollar then!" "By Jabers!" all unanimously joined and rush they ran back again all together but one got before the rest and throwing himself at my feet clasping my knees looked up and by the pale moonlight I saw the eager look —"Your Honor! Would there be any one in all the Virgin Islands ever did ye an ill turn (the rascal!) youd wish to be revenged of? Tell me—Tell us this minute! Youve only to spake the word and with all the pleasure in life we'll *bate* him dead for ye—We'll *do* him for you now and God bless you forever. Ye have only to say the word."' Captain Napier said he was sure they would with all the pleasure in life as they swore have that instant done his bidding, if he had bid them murder any man in the country or they would have set fire to any house he had but pointed to—Paddy forever! This *gratitude of revenge* is characteristically Irish *entirely* and whether a virtue or a vice or a mixture—the *materials* for both or either who shall decide . . .

I went with Mrs. Marcet and Mrs. E Romilly in their carriage (gratis) on friday last to see a pauper school at Battersea[1] established by a certain Dr. Kay a poor law Commissioner who has travelled in Switzerland and Italy and everywhere and gathered from Pestalozzis and Fellenbergs and Werly's every creatures best about schools. It would take far more time than I have to tell about it all—This for home talk—But I will say that the classes for teaching mechanics and arithmetic I thought very good and the boys called upon to explain the *resolution of forces—advantages gained by system of pullies*—levers &c—clear and of practical use. These boys are educating for masters of other schools. They looked healthy and happy—The classes for learning gardening and agriculture good—Entertaining accounts by master of agricultural-different processes in different parts of the world—Rice cultivation—Irrigation—India &c &c. Dr. Kay is rather too enthusiastic a man—His mother a neat Hans Holbein looking woman with steadfast eye upon him as he talks and other eye upon household affairs which she makes daughter-genteel despatch nicely doing the honors, engaging to

[1] Battersea training college for pupil teachers was founded 1839–40 by James Kay (later Kay-Shuttleworth) and E. Carleton Tufnell.

luncheon &c. He had been reading this morning he told us Hamlet to the young men to waken their imaginations! Mrs. Marcet's good sense *squeeled* directly as if trodden upon 'Oh! Oh!! Mr. Kay! How could they possibly comprehend Hamlet when all our best critics are not able they own to understand what Shakespear meant or should mean?' I thought of Francis's Essay on the character of Hamlet[1] but held my peace for it was right to do so to keep the peace between the high flying over-zeal of young Dr. Kay and the flat downright good sense of old Mrs. Marcets experience.

After the lessons on mechanics and algebra there was luncheon—very necessary to poor me. At luncheon 2 masters somewhat formal and pedantic and an entertaining Ignoramus Maltese novice who is learning to be a master I believe that he may go forth and teach school in his own Island. He spoke fair and looked black—black-handsome. He told us in broken English which he had learned wonderfully well in a few months that the native Maltese have no *written* language—of their own-own —no alphabet even. The upper classes all speak Italian—The lower classes a sort of Patois gibberish supposed to be derived from *Arabic* but how it came there Lord Knows and Learned men dispute without ever being or having been able to settle . . . Then he spoke of his own sisters twain. I asked if they ever wrote to him and in what language. 'They cannot either of them my sisters write nor read but they write to me in Italian regularly by the hand of a secretario.' And then Miss Kay jumped up and ran from table to side table and brought bandbox full of artificial flowers and beautiful lace—all made by these two sisters Maltese—The lace exquisite! He motioned with his great hands shewing how they worked on their cushions *with their strings and leads*. 'Bobbins' said I. 'Bobbins!' said he catching with delight in his eyes at the right name recognised quick and he gave me a bow—and compliments followed on *my* works— But I am not clean sure he had ever heard my name before, tho he vowed he had seen my books—on tables—and with good prompting by standers by made out something about Italian Early Lessons[2]—translations—and hoped for more and I finished

[1] Published in *New Monthly Magazine*, xxix (1830), 327–36.
[2] Bianca Milesi Mojou had published a translation of *Early Lessons* in 1834.

and relieved him greatly by recommending an Italian translation of Mrs. Barbaulds Hymns[1] which Mrs. Marcet and Mrs. Edward Romilly knew well and agreed with me seemed born in Italian—the sense and sound suit so well.

Luncheon ended and dolls and artificial flowers removed we went out of glass door on green lawn and down the broad gravel walks we saw running rejoicing and shouting to each other happily a troop of boys—taking their hour of sweet liberty and some were swinging and jumping at their gymnastics. Full tilt I met running les jambes au Cou a lump of a boy about 11 or 12 years old a New Zealander boy with large head and frizzled black hair and face as yellow as dirty gold and eyes as keen savage as ever you saw in print or drawing—very like the head of *Button* that Fanny copied from Fitzroys voyage (or Darwins delightful).[2] I stopped my full tilt running Zealander to talk and try to get something out of him about his happiness or unhappiness in his civilised life but he was so shy and so stupid that I could get nothing out of him but Aye or No and his eyes askance would never look at me. So I let him run off—A savage he was and a savage he is and a savage he will be and theres an end of that . . .

To Mrs. Edgeworth

Friday, 19 March 1841

Since I last wrote my sixteen paged epistle nothing worthy of note or capable of entertaining you my dears has occurred excepting two morning visits from Lover. He appears to much greater advantage quite in private than in public drawing room exhibition—much less vulgar—he has [?no] conceit or affectation—he is truly humourous and exquisitely Irish without

[1] A. L. Barbauld, *Hymns in Prose for Children* (1781). There were two Italian versions, both published in London: *Inni giovenili* (1819) and *Inni per la gioventù* (1838).

[2] Jemmy Button was a boy taken to England from Tierra del Fuego on the first voyage of the *Beagle*, given a brief English education and taken back home on the second voyage in 1833. The effects of education wore off very rapidly (Fitzroy, *Narrative of the Surveying Voyages of His Majesty's Ships 'Adventure' and 'Beagle' between 1826 and 1836* (1839), ii, illustration facing p. 324).

exaggeration of tone or manner. In public he is obliged to exaggerate brogue for English auditors who not understanding the real Irish humor seize the brogue as a sign for laughing *at* more than *with* and enjoy the depreciation what they think the inferiority of the Irish instead of perceiving the *wit* and the *blunder* in which there is always *very* near a meaning which they are very *far* from seizing or being able to catch or to have and to hold. Lover sang (on St. Patricks birthday) St. Patricks Birthday. '*Why it was the 17th*—Because it could not be settled whether he was born on 8th or 9th—Whether the clock was too slow or the child too quick. So upon a reference to the priest it was settled that the Saints birthday should be 8 and 9 both together the *17th*. Blessings on the day! And one day it should be for you know it is only twins has two birthdays.' But *singing* is very different from *saying* and you must hear Lover to do him justice. When you come here Dear mother you will hear him I hope. He has promised me that you shall . . .

To the family at Edgeworthstown

Thursday (thermometer 56), 23 March 1841
Before breakfast True time! *only* time in Town
Coffee up and Coffee down

My dear friends all great and small including baby whom you never mention now at all! I had not time yesterday to bring up my history of my country visits.

Primis—Bought a new bonnet—much wanted as my black velvet rather the worse for 2 winters wear when I began my London campaign had grown rusty-fusty and past all enduring. The new one is lovely!—and grey as its wearer and Fanny likes it and thats enough.

In the family coach that came for me[1] was Madame Brihl a governess flat backed, stedfast and demure German, educated at Paris and all proper—'hors les p-s and b-s and c-s' which could not pass surely on the Countess de Salis's delicate ear for true Parisian. But she *has her cheap* as she afterwards explained to me upon condition of placing her well with some High and Mighty

[1] The coach was to take ME to stay with her old friend the Countess de Salis at the latter's country house, Dawley Lodge, nr. Hillingdon, Middlesex.

fashionable when she has done with her (I do like people that are always in character).

Besides this governess who on the back seat sat beside my nice new varnished black cap box (like Honoras and bought by Captain Beaufort) three ladies occupied the front (which I believe is the back). The 3 ladies were Mademoiselle de Salis—*Harriet—miscalled Haddy!*—a cordial simple open hearted, rosy, dairy faced fat lump of a good girl as ever you saw, that does infinite credit to her mother's education though perhaps she does not think that and you would never have expected it nor should I. *Haddy* has quite country-sunshine in her face and I am sure in her heart but she is monstrous large in every direction for 16 and how she is to be laced down that it mayn't bulge out at the sides or before I cannot imagine, nor how she is to be kept back to look right *17 only* when she comes out. But the Countess who understands these things assures me that it will all do right for that Haddy grows thinner every year and will be the right size by the right time *and* she means to take her and herself off (and leave the governess on or off the pavé) in June next for a twelvemonth at least, out of London sight, to finish her in the palace of some Italian prince and the Castle of some German or Swiss Count whose names you will excuse me. And admire my dear mother how well all this is settled for observe you they will live at free cost for that twelvemonth (bating the journey).

The second person on the back seat was myself bodkin, sitting back with feet just apparent at edge of cushion . . .

I spare you the description of Dawley Lodge house and furniture Francis having seen it all and he might catch me tripping or painting the house plus belle que la verité. But I must say one word about the conservatory into which the windows and doors of the drawing room open wide. I am sure that half a quarter of a mile well matted since Francis saw and smelt them has been added to their scented length and as I walked breathing all the perfumes of Arabia or better far of the Cape and South America I at every step broke the tenth commandment!—for I coveted everything I saw or smelt of my neighbours good—not for myself indeed but for you dear mother who if I could have got them all would not have known where upon *earth* or in greenhouse to have put them all. Nevertheless you are to have as many as ever you please or can carry home with you in due season—cuttings and layers and seeds. I spared not begging and to do Harriet de Salis (for now she turned into the Harriet of former times) she was as ready to give you as I could be to beg for you and thats saying a great deal. Tell my own Harriet that the question '*Emballe t'il*' was forever on my lip till we got out of Green and Hot houses. But before we got out came in 'the first Botanist in Europe—Miss E—give me leave—Doctor Lindley—You know his works?' Not i—but U mother and all of You or *Yees* have seen all his superb colored plates[1] of Epiphytes or air plants of which Humboldt gives such fine accounts.[2]

My Countess who has ever a thrifty mind—one eye ever on business even when the other is on pleasure bent always invites Lindley down to her *select* parties which he loves (Champagne inclusive) and he in return must review her hot houses and give advice gratis, also curious and rich and rare plants and flowers and fruits that money alone could not purchase. He is President of Horticultural Society and has got into *fine* Society and figures away in it, a London diner-out and what not tho the son of a gardener or shoemaker I'm not sure which and no matter . . .

Afterwards when I became hand and glove with this Dr. Lindley I talked to him of Dr. Brown the next best great Botanist (I had always heard from Captain Beaufort at whose house I met him the *first*) and he too you know as well as Sir William Hooker had said well for Pakenham so we had plenty of mutually interesting conversation. But presently I advised myself to speak of the *Onion* said to have been found in the Mummy's hands and to have sprouted and grown after being thousands of years buried—Also of the raspberry seeds found in the coffin buried in the English Barrow concerning the coming to life of which I had heard Brown questioned and quizzed a few days before this by Mrs. Guillemard at Mrs. Beauforts party as I think I mentioned to you. But whether I did or not—by mentioning the same now I got into the wrong box for my first Botanist in Europe turned

[1] *Sertum orchidaceum* by Dr. Lindley was published in 1838.

[2] *Personal Narrative of Travels to the Equinoctial Regions of the New Continent during the years 1799–1804*, by A. de Humboldt and A. Bonpland, trans. H. M. Williams (1821).

quick upon me and exclaimed 'I can answer for the raspberries Ma'am. I saw them—I have them alive. As to the Onion and the mummy case that *was* a hoax upon Brown no doubt.' Then he averred that tho not witness present he knew the voucher of the fact a man of undoubted veracity and of infallibly good sight who saw the barrow when first opened and the seeds (either *in* or *out* of the stomach of the man I never could understand or in delicacy ascertain which) and the seeds *'in their boggish stuff'* as Dr. Lindley said were brought exactly as they were found to him and he saw that they were raspberry seeds and he put them in ground and they grew and have grown to real raspberry bushes and I am to have a green leaf from one of them so soon as it unfolds . . . There is an end of all I have to tell you about Dr. Lindley except that he is a Catholic which I found out next morning being sunday by his not going to church with us but to Chapel and he blushed Oh how he blushed when before *the company* the Countess called him a good Catholic and thought she said he would not object to going to the church door with us. But he slid off his own way—and no more about him . . .

But I have not got through sunday yet quite. After church and a good sermon and a good early dinner the youngsters went their own ways walking and boating and the Countess mean time had the grace to sit with me the while talking most agreeably Economy (not political) Literature, not too deep and gossip-fashionable, with quantum suff: of scandal but not by any means ill natured tout au contraire—the strait laced might say rather too easy—But all the more entertaining both to sinners and saints I ween and we were tete a tete, in a bower apart—In the middle of the length of the conservatories there is a trelliced bower overhanging a low green calico cushioned sofa on which we sat at our ease and where on week days [Haddy] is used to take her lessons in botany—history and morality no doubt . . .

And now to finish the everlasting history of this visit. How do you think we finished sunday evening? With prayers you will say Madam to be sure. Yes—And after a good and very nicely given little rebuke to her young Etonian boy for speaking rather irreverently of the lengthy prayers at Eton and begging his mamma would give short prayers and after all this and after his reading the lessons for the day to his self in German (finger on each verse pointing as Haddy read in English and called out the numbers on each verse) I ask you after all this when we rose from our knees and returned from prayer room to drawing room —What do you think saw we and heard we next? In the inner drawing room a table covered with green cloth—lights placed as for a stage exhibition and cups and ball and all preparations for playing conjurors tricks and from the side door slipped in my young Etonian with his conjurors wand in hand and his elder brother for his Coadjutor. And we were all ranged in two rows as audience and spectators and numbers of conjurors tricks—some of them excellent in their kind were played and between times Musick—(not sacred) by the young ladies—very good—and Haddys governess at her back and playing too if I do not disremember. The secrets of these conjuring tricks had been bought and bought at high price they say by the young Etonian for it is now the high fashion at Eton to buy and play conjurors tricks—better than brandy methinks—I don't know whether so good as pugilistics—Doctors differ. But those whom the old song 'deemed it Sabbath breaking to go without a pudding' ought methinks deem it as well to go without the conjuring tricks so close upon the prayers on Sunday Evening. I must not be uncharitable—this boy was very goodnatured to me and went on the rail road with me next morning to take care of me and my bag and box to meet the Miss O Beirnes. N B—There was a poor woman in the railroad coach for the first time whom Lady Canning heard muttering low to herself all the time

Great box! Little box! Bandbox bag!

which she called out loud that all the guards might hear when she came to the last station . . .

To Harriet Butler

19 April 1841

. . . It [Sunday] is the only day when he [Lord Jeffrey] can pay visits in the morning and it does not hurt his conscience nor do I find that even very good people here in London town make any more scruple of visiting after church on a Sunday more than they used to do in former days long syne when I was young—

and little sins had not grown into great sins as in these days nor —vice versa—great sins into little or no account—in fashionable ritual.

Last evening—Sunday. Doctor Holland dropped in just as I was making tea tete a tete with Lestock and what do you think was the first thing he did? He offered to make tea for us. He made the most audacious assertion—the most *astonishing*—That gentlemen always make tea better than ladies! 'I tell Mrs. Holland she does not know how to make tea.' I questioned him as to this theory and as to the difference of his practise. 'There now now! You do wrong.' 'How! In putting water into the teapot to heat it?' 'No but in pouring out that water—You neglect to pour out the last drops—the water that has condensed at the top of the lid and trickled downwards to the bottom—a cold spoonful that spoils the first infusion. Then you put in you ladies I mean always too much or too little water &c &c. You judge of sugar by lumps—so many lumps for each cup leaving out size and quality of sugar.' In short he went on with a long list of faults. Fanny when I reported this to her observed that the Duke of Wellington was more modest about teamaking but fully as conscious of the difficulty of the operation. At his breakfasts you know he has tea pot—tea and groceries as you please for each guest to please themselves if they can. Dr. Holland told us that he was just come from his father in law Sydney Smiths tea table where he left his wife God help her! making tea for Sydney Smith, Rogers—Moore Macaulay and Lord Jeffrey. I dare say these great wits ill met were not an agreeable party. Two of them you know had fought a duel in days of yore. Sydney Smith says of Macaulay 'There are flashes of silence in his conversation which are very agreeable.'

To Harriet Butler

[? 20 April 1841]

. . . [Dr. Ashburner] was led to reviewing Sir J Mackintoshs metaphysical intellectual and moral character—and the Doctor told as he sat beside Fanny's bed many anecdotes of his life in India which too fully proved what I had often heard rumoured that his integrity as a judge in India was not intact and the ermine not unspotted not clean. Ashburner was there at the time and knew both the on dits and the behind the curtains. In grave cases where robbers and murderers were to be punished or acquitted by the sign manual of the Judge—In cases where 'He who allows oppression shares the crime'—Mackintosh, from sheer indolence and mere carelessness lying on a sofa unwilling to put aside some book he was reading and noting with his happy pencil signed with his too ready pen the papers that were put before him and rather than be at the trouble of reading and examining acquitted.[1] This subjected him to violent reproach and left his character tarnished dreadfully. It was proved that Lady Mackintosh had received shawls and pearls—not absolutely to intercede in this particular case but from the parties concerned and others. Those who thought worst of Sir James of course cried 'Bribery!—convicted.' Those who thought best could only say 'Sad indolence and inattention to his duty.' It seems to me to have been with Mackintosh much as with Bacon. He let the bribes be taken—either did not see or chose to shut his eyes. How very painful it is to be forced to think that the wisest and the wittiest *can* be the meanest! When moral is separated from intellectual greatness how it sinks!—falls to rise no more! v Bonaparte &c. . . .

To Fanny Wilson

11 Gloucester Place,[2] Tuesday, 25 May 1841

. . . Lestock came with me to breakfast *here* at 8 oclock and then he took Honora and Captain Beaufort and me to the Polytechnic and we all had our likenesses taken and I will tell you no more lest I should some way or other cause you disappointment. For my own part my object is secure for I have done my dear what you wished. It is a wonderful mysterious operation. You are taken from one room into another up stairs and down and you see various people whispering and hear them in

[1] Sir James Mackintosh disliked passing a death sentence from principle rather than from indolence.

[2] The home of Francis Beaufort and his second wife Honora Edgeworth.

neighboring passages and rooms unseen and the whole apparatus and stool on high platform under a glass dome casting a *snap-dragon blue* light making all look like spectres and the men in black gliding about like &c. I have not time to tell you more of that . . .[1]

To M. Pakenham Edgeworth

Collingwood, 26 November 1843

. . . We are very happy here. Herschel and Lady Herschel are so kind and agreeable and he gives us so much of his time to us, conversing or shewing us all that is most interesting. He shewed us yesterday a great number of his Daguerreotypes in all the varied states—where the *light* was first darkness and then in the next state where after lying by some time the dark turns to light and then where it all fades away and seemingly leaves no trace behind—and then when upon certain incantations or applications it all returns. He shewed us a Daguerreotype of the stand of the great instrument before it was taken down.[2] He told us that the impression of that frame as it stood was so strong on his eyes that when it was gone he some time afterwards *saw* it in its place so plainly before him that he thought he could have touched it. *There it is still!* I never saw so sensitive a person—almost too much for his health. He complains—no he never *complains*, but he told us of a strange delusion or disease of his sight which comes on at night sometimes when he is sitting up reading. The farthest part of the room vanishes and by degrees the circuit of sight diminishes so that he can at last see only the table before him and just the space occupied by the candles. This should warn him not to *overwork* and it does warn Lady Herschel to take all means to prevent his overstraining his great faculties. With this view I am not ashamed as I must otherwise have been of the

[1] See frontispiece for ME's portrait. The studio had been opened by Richard Beard on 23 Mar. There exist three later daguerreotypes, two of 1843 and one undated. These together with the Adam Buck portrait in the Edgeworth family group of 1789 (Butler, *The Black Book of Edgeworthstown* (1926), illustration facing p. 166) are the only formal portraits ever made of ME, though there are a few rough sketches. The portrait at the beginning of Augustus Hare's *Life and Letters* (1894) is imaginary, based on an engraving from a magazine (*Mem.* i. 222–3).

[2] His father's great telescope at Slough.

time he gives up to us. He has shewn us innumerable drawings he took at the Cape—1835—of the spots in the sun and their *changes* unaccountable! from day to day. He is now hard at work preparing his account of his observations at the Cape.[1] He reproaches himself very much for having been led away by the Daguerreotype enchanting pursuit too long from this duty. . . .

To M. Pakenham Edgeworth

[n.d.]

. . . One of Sir John's sketches was of a burning wood opposite to their house on a high hill and slope. The servants rushed into their dining room and called out Mountain on fire. Lady Herschel hurried off the children all to a garden house. The roof which was of thatch on their dwelling house was all torn off and the people in crowds then ran out to the burning wood which was coming down the hill with all speed and with all force and with whatever *sticks* or stones or irons or bushes actually *beat* out the fire—The bushes doing the work best! A few days afterwards the whole mountain side was covered with most beautiful flowers of all hues (and all of names unknown to me) Gladiolis and red and white Watsonia—plain and striped only bring some conception of the bright colors to my minds eye. Lady Herschel says the profusion is indescribable and inconcievable to those who have not seen the like. The rich manure of the ashes of the trees and the sudden removal of the oppressive shade produced this burst and blow of vegetable life and bloom . . .

To Harriet Butler

1 North Audley Street, 3 December 1843

. . . As well as I can remember I told my and your mother all about our dinner on gold plate (stupid nevertheless) at Bedgebury

[1] J. Herschel, *Results of Astronomical Observations . . . at the Cape of Good Hope* (1847).

with Sir Robert Peels sister and all to boot—and Alexander Hope uglier than sin and his father and Lady Mildred granddaughter of the Lady Salisbury who was burnt &c &c. The visit ended with a gracious cold kiss from Lady Beresford to me and a warm shake hands from her goodnatured Marshal with his one effective hand and a most pressing invitation to come again enforced by pressure kind of that hand. 'Pray come back and let me shew you this place by daylight and come to stay some time.' But I shall not for (between you and I my dear Harriet and please so to keep it for I have not let it out to any at home) I do not think that Lady Beresford paid even proper attention to Fanny tho she had asked her to dinner—she scarcely spoke to her. It is nonsense to feel or see or mention this even to you—But you know Mrs. Hope's draw-up look and will understand and it will account for my never-go-there-no-more determination—Contrary to the half promise I had made Lady Beresford in answer to her warm reception of myself. She is altered—not absolutely in good nature—but she is grown fat and flaccid mind and body. There never was much in there and now there's nothing and she is out of my line. Town or country mouse I don't want to see more of the like. I have drawn and shall keep to this line. I dine only with *old friends*. In my 76th and in a month my 77th year this is surely unanswerable and becoming —and whether or not I will abide by it—I am ashamed of writing so much about Lady Beresford and nonsense . . .

. . . It is droll enough that *Robinson* should scoff at me for having lost my judgment taken in by Sir *John* Herschel's *elegance* when neither I nor anybody else that had ever seen elegance either in or out of the fashionable world could ever think him elegant or concieve that he made any pretence to elegance. Refined he is highly in sentiment and conversation and sensitive far far too much for health or happiness—mimosa sensitiveness that shrinks from every touch not merely of blame, but even from the very intimacy he most wishes to have. Captain Beaufort well observed 'Herschels great want in life is *sympathy* and yet he repels it. His shyness or reserve of manner is so great even to me', said Captain Beaufort 'that I cannot get at him and am tired of trying.' I can only say it was not so with us. The light within burst through the dark visage and in the 4 days we learned more of his character than I have done with others in 4 years—and there was more to learn. He is on the verge of the dreadful danger of over wrought intellect—over excited sensibility. In his earlier life when disappointed in love he shut himself up in darkness for I don't know how many weeks and would let not mortal see him and even of later times when vexed in friendship or when scientific things go wrong he betakes himself to darkness and solitude and in abstraction shuts himself up from the external universe. Very very dangerous! Solitary confinement even to the innocent—and even to the stupid a very hazardous experiment! Lady Herschel, who you may be sure did not tell me any thing of all this—is as we could percieve well aware of the precarious state of health and the delicate dealing necessary with such nerves. She is a most amiable highly cultivated, unpresuming sensible woman who does all that can be done by affection and intelligence and sympathy and care or efforts to divert his mind and draw him from intense application and divert him from all painful thoughts . . .

And now I must go and dress myself—very little—Only to drink tea at Dr. Hollands—*petit comité* only their two selves and Mrs. Hollands father, you know Sydney Smith. Good bye—I have not another idea but I *shall have* plenty—soon.

Monday morning—up at 5 minutes before seven—
candles—and coffee for one—Very well and slept
like a top my dear Harriet Thank you—

We had a very pleasant evening I need scarcely say but *to Boswell* Sydney Smith would out Boswell-Boswell and is past my powers and your wishes I am sure my dear so I will leave *that*—*there*. Sydney Smith had not his merryandrew jacket on, outside at least over his canonicals tho' now and then it peeped from underneath unbecomingly I thought but not to say indecently—Fanny says much less than usual. He had his learned and reverend sock on and talked much of Churches Catholic and Protestant and applied to me for information as to the state of Catholic priests *in my opinion*. My opinion I told him I thought could be worth little or nothing on the question to him. The facts which had actually come within my own knowledge in our own neighborhood and County or in others within my reach and means of verification I willingly and truly (I trust) told him but these facts did not accord at all with his preconcieved notion of their oppressed, depressed state diabolically treated by the protestant church, protestant landlords and protestant and Tory Government. He civilly waived aside my evidence and looked 'You may go down off the table, where I only set you up when I thought you were on my side.' 'Six millions O Connell says seven trampled upon still by one—notwithstanding this talk of emancipation. There must be a *reformation* and redress of grievances.' 'Reformation! Of what—or of who or of whom' I simply asked 'Redress of grievances? What and which be they?' 'The Catholics should have an established Church.' '*An* would turn into *the*.' 'Well and where would be the harm or the injustice seeing they are the majority?' I did not ask '*What constitutes the majority?*' I was afraid of setting the Abbe Sieyès[1] and Sydney Smith *at it* lest the whole French Revolution should come upon my head. I saw I need not must not go to spiritual considerations either so keeping to temporalities I merely begged his Reverence would consider that we poor Protestants had bodies to be saved and did not like, only one million as we are, to be trampled upon by seven and to have our Church pulled down about our ears and our clergy to be buried under the rubbish and their church lands and our estates taken from us. He scoffed at such suppositions but I appealed to his own knowledge of history recording the encroaching and predominating nature or art of Cats &c &c. 'But without looking to remote consequences' he replied 'We must do what justice and *humanity* requires.' And then he shewed that he was utterly mistaken and misinformed as to the present state of the priesthood in Ireland and revenue of the Catholic Church. What so unjust and unjustifiable as their church paying tithes to another in which they don't believe—Ireland never will—never can—never ought to be quiet under such a grievance. He seemed convinced that the Irish priests have not enough to keep body and soul together. He would not listen (except with civil sneer) to any of my poor little *facts* but Dr. Holland put him down with Lord Lansdowne's name and

[1] Count (Abbé) Emmanuel Joseph Sieyès, '*Qu'est-ce que le tiers état?*' (1789). It furnished a programme for the popular leaders in the initial stages of the French Revolution.

authority—added his own observations in going thro' Ireland lately. Lord Lansdowne says that the average salary of the Irish priest is £290 per Annum and average of Prot—£120 or £130. Sydney Smith was staggered by this and said he must inquire further. Meanwhile he asked me whether the Cat priests are a moral, sober well conducted people. To moral and sober, I gave good and I trust true testimony—as clergy formerly especially ere they took to politics zealous and excellent parish priests—as to well conducted in politics and elections and so forth and Repeal agitations vide Bishop [O'] Higgins—and hear him—Hear him. I told of his don't be antici*pa*ting and the rich brogue gave him some idea of the manners and whether they were fit to sit at good mens tables &c—which he was curious to know.

Laughing at brogue (how easy!) led him on to his own merrier mood, and he told good anecdote of a conversation with Bishop Doyle in former days—beginning with 'My Lord' (propitiously and propitiatingly) 'Don't you think that it would be a good thing if your clergy were paid by the State?' Bishop Doyle assured him that it would never do—such an offer could never be accepted (much the same tone now taken). 'But suppose there were lodged in Bank for all you clergy at an average £100 a year (I think Sydney said or £150)—and suppose five per cent for arrears allowed.' *'Ah Mr. Smith you have a way of putting things'* was the honest Bishops reply. Delightful laugh went round the tea table. This was just a parallel case to the French virtuous ladys answer when the offer supposed came up to her price *Ah c'est beaucoup.*

There the religious, Irish conversation closed—Much about O Connell—all of which Sydney Smith scarcely knows what to make he says. Dr. Holland and I helped him a little. Lying and Cowardice Sydney was perfectly aware of 'But still—still has not he a real enthusiasm for his religion and his country?' turning to me. I could only say that I did believe him to be a sincere bigotted Catholic—yet I could not say enthusiastic for I took a distinction between bigotry bred in a man and enthusiasm natural and genuine. However that be between God and him and his conscience—no right to judge—no means of ascertaining —But by his works you may judge of his patriotism or his selfishness. Then we went through his history—Catholic rents[1] —debts paid—College fines—money in funds for him—wrested wrenched from the hands of poor not vile peasants &c &c. Sydney staggered again more and more and indeed by recollecting a lie—uncourteous—absolute—unblushing—base which O Connell had uttered and published of his reverend self. 'He said that when I was asked whether I would swear that I believed the 39 Articles I answered certainly and that I only wished there were 3 or five hundred more.' This lie against himself struck Sydney Smith more than all the rest and he seemed right glad to repudiate him.

Then branched off to literature and Diners out in Town and they settled that since Mackintosh is gone there is not a Converser in London worth hearing. Many were proposed but all rejected by Sydney with the banishing back of his hand—excommunicating from good society. Rogers,—Oh no poor Sam—and Sydney told a story of a poor stranger Irish country lady to whom at dinner he was telling the names of the company and naming Rogers—who was opposite—she exclaimed 'Oh! do I see *Rogers*!' Then Sydney sly asked who or what she took his self to be? 'A bishop perhaps. But no where's your little apron?' Macaulay was next named. Sydney Smith has a very high opinion of his talents and of his style of writing essays and Reviews —but no converser no no. 'Flashes of silence agreeable' you recollect Harriet and so did I and low down said and Sydney heard and smiled—Asked if I had ever seen or heard. Yes once and but once when first he came out—at a dinner at Lord Lansdowne's—I thought he must by this time have learned better tact and better management of his amour propre or vanity than then he had. Holland quite agreed. Sydney to my astonishment declares he acquits Macaulay of all vanity—Thinks he only pours out talk and listens to no other mortal man or woman only because he cannot help pouring out. 'Did you ever see a beer barrel burst Miss E? Well Macaulay bursts like a beer barrel and it all comes over you but he can't help it. He really has no wish to shew off.' I had a great mind to ask whether he ever bursts

[1] The funds raised to support various societies founded by O'Connell, chiefly for the Repeal of the Union, but also for the protection of the voting rights of the forty-shilling freeholders, the reform of corporations and the adjustment of tithes.

in private—in his own room alone. Why burst always in public? But as I am to meet Macaulay in a few days by particular desire at Dr. Hollands and Sydney to be by I thought it was well to keep myself safe—So no more said I but chimed in admiration of his talents—Life of Addison[1] especially (tho no review of poor Miss A).

Sydney was exceedingly goodnatured and absolutely kind to me—suggested to Dr. and Mrs. Holland who they might have to meet and please me dinner and evening. 'Senior now Senior by all means. I have just been reading of his the best thing I ever read on present state of Ireland—Diseases and cures. Is it not Holland? It is an article for the next number of the Edinburgh Review[2]—Admirable. I will send it to you Miss E—under the rose—worthy of it! But (turning to his daughter) do not have Senior and Macaulay for her same night—or day—One at a time or they would be too much.' He has not been so long a London diner out and giver of dinners without learning all the requisites for making people and things go off well.

I forgot to mention his admiration of Herschel 'acknowledged first man of science'—of whom he knows nothing but his Essay on Nat Philosophy[3]—style admirable!—and then Mrs. Somerville—Her Introduction[4] to all those things about Light and stars and nebulae of which I know nought said Sydney, but her style clear and excellent—But as to herself I never could get anything out of her beyond what you might get from any sempstress. She avoids all depth in converse—and no pretty superficial—very amiable no doubt. I'd bear the husband for her—thats all I can say. Where is she?

This is his light style. Then to gratify me I am sure he asked for Bushe or rather of Bushe—knew he was dead. I short as I could put in—no *éloge*[5]—but of manner of conversation gave some idea and mentioned his constant polite *benevolent* attention

[1] Review of *The Life of Joseph Addison* by Lucy Aikin (1843), *Edinburgh Review*, lxxviii (1843).

[2] *Edinburgh Review*, lxxix (1844).

[3] J. Herschel, *A Preliminary Discourse on the Study of Natural Philosophy* (Lardner's *Cabinet Encyclopaedia*, 1830).

[4] Mary Somerville, *The Mechanism of the Heavens* (1831).

[5] The laudatory discourse pronounced on deceased members of the Académie française, Académie des Sciences, etc.

to others—especially to bring forward the young. Sydney thought I meant young ladies. 'Oh I hate em I hate em—in conversation can't abide em—can't can't! So green so jejeune so flaccid—never speak to them—can't can't.'

If Richard should be amused with anything herein contained beg that he will pay me directly by telling me what proportion of tithe the Catholics now pay to the Protestant Church. As far as I could recollect—but I did not dare to assert because I was not sure—The landlord now pays all the tithe—Composition—Rent Charge—which we add to the rent named in lease—in fact as part of the rent and then it is paid half yearly by the tenant. But the composition tithe has taken one quarter of the whole from the Protestant clergy as the *price* for the security of the landlords payment? Have not the Catholic tenants been relieved of the weight of this fourth part which formerly they did pay? . . .

To Mrs. Edgeworth

[? January, 1844]

. . . You may wonder that I venture to talk of Bentham[1] so much and his pedantic gibberish codification letters in mixed company, but leaving the codification utility or inutility and the gibberish aside there is a vast quantity of gossip and some love letters—some nauseous, some beautiful which are fine subjects of interest to ladies *and* gentlemen—For instance the letters from and to Miss Fox and the curiosity of the many to know whether the stars or blanks mean Miss Fox or not—and then the pride of the few who can read aright and have been behind the scenes and can vouch for such anecdotes as the keys put into the pocket—screen overturned—feet of feathers gliding away &c &c. Ma'am if you dont know of all these things Heaven help ye. I do and make my profit of them. I believe that the Atheneum did not give you the odious twaddle epistle which Bentham addressed in his 81st year to Miss XXX 'with all the trophies of his former loves'—a letter which almost killed Miss Fox with shame they say and for publishing which that Bowring ought to be hanged drawn and quartered—And hanged drawn and quar-

[1] Bentham, *Collected Works*, ed. J. Bowring (1843), x and xi.

tered a hundred times over for 100 other high treasons against social confidence of which he has been guilty in this Life. What do you think of his publishing every word of a most private conversation confession of Bentham's anent these foolish, doating love-affairs, which he had taken previously to his beginning to tell, a certificate from said *John Bowring* in writing regularly signed, that he would never divulge what Bentham was about to tell him nor even ever recur to the subject nor ever question him upon it without permission. Can you concieve? But you cant and I am very foolish to ask you. Bowring is a much worse kind of Boswell—venemous—treacherous. You may wonder that it was worth while to Boswell-Bentham but notwithstanding all Benthams pedantry and tiresomeness-gibberish-osity-ness he could write with admirable clear brevity whenever he thought proper had made himself master of many subjects of the greatest interest to all human creatures. This was felt and acknowledged by the most distinguished, good and bad, the most celebrated and the most notorious in all countries in the civilized world—beginning with England Ireland Wales Then going on to France Spain Italy all Europe and All America. As Hallam told me a learned Italian said to him 'Your English Bentham has in all countries except England a really Colossal reputation.' . . .

To Mrs. Edgeworth

[January 1844]

. . . We went yesterday to Kensington Gore to see dear Lady Elizabeth Whitbread and to inquire for Julia Grant. We found Lady Elizabeth in her room downstairs in the same armchair, by the same window looking out upon the pretty shrubs and the water and ducks and swan and maid feeding them and all of old continued habits of life and cheerful flowers beautiful Camelias scarlet and white as used to be—But she herself so sad! 'Julia is dying. She cannot last many days perhaps not hours.' Nothing can surpass the true tenderness of Lady Elizabeth to this her faithful old gentle sincere friend. Well did she keep her promise to Mr. Whitbread never to leave his wife and well for her that she did—even for her own sake in her own last moments.

Agnes Baillie has been ill but has recovered sufficiently to hope to come to Town next week and to meet us at Mrs. Baillies. Heaven grant! These illnesses and imminent perils and deaths are the more striking and awful I feel in a bustling capital city than they would be I think in the country and surrounded by one's own family—sympathising friends and one's own guardian angels as it were. There is something shocking immediately after the tidings of death in seeing the bustling the struggling in the crowded streets and the fine carriages and the unthinking mortals who care nothing for one another dead or alive—and they might say so much the better for we are saved unavailing thought and anguish. And yet I would rather have the thought and even the anguish for without pain no pleasure for the heart—certainly true—and no prayer for indifference for me. These Memento mori come with some force home to me at 76 . . . I pray most earnestly and devoutly to God as my father did before me that my body may not survive my mind and that I may never be a sad spectacle to my most dear excellent friends—that I may leave a tender not unpleasing recollection in their hearts and not give them more pain or of a different sort from that which I know they will feel at losing me—their loved—their petted one. My dearest mother tho I have written this and feel it truly yet I am not in the least melancholy or apprehensive—or unprepared or afraid of dying (and moreover have a strong hope that we shall meet again and walk in my garden once more together &c &c). As to the rest, I am truly resigned and trust to the goodness of my Creator living or dying . . .

To Mrs. Edgeworth

1 North Audley St., 2 February 1844

. . . Opening of Parliament.[1] The first view of the house struck me as not nearly so good or grand as the old house but my mouth was stopped with 'pro tempore only you know'. We

[1] The old Houses of Parliament had been burnt down in 1834. The House of Lords was at this date sitting in the Painted Chamber, while the Commons occupied the patched-up House of Lords. The new House of Lords did not come into use until 1847.

came at a side door—scarlet—for even the doors must be scarlet it seems—barely 80 feet long this slip of a Hall—a gallery of many tiers at the farthest end opposite the raised platform (*dais* I should say I suppose) on which great gilt crimson armchair commonly called throne stood empty—gaping for her Majesty —and a few steps lower a chair for Prince Albert.

The sides of the room of course you see as we saw lined with scarlet benches 5 or 6 deep—and a great table scarlet covered —3 or 4 chandeliers—not one handsome—no lights but sunlight broad and bright. We paused soon as we had cleared the scarlet door way and considered about the way we should go (Mrs. Hamilton Gray and sister I forgot to say had not been ready when we called for them so that we 3 were by ourselves ignoramuses—not in the bliss but in the puzzle of ignorance . . . For the present we were half lured half urged or civilly bullied on by the officer in waiting till we found ourselves at the foot of an ignominiously narrow staircase narrow I protest as that leading to my own room at home and up there was no help for it crowds of well dressed as ourselves before and behind pushing up and on we were fain or forced to go—on my right the wall on my left benches filled with seated ladies—and the man at the bottom of the staircase squeezed into the corner of the banisters looking up piteously perspiring and calling out 'On on ladies if you please—do not stop the way—Room enough above if you'll only go on.'

But there was one objection to going on—there were no seats above—and instinct taught us that if we stopped where we were we might at the last gasp make seats of the stairs under our footing. So we made ourselves small—no great effort on my part—and taking to the wall we left a scarcely practicable pass for the one by one passengers who less wary and more obedient than ourselves passed up to the highmost void. Fanny feared much for me that I should never be able to stand it and somehow or other my name was pronounced loud that the side benches heard, and one of the old Miss Sothebys not the ugliest but certainly the most goodnatured hearing stretched out at sides her fat cordial arm to me 'Miss Edgeworth glad! proud! glad! come on come in. We'll squeeze room for you between myself here and my friend Miss FitzHugh'—and squeeze and *scrudge* they did till I was bodkin'd betwixt them two but never touched the bench I should have sat upon till long after taking my seat. They began to tell who was who above about and underneath while I cast back a longing lingering look up the stairs where I had left my sisters twain. 'No no that I can't do for you!' quoth Mrs. Sotheby. 'That's impossible.' So that hope killed off I took to making the best of my own selfish position and surveyed all beneath me from the black heads of the Reporter gentlemen with their pencils and papers before them on the form and desk immediately below me in the front of our gallery to the depths of the Hall below through its long extent. On the table sprawling and stretching in the midst—with the feathered lappet-ed and jewel'd peeresses on the right and foreign eminences and Excellenzas on the left—were the long robed ermined judges laying their wigs together and shaking hands—tails of wigs many curl tailed on their backs—and the wigs jointly and severally looked like so many vast white and grey birds nests from Brobdignag with a black hole at the top of each for the birds to creep out or in. But this which seemed unto me a black hole size of half a crown—use inconcievable! I have since learned from good authority is a round piece of black silk or black something the sign or badge of the wearer of the wigs' being a Serjeant at law —which all the Judges of the land are by necessity and law before they become Judges or in the act of becoming such. Be this as it may—More and more and more scarlet ermined dignitaries and nobles bred and born swarmed into the Hall and I learned from my learned neighbor Miss Sotheby's instructions to her young nieces and protegees above me that each row of Ermine has its meaning and its heraldic value—One horizontal row on top of the mantle a baron—2—an Earl—3 a Marqu*is* or q*uess* 4 a Duke and for aught I heard 5 a Prince.

But of all this dear Madam you have known no doubt since the day you were suckled or sucked tho new to me Heaven help me at 76. Then the Wigs and gentlemen all noble did their bows or Cowtoos to the throne—Empty chair—Empty ceremony—old style—very good. Then in at the scarlet door came fluttering with white ribbon shoulder knots and streamers flying in all directions a full broad scarlet-5 rowed-ermined figure with high bald forehead, facetious face, and jovial, hail fellow well-met personage, princely withal—His Royal Highness the Duke of Cambridge—and the sidelong peeress benches stretched their fair hands and he his ungloved Royal hastily here—there and everywhere and chattering so loud and long he went on, his facetious Highness, that even we in gallery remote could hear the Ha! Ha! Haw! that followed ever and anon and blessed ourselves and feared we should not hear the Queen—But it was said that he would be silent when the Queen came and so it proved.

The guns were heard—Once—twice—and at the second discharge all were silent as mice. Even his Highness of Cambridge ceased to rustle and flutter and he stood nobly still. Enter the crown and cushion and sword of state and mace and all—vide newspaper—as you have seen—*And* the Queen leaning on Prince Alberts arm—ladies trainbearing etc. She did not go up the steps of her throne well—caught her foot and stumbled against the edge of the footstool in front which was too high. She did not seat herself in a decided Queen like manner, and after sitting down paltered too much with drapery arranging her petticoats at sides in the way in which Frenchwomen do and may do gracefully but which no Englishwoman born does gracefully and which ill becomes an English Queen. That footstool was much too high! Her knees were crumpled up and her figure short enough already was foreshortened as she sat and her drapery did not cover or come to the edge of the stool. As my neighbor Miss Fitzhugh—who I suspect belonged to the stage by her nice observations on scenic effect—'Very bad effect! That drapery should have been lengthened to throw over the stool and give length to her figure.' However and nevertheless, the better half of her looked perfectly ladylike and Queenlike—Her head finely shaped and well held on her shoulders—The likeness of a queenly crown that diadem of diamond—beautifully fair the neck and arms and the arms moved gracefully, and never too much—quite naturally and easily. I *might* romance or fable to you and moralize about her countenance and temper good or bad, but truth insists upon my confessing that I could not at the distance at which I was (and the chandeliers interfering sadly) see her Royal countenance plainly as Francis did on Windsor terrace and cannot say whether she looked smilingly even or not but I heard those beside me declaring she looked divinely gracious. There was dead silence—a more sublime effect and more of Majesty implied in that moments silence than in all the magnificence around. She spoke—low and well—desiring My Lords and Gentlemen to be seated. I omitted to notice the entrance of the Speaker and house of Commons from beneath our gallery which in truth I did not see but only knew that my Gentlemen were there.

The Queen then received from the Lord in waiting her speech and read. Her voice clear and perfectly distinct was heard by us ultimate auditors. It was not quite so fine a voice as I had expected. It had not the full rich tones, nor the varied powers and inflexions of a perfect voice for reading nor did she read so well as I had been taught to expect. She read with good sense as if she perfectly understood but did not fully or warmly feel what she was reading. It was more a girls well read lesson than a Queen pronouncing her speech. She did not lay emphasis sufficient to mark the gradations of importance in the objects and she did not make pauses enough. The best pronounced paragraphs were those about France and Ireland—her firm determination to maintain inviolate the legislative union[1]—and '*I am resolved to act in strict conformity with this declaration*' she pronounced strongly—con amore well. But she shewed less confidence in reading about the suspension of the Elective franchise[2]—that whole passage is indeed in too much detail. Even Harriet could not have read it well and for the writers sake would have slurred but a queen has not the privilege of slurring. Emphasis and soul were wanting in the conclusion where they were called for when she said 'In full confidence in your loyalty and wisdom and with an earnest prayer to Almighty God' . . .

Upon the whole I was disappointed and all the exaggerations of praise I heard bursting all round me afterwards made me feel more of the dull cold ear. Her Majestys exit I was much pleased to look at—it was so graceful and gracious and then and there she took time enough for all her motions—noticing all properly

[1] Between Great Britain and Ireland.

[2] The Queen said that the revision of the law of registration of voters in Ireland, together with other causes, might produce a diminution in the number of county voters there and it might be advisable to consider means to counter this.

—from 'My dear Uncle'—words distinctly heard as she passed the Duke of Cambridge—to the last expecting curtsying fair one at the door way. Vanished the Queen—the buz—the noise—the clatter rose and all were in motion and the tide of scarlet and ermine flowed and ebbed and there were the benches left below and the table and the empty chair of state—and after an immense while the throngs of people bonneted and shawled came forth from all the side niches and windows and down from the upper gallery's space and places unseen unknown gave up their occupants and all the outward Halls were filled with the living mass as we looked down upon them from the back antichamber-hall steps one sea of heads . . .

To Mrs. Edgeworth

Collingwood, before breakfast, 8 April 1844

As fine a sunshining day as ever you saw or felt and from my window I see a beautiful lawn and flower beds like your own on the green grass near the house and two children rolling that grass plot and I hear their dear happy voices and their fathers along with them. It is impossible to be more comfortable or to have been more cordially received than we have been by these kind friends. An immensity of trouble Lady Herschel and Sir John have taken (without shewing it) to receive us. They have given up their own bedchamber and dressing room to Fanny and Lestock and put up a bed for me in the next room because they thought I should like to be within reach of Fanny and the nice room I am in is Herschels own study or working room with all his instruments put away in glass cases and presses in the corner and his clock and books and all his things left! How very very kind and I can only say we do feel it and are most grateful and do not find gratitude a bit a burthen. It is only the black gentlemen and the like who feel that way.

Lord and Lady Adare are here—He no great shakes but a sincere admirer of the stars—double or single—and a tolerable measurer of their brightness. She I mean her Ladyship (who was an Elliot Mintos daughter Mintos sister) is a very well informed accomplished woman paints and plays divinely I hear and is a great historian withal and withal has not a grain of affectation or pretension . . . Besides the Lord and the Lady here is a baronet Sir Edward Ryan (Irish) who was Chief Justice or judge at Calcutta—went for his health to the Cape and found health and Herschel there and liked them both and Lady Herschel into the bargain—because he could not help it—nobody can. Sir E Ryan is very good natured and good humored and has beautiful white teeth and laughs much I do him the justice to believe without the least thought of shewing them. Besides Sir Edward here is Mr. Stewart a brother of Lady Herschels who met us at the end of the Railway on Saturday—got on the box and drove on with us here. Very happy we were to serve his turn as well as our own with the Herschel carriage and fine horses (that won't stand still).

Besides the beforementioned here is one whom I am right glad to see—I mean to *Hear* for he is much better to hear than to *see*—for he has an empurpled and embossed face and a nose as large and bursting looking and pumpled as a ripe fig largest end foremost—and 'spite of all that this can do to make the outward man forbid' no sooner does he begin to speak no sooner does the inner man come out than you forget all about his face nor even see his Scratch wig which before you might have marked was a world too small for his great head—and a little like that which Elwes[1] picked out of the gutter supposed to have been the cast wig of an old beggarman. And this gentleman's name which I am sure you by this time are longing to know is Jones—*Jones on Rent*—And I have attacked and plagued and gratified him by plaguing him to write a new volume. He says that he is going to do better, that he is about to publish lectures on political economy. You know the business of his life is to read Lectures on Political Economy at Haileybury. He has the place which Mackintosh had there and fills it if not as brilliantly full as usefully to the young men or boys. Perhaps what he says to some of these only goes in at one ear and out at the other but what is written remains and will remain graven on better than tablets of brass. Jones and Herschel are very fond of one another—capable of admiration pure from envy—often differing but

[1] John Elwes, the miser (1714–89). His *Life* by Major Edward Topham came out in 1799 and ran through many editions.

always agreeing to differ like Malthus and Ricardo who hunted together delightfully in search of Truth and huzzaed when they found her on whichever side she was and without caring who found her first. Indeed I have seen them put both their able hands to the windlass to drag her up from the bottom of that well in which she so strangely loves to dwell . . .

It was Fanny's declining health and the death in 1846 of her brother Francis, the agent at Edgeworthstown, which prevented further journeys. Fanny died in 1848 but Maria was still active enough to organize relief work in the Great Famine. She lived on at Edgeworthstown with her stepmother and Francis's young family until May 1849.

always [illegible] to dislike [illegible] and [illegible] [illegible] for their [illegible] in search of Truth, [illegible] [illegible] whichever side she [illegible] and [illegible] [illegible] [illegible] [illegible] to the [illegible] [illegible] the bottom of that well in which she so strangely loves to dwell.

It was Hardy's dedication [illegible] [illegible] [illegible] [illegible] brother [illegible] [illegible] [illegible] [illegible] [illegible] [illegible] [illegible] [illegible] enough to [illegible] in the Great [illegible] [illegible] [illegible] [illegible] [illegible] 1894.

INDEX OF PLACES

* Indicates address of a letter

BIOGRAPHICAL INDEX

Note. The biographical details given here are meant only to identify the persons concerned and to explain the references in the letters. Persons who only occur in lists are not included.

Biographical Index

Beaufort, the Revd. Daniel Augustus, *see* ME's Family Circle, xxxiii, xxxvi, xl, 4, 46, 60, 136, 139, 196, 291, 295, 367; letter to, 217
Beaufort, Frances Anne, *see* Edgeworth
Beaufort, Captain Francis, *see* ME's Family Circle, xxii, xxxiv, xxxvi, 4, 45, 75, 107, 109, 121, 126, 128–9, 136, 139–40, 147, 183, 193, 307, 318, 345, 357–9, 364, 366, 368, 372, 376, 383, 405–11, 413, 415–20, 424, 433, 435, 442, 479, 522, 535, 546, 566, 588, 589, 593, 596
Beaufort, Harriet, *see* ME's Family Circle, xxxvi, 211, 256, 312, 321, 388, 570; letter to, 307
Beaufort, Louisa, *see* ME's Family Circle, xxxvii, 196, 219, 238, 248, 387, 423, 446, 461, 570; letter to, 376
Beaufort, Mrs. Mary, *see* ME's Family Circle, xxxvi, 73, 415, 485
Beaufort, the Revd. William, *see* ME's Family Circle, xix n., xxxvi, 139, 218
Beaumont, —, 505
Beddoes, Anna Frances Emily, *see* ME's Family Circle, xxxiii, 78
Beddoes, Anna Maria, *see* ME's Family Circle, xxxiii, xl, 1, 64, 73–4, 76–8, 80–1, 155, 423
Beddoes, Henry, *see* ME's Family Circle, xxxiii, 77, 129
Beddoes, Mary, *see* ME's Family Circle, xxxiii, 78
Beddoes, Dr. Thomas (1760–1808), of the Pneumatic Institution, Bristol; husband of Anna Edgeworth, xxxiii, 330 n.
Beddoes, Thomas Lovell, *see* ME's Family Circle, xxxiii, 77, 129, 155, 247, 248
Bedford, Georgiana, Duchess of (d. 1853), w. of 6th Duke and dau. of 4th Duke of Gordon, 193
Bedford, John Russell, 6th Duke of (1766–1839), whig Lord Lieut. of Ireland 1806–7; early patron of Joseph Lancaster (q.v.), 58, 67, 193
Belgrave, Lady Elizabeth, *see* Gower
Bell, Andrew (1753–1832), founder of the school system sponsored by the National Soc. for promoting the education of the poor (Anglican), 57, 566
Bell, Charles, later Sir (1774–1842), anatomist, and his w. Marion, dau. of Charles Shaw, 311
Bennet, Hon. Henry Grey, M.P. (1777–1836), 2nd s. of 4th Earl of Tankerville, 166, 370–1
Bennet, Lady Mary (d. 1861), dau. of 4th Earl of Tankerville; m. (1831) Sir Charles Monck Bt. (q.v.), 296
Bennet, the Revd. —, chaplain at Millbank Penitentiary, 386
Bentham, Jeremy (1748–1832), utilitarian philosopher and writer on jurisprudence, xxii, 50, 69, 232, 325, 602–3
Beresford, Lady, *see* Hope, Mrs. Louisa
Beresford, William, Viscount (1768–1854), m. the Hon. Mrs. Hope (q.v.), 596
Berry, Agnes (1764–1852) and Mary (1763–1852), friends of Horace Walpole. Mary Berry, with her father, edited Walpole's literary remains, xx n., xxviii, 51, 60–1, 66, 117, 184, 196, 573
Bertrand, Henri Gratien, General Count (1773–1844), companion of Napoleon on Elba and St. Helena, 351
Bessborough, Henrietta Frances, Countess of (1761–1821), w. of 3rd Earl and dau. of 1st Earl Spencer, 54, 281
Bicknell, Mrs. Sabrina, one of two orphans brought up by Thomas Day (q.v.) as a possible future wife; married James Bicknell, his friend, and in her widowhood was housekeeper to Dr. Burney, xxxix, 109–10, 121–2
Bicknell, —, lawyer, son of Mrs. Sabrina Bicknell, 121–2
Biddulph, the Revd. Zachary Henry (b. *c.* 1792), Fellow of Magdalen Coll., Oxford, 220, 222, 247–8
Bigge, John Thomas (1780–1843), commissioner of inquiry at Botany Bay to examine the effectiveness of transportation as a deterrent, 372

Brown, Lancelot ('Capability') (1715–1783), landscape gardener, 73
Brown, Robert, F.R.S. (1773–1858), botanist, *589–90*
Browne, Dominick, M.P., later Lord Oranmore (1787–1860), 487
Brownlow, Isabella, dau. of Lieut.-Col. Charles Brownlow of Lurgan; m. (1818) Roderick Macneill of Barra, 78
Brownrigg, Lieut-Col. Robert James (1790–1822), m. Emma, dau. of Major Colebrooke Nisbet, 181, 412
Brunel, Marc Isambard (1769–1849), civil engineer; patented machinery for making ships' blocks in 1799 and built mills with improved machinery at Battersea 1804–12: *65*, 203
Buckingham, Richard Grenville, Marquess of (1776–1839), cr. Duke 1822: *355*
Bull, Mrs., lodging house keeper, *354–5*
Bunbury, Sir Charles, Bt., M.P. (1740–1821), befriended Mrs. Inchbald (q.v.) in her later years, 100
Bunbury, Sir Henry Edward, Bt., M.P. (d. 1860), under sec. for war 1809–16; m. Louisa Emilia, dau. of Hon. H. E. Fox, 100
Burdett, Sir Francis, Bt. (1770–1844); M.P. for Westminster 1807–37: 106
Burford, William Aubrey Beauclerk, Earl of, later 9th Duke of St. Albans (1801–49), *296–7*
Burney, Dr. C. (1726–1814), met the Edgeworths 1799: xxxix, 60
Burrell, —, friend of the Carr family (q.v.), 307
Burrowes, Elizabeth, dau. of Col. Thomas Burrowes of Dangan Castle and his 2nd w. Frances Beresford, sister of Mrs. Hope (q.v.), 195, 199, *296*, *362*, *377*, *393*
Bury, Lady Charlotte (1775–1861), dau. of 5th Duke of Argyll and w. of the Revd. E. J. Bury; lady in waiting to Queen Caroline; novelist, *448–9*, 485
Bushe, Mrs. Anne, w. of C. K. Bushe and dau. of John Crampton, *56*, 318
Bushe, Charles Kendal (1767–1843), solicitor general and later (1822) chief justice of king's bench in Ireland; the original of the lord chief justice in ME's novel *Patronage*, 310, 318, *601*
Bushe, John, s. of the above, *136*
Busk, Robert (1768–1835), merchant of St. Petersburg, *174–5*
Bute, John Stuart, 2nd Marquess of (1793–1848), 337
Butler, Mrs. A. G., dau. of M. P. Edgeworth, xxx
Butler, the Revd. George (1774–1853), headmaster of Harrow and later Dean of Peterborough, 398
Butler, Harriet, *see* Edgeworth
Butler, the Revd. Richard, *see* ME's Family Circle, xxxv, 423, *556*, *561*, *575*, 602
Butler, the Revd. Dr. Richard, father of Richard Butler (above), 489, *516*
Butt, the Revd. Thomas, nephew of the Revd. George Butt (1741–95) and curate at Trentham; m. —, wid. of James Edwards, bookseller. Dr. G. Butt and his w. and daughters (later the authoresses Mrs. Sherwood and Mrs. Cameron) were friends of Mary Sneyd (*see* ME's Family Circle), 157, *568*
Buxton, Thomas Fowell, M.P., later Sir (1786–1845), philanthropist and penal reformer, 118, 123, *166*, 183, 185
Byron, Ada (1815–52), dau. of Lord Byron, 445
Byron, Anne Isabella, Lady (d. 1860), dau. of Sir R. Milbanke; m. Lord Byron 1815 and separated from him 1816: *59*, *66*, 114, 120, 401, *463–5*
Byron, George Gordon, Lord (1788–1824), xxv, 1, 51, 54, 61, 65 n., 84, *96*, 114–15, 168, 230, 339, *463–5*, 478, 482, 484–5, *512–13*

Callcott, Augustus Wall, R.A., later Sir (1779–1844), 341, *345–7*, 367, 444, 511
Callcott, Mrs. Maria, later Lady (1785–1842), *née* Dundas; m. (1) Capt. Thomas Graham R.N. (2) A. W.

Chantrey, Francis Leggatt (*cont.*): cousin Mary Anne Wale, 177, 182, 456, 462, 478, 517–19, 530, 551–2, 561
Charleville, Catherine Maria, Countess of, w. of 1st Earl of Charleville and dau. of T. W. Dawson of Kinscaly, Co. Dublin, 66, 511–12
Charlotte, Princess, only child of George IV, 14
Charlotte Sophia, Queen (1744–1818), w. of George III, 14, 79, 128
Chawner, Miss, Irish artist, 481
Chenevix, Richard, F.R.S. (1774–1830), chemist; brother of the Edgeworths' neighbour Mrs. Tuite of Sonna; m. 1812 Countess de Rouault, 316, 322 n., 325 n., 352
Choiseul-Gouffier, Duc de (1752–1817), diplomat and archaeologist; author of *Voyage pittoresque de la Grèce* (1782), 44
Cholmondeley, Mrs. Caroline Elizabeth (d. 1818), 3rd dau. of Nicholas Smythe of Condover, Salop, and w. of Charles Cholmondeley of Overleigh, Chester; schoolfellow of ME, 21
Cholmondeley, Charles, of Overleigh, Chester (1770–1846), brother of 1st Lord Delamere, 212
Churchill, —, printer, 47
Cipriani, Giovanni Battista, R.A. (1729–85), historical painter and engraver, 34
Clare, Anne, Countess of (d. 1844), w. of 1st Earl and dau. of R. C. Whaley, 188, 193, 393
Clarence, William, Duke of, *see* William IV
Clarendon, Thomas Villiers, 2nd Earl of (1753–1824), 398
Clark, Sir James (1788–1870), court physician, 573
Clarke, the Revd. Edward Daniel (1769–1822), traveller and collector; professor of mineralogy, Cambridge; published his *Travels* 1810–23; m. Angelica, dau. of Sir W. B. Rush, 35, 40–1, 43–5, 48
Clerk, William, of Eldin, friend of Walter Scott, 366–7
Clifford, Mrs. (d. 1814), of Perrystone Court, Herefs.; had known RLE during his residence at Hare Hatch, Berks., 74, 510
Clisson, —, American associated with Liberian colonization, 580–1
Clutterbuck, Mrs. Henrietta, w. of Thomas Clutterbuck and dau. of David Ricardo (q.v.), 266, 284, 287
Clutterbuck, Thomas, of Widcombe House, Bath, and Hardenhuish Park, 284, 287, 302
Cobbe, —, Irish neighbour of the Edgeworths, 209, 272
Cobbett, William (1762–1835), 331
Cockerell, Charles Robert, R.A. (1788–1863), architect; friend of Captain Francis Beaufort, (q.v.), 188, 396–7
Cocks, (Col.), Major Edward Charles Cocks, s. of 1st Earl Somers; killed at assault of Burgos 1812: 73
Codrington, William (1790–1842), of Wroughton, Wilts., 145, 153
Coffey, Molly, servant of Mrs. Ruxton (q.v.), 144
Colebrooke, Major William Macbean George, later Sir (1787–1870), soldier and colonial governor, 281, 285, 289, 376
Collier, —, tutor to Vladimir Davidoff (q.v.), 450–1
Collins, Mary, servant, 232–3, 236
Copleston, the Revd. Edward (1776–1849), Provost of Oriel Coll., Oxford 1814–28; later Bishop of Llandaff and Dean of St. Paul's, 247, 546
Corbin, —, American, 531
Cork and Orrery, Isabella, Countess of (d. 1843), w. of 8th Earl and dau. of William Poyntz of Midgeham; well-known hostess of her day, xxviii, 67
Cornwall, Barry, *see* Proctor
Corrie, the Revd. John, pres. of Birmingham Philosophical Institute, 177–8
Corrie, —, ? Josiah, resident agent of Birmingham and London Rly. Co. and w., 560
Cottu, Charles (1778–1849), French judge; author of *Réflexions sur l'état*

actuel du jury de la liberté individuelle et des prisons (1818) and *De l'administration de la justice criminelle en Angleterre* (1820), 82–4, 439–40

Courtop, —, ? George Courthope (1767–1835) of Whiligh, Sussex, 435

Cowper, Amelia, Countess (d. 1869), w. of 5th Earl and dau. of 1st Viscount Melbourne, 378

Cowper, William (1731–1800), poet, 102, 169

Coxe, —, 'of the Museum', 365

Crabbe, the Revd. George (1754–1832), poet; chaplain to the Duke of Rutland, 123, 150, 168–9, 283–4

Crampton, Sir Philip (1777–1858), Irish surgeon and an old family friend of the Edgeworths, xxviii n., 446, 456

Creed, —, sec. of London and Birmingham Rly. Co., 443, 446, 452, 457, 546, 571

Crewe, Frances Anne, later Lady (d. 1818), w. of 1st Lord Crewe and dau. of Fulke Greville of Wilbury; well-known Whig hostess. The Edgeworths had known her sister-in-law at Pakenham Hall, 51, 52, 54, 169

Cripps, John Marten (d. 1853), travelling companion of Dr. E. D. Clarke (q. v.); presented marbles to Cambridge Univ.; m. Charlotte, dau. of Sir W. B. Rush, 40–1

Cripps, Joseph, M.P. for Cirencester (ME wrongly says Gloucester), 261

Croker, John Wilson, M.P. (1780–1857), xxxiii n., 573–4

Crumpe, Miss (*fl.* 1823, 1829), novelist, and her mother, 529, 533–4

Cunliffe, Mrs. Emma (d. 1850), w. of Foster Cunliffe and dau. of 1st Lord Crewe, 397

Cunliffe, Harriet, Lady (d. 1830), w. of Sir Foster Cunliffe Bt., 397

Cunningham, Col. Francis (d. 1816), s. of Sir William Augustus Cunningham Bt. of Milncraig; m. 1805 Jane, dau. of Sir John Whitefoord Bt., 147–8

Currie, Mrs., 76

Czartorinska, Princess Isabella, *née* Flemming (1743–1845), w. of Prince Adam Czartorinski, 470

D'Arblay, Madame (Fanny Burney) (1752–1840). Lived in France 1802–12: 60

Darnley, Elizabeth, Countess of, w. of 4th Earl and dau. of Rt. Hon. William Brownlow of Lurgan, 51–2, 67, 189, 193, 327, 401

Dartmouth, Frances, Countess of (d. 1838), w. of 3rd Earl and dau. of 1st Earl of Aylesford, 171

Darwin, Charles, F.R.S. (1809–82), 571–2

Darwin, Edward (1782–1829), eldest s. of Dr. Erasmus Darwin by his 2nd w., 21–2

Darwin, Mrs. Elizabeth, *née* Collier, 2nd w. of Dr. Erasmus Darwin and wid. of Edward Sacheverell Pole of Radbourne, xxxix, 29, 154–5

Darwin, Mrs. Emma, w. of Charles Darwin and dau. of Josiah Wedgwood jr., 571–2

Darwin, Dr. Erasmus (1731–1802), of Lichfield and Derby; author of *The Botanic Garden* (1789–92) and *The Temple of Nature* (1803); member of the Lunar Soc. of Birmingham and an old friend of RLE, xviii, 11, 13, 22, 121, 142, 154–5, 177, 208

Darwin, John, s. of Dr. Erasmus Darwin by his 2nd w., 154–5

Darwin, Dr. Robert (1766–1848), of Shrewsbury, eldest s. of Dr. Erasmus Darwin and father of Charles Darwin, 4, 16, 21, 554

Darwin, (Sir) (Francis) Sacheverell (1786–1856), eldest s. of Dr. Erasmus Darwin by his 2nd w., 21

Dashwood, Miss, friend of Anna Beddoes (q.v.), 181

Davidoff, Vladimir (d. 1882), traveller in Greece and Near East, 450–1

Davie, the Revd. J. (1777–1813), Master of Sidney Sussex Coll., Cambridge, and vice-chancellor of Cambridge Univ. 1812–13: 36–7

Davies, Captain, 'of the Countess', 76

Davy, Sir Humphrey, F.R.S. (1778–

Edgeworth, (Charles) Sneyd, *see* ME's Family Circle, xxxiv, xl, *23–5*, *29*, *205*, *415*, *429–32*, *466*, *526*, *530*, *535*, *541–2*, *569*; letters to, 32, 47, 150

Edgeworth, Sophy I (b. and d. 1784), xl

Edgeworth, Sophy II, *see* ME's Family Circle, xxxv, xl, *164*, *248*, *414*, *503*

Edgeworth, Thomas Day (1789–92), xl

Edgeworth, William I (1788–90), xl

Edgeworth, William II, *see* ME's Family Circle, xxxiv, xl, *4*, *5*, *25–6*, *28*, *37*, *75*, *122*, *240*, *245*, *308*, *398*

Edgeworth de Firmont, Abbé Henry Essex (1745–1807), confessor to Louis XVI on the scaffold, xxxiv, *66*

Edmonstone, —, ? Neil Benjamin (1765–1841), Indian civilian, *473*

Elers, Anna Maria, *see* Edgeworth

Elers, Paul (*c.* 1699–1781), grandfather of ME, xxxii

Ellice, Edward, M.P. (1810–80), 180, 182, 339

Ellice, Lady Hannah Althaea, dau. of 1st Earl Grey and w. of Edward Ellice; sister of Lady Elizabeth Whitbread (q.v.), 180–2, 339, 412

Elliott, Charles; and his mother, 472–3

Ellis, George James Welbore Agar, M.P. (1797–1833), 187, 193

Ellis, —, *76*

Elphin, Bishop of, *see* Law

Elphinstone, Frances, Lady (d. 1858), w. of Sir Richard Elphinstone and dau. of John Warburton; sister of Henry Warburton (q.v.), 389–90

Enghien, Louis Antoine Henri de Bourbon, Duc d' (1772–1804), last of the Condé family; arrested on neutral territory and, after trial for alleged complicity in Cadoudal's plot, shot at Vincennes, 21 March 1804: 2

Englefield, Sir Henry, F.S.A., F.R.S. (1752–1822), grandfather of Mrs. G. E. Strickland (q.v.), xxviii, 393–4

Ennismore, Richard Hare, Viscount (1773–1827), eldest s. of 1st Earl of Listowel, 397

Essington, Samuel, former Edgeworthstown servant; hotel keeper at Gt. Malvern, 72–3

Evelyn, John (d. 1827), succeeded to family estate at Wotton 1817: 200–1

Ewart, Peter (1767–1842), Manchester cotton spinner and engineer; an early member of the Manchester Literary and Philosophical Soc., 19

Fanshawe, Catherine Maria (1765–1834), poetess; author of the riddle ' 'Twas whispered in heaven, 'twas muttered in hell . . .'; and her sisters, *51*, 183–4, 188, 192–3

Farington, Joseph, R.A. (1747–1821), landscape painter and diarist. For his meeting with ME see *Farington Diary*, viii (1928), *216*: 184

Farish, the Revd. William (1774–1837), professor of chemistry, Cambridge 1794–1813; Jacksonian professor 1813–37; had a special interest in the application of science to industry, 33, 38–42

Farnham, Lady, probably Grace, dau. of Thomas Cuffe, wid. of 2nd Earl, 87, 481, *553*, *556*

Farquhar, Robert Townsend, later Sir (1776–1830), governor of Mauritius 1812–23: 185

Farquhar, Sir Walter (d. 1819), physician to the Prince Regent, 61

Farren, William (1786–1861), actor; excelled in old men's parts, 541

Fawcett, —, ? the Revd. James (1752–1831), Norrisian professor of divinity, Cambridge 1795–1815: 67

Fay, Leontine, actress, *546*

Fazakerley, J. N., M.P. (*c.* 1788–1852), *225*, *228–9*, 439

Fellenberg, Philippe Emanuel (1771–1844), Swiss educationalist, 584

Fellowes, Mrs., housekeeper at Blenheim, *246–7*

Ferriar, John, M.D. (1761–1815), physician to Manchester Infirmary; author of medical and literary works, 15

Fielding, Captain Charles, later Admiral (1780–1837), *225*

Fielding, Lady Elizabeth, w. of Capt. Charles Fielding and dau. of 2nd Earl of Ilchester, *225*, *229*, 438

Fingall, Arthur James Plunkett, 8th

(? Harriet, m. the Revd. R. W. Wake), *66*

Gray, Mrs. Caroline Hamilton (d. 1887), *née* Johnstone, w. of the Revd. J. Hamilton Gray; learned authoress, *605*

Greatheed, Anne Caroline, granddaughter and heir of Bertie Greatheed of Guys Gliffe, Warws.; m. 1822 Charles Percy, 8th s. of 2nd Lord Lovaine, *369*

Greaves, Mrs. and Miss, of Lichfield; probably relatives of Mrs. Maria Sneyd (q.v.), *22–3*, 172, 211

Greenough, George Bellas, M.P. (1778–1855), geographer and geologist; visited Edgeworthstown 1806, 1813: 297, 401, 425

Grenville, Anne, Lady (d. 1864), w. of Lord Grenville and dau. of Thomas Pitt, 1st Lord Camelford, *89–91*

Grenville, Rt. Hon. Thomas, M.P. (1755–1846), brother of Lord Grenville; took part in peace negotiations after War of American Independence; book collector; left his library to the British Museum, *86–8*, *90*, *92*, *94–5*, 101

Grenville, William Wyndham Grenville, Lord (1759–1834), *86–9*, *91*, 102, 222, *319–20*, 418, 504

Greville, Mrs., sister-in-law of Lady Crewe (q.v.), probably Meliora, w. of Captain W. F. Greville and dau. of Hon. and Revd. R. Southwell, 169

Greville, the Misses, ? daughters of Lady Crewe's brother W. F. Greville, *54*

Grey, Charles, 2nd Earl (1764–1845), Reform Bill Prime Minister, 70, 109, 203–4, *395–6*

Grey, Elizabeth, Countess (d. 1822), wid. of 1st Earl Grey and dau. of George Grey of Howick, 181, 335, 346

Grey, Lady Elizabeth, dau. of 2nd Earl Grey, *505*

Grey, Mary Elizabeth, Countess (d. 1861), w. of 2nd Earl Grey and dau. of 1st Lord Ponsonby, 70, *204–5*, 397

Grey, Mary, Lady (d. 1858), w. of Captain Sir George Grey (brother of 2nd Earl), resident commissioner of Portsmouth dockyard; sister of Samuel Whitbread sr. (q.v.), *406–7*

Griffiths, Mrs. Mary (d. 1877), of Philadelphia and Charlieshope, N.J.; authoress; aunt to Gerard Ralston (q.v.), *345*

Griffiths, Mrs., *46*, 130

Grogan, Nathaniel (d. 1807?), painter of Irish life, 358

Guiccioli, Teresa, Countess, mistress of Lord Byron (q.v.), 484, *512–13*

Guillemard, Mrs. Mary, w. of W. Guillemard and dau. of the Revd. E. Giddy; sister of Davies Gilbert (Giddy) (q.v.), 78, *80–2*, 512, 530, *589*

Gurney, —, ? John Joseph Gurney (1788–1847), philanthropist and the most eminent of Elizabeth Fry's brothers, 118

Gwatkin, Richard Lovell, m. 1781 Theophila, dau. of John Palmer and niece of Sir Joshua Reynolds, 503, *506–7*

Gwydyr, Clementina, Lady, w. of 2nd Lord Gwydyr and dau. of Lord Perth, *362–3*, 378

Haldimand, Anthony Francis (1741–1817), merchant banker, 63

Hales, —, former envoy to Sweden and Denmark, 252, *254–5*

Halford, Sir Henry, Bt. (1766–1844), physician to George IV and William IV and Queen Victoria, 499

Hall, Captain Basil (1788–1844), m. Margaret, dau. of Sir J. Hunter; author of many travel books with which ME give him critical assistance, 468, 478, 508, 522, 532, *546*

Hallam, Henry (1777–1859), historian, *54*, 225, *228–9*, 397, 523, 603

Hamilton, Mrs. Caroline (d. 1854), dau. of 2nd Lord Longford and w. of Henry Hamilton, s. of Rt. Hon. Sackville Hamilton, formerly chief sec. for Ireland; sister of the Duchess of Wellington (q.v.), 49, 142

Hamilton, Catherine (Kitty), dau. of James Hamilton of Brown Hall, Co.

Hamilton, Catherine (*cont.*): Donegal, and Helen (d. 1807), the Duchess of Wellington's sister, 299
Hamilton, William Richard, M.P. (1777–1859), antiquary and diplomat; under sec. for foreign affairs 1809–22: 188
Hamilton, Sir William Rowan, F.R.S. (1805–65), mathematician, xxvii
Hamilton, Col., and w., of Heldersham (? Hilderston) Hall, 244
Hammersley, —, 188
Hamond, Elton (1786–1820), literary hanger-on; visited Edgeworthstown 1807 and corresponded with ME 1808–11; an aquaintance of C. S. Edgeworth; committed suicide, 119
Hamond, Miss, sister of Elton Hamond; lived many years with Mrs. Barbauld (q.v.), 119
Harcourt, Miss, dau. of Edward Vernon Harcourt, Archbishop of York, 282
Hardwicke, Philip Yorke, 3rd Earl of (1757–1834), Lord Lieut. of Ireland 1801–6; m. Elizabeth, dau. of 5th Earl of Balcarres, *51*, *52*
Hare, Augustus J. C. (1834–1903), editor of *Life and Letters of ME* (1894), xxx
Hare, the Revd. J. C., Fellow of Trinity Coll. Cambridge, *136–7*, *155*
Harness, the Revd. William (1790–1869), author, *195*, *199*, *200–1*, *369*, *377*, *391*
Harrowby, Dudley Ryder, 1st Earl of (1762–1847), *156*, 187–8, 191–2
Harrowby, Susan, Countess of (d. 1838), w. of 1st Earl and dau. of 1st Marquess of Stafford, *156*, 184, 187–8, 192–3, *369*, *405*
Haughton, Moses (1772?–1848?), miniaturist and engraver, *551–2*
Hawtrey, the Revd. Edward Craven (1789–1862), headmaster of Eton, *572–5*
Hay, Robert (1799–1863), egyptologist and traveller, *255*
Hay, Robert William (1786–1861), under sec. colonial office, 485–6, *510*
Haygarth, Dr. John, F.R.S. (1740–1827), author of *Plan to exterminate smallpox* (1793); Bath physician, 83
Haygarth, William, author of *Greece, a poem* (1814), and *Panoramic View of Athens, illustrated* (1817), 83
Heaphy, Thomas (1775–1835), water colour painter; founder of Royal Soc. of Artists, 203
Henderson, —, dentist, *124–5*
Herschel, Caroline Emilia Mary, dau. of J. F. Herschel, *503*
Herschel, John Frederick, later 1st Bt., F.R.S. (1792–1871), astronomer, xxiv, 411–12, 442, 471, *500–2*, *505–6*, *508*, *538*, *594–5*, *596–7*, 601, *609–10*
Herschel, Mrs. Margaret, later Lady, w. of J. F. Herschel and dau. of the Revd. A. Stewart, *500–3*, *505*, *594–5*, *597*, *609–10*
Herschel, Sir William, F.R.S. (1738–1822), astronomer, xxxviii, 411–12
Hertford, Isabella Anne, Marchioness of (d. 1836), dau. of 9th Viscount Irvine and w. of 2nd Marquess; reputed mistress of the Prince Regent, *51*, *55*
Hervey, Mrs., *502*
Hesketh, Sir Thomas Dalrymple, Bt. (1777–1842), founder of a school at Rufford, Lancs., *385*
Hesketh, Miss, dau. of the above, *385*
Hesse Homburg, Elizabeth, Princess of, 3rd dau. of George III; m. 1818 Frederick, Landgrave and Prince of Hesse Homburg, 79, 100
Heytesbury, William A'Court, 1st Lord (1779–1860), ambassador at St. Petersburg, 1828–32: 450
Hinds, —, agent at Edgeworthstown, 427
Hitchings, —, ? the Revd. R. W. Hitchins (1764–1827), Fellow of Exeter Coll., Oxford, and rector of Baverstock, Wilts., 201
Hoare, Charles (d. 1851), 2nd s. of Sir R. Hoare, Bt.; banker, xv
Hoare, Mrs. Frances Dorothea, w. of Charles Hoare and dau. of Sir G. Robinson, Bt.; a schoolfriend of ME, xv, xxxviii, 1, 62
Hoare, Prince (1755–1834), artist and author, 372

Jersey, Frances, Countess of, *née* Twysden (d. 1821), w. of 4th Earl; reputed mistress of the Prince Regent, *56*
Jersey, Sarah, Countess of (d. 1867), w. of 5th Earl and dau. of Robert Child of Osterley Park, 189, 193, 342
Johnson, Joseph (1738–1809), the Edgeworths' first publisher, xxxix, 46 n.
Johnstone, —, prospective tenant, 426–7
Jones, Anna Maria, Lady, wid. of Sir William Jones (friend of Thomas Day) and dau. of Jonathan Shipley, Bishop of St. Asaph; aunt of the Revd. J. C. Hare (q.v.), 136, 155
Jones, the Revd. Richard (1790–1850), political economist; successor to T. R. Malthus (q.v.) as professor of political economy at E. India Coll., Haileybury, 478–9, 489, 514, 516–17, 520–1, 610–11
Jordan, Mrs. Dorothy (1762–1816), *née* Bland, actress and mistress to the Duke of Clarence, later William IV, 462
Josephine, Empress (1763–1814), 1st w. of Napoleon; divorced 1809: 3, 349, 497

Kater, Captain Henry, F.R.S. (1777–1835), physicist and surveyor, xxiii, 321, 382–3, 387, 389, 396–8, 411–13
Kater, Mrs. Mary Frances, *née* Reeve, w. of Henry Kater, xxiii, 387–9, 411–13
Kay, Dr. James Phillips, later Sir James Kay-Shuttleworth Bt. (1804–77), assistant poor law commissioner; first sec. of committee of council on education 1839–49; joint founder of Battersea training coll. for pupil teachers 1839–40: 522, 584–5
Kaye, John, Bishop of Lincoln (1783–1853), 457
Keating(e), Maria, dau. of the Revd. — Keating (below), 564
Keating, the Revd. —, incumbent of Edgeworthstown, 6
Keir, Amelia, *see* Moilliet
Keir, James, F.R.S. (1735–1820), chemist; member of the Lunar Soc. of Birmingham; author of a memoir of Thomas Day (q.v.), xviii, xxxviii, 122, 174, 232
Kemble, Charles (1775–1854), actor, 392
Kemble, John Philip (1757–1823), actor, 396
Kendal, —, incendiary, 42
Kennedy & Co., nurserymen, 3
Kennedy, Mrs. Sophia (d. 1879), w. of Rt. Hon. T. F. Kennedy and dau. of Sir S. Romilly (q.v.), 139, 368, 439
Kent, Edward, Duke of (1767–1820), 4th s. of George III and father of Queen Victoria, 57–8
Keppel, George Thomas, later 6th Earl of Albemarle (1799–1891), 545–6
Kerry, William Thomas, Lord (1811–36), elder s. of Lord Lansdowne (q.v.), 84–5, 226
Kiernan, Anne, housemaid, 436
King, Emmeline, *see* Edgeworth
King or König, John (d. 1846), *see* ME's Family Circle, xxxii, 75
King, Peter King, Lord (1766–1833), author, 193, 485
King, Captain, 429, 435
Kingston, Mr. and Mrs., 65
Kirkland, Mr. and Miss, 489
Knight, Henry Gally (1786–1846), writer on architecture; m. Henrietta, dau. of A. H. Eyre of the Grove, Notts., 101–2, 368, 509, 511
Knight, Richard Payne (1760–1824), author of *The Landscape* (1796) and *Analytical inquiry into the principles of taste* (1808), 73, 377
Kutaslo, Prince, almost certainly Prince Peter Borisovich Kozlovsky (1783–1840), Russian diplomat, 66

Lamb, Lady Caroline (d. 1828), w. of William Lamb, later 3rd Lord Melbourne, and dau. of Earl of Bessborough, 105–7
Lancaster, Joseph (1778–1838), founder of the schools system run by the non-sectarian Royal Lancasterian Soc., 57

Lister, Thomas, of Armitage Park, Staffs.; m. as his 2nd w. Mary Grove, dau. of William Grove and Lucy Sneyd, sister of Mrs. Honora and Mrs. Elizabeth Edgeworth, 24
Lister, Thomas Henry (1800–42), s. of Thomas Lister of Armitage Park; novelist and dramatist; author of *Granby* (1826); m. Theresa Villiers, sister of 4th Earl of Clarendon, 553, 555
Liston, John (1776?–1846), actor, 541
Listowel, Anne, Countess of (d. 1859), 2nd w. of 1st Earl and dau. of John Latham of Meldrum, Co. Tipperary, 357–8, 381, 397
Listowel, William Hare, 1st Earl of (1751–1837), 358, 381
Littleton, Mr. and Mrs., ? Edward John Walhouse Littleton of Teddesley Park, Staffs. (1791–1863), later 1st Lord Hatherton; m. 1812 Hyacinthe Mary, natural dau. of Marquess Wellesley (q.v.), 154
Liverpool, Robert Banks, 2nd Earl of (1770–1828), 1st Lord of the Treasury 1812–27; m. (1) Lady Louisa Hervey (d. 1821), (2) Mary, dau. of Charles Chester, 270, 356
Lloyd, —, bookseller, of Harley St., 361
Lock, William (1804–32), s. of William Lock (1767–1847) of Norbury Park, Surrey; a well-known amateur painter, 297
Lock, Mrs., 346
Lockhart, Charlotte Harriet Jane (d. 1858), dau. of J. G. and Sophia Lockhart, 448, 466
Lockhart, John ('Hugh Littlejohn') (1821–32), elder s. of J. G. and Sophia Lockhart, 448, 461, 465, 522
Lockhart, John Gibson (1794–1854), son-in-law and biographer of Sir Walter Scott: editor of *Quarterly Review*; acted as intermediary with Bentley over the publication of ME's *Helen* (1834), 444, 447–8, 460, 462–5, 484–5, 494, 522, 531, 577
Lockhart, Mrs. (Charlotte) Sophia (d. 1837), w. of J. G. Lockhart and elder dau. of Sir Walter Scott, 447–8, 450, 459–61, 465–7, 486, 522–3, 529
Lockhart, Walter Scott (1827–53), younger s. of J. G. and Sophia Lockhart, 448
Londonderry, Charles William Stewart, 3rd Marquess of (1778–1829), 537
Londonderry, Emily, Marchioness of (1772–1829), w. of 2nd Marquess and dau. of 2nd Earl of Buckinghamshire, xxiii, 380–1, 390
Londonderry, Robert Stewart, 2nd Marquess of (1769–1822), better known as Lord Castlereagh, 270, 370, 380–1
Longford, Edward Michael Pakenham, 2nd Lord (1743–92), friend and cousin of RLE and a near neighbour, 185, 190
Loring, Captain, ? John Wentworth, R.N., 406
Louis Philippe, King of France, 438, 441
Lover, Samuel (1797–1868), Irish song writer, novelist and painter, 586–7
Lowe, Lieut.-Gen. Sir Hudson (1769–1844), governor of St. Helena, 351
Lowndes, William Thomas (d. 1843), bibliographer; nephew of Mrs. Thomas Day, 227
Lowther, Mrs., *née* Palmer; sister of Mrs. Gwatkin (q.v.), 531–2
Ludolf, Count, ambassador from Naples, and w., 253, 255–6
Lushington, Mrs. Sarah (d. 1839), w. of Charles Lushington M.P. and dau. of Joseph Gascoigne; author of *A Journey from Calcutta to Europe 1827–8* (1829), 536, 542
Lushington, Mrs. Sarah Grace (d. 1837), w. of Dr. S. Lushington, *see* Carr
Lushington, Dr. Stephen, M.P. (1782–1873), legal adviser and executor to Queen Caroline, 301, 306–7, 311–12, 371, 490, 536
Luttrell, Henry (1765?–1851), wit and poet; author of *Advice to Julia, a Letter in Rhyme* (1820), 272, 397, 529
Lyndhurst, Sarah, Lady (d. 1834), w. of 1st Lord Lyndhurst and dau. of Charles Bransden, 485–6, 488, 510

Lyon, Sir James (1775–1842) and w., dau. of Edward Coxe, 406, 411
Lyster, Mrs. Helena, w. of Matthew Lyster of New Park, Co. Roscommon, and mother of Mrs. Elizabeth Smythe of Barbavilla, Co. Westmeath, 239
Lyster, the Revd. James, curate at Edgeworthstown and son in law of — Keating, vicar for 30 years, xxxiii n.
Lyttelton, Lady Sarah, w. of Hon. W. Lyttelton, later 3rd Lord Lyttelton, and dau. of 2nd Earl Spencer, 54

Macan, —, ? Thomas, brother of Turner Macan; d. unm. in India, 287–8
Macan, Turner, of Carriff, Co. Armagh (d. 1835), 287–8
Macaulay, Thomas Babington, later 1st Lord (1800–59), 488, 592, 600–1
Macdonald, —, 270
McGregor, Miss, sister of Mrs. James Watt sr. (q.v.), 216–17
MacHugh, Miss, 607
Mackintosh, Catherine, Lady, 2nd w. of Sir J. Mackintosh and dau. of John Allen of Cresselly, 328, 334, 354, 593
Mackintosh, Sir James, M.P. (1765–1832), philosopher and historian; Indian judge 1804–11; professor of law and general politics at E. India Coll., Haileybury, xxii, 50–1, 57, 65–6, 74, 176 n., 227, 327–8, 331–4, 338, 345, 354–5, 405, 478–81, 493, 523, 592–3, 600
Mackintosh, Robert James (1806–64), s. of Sir J. Mackintosh, 331–2
Mackintosh, Miss, dau. of Sir J. Mackintosh, 334, 354, 478
Mackintosh, Mr., 503
Macklin, Charles (1697?–1797), actor and stage-manager, 541
McLane, Louis (1786–1857), American ambassador in London 1829–31, and w. (Catherine Mary, dau. of Robert Milligan), 494, 496
McNeill, Roderick, of Barra, m. Isabella Brownlow (q.v.), 78
Mahon, Charles James Patrick, The O'Gorman Mahon (1800–91), Irish politician, 480
Mahon, Philip Henry, Lord (1805–75), later 5th Earl Stanhope, historian; grandson of Lord Carrington (q.v.), 509, 531, 546
Malcolm, Sir John (1769–1833), Indian administrator and diplomat; wrote on Persia and India, 486, 488, 573
Maling, Mrs. Harriet (d. 1825), w. of Admiral T. J. Maling and dau. of Erasmus Darwin (q.v.), 155
Mallet, J. L., sec. to the audit board; m. Frances Merivale, dau. of J. L. Merivale of Windmill Hill, Hampstead, 68, 129, 183, 455
Malone, Catherine (Kitty), sister of Lord Sunderlin (q.v.), 87
Maltby, Francis Newcombe (d. 1877), Indian civil servant 1831–62: 437
Malthus, Mrs. Harriet, w. of the Revd. T. R. Malthus and dau. of J. Eckershall of Claverton House, 63–4, 525
Malthus, the Revd. Thomas Robert (1766–1834), author of *Essay on Population* (1798) and *The Nature and Progress of Rent* (1815); professor of history and political economy at E. India Coll., Haileybury; met RLE at Joseph Johnson's (q.v.) in 1805: xxiii, 63–5, 328–9, 331, 334, 338, 423, 437, 489, 611
Manning, William, of Coombe Bank, Sevenoaks; M.P. for Lymington (ME wrongly says Oxford); m. Elizabeth, sister of Lord Carrington (q.v.), 252, 517
Mansfield, William Murray, 3rd Earl of (1777–1840), 537
Mansfield, Miss, 523
Mansfield, Mr. and Mrs., 447
Marcet, Alexander John Gaspard, M.D. (1770–1822), physician and chemical lecturer at Guys Hospital; professor of chemistry at Geneva 1819: 129, 309, 315, 321
Marcet, Mrs. Jane (1769–1858), *née* Haldimand, w. of Dr. Alexander Marcet; writer of children's books and popular scientific textbooks, xxiii, xxiv, 63–4, 68, 129, 183, 185,

280, 308–10, 312–13, 315, 321–4, 326, 359, 361, 363–4, 383, 389, 397, 498, 509, 579, 584–5
Marcet, Sophia, *see* Romilly
Marie Antoinette, Queen, w. of Louis XVI and archduchess of Austria, 2
Marie Louise, Empress, w. of Napoleon and archduchess of Austria, 2, 497
Marsden, William (1754–1836), orientalist, 566
Marshall, John, of Leeds and Hallsteads; friend of Wordsworth, 452–3
Martin, —, ? Robert Montgomery (1803?–1868), writer on Indian and colonial history and statistics, 532
Massereene, Harriet, Viscountess (d. Jan. 1831), dau.-in-law of RLE's old friend John Foster, Lord Oriel, 490
Mathew, Father Theobald (1790–1856), leader of Irish temperance movement, 575
Mathews, Charles (1776–1835), actor, 541
Mayo, Dr. Thomas (1790–1856), president of Royal Coll. of Physicians; eldest s. of John Mayo; succeeded to his father's lucrative practice in Tunbridge Wells. Both Mayos had care of William and C. S. Edgeworth at different periods, 526
Meath, Bishop of, *see* Alexander *and* O'Beirne
Melville, Lady Catherine, w. of John White Melville and dau. of 5th Duke of Leeds, 286
Meryon, Dr. Charles Lewis (1783–1877), physician and biographer of Lady Hester Stanhope (q.v.), 357
Milbanke, Anne Isabella, *see* Byron
Milbanke, Judith, Lady (d. 1822), w. of Sir Ralph Milbanke; mother of Lady Byron (q.v.), 59, 66
Miles, John, bookseller and publisher; nephew of the Edgeworths' first publisher Joseph Johnson and for a short time partner of Rowland Hunter (q.v.), 46 n., 47
Mill, James (1773–1836), utilitarian philosopher, 185, 266
Milligan, Mrs. Elizabeth Margaret (d. 1876), w. of Robert Millligan (d. 1875), West India merchant; dau. of Dr. Matthew Baillie, 117, 454
Milligan, Jean, *see* Hughan
Milman, the Revd. Henry Hart (1791–1868), author of, *inter alia, The Martyr of Antioch* (1822), 382
Milne, —, ? Joshua, actuary, 530
Moffat, Robert (1795–1883), missionary in Africa, 581–3
Moilliet, Mrs. Amelia (1780–1857), w. of J. L. Moilliet and dau. of James Keir (q.v.), xviii, xxi, 172, 175, 178, 210, 232–4, 237, 243–5, 422, 552, 559, 562–5, 567
Moilliet, Emily (Amelia), dau. of J. L. Moilliet; m. Samuel Knight, 172, 210, 243, 422, 551–2
Moilliet, James (1806–78), s. of J. L. Moilliet, xviii, 237, 422, 549–50, 552–3, 562, 565–6
Moilliet, John Lewis sr. (1780–1857), banker of Birmingham; of Swiss origin and had also a house in Switzerland at Pregny, xviii, xxi, 172–3, 175, 177–8, 215, 233, 237, 243–5, 249, 418, 422, 548–52, 561, 565, 567–8
Moilliet, John Lewis jr. (b. 1803), s. of J. L. Moilliet, 233, 405
Moilliet, Susan, dau. of J. L. Moilliet, 210, 422, 559, 562–3, 565, 567
Moilliet, Theodore, s. of J. L. Moilliet, and his w. Louisa, 210, 562, 567
Moira, Francis Rawdon, 2nd Earl of and 1st Marquess of Hastings (1754–1836), soldier and politician; governor general of Bengal 1813–22. His mother had befriended ME when she first came to Ireland, 30–1
Monck, Sir Charles, Bt. (1799–1867), 204
Monck, Lady Elizabeth, w. of Henry Monck of Fowre, Co. Westmeath, and dau. of 2nd Earl of Arran, 55
Montagu, Mrs. Elizabeth (1720–1800), blue stocking, 387
Monteagle, Lord, *see* Spring Rice
Montgomery, Col. Hugh (d. 1838), of Blessingbourne, Co. Tyrone; m. Dolores Pink of Malaga, 113–14

Nimmo, Alexander (1783–1832), engineer of western district of Ireland, where he built bridges, roads, and harbours, 576
Nisbet, Mrs., w. of General Colebrooke Nisbet and mother of Mrs. Brownrigg (q.v.), 181, 261, 412
North, John Henry, of Merrion Sq., Dublin; M.P. for Dublin University etc.; m. Letitia, sister of John Leslie Foster (q.v.), 488
Nugent, George Grenville, Lord (1789–1850), 2nd s. of Mary Elizabeth, Marchioness of Buckingham (cr. 1800 Baroness Nugent); m. Anne Lucy, dau. of Hon. General Vere Poulett, 491–2, 497, 509–10
Nugent, Mrs., 83

Oakley, Lady, ? w. of Sir Charles Oakley Bt., 22
O'Beirne, Mrs. Jane, w. of Bishop of Meath and dau. of Hon. Francis Stuart, 284, 341, 406
O'Beirne, Thomas Lewis, Bishop of Meath (1748?–1823), convert to Protestantism; chaplain and private sec. to Duke of Portland and Lord Fitzwilliam when Lords Lieut. of Ireland 1782 and 1794; Bishop of Ossory 1795; Bishop of Meath 1798; pamphleteer; an old friend of the Edgeworths, 92, 339
O'Connell, Daniel (1775–1845), 'the Liberator', 457, 467, 471, 598–9
Ogden (? Oakden), —, and w., 138, 280–1
O'Higgins, William, Roman Catholic Bishop of Ardagh 1829–53: 599
Opie, Mrs. Amelia (1769–1853), *née* Alderson; novelist, 51
Ord, Mrs. Mary, w. of William Ord and dau. of the Revd. J. Scott, 225, 229
Ord, William, M.P. (*c.* 1781–1855), of Farnham and Whitfield Hall, Northumberland, 225, 382
Ord, William (*c.* 1803–38), s. of William Ord, M.P., 225, 382, 523
Osborne, Lord Francis (1797–1850), later Lord Godolphin, 41
Pakenham, Lady Elizabeth (d. 1818), dau. of 1st Lord Longford, 3, 59
Pakenham, the Hon. and Revd. Henry (1787–1863), 5th s. of the Edgeworths' friend and neighbour Lord Longford; later Dean of St. Patrick's, Dublin; m. 1822 Eliza Catherine Sandford, dau. of 2nd Lord Mountsandford, 142, 285
Pakenham, Kitty, *see* Duchess of Wellington
Pakenham, Admiral the Hon. Sir Thomas (1757–1836), 2nd s. of 1st Lord Longford, 54, 300, 325, 487
Pallmer, Mrs., servant of Anna Beddoes at Bath, 77
Palmer, Horsley, s. of partner of L. P. Wilson, sr. (q.v.), and w., 530
Palmerston, Henry John Temple, Viscount (1784–1865), 193, 578–9
Paris, John Ayrton, M.D. (1785–1856), medical and scientific author; biographer of Davy, 490
Parkinson, John, dentist, 124
Parr, the Revd. Samuel (1747–1825), classical scholar and schoolmaster, 65–6
Parsons, John (1761–1819), Bishop of Peterborough and Master of Balliol Coll., Oxford, 222
Patterson, Mrs. Elizabeth (1785–1879), w. of Jerome Bonaparte, Napoleon's brother, 349
Paul, Sir George, Bt. (1746–1820), philanthropist, especially concerned with the improvement of Gloucestershire prisons, 82–3
Pearce, —, ? Henry Robert (1785–1843), natural s. of James Hare (1749–1804), wit and friend of C. J. Fox, 357
Peel, Robert, later 2nd Bt. (1788–1850), 354, 370, 405, 433, 434, 495, 531
Pembroke, Catherine, Countess of (d. 1856), w. of 11th Earl and dau. of Simon, Count Woronzow, 292–4
Pepys, Sir William Weller, Bt. (d. 1825), 386–7
Pepys, —, s. of Sir W. Pepys, 387

Reynolds, Sir Joshua (1723–92), 59, 65, 503, 506–7, 532
Ricardo, Bertha, dau. of David Ricardo, 257, 263, 265, 267–8
Ricardo, David, M.P. (1772–1823), economist, xxiii, xxiv, 226–7, 256–7, 259–69, 271–2, 279, 333, 340, 354, 362–4, 365–6, 372, 396, 398, 411, 611
Ricardo, Fanny, dau. of D. Ricardo; m. Edward Austen, cloth manufacturer, 258–9, 264, 266
Ricardo, Mrs. Harriett, w. of Osman Ricardo and dau. of R. H. Mallory of Woodcote, Warws., 256–7, 265–8, 530, 541
Ricardo, Henrietta, *see* Clutterbuck
Ricardo, Mary, dau. of D. Ricardo, 257, 262, 265, 267–8, 541
Ricardo, Mortimer (1807–76), s. of D. Ricardo, 265
Ricardo, Osman, M.P. (1795–1881), eldest s. of D. Ricardo, 256–7, 264, 530, 541
Ricardo, Priscilla, dau. of D. Ricardo and w. of Anthony Austen, 259
Ricardo, Mrs. Priscilla Anne, w. of D. Ricardo and dau. of Edward Wilkinson, 256–7, 259–60, 264, 266–7, 365–6, 541
Rice, *see* Spring Rice
Richardson, John (1780–1864), solicitor; friend of Sir Walter Scott, 311
Richmond, Charles Lennox, 4th Duke of (1764–1819), Lord Lieut. of Ireland 1806–13: 102
Roberts, Miss, dressmaker, 181
Robinson, Fanny, *see* Hoare
Robinson, Dr. T. R., *see* ME's Family Circle, xxxv
Rocca, Albert Jean Michel (1788–1818) of Geneva; m. 1816 Madame de Stael (q.v.), 96
Roe or Row, Captain, 289
Rogers, Samuel (1763–1855), banker and poet; published *The Pleasures of Memory* 1792; met the Edgeworths in Paris 1802–3: xxiv n., xxviii, xxxiii n., 69, 347, 485, 490, 496, 509–10, 529, 531, 592, 600
Roget, Mrs. and Miss, w. and sister of Peter Mark Roget (1779–1869), author of the *Thesaurus*. Roget was a friend of Lovell Edgeworth, 64
Rolfe, Robert Monsey, M.P., later Lord Cranworth (1790–1868); m. Laura Carr (q.v.), 307–8, 362
Romilly, Edward, M.P. (1804–70), 3rd s. of Sir S. Romilly, 509
Romilly, Sir Samuel, M.P. (1757–1818), Whig law reformer; m. Anne, dau. of Francis Garbett of Knill Court, Herefs.; correspondents of the Edgeworths, xxii, 1, 14, 60–1, 65, 74, 106, 137–9, 166, 182, 194, 271, 482, 484, 513
Romilly, Mrs. Sophia (d. 1877), w. of Edward Romilly and dau. of Dr. and Mrs. Marcet (q.v.), 509, 584, 586
Roscoe, Mrs. Jane, w. of William Roscoe and dau. of William Griffies of Liverpool, 10–11, 13, 48
Roscoe, William, M.P. (1753–1831), Liverpool banker, historian, poet, and collector; author of *Leo Xth* (1805), 10–15
Roscoe, William Stanley (1782–1843), s. of William Roscoe; banker, poet and authority on Italian literature, 13
Rothes, Charlotte Julia, Countess of (d. 1846), 2nd w. of 10th Earl and dau. of Col. John Campbell, 199, 297–8
Rothwell, Richard (1799–1853), s. of Thomas Rothwell of Rockfield, Co. Meath, and stepson of Letitia Corry, niece to ME's uncle by marriage, John Ruxton (q.v.), 178, 248
Rous, Mrs., of Harp Inn, Conway, 7
Rowan, Archibald Hamilton (1751–1834), United Irishman; fled to America after escaping from prison 1794; pardoned and returned to Ireland 1803: 348
Roy, Rammohun (1774–1833), Indian theistical reformer; spent last two years of life in England, 546
Rumford, Benjamin Thompson, Count (1753–1814), scientist and administrator both in England and in Bavaria: m. as his 2nd w. the wid. of the chemist Lavoisier, 175

Rush, Angelica, *see* Clarke
Rush, Charlotte, *see* Cripps
Russell, Lord John, 436, 439
Russell, the Revd. John (1787–1863), headmaster of Charterhouse 1811–32; s. of RLE's tutor at Corpus Christi Coll., Oxford, 109, 129, 155, 220, 314, 338–9
Russell, the Revd. William (*c.* 1788–1831), Fellow of Magdalen Coll., Oxford; brother of the above, 220, 247
Russell, Mrs. 'of Northumberland', either Anne (*née* Milbanke), w. of William Russell of Brancepeth, coal owner, or Elizabeth (*née* Tennyson), dau. of his son Matthew, 40
Rutland, Elizabeth, Duchess of (d. 1825), w. of 5th Duke and dau. of 5th Earl of Carlisle, 61–2, 378
Rutland, Mary Isabella, Duchess of (d. 1831), w. of 4th Duke and dau. of 4th Duke of Beaufort; member of Prince of Wales's circle, 56
Ruxton (Fitzherbert), Elizabeth (Bess), *see* ME's Family Circle, xxxvi, 48, 52 n., 145 n.
Ruxton, John, *see* ME's Family Circle, xxxvi, 53, 130
Ruxton, Mrs. Margaret, *see* ME's Family Circle, xxii, xxiii, xxix, xxxvi, xl, 48, 60, 202, 233, 260, 348, 358, 388; letters to, 9, 72, 82, 130, 158, 181, 184, 251, 280, 338, 340, 362, 389
Ruxton, Margaret, *see* ME's Family Circle, xxxvi, 147
Ruxton (Fitzherbert), Richard, *see* ME's Family Circle, xxxvi, 242
Ruxton Sophy, *see* ME's Family Circle, xxviii, xxxiii, xxxvi, 68, 221; letters to, 49, 101, 142, 191, 270, 303, 323, 436, 440, 491
Ryan, Sir Edward, F.R.S. (1793–1873), Chief justice, Calcutta and Presidency of Bengal, 610
Ryder, Lady Mary, 2nd dau. of 1st Earl of Harrowby, 156

Salisbury, Bishop of, *see* Fisher
Salisbury, James Brownlow Cecil, 2nd Marquess of (1791–1868), 537
Salisbury, Mary, Marchioness of (1750–1835), w. of 1st Marquess and dau. of 1st Marquess of Downshire (cr. Earl of Hillsborough 1772, Marquess of Downshire 1789), 326–7
Sandford, Daniel Keyte, later Sir (1798–1838), professor of Greek, Glasgow University 1821: 247
Sandon, Dudley Ryder, Viscount (1798–1882), eldest s. of 1st Earl of Harrowby, 405
Saurin, William (1757–?1839), attorney general for Ireland; removed from his post by Marquess Wellesley for anti-Catholic agitation, 319
Scarlett, James, M.P., later 1st Lord Abinger (1769–1844), attorney general 1827–8 and 1829–30; law reformer, 439–40
Scoresby, the Revd. William (1789–1857), formerly whaling captain; chaplain of the floating chapel for mariners, Liverpool; author of *Account of the Arctic Regions* (1820) and contributions to scientific journals, 420
Scott, Anne (1803–33), younger dau. of Sir Walter Scott, 460
Scott, Charles (1805–41), younger s. of Sir Walter Scott, 577–9
Scott, Mrs. E., of Danesfield, nr. Marlow; wid. of Robert Scott (d. 1808), 376
Scott, Sir Walter (1771–1832), xxiv, xxviii, xxxv, 142, 168, 261, 303, 323–4, 341–2, 366–7, 426, 447–8, 456, 462, 489–90, 492, 558, 566, 573
Scott, Mrs., of Kilkenny, 61
Scott, —, s. of the Revd. James Scott of Itchenstoke, Hants; consul at Venice, 121
Sebright, Frederica Anne Saunders (d. 1864), dau. of Sir J. Sebright, 200, 308, 321–2, 325–6, 332
Sebright, Sir John, Bt., M.P. (1767–1846), whig politician; agriculturist; author of books on animals, 129, 316, 320, 323–6, 370
Sedgwick, Adam (1785–1875), professor of geology, Cambridge; president of Geological Soc. 1831: 484

Smith, Thomas (d. 1822), of Easton Grey, Glos.; visited Edgeworthstown 1815: *226–7*, 258, *261–3*, *267–70*, 274, 411

Smith, Mrs., w. of Thomas Smith of Easton Grey and step-daughter of Mrs. Chandler of Gloucester (q.v.), *227–8*, 231, 258, *270–1*, *278–9*, 411

Smith, —, tutor of Thomas Hope's sons, 498

Sneyd, Charlotte, see ME's Family Circle, xix, xxxvi, xxxvii, 7, 9, 140–1, 147, 163, 186, 232, 291, 395, 399; letters to, 16, 180, 300

Sneyd, Major Edward, of Byrkley Lodge, Staffs., xix, xxxii

Sneyd, Edward (1755–1832), s. of Major Edward Sneyd and brother of Mrs. Honora and Mrs. Elizabeth Edgeworth, xviii–xix, 17–18, 23–4, 66, 101, 148, 150, 154, 157, 160, *554–6*

Sneyd, Elizabeth, *see* Edgeworth

Sneyd, Emma (d. 1858), dau. of Edward Sneyd, xix, 7, 16–17, 24–5, *65–6*, 143, 146, 148, 150, 157, 160, 167–8, 171, 544, *554–6*, 558

Sneyd, Harriet, ? dau. of Walter Sneyd of Keele, 261

Sneyd, Honora, *see* Edgeworth

Sneyd, J., of Keele, 150, 156

Sneyd, the Revd. John (1766–1835), of Elford; friend and correspondent of Canning, 140–1, 150–1, 278, *553–4*, 558

Sneyd, Mrs. Maria, w. of Edward Sneyd and dau. of Joseph Greaves of Aston, Derbyshire, xix, 16–17, 23–5, 61, *65–6*, 140, 146, 148, 150, 153–4, 157, 160, *162–5*, 167, 170–1, 544, *554–6*, 558

Sneyd, Mary, see ME's Family Circle, xix, xxxvi, 48, 140–1, 147, 162, 232, 238, 291, 298, 400, 420, 485, 517, 542, *555–6*; letters to, 1, 72, 180

Sneyd, —, 'not of Keele', 298

Somers, John Somers Cocks, 1st Earl (1760–1841); m. Margaret, dau. of the Revd. T. R. Nash, 73

Somerset, Charlotte, Duchess of (d. 1827), w. of 11th Duke and dau. of 9th Duke of Hamilton and Brandon, 51

Somerville, John, 15th Lord (1765–1819), agricultural expert; early patron of Joseph Lancaster (q.v.), 51, 53

Somerville, Mrs. Mary (1780–1872), w. of William Somerville and dau. of Sir W. G. Fairfax; scientific writer, xxiii–xxiv, 321–4, 361–2, 366–7, 382, 387–9, 530, 601

Somerville, Dr. William (1771–1860), 321–2, 324, 367

Sophia, Princess (1777–1848), 5th dau. of George III, 127

Sotheby, Mrs. Mary, w. of William Sotheby (1757–1833), author; dau. of Ambrose Isted of Ecton, Northants., 398, 405, 523, *605–6*

South, James, later Sir (1785–1865), astronomer, *532–3*, *546*

Southey, Robert (1774–1843), 443

Sparks, Jared (1789–1866), professor of ancient and modern history and later president of Harvard; ed. *The Writings of George Washington* (1834–7), 580

Spencer, George John, 2nd Earl (1758–1834), 1st lord of the admiralty 1794–1801; home sec. 1806–7: 53

Spencer, Lady Georgiana (d. 1823), dau. of Earl Spencer; m. Lord George Quin, 53

Spencer, Harriet Caroline, dau. of W. R. Spencer and w. of Count Charles Westerholt, 394

Spencer, Lavinia, Countess (d. 1831), w. of 2nd Earl and dau. of 1st Earl of Lucan, xix, *53*, 108, *135–6*, 139

Spencer, William Robert (1769–1834), poet and wit; m. Susan, wid. of Count Spreti and dau. of Count Tenison Walworth, 301, *394–5*

Spring Rice, Lady Theodosia (d. 1839), w. of Thomas Spring Rice and dau. of 1st Earl of Limerick, 401–2, 441, 461, 467

Spring Rice, Thomas, M.P., later Lord Monteagle (1790–1866), sec. to the treasury 1830–4; chancellor

traveller; known to have been in England Dec. 1830–June 1831; unrelated to Ivan Turganiev the novelist, 480, 492
Turner, —, banker, 439, 441
Tyerman, — and w., owners of 10 Holles St., 360, 371, 412

Van de Weyer, Jean Sylvain, Baron (1802–74), Belgian politician and diplomat prominent in establishment of Belgian state in 1831; m. Elizabeth Anne Sturges, dau. of Joshua Bates of Barings bank, 573–4
Vane, Frances Anne, Lady (1713–88), 387
Vansittart, Nicholas, M.P., later Lord Bexley (1766–1851), secretary for Ireland 1805; chancellor of the exchequer 1812–23: 370
Vaudreuil, Alfred, Vicomte de (1799–1834), 1st sec. at French embassy in London, 440
Vennelock, Elizabeth, servant, 360
Vernon, Alice Lucy, Lady (d. 1827), 2nd w. of 3rd Lord Vernon and dau. of Sir John Whitefoord, Bt., 147
Vernon, Elizabeth (d. 1830), dau. of Dowager Countess of Upper Ossory and Richard Vernon of Hilton, Staffs.; step-aunt to Lord Holland and Caroline Fox (q.v.), with the latter of whom she lived at Little Holland House, 225, 280–1
Vernon, Hon. George (1779–1835), eldest s. of 3rd Lord Vernon, 146, 149, 178, 248
Vernon, Mrs. Granville, ? Frances Julia, w. of Granville Harcourt Vernon of Grove Hall, Notts., s. of Lord Vernon's brother the Archbishop of York, 144
Vernon, Henry, 3rd Lord, *see* Sedley
Vernon, Hon. Henry (d. 1845), 2nd s. of 3rd Lord Vernon, 146, 148, 154
Vernon, Hon. John (1798–1875), 3rd s. of Lord Vernon, 149
Vernon, Miss, *see* Harcourt
Victoria, Queen, 607–9
Vince, Dr. Samuel, F.R.S. (1749–1821), professor of astronomy, Cambridge, 36
Waddington, Mrs., niece of Mrs. Delany, 563
Waite, George (d. 1820), dentist, 124, 128–9, 346
Wakefield, Edward (1774–1854), author of *Ireland: statistical and political* (1812), 46, 56, 58, 266
Waldegrave, Captain, ? William (1796–1838), 2nd s. of Lord Radstock, 380
Waller, Belinda and Jane and their parents, 265
Waller, Elizabeth, *see* ME's Family Circle, xxxvii; letter to, 139
Waller, Major and Mrs., 265
Walpole, the Revd. Robert (1781–1856), classical scholar and traveller; published *Memoirs relating to Turkey* (2nd ed. 1818) and *Travels in various countries of the East* (1820), the latter including travels by Morritt, Sibthorpe and Hunt with notes by Walpole; completed last vol. of E. D. Clarke's *Travels*, 44–5
Walsham, John Garbett (d. 1819), brother of Lady Romilly, 138
Walsingham, George de Grey, 3rd Lord (1776–1831); m. Matilda, dau. of Paul Methuen of Corsham, Wilts., 528
Warburton, Henry, M.P. (1784?–1858), philosophical radical; friend of Ricardo and Wollaston, xxiii, 270, 383, 389–90
Ward, Robert Plumer, M.P. (1765–1846), novelist and politician, 333, 531
Waterpark, Juliana, Lady (d. 1847), w. of 2nd Lord Waterpark and dau. of Thomas Cooper of Mullimast Castle, Co. Kildare, 146
Waterson, Mrs., 4
Watkinson, the Revd. Robert (1775–1869), housemaster at Charterhouse, 329, 338
Watt, Mrs. Anne (d. 1832), 2nd w. of James Watt sr. and dau. of — McGregor, 177–8, 214–15, 552
Watt, James sr. (1736–1819), inventor of the steam engine, xvii, xxiv, 65, 176–8, 214–16
Watt, James jr. (1769–1848), engineer, s. of the above, 65, 214–15, 217, 552

Wilkinson, Josiah Henry, s. of Edward Wilkinson and brother-in-law of David Ricardo (q.v.), *365–6*
Wilkinson, Miss, Bath dressmaker, *284–5*
Wilkinson, Mrs., companion to Mrs. Siddons (q.v.), 391
William IV, 100, *462*, *503–4*, *537*
Willing, —, ? son of Thomas Willing (1731–1821), Philadelphia banker, *530*
Wilmot, Mrs. Barbarina, m. (1) V. H. Wilmot, (2) Thomas, 20th Lord Dacre; dau. of Sir Chaloner Ogle, 71
Wilson, Alicia, *see* Beaufort
Wilson, Captain John, brother of Lestock Wilson jr., 130, 139, *522*, *524*, *535*
Wilson, Lestock Peach sr., E. India merchant, of The Grove, Epping, and w. (*née* Boileau); parents of Alicia, John and Lestock Peach Wilson jr., *46* n., *126*, 128, 130
Wilson, Lestock Peach jr., *see* ME's Family Circle: xxxv, 108–10, 123, 125, 129–30, 152, 183, 414–611 *passim*
Wilson, Miss, sister or aunt of L. P. Wilson jr., 184
Wilson, Mr. and Miss, cousins of J. G. Lockhart (q.v.), 461–2
Windham, William, M.P. (1750–1810), sec. for war under Pitt 1794–1801; held war and colonial office under Lord Grenville 1806–7: 100, 228
Wollaston, William Hyde, F.R.S. (1766–1828), physiologist, chemist, and physicist, xxiii–xxiv, 129, 271, 308, 321–2, 324, 326, 352, 362, 382–3, 387–8, 398, 405
Woodhouse, John Chappell (*c.* 1750–1833), Dean of Lichfield, 22
Wordsworth, William (1770–1850), and fam., 452–3, *455–6*
Woronzow, Isemen (1744–1832), Russian ambassador in London for 20 years, 293
Woronzow, General Michael (1782–1856), 293
Worthington, Mr., quarry master, and his w. and s., 4–6, 240–1
Wortley, Lady Caroline (d. 1876), dau. of 1st Lord Wharncliffe, 151
Wren, Christopher (*c.* 1776–1828), of Wroxall Abbey, Warws., and w., 218–19
Wren, Miss, relative of the above; lived with family of Lewis O'Beirne, Bishop of Meath (q.v.), 218
Wyatt, James (1746–1813), architect, 207, 247
Wyse, Madame Letitia, dau. of Lucien Bonaparte, Prince of Canino, and w. of Thomas Wyse; notorious for her unbalanced and scandalous behaviour in Ireland in the later 1820s.; sister of Lady Dudley Stuart (q.v.), 492

Young, Anna Louisa, w. of Sir William Lawrence Young, Bt., step-nephew of Robert and Thomas Talbot (q.v.), 253

PRINTED IN GREAT BRITAIN
AT THE UNIVERSITY PRESS, OXFORD
BY VIVIAN RIDLER
PRINTER TO THE UNIVERSITY